Collected Fiction: 1931–1936

H. P. LOVECRAFT

Collected Fiction

A VARIORUM EDITION

VOLUME 3: 1931–1936

Edited by S. T. Joshi

Hippocampus Press

New York

First Paperback Edition.

Published by Hippocampus Press
P.O. Box 641, New York, NY 10156.
http://www.hippocampuspress.com

Cover design and cover artwork by Fergal Fitzpatrick. For the cover of
volume three, Mr. Fitzpatrick has used *the ancient and the permanent* as his
conceptual departure.

"I should describe mine own nature as tripartite, my interests consisting of
three parallel and dissociated groups—(a) Love of the strange and the
fantastic. (b) Love of the abstract truth and of scientific logick. (c) Love of
the ancient and the permanent. Sundry combinations of these three strains
will probably account for all my odd tastes and eccentricities."
—H. P. Lovecraft to Rheinhart Kleiner (7 March 1920)

Portrait of H. P. Lovecraft, June 1934.
Photo of S. T. Joshi by Emily Marija Kurmis.

Hippocampus Press logo designed by Anastasia Damianakos.

1 3 5 7 9 8 6 4 2

ISBN: 978-1-61498-111-4

Contents

Introduction

As in the case of the stories in Volume 2 of this edition, every story in this volume (with the exception of the fragment "The Book") appeared in pulp magazines without prior publication in amateur journals; and for every one of the stories (with the exception of "The Haunter of the Dark"), Lovecraft's A.Ms. or T.Ms. or both survive. Nevertheless, the textual problems surrounding some of the tales are as formidable as for any of Lovecraft's work, prose or verse.

The crux of the difficulty lies in the two works—*At the Mountains of Madness* and "The Shadow out of Time"—published in *Astounding Stories,* a science fiction pulp magazine with whose editor, F. Orlin Tremaine, Lovecraft had no prior relationship. Accordingly, he was unable to insist on the printing of his tales in a relatively unaltered manner, with the result that both stories were heavily edited (with about 1000 words omitted from *At the Mountains of Madness* at various points in the text, especially the end). Further textual confusion results from the loss of critical components of the textual transmission process—for *At the Mountains of Madness,* the T.Ms. actually submitted to *Astounding,* which must have borne some revisions by Lovecraft; for "The Shadow out of Time," Barlow's T.Ms. submitted to *Astounding,* which clearly contained numerous transcriptional errors. The latter loss is of lesser consequence, since the providential discovery of Lovecraft's A.Ms. in 1994 makes the job of textual restoration much simpler than that for *At the Mountains of Madness,* where there will always be uncertainty as to which variants between Lovecraft's original T.Ms. and the *Astounding* text are the result of editorial alterations by Tremaine's staff and which are Lovecraft's own revisions.

Given these difficulties, it is not surprising that the initial Arkham House texts of these two works are riddled with errors; even my first corrected text of "The Shadow out of Time" (published in 1984), could only correct obvious errors such as the Americanisation of Lovecraft's British spellings. (Some years earlier I had prepared a conjectural restoration of the clearly erroneous paragraphing in the tale, in consultation with other scholars; but, although it turned out that many of my restorations proved to be accurate, it was properly decided that I had no authority to print such a text in the absence of detailed textual notes indicating my revisions.) Conversely, the Arkham House texts of "The Shadow over Innsmouth" and "The Dreams in the Witch House" are on the whole accurate. That for "The Thing on the Doorstep" is very poor, chiefly because the unnamed typist who had prepared the T.Ms. for Lovecraft made numerous serious mistakes in transcribing the text, and Arkham House chose not to prepare a text from the A.Ms.

In the Appendix are printed works that, in my judgment, do not constitute stories in the fullest sense of the term, but which have frequently been reprinted in editions of Lovecraft's tales and are therefore of interest. These include Lovecraft's very early juvenilia, written in the period 1897–1902; the dream-accounts "The Very Old Folk" (taken from a letter to Donald Wandrei) and "The Evil Clergyman" (taken from a letter—apparently lost or not extant—to Bernard Austin Dwyer); the discarded draft of "The Shadow over Innsmouth"; the very brief humorous squib "Cigarette Characterizations"; and a story fragment that August Derleth used, with considerable alterations, in *The Lurker at the Threshold* (1945).

Abbreviations used in the notes are as follows:

A.Ms.   autograph manuscript
ES   *Essential Soltiude: The Letters of H. P. Lovecraft and August Derleth* (2008)
JHL   John Hay Library, Brown University (Providence, RI)
OFF   *O Fortunate Floridian: H. P. Lovecraft's Letters to R. H. Barlow* (2007)
om.   omitted
SL   *Selected Letters* (1965–76; 5 vols.)
T.Ms.   typed manuscript

—S. T. JOSHI

Collected Fiction: 1931–1936

At the Mountains of Madness

I.

I am forced into speech because men of science have refused to follow my advice without knowing why. It is altogether against my will that I tell my reasons for opposing this contemplated invasion of the antarctic—with its vast fossil-hunt[a] and its wholesale boring and melting of the ancient ice-cap—and[b] I am the more reluctant because my warning may be in vain.[c] Doubt of the real facts, as I must reveal them, is inevitable; yet[d] if I suppressed what will seem extravagant and incredible there would be nothing left. The hitherto withheld photographs, both ordinary and aërial, will count in my favour;[e] for

Editor's Note: The extremely involved textual problems surrounding this work have been discussed in my article "Textual Problems in *At the Mountains of Madness,*" *Crypt of Cthulhu* No. 75 (Michaelmas 1990): 16–21. I can here do no more than outline the central issues. HPL's original A.Ms. and T.Ms. survive; but after the tale was rejected by *Weird Tales* in the summer of 1931, the T.Ms. lay dormant for years. Through the services of agent Julius Schwartz, the tale was accepted by *Astounding Stories* and published in the February, March, and April 1936 issues. HPL, however, had manifestly revised certain portions of his original T.Ms. (a carbon of which was probably sent by Schwartz to *Astounding*), especially in regard to the hypothesis that the Antarctic continent was actually two land masses separated by a frozen sea—a hypothesis disproved by explorations in 1934–35. But there are thousands of other divergences between the original T.Ms. and the *Astounding* text, raising the question as to how many of these changes are also deliberate revisions by HPL or alterations by the *Astounding* editors. I have concluded that the great majority of these divergences are editorial, and that the original T.Ms. should in nearly all instances be followed.

[a] fossil-hunt] fossil hunt C, D
[b] ice-cap—and] ice caps. And C, D
[c] vain.] vain. ¶ C, D
[d] yet] yet, C[c], D
[e] favour;] favor, C, D

they are damnably vivid and graphic. Still, they will be doubted because of the great lengths to which clever fakery can be carried. The ink drawings, of course, will be jeered at as obvious impostures;[a] notwithstanding a strangeness of[b] technique which art experts ought to remark and puzzle over.

In the end I must rely on the judgment and standing of the few scientific leaders who have, on the one hand, sufficient independence of thought to weigh my data on its own hideously convincing merits or

HPL himself, when he noted the extent of the alterations (chiefly in the third segment), specified the nature of some of the changes in a letter to R. H. Barlow (*OFF* 335f.)—excess punctuation, the breaking up of his long paragraphs into two or more shorter paragraphs, alterations of scientific terms, etc. He went on to state that he spent days in preparing three "corrected" copies of the issues of *Astounding*, adding omitted passages and fixing erroneous paragraphing in pencil and scraping off excess punctuation with a razor. However, it becomes evident that HPL failed to correct a substantial number of errors—e.g., the Americanisation of his British spellings, elimination of hyphens in compound words, the erroneous capitalisation of species names (e.g., "shoggoth"), and so on—either because he did not notice them or because he could not be bothered to do so. I believe that two small passages in Section III (the first instalment) omitted by *Astounding* were not restored in HPL's "corrected" copies because he failed to notice their omission. Also, because HPL was correcting the story using the A.Ms. rather than the T.Ms. (which was at the time unavailable to him), he unwittingly restored erroneous readings from his A.Ms. that he himself had revised when preparing his original T.Ms. These "corrected" copies of *Astounding* are, therefore, only of minimal assistance in the restoration of the text.

August Derleth of Arkham House, when preparing the text for publication in *The Outsider and Others* (1939), used these corrected copies, since he knew that the printed text was severely corrupt. Although this text is therefore superior to the *Astounding* text, at least in terms of paragraphing and other details, it still contains thousands of apparent errors. There seems little option to following the original T.Ms. except in instances where demonstrable revisions occurred (in at least one passage, HPL appears to have added a sentence in the carbon submitted to *Astounding*, correcting a printing error in his "corrected" copies). Even such a text can only be considered provisional.

Texts: A = A.Ms. (JHL); B = T.Ms. (JHL); C = *Astounding Stories* 16, No. 6 (February 1936): 8–32; 17, No. 1 (March 1936): 125–55; 17, No. 2 (April 1936): 132–50; C^c = HPL's corrections in his copies of the *Astounding* serialisation (JHL); D = *At the Mountains of Madness and Other Novels* (Arkham House, 1964), 1–100. Copy-text: B (with some readings from C and C^c).

[a] impostures;] impostures, D
[b] of] and B, C^c

in the light of certain primordial and highly baffling myth-cycles;[a] and on the other hand, sufficient influence to deter the exploring world in general from any rash and overambitious programme[b] in the region of those mountains of madness.[c] It is an unfortunate fact that relatively obscure men like myself and my associates, connected only with a small university, have little chance of making an impression where matters of a wildly bizarre or highly controversial nature[d] are concerned.

It is further against us that we are not, in the strictest sense, specialists in the fields which came primarily to be concerned. As a geologist[e] my object in leading the Miskatonic University Expedition was wholly that of securing deep-level specimens of rock and soil from various parts of the antarctic continent, aided by the remarkable drill devised by Prof.[f] Frank H. Pabodie of our engineering department.[g] I had no wish to be a pioneer in any other field than this;[h] but I did hope that the use of this new mechanical appliance at different points along previously explored paths would bring to light materials of a sort hitherto unreached by the ordinary methods of collection.[i] Pabodie's drilling apparatus, as the public already knows from our reports, was unique and radical in its lightness, portability, and capacity to combine the ordinary artesian[j] drill principle with the principle of the small circular rock drill in such a way as to cope quickly with strata of varying hardness.[k] Steel head, jointed rods, gasoline motor, collapsible wooden derrick, dynamiting paraphernalia, cording, rubbish-removal auger, and sectional piping for bores five inches wide and up to 1000[l] feet deep all formed, with needed accessories, no greater load than three seven-dog

[a] myth-cycles;] myth cycles; C, D
[b] overambitious programme] over-ambitious programme A, B; over-/ambitious program C; over ambitious program D
[c] madness.] madness. ¶ C[c]
[d] nature] natures C[c]
[e] geologist] geologist, C, D
[f] Prof.] Professor C, D
[g] department.] department. ¶ C[c]
[h] this;] this, C, D
[i] collection.] collection. ¶ C, D
[j] artesian] Artesian C[c]
[k] hardness.] hardness. ¶ C[c]
[l] 1000] one thousand C, D

sledges could carry; this being[a] made possible by the clever aluminum alloy of which most of the metal objects were fashioned.[b] Four large Dornier aëroplanes, designed especially for the tremendous altitude flying necessary on the antarctic plateau and with added fuel-warming and quick-starting devices worked out by Pabodie, could transport our entire expedition from a base at the edge of the great ice barrier to various suitable inland points, and from these points a sufficient quota of dogs would serve us.

We planned to cover as great an area as one antarctic season—or longer, if absolutely necessary—would permit, operating mostly in the mountain ranges and on the plateau south of Ross Sea; regions explored in varying degree by Shackleton, Amundsen, Scott, and Byrd. With frequent changes of camp, made by aëroplane and involving distances great enough to be of geological significance, we expected to unearth a quite unprecedented amount of material;[c] especially in the pre-Cambrian strata of which so narrow a range of antarctic specimens had previously been secured.[d] We wished also to obtain as great as possible a variety of the upper fossiliferous rocks, since the primal life-history[e] of this bleak realm of ice and death is of the highest importance to our knowledge of the earth's past. That the antarctic continent was once temperate and even tropical, with a teeming vegetable and animal life of which the lichens, marine fauna, arachnida,[f] and penguins of the northern edge are the only survivals, is a matter of common information; and we hoped to expand that information in variety, accuracy, and detail. When a simple boring revealed fossiliferous signs, we would enlarge the aperture by blasting[g] in order to get specimens of suitable size and condition.

Our borings, of varying depth according to the promise held out by the upper soil or rock, were to be confined to exposed or nearly exposed[h] land surfaces—these inevitably being slopes and ridges because of the

[a] carry; this being] carry. This was C, D
[b] fashioned.] fashioned. ¶ C[c]
[c] material;] material— C, D
[d] secured.] secured. ¶ C[c]
[e] life-history] life history C, D
[f] arachnida,] arachnidae, B
[g] blasting] blasting, C, D
[h] exposed . . . exposed] exposed, . . . exposed, C, D

mile or two-mile thickness of solid ice overlying the lower levels.[a] We could not afford to waste drilling depth on[b] any considerable amount of mere[c] glaciation, though Pabodie had worked out a plan for sinking copper electrodes in thick clusters of borings and melting off limited areas of ice with current from a gasoline-driven dynamo.[d] It is this plan—which we could not put into effect except experimentally on an expedition such as ours—that the coming Starkweather-Moore Expedition proposes to follow[e] despite the warnings I have issued since our return from the antarctic.

The public knows of the Miskatonic Expedition through our frequent wireless reports to the *Arkham Advertiser* and Associated Press, and through the later articles of Pabodie and myself. We consisted of four men from the University—Pabodie, Lake of the biology department, Atwood of the physics department (also a meteorologist),[f] and I[g] representing geology and having nominal command—besides sixteen assistants:[h] seven graduate students from Miskatonic and nine skilled mechanics.[i] Of these sixteen, twelve were qualified aëroplane pilots, all but two of whom were competent wireless operators. Eight of them understood navigation with compass and sextant, as did Pabodie, Atwood,[j] and I. In addition, of course, our two ships—wooden ex-whalers,[k] reinforced for ice conditions and having auxiliary steam—were fully manned.[l] The Nathaniel Derby Pickman Foundation, aided by a few special contributions, financed the expedition; hence our preparations were extremely thorough[m] despite the absence of great publicity.[n] The

[a] levels.] levels. ¶ C[c]
[b] depth on] the depth of D
[c] mere] more C[c]
[d] dynamo.] dynamo. ¶ C[c]
[e] follow] follow, C, D
[f] department (. . .),] department, (. . .) B; department—. . .— A, C, D
[g] I] myself, C, D
[h] assistants;] assistants: C, D
[i] mechanics.] mechanics. ¶ C[c]
[j] Atwood,] Daniels, A; Atwood B, C, D
[k] ex-whalers,] exwhalers, C
[l] manned.] manned. C[c]
[m] thorough] thorough, C, D
[n] publicity.] publicity. ¶ C[c]

dogs, sledges, machines, camp materials, and unassembled parts of our five planes were delivered in Boston, and there our ships were loaded.[a] We were marvellously[b] well-equipped for our specific purposes, and in all matters pertaining to supplies, regimen, transportation, and camp construction we profited by the excellent example of our many recent and exceptionally brilliant predecessors. It was the unusual number and fame of these predecessors which made our own expedition—ample though it was—so little noticed by the world at large.

As the newspapers told, we sailed from Boston Harbour[c] on September 2, 1930;[d] taking a leisurely course down the coast and through the Panama Canal, and stopping at Samoa and Hobart, Tasmania, at which latter place we took on final supplies.[e] None of our exploring party had ever been in the polar regions before, hence we all relied greatly on our ship captains—J. B. Douglas, commanding the brig *Arkham,* and serving as commander of the sea party,[f] and Georg Thorfinnssen, commanding the barque *Miskatonic*—both veteran whalers in antarctic waters.[g] As we left the inhabited world behind the sun sank lower and lower in the north, and stayed longer and longer above the horizon each day. At about 62° South Latitude we sighted our first icebergs—table-like[h] objects with vertical sides—and just before reaching the Antarctic Circle,[i] which we crossed on October 20th[j] with appropriately quaint ceremonies, we were considerably troubled with field ice.[k] The falling temperature bothered me considerably after our long voyage through the tropics, but I tried to brace up for the worse rigours[l] to come. On many occasions the curious

[a] loaded.] loaded. ¶ Cᶜ
[b] marvellously] marvelously C, D
[c] Harbour] Harbor C, D
[d] 2, 1930;] 2nd, 1930, C, D
[e] supplies.] supplies. ¶ Cᶜ
[f] party,] party D
[g] waters.] waters. ¶ A, C, D
[h] table-like] tablelike C, D
[i] Antarctic Circle,] antarctic circle, C, D
[j] 20th] 20 A, B
[k] ice.] ice. ¶ Cᶜ
[l] rigours] rigors C, D

atmospheric effects enchanted me vastly; these including[a] a strikingly vivid mirage—the first I had ever seen—in which distant bergs became the battlements of unimaginable cosmic castles.

Pushing through the ice, which was fortunately neither extensive nor thickly packed, we regained open water at South Latitude 67°, East Longitude 175°. On the morning of October 26th[b] a strong "land blink"[c] appeared on the south, and before noon we all felt a thrill of excitement at beholding a vast, lofty, and snow-clad mountain chain which opened out and covered the whole vista ahead. At last we had encountered an outpost of the great unknown continent and its cryptic world of frozen death.[d] These peaks were obviously the Admiralty Range discovered by Ross, and it would now be our task to round Cape Adare and sail down the east coast of Victoria Land to our contemplated base on the shore of McMurdo Sound[e] at the foot of the volcano Erebus in South Latitude 77° 9′.

The last lap of the voyage was vivid and fancy-stirring, great[f] barren peaks of mystery looming[g] up constantly against the west as the low northern sun of noon or the still lower horizon-grazing southern sun of midnight poured its hazy reddish rays over the white snow, bluish ice and water lanes,[h] and black bits of exposed granite slope.[i] Through the desolate summits swept raging[j] intermittent gusts of the terrible antarctic wind;[k] whose cadences sometimes held vague suggestions of a wild and half-sentient musical piping, with notes extending over a wide range, and which for some subconscious mnemonic reason seemed to me disquieting and even dimly terrible.[l] Something about the scene reminded

[a] including] included C[c]
[b] 26th] 26 A
[c] "land blink"] land blink C, D
[d] death.] death. ¶ C[c]
[e] Sound] Sound, C, D
[f] fancy-stirring, great] fancy-stirring. Great C, D
[g] looming] loomed C, D
[h] water lanes,] water-lanes, A, B
[i] slope.] slope. ¶ C[c]
[j] raging] raging, C, D
[k] wind;] wind, C[c]
[l] terrible.] terrible. ¶ C[c]

me of the strange and disturbing Asian paintings of Nicholas Roerich, and of the still stranger and more disturbing descriptions of the evilly fabled plateau of Leng which occur in the dreaded "Necronomicon"[a] of the mad Arab Abdul Alhazred. I was rather sorry, later on, that I had ever looked into that monstrous book at the college library.

On the seventh[b] of November, sight of the westward range having been temporarily lost, we passed Franklin Island; and the next day descried the cones of Mts. Erebus and Terror on Ross Island ahead, with the long line of the Parry Mountains beyond. There now stretched off to the east the low, white line of the great ice barrier;[c] rising perpendicularly to a height of 200[d] feet like the rocky cliffs of Quebec, and marking the end of southward navigation.[e] In the afternoon we entered McMurdo Sound and stood off the coast in the lee of smoking Mt. Erebus. The scoriac[f] peak towered up some 12,700[g] feet against the eastern sky, like a Japanese print of the sacred Fujiyama;[h] while beyond it rose the white, ghost-like[i] height of Mt. Terror, 10,900[j] feet in altitude, and now extinct as a volcano.[k] Puffs of smoke from Erebus came intermittently, and one of the graduate assistants—a brilliant young fellow named Danforth—pointed out what looked like lava on the snowy slope;[l] remarking that this mountain, discovered in 1840, had undoubtedly been the source of Poe's image when he wrote seven years later of[m]

"—the lavas that restlessly roll
Their sulphurous currents down Yaanek

[a] "Necronomicon"] *Necronomicon* A, B, C, D
[b] seventh] 7th A, B, C, D
[c] barrier;] barrier, C, D
[d] 200] two hundred C, D
[e] navigation.] navigation. ¶ C[c]
[f] scoriac] scoriaceous C[c]
[g] 12,700] twelve thousand seven hundred C; twelve thousand, seven hundred D
[h] Fujiyama;] Fujiyama, C, D
[i] ghost-like] ghostlike A, B, C, D
[j] 10,900] ten thousand nine hundred C; ten thousand, nine hundred D
[k] volcano.] volcano. ¶ C[c]
[l] slope;] slope, C, D
[m] later of] later: C, D

In the ultimate climes of the pole—
That groan as they roll down Mount Yaanek
In the realms of the boreal pole."[a]

Danforth[b] was a great reader of bizarre material, and had talked a good deal of Poe. I was interested myself because of the antarctic scene of Poe's only long story—the disturbing and enigmatical "Arthur Gordon Pym".[c] On the barren shore, and on the lofty ice barrier in the background, myriads[d] of grotesque penguins squawked and flapped their fins;[e] while many fat seals were visible on the water, swimming or sprawling across large cakes of slowly drifting ice.

Using small boats, we effected a difficult landing on Ross Island shortly after midnight[f] on the morning of the 9th, carrying a line of cable from each of the ships and preparing to unload supplies by means of a breeches-buoy arrangement.[g] Our sensations on first treading antarctic[h] soil were poignant and complex, even though at this particular point the Scott and Shackleton expeditions had preceded us.[i] Our camp on the frozen shore below the volcano's slope was only a provisional one;[j] headquarters being kept aboard the *Arkham*. We landed all our drilling apparatus, dogs, sledges, tents, provisions, gasoline tanks, experimental ice-melting outfit, cameras[k] both ordinary and aërial, aëroplane parts, and other accessories, including three small portable wireless outfits (besides those in the planes)[l] capable of communicating with the *Arkham's* large outfit from any part of the antarctic continent that we would be likely to visit.[m] The ship's outfit, communicating with the

[a] "—the . . . pole."] —*the . . . pole.* D
[b] Danforth] ¶ Danforth C[c], D
[c] "Arthur Gordon Pym".] *Arthur Gordon Pym.* C, D
[d] myriads] myriad C
[e] fins;] fins, C, D
[f] midnight] midnight, C[c]
[g] arrangement.] arrangement. ¶ C[c]
[h] antarctic] Antarctic D
[i] us.] us. ¶ C[c]
[j] one;] one, C, D
[k] cameras] cameras, C, D
[l] outfits (. . .)] outfits—. . .— C, D
[m] visit.] visit. ¶ C[c]

outside world, was to convey press reports to the *Arkham Advertiser's* powerful wireless station on Kingsport Head, Mass.[a] We hoped to complete our work during a single antarctic summer; but if this proved impossible we would winter on the *Arkham,* sending the *Miskatonic* north before the freezing of the ice for another summer's supplies.

I need not repeat what the newspapers have already published about our early work: of our ascent of Mt. Erebus; our successful mineral borings at several points on Ross Island and the singular speed with which Pabodie's apparatus accomplished them, even through solid rock layers; our provisional test of the small ice-melting equipment; our perilous ascent of the great barrier with sledges and supplies; and our final assembling of five huge aëroplanes at the camp atop the barrier. The health of our land party—twenty men and 55[b] Alaskan sledge dogs—was remarkable, though of course we had so far encountered no really destructive temperatures or windstorms.[c] For the most part, the thermometer varied between zero and 20° or 25° above, and our experience with New England winters had accustomed us to rigours[d] of this sort. The barrier camp was semi-permanent,[e] and destined to be a storage cache for gasoline, provisions, dynamite, and other supplies.[f] Only four of our planes were needed to carry the actual exploring material, the fifth being left with a pilot and two men from the ships[g] at the storage cache to form a means of reaching us from the *Arkham* in case all our exploring planes were lost.[h] Later, when not using all the other planes for moving apparatus, we would employ one or two in a shuttle transportation service between this cache and another permanent base on the great plateau from 600 to 700[i] miles southward, beyond Beardmore Glacier.[j] Despite the almost unanimous accounts of

[a] Mass.] Massachusetts. D
[b] 55] fifty-five C, D
[c] windstorms.] windstorms. ¶ C[c]
[d] rigours] rigors C, D
[e] semi-permanent,] semipermanent, C[c]
[f] supplies.] supplies. ¶ C, D
[g] men . . . ships] men, . . . ships, C[c]
[h] lost.] lost. ¶ C[c]
[i] 600 to 700] six hundred to seven hundred C, D
[j] Glacier.] Glacier. ¶ C[c]

appalling winds and tempests that pour down from the plateau, we determined to dispense with intermediate bases;[a] taking our chances in the interest of economy and probable efficiency.

Wireless reports have spoken of the breath-taking four-hour non-stop[b] flight of our squadron on November 21st over the lofty shelf ice, with vast peaks rising on the west, and the unfathomed silences echoing to the sound of our engines.[c] Wind troubled us only moderately, and our radio compasses helped us through the one opaque fog we encountered. When the vast rise loomed ahead, between Latitudes 83° and 84°, we knew we had reached Beardmore Glacier, the largest valley glacier in the world, and that the frozen sea was now giving place to a frowning and mountainous coast-line.[d] At last we were truly entering the white, aeon-dead world of the ultimate south, and even[e] as we realised[f] it we saw the peak of Mt. Nansen in the eastern distance, towering up to its height of almost 15,000[g] feet.

The successful establishment of the southern base above the glacier in Latitude 86° 7′, East Longitude 174° 23′, and the phenomenally rapid and effective borings and blastings made at various points reached by our sledge trips and short aëroplane flights, are matters of history; as is the arduous and triumphant ascent of Mt. Nansen by Pabodie and two of the graduate students—Gedney and Carroll—on December 13–15th.[h] We were some 8500[i] feet above sea-level, and when[j] experimental drillings revealed solid ground only twelve feet down through the snow and ice at certain points, we made considerable use of the small melting apparatus and sunk bores and performed dynamiting at many places[k] where no previous explorer had ever thought of

---

[a] bases;] bases, C, D
[b] breath-taking . . . non-stop] breathtaking, four-hour, nonstop [non-/stop D] C, D
[c] engines.] engines. ¶ C[c]
[d] coast-line.] coast line. ¶ C [*paragraphing error corrected by HPL*]; coast line. D
[e] south, and even] south. Even C, D
[f] realised] realized C, D
[g] 15,000] fifteen thousand C, D
[h] 13–15th.] 13–15. A, D; 13th to 15th. ¶ C [*corr. by HPL to* 13–15.]
[i] 8500] eight thousand five hundred C; eight thousand, five hundred D
[j] sea-level, and when] sea-level. When C[c]
[k] places] places, C[c]

securing mineral specimens.[a] The pre-Cambrian granites and beacon sandstones thus obtained confirmed our belief that this plateau was homogeneous[b] with the great bulk of the continent to the west, but somewhat different from the parts lying eastward below South America—which we then thought to form a separate and smaller continent divided from the larger one by a frozen junction of Ross and Weddell Seas, though Byrd has since disproved the hypothesis.[c]

In certain of the sandstones, dynamited and chiselled[d] after boring revealed their nature, we found some highly interesting fossil markings and fragments—[e]notably ferns, seaweeds, trilobites, crinoids, and such molluscs[f] as linguellae and gasteropods—[g]all of which seemed of real significance in connexion[h] with the region's primordial history. There was also a queer triangular, striated marking about a foot in greatest diameter[i] which Lake pieced together from three fragments of slate brought up from a deep-blasted[j] aperture.[k] These fragments came from a point to the westward, near the Queen Alexandra Range; and Lake, as a biologist, seemed to find their curious marking unusually puzzling and provocative, though to my geological eye it looked not unlike some of the ripple effects reasonably common in the sedimentary rocks.[l] Since slate is no more than a metamorphic formation into which a sedimentary stratum is pressed, and since the pressure itself produces odd distorting effects on any markings which may exist, I saw no reason for extreme wonder over the striated depression.

[a] specimens.] specimens. ¶ Cc
[b] homogeneous] homogeneous, C, D
[c] somewhat . . . hypothesis.] radically different from the parts lying eastward below South America, which in all probability form a separate and smaller continent divided from the larger by a frozen junction of Ross and Weddell Seas. A, B; somewhat . . . report. Cc
[d] chiselled] chiseled C, D
[e] fragments—] fragments; A, B, C, D
[f] molluscs] mollusks C, D
[g] gasteropods—] gasteropods; A, B; gastropods— C, D
[h] connexion] connection C, D
[i] marking . . . diameter] marking, . . . diameter, C, D
[j] deep-blasted] deep blasted A, B
[k] aperture.] aperture. ¶ Cc
[l] rocks.] rocks. ¶ Cc

On January 6,[a] 1931, Lake, Pabodie, Danforth,[b] all six of the students, four mechanics, and myself flew directly over the south pole in two of the great planes, being forced down once by a sudden high wind which fortunately[c] did not develop[d] into a typical storm. This was, as the papers have stated, one of several observation flights;[e] during others of which we tried to discern new topographical features in areas unreached by previous explorers.[f] Our early flights were disappointing in this latter respect;[g] though they afforded us some magnificent examples of the richly fantastic and deceptive mirages of the polar regions, of which our sea voyage had given us some brief foretastes.[h] Distant mountains floated in the sky as enchanted cities, and often the whole white world would dissolve into a gold, silver, and scarlet land of Dunsanian dreams and adventurous expectancy under the magic of the low midnight sun.[i] On cloudy days we had considerable trouble in flying,[j] owing to the tendency of snowy earth and sky to merge into one mystical opalescent void with no visible horizon to mark the junction of the two.

At length we resolved to carry out our original plan of flying 500[k] miles eastward with all four exploring planes and establishing a fresh sub-base at a point which would probably be on the smaller continental division, as we mistakenly conceived it.[l] Geological specimens obtained there would be desirable for purposes of comparison.[m] Our health so far had remained excellent;[n] lime-juice[o] well offsetting the steady diet of tinned and salted food, and temperatures generally above zero

---

[a] 6,] 6th, B
[b] Danforth] Daniels A, B, C, C[c], D
[c] wind which fortunately] wind, which, fortunately, C, D
[d] develop] develope D
[e] flights;] flights, C, D
[f] explorers.] explorers. ¶ C[c]
[g] respect;] respect, C, D
[h] foretastes.] foretastes. ¶ C[c]
[i] sun.] sun. ¶ C[c]
[j] flying,] flying D
[k] 500] five hundred C, D
[l] division, as . . . it.] division. A, B
[m] comparison.] comparison. ¶ C[c]
[n] excellent;] excellent, B; excellent— C, D
[o] lime-juice] lime juice C, D

enabling us to do without our thickest furs.[a] It was now midsummer, and with haste and care we might be able to conclude work by March and avoid a tedious wintering through the long antarctic night. Several savage windstorms had burst upon us from the west, but we had escaped damage through the skill of Atwood in devising rudimentary aëroplane shelters and windbreaks of heavy snow blocks, and reinforcing the principal camp buildings with snow. Our good luck and efficiency had indeed been almost uncanny.

The outside world knew, of course, of our programme,[b] and was told also of Lake's strange and dogged insistence on a westward—or rather, northwestward—prospecting trip before our radical shift to the new base.[c] It seems that he had pondered a great deal, and with alarmingly radical daring,[d] over that triangular striated[e] marking in the slate; reading into it certain contradictions in Nature[f] and geological period which whetted his curiosity to the utmost, and made him avid to sink more borings and blastings in the west-stretching formation to which the exhumed fragments evidently belonged.[g] He was strangely convinced that the marking was the print of some bulky, unknown, and radically unclassifiable organism of considerably advanced evolution, notwithstanding that the rock which bore it was of so vastly ancient a date—Cambrian if not actually pre-Cambrian—as to preclude the probable existence not only of[h] all highly evolved life, but of any life at all above the unicellular or at most the trilobite stage. These fragments, with their odd marking, must have been 500[i] million to a thousand million years old.

[a] furs.] furs. ¶ C[c]
[b] programme,] program, C, D
[c] base.] base. ¶ C[c]
[d] deal, . . . daring,] deal . . . daring B, C[c]
[e] striated] straited D
[f] Nature] nature A, B, C, D
[g] belonged.] belonged. ¶ C[c]
[h] of] on B, C[c]
[i] 500] five hundred C, D

II.

Popular imagination, I judge, responded actively to our wireless bulletins of Lake's start northwestward into regions never trodden by human foot or penetrated by human imagination;[a] though we did not mention his wild hopes of revolutionising[b] the entire sciences of biology and geology.[c] His preliminary sledging and boring journey of January 11–18th[d] with Pabodie and five others—marred by the loss of two dogs in an upset when crossing one of the great pressure-ridges[e] in the ice—had brought up more and more of the archaean[f] slate; and even I was interested by the singular profusion of evident fossil markings in that unbelievably ancient stratum. These markings, however, were of very primitive life-forms[g] involving no great paradox except that any life-forms[h] should occur in rock as definitely pre-Cambrian as this seemed to be; hence I still failed to see the good sense of Lake's demand for an interlude in our time-saving programme[i]—an interlude requiring the use of all four planes, many men, and the whole of the expedition's mechanical apparatus.[j] I did not, in the end, veto the plan;[k] though I decided not to accompany the northwestward party despite Lake's plea for my geological advice. While they were gone, I would remain at the base with Pabodie and five men and work out final plans for the eastward shift. In preparation for this transfer[l] one of the planes had begun to move up a good gasoline supply from McMurdo Sound; but this could wait temporarily. I kept with me one sledge and nine dogs, since it is unwise to be at any time without possible transportation in an utterly tenantless world of aeon-long death.

[a] imagination;] imagination, C, D
[b] revolutionising] revolutionizing C, D
[c] geology.] geology. ¶ C[c]
[d] 11–18th] 11–18 A; 11th to 18th C, D
[e] pressure-ridges] pressure ridges C, D
[f] archaean] Archaean C, D
[g] life-forms] life forms C, D
[h] life-forms] life forms C, D
[i] programme] program C, D
[j] apparatus.] apparatus. ¶ C[c]
[k] plan;] plan, C, D
[l] transfer] transfer, C, D

Lake's sub-expedition[a] into the unknown, as everyone[b] will recall, sent out its own reports from the short-wave[c] transmitters on the planes; these being simultaneously picked up by our apparatus at the southern base and by the *Arkham* at McMurdo Sound, whence they were relayed to the outside world on wave-lengths[d] up to 50[e] metres. The start was made January 22[f] at 4 a.m.;[g] and the first wireless message we received came only two hours later, when Lake spoke of descending and starting a small-scale ice-melting and bore at a point some 300[h] miles away from us. Six hours after that a second and very excited message told of the frantic, beaver-like[i] work whereby a shallow shaft had been sunk and blasted;[j] culminating in the discovery of slate fragments with several markings approximately like the one which had caused the original puzzlement.

Three hours later a brief bulletin announced the resumption of the flight in the teeth of a raw and piercing gale; and when I despatched[k] a message of protest against further hazards, Lake replied curtly that his new specimens made any hazard worth taking.[l] I saw that his excitement had reached the point of mutiny, and that I could do nothing to check this headlong risk of the whole expedition's success; but it was appalling to think of his plunging deeper and deeper into that treacherous and sinister white immensity of tempests and unfathomed mysteries which stretched off for some 1500[m] miles to the half-known, half-suspected coast-line[n] of Queen Mary and Knox Lands.

Then, in about an hour and a half more, came that doubly excited

---

[a] sub-expedition] subexpedition C, D
[b] everyone] every one C, D
[c] short-wave] short-/wave C; shortwave D
[d] wave-lengths] wave lengths C, D
[e] 50] fifty C, D
[f] 22] 22nd C, D
[g] a.m.;] a. m.; C; A.M.; D
[h] 300] three hundred C, D
[i] beaver-like] beaverlike C
[j] blasted;] blasted, C, D
[k] despatched] dispatched C, D
[l] taking.] taking. ¶ Cc
[m] 1500] fifteen hundred C, D
[n] coast-line] coast line C, D

message from Lake's moving plane[a] which almost reversed my sentiments and made me wish I had accompanied the party.[b]

"10:05 p.m.[c] On the wing. After snowstorm, have spied mountain range ahead higher than any hitherto seen. May equal Himalayas[d] allowing for height of plateau. Probable Latitude 76° 15′, Longitude 113° 10′ E. Reaches far as can see to right and left. Suspicion of two smoking cones. All peaks black and bare of snow. Gale blowing off them impedes navigation."

After that Pabodie, the men, and I hung breathlessly over the receiver. Thought of this titanic mountain rampart 700[e] miles away inflamed our deepest sense of adventure; and we rejoiced that our expedition, if not ourselves personally, had been its discoverers. In half an hour Lake called us again.[f]

"Moulton's plane forced down on plateau in foothills, but nobody hurt and perhaps can repair. Shall transfer essentials to other three for return or further moves if necessary, but no more heavy plane travel needed just now. Mountains surpass anything in imagination. Am going up scouting in Carroll's plane, with all weight out. You[g] can't imagine anything like this. Highest peaks must go over 35,000[h] feet. Everest out of the running. Atwood to work out height with theodolite while Carroll and I go up. Probably wrong about cones, for formations look stratified. Possibly pre-Cambrian slate with other strata mixed in. Queer skyline[i] effects—regular sections of cubes clinging to highest peaks. Whole thing marvellous[j] in red-gold light of low sun. Like land of mystery in a dream or gateway to forbidden world of untrodden wonder. Wish you were here to study."

Though it was technically sleeping-time,[k] not one of us listeners thought for a moment of retiring. It must have been a good deal the same

---

[a] plane] plane, C, D
[b] party.] party: C, D
[c] p.m.] p. m. C; P.M. D
[d] Himalayas] Himalayas, C, D
[e] 700] seven hundred C, D
[f] again.] again: C, D
[g] out. You] out. ¶ "You C[c], D
[h] 35,000] thirty-five thousand C, D
[i] skyline] sky line C, D
[j] marvellous] marvelous C, D
[k] sleeping-time,] sleeping time, C, D

at McMurdo Sound, where the supply cache and the *Arkham* were also getting the messages; for Capt.[a] Douglas gave out a call congratulating everybody on the important find, and Sherman, the cache operator, seconded his sentiments. We were sorry, of course, about the damaged aëroplane;[b] but hoped it could be easily mended. Then, at 11 p.m.,[c] came another call from Lake.[d]

"Up with Carroll over highest foothills. Don't dare try really tall peaks in present weather, but shall later. Frightful work climbing, and hard going at this altitude, but worth it. Great range fairly solid, hence can't get any glimpses beyond. Main summits exceed Himalayas, and very queer. Range looks like pre-Cambrian slate, with plain signs of many other upheaved strata. Was wrong about volcanism. Goes farther in either direction than we can see. Swept clear of snow above about 21,000 feet. Odd[e] formations on slopes of highest mountains. Great low square blocks with exactly vertical sides, and rectangular lines of low[f] vertical ramparts, like the old Asian castles clinging to steep mountains in Roerich's paintings. Impressive from distance. Flew close to some, and Carroll thought they were formed of smaller separate pieces, but that is probably weathering. Most edges crumbled and rounded off as if exposed to storms and climate changes for millions of years. Parts,[g] especially upper parts, seem to be of lighter-coloured[h] rock than any visible strata on slopes proper, hence an[i] evidently crystalline origin. Close flying shews[j] many cave-mouths,[k] some unusually regular in outline, square or semicircular.[l] You must come and investigate. Think I saw rampart[m]

[a] Capt.] Captain C, D
[b] aëroplane;] aëroplane, C, D
[c] 11 p.m.,] eleven p. m., C; 11 P.M., D
[d] Lake.] Lake: C, D
[e] 21,000 feet. Odd] twenty-one thousand feet. ¶ "Odd C, D
[f] low] low, C, D
[g] years. Parts,] years. ¶ "Parts, C, D
[h] lighter-coloured] lighter coloured A, B; lighter-colored C, D
[i] an] of D
[j] shews] shows B, C, D [*A illegible*]
[k] cave-mouths,] cave mouths, C, D
[l] semicircular.] semi-circular. D
[m] rampart] rampant D

squarely on top of one peak. Height seems about 30,000 to 35,000[a] feet. Am up 21,500[b] myself, in devilish[c] gnawing cold. Wind whistles and pipes through passes and in and out of caves, but no flying danger so far."

From then on for another half-hour[d] Lake kept up a running fire of comment, and expressed his intention of climbing some of the peaks on foot. I replied that I would join him as soon as he could send a plane, and that Pabodie and I would work out the best gasoline plan—just where and how to concentrate our supply in view of the expedition's altered character.[e] Obviously, Lake's boring operations, as well as his aëroplane activities, would need a great deal delivered for the new base which he was[f] to establish at the foot of the mountains; and it was possible that the eastward flight might not be made after all[g] this season. In connexion[h] with this business I called Capt.[i] Douglas and asked him to get as much as possible out of the ships and up the barrier with the single dog-team[j] we had left there. A direct route across the unknown region between Lake and McMurdo Sound was what we really ought to establish.

Lake called me later to say that he had decided to let the camp stay where Moulton's plane had been forced down, and where repairs had already progressed somewhat. The ice-sheet[k] was very thin, with dark ground here and there visible, and he would sink some borings and blasts at that very point before making any sledge trips or climbing expeditions.[l] He spoke of the ineffable majesty of the whole scene, and the queer state of his sensations at being in the lee of vast[m] silent

[a] 30,000 to 35,000] thirty thousand to thirty-five thousand C, D
[b] 21,500] twenty-one thousand five hundred C; twenty-one thousand, five hundred D
[c] devilish] devilish, C, D
[d] half-hour] half hour C, D
[e] character.] character. ¶ C[c]
[f] need . . . was] require a great deal for the new base which he planned D
[g] made after all] made, after all, C, D
[h] connexion] connection C, D
[i] Capt.] Captain C, D
[j] dog-team] dog team C, D
[k] ice-sheet] ice sheet A, B, C, D
[l] expeditions.] expeditions. ¶ C[c]
[m] vast] vast, C, D

pinnacles[a] whose ranks shot up like a wall reaching the sky at the world's rim.[b] Atwood's theodolite observations had placed the height of the five tallest peaks at from 30,000 to 34,000[c] feet.[d] The windswept nature of the terrain clearly disturbed Lake, for it argued the occasional existence of prodigious gales[e] violent beyond anything we had so far encountered. His camp lay a little more than five miles from where the higher foothills abruptly rose.[f] I could almost trace a note of subconscious alarm in his words—flashed across a glacial void of 700[g] miles—as he urged that we all hasten with the matter and get the strange[h] new region disposed of as soon as possible. He was about to rest now, after a continuous day's work of almost unparalleled[i] speed, strenuousness, and results.

In the morning I had a three-cornered wireless talk with Lake and Capt.[j] Douglas at their widely separated bases; and it[k] was agreed that one of Lake's planes would come to my base for Pabodie, the five men, and myself, as well as for all the fuel it could carry. The rest of the fuel question, depending on our decision about an easterly trip, could wait for a few days;[l] since Lake had enough for immediate camp heat and borings.[m] Eventually the old southern base ought to be restocked;[n] but if we postponed the easterly trip we would not use it till the next summer, and meanwhile[o] Lake must send a plane to explore a direct route between his new mountains and McMurdo Sound.

[a] pinnacles] pinnacles, C[c]

[b] rim.] rim. ¶ C[c]

[c] 30,000 to 34,000] thirty thousand to thirty-four thousand C, D

[d] feet.] feet. ¶ C[c]

[e] gales] gales, C, D

[f] abruptly rose.] rose abruptly. ¶ C [*paragraphing error only corr. by HPL*]; rose abruptly. D

[g] 700] seven hundred C, D

[h] strange] strange, C, D

[i] unparalleled] unparallelled A, B

[j] Capt.] Captain C, D

[k] bases; and it] bases. It C, D

[l] days;] days, C, D

[m] borings.] borings. ¶ C[c]

[n] restocked;] restocked, C; restocked D

[o] and meanwhile] and, meanwhile, C, D

Pabodie and I prepared to close our base for a short or long period, as the case might be. If we wintered in the antarctic we would probably fly straight from Lake's base to the *Arkham* without returning to this spot. Some of our conical tents had already been reinforced by blocks of hard snow, and now we decided to complete the job of making a permanent Esquimau[a] village. Owing to a very liberal tent supply, Lake had with him all that his base would need[b] even after our arrival. I wirelessed that Pabodie and I would be ready for the northwestward move after one day's work and one night's rest.

Our labours,[c] however, were not very steady after 4 p.m.;[d] for about that time Lake began sending in the most extraordinary and excited messages. His working day had started unpropitiously;[e] since an aëroplane survey of the nearly exposed[f] rock surfaces shewed[g] an entire absence of those archaean[h] and primordial strata for which he was looking, and which formed so great a part of the colossal peaks that loomed up at a tantalising[i] distance from the camp.[j] Most of the rocks glimpsed were apparently Jurassic and Comanchian sandstones and Permian and Triassic schists, with now and then a glossy black outcropping suggesting a hard and slaty coal.[k] This rather discouraged Lake, whose plans all hinged on unearthing specimens more than 500[l] million years older. It was clear to him that in order to recover the archaean[m] slate vein in which he had found the odd markings, he would have to make a long sledge trip from these foothills to the steep slopes of the gigantic mountains themselves.

He had resolved, nevertheless, to do some local boring as part of the

---

[a] Esquimau] *om.* C, D
[b] need] need, C, D
[c] labours,] labors, C, D
[d] 4 p.m.;] four p. m., C; 4 P.M., D
[e] unpropitiously;] unpropitiously, C, D
[f] nearly exposed] nearly-exposed D
[g] shewed] showed B, C, D
[h] archaean] Archaean C, D
[i] tantalising] tantalizing C, D
[j] camp.] camp. ¶ C[c]
[k] coal.] coal. ¶ C[c]
[l] 500] five hundred C, D
[m] archaean] Archaean C, D

expedition's general programme;[a] hence[b] set up the drill and put five men to work with it while the rest finished settling the camp and repairing the damaged aëroplane. The softest visible rock—a sandstone about a quarter of a mile from the camp—had been chosen for the first sampling; and the drill made excellent progress without much supplementary blasting.[c] It was about three hours afterward, following the first really heavy blast of the operation, that the shouting of the drill crew was heard; and that young Gedney—the acting foreman—rushed into the camp with the startling news.

They had struck a cave. Early in the boring the sandstone had given place to a vein of Comanchian limestone[d] full of minute fossil cephalopods, corals, echini, and spirifera, and with occasional suggestions of siliceous sponges and marine vertebrate bones—the latter probably of teliosts,[e] sharks, and ganoids.[f] This in itself[g] was important enough, as affording the first vertebrate fossils the expedition had yet secured; but when shortly afterward the drill-head[h] dropped through the stratum into apparent vacancy, a wholly new and doubly intense wave of excitement spread among the excavators.[i] A good-sized blast had laid open the subterrene[j] secret; and now, through a jagged aperture perhaps five feet across and three feet thick, there yawned before the avid searchers a section of shallow limestone hollowing worn more than fifty million years ago by the trickling ground waters of a bygone tropic world.

The hollowed layer was not more than seven or eight feet deep,[k] but extended off indefinitely in all directions and had a fresh, slightly moving air which suggested its membership in an extensive subterranean system. Its roof and floor were abundantly equipped with large stalactites and

---

[a] programme;] program; C, D
[b] hence] hence, he C; hence he D
[c] blasting.] blasting. ¶ C[c]
[d] limestone] limestone, C, D
[e] teliosts,] teleosts, D
[f] ganoids.] ganoids. ¶ C[c]
[g] This in itself] This, in itself, C[c], D
[h] drill-head] drill head C, D
[i] excavators.] excavators. ¶ C[c]
[j] subterrene] subterrane C[c]
[k] deep,] deep D

stalagmites, some of which met in columnar form; but[a] important above all else was the vast deposit of shells and bones[b] which in places nearly choked the passage. Washed down from unknown jungles of Mesozoic tree-ferns[c] and fungi, and forests of Tertiary[d] cycads, fan-palms,[e] and primitive angiosperms, this osseous medley contained representatives of more Cretaceous, Eocene,[f] and other animal species than the greatest palaeontologist[g] could have counted or classified in a year. Molluscs, crustacean armour,[h] fishes, amphibians, reptiles, birds, and early mammals—great and small, known and unknown.[i] No wonder Gedney ran back to the camp shouting, and no wonder everyone[j] else dropped work and rushed headlong through the biting cold to where the tall derrick marked a new-found gateway to secrets of inner earth and vanished aeons.

When Lake had satisfied the first keen edge of his curiosity he scribbled a message in his notebook and had young Moulton run back to the camp to despatch[k] it by wireless. This was my first word of the discovery, and it told of the identification of early shells, bones of ganoids and placoderms, remnants of labyrinthodonts and thecodonts,[l] great mososaur[m] skull fragments, dinosaur vertebrae and armour-plates,[n] pterodactyl teeth and wing-bones,[o] archaeopteryx debris,[p] Miocene[q] sharks' teeth, primitive bird-skulls, and skulls, vertebrae, and other[r] bones of archaic mammals

---

[a] form; but] form. ¶ But C[c]; form: but D

[b] bones] bones, C[c], D

[c] Mesozoic tree-ferns] mesozoic tree-terns A, B; Mesozoic tree ferns C, D

[d] Tertiary] tertiary A, B

[e] fan-palms,] fan palms, D

[f] Cretaceous, Eocene,] cretaceous, eocene, A, B

[g] palaeontologist] paleontologist C, D

[h] Molluscs, . . . armour,] Mollusks, . . . armor, C, D

[i] unknown.] unknown. ¶ C[c]

[j] everyone] every one C, D

[k] despatch] dispatch C, D

[l] labyrinthodonts and thecodonts,] labyrinthodonta and thecoïidea, C[c]

[m] mososaur] mosasaur C, D

[n] armour-plates,] armor plates, C, D

[o] wing-bones,] wing bones, C, D

[p] archaeopteryx debris,] Archaeopteryx débris, C; Archaeopteryx debris, D

[q] Miocene] miocene A, B

[r] bird-skulls, . . . other] bird skulls, and other D

such as palaeotheres,[a] xiphodons,[b] dinocerases,[c] eohippi, oreodons,[d] and titanotheres.[e] There was nothing as recent as a mastodon, elephant, true camel, deer, or bovine animal; hence Lake concluded that the last deposits had occurred during the Oligocene age,[f] and that the hollowed stratum had lain in its present dried, dead, and inaccessible state for at least thirty million years.

On the other hand, the prevalence of very early life-forms[g] was singular in the highest degree. Though the limestone formation was, on the evidence of such typical imbedded fossils as ventriculites, positively and unmistakably Comanchian and not a particle earlier;[h] the free fragments in the hollow space included a surprising proportion from organisms hitherto considered as peculiar to far older periods—even rudimentary fishes, molluscs,[i] and corals as remote as the Silurian or Ordovician.[j] The inevitable inference was that in this part of the world there had been a remarkable and unique degree of continuity between the life of over 300[k] million years ago and that of only thirty million years ago. How far this continuity had extended beyond the Oligocene age[l] when the cavern was closed,[m] was of course past all speculation. In any event, the coming of the frightful ice in the Pleistocene some 500,000[n] years ago—a mere yesterday as compared with the age of this cavity—must have put an end to any of the primal forms which had locally managed to outlive their common terms.

---

[a] palaeotheres,] Palaeotheres, C
[b] xiphodons,] Xiphodon, C, D
[c] dinocerases,] *om.* C, D
[d] eohippi, oreodons,] Eohippi, Oreodons, C, D
[e] titanotheres.] Titanotheriidae. ¶ C[c]
[f] age,] Age, C, D
[g] life-forms] life forms C, D
[h] earlier;] earlier, D
[i] molluscs,] mollusks, C, D
[j] Ordovician.] Ordovician. ¶ C[c]
[k] 300] three hundred A, B, C, D
[l] age] Age C, D
[m] closed,] closed C, D
[n] 500,000] five hundred thousand C, D

Lake was not content to let his first message stand, but had another bulletin written and despatched[a] across the snow to the camp before Moulton could get back. After that Moulton stayed at the wireless in one of the planes;[b] transmitting to me—and to the *Arkham* for relaying to the outside world—the frequent postscripts which Lake sent him by a succession of messengers.[c] Those who followed the newspapers will remember the excitement created among men of science by that afternoon's reports—reports which have finally led, after all these years,[d] to the organisation[e] of that very Starkweather-Moore Expedition which I am so anxious to dissuade from its purposes. I had better give the messages literally as Lake sent them, and as our base operator McTighe translated them from his[f] pencil shorthand.[g]

"Fowler makes discovery of highest importance in sandstone and limestone fragments from blasts. Several distinct triangular striated prints like those in archaean[h] slate, proving that source survived from over 600[i] million years ago to Comanchian times without more than moderate morphological changes and decrease in average size.[j] Comanchian prints apparently more primitive or decadent, if anything, than older ones. Emphasise[k] importance of discovery in press. Will mean to biology what Einstein has meant to mathematics and physics. Joins up with my previous work and amplifies conclusions. Appears[l] to indicate, as I suspected, that earth has seen whole cycle or cycles of organic life before known one that begins with archaeozoic[m] cells. Was evolved and specialised[n] not later than[o] thousand million years ago, when planet was young and recently

[a] despatched] dispatched C, D
[b] planes;] planes, C, D
[c] messengers.] messengers. ¶ C[c]
[d] reports—. . . years,] reports—reports leading A, B
[e] organisation] organization C, D
[f] his] the D
[g] shorthand.] shorthand: C, D
[h] archaean] Archaean D
[i] 600] six hundred C, D
[j] size.] size, D
[k] Emphasise] Emphasize C, D
[l] Appears] ¶ Appears C; ¶ "Appears D
[m] archaeozoic] Archaeozoic C, D
[n] specialised] specialized C, D
[o] than] than a C, D

uninhabitable for any life-forms[a] or normal protoplasmic structure. Question arises when, where, and how development took place."[b]

"Later. Examining certain skeletal fragments of large land and marine saurians and primitive mammals, find singular local wounds or injuries to bony structure not attributable to any known predatory or carnivorous animal of any period. Of two sorts—straight, penetrant bores, and apparently hacking incisions. One or two cases of cleanly severed bone.[c] Not many specimens affected. Am sending to camp for electric torches. Will extend search area underground by hacking away stalactites."[d]

"Still later. Have found peculiar soapstone fragment about six inches across and an inch and a half thick, wholly unlike any visible local formation. Greenish,[e] but no evidences to place its period. Has curious smoothness and regularity. Shaped like five-pointed star with tips broken off, and signs of other cleavage at inward angles and in centre of surface. Small, smooth depression in centre[f] of unbroken surface. Arouses much curiosity as to source and weathering. Probably some freak of water action. Carroll, with magnifier, thinks he can make out additional markings of geologic significance. Groups of tiny dots in regular patterns. Dogs growing uneasy as we work, and seem to hate this soapstone. Must see if it has any peculiar odour.[g] Will report again when Mills gets back with light and we start on underground area."[h]

"10:15 p.m.[i] Important discovery. Orrendorf and Watkins, working underground at 9:45 with light, found monstrous barrel-shaped fossil of wholly unknown nature; probably vegetable unless overgrown specimen of unknown marine radiata. Tissue evidently preserved by mineral salts. Tough

[a] life-forms] life forms C, D
[b] "Fowler . . . place."] Fowler . . . place. C
[c] bone.] bones. C, D
[d] "Later. . . . stalactites."] Later. . . . stalactites. C
[e] formation. Greenish,] formation—greenish, C, D
[f] centre . . . centre] center . . . center C, D
[g] odour.] odor. C, D
[h] "Still . . . area."] Still . . . area. C
[i] p.m.] p. m. C; P.M. D

as leather, but astonishing flexibility retained in places. Marks of broken-off[a] parts at ends and around sides. Six feet end to end, 3.5 feet central diameter, tapering to 1[b] foot at each end. Like a barrel with five bulging ridges in place of staves. Lateral breakages, as of thinnish stalks, are at equator in middle of these ridges. In furrows between ridges are curious growths. Combs[c] or wings that fold up and spread out like fans. All greatly damaged but one, which gives almost 7-foot[d] wing spread. Arrangement reminds one of certain monsters of primal myth, especially fabled Elder Things in 'Necronomicon'. These[e] wings seem to be membraneous,[f] stretched on framework[g] of glandular tubing. Apparent minute orifices in frame tubing at wing tips. Ends of body shrivelled,[h] giving no clue to interior or to what has been broken off there. Must dissect when we get back to camp. Can't decide whether vegetable or animal. Many features obviously of almost incredible primitiveness. Have set all hands cutting stalactites and looking for further specimens. Additional scarred bones found, but these must wait. Having trouble with dogs. They can't endure the new specimen, and would probably tear it to pieces if we didn't keep it at a distance from them."[i]

"11:30 p.m.[j] Attention, Dyer, Pabodie, Douglas. Matter of highest—I might say transcendent—importance. *Arkham* must relay to Kingsport Head Station at once. Strange barrel growth is the archaean[k] thing that left prints in rocks. Mills, Boudreau, and Fowler discover cluster of thirteen more at underground point forty feet from aperture. Mixed with curiously rounded and configured soapstone fragments smaller than one previously found— star-shaped[l] but no marks of breakage except at some of the points. Of[m] organic specimens, eight apparently perfect, with all appendages. Have

[a] broken-off] broken off A, B
[b] 3.5 . . . 1] three and five tenths . . . one C; three and five-tenths . . . one D
[c] growths. Combs] growths—combs C, D
[d] 7-foot] seven-foot C, D
[e] 'Necronomicon'. These] *Necronomicon.* These A, B; *Necronomicon.* ¶ These C; *Necronomicon.* ¶ "There D
[f] membraneous,] membranous, C[c], D
[g] framework] frame work D
[h] shrivelled,] shriveled, C, D
[i] 10:15 . . . them."] 10:15 . . . them. C
[j] "11:30 p.m.] 11:30 p. m. C; 11:30 P.M. D
[k] archaean] Archaean D
[l] star-shaped] star-shaped, C, D
[m] Of] ¶ Of C; ¶ "Of D

brought all to surface, leading off dogs to distance. They cannot stand the things. Give close attention to description and repeat back for accuracy. Papers must get this right.

"Objects[a] are eight feet long all over. Six-foot[b] five-ridged barrel torso 3.5 feet central diameter, 1[c] foot end diameters. Dark grey,[d] flexible, and infinitely tough. Seven-foot membraneous[e] wings of same colour,[f] found folded, spread out of furrows between ridges. Wing framework tubular or glandular, of lighter grey,[g] with orifices at wing tips. Spread wings have serrated edge. Around equator, one at central apex of each of the five vertical, stave-like ridges,[h] are five systems of light-grey[i] flexible arms or tentacles found tightly folded to torso but expansible to maximum length of over 3[j] feet. Like arms of primitive crinoid. Single stalks 3[k] inches diameter branch after 6[l] inches into five sub-stalks,[m] each of which branches after 8[n] inches into five[o] small, tapering tentacles or tendrils, giving each stalk a total of 25[p] tentacles.

"At[q] top of torso blunt[r] bulbous neck of lighter grey[s] with gill-like suggestions[t] holds yellowish five-pointed starfish-shaped apparent head covered with 3-inch[u] wiry cilia of various prismatic colours. Head[v] thick

---

[a] "Objects] Objects C
[b] Six-foot] Six-foot, C, D
[c] 3.5 . . . 1] three and five tenths . . . one C; three and five-tenths . . . one D
[d] grey,] gray, C, D
[e] membraneous] membranous C, D
[f] colour,] color, C, D
[g] grey,] gray, C, D
[h] stave-like ridges,] stavelike ridges, C; stave-like ridges D
[i] light-grey] light grey A, B; light gray C; light-gray D
[j] 3] three C, D
[k] 3] three A, B, C, D
[l] 6] six C, D
[m] sub-stalks,] substalks, C, D
[n] 8] eight C, D
[o] five] *om.* D
[p] 25] twenty-five C, D
[q] "At] At C
[r] blunt] blunt, C, D
[s] grey] gray C, D
[t] suggestions] suggestions, C, D
[u] 3-inch] three-inch C, D
[v] colours. Head] colors. ¶ Head C; colors. ¶ "Head D

and puffy, about 2[a] feet point to point, with 3-inch[b] flexible yellowish tubes projecting from each point. Slit in exact centre[c] of top probably breathing aperture. At end of each tube is spherical expansion where yellowish membrane rolls back on handling to reveal glassy, red-irised globe, evidently an eye. Five[d] slightly longer reddish tubes start from inner angles of starfish-shaped head and end in sac-like[e] swellings of same colour which upon pressure[f] open to bell-shaped orifices 2[g] inches maximum diameter and lined with sharp[h] white tooth-like projections. Probable[i] mouths. All these tubes, cilia, and points of starfish-head[j] found folded tightly down; tubes and points clinging to bulbous neck and torso. Flexibility surprising despite vast toughness.

"At[k] bottom of torso[l] rough but dissimilarly functioning counterparts of head arrangements exist. Bulbous light-grey pseudo-neck,[m] without gill suggestions, holds greenish five-pointed starfish-arrangement.[n] Tough,[o] muscular arms 4 feet long and tapering from 7[p] inches diameter at base to about 2.5[q] at point. To each point is attached small end of a greenish five-veined membraneous[r] triangle 8 inches long and 6[s] wide at farther end. This is the paddle, fin, or pseudo-foot[t] which has made prints in rocks from a thousand million to 50 or 60[u] million years old. From[v] inner

[a] 2] two C, D
[b] 3-inch] three-inch C, D
[c] centre] center C, D
[d] Five] ¶ Five C; ¶ "Five D
[e] sac-like] saclike C, D
[f] colour . . . pressure] color which, upon pressure, C, D
[g] 2] two C, D
[h] sharp] sharp, C, D
[i] projections. Probable] projections—probable C; projections—probably D
[j] starfish-head] starfish-head, A, B; starfish head, C, D
[k] "At] At C
[l] torso] torso, C, D
[m] light-grey pseudo-neck,] light-gray pseudoneck, C, D
[n] starfish-arrangement.] starfish arrangement. C, D
[o] Tough,] ¶ Tough, C; ¶ "Tough, D
[p] 4 . . . 7] four . . . seven C, D
[q] 2.5] two and five tenths C; two and five-tenths D
[r] membraneous] membranous D
[s] 8 . . . 6] eight . . . six C, D
[t] pseudo-foot] pseudofoot C, D
[u] 50 or 60] fifty or sixty C, D
[v] From] ¶ From C; ¶ "From D

angles of starfish-arrangement[a] project 2-foot[b] reddish tubes tapering from 3 inches diameter at base to 1[c] at tip. Orifices at tips. All these parts infinitely tough and leathery, but extremely flexible. Four-foot arms with paddles undoubtedly used for locomotion of some sort, marine or otherwise. When moved, display suggestions of exaggerated muscularity. As found, all these projections tightly folded over pseudo-neck[d] and end of torso, corresponding to projections at other end.

"Cannot[e] yet assign positively to animal or vegetable kingdom, but odds now favour[f] animal. Probably represents incredibly advanced evolution of radiata without loss of certain primitive features. Echinoderm resemblances unmistakable despite local contradictory evidences. Wing[g] structure puzzles in view of probable[h] marine habitat, but may have use in water navigation. Symmetry is curiously vegetable-like,[i] suggesting vegetable's essentially[j] up-and-down structure rather than animal's fore-and-aft structure. Fabulously early date of evolution, preceding even simplest archaean protozoa[k] hitherto known, baffles all conjecture as to origin.

"Complete[l] specimens have such uncanny resemblance to certain creatures of primal myth that suggestion of ancient existence outside antarctic becomes inevitable. Dyer and Pabodie have read 'Necronomicon'[m] and seen Clark Ashton Smith's nightmare paintings based on text, and will understand when I speak of Elder Things supposed to have created all earth-life[n] as jest or mistake. Students have always thought conception formed from morbid imaginative treatment of very ancient tropical radiata. Also like prehistoric folklore things Wilmarth has spoken of—Cthulhu cult appendages, etc.

"Vast[o] field of study opened. Deposits probably of late Cretaceous or

[a] starfish-arrangement] starfish arrangement C, D
[b] 2-foot] two-foot C, D
[c] 3 . . . 1] three . . . one A, B, C, D
[d] pseudo-neck] pseudoneck C, D
[e] "Cannot] Cannot C
[f] favour] favor C, D
[g] Wing] ¶ Wing C; ¶ "Wing D
[h] probable] probably B
[i] vegetable-like,] vegetablelike, C, D
[j] essentially] essential C, D
[k] archaean protozoa] archaean Protozoa C; Archaean protozoa D
[l] "Complete] Complete C
[m] 'Necronomicon'] *Necronomicon* A, B, C, D
[n] earth-life] earth life C, D
[o] "Vast] Vast C

early Eocene period, judging from associated specimens. Massive stalagmites deposited above them. Hard work hewing out, but toughness prevented damage. State of preservation miraculous, evidently owing to limestone action. No more found so far, but will resume search later. Job now to get fourteen[a] huge specimens to camp without dogs, which bark furiously and can't be trusted near them. With[b] nine men—three left to guard the dogs—we ought to manage the three sledges fairly well, though wind is bad. Must establish plane communication with McMurdo Sound and begin shipping material. But I've got to dissect one of these things before we take any rest. Wish I had a real laboratory here. Dyer better kick himself for having tried to stop my westward trip. First the world's greatest mountains, and then this. If this last isn't the high spot of the expedition, I don't know what is. We're made scientifically. Congrats, Pabodie, on the drill that opened up the cave. Now will *Arkham* please repeat description?"[c]

The sensations of Pabodie and myself at receipt of this report were almost beyond description, nor were our companions much behind us in enthusiasm. McTighe, who had hastily translated a few high spots as they came from the droning receiving set, wrote out the entire message from his shorthand version[d] as soon as Lake's operator signed off.[e] All appreciated the epoch-making significance of the discovery, and I sent Lake congratulations as soon as the *Arkham's* operator had repeated back the descriptive parts as requested; and my example was followed by Sherman from his station at the McMurdo Sound supply cache, as well as by Capt.[f] Douglas of the *Arkham*.[g] Later, as head of the expedition, I added some remarks to be relayed through the *Arkham* to the outside world. Of course, rest was an absurd thought amidst this excitement; and my only wish was to get to Lake's camp as quickly as I could. It disappointed me when he sent word that a rising mountain gale made early aërial travel impossible.

But within an hour and a half interest again rose to banish

---

[a] fourteen] 14 A, B
[b] With] ¶ With C; ¶ "With D
[c] description?"] description? C
[d] version] version, C[c]
[e] off.] off. ¶ C[c]
[f] Capt.] Captain C, D
[g] *Arkham.*] *Arkham.* ¶ C[c]

disappointment. Lake was sending more messages, and[a] told of the completely[b] successful transportation of the fourteen great specimens to the camp. It had been a hard pull, for the things were surprisingly heavy; but nine men had accomplished it very neatly. Now some of the party were hurriedly building a snow corral at a safe distance from the camp, to which the dogs could be brought for greater convenience in feeding. The specimens were laid out on the hard snow near the camp, save for one on which Lake was making crude attempts at dissection.

This dissection seemed to be a greater task than had been expected; for[c] despite the heat of a gasoline stove in the newly raised[d] laboratory tent, the deceptively flexible tissues of the chosen specimen—a powerful and intact one—lost nothing of their more than leathery toughness. Lake was puzzled as to how he might make the requisite incisions without violence destructive enough to upset all the structural niceties he was looking for.[e] He had, it is true, seven more perfect specimens; but these were too few to use up recklessly unless the cave might later yield an unlimited supply. Accordingly he removed the specimen and dragged in one which, though having remnants of the starfish-arrangements[f] at both ends, was badly crushed and partly disrupted along one of the great torso furrows.

Results, quickly reported over the wireless, were baffling and provocative indeed. Nothing like delicacy or accuracy was possible with instruments hardly able to cut the anomalous tissue, but the little that was achieved left us all awed and bewildered.[g] Existing biology would have to be wholly revised, for this thing was no product of any cell-growth science knows about. There had been scarcely any mineral replacement, and despite an age of perhaps forty million years the internal organs were wholly intact. The leathery, undeteriorative, and almost indestructible quality was an inherent attribute of the thing's form of organisation;[h]

---

[a] Lake . . . and] Lake, sending more messages, C, D

[b] completely] *om.* A, B [*revision by HPL in C?*]

[c] expected; for] expected, for, C, D

[d] newly raised] newly-raised B

[e] for.] for. ¶ C[c]

[f] starfish-arrangements] starfish arrangements A, B, C, D

[g] bewildered.] bewildered. ¶ C[c]

[h] organisation;] organization, C, D

and pertained to some palaeogean[a] cycle of invertebrate evolution utterly beyond our powers of speculation.[b] At first all that Lake found was dry, but as the heated tent produced its thawing effect, organic moisture of pungent and offensive odour[c] was encountered toward the thing's uninjured side. It was not blood, but a thick, dark-green[d] fluid apparently answering the same purpose. By the time Lake reached this stage all 37[e] dogs had been brought to the still uncompleted corral near the camp;[f] and even at that distance set up a savage barking and show of restlessness at the acrid, diffusive smell.

Far from helping to place the strange entity, this provisional dissection merely deepened its mystery. All guesses about its external members had been correct, and on the evidence of these one could hardly hesitate to call the thing animal;[g] but internal inspection brought up so many vegetable evidences that Lake was left hopelessly at sea. It had digestion and circulation, and eliminated waste matter through the reddish tubes of its starfish-shaped base.[h] Cursorily, one would say that its respiratory apparatus handled oxygen rather than carbon dioxide; and there were odd evidences of air-storage[i] chambers and methods of shifting respiration from the external orifice to at least two other fully developed breathing-systems[j]—gills and pores.[k] Clearly, it was amphibian and probably adapted to long airless hibernation-periods[l] as well. Vocal organs seemed present in connexion[m] with the main respiratory system, but they presented anomalies beyond immediate solution. Articulate speech, in the sense of syllable-utterance,[n] seemed barely

[a] palaeogean] paleocene C [*corr. by HPL to* paleogean]; paleogean D
[b] speculation.] speculation. ¶ C[c]
[c] odour] odor C, D
[d] dark-green] dark green A, B
[e] 37] thirty-seven C, D
[f] camp;] camp, C, D
[g] animal;] animal, C[c]
[h] base.] base. ¶ C[c]
[i] air-storage] air storage A, B
[j] breathing-systems] breathing systems C, D
[k] pores.] pores. ¶ C[c]
[l] hibernation-periods] hibernation periods C, D
[m] connexion] connection C, D
[n] syllable-utterance,] syllable utterance, C, D

conceivable;[a] but musical piping notes covering a wide range were highly probable. The muscular system was almost preternaturally[b] developed.

The nervous system was so complex and highly developed as to leave Lake aghast. Though excessively primitive and archaic in some respects, the thing had a set of ganglial[c] centres[d] and connectives arguing the very extremes of specialised[e] development.[f] Its five-lobed brain was surprisingly advanced;[g] and there were signs of a sensory equipment, served in part through the wiry cilia of the head, involving factors alien to any other terrestrial organism. Probably it had[h] more than five senses, so that its habits could not be predicted from any existing analogy.[i] It must, Lake thought, have been a creature of keen sensitiveness and delicately differentiated functions in its primal world;[j] much like the ants and bees of today.[k] It reproduced like the vegetable cryptogams,[l] especially the pteridophytes;[m] having spore-cases[n] at the tips of the wings and evidently developing from a thallus or prothallus.

But to give it a name at this stage was mere folly. It looked like a radiate, but was clearly something more. It was partly vegetable, but had three-fourths of the essentials of animal structure. That it was marine in origin, its symmetrical contour and certain other attributes clearly indicated; yet one could not be exact as to the limit of its later adaptations. The wings, after all, held a persistent suggestion of the aërial.[o] How it could have undergone its tremendously complex evolution on a

[a] conceivable;] conceivable, C, D
[b] preternaturally] pre-/naturally C; prematurely D
[c] ganglial] gangliar C[c]
[d] centres] centers C, D
[e] specialised] specialized C, D
[f] development.] development. ¶ C[c]
[g] advanced;] advanced, C, D
[h] had] has D
[i] analogy.] analogy. ¶ C[c]
[j] world;] world— C, D
[k] today.] to-day. C
[l] cryptogams,] crytogams, D
[m] pteridophytes;] pteridophyta, C; Pteridophyta, D
[n] spore-cases] spore cases C, D
[o] aërial.] aërial. ¶ C[c]

new-born earth in time to leave prints in archaean[a] rocks was so far beyond conception as to make Lake whimsically recall the primal myths about Great Old Ones who filtered down from the stars and concocted earth-life[b] as a joke or mistake; and the wild tales of cosmic hill things from Outside[c] told by a folklorist colleague in Miskatonic's English department.

Naturally, he considered the possibility of the pre-Cambrian prints'[d] having been made by a less evolved ancestor of the present specimens;[e] but quickly rejected this too facile[f] theory upon considering the advanced structural qualities of the older fossils. If anything, the later contours shewed[g] decadence rather than higher evolution.[h] The size of the pseudo-feet[i] had decreased, and the whole morphology seemed coarsened and simplified. Moreover, the nerves and organs just examined[j] held singular suggestions of retrogression from forms still more complex. Atrophied and vestigial parts were surprisingly prevalent. Altogether, little could be said to have been solved; and Lake fell back on mythology for a provisional name—jocosely dubbing his finds "The Elder Ones".[k]

At about 2:30 a.m.,[l] having decided to postpone further work and get a little rest, he covered the dissected organism with a tarpaulin, emerged from the laboratory tent, and studied the intact specimens with renewed interest.[m] The ceaseless antarctic sun had begun to limber up their tissues a trifle, so that the head-points[n] and tubes of two

---

[a] archaean] Archaean D
[b] earth-life] earth life C, D
[c] Outside] outside C, D
[d] prints'] prints B, C[c], D
[e] specimens;] specimens, C, D
[f] too facile] too-facile C, D
[g] shewed] showed B, C, D [*A illegible*]
[h] evolution.] evolution. ¶ C[c]
[i] pseudo-feet] pseudofeet C, D
[j] organs . . . examined] organs, . . . examined, C[c]
[k] Ones".] Ones." C, D
[l] 2:30 a.m.,] two-thirty a. m., C; two-thirty A.M., D
[m] interest.] interest. ¶ C[c]
[n] head-points] head points C, D

or three shewed[a] signs of unfolding; but Lake did not believe there was any danger of immediate decomposition in the almost sub-zero[b] air. He did, however, move all the undissected specimens closer[c] together and throw a spare tent over them in order to keep off the direct solar rays. That would also help to keep their possible scent away from the dogs, whose hostile unrest was really becoming a problem[d] even at their substantial distance and behind the higher and higher snow walls which an increased quota of the men were hastening to raise around their quarters.[e] He had to weight down the corners of the tent-cloth[f] with heavy blocks of snow to hold it in place amidst the rising gale, for the titan mountains seemed about to deliver some gravely severe blasts. Early apprehensions about sudden antarctic[g] winds were revived, and under Atwood's supervision precautions were taken to bank the tents, new dog-corral,[h] and crude aëroplane shelters with snow[i] on the mountainward side. These latter shelters, begun with hard snow blocks during odd moments, were by no means as high as they should have been; and Lake finally detached all hands from other tasks to work on them.

It was after four when Lake at last prepared to sign off and advised us all to share the rest period his outfit would take when the shelter walls were a little higher. He held some friendly chat with Pabodie over the ether, and repeated his praise of the really marvellous[j] drills that had helped him make his discovery. Atwood also sent greetings and praises.[k] I gave Lake a warm word of congratulation, owning up that he was right about the western trip;[l] and we all agreed to get in touch by wireless at

[a] shewed] showed B, C, D
[b] sub-zero] subzero C; sub-/zero D
[c] closer] close D
[d] problem] problem, C, D
[e] quarters.] quarters. ¶ C[c]
[f] tent-cloth] tent cloth C, D
[g] antarctic] Antarctic D
[h] dog-corral,] dog corral, C, D
[i] snow] snow, C[c]
[j] marvellous] marvelous C, D
[k] praises.] praises. ¶ C[c]
[l] trip;] trip, C, D

ten in the morning. If the gale was then over, Lake would send a plane for the party at my base. Just before retiring I despatched[a] a final message to the *Arkham*[b] with instructions about toning down the day's news for the outside world, since the full details seemed radical enough to rouse a wave of incredulity until further substantiated.

III.

None of us, I imagine, slept very heavily or continuously that morning; for both[c] the excitement of Lake's discovery and the mounting fury of the wind were against such a thing. So savage was the blast,[d] even where we were, that we could not help wondering how much worse it was at Lake's camp, directly under the vast unknown peaks that bred and delivered it.[e] McTighe was awake at ten[f] o'clock and tried to get Lake on the wireless, as agreed, but some electrical condition in the disturbed air to the westward seemed to prevent communication. We did, however, get the *Arkham,* and Douglas told me that he had likewise been vainly trying to reach Lake. He had not known about the wind, for very little was blowing at McMurdo Sound[g] despite its persistent rage where we were.

Throughout the day we all listened anxiously and tried to get Lake at intervals, but invariably without results. About noon a positive frenzy of wind stampeded out of the west, causing us to fear for the safety of our camp; but it eventually died down, with only a moderate relapse at 2 p.m.[h] After three[i] o'clock it was very quiet, and we redoubled our efforts to get Lake. Reflecting that he had four planes, each provided with an excellent short-wave outfit, we could not imagine any ordinary accident capable of crippling all his wireless equipment at

---

[a] despatched] dispatched C, D
[b] *Arkham*] *Arkham,* C[c]
[c] morning; for both] morning. Both C, D
[d] blast,] blast B, C[c]
[e] it.] it. ¶ C[c]
[f] ten] 10 A, B
[g] Sound] Sound, C, D
[h] 2 p.m.] two p. m. ¶ C [*paragraphing error corr. by HPL*]; 2 P.M. D
[i] three] 3 A, B

once. Nevertheless the stony silence continued;[a] and when we thought of the delirious force the wind must have had in his locality we could not help making the most direful conjectures.

By six[b] o'clock our fears had become intense and definite, and after a wireless consultation with Douglas and Thorfinnssen I resolved to take steps toward investigation. The fifth aëroplane, which we had left at the McMurdo Sound supply cache with Sherman and two sailors, was in good shape and ready for instant use; and it seemed that the very emergency for which it had been saved was now upon us.[c] I got Sherman by wireless and ordered him to join me with the plane and the two sailors at the southern base as quickly as possible;[d] the air conditions being apparently highly favourable.[e] We then talked over the personnel of the coming investigation party;[f] and decided that we would include all hands, together with the sledge and dogs which I had kept with me. Even so great a load would not be too much for one of the huge planes built to our especial[g] orders for heavy machinery transportation. At intervals I still tried to reach Lake with the wireless, but all to no purpose.

Sherman, with the sailors Gunnarsson and Larsen, took off at 7:30;[h] and reported a quiet flight from several points on the wing. They arrived at our base at midnight, and all hands at once discussed the next move. It was risky business sailing over the antarctic in a single aëroplane without any line of bases, but no one drew back from what seemed like the plainest necessity. We turned in at two[i] o'clock for a brief rest after some preliminary loading of the plane, but were up again in four hours to finish the loading and packing.

At 7:15 a.m.,[j] January 25th,[k] we started flying northwestward under

[a] continued;] continued, C, D
[b] six] 6 A, B
[c] us.] us. ¶ C[c]
[d] possible;] possible, C, D
[e] favourable.] favorable. C, D
[f] party;] party, C, D
[g] especial] special C, D
[h] 7:30;] seven thirty; C; seven-thirty; D
[i] two] 2 A, B
[j] 7:15 a.m.,] seven fifteen a. m., C; 7:15 A.M., D
[k] 25th,] 25, A

McTighe's pilotage with ten men, seven[a] dogs, a sledge, a fuel and food supply, and other items including the plane's wireless outfit. The atmosphere was clear, fairly quiet, and relatively mild in temperature;[b] and we anticipated very little trouble in reaching the latitude and longitude designated by Lake as the site of his camp. Our apprehensions were over what we might find, or fail to find, at the end of our journey;[c] for silence continued to answer all calls despatched[d] to the camp.

Every incident of that four-and-a-half-hour flight is burned into my recollection because of its crucial position in my life. It marked my loss, at the age of fifty-four,[e] of all that peace and balance which the normal mind possesses through its accustomed conception of external Nature and Nature's[f] laws.[g] Thenceforward the ten of us—but the student Danforth and myself above all others—were to face a hideously amplified world of lurking horrors which nothing can erase from our emotions, and which we would refrain from sharing with mankind in general if we could. The newspapers have printed the bulletins we sent from the moving plane;[h] telling of our non-stop[i] course, our two battles with treacherous upper-air gales, our glimpse of the broken surface where Lake had sunk his mid-journey shaft three days before, and our sight of a group of those strange fluffy snow-cylinders[j] noted by Amundsen and Byrd as rolling in the wind across the endless leagues of frozen plateau.[k] There came a point, though, when our sensations could not be conveyed in any words the press would understand;[l] and a later[m] point when we had to adopt an actual rule of strict censorship.

---

[a] ten . . . seven] 10 . . . 7 A, B
[b] temperature;] temperature, C, D
[c] journey;] journey, C, D
[d] despatched] dispatched C, D
[e] fifty-four,] 54, A, B
[f] Nature and Nature's] nature and nature's A, B, C, D
[g] laws.] laws. ¶ Cc
[h] plane;] plane, C, D
[i] non-stop] nonstop C, D
[j] snow-cylinders] snow cylinders C, D
[k] plateau.] plateau. ¶ Cc
[l] understand;] understand, C, D
[m] later] latter D

The sailor Larsen was first to spy the jagged line of witch-like[a] cones and pinnacles ahead, and his shouts sent everyone[b] to the windows of the great cabined plane. Despite our speed, they were very slow in gaining prominence; hence we knew that they must be infinitely far off, and visible only because of their abnormal height.[c] Little by little, however, they rose grimly into the western sky; allowing us to distinguish various bare, bleak, blackish summits, and to catch the curious sense of phantasy[d] which they inspired as seen in the reddish antarctic light against the provocative background of iridescent ice-dust clouds. In the whole spectacle there was a persistent, pervasive hint of stupendous secrecy and potential revelation;[e] as if these stark, nightmare spires marked the pylons of a frightful gateway into forbidden spheres of dream, and complex gulfs of remote time, space, and ultra-dimensionality.[f] I could not help feeling that they were evil things—mountains of madness whose farther slopes looked out over some accursed ultimate abyss.[g] That seething, half-luminous cloud-background[h] held ineffable suggestions of a vague, ethereal *beyondness*[i] far more than terrestrially spatial;[j] and gave appalling reminders of the utter remoteness, separateness, desolation, and aeon-long death of this untrodden and unfathomed austral world.

It was young Danforth who drew our notice to the curious regularities of the higher mountain skyline[k]—regularities like clinging fragments of perfect cubes, which Lake had mentioned in his messages, and which indeed justified his comparison with the dream-like[l] suggestions of primordial temple-ruins[m] on cloudy Asian mountaintops

---

[a] witch-like] witchlike A, B, C, D
[b] everyone] every one C
[c] height.] height. ¶ C[c]
[d] phantasy] fantasy D
[e] revelation;] revelation. It was C, D
[f] ultra-dimensionality.] ultradimensionality. C, D
[g] abyss.] abyss. ¶ C[c]
[h] cloud-background] cloud background C, D
[i] *beyondness*] beyondness C, D
[j] spatial;] spatial, C, D
[k] skyline] sky line C, D
[l] dream-like] dreamlike A, B, C, D
[m] temple-ruins] temple ruins, C, D [*comma removed by HPL in C*]

so subtly and strangely painted by Roerich.[a] There was indeed something hauntingly Roerich-like[b] about this whole unearthly continent of mountainous mystery. I had felt it in October when we first caught sight of Victoria Land, and I felt it afresh now. I felt, too, another wave of uneasy consciousness of archaean[c] mythical resemblances;[d] of how disturbingly this lethal realm corresponded to the evilly famed plateau of Leng in the primal writings.[e] Mythologists have placed Leng in Central Asia;[f] but the racial memory of man—or of his predecessors—is long, and it may well be that certain tales have come down from lands and mountains and temples of horror earlier than Asia and earlier than any human world we know.[g] A few daring mystics have hinted at a pre-Pleistocene origin for the fragmentary Pnakotic Manuscripts, and have suggested that the devotees of Tsathoggua were as alien to mankind as Tsathoggua itself.[h] Leng, wherever in space or time it might brood, was not a region I would care to be in or near;[i] nor did I relish the proximity of a world that had ever bred such ambiguous and archaean[j] monstrosities as those Lake had just mentioned. At the moment I felt sorry that I had ever read the abhorred "Necronomicon",[k] or talked so much with that unpleasantly erudite folklorist Wilmarth at the university.

This mood undoubtedly served to aggravate my reaction to the bizarre mirage which burst upon us from the increasingly opalescent zenith as we drew near the mountains and began to make out the cumulative undulations of the foothills. I had seen dozens of polar mirages during the preceding weeks, some of them quite as uncanny and fantastically vivid as the present sample;[l] but this one had a wholly

---

[a] Roerich.] Roerich. ¶ C^c
[b] Roerich-like] Roerichlike C
[c] archaean] Archaean D
[d] resemblances;] resemblances, C^c
[e] writings.] writings. ¶ C^c
[f] Asia;] Asia, C^c
[g] know.] know. ¶ C^c
[h] itself.] itself. ¶ C^c
[i] near;] near, C, D
[j] archaean] Archaean D
[k] "Necronomicon",] *Necronomicon,* A, B, C, D
[l] sample;] sample, C^c

novel and obscure quality of menacing symbolism, and I shuddered as the seething labyrinth of fabulous walls and towers and minarets loomed out of the troubled ice-vapours[a] above our heads.

The effect was that of a Cyclopean[b] city of no architecture known to man or to human imagination, with vast aggregations of night-black masonry embodying monstrous perversions of geometrical laws and attaining the most grotesque extremes of sinister bizarrerie.[c] There were truncated cones, sometimes terraced or fluted, surmounted by tall cylindrical shafts here and there bulbously enlarged and often capped with tiers of thinnish scalloped discs;[d] and strange,[e] beetling, table-like[f] constructions suggesting piles of multitudinous rectangular slabs or circular plates or five-pointed stars with each one overlapping the one beneath.[g] There were composite cones and pyramids either alone or surmounting cylinders or cubes or flatter truncated cones and pyramids, and occasional needle-like[h] spires in curious clusters of five.[i] All of these febrile structures seemed knit together by tubular bridges crossing from one to the other at various dizzy heights, and the implied scale of the whole was terrifying and oppressive in its sheer giganticism.[j] The general type of mirage was not unlike some of the wilder forms observed and drawn by the arctic[k] whaler Scoresby in 1820;[l] but at this time and place, with those dark, unknown mountain peaks soaring stupendously ahead, that anomalous elder-world discovery in our minds, and the pall of probable disaster enveloping the greater part of our expedition, we all seemed to find in it a taint of latent malignity and infinitely evil portent.

I was glad when the mirage began to break up, though in the

---

[a] ice-vapours] ice vapors C, D

[b] Cyclopean] cyclopean A, B

[c] laws . . . bizarrerie.] laws. C, D

[d] discs;] disks, C; disks; D [*comma changed to semicolon by HPL in C*]

[e] strange,] strange D

[f] table-like] tablelike C; table-/like D

[g] beneath.] beneath. ¶ C[c]

[h] needle-like] needlelike C

[i] five.] five. ¶ C[c]

[j] giganticism.] gigantism. ¶ C [*paragraphing error corr. by HPL*]; gigantism. D

[k] arctic] Arctic A, B

[l] 1820;] 1820, C, D

process the various nightmare turrets and cones assumed distorted[a] temporary forms of even vaster hideousness. As the whole illusion dissolved to churning opalescence[b] we began to look earthward again, and saw that our journey's end was not far off.[c] The unknown mountains ahead rose dizzyingly[d] up like a fearsome rampart of giants, their curious regularities shewing[e] with startling clearness even without a field-glass.[f] We were over the lowest foothills now, and could see amidst the snow, ice, and bare patches of their main plateau a couple of darkish spots which we took to be Lake's camp and boring.[g] The higher foothills shot up between five and six miles away, forming a range almost distinct from the terrifying line of more than Himalayan peaks beyond them. At length Ropes—the student who had relieved McTighe at the controls—began to head downward toward the left-hand dark spot whose size marked it as the camp. As he did so, McTighe sent out the last uncensored wireless message the world was to receive from our expedition.

Everyone,[h] of course, has read the brief and unsatisfying bulletins of the rest of our antarctic sojourn.[i] Some hours after our landing we sent a guarded report of the tragedy we found, and reluctantly announced the wiping out of the whole Lake party by the frightful wind of the preceding day, or of the night before that. Eleven known dead, young Gedney missing.[j] People pardoned our hazy lack of details through realisation[k] of the shock the sad event must have caused us, and believed us when we explained that the mangling action of the wind had rendered all eleven bodies unsuitable for transportation outside.[l] Indeed, I flatter myself that even in the midst of our distress, utter bewilderment, and soul-clutching horror, we scarcely went beyond

[a] distorted] distorted, C, D
[b] opalescence] opalescence, C[c]
[c] off.] off. ¶ C[c]
[d] dizzyingly] dizzily C, D
[e] shewing] showing B, C, D
[f] field-glass.] field glass. C, D
[g] boring.] boring. ¶ C[c]
[h] Everyone,] Every one, C
[i] sojourn.] sojourn. ¶ C[c]
[j] Eleven . . . missing.] There were eleven known dead, young Gedney was missing. C[c]
[k] realisation] realization C, D
[l] outside.] outside. ¶ C[c]

the truth in any specific instance. The tremendous significance lies in what we dared not tell—[a]what I would not tell now but for the need of warning others off from nameless terrors.

It is a fact that the wind had wrought[b] dreadful havoc. Whether all could have lived through it, even without the other thing, is gravely open to doubt. The storm, with its fury of madly driven ice-particles,[c] must have been beyond anything our expedition had encountered before.[d] One aëroplane shelter—all, it seems, had been left in a far too flimsy and inadequate state—was nearly pulverised;[e] and the derrick at the distant boring was entirely shaken to pieces.[f] The exposed metal of the grounded planes and drilling machinery was bruised into a high polish, and two of the small tents were flattened despite their snow banking. Wooden surfaces left out in the blast[g] were pitted and denuded of paint, and all signs of tracks in the snow were completely obliterated.[h] It is also true that we found none of the archaean[i] biological objects in a condition to take outside as a whole. We did gather some minerals from a vast[j] tumbled pile, including several of the greenish soapstone fragments whose odd five-pointed rounding and faint patterns of grouped dots caused so many doubtful comparisons;[k] and some fossil bones, among which were the most typical of the curiously injured specimens.[l]

None of the dogs survived, their hurriedly built snow enclosure[m] near the camp being almost wholly destroyed. The wind may have done that, though the greater breakage[n] on the side next the camp, which

[a] tell—] tell; C, D
[b] wrought] brought D
[c] madly driven ice-particles,] madly-driven ice-particles, A, B; madly driven ice particles, C, D
[d] before.] before. ¶ C[c]
[e] pulverised;] pulverized; C; pulverized— D
[f] pieces.] pieces. ¶ C[c]
[g] blast] blaster D
[h] obliterated.] obliterated. ¶ C[c]
[i] archaean] Archaean D
[j] vast] vast, C, D
[k] comparisons;] comparisons, C[c]
[l] specimens.] speciments. D
[m] enclosure] inclosure C, D
[n] breakage] breakage, C[c]

was not the windward one, suggests an outward leap or break of the frantic beasts themselves.[a] All three sledges were gone, and we have tried to explain that the wind may have blown them off into the unknown. The drill and ice-melting machinery at the boring were too badly damaged to warrant salvage, so we used them to choke up that subtly disturbing gateway to the past which Lake had blasted.[b] We likewise left at the camp the two most shaken-up[c] of the planes; since our surviving party had only four real pilots—Sherman, Danforth, McTighe, and Ropes—in all, with Danforth in a poor nervous shape to navigate. We brought back all the books, scientific equipment, and other incidentals we could find, though much was rather unaccountably blown away. Spare tents and furs were either missing or badly out of condition.

It was approximately 4 p.m.,[d] after wide plane cruising had forced us to give Gedney up for lost, that we sent our guarded message to the *Arkham* for relaying; and I think we did well to keep it as calm and non-committal[e] as we succeeded in doing.[f] The most we said about agitation concerned[g] our dogs, whose frantic uneasiness near the biological specimens was to be expected from poor Lake's accounts. We did not mention, I think, their display of the same uneasiness when sniffing around the queer greenish soapstones and certain other objects in the disordered region;[h] objects including scientific instruments, aëroplanes, and machinery[i] both at the camp and at the boring, whose parts had been loosened, moved, or otherwise tampered with by winds that must have harboured[j] singular curiosity and investigativeness.

About the fourteen biological specimens we were pardonably indefinite. We said that the only ones we discovered were damaged, but

[a] themselves.] themselves. ¶ C^c
[b] blasted.] blasted. ¶ C^c
[c] shaken-up] shaken up C, D
[d] 4 p.m.,] four p. m., C; 4 P.M., D
[e] non-committal] non-/committal B; noncommittal C, D
[f] doing.] doing. ¶ C^c
[g] concerned] conerned D
[h] region;] region— C, D
[i] machinery] machinery, C, D
[j] harboured] harbored C, D

that enough was left of them to prove Lake's description wholly and impressively accurate. It was hard work keeping our personal emotions out of this matter—and we did not mention numbers or say exactly how we had found those which we did find. We had by that time agreed not to transmit anything suggesting madness on the part of Lake's men, and it surely looked like madness to find six imperfect monstrosities carefully buried upright in nine-foot snow graves under five-pointed mounds punched over with groups of dots in patterns exactly like[a] those on the queer greenish soapstones dug up from Mesozoic or Tertiary[b] times. The eight perfect specimens mentioned by Lake seemed to have been completely[c] blown away.

We were careful, too, about the public's general peace of mind; hence Danforth and I said little about that frightful trip over the mountains the next day. It was the fact that only a radically lightened plane could possibly cross a range of such height which mercifully limited that scouting tour to the two of us.[d] On our return at 1 a.m.[e] Danforth was close to hysterics, but kept an admirably stiff upper lip. It took no persuasion to make him promise not to shew[f] our sketches and the other things we brought away in our pockets, not to say anything more to the others than what we had agreed to relay outside, and to hide our camera films for private development later on; so that part of my present story will be as new to Pabodie, McTighe, Ropes, Sherman, and the rest as it will be to the[g] world in general. Indeed—[h]Danforth is closer-mouthed[i] than I;[j] for he saw—or thinks he saw—[k]one thing he will not tell even me.

---

[a] like] *om.* D
[b] Mesozoic or Tertiary] mesozoic or tertiary A, B
[c] completely] *om.* A, B [*presumably added by HPL in TMS sent to C*]
[d] us.] us. ¶ C^c
[e] 1 a.m.] one a. m., C; 1 A.M., D
[f] shew] show A, B, C, D
[g] the] that B, C^c
[h] Indeed—] Indeed, D
[i] closer-mouthed] closer mouthed C, D
[j] I;] I: B, C, D
[k] saw—. . . saw—] saw . . . saw B; saw, . . . saw, C, D

As all know, our report included a tale of a hard ascent;[a] a confirmation of Lake's opinion that the great peaks are of archaean[b] slate and other very primal crumpled strata unchanged since at least middle Comanchian times;[c] a conventional comment on the regularity of the clinging cube and rampart formations;[d] a decision that the cave-mouths[e] indicate dissolved calcareous veins;[f] a conjecture that certain slopes and passes would permit of the scaling and crossing of the entire range by seasoned mountaineers;[g] and a remark that the mysterious other side holds a lofty and immense super-plateau[h] as ancient and unchanging as the mountains themselves—20,000[i] feet in elevation, with grotesque rock formations protruding through a thin glacial layer and with low gradual foothills between the general plateau surface and the sheer precipices of the highest peaks.

This body of data is in every respect true so far as it goes, and it completely satisfied the men at the camp. We laid our absence of sixteen hours—a longer time than our announced flying, landing, reconnoitring,[j] and rock-collecting programme[k] called for—to a long mythical spell of adverse wind conditions;[l] and told truly of our landing on the farther foothills.[m] Fortunately our tale sounded realistic and prosaic enough not to tempt any of the others into emulating our flight. Had any tried to do that, I would have used every ounce of my persuasion to stop them—and I do not know what Danforth would have done.[n] While we were gone, Pabodie, Sherman, Ropes, McTighe,

[a] ascent;] ascent— C, D
[b] archaean] Archaean D
[c] times;] time, C^c
[d] formations;] formations, C^c
[e] cave-mouths] cave mouths C, D
[f] veins;] veins, C^c
[g] mountaineers;] mountaineers, C^c
[h] super-plateau] superplateau C, D
[i] 20,000] twenty thousand C, D
[j] reconnoitring,] reconnoitering, C, D
[k] programme] program C, D
[l] conditions;] conditions, C, D
[m] foothills.] foothills. ¶ C^c
[n] done.] done. ¶ C^c

and Williamson had worked like beavers over Lake's two best planes;[a] fitting them again for use[b] despite the altogether unaccountable juggling of their operative mechanism.

We decided to load all the planes the next morning and start back for our old base as soon as possible. Even though indirect, that was the safest way to work toward McMurdo Sound; for a straight-line[c] flight across the most utterly unknown stretches of the aeon-dead continent would involve many additional hazards.[d] Further exploration was hardly feasible in view of our tragic decimation and the ruin of our drilling machinery; and the[e] doubts and horrors around us—which we did not reveal—made us wish only to escape from this austral world of desolation and brooding madness as swiftly as we could.

As the public knows, our return to the world was accomplished without further disasters. All planes reached the old base on the evening of the next day—January 27th[f]—after a swift non-stop[g] flight; and on the 28th we made McMurdo Sound in two laps, the one pause being very brief, and occasioned by a faulty rudder[h] in the furious wind over the ice-shelf[i] after we had cleared the great plateau.[j] In five days more[k] the *Arkham* and *Miskatonic,* with all hands and equipment on board, were shaking clear of the thickening field ice and working up Ross Sea[l] with the mocking mountains of Victoria Land looming westward against a troubled antarctic sky and twisting the wind's wails into a wide-ranged musical piping which chilled my soul to the quick.[m] Less than a fortnight later we left the last hint of polar land behind us,[n] and

[a] planes;] planes, C, D
[b] use] use, C[c]
[c] straight-line] straightline D
[d] hazards.] hazards. ¶ C[c]
[e] machinery; and the] machinery. The C, D
[f] 27th] 27 A
[g] non-stop] non-/stop C; nonstop D
[h] rudder] rudder, C[c]
[i] ice-shelf] ice shelf A, B, C, D
[j] plateau.] plateau. ¶ C[c]
[k] more] more, C, D
[l] Sea] Sea, C[c]
[m] quick.] quick. ¶ C[c]
[n] us,] us D

thanked heaven that we were clear of a haunted, accursed realm where life and death, space and time, have made black and blasphemous alliances in the unknown epochs since matter first writhed and swam on the planet's scarce-cooled crust.

Since our return we have all constantly worked to discourage antarctic exploration, and have kept certain doubts and guesses to ourselves with splendid unity and faithfulness. Even young Danforth, with his nervous breakdown, has not flinched or babbled to his doctors—indeed,[a] as I have said, there is one thing he thinks he alone saw which he will not tell even me, though I think it would help his psychological state if he would consent to do so. It might explain and relieve much, though perhaps the thing was no more than the delusive aftermath of an earlier shock. That is the impression I gather after those rare[b] irresponsible moments when he whispers disjointed things to me—things which he repudiates vehemently as soon as he gets a grip on himself again.

It will be hard work deterring others from the great white south, and some of our efforts may directly harm our cause by drawing inquiring notice. We might have known from the first that human curiosity is undying, and that the results we announced would be enough to spur others ahead on the same age-long pursuit of the unknown.[c] Lake's reports of those biological monstrosities had aroused naturalists and palaeontologists to the highest pitch;[d] though we were sensible enough not to shew[e] the detached parts we had taken from the actual buried specimens, or our photographs of those specimens as they were found. We also refrained from shewing[f] the more puzzling of the scarred bones and greenish soapstones; while Danforth and I have closely guarded the pictures we took or drew on the super-plateau[g] across the range, and the crumpled things we smoothed, studied in terror, and brought away in our pockets.[h] But now that Starkweather-Moore party is

---

[a] doctors—indeed,] doctors. ¶ Indeed, C[c]
[b] rare] rare, C, D
[c] unknown.] unknown. ¶ C[c]
[d] pitch;] pitch, C, D
[e] shew] show B, C, D
[f] shewing] showing B, C, D
[g] super-plateau] superplateau C, D
[h] pockets.] pockets. ¶ C[c]

organising,[a] and with a thoroughness far beyond anything our outfit attempted. If[b] not dissuaded, they will get to the innermost nucleus of the antarctic and melt and bore till they bring up that which may end the world we know.[c] So I must break through all reticences at last—even about that ultimate[d] nameless thing beyond the mountains of madness.

IV.

It is only with vast hesitancy and repugnance that I let my mind go back to Lake's camp and what we really found there—and to that other thing beyond the frightful mountain wall.[e] I am constantly tempted to shirk the details, and to let hints stand for actual facts and ineluctable deductions. I hope I have said enough already to let me glide briefly over the rest; the rest, that is, of the horror at the camp.[f] I have told of the wind-ravaged[g] terrain, the damaged shelters, the disarranged machinery, the varied uneasinesses[h] of our dogs, the missing sledges and other items, the deaths of men and dogs, the absence of Gedney, and the six insanely buried biological specimens, strangely sound in texture for all their structural injuries, from a world forty million years dead. I do not recall whether I mentioned that upon checking up the canine bodies we found one dog missing. We did not think much about that till later—indeed, only Danforth and I have thought of it at all.

The principal things I have been keeping back relate to the bodies, and to certain subtle points which may or may not lend a hideous and incredible kind of rationale to the apparent chaos.[i] At the time[j] I tried to keep the men's minds off those points; for it was so much simpler—so much more normal—to lay everything to an outbreak of

---

[a] organising,] organizing, C, D
[b] attempted. If] attempted—if C[c]
[c] may end . . . know.] we know may end the world. C, D
[d] ultimate] ultimate, C, D
[e] frightful mountain wall.] B; mountains of madness. A, D; awful mountain wall. C [*corr. by HPL to* mountains of madness.]
[f] I am . . . camp.] *om.* ¶ C[c]
[g] wind-ravaged] wind ravaged D
[h] uneasinesses] uneasiness C[c]
[i] chaos.] chaos. ¶ C[c]
[j] time] time, C, D

madness on the part of some of Lake's party. From the look of things, that daemon[a] mountain wind must have been enough to drive any man mad in the midst of this centre[b] of all earthly mystery and desolation.

The crowning abnormality, of course, was the condition of the bodies—men and dogs alike. They had all been in some terrible kind of conflict, and were torn and mangled in fiendish and altogether inexplicable ways. Death, so far as we could judge, had in each case come from strangulation or laceration.[c] The dogs had evidently started the trouble, for the state of their ill-built corral bore witness to its forcible breakage from within. It had been set some distance from the camp because of the hatred of the animals for those hellish archaean[d] organisms, but the precaution seemed to have been taken in vain. When left alone in that monstrous wind behind flimsy walls of insufficient height[e] they must have stampeded—whether from the wind itself, or from some subtle, increasing odour[f] emitted by the nightmare specimens, one could not say. Those specimens, of course, had been covered with a tent-cloth; yet the low antarctic sun had beat steadily upon that cloth, and Lake had mentioned that solar heat tended to make the strangely sound and tough tissues of the things relax and expand. Perhaps the wind had whipped the cloth from over them, and jostled them about in such a way that their more pungent olfactory qualities became manifest despite their unbelievable antiquity.[g]

But whatever had happened, it was hideous and revolting enough. Perhaps I had better put squeamishness aside and tell the worst at last—though with a categorical statement of opinion, based on the first-hand observations and most rigid deductions of both Danforth and myself, that the then missing Gedney was in no way responsible for the loathsome horrors we found.[h] I have said that the bodies were frightfully mangled. Now I must add that some were incised and

---

[a] daemon] demon C, D
[b] centre] center C, D
[c] laceration.] laceration. ¶ C[c]
[d] archaean] Archaean D
[e] wind . . . height] wind, . . . height, C, D
[f] odour] odor C, D
[g] Those . . . antiquity.] *om.* C, D
[h] found.] found. ¶ C[c]

subtracted from in the most curious, cold-blooded, and inhuman fashion. It was the same with dogs and men. All the healthier, fatter bodies, quadrupedal or bipedal, had had their most solid masses of tissue cut out and removed, as by a careful butcher; and around them was a strange sprinkling of salt—taken from the ravaged provision-chests[a] on the planes—which conjured up the most horrible associations.[b] The thing had occurred in one of the crude aëroplane shelters from which the plane had been dragged out, and subsequent winds had effaced all tracks which could have supplied any plausible theory. Scattered bits of clothing, roughly slashed from the human incision-subjects,[c] hinted no clues.[d] It is useless to bring up the half-impression[e] of certain faint snow-prints[f] in one shielded corner of the ruined enclosure[g]—because that impression did not concern human prints at all, but was clearly mixed up with all the talk of fossil prints which poor Lake had been giving throughout the preceding weeks. One had to be careful of one's imagination in the lee of those overshadowing mountains of madness.

As I have indicated, Gedney and one dog turned out to be missing in the end. When we came on that terrible shelter we had missed two dogs and two men; but the fairly unharmed dissecting tent, which we entered after investigating the monstrous graves, had something to reveal.[h] It was not as Lake had left it, for the covered parts of the primal monstrosity had been removed from the improvised table. Indeed, we had already realised[i] that one of the six imperfect and insanely buried things we had found—the one with the trace of a peculiarly hateful odour[j]—must represent the collected sections of the entity

---

[a] provision-chests] provision chests C, D
[b] associations.] associations. ¶ C[c]
[c] incision-subjects,] incision subjects, C, D
[d] clues.] clues. ¶ C[c]
[e] half-impression] half impression C, D
[f] snow-prints] snow prints C, D
[g] enclosure] inclosure C, D
[h] reveal.] reveal. ¶ C[c]
[i] realised] realized C, D
[j] odour] odor C, D

which Lake had tried to analyse.[a] On and around that laboratory table were strown[b] other things, and it did not take long for us to guess that those things were the carefully[c] though oddly and inexpertly dissected parts of one man and one dog. I shall spare the feelings of survivors by omitting mention of the man's identity.[d] Lake's anatomical instruments were missing, but there were evidences of their careful cleansing. The gasoline stove was also gone, though around it we found a curious litter of matches. We buried the human parts beside the other ten men, and the canine parts with the other 35[e] dogs. Concerning the bizarre smudges on the laboratory table, and on the jumble of roughly handled illustrated books scattered near it, we were much too bewildered to speculate.

This formed the worst of the camp horror, but other things were equally perplexing. The disappearance of Gedney, the one dog, the eight uninjured biological specimens, the three sledges, and certain instruments, illustrated technical and scientific books, writing materials, electric torches and batteries, food and fuel, heating apparatus, spare tents, fur suits, and the like, was utterly beyond sane conjecture; as were likewise the spatter-fringed ink-blots[f] on certain pieces of paper, and the evidences of curious alien fumbling and experimentation around the planes and all other mechanical devices both at the camp and at the boring. The dogs seemed to abhor this oddly disordered machinery.[g] Then, too, there was the upsetting of the larder, the disappearance of certain staples, and the jarringly comical heap of tin cans pried open in the most unlikely ways and at the most unlikely places. The profusion of scattered matches, intact, broken, or spent, formed another minor enigma;[h] as did the two or three tent-cloths[i] and fur suits which we found lying about with peculiar and unorthodox slashings conceivably

[a] analyse.] analyze. ¶ C [*paragraphing error corr. by HPL*]; analyze. D
[b] strown] strewn C, D
[c] carefully] carefully, C
[d] identity.] identity. ¶ C[c]
[e] 35] thirty-five C, D
[f] spatter-fringed ink-blots] spatter-fringed ink blots C; spatterfringed ink blots D
[g] machinery.] machinery. ¶ C[c]
[h] enigma;] enigma— C, D
[i] tent-cloths] tent cloths C, D

due to clumsy efforts at unimaginable adaptations.[a] The maltreatment of the human and canine bodies, and the crazy burial of the damaged archaean[b] specimens, were all of a piece with this apparent disintegrative madness. In view of just such an eventuality as the present one, we carefully photographed all the main evidences of insane disorder at the camp; and shall use the prints to buttress our pleas against the departure of the proposed Starkweather-Moore Expedition.

Our first act after finding the bodies in the shelter was to photograph and open the row of insane graves with the five-pointed snow mounds. We could not help noticing the resemblance of these monstrous mounds, with their clusters of grouped dots, to poor Lake's descriptions of the strange greenish soapstones; and when we came on some of the soapstones themselves in the great mineral pile we found the likeness very close indeed.[c] The whole general formation, it must be made clear, seemed abominably suggestive of the starfish-head[d] of the archaean[e] entities; and we agreed that the suggestion must have worked potently upon the sensitised[f] minds of Lake's overwrought party. Our own first sight of the actual buried entities formed a horrible moment, and sent the imaginations of Pabodie and myself back to some of the shocking primal myths we had read and heard. We all agreed that the mere sight and continued presence of the things must have coöperated with the oppressive polar solitude and daemon mountain wind in driving Lake's party mad.[g]

For madness—centreing[h] in Gedney as the only possible surviving agent—was the explanation spontaneously adopted by everybody so far as spoken utterance was concerned; though I will not be so naive[i] as to deny that each of us may have harboured[j] wild guesses which

[a] adaptations.] adaptations. ¶ C^c
[b] archaean] Archaean C, D
[c] indeed.] indeed. ¶ C^c
[d] starfish-head] starfish head C, D
[e] archaean] Archaean D
[f] sensitised] sensitized C, D
[g] Our . . . mad.] *om.* C, D
[h] centreing] centering C, D
[i] naive] naïve C, D
[j] harboured] harbored C, D

sanity forbade him to formulate completely.[a] Sherman, Pabodie, and McTighe made an exhaustive aëroplane cruise over all the surrounding territory in the afternoon, sweeping the horizon with field-glasses[b] in quest of Gedney and of the various missing things; but nothing came to light.[c] The party reported that the titan barrier range extended endlessly to right and left alike, without any diminution in height or essential structure. On some of the peaks, though, the regular cube and rampart formations were bolder and plainer;[d] having doubly fantastic similitudes to Roerich-painted Asian hill ruins. The distribution of cryptical cave-mouths[e] on the black snow-denuded summits seemed roughly even as far as the range could be traced.

In spite of all the prevailing horrors we were left with enough sheer scientific zeal and adventurousness to wonder about the unknown realm beyond those mysterious mountains.[f] As our guarded messages stated, we rested at midnight after our day of terror and bafflement;[g] but not without a tentative plan for one or more range-crossing altitude flights in a lightened plane with aërial camera and geologist's outfit, beginning the following morning.[h] It was decided that Danforth and I try it first, and we awaked at 7 a.m.[i] intending an early trip; though[j] heavy winds—mentioned in our brief bulletin to the outside world—delayed our start till nearly nine[k] o'clock.

I have already repeated the non-committal[l] story we told the men at camp—and relayed outside—after our return sixteen hours later. It is now my terrible duty to amplify this account by filling in the merciful blanks with hints of what we really saw in that[m] hidden trans-

[a] completely.] completely. ¶ C[c]
[b] field-glasses] field glasses B, C, D
[c] light.] light. ¶ C[c]
[d] plainer;] plainer, C, D
[e] cave-mouths] cave mouths C, D
[f] mountains.] mountains. ¶ C[c]
[g] bafflement;] bafflement— C, D
[h] morning.] morning. ¶ C[c]
[i] 7 a.m.] seven a. m. C; 7 A.M. D
[j] trip; though] flight; however, D
[k] nine] 9 A, B
[l] non-committal] noncommittal C, D
[m] that] the D

montane[a] world—hints of the revelations which have finally driven Danforth to a nervous collapse.[b] I wish he would add a really frank word about the thing which he thinks he alone saw—even though it was probably a nervous delusion—and which was perhaps the last straw that put him where he is; but he is firm against that. All I can do is to repeat his later disjointed whispers about what set him shrieking as the plane soared back through the wind-tortured mountain pass after that real and tangible shock which I shared.[c] This will form my last word. If the plain signs of surviving elder horrors in what I disclose be not enough to keep others from meddling with the inner antarctic—or at least from prying too deeply beneath the surface of that ultimate waste of forbidden secrets and unhuman,[d] aeon-cursed desolation—the responsibility for unnamable and perhaps immensurable[e] evils will not be mine.

Danforth and I, studying the notes made by Pabodie in his afternoon flight and checking up with a sextant, had calculated that the lowest available pass in the range lay somewhat to the right of us, within sight of camp, and about 23,000 or 24,000[f] feet above sea-level.[g] For this point, then, we first headed in the lightened plane as we embarked on our flight of discovery. The camp itself, on foothills which sprang from a high continental plateau, was some 12,000[h] feet in altitude; hence the actual height increase necessary was not so vast as it might seem. Nevertheless we were acutely conscious of the rarefied air and intense cold as we rose; for on account of visibility conditions[i] we had to leave the cabin windows open. We were dressed, of course, in our heaviest furs.

As we drew near the forbidding peaks, dark and sinister above the line of crevasse-riven snow and interstitial glaciers, we noticed more and

---

[a] trans-montane] transmontane C, D

[b] collapse.] collapse. ¶ C[c]

[c] shared.] shared. ¶ C[c]

[d] unhuman,] un-human, A, B; un-/human, C; inhuman, D

[e] immensurable] immeasurable C, D

[f] 23,000 or 24,000] twenty-three thousand or twenty-four thousand C, D

[g] sea-level.] sea level. C, D

[h] 12,000] twelve thousand C, D

[i] for . . . conditions] for, . . . conditions, C, D

more the curiously regular formations clinging to the slopes; and thought again of the strange Asian paintings of Nicholas Roerich.[a] The ancient and wind-weathered rock strata fully verified all of Lake's bulletins, and proved that these hoary[b] pinnacles had been towering up in exactly the same way since a surprisingly early time in earth's history—perhaps over fifty million years. How much higher they had once been, it was futile to guess; but everything about this strange region pointed to obscure atmospheric influences unfavourable[c] to change, and calculated to retard the usual climatic processes of rock disintegration.

But it was the mountainside tangle of regular cubes, ramparts, and cave-mouths[d] which fascinated and disturbed us most. I studied them with a field-glass[e] and took aërial photographs whilst[f] Danforth drove; and at times[g] relieved him at the controls—though my aviation knowledge was purely an amateur's—in order to let him use the binoculars.[h] We could easily see that much of the material of the things was a lightish archaean[i] quartzite, unlike any formation visible over broad areas of the general surface; and that their regularity was extreme and uncanny to an extent which poor Lake had scarcely hinted.

As he had said, their edges were crumbled and rounded from untold aeons of savage weathering; but their preternatural solidity and tough material had saved them from obliteration. Many parts, especially those closest to the slopes, seemed identical in substance with the surrounding rock surface.[j] The whole arrangement looked like the ruins of Machu Picchu in the Andes, or the primal foundation-walls[k]

[a] Roerich.] Roerich. ¶ C[c]
[b] hoary] *om.* C, D
[c] unfavourable] unfavorable C, D
[d] cave-mouths] cave mouths C, D
[e] field-glass] field glass C, D
[f] whilst] while C, D
[g] times] times I C, D
[h] binoculars.] binoculars. ¶ C[c]
[i] archaean] Archaean D
[j] surface.] surface. ¶ C[c]
[k] foundation-walls] foundation walls C, D

of Kish as dug up by the Oxford–Field[a] Museum Expedition in 1929; and both Danforth and I obtained that occasional impression of *separate Cyclopean blocks*[b] which Lake had attributed to his flight-companion Carroll.[c] How to account for such things in this place was frankly beyond me, and I felt queerly humbled as a geologist. Igneous formations often have strange regularities—like the famous Giants' Causeway in Ireland—but this stupendous range, despite Lake's original suspicion of smoking cones, was above all else non-volcanic[d] in evident structure.

The curious cave-mouths,[e] near which the odd formations seemed most abundant, presented another[f] albeit a lesser puzzle because of their regularity of outline. They were, as Lake's bulletin had said, often approximately square or semicircular; as if the natural orifices had been shaped to greater symmetry by some magic hand. Their numerousness and wide distribution were remarkable, and suggested that the whole region was honeycombed with tunnels dissolved out of limestone strata.[g] Such glimpses as we secured did not extend far within the caverns, but we saw that they were apparently clear of stalactites and stalagmites. Outside, those parts of the mountain slopes adjoining the apertures seemed invariably smooth and regular; and Danforth thought that the slight cracks and pittings of the weathering tended toward unusual patterns.[h] Filled as he was with the horrors and strangenesses discovered at the camp, he hinted that the pittings vaguely resembled those baffling groups of dots sprinkled over the primeval[i] greenish soapstones, so hideously duplicated on the madly conceived snow mounds above those six buried monstrosities.

We had risen gradually in flying over the higher foothills and along toward the relatively low pass we had selected. As we advanced we occasionally looked down at the snow and ice of the land route,

[a] Oxford–Field] Oxford Field D
[b] *separate . . . blocks*] separate *cyclopean blocks* A, B; separate Cyclopean blocks C, D
[c] Carroll.] Carroll. ¶ Cᶜ
[d] non-volcanic] nonvolcanic C, D
[e] cave-mouths,] cave mouths, C, D
[f] another] another, Cᶜ
[g] strata.] strata. ¶ Cᶜ
[h] patterns.] patterns. ¶ Cᶜ
[i] primeval] primaeval B

wondering whether we could have attempted the trip with the simpler equipment of earlier days.[a] Somewhat to our surprise we saw that the terrain was far from difficult as such things go; and that despite the crevasses and other bad spots it would not have been likely to deter the sledges of a Scott, a Shackleton, or an Amundsen. Some of the glaciers appeared to lead up to wind-bared passes with unusual continuity, and upon reaching our chosen pass we found that its case formed no exception.

Our sensations of tense expectancy as we prepared to round the crest and peer out over an untrodden world can hardly be described on paper; even though we had no cause to think the regions beyond the range essentially different from those already seen and traversed. The touch of evil mystery in these barrier mountains, and in the beckoning sea of opalescent sky glimpsed betwixt their summits, was a highly subtle and attenuated matter not to be explained in literal words. Rather was it an affair of vague psychological symbolism and aesthetic association—a thing mixed up with exotic poetry and paintings, and with archaic myths lurking in shunned and forbidden volumes.[b] Even the wind's burden held a peculiar strain of conscious malignity; and for a second it seemed that the composite sound included a bizarre musical whistling[c] or piping over a wide range as the blast swept in and out of the omnipresent and resonant cave-mouths.[d] There was a cloudy note of reminiscent repulsion in this sound, as complex and unplaceable as any of the other dark impressions.

We were now, after a slow ascent, at a height of 23,570[e] feet according to the aneroid; and had left the region of clinging snow definitely below us. Up here were only dark, bare rock slopes and the start of rough-ribbed glaciers—but with those provocative cubes, ramparts, and echoing cave-mouths[f] to add a portent of the unnatural,

---

[a] days.] days. ¶ C^c
[b] volumes.] volumes. ¶ C^c
[c] whistling] whistling, C^c
[d] cave-mouths.] cave mouths. C, D
[e] 23,570] twenty three thousand five hundred and seventy C; twenty-three thousand, five hundred and seventy D
[f] cave-mouths] cave mouths C, D

the fantastic, and the dream-like.[a] Looking along the line of high peaks, I thought I could see the one mentioned by poor Lake, with a rampart exactly on top. It seemed to be half-lost[b] in a queer antarctic haze;[c] such a haze, perhaps, as had been responsible for Lake's early notion of volcanism.[d] The pass loomed directly before us, smooth and windswept between its jagged and malignly frowning pylons. Beyond it was a sky fretted with swirling vapours[e] and lighted by the low polar sun—the sky of that mysterious farther realm upon which we felt no human eye had ever gazed.

A few more feet of altitude and we would behold that realm. Danforth and I, unable to speak except in shouts amidst the howling, piping wind that raced through the pass and added to the noise of the unmuffled engines, exchanged eloquent glances. And then, having gained those last few feet, we did indeed stare across the momentous divide and over the unsampled secrets of an elder and utterly alien earth.

V.

I think that both of us simultaneously cried out in mixed awe, wonder, terror, and disbelief in our own senses as we finally cleared the pass and saw what lay beyond. Of course[f] we must have had some natural theory in the back of our heads to steady our faculties for the moment. Probably we thought of such things as the grotesquely weathered stones of the Garden of the Gods in Colorado, or the fantastically symmetrical wind-carved rocks of the Arizona desert. Perhaps we even half thought[g] the sight a mirage like that we had seen the morning before on first approaching those mountains of madness.[h] We must have had some such normal notions to fall back upon as our eyes swept that limitless, tempest-scarred plateau and grasped the almost

[a] dream-like.] dreamlike. A, B, D; dreamlike. ¶ C [*paragraphing error corr. by HPL*]

[b] half-lost] half lost C, D

[c] haze;] haze— C, D

[d] volcanism.] volcanism. ¶ C[c]

[e] vapours] vapors C, D

[f] course] course, C, D

[g] half thought] half-thought A, B

[h] madness.] madness. ¶ C[c]

endless labyrinth of colossal, regular, and geometrically eurhythmic[a] stone masses which reared their crumbled and pitted crests above a glacial sheet not more than 40 or 50[b] feet deep at its thickest, and in places obviously thinner.

The effect of the monstrous sight was indescribable, for some fiendish violation of known natural law seemed certain at the outset. Here, on a hellishly ancient table-land fully 20,000[c] feet high, and in a climate deadly to habitation since a pre-human[d] age not less than 500,000[e] years ago, there stretched nearly to the vision's limit a tangle of orderly stone which only the desperation of mental self-defence[f] could possibly attribute to any but a conscious and artificial cause.[g] We had previously dismissed, so far as serious thought was concerned, any theory that the cubes and ramparts of the mountainsides were other than natural in origin. How could they be otherwise, when man himself could scarcely have been differentiated from the great apes at the time when this region succumbed to the present unbroken reign of glacial death?

Yet now the sway of reason seemed irrefutably shaken, for this Cyclopean maze of squared, curved, and angled blocks had features which cut off all comfortable refuge. It was, very clearly, the blasphemous city of the mirage in stark, objective, and ineluctable reality. That damnable portent had had a material basis after all—there had been some horizontal stratum of ice-dust[h] in the upper air, and this shocking stone survival had projected its image across the mountains according to the simple laws of reflection. Of course[i] the phantom had been twisted and exaggerated, and had contained things which the real source did not contain; yet now, as we saw that real source, we thought it even more hideous and menacing than its distant image.

[a] eurhythmic] eurythmic A, B, C, D
[b] 40 or 50] forty or fifty C, D
[c] 20,000] twenty thousand C, D
[d] pre-human] prehuman C, D
[e] 500,000] five hundred thousand C, D
[f] self-defence] self-defense C, D
[g] cause.] cause. ¶ C[c]
[h] ice-dust] ice dust C, D
[i] course] course, C, D

Only the incredible, unhuman massiveness of these vast stone towers and ramparts had saved the frightful thing from utter annihilation in the hundreds of thousands—perhaps millions—of years it had brooded there amidst the blasts of a bleak upland. "Corona Mundi . . .[a] Roof of the World . . ."[b] All sorts of fantastic phrases sprang to our lips as we looked dizzily down at the unbelievable spectacle.[c] I thought again of the eldritch primal myths that had so persistently haunted me since my first sight of this dead antarctic world—of the daemoniac[d] plateau of Leng, of the Mi-Go, or Abominable Snow-Men[e] of the Himalayas, of the Pnakotic Manuscripts with their pre-human[f] implications, of the Cthulhu cult, of the "Necronomicon",[g] and of the Hyperborean legends of formless Tsathoggua and the worse than formless star-spawn[h] associated with that semi-entity.[i]

For boundless miles in every direction the thing stretched off with very little thinning; indeed, as our eyes followed it to the right and left along the base of the low, gradual foothills which separated it from the actual mountain rim, we decided that we could see no thinning at all except for an interruption at the left of the pass through which we had come. We had merely struck, at random, a limited part of something of incalculable extent.[j] The foothills were more sparsely sprinkled with grotesque stone structures, linking the terrible city to the already familiar cubes and ramparts which evidently formed its mountain outposts. These latter, as well as the queer cave-mouths,[k] were as thick on the inner as on the outer sides of the mountains.

The nameless stone labyrinth consisted, for the most part, of walls

[a] Mundi . . .] Mundi— C, D

[b] World . . ."] World—" C, D

[c] spectacle.] spectacle. ¶ C[c]

[d] daemoniac] demonic C [*corr. by HPL to* demoniac]; demoniac D

[e] Abominable Snow-Men] Abominable Snow Men C; abominable Snow Men D

[f] pre-human] prehuman C, D

[g] "Necronomicon",] *Necronomicon,* A, B, C, D

[h] star-spawn] star spawn C, D

[i] semi-entity.] semientity. C, D

[j] extent.] extent. ¶ C[c]

[k] cave-mouths,] cave mouths, C, D

from 10 to 150[a] feet in ice-clear height, and of a thickness varying from five to ten feet. It was composed mostly of prodigious blocks of dark primordial slate, schist, and sandstone—blocks in many cases as large as 4 × 6 × 8 feet—though in several places it seemed to be carved out of a solid, uneven bed-rock[b] of pre-Cambrian slate.[c] The buildings were far from equal in size;[d] there being innumerable honeycomb-arrangements[e] of enormous extent as well as smaller separate structures.[f] The general shape of these things tended to be conical, pyramidal, or terraced; though there were many perfect cylinders, perfect cubes, clusters of cubes, and other rectangular forms, and a peculiar sprinkling of angled edifices whose five-pointed ground plan roughly suggested modern fortifications. The builders had made constant and expert use of the principle of the arch, and domes had probably existed in the city's heyday.

The whole tangle was monstrously weathered, and the glacial surface from which[g] the towers projected was strown[h] with fallen blocks and immemorial debris.[i] Where the glaciation was transparent we could see the lower parts of the gigantic piles, and[j] noticed the ice-preserved stone bridges which connected the different towers at varying distances above the ground. On the exposed walls we could detect the scarred places where other and higher bridges of the same sort had existed.[k] Closer inspection revealed countless largish windows; some of which were closed with shutters of a petrified material originally wood, though most gaped open in a sinister and menacing fashion.[l] Many of the ruins, of course, were roofless, and with uneven though wind-

---

[a] 10 to 150] ten to one hundred and fifty C, D
[b] bed-rock] bed rock C, D
[c] slate.] slate. ¶ C[c]
[d] size;] size, C, D
[e] honeycomb-arrangements] honeycomb arrangements A, B, C, D
[f] structures.] structures. ¶ C[c]
[g] which] where C[c]
[h] strown] strewn C, D
[i] debris.] débris. C
[j] and] and we C, D
[k] existed.] existed. ¶ C[c]
[l] fashion.] fashion. ¶ C[c]

rounded upper edges; whilst others, of a more sharply conical or pyramidal model or else protected by higher surrounding structures, preserved intact outlines despite the omnipresent crumbling and pitting. With the field-glass[a] we could barely make out what seemed to be sculptural decorations in horizontal bands—decorations including those curious groups of dots whose presence on the ancient soapstones now assumed a vastly larger significance.

In many places the buildings were totally ruined and the ice-sheet[b] deeply riven from various geologic causes. In other places the stonework was worn down to the very level of the glaciation. One broad swath, extending from the plateau's interior to a cleft in the foothills about a mile to the left of the pass we had traversed, was wholly free from buildings; and[c] probably represented, we concluded, the course of some great river which in Tertiary[d] times—millions of years ago—had poured through the city and into some prodigious subterranean abyss of the great barrier range. Certainly, this was above all a region of caves, gulfs, and underground secrets beyond human penetration.

Looking back to our sensations, and recalling our dazedness at viewing this monstrous survival from aeons we had thought pre-human,[e] I can only wonder that we preserved the semblance of equilibrium[f] which we did. Of course[g] we knew that something—chronology, scientific theory, or our own consciousness—was woefully awry; yet we kept enough poise to guide the plane, observe many things quite minutely, and take a careful series of photographs which may yet serve both us and the world in good stead.[h] In my case, ingrained scientific habit may have helped; for above all my bewilderment and sense of menace there burned a dominant curiosity to fathom more of this age-old secret—to know what sort of beings had built and lived in this incalculably gigantic place, and what relation to the general world of

[a] field-glass] field glass C, D
[b] ice-sheet] ice sheet C, D
[c] buildings; and] buildings. It C, D
[d] Tertiary] tertiary A, B
[e] pre-human,] prehuman, C, D
[f] equilibrium] equilibrium, D
[g] course] course, C, D
[h] stead.] stead. ¶ C[c]

its time or of other times so unique a concentration of life could have had.

For this place could be no ordinary city. It must have formed the primary nucleus and centre[a] of some archaic and unbelievable chapter of earth's history whose outward ramifications, recalled only dimly in the most obscure and distorted myths, had vanished utterly amidst the chaos of terrene convulsions long before any human race we know had shambled out of apedom. Here sprawled a palaeogean[b] megalopolis compared with which the fabled Atlantis and Lemuria, Commoriom and Uzuldaroum, and Olathoë in the land of Lomar are recent things of today[c]—not even of yesterday; a megalopolis ranking with such whispered pre-human[d] blasphemies as Valusia, R'lyeh, Ib in the land of Mnar, and the Nameless City of Arabia Deserta.[e] As we flew above that tangle of stark titan[f] towers my imagination sometimes escaped all bounds and roved aimlessly in realms of fantastic associations—even weaving links betwixt this lost world and some of my own wildest dreams concerning the mad horror at the camp.

The plane's fuel-tank,[g] in the interest of greater lightness, had been only partly filled; hence we now had to exert caution in our explorations. Even so, however, we covered an enormous extent of ground—or rather, air—after swooping down to a level where the wind became virtually negligible.[h] There seemed to be no limit to the mountain range,[i] or to the length of the frightful stone city which bordered its inner foothills. Fifty miles of flight in each direction shewed[j] no major change in the labyrinth of rock and masonry that clawed up corpse-like[k] through the eternal ice.[l] There were, though, some highly absorbing

---

[a] centre] center C, D
[b] palaeogean] Palaeogaean C [*corr. by HPL to* palaeogaean], D
[c] today] to-day C
[d] pre-human] prehuman C, D
[e] Deserta.] Deserta. ¶ C[c]
[f] titan] Titan A, B, C
[g] fuel-tank,] fuel tank, C, D
[h] negligible.] negligible. ¶ C[c]
[i] mountain range,] mountain-range, A, B
[j] shewed] showed B, C, D
[k] corpse-like] corpselike A, B, C, D
[l] ice.] ice. ¶ C[c]

diversifications; such as the carvings on the canyon where that broad river had once pierced the foothills and approached its sinking-place[a] in the great range.[b] The headlands at the stream's entrance had been boldly carved into Cyclopean pylons; and something about the ridgy, barrel-shaped designs stirred up oddly vague, hateful, and confusing semi-remembrances[c] in both Danforth and me.

We also came upon several star-shaped open spaces, evidently public squares;[d] and noted various undulations in the terrain. Where a sharp hill rose, it was generally hollowed out into some sort of rambling stone edifice; but there were at least two exceptions. Of these latter, one was too badly weathered to disclose what had been on the jutting eminence, while the other still bore a fantastic conical monument carved out of the solid rock and roughly resembling such things as the well-known Snake Tomb in the ancient valley of Petra.

Flying inland from the mountains, we discovered that the city was not of infinite width, even though its length along the foothills seemed endless. After about thirty miles the grotesque stone buildings began to thin out, and in ten more miles we came to an unbroken waste virtually without signs of sentient artifice. The course of the river beyond the city seemed marked by a broad[e] depressed line;[f] while the land assumed a somewhat greater ruggedness, seeming to slope slightly upward as it receded in the mist-hazed west.

So far we had made no landing, yet to leave the plateau without an attempt at entering some of the monstrous structures would have been inconceivable. Accordingly[g] we decided to find a smooth place on the foothills near our navigable pass, there grounding the plane and preparing to do some exploration on foot.[h] Though these gradual slopes were partly covered with a scattering of ruins, low flying soon

[a] sinking-place] sinking place C, D
[b] range.] range. ¶ C[c]
[c] semi-remembrances] semiremembrances C
[d] squares;] squares, C, D
[e] broad] broad, C, D
[f] line;] line, C, D
[g] Accordingly] Accordingly, C[c], D
[h] foot.] foot. ¶ C[c]

disclosed an ample number of possible landing-places.[a] Selecting that nearest to the pass, since our next[b] flight would be across the great range and back to camp, we succeeded about 12:30 p.m.[c] in coming down[d] on a smooth, hard snowfield[e] wholly devoid of obstacles and well adapted to a swift and favourable takeoff[f] later on.

It did not seem necessary to protect the plane with a snow banking for so brief a time and in so comfortable an absence of high winds at this level; hence we merely saw that the landing skis were safely lodged, and that the vital parts of the mechanism were guarded against the cold.[g] For our foot journey we discarded the heaviest of our flying furs, and took with us a small outfit consisting of pocket compass, hand camera, light provisions, voluminous notebooks and paper, geologist's hammer and chisel, specimen-bags,[h] coil of climbing rope, and powerful electric torches with extra batteries; this equipment having been carried in the plane on the chance that we might be able to effect a landing, take ground pictures, make drawings and topographical sketches, and obtain rock specimens from some bare slope, outcropping, or mountain cave.[i] Fortunately we had a supply of extra paper to tear up, place in a spare specimen-bag,[j] and use on the ancient principle of hare-and-hounds[k] for marking our course in any interior mazes we might be able to penetrate. This had been brought in case we found some cave system with air quiet enough to allow such a rapid and easy method in place of the usual rock-chipping method of trail-blazing.[l]

Walking cautiously downhill over the crusted snow toward the stupendous stone labyrinth that loomed against the opalescent west,

[a] landing-places.] landing places. A, B, C, D
[b] next] *om.* D
[c] 12:30 p.m.] twelve thirty p. m. C; 12:30 P.M. D
[d] coming down] effecting a landing D
[e] snowfield] snow field C, D
[f] favourable takeoff] favorable take-off C, D
[g] cold.] cold. ¶ C^c
[h] specimen-bags,] specimen bags, C, D
[i] cave.] cave. ¶ C^c
[j] specimen-bag,] specimen bag, C, D
[k] hare-and-hounds] hare and hounds C, D
[l] trail-blazing.] trail blazing. C, D

we felt almost as keen a sense of imminent marvels as we had felt on approaching the unfathomed mountain pass four hours previously.[a] True, we had become visually familiar with the incredible secret concealed by the barrier peaks; yet the prospect of actually entering primordial walls reared by conscious beings perhaps millions of years ago—before any known race of men could have existed—was none the less awesome and potentially terrible in its implications of cosmic abnormality.[b] Though the thinness of the air at this prodigious altitude made exertion somewhat more difficult than usual;[c] both Danforth and I found ourselves bearing up very well, and felt equal to almost any task which might fall to our lot.[d] It took only a few steps to bring us to a shapeless ruin worn level with the snow, while ten or fifteen rods farther on there was a huge[e] roofless rampart still complete in its gigantic five-pointed outline[f] and rising to an irregular height of ten or eleven feet. For this latter we headed; and when at last we were able actually[g] to touch its weathered Cyclopean blocks, we felt that we had established an unprecedented and almost blasphemous link with forgotten aeons normally closed to our species.

This rampart, shaped like a star and perhaps 300[h] feet from point to point, was built of Jurassic sandstone blocks of irregular size, averaging 6 × 8 feet in surface. There was a row of arched loopholes or windows about four feet wide and five feet high;[i] spaced quite symmetrically along the points of the star and at its inner angles, and with the bottoms about four feet from the glaciated surface.[j] Looking through these, we could see that the masonry was fully five feet thick, that there were no partitions remaining within, and that there were traces of banded carvings

[a] previously.] previously. ¶ Cᶜ
[b] abnormality.] abnormality. ¶ Cᶜ
[c] usual;] usual, C, D
[d] lot.] lot. ¶ Cᶜ
[e] huge] huge, C, D
[f] outline] outline, B, Cᶜ
[g] able actually] actually able C, D
[h] 300] three hundred C, D
[i] high;] high, C, D
[j] surface.] surface. ¶ Cᶜ

or bas-reliefs[a] on the interior walls;[b] facts we had indeed guessed before, when flying low over this rampart and others like it. Though lower parts must have originally existed, all traces of such things were now wholly obscured by the deep layer of ice and snow at this point.

We crawled through one of the windows and vainly tried to decipher the nearly effaced mural designs, but did not attempt to disturb the glaciated floor. Our orientation flights had indicated that many buildings in the city proper were less ice-choked, and that we might perhaps find wholly clear interiors leading down to the true ground level if we entered those structures still roofed at the top.[c] Before we left the rampart we photographed it carefully, and studied its mortarless Cyclopean masonry with complete bewilderment. We wished that Pabodie were present, for his engineering knowledge might have helped us guess how such titanic blocks could have been handled in that unbelievably remote age when the city and its outskirts were built up.

The half-mile walk downhill to the actual city, with the upper wind shrieking vainly and savagely through the skyward peaks in the background, was something whose[d] smallest details will always remain engraved on my mind. Only in fantastic nightmares could any human beings but Danforth and me conceive such optical effects.[e] Between us and the churning vapours[f] of the west lay that monstrous tangle of dark stone towers;[g] its outré and incredible forms impressing us afresh at every new angle of vision. It was a mirage in solid stone, and were it not for the photographs I would still doubt that such a thing could be. The general type of masonry was identical with that of the rampart we had examined; but the extravagant shapes which this masonry took in its urban manifestations were past all description.

Even the pictures illustrate only one or two phases of its infinite bizarrerie,[h] endless variety, preternatural massiveness, and utterly alien

[a] bas-reliefs] basreliefs C
[b] walls;] walls— C, D
[c] top.] top. ¶ Cᶜ
[d] whose] of which the C, D
[e] effects.] effects. ¶ Cᶜ
[f] vapours] vapors C, D
[g] towers;] towers, C, D
[h] infinite bizarrerie,] *om.* C, D

exoticism. There were geometrical forms for which an Euclid could[a] scarcely find a name—cones of all degrees of irregularity and truncation; terraces of every sort of provocative disproportion; shafts with odd bulbous enlargements; broken columns in curious groups;[b] and five-pointed or five-ridged arrangements of mad grotesqueness.[c] As we drew nearer we could see beneath certain transparent parts of the ice-sheet,[d] and detect some of the tubular stone bridges that connected the crazily sprinkled structures at various heights. Of orderly streets there seemed to be none, the only broad open swath being a mile to the left, where the ancient river had doubtless flowed through the town into the mountains.

Our field-glasses[e] shewed[f] the external[g] horizontal bands of nearly effaced sculptures and dot-groups[h] to be very prevalent, and we could half imagine[i] what the city must once have looked like—even though most of the roofs and tower-tops[j] had necessarily perished.[k] As a whole, it had been a complex tangle of twisted lanes and alleys;[l] all of them deep canyons, and some little better than tunnels because of the overhanging masonry or overarching bridges.[m] Now, outspread below us, it loomed like a dream-phantasy[n] against a westward mist through whose northern end the low, reddish antarctic sun of early afternoon was struggling to shine; and when for a moment[o] that sun encountered a denser obstruction and plunged the scene into temporary shadow, the effect was subtly menacing in a way I can never hope to depict. Even

[a] could] would D
[b] truncation; . . . disproportion; . . . enlargements; . . . groups;] truncation, . . . disproportion, . . . enlargements, . . . groups, C, D
[c] grotesqueness.] grotesqueness. ¶ C[c]
[d] ice-sheet,] ice sheet, C, D
[e] field-glasses] field glasses C, D
[f] shewed] showed B, C, D
[g] external] external, C, D
[h] dot-groups] dot groups C, D
[i] half imagine] half-imagine A, B
[j] tower-tops] tower tops C, D
[k] perished.] perished. ¶ C[c]
[l] alleys;] alleys, C, D
[m] bridges.] bridges. ¶ C[c]
[n] dream-phantasy] dream phantasy C; dream fantasy D
[o] when . . . moment] when, . . . moment, C, D

the faint howling and piping of the unfelt wind in the great mountain passes behind us took on a wilder note of purposeful malignity.[a] The last stage of our descent to the town was unusually steep and abrupt, and a rock outcropping at the edge where the grade changed led us to think that an artificial terrace had once existed there. Under the glaciation, we believed, there must be a flight of steps or its equivalent.

When at last we plunged into the labyrinthine[b] town itself, clambering over fallen masonry and shrinking from the oppressive nearness and dwarfing height of omnipresent crumbling and pitted walls, our sensations again became such that I marvel at the amount of self-control we retained.[c] Danforth was frankly jumpy, and began making some offensively irrelevant speculations about the horror at the camp—which I resented all the more because I could not help sharing certain conclusions forced upon us by many features of this morbid survival from nightmare antiquity.[d] The speculations worked on his imagination, too; for in one place—where a debris-littered[e] alley turned a sharp corner—he insisted that he saw faint traces of ground markings which he did not like; whilst elsewhere he stopped to listen to a subtle[f] imaginary sound from some undefined point—a muffled musical piping, he said, not unlike that of the wind in the mountain caves[g] yet somehow disturbingly different.[h] The ceaseless *five-pointedness* [i] of the surrounding architecture and of the few distinguishable mural arabesques had a dimly sinister suggestiveness we could not escape;[j] and gave us a touch of terrible subconscious certainty concerning the primal entities which had reared and dwelt in this unhallowed place.

Nevertheless[k] our scientific and adventurous souls were not wholly

---

[a] malignity.] malignity. ¶ C^c
[b] labyrinthine] *om.* C, D
[c] retained.] retained. ¶ C^c
[d] antiquity.] antiquity. ¶ C^c
[e] debris-littered] débris-littered C
[f] subtle] subtle, C, D
[g] caves] caves, C, D
[h] different.] different. ¶ C^c
[i] *five-pointedness*] five-pointedness C, D
[j] escape;] escape, C, D
[k] Nevertheless] Nevertheless, C, D

dead;[a] and we mechanically carried out our programme[b] of chipping specimens from all the different rock types represented in the masonry. We wished a rather full set in order to draw better conclusions regarding the age of the place.[c] Nothing in the great outer walls seemed to date from later than the Jurassic and Comanchian[d] periods, nor was any piece of stone in the entire place of a greater recency than the Pliocene age.[e] In stark certainty, we were wandering amidst a death which had reigned at least 500,000[f] years, and in all probability even longer.

As we proceeded through this maze of stone-shadowed twilight we stopped at all available apertures to study interiors and investigate entrance possibilities. Some were above our reach, whilst others led only into ice-choked ruins as unroofed and barren as the rampart on the hill.[g] One, though spacious and inviting, opened on a seemingly bottomless abyss without visible means of descent. Now and then we had a chance to study the petrified wood of a surviving shutter, and were impressed by the fabulous antiquity implied in the still discernible grain. These things had come from Mesozoic[h] gymnosperms and conifers—especially Cretaceous cycads—and from fan-palms[i] and early angiosperms of plainly Tertiary[j] date. Nothing definitely later than the Pliocene could be discovered.[k] In the placing of these shutters—whose edges shewed[l] the former presence of queer and long-vanished hinges—usage seemed to be varied;[m] some being on the outer and some on the inner side of the deep embrasures. They seemed to have become wedged in place, thus surviving the rusting of their former and probably metallic fixtures and fastenings.

[a] dead;] dead, C, D
[b] programme] program C, D
[c] place.] place. ¶ C[c]
[d] Comanchian] Comanchean C[c]
[e] age.] Age. C, D
[f] 500,000] five hundred thousand C, D
[g] hill.] hill. ¶ C[c]
[h] Mesozoic] mesozoic A, B
[i] fan-palms] fan palms C, D
[j] Tertiary] tertiary A, B
[k] discovered.] discovered. ¶ C[c]
[l] shewed] showed B, C, D
[m] varied;] varied— C, D

After a time we came across a row of windows—in the bulges of a colossal five-ridged[a] cone of undamaged apex—which led into a vast, well-preserved room with stone flooring; but these were too high in the room to permit of[b] descent without a rope. We had a rope with us, but did not wish to bother with this twenty-foot drop unless obliged to—especially in this thin plateau air where great demands were made upon the heart action.[c] This enormous room was probably a hall or concourse of some sort, and our electric torches shewed[d] bold, distinct, and potentially startling sculptures arranged round the walls in broad, horizontal bands separated by equally broad strips of conventional arabesques. We took careful note of this spot, planning to enter here unless a more easily gained interior were[e] encountered.

Finally, though, we did encounter exactly the opening we wished; an archway about six feet wide and ten feet high, marking the former end of an aërial bridge which had spanned an alley about five feet above the present level of glaciation. These archways, of course, were flush with upper-story floors;[f] and in this case one of the floors still existed.[g] The building thus accessible was a series of rectangular terraces on our left facing westward. That across the alley, where the other archway yawned, was a decrepit cylinder with no windows and with a curious bulge about ten feet above the aperture. It was totally dark inside, and the archway seemed to open on a well of illimitable emptiness.

Heaped debris[h] made the entrance to the vast left-hand building doubly easy, yet for a moment we hesitated before taking advantage of the long-wished chance. For though we had penetrated into this tangle of archaic mystery, it required fresh resolution to carry us actually inside a complete and surviving building of a fabulous elder world whose nature was becoming more and more hideously plain to us.[i] In the end,

[a] five-ridged] five-edged C, D
[b] of] *om.* C, D
[c] action.] action. ¶ C[c]
[d] shewed] showed B, C, D
[e] were] was C[c]
[f] floors;] floors, C, D
[g] existed.] existed. ¶ C[c]
[h] debris] débris C
[i] us.] us. ¶ C[c]

however, we made the plunge;[a] and scrambled up over the rubble into the gaping embrasure. The floor beyond was of great slate slabs, and seemed to form the outlet of a long, high corridor with sculptured walls.

Observing the many inner archways which led off from it, and realising[b] the probable complexity of the nest of apartments within, we decided that we must begin our system of hare-and-hound trail-blazing.[c] Hitherto our compasses, together with frequent glimpses of the vast mountain range between the towers in our rear, had been enough to prevent our losing our way; but from now on, the artificial substitute would be necessary.[d] Accordingly we reduced our extra paper to shreds of suitable size, placed these in a bag to be carried by Danforth, and prepared to use them as economically as safety would allow. This method would probably gain us immunity from straying, since there did not appear to be any strong air-currents[e] inside the primordial masonry. If such should develop, or if our paper supply should give out, we could of course fall back on the more secure though more tedious and retarding method of rock-chipping.[f]

Just how extensive a territory we had opened up, it was impossible to guess without a trial. The close and frequent connexion[g] of the different buildings made it likely that we might cross from one to another on bridges underneath the ice[h] except where impeded by local collapses and geologic rifts, for very little glaciation seemed to have entered the massive constructions.[i] Almost all the areas of transparent ice had revealed the submerged windows as tightly shuttered, as if the town had been left in that uniform state until the glacial sheet came to crystallise[j] the lower part for all succeeding time. Indeed, one gained a curious impression that this place had been deliberately closed and deserted in

---

[a] plunge;] plunge, C, D
[b] realising] realizing C, D
[c] hare-and-hound trail-blazing.] hare-and-hound trail blazing. C, D
[d] necessary.] necessary. ¶ C[c]
[e] air-currents] air currents C, D
[f] rock-chipping.] rock chipping. C. D
[g] connexion] connection C, D
[h] ice] ice, C[c], D
[i] constructions.] constructions. ¶ C[c]
[j] crystallise] crystallize C, D

some dim, bygone aeon, rather than overwhelmed by any sudden calamity or even gradual decay. Had the coming of the ice been foreseen, and had a nameless population left en masse[a] to seek a less doomed abode?[b] The precise physiographic conditions attending the formation of the ice-sheet[c] at this point would have to wait for later solution. It had not, very plainly, been a grinding drive. Perhaps the pressure of accumulated snows had been responsible;[d] and perhaps some flood from the river, or from the bursting of some ancient glacial dam in the great range, had helped to create the special state now observable. Imagination could conceive almost anything in connexion[e] with this place.[f]

VI.

It would be cumbrous to give a detailed, consecutive account of our wanderings inside that cavernous, aeon-dead honeycomb of primal masonry;[g] that monstrous lair of elder secrets which now echoed for the first time, after uncounted epochs, to the tread of human feet.[h] This is especially true because so much of the horrible drama and revelation came from a mere study of the omnipresent mural carvings. Our flashlight photographs of those carvings will do much toward proving the truth of what we are now disclosing, and it is lamentable that we had not a larger film supply with us. As it was, we made crude notebook sketches of certain salient features after all our films were used up.

The building which we had entered was one of great size and elaborateness, and gave us an impressive notion of the architecture of that nameless geologic past. The inner partitions were less massive than the outer[i] walls, but on the lower levels were excellently preserved.

---

[a] en masse] *en masse* C, D
[b] abode?] abode? ¶ C^c
[c] ice-sheet] ice sheet B, C, D; *om.* A [*see below*]
[d] responsible;] responsible, C, D
[e] connexion] connection C, D
[f] The precise . . . place.] *om.* A
[g] masonry;] masonry— C, D
[h] feet.] feet. ¶ C^c
[i] outer] uter C^c

Labyrinthine complexity, involving curiously irregular differences[a] in floor levels, characterised[b] the entire arrangement; and we should certainly have been lost at the very outset but for the trail of torn paper left behind us.[c] We decided to explore the more decrepit upper parts first of all, hence climbed aloft in the maze for a distance of some 100[d] feet, to where the topmost tier of chambers yawned snowily and ruinously open to the polar sky. Ascent was effected over the steep, transversely ribbed stone ramps or inclined planes which everywhere served in lieu of stairs.[e] The rooms we encountered were of all imaginable shapes and proportions, ranging from five-pointed stars to triangles and perfect cubes. It might be safe to say that their general average was about 30 × 30 feet in floor area, and 20[f] feet in height;[g] though many larger apartments existed.[h] After thoroughly examining the upper regions and the glacial level we descended story by story[i] into the submerged part, where indeed we soon saw we were in a continuous maze of connected chambers and passages probably leading over unlimited areas outside this particular building.[j] The Cyclopean massiveness and giganticism[k] of everything about us became curiously oppressive; and there was something vaguely but deeply unhuman in all the contours, dimensions, proportions, decorations, and constructional nuances of the blasphemously archaic stonework. We soon realised from what the carvings revealed[l] that this monstrous city was many million years old.

We cannot yet explain the engineering principles used in the anomalous balancing and adjustment of the vast rock masses, though

[a] differences] difference D
[b] characterised] characterized C, D
[c] us.] us. ¶ C[c]
[d] 100] one hundred C, D
[e] stairs.] stairs. ¶ C[c]
[f] 20] twenty C
[g] height;] height, C, D
[h] existed.] existed. ¶ C[c]
[i] descended . . . story] descended, . . . story, C, D
[j] building.] building. ¶ C[c]
[k] giganticism] gigantism D
[l] realised . . . revealed] realized, . . . revealed, C, D

the function of the arch was clearly much relied on. The rooms we visited were wholly bare of all portable contents, a circumstance which sustained our belief in the city's deliberate desertion. The prime decorative feature was the almost universal system of mural sculpture;[a] which tended to run in continuous horizontal bands three feet wide and arranged from floor to ceiling in alternation with bands of equal width given over to geometrical arabesques.[b] There were exceptions to this rule of arrangement, but its preponderance was overwhelming. Often, however, a series of smooth cartouches containing oddly patterned groups of dots would be sunk along one of the arabesque bands.

The technique, we soon saw, was mature, accomplished, and aesthetically evolved to the highest degree of civilised mastery;[c] though utterly alien in every detail to any known art tradition of the human race. In delicacy of execution no sculpture I have ever seen could approach it. The minutest details of elaborate vegetation, or of animal life, were rendered with astonishing vividness despite the bold scale of the carvings; whilst the conventional designs were marvels of skilful[d] intricacy.[e] The arabesques displayed a profound use of mathematical principles, and were made up of obscurely symmetrical curves and angles based on the quantity of five.[f] The pictorial bands followed a highly formalised[g] tradition, and involved a peculiar treatment of perspective;[h] but had an artistic force that moved us profoundly notwithstanding the intervening gulf of vast geologic periods.[i] Their method of design hinged on a singular juxtaposition of the cross-section[j] with the two-dimensional silhouette, and embodied an analytical psychology beyond that of any known race of antiquity. It is useless to try to compare this art with any represented in our museums.

[a] sculpture;] sculpture, C, D
[b] arabesques.] arabesques. ¶ Cᶜ
[c] civilised mastery;] civilized mastery, C, D
[d] skilful] skillful C, D
[e] intricacy.] intricacy. ¶ Cᶜ
[f] five.] five. ¶ Cᶜ
[g] formalised] formalized C, D
[h] perspective;] perspective, C, D
[i] periods.] periods. ¶ Cᶜ
[j] cross-section] cross section C, D

Those who see our photographs will probably find its closest analogue in certain grotesque conceptions of the most daring futurists.

The arabesque tracery consisted altogether of depressed lines[a] whose depth on unweathered walls varied from one to two inches. When cartouches with dot-groups[b] appeared—evidently as inscriptions in some unknown and primordial language and alphabet—the depression of the smooth surface was perhaps an inch and a half, and of the dots perhaps a half-inch[c] more. The pictorial bands were in counter-sunk[d] low relief, their background being depressed about two inches from the original wall surface.[e] In some specimens marks of a former colouration[f] could be detected, though for the most part the untold aeons had disintegrated and banished any pigments which may have been applied. The more one studied the marvellous[g] technique the more one admired the things. Beneath their strict conventionalisation[h] one could grasp the minute and accurate observation and graphic skill of the artists; and indeed, the very conventions themselves served to symbolise[i] and accentuate the real essence or vital differentiation of every object delineated.[j] We felt, too, that besides these recognisable[k] excellences there were others lurking beyond the reach of our perceptions. Certain touches here and there gave vague hints of latent symbols and stimuli which another mental and emotional background, and a fuller or different sensory equipment, might have made of profound and poignant significance to us.

The subject-matter[l] of the sculptures obviously came from the life of the vanished epoch of their creation, and contained a large proportion

---

[a] lines] lines, C, D
[b] dot-groups] dot groups C, D
[c] half-inch] half inch C, D
[d] counter-sunk] countersunk C, D
[e] surface.] surface. ¶ C[c]
[f] colouration] coloration C, D
[g] marvellous] marvelous C, D
[h] conventionalisation] conventionalization C, D
[i] symbolise] symbolze C, D
[j] delineated.] delineated. ¶ C[c]
[k] recognisable] recognizable C, D
[l] subject-matter] subject matter C, D

of evident history. It is this abnormal historic-mindedness of the primal race—a chance circumstance operating, through coincidence, miraculously in our favour[a]—which made the carvings so awesomely informative to us, and which caused us to place their photography and transcription above all other considerations.[b] In certain rooms the dominant arrangement was varied by the presence of maps, astronomical charts, and other scientific designs on[c] an enlarged scale—these things giving a naive[d] and terrible corroboration to what we gathered from the pictorial friezes and dados.[e] In hinting at what the whole revealed, I can only hope that my account will not arouse a curiosity greater than sane caution on the part of those who believe me at all. It would be tragic if any were to be allured to that realm of death and horror by the very warning meant to discourage them.

Interrupting these sculptured walls were high windows and massive twelve-foot doorways; both now and then retaining the petrified wooden planks—elaborately carved and polished—of the actual shutters and doors. All metal fixtures had long ago vanished, but some of the doors remained in place and had to be forced aside as we progressed from room to room.[f] Window-frames[g] with odd transparent panes—mostly elliptical—survived here and there, though in no considerable quantity. There were also frequent niches of great magnitude, generally empty, but once in a while containing some bizarre object carved from green soapstone which was either broken or perhaps held too inferior to warrant removal.[h] Other apertures were undoubtedly connected with bygone mechanical facilities—heating, lighting, and the like—of a sort suggested in many of the carvings. Ceilings tended to be plain, but had sometimes been inlaid with green soapstone or other tiles, mostly fallen now. Floors were also paved with such tiles, though plain stonework predominated.

[a] favour] favor C, D
[b] considerations.] considerations. ¶ C^c
[c] on] of D
[d] naive] naïve C, D
[e] dados.] dadoes. D
[f] room.] room. ¶ C^c
[g] Window-frames] Window frames C, D
[h] removal.] removal. ¶ C^c

As I have said, all furniture and other moveables[a] were absent; but the sculptures gave a clear idea of the strange devices which had once filled these tomb-like,[b] echoing rooms. Above the glacial sheet the floors were generally thick with detritus, litter, and debris;[c] but farther down this condition decreased.[d] In some of the lower chambers and corridors there was little more than gritty dust or ancient incrustations, while occasional areas had an uncanny air of newly swept[e] immaculateness. Of course, where rifts or collapses had occurred, the lower levels were as littered as the upper ones.[f] A central court—as in other structures we had seen from the air[g]—saved the inner regions from total darkness; so that we seldom had to use our electric torches in the upper rooms except when studying sculptured details. Below the ice-cap,[h] however, the twilight deepened; and in many parts of the tangled ground level[i] there was an approach to absolute blackness.

To form even a rudimentary idea of our thoughts and feelings as we penetrated this aeon-silent maze of unhuman masonry one must correlate a hopelessly bewildering chaos of fugitive moods, memories, and impressions. The sheer appalling antiquity and lethal desolation of the place were enough to overwhelm almost any sensitive person, but added to these elements were the recent unexplained horror at the camp, and the revelations all too soon effected by the terrible mural sculptures around us.[j] The moment we came upon a perfect section of carving, where no ambiguity of interpretation could exist, it took only a brief study to give us the hideous truth—a truth which it would be naive[k] to claim Danforth and I had not independently suspected before, though we had carefully refrained from even hinting it to each

---

[a] moveables] movables C, D
[b] tomb-like,] tomblike, C, D
[c] debris;] débris, C; debris, D
[d] decreased.] decreased. ¶ Cᶜ
[e] newly swept] newly-swept A, B
[f] ones.] ones. ¶ Cᶜ
[g] as in . . . air] as we had seen in other structures, from the air Cᶜ
[h] ice-cap,] ice cap, C, D
[i] ground level] ground-level A, B
[j] us.] us. ¶ Cᶜ
[k] naive] naïve C, D

other. There could now be no further merciful doubt about the nature of the beings which had built and inhabited this monstrous dead city millions of years ago, when man's ancestors were primitive archaic mammals, and vast dinosaurs[a] roamed the tropical steppes of Europe[b] and Asia.

We had previously clung to a desperate alternative and insisted—each to himself—that the omnipresence of the five-pointed motif meant only some cultural or religious exaltation of the archaean[c] natural object which had so patently embodied the quality of five-pointedness; as the decorative motifs of Minoan Crete exalted the sacred bull, those of Egypt the scarabaeus, those of Rome the wolf and the eagle, and those of various savage tribes some chosen totem-animal.[d] But this lone refuge was now stripped from us, and we were forced to face definitely the reason-shaking realisation[e] which the reader of these pages has doubtless long ago anticipated. I can scarcely bear to write it down in black and white even now, but perhaps that will not be necessary.

The things once rearing and dwelling in this frightful masonry in the age of dinosaurs were not indeed dinosaurs,[f] but far worse. Mere dinosaurs[g] were new and almost brainless objects—but the builders of the city were wise and old, and had left certain traces in rocks even then laid down well-nigh[h] a thousand million years . . .[i] rocks laid down before the true life of earth had advanced beyond plastic groups of cells . . .[j] rocks laid down before the true life of earth had existed at all.[k] They were the makers and enslavers of that life, and above all doubt the originals of the fiendish elder myths which things like the Pnakotic

---

[a] dinosaurs] Dinosaurio C[c]
[b] Europe] America A, B
[c] archaean] Archaean D
[d] totem-animal.] totem animal. ¶ C [*paragraphing error corr. by HPL*]; totem animal. D
[e] realisation] realization C, D
[f] dinosaurs . . . dinosaurs,] Dinosauria . . . Dinosauria, C[c]
[g] dinosaurs] Dinosauria C[c]
[h] well-nigh] well nigh C, D
[i] years . . .] years— C, D
[j] cells . . .] cells— C, D
[k] all.] all. ¶ C[c]

Manuscripts and the "Necronomicon"[a] affrightedly hint about. They were the Great Old Ones[b] that had filtered down from the stars when earth was young—the beings whose substance an alien evolution had shaped, and whose powers were such as this planet had never bred. And to think that only the day before Danforth and I had actually looked upon fragments of their millennially fossilised substance . . .[c] and that poor Lake and his party had seen their complete outlines. . . .[d]

It is of course[e] impossible for me to relate in proper order the stages by which we picked up what we know of that monstrous chapter of pre-human[f] life. After the first shock of the certain revelation[g] we had to pause a while to recuperate, and it was fully three[h] o'clock before we got started on our actual tour of systematic research.[i] The sculptures in the building we entered were of relatively late date—perhaps two million years ago—as checked up by geological, biological, and astronomical features;[j] and embodied an art which would be called decadent in comparison with that of specimens we found in older buildings[k] after crossing bridges under the glacial sheet.[l] One edifice hewn from the solid rock seemed to go back forty or possibly even fifty million years—to the lower Eocene or upper Cretaceous—and contained bas-reliefs of an artistry surpassing anything else, with one tremendous exception, that we encountered. That was, we have since agreed, the oldest domestic structure we traversed.

Were it not for the support of those flashlights soon to be made public, I would refrain from telling what I found and inferred, lest I be confined as a madman. Of course, the infinitely early parts of the

[a] "Necronomicon"] *Necronomicon* A, B, C, D
[b] Great Old Ones] great "Old Ones" C, D
[c] fossilised substance . . .] fossilized substance— C, D
[d] outlines. . . .] outlines— C, D
[e] is of course] is, of course, C[c]
[f] pre-human] prehuman C; pre-/human D
[g] revelation] revelation, C[c]
[h] three] 3 A
[i] research.] research. ¶ C[c]
[j] features;] features— C, D
[k] buildings] buildings, C[c]
[l] sheet.] sheet. ¶ C[c]

patchwork[a] tale—representing the pre-terrestrial[b] life of the star-headed beings on other planets, and in other galaxies, and in other universes—can readily be interpreted as the fantastic mythology of those beings themselves; yet such parts sometimes involved designs and diagrams so uncannily close to the latest findings of mathematics and astrophysics that I scarcely know what to think. Let others judge when they see the photographs I shall publish.

Naturally, no one set of carvings which we encountered told more than a fraction of any connected story;[c] nor did we even begin to come upon the various stages of that story in their proper order. Some of the vast rooms were independent units so far as their designs were concerned, whilst in other cases a continuous chronicle would be carried through a series of rooms and corridors.[d] The best of the maps and diagrams were on the walls of a frightful abyss below even the ancient ground level—a cavern perhaps 200 feet square and 60[e] feet high, which had almost undoubtedly been an educational centre[f] of some sort.[g] There were many provoking repetitions of the same material in different rooms and buildings;[h] since certain chapters of experience, and certain summaries or phases of racial history, had evidently been favourites[i] with different decorators or dwellers. Sometimes, though, variant versions of the same theme proved useful in settling debatable points and filling in[j] gaps.

I still wonder that we deduced so much in the short time at our disposal. Of course, we even now have only the barest outline;[k] and much of that was obtained later on from a study of the photographs

---

[a] patchwork] patch-/work B, D
[b] pre-terrestrial] preterrestrial C, D
[c] story;] story, C, D
[d] corridors.] corridors. ¶ C[c]
[e] 200 . . . 60] two hundred . . . sixty C, D
[f] centre] center C, D
[g] sort.] sort. ¶ C[c]
[h] buildings;] buildings, C, D
[i] favourites] favorites C, D
[j] in] up C, D [in *typed over* up *in* B]
[k] outline;] outline— C, D

and sketches we made.[a] It may be the effect of this later study—the revived memories and vague impressions acting in conjunction with his general sensitiveness and with that final supposed horror-glimpse whose essence he will not reveal even to me—which has been the immediate source of Danforth's present breakdown.[b] But it had to be; for we could not issue our warning intelligently without the fullest possible information, and the issuance of that warning is a prime necessity. Certain lingering influences in that unknown antarctic world of disordered time and alien natural law make it imperative that further exploration be discouraged.

VII.

The full story, so far as deciphered, will eventually[c] appear in an official bulletin of Miskatonic University. Here I shall sketch only the salient high lights[d] in a formless, rambling way. Myth or otherwise, the sculptures told of the coming of those star-headed things to the nascent, lifeless earth out of cosmic space—their coming, and the coming of many other alien entities such as at certain times embark upon spatial pioneering.[e] They seemed able to traverse the interstellar ether on their their vast membraneous[f] wings—thus oddly confirming some curious[g] hill folklore long ago told me by an antiquarian colleague. They had lived under the sea a good deal, building fantastic cities and fighting terrific battles with nameless adversaries by means of intricate devices employing unknown principles of energy.[h] Evidently their scientific and mechanical knowledge far surpassed man's today,[i] though they made use of its more widespread and elaborate forms only when

---

[a] made.] made. ¶ C[c]
[b] breakdown.] breakdown. ¶ C[c]
[c] eventually] shortly A, B [*probably a revision by HPL*]
[d] high lights] highlights C, D
[e] pioneering.] pioneering. ¶ C[c]
[f] membraneous] membranous C, D
[g] curious] curius D
[h] energy.] energy. ¶ C[c]
[i] today,] to-day, C

obliged to.[a] Some of the sculptures suggested that they had passed through a stage of mechanised[b] life on other planets, but had receded upon finding its effects emotionally unsatisfying. Their preternatural toughness of organisation[c] and simplicity of natural wants made them peculiarly able to live on a high plane without the more specialised[d] fruits of artificial manufacture, and even without garments[e] except for occasional protection against the elements.

It was under the sea, at first for food and later for other purposes, that they first created earth-life[f]—using available substances according to long-known methods.[g] The more elaborate experiments came after the annihilation of various cosmic enemies. They had done the same thing on other planets;[h] having manufactured not only necessary foods, but certain multicellular protoplasmic masses capable of moulding[i] their tissues into all sorts of temporary organs under hypnotic influence and thereby forming ideal slaves to perform the heavy work of the community.[j] These viscous masses were without doubt what Abdul Alhazred whispered about as the "shoggoths"[k] in his frightful "Necronomicon",[l] though even that mad Arab had not hinted that any existed on earth except in the dreams of those who had chewed a certain alkaloidal herb.[m] When the star-headed Old Ones on this planet had synthesised[n] their simple food forms and bred a good supply of shoggoths,[o] they allowed other cell-groups[p] to develop into

[a] to.] to. ¶ C[c]
[b] mechanised] mechanized C, D
[c] organisation] organization C, D
[d] specialised] specialized C, D
[e] garments] garments, C, D
[f] earth-life] earth life C, D
[g] methods.] methods. ¶ C[c]
[h] planets;] planets, C, D
[i] moulding] molding C, D
[j] community.] community. ¶ C[c]
[k] "shoggoths"] "Shoggoths" C, D
[l] "Necronomicon",] *Necronomicon,* A, B, C, D
[m] herb.] herb. ¶ C[c]
[n] synthesised] synthesized C, D
[o] shoggoths,] Shoggoths, C, D
[p] cell-groups] cell groups C, D

other forms of animal and vegetable life for sundry purposes;[a] extirpating any whose presence became troublesome.

With the aid of the shoggoths,[b] whose expansions could be made to lift prodigious weights, the small, low cities under the sea grew to vast and imposing labyrinths of stone not unlike those which later rose on land. Indeed, the highly adaptable Old Ones had lived much on land in other parts of the universe, and probably retained many traditions of land construction.[c] As we studied the architecture of all these sculptured palaeogean[d] cities, including that whose aeon-dead corridors we were even then traversing, we were impressed by a curious coincidence which we have not yet tried to explain, even to ourselves. The tops of the buildings, which in the actual city around us had of course[e] been weathered into shapeless ruins ages ago, were clearly displayed in the bas-reliefs;[f] and shewed[g] vast clusters of needle-like[h] spires, delicate finials on certain cone and pyramid apexes, and tiers of thin, horizontal scalloped discs[i] capping cylindrical shafts. This was exactly what we had seen in that monstrous and portentous mirage, cast by a dead city whence such skyline[j] features had been absent for thousands and tens of thousands of years, which loomed on our ignorant eyes across the unfathomed mountains of madness as we first approached poor Lake's ill-fated camp.

Of the life of the Old Ones, both under the sea and after part of them migrated to land, volumes could be written. Those in shallow water had continued the fullest use of the eyes at the ends of their five main head tentacles, and had practiced the arts of sculpture and of writing in quite the usual way—the writing accomplished with a stylus

---

[a] purposes;] purposes, C, D
[b] shoggoths,] Shoggoths, C, D
[c] construction.] construction. ¶ C[c]
[d] palaeogean] Palaeogaean C [corr. by HPL to palaeogaean]
[e] had of course] had, of course, C, D
[f] bas-reliefs;] bas-reliefs, C, D
[g] shewed] showed B, C, D
[h] needle-like] needlelike C
[i] discs] disks C, D
[j] skyline] sky-line C, D

on waterproof waxen surfaces.[a] Those lower down in the ocean depths, though they used a curious phosphorescent organism to furnish light, pieced out their vision with obscure special senses operating through the prismatic cilia on their heads—senses which rendered all the Old Ones partly independent of light in emergencies. Their forms of sculpture and writing had changed curiously during the descent, embodying certain apparently chemical coating processes—probably to secure phosphorescence—which the bas-reliefs could not make clear to us.[b] The beings moved in the sea partly by swimming—using the lateral crinoid arms—and partly by wriggling with the lower tier of tentacles containing the pseudo-feet.[c] Occasionally they accomplished long swoops with the auxiliary use of two or more sets of their fan-like[d] folding wings.[e] On land they locally used the pseudo-feet,[f] but now and then flew to great heights or over long distances with their wings. The many slender tentacles into which the crinoid arms branched were infinitely delicate, flexible, strong, and accurate in muscular-nervous coördination;[g] ensuring the utmost skill and dexterity in all artistic and other manual operations.

The toughness of the things was almost incredible. Even the terrific pressures[h] of the deepest sea-bottoms[i] appeared powerless to harm them. Very few seemed to die at all except by violence, and their burial-places[j] were very limited. The fact[k] that they covered their vertically inhumed dead with five-pointed inscribed mounds set up thoughts in Danforth and me which made a fresh pause and recuperation necessary after the sculptures revealed it.[l] The beings multiplied by means of

[a] surfaces.] surfaces. ¶ C[c]
[b] us.] us. ¶ C[c]
[c] pseudo-feet.] pseudofeet. C, D
[d] fan-like] fanlike A, B, D; fan-/like C
[e] wings.] wings. ¶ C[c]
[f] pseudo-feet,] pseudo-/feet, C; pseudofeet, D
[g] coördination;] coördination— C, D
[h] pressures] pressure C, D
[i] sea-bottoms] sea bottoms C, D
[j] burial-places] burial places A, B, C, D
[k] fact] facts C
[l] it.] it. ¶ C[c]

spores—like vegetable pteridophytes[a] as Lake had suspected—but[b] owing to their prodigious toughness and longevity, and consequent lack of replacement needs, they did not encourage the large-scale development of new prothalli[c] except when they had new regions to colonise.[d] The young matured swiftly, and received an education evidently beyond any standard we can imagine. The prevailing intellectual and aesthetic life was highly evolved, and produced a tenaciously enduring set of customs and institutions which I shall describe more fully in my coming monograph. These varied slightly according to sea or land residence, but had the same foundations and essentials.

Though able, like vegetables, to derive nourishment from inorganic substances;[e] they vastly preferred organic and especially animal food. They ate uncooked marine life under the sea, but cooked their viands on land. They hunted game and raised meat herds—slaughtering with sharp weapons whose odd marks on certain fossil bones our expedition had noted.[f] They resisted all ordinary temperatures marvellously;[g] and in their natural state could live in water down to freezing. When the great chill of the Pleistocene drew on, however—nearly a million years ago—the land dwellers had to resort to special measures[h] including artificial heating;[i] until at last[j] the deadly cold appears to have driven them back into the sea.[k] For their prehistoric flights through cosmic space, legend said, they had[l] absorbed certain chemicals and became almost independent of eating, breathing, or heat conditions;[m] but by the time of the great cold they had lost track of the method. In any case[n] they

[a] pteridophytes] pteridophyta, C[c]; pteridophytes, D
[b] but] but, C[c], D
[c] prothalli] prothallia C[c], D
[d] colonise.] colonize. ¶ C [*paragraphing error corr. by HPL*]; colonize. D
[e] substances;] substances, D
[f] noted.] noted. ¶ C[c]
[g] marvellously;] marvelously, C, D
[h] measures] measures, C, D
[i] heating;] heating— C, D
[j] until at last] until, at last, C[c]
[k] sea.] sea. ¶ C[c]
[l] had] *om.* D
[m] conditions;] conditions— C, D
[n] case] case, B, C[c]

could not have prolonged the artificial state indefinitely without harm.

Being non-pairing and semi-vegetable[a] in structure, the Old Ones had no biological basis for the family phase of mammal life;[b] but seemed to organise[c] large households on the principles of comfortable space-utility and—as we deduced from the pictured occupations and diversions of co-dwellers[d]—congenial mental association.[e] In furnishing their homes they kept everything in the centre[f] of the huge rooms, leaving all the wall spaces free for decorative treatment. Lighting, in the case of the land inhabitants, was accomplished by a device probably electro-chemical in nature.[g] Both on land and under water they used curious tables, chairs,[h] and couches like cylindrical frames—for they rested and slept upright with folded-down tentacles—and racks for the hinged sets of dotted surfaces forming their books.

Government was evidently complex and probably socialistic, though no certainties in this regard could be deduced from the sculptures we saw. There was extensive commerce, both local and between different cities;[i] certain small, flat counters, five-pointed and inscribed, serving as money. Probably the smaller of the various greenish soapstones found by our expedition were pieces of such currency.[j] Though the culture was mainly urban, some agriculture and much stock-raising[k] existed. Mining and a limited amount of manufacturing were also practiced. Travel was very frequent, but permanent migration seemed relatively rare except for the vast colonising[l] movements by which the race expanded.[m] For personal locomotion no external aid

[a] non-pairing and semi-vegetable] nonpairing and semivegetable C, D
[b] life;] life, C, D
[c] organise] organize C, D
[d] co-dwellers] codwellers C
[e] association.] association. ¶ C[c]
[f] centre] center C, D
[g] nature.] nature. ¶ C[c]
[h] chairs,] chairs A, B, C, D
[i] cities; cities— C, D
[j] currency.] currency. ¶ C[c]
[k] stock-raising] stock raising C, D
[l] colonising] colonizing C, D
[m] expanded.] expanded. ¶ C[c]

was used;[a] since in land, air, and water movement alike the Old Ones seemed to possess excessively vast capacities for speed. Loads, however, were drawn by beasts of burden—shoggoths[b] under the sea, and a curious variety of primitive vertebrates in the later years of land existence.

These vertebrates, as well as an infinity of other life-forms[c]—animal and vegetable, marine, terrestrial, and aërial—were the products of unguided evolution acting on life-cells[d] made by the Old Ones[e] but escaping beyond their radius of attention. They had been suffered to develop unchecked because they had not come in conflict with the dominant beings. Bothersome forms, of course, were mechanically exterminated.[f] It interested us to see in some of the very last and most decadent sculptures a shambling[g] primitive mammal, used sometimes for food and sometimes as an amusing buffoon by the land dwellers, whose vaguely simian and human foreshadowings were unmistakable. In the building of land cities the huge stone blocks of the high towers were generally lifted by vast-winged pterodactyls of a species heretofore unknown to palaeontology.[h]

The persistence with which the Old Ones survived various geologic changes and convulsions of the earth's crust was little short of miraculous. Though few or none of their first cities seem to have remained beyond the archaean age,[i] there was no interruption in their civilisation[j] or in the transmission of their records.[k] Their original place of advent to the planet was the Antarctic Ocean, and it is likely that they came not long after the matter forming the moon was wrenched from the neighbouring[l] South Pacific. According to one of the

[a] used;] used, C, D
[b] shoggoths] Shoggoths C, D
[c] life-forms] life forms C, D
[d] life-cells] life cells C, D
[e] Ones] Ones, C, D
[f] exterminated.] exterminated. ¶ C[c]
[g] shambling] shambling, C, D
[h] palaeontology.] paleontology. C, D
[i] archaean age,] Archaean Age, C, D
[j] civilisation] civilization C, D
[k] records.] records. ¶ C[c]
[l] neighbouring] neighboring C, D

sculptured maps,[a] the whole globe was then under water, with stone cities scattered farther and farther from the antarctic as aeons passed.[b] Another map shews[c] a vast bulk of dry land around the south pole, where it is evident that some of the beings made experimental settlements[d] though their main centres[e] were transferred to the nearest sea-bottom.[f] Later maps, which display this[g] land mass as cracking and drifting, and sending certain detached parts northward, uphold in a striking way the theories of continental drift lately advanced by Taylor, Wegener, and Joly.

With the upheaval of new land in the South Pacific[h] tremendous events began. Some of the marine cities were hopelessly shattered, yet that was not the worst misfortune. Another race—a land race of beings shaped like octopi and probably corresponding to the[i] fabulous pre-human[j] spawn of Cthulhu—soon began filtering down from cosmic infinity and precipitated a monstrous war which for a time drove the Old Ones wholly back to the sea—a colossal blow in view of the increasing land settlements. Later[k] peace was made, and the new lands were given to the Cthulhu spawn whilst the Old Ones held the sea and the older lands. New land cities were founded—the greatest of them in the antarctic, for this region of first arrival was sacred.[l] From then on, as before, the antarctic remained the centre[m] of the Old Ones' civilisation, and all the discoverable[n] cities built there by the Cthulhu spawn were blotted out.[o] Then suddenly[p] the lands of the Pacific sank

[a] maps,] maps D
[b] passed.] passed. ¶ C[c]
[c] shews] shows B, C, D
[d] settlements] settlements, C, D
[e] centres] centers, C, D
[f] sea-bottom.] sea bottom. ¶ C [*paragraphing error corr. by HPL*]; sea bottom. D
[g] this] the D
[h] Pacific] Pacific, C[c]
[i] the] *om.* D
[j] pre-human] prehuman C; pre-/human D
[k] settlements. ¶ Later] settlements. ¶ Later, C[c]
[l] sacred.] sacred. ¶ C[c]
[m] centre] center C, D
[n] discoverable] *om.* C, D
[o] out.] out. ¶ C[c]
[p] Then suddenly] Then, suddenly, C[c]

again, taking with them the frightful stone city of R'lyeh and all the cosmic octopi, so that the Old Ones were again supreme on the planet[a] except for one shadowy fear about which they did not like to speak.[b] At a rather later age their cities dotted all the land and water areas of the globe—hence the recommendation in my coming monograph that some archaeologist make systematic borings with Pabodie's type of apparatus in certain widely separated regions.

The steady trend down the ages was from water to land;[c] a movement encouraged by the rise of new land masses, though the ocean was never wholly deserted. Another cause of the landward movement was the new difficulty in breeding and managing the shoggoths[d] upon which successful sea-life[e] depended.[f] With the march of time, as the sculptures sadly confessed, the art of creating new life from inorganic matter had been lost;[g] so that the Old Ones had to depend on the moulding[h] of forms already in existence. On land the great reptiles proved highly tractable; but the shoggoths[i] of the sea, reproducing by fission and acquiring a dangerous degree of accidental intelligence, presented for a time a formidable problem.

They had always been controlled through the hypnotic suggestion[j] of the Old Ones, and had modelled[k] their tough plasticity into various useful temporary limbs and organs; but now their self-modelling[l] powers were sometimes exercised independently, and in various imitative forms implanted by past suggestion.[m] They had, it seems, developed a semi-stable[n] brain whose separate and occasionally stubborn

[a] planet] planet, C[c]
[b] speak.] speak. ¶ C[c]
[c] land;] land— C, D
[d] shoggoths] Shoggoths C, D
[e] sea-life] sea life C, D
[f] depended.] depended. ¶ C[c]
[g] lost;] lost, C, D
[h] moulding] molding C, D
[i] shoggoths] Shoggoths C, D
[j] suggestion] suggestions D
[k] modelled] modeled C, D
[l] self-modelling] self-modeling C, D
[m] suggestion.] suggeston. D
[n] semi-stable] semistable C, D

volition echoed the will of the Old Ones without always obeying it.[a] Sculptured images of these shoggoths[b] filled Danforth and me with horror and loathing. They were normally shapeless entities composed of a viscous jelly which looked like an agglutination of bubbles;[c] and each averaged about fifteen feet in diameter when a sphere. They had, however, a constantly shifting shape and volume;[d] throwing out temporary developments or forming apparent organs of sight, hearing, and speech in imitation of their masters, either spontaneously or according to suggestion.

They seem to have become peculiarly intractable toward the middle of the Permian age,[e] perhaps 150[f] million years ago, when a veritable war of re-subjugation[g] was waged upon them by the marine Old Ones. Pictures of this war, and of the headless, slime-coated fashion in which the shoggoths[h] typically left their slain victims, held a marvellously[i] fearsome quality despite the intervening abyss of untold ages.[j] The Old Ones had used curious weapons of molecular[k] disturbance against the rebel entities, and in the end had achieved a complete victory. Thereafter the sculptures shewed[l] a period in which shoggoths[m] were tamed and broken by armed Old Ones as the wild horses of the American west were tamed by cowboys.[n] Though during the rebellion the shoggoths[o] had shewn[p] an ability to live out of water, this transition

[a] it.] it. ¶ C[c]
[b] shoggoths] Shoggoths C, D
[c] bubbles;] bubbles, C, D
[d] volume;] volume— C, D
[e] age,] Age, C, D
[f] 150] one hundred and fifty C, D
[g] re-subjugation] resubjugation C, D
[h] shoggoths] Shoggoths C, D
[i] marvellously] marvelously C, D
[j] ages.] ages. ¶ C[c]
[k] molecular] molecular and atomic D
[l] shewed] showed B, C, D
[m] shoggoths] Shoggoths C, D
[n] cowboys.] cowboys. ¶ C[c]
[o] shoggoths] Shoggoths C, D
[p] shewn] shown B, C, D

was not encouraged;[a] since their usefulness on land would hardly have been commensurate with the trouble of their management.

During the Jurassic age[b] the Old Ones met fresh adversity in the form of a new invasion from outer space—this time by half-fungous, half-crustacean creatures from a planet identifiable as the remote and recently discovered Pluto; creatures[c] undoubtedly the same as those figuring in certain whispered hill legends of the north, and remembered in the Himalayas as the Mi-Go, or Abominable Snow-Men.[d] To fight these beings the Old Ones attempted, for the first time since their terrene advent, to sally forth again into the planetary ether; but despite all traditional preparations[e] found it no longer possible to leave the earth's atmosphere. Whatever the old secret of interstellar travel had been, it was now definitely lost to the race.[f] In the end the Mi-Go drove the Old Ones out of all the northern lands, though they were powerless to disturb those in the sea. Little by little the slow retreat of the elder race to their original antarctic habitat was beginning.

It was curious to note from the pictured battles that both the Cthulhu spawn and the Mi-Go seem to have been composed of matter more widely different from that which we know than was the substance of the Old Ones. They were able to undergo transformations and reintegrations impossible for their adversaries, and seem therefore to have originally come from even remoter gulfs of cosmic space.[g] The Old Ones, but for their abnormal toughness and peculiar vital properties, were strictly material, and must have had their absolute origin within the known space-time continuum;[h] whereas the first sources of the other beings can only be guessed at with bated breath. All this, of course, assuming that the non-terrestrial[i] linkages and the

---

[a] encouraged;] encouraged— C, D

[b] age] Age C, D

[c] creatures . . . creatures] creatures—creatures C, D

[d] Abominable Snow-Men.] Abominable Snow Men. ¶ C [*paragraphing error corr. by HPL*]; abominable Snow Men. D

[e] but . . . preparations] but, . . . preparations, C [*second comma removed by HPL*], D

[f] race.] race. ¶ C[c]

[g] space.] space. ¶ C[c]

[h] continuum;] continuum— C, D

[i] non-terrestrial] nonterrestrial C

anomalies ascribed to the invading foes are not pure mythology. Conceivably, the Old Ones might have invented a cosmic framework to account for their occasional defeats;[a] since historical interest and pride obviously formed their chief psychological element. It is significant that their annals failed to mention many advanced and potent races of beings whose mighty cultures and towering cities[b] figure persistently in certain obscure legends.[c]

The changing state of the world through long geologic ages appeared with startling vividness in many of the sculptured maps and scenes. In certain cases existing science will require revision, while in other cases its bold deductions are magnificently confirmed.[d] As I have said, the hypothesis of Taylor, Wegener, and Joly that all the continents are fragments of an original antarctic land mass which cracked from centrifugal force and drifted apart over a technically viscous lower surface—an hypothesis suggested by such things as the complementary[e] outlines of Africa and South America, and the way the great mountain chains are rolled and shoved up—receives striking support from this uncanny source.

Maps evidently shewing[f] the Carboniferous world[g] of a[h] hundred million or more years ago displayed significant rifts and chasms destined later to separate Africa from the once continuous realms of Europe (then the Valusia of hellish[i] primal legend), Asia, the Americas, and the antarctic continent.[j] Other charts—and most significantly one in connexion[k] with the founding fifty million years ago of the vast dead city around us—shewed[l] all the present continents well

---

[a] defeats;] defeats, C, D
[b] cities] ethics C[c] [*see below*]
[c] It is . . . legends.] *om.* A, B [*Presumably a handwritten addition by HPL in the T.Ms. sent to C; hence the curious transcriptional error* ethics *for* cities *above.*]
[d] confirmed.] confirmed. ¶ C[c]
[e] complementary] complimentary C[c]
[f] shewing] showing B, C, D
[g] world] *om.* B, C[c]
[h] a] an A, B, C, D
[i] hellish] *om.* C, D
[j] continent.] continent. ¶ C[c]
[k] connexion] connection C, D
[l] shewed] showed B, C, D

differentiated. And in the latest discoverable specimen—dating perhaps from the Pliocene age[a]—the approximate world of today[b] appeared quite clearly despite the linkage of Alaska with Siberia, of North America with Europe through Greenland, and of South America with the[c] antarctic continent through Graham Land.[d] In the Carboniferous map the whole globe—ocean floor and rifted land mass alike—bore symbols of the Old Ones' vast stone cities, but in the later charts the gradual recession toward the antarctic became very plain.[e] The final Pliocene specimen shewed[f] no land cities except on the antarctic continent and the tip of South America, nor any ocean cities north of the fiftieth parallel of South Latitude. Knowledge and interest in the northern world, save for a study of coast-lines[g] probably made during long exploration flights on those fan-like[h] membraneous[i] wings, had evidently declined to zero among the Old Ones.

Destruction of cities through the upthrust of mountains, the centrifugal rending of continents, the seismic convulsions of land or sea-bottom,[j] and other natural causes was a matter of common record; and it was curious to observe how fewer and fewer replacements were made as the ages wore on.[k] The vast dead megalopolis that yawned around us seemed to be the last general centre[l] of the race;[m] built early in the Cretaceous age[n] after a titanic earth-buckling had[o] obliterated a

[a] age] Age C, D
[b] today] to-day C
[c] the] a still undiscovered A, B
[d] Land.] Land. ¶ C[c]
[e] plain.] plain. ¶ C[c]
[f] shewed] showed B, C, D
[g] coast-lines] coast lines A, B, C, D
[h] fan-like] fanlike A, B, C, D
[i] membraneous] membranous C[c], D
[j] sea-bottom,] sea bottom, C, D
[k] on.] on. ¶ C[c]
[l] centre] center C, D
[m] race;] race— C, D
[n] age] Age C, D
[o] earth-buckling had] earth-buckling—the one which had sundered the antarctic continent and joined Ross and Weddell Seas—had A, B; earth buckling had C, D

still vaster predecessor not far distant.[a] It appeared that this general region was the most sacred spot of all, where reputedly the first Old Ones had settled on a primal sea-bottom.[b] In the new city—many of whose features we could recognise[c] in the sculptures, but which stretched fully a[d] hundred miles along the mountain range in each direction beyond the farthest limits of our aërial survey—there were reputed to be preserved certain sacred stones forming part of the first sea-bottom city, which were[e] thrust up to light after long epochs in the course of the general crumpling[f] of strata.

VIII.

Naturally, Danforth and I studied with especial[g] interest and a peculiarly personal sense of awe everything pertaining to the immediate district in which we were. Of this local material there was naturally a vast abundance; and on[h] the tangled ground level of the city we were lucky enough to find a house of very late date whose walls, though somewhat damaged by a neighbouring[i] rift, contained sculptures of decadent workmanship carrying the story of the region[j] much beyond the period of the[k] Pliocene map[l] whence we derived our last general glimpse of the pre-human[m] world. This was the last place we examined in detail, since what we found there gave us[n] a fresh[o] immediate objective.

[a] distant.] distant. ¶ C^c
[b] sea-bottom.] sea bottom. C, D
[c] recognise] recognize C, D
[d] a] an A, B
[e] were] *om.* D
[f] crumpling] crumbling D
[g] especial] special C^c
[h] abundance; and on] abundance. ¶ On C^c
[i] neighbouring] neighboring C, D
[j] region] region, C^c
[k] period of the] *om.* A, B, C^c
[l] map] map, C
[m] pre-human] prehuman C, D
[n] gave us] set us upon A, B; set upon us C^c
[o] fresh] fresh, C

Certainly, we were in one of the strangest, weirdest, and most terrible of all the corners of earth's globe. Of all existing lands it was infinitely the most ancient; and the[a] conviction grew upon us that this hideous upland must indeed be the fabled nightmare plateau of Leng which even the mad author of the "Necronomicon"[b] was reluctant to discuss.[c] The great mountain chain was tremendously long—starting as a low range at Luitpold Land on the coast of Weddell Sea and virtually crossing the entire continent. The really high part stretched in a mighty arc from about Latitude 82°, E. Longitude 60° to Latitude 70°, E. Longitude 115°, with its concave side toward our camp and its seaward end in the region of that long, ice-locked coast whose hills were glimpsed by Wilkes and Mawson at the Antarctic Circle.[d]

Yet even more monstrous exaggerations of Nature[e] seemed disturbingly close at hand. I have said that these peaks are higher than the Himalayas, but the sculptures forbid me to say that they are earth's highest. That grim honour[f] is beyond doubt reserved for something which half the sculptures hesitated to record at all, whilst others approached it with obvious repugnance and trepidation.[g] It seems that there was one part of the ancient land—the first part that ever rose from the waters after the earth had flung off the moon and the Old Ones had seeped down from the stars—which had come to be shunned as vaguely and namelessly evil. Cities built there had crumbled before their time, and had been found suddenly deserted.[h] Then when the first great earth-buckling[i] had convulsed the region in the Comanchian age,[j] a frightful line of peaks had shot suddenly up amidst the most

---

[a] ancient; and the] ancient. The C, D
[b] "Necronomicon"] *Necronomicon* A, B, C, D
[c] discuss.] discuss. ¶ C[c]
[d] Antarctic Circle.] antarctic circle. C, D
[e] Nature] nature A, B, C, D
[f] honour] honor C, D
[g] trepidation.] trepidation. ¶ C[c]
[h] deserted.] deserted. ¶ C[c]
[i] earth-buckling] earth buckling C, D
[j] Comanchian age,] Comanchean Age, C [Comanchean *corr. by HPL*], Comanchian Age, D

appalling din and chaos—and earth had received her loftiest and most terrible mountains.

If the scale of the carvings was correct, these abhorred things must have been much over 40,000[a] feet high—radically vaster than even the shocking mountains of madness we had crossed. They extended, it appeared,[b] from about Latitude 77°, E. Longitude 70° to Latitude 70°, E. Longitude 100°—less than 300[c] miles away from the dead city, so that we would have spied their dreaded summits in the dim western distance had it not been for that vague[d] opalescent haze. Their northern end must likewise be visible from the long Antarctic Circle[e] coast-line[f] at Queen Mary Land.

Some of the Old Ones, in the decadent days, had made strange prayers to those mountains;[g] but none ever went near them or dared to guess what lay beyond. No human eye had ever seen them, and as I studied the emotions conveyed in the carvings I prayed that none ever might.[h] There are protecting hills along the coast beyond them—Queen Mary and Kaiser Wilhelm Lands—and I thank heaven[i] no one has been able to land and climb those hills. I am not as sceptical about old tales and fears as I used to be, and I do not laugh now at the pre-human[j] sculptor's notion that lightning paused meaningfully now and then at each of the brooding crests, and that an unexplained glow shone from one of those terrible pinnacles all through the long polar night. There may be a very real and very monstrous meaning in the old Pnakotic whispers about Kadath in the Cold Waste.

But the terrain close at hand was hardly less strange, even if less namelessly accursed. Soon after the founding of the city the great mountain range became the seat of the principal temples, and many

---

[a] 40,000] forty thousand C, D
[b] extended, it appeared,] extended it appeared D
[c] 300] three hundred C, D
[d] vague] vague, C, D
[e] Antarctic Circle] antarctic circle C, D
[f] coast-line] coast line A, B, C, D
[g] mountains;] mountains— C, D
[h] might.] might. ¶ C[c]
[i] heaven] Heaven A, B, C, D
[j] pre-human] prehuman C, D

carvings shewed[a] what grotesque and fantastic towers had pierced the sky where now we saw only the curiously clinging cubes and ramparts.[b] In the course of ages the caves had appeared, and had been shaped into adjuncts of the temples. With the advance of still later epochs all the limestone veins of the region were hollowed out by ground waters, so that the mountains, the foothills, and the plains below them were a veritable network of connected caverns and galleries. Many graphic sculptures told of explorations deep underground, and of the final discovery of the Stygian sunless sea that lurked at earth's bowels.

This vast nighted gulf had undoubtedly been worn by the great river which flowed down from the nameless and horrible westward mountains, and which had formerly turned at the base of the Old Ones' range and flowed beside that chain into the Indian Ocean between Budd and Totten Lands on Wilkes's coast-line.[c] Little by little it had eaten away the limestone hill base at its turning, till at last its sapping currents reached the caverns of the ground waters and joined with them in digging a deeper abyss. Finally its whole bulk emptied into the hollow hills and left the old bed toward the ocean dry. Much of the later city as we now found it had been built over that former bed. The Old Ones, understanding what had happened, and exercising their always keen artistic sense, had carved into ornate pylons those headlands of the foothills where the great stream began its descent into eternal darkness.

This river, once crossed by scores of noble stone bridges, was plainly the one whose extinct course we had seen in our aëroplane survey. Its position in different carvings of the city helped us to orient ourselves to the scene as it had been at various stages of the region's age-long, aeon-dead history;[d] so that we were able to sketch a hasty but careful map of the salient features—squares, important buildings, and the like—for guidance in further explorations.[e] We could soon reconstruct in fancy the whole stupendous thing as it was a million or

---

[a] shewed] showed B, C, D

[b] ramparts.] ramparts. ¶ C[c]

[c] coast-line.] coast line. B, C, D

[d] history;] history, C, D

[e] explorations.] explorations. ¶ C[c]

ten million or fifty million years ago, for the sculptures told us exactly what the buildings and mountains and squares and suburbs and landscape setting and luxuriant Tertiary[a] vegetation had looked like.[b] It must have had a marvellous[c] and mystic beauty, and as I thought of it I almost forgot the clammy sense of sinister oppression with which the city's inhuman age and massiveness and deadness and remoteness and glacial twilight had choked and weighed on my spirit. Yet[d] according to certain carvings the denizens of that city had themselves known the clutch of oppressive terror; for there was a sombre[e] and recurrent type of scene in which the Old Ones were shewn[f] in the act of recoiling affrightedly from some object—never allowed to appear in the design—found in the great river and indicated as having been washed down through waving, vine-draped cycad-forests[g] from those horrible westward mountains.

It was only in the one late-built house with the decadent carvings that we obtained any foreshadowing of the final calamity leading to the city's desertion. Undoubtedly there must have been many sculptures of the same age elsewhere, even allowing for the slackened energies and aspirations of a stressful and uncertain period; indeed, very certain evidence of the existence of others came to us shortly afterward. But this was the first and only set we directly encountered.[h] We meant to look farther later on; but as I have said, immediate conditions dictated another present objective. There would, though, have been a limit— for after all hope of a long future occupancy of the place had perished among the Old Ones, there could not but have been a complete cessation of mural decoration. The ultimate blow, of course, was the coming of the great cold which once held most of the earth in thrall, and which has never departed from the ill-fated poles—the great cold

---

[a] Tertiary] tertiary A, B
[b] like.] like. ¶ C^c
[c] marvellous] marvelous C, D
[d] spirit. Yet] spirit. ¶ Yet, C^c
[e] sombre] somber C, D
[f] shewn] shown B, C, D
[g] cycad-forests] cycad forests C, D
[h] encountered.] encountered. ¶ C^c

that, at the world's other extremity, put an end to the fabled lands of Lomar and Hyperborea.

Just when this tendency began in the antarctic it would be hard to say in terms of exact years. Nowadays we set the beginning of the general glacial periods at a distance of about 500,000[a] years from the present, but at the poles the terrible scourge must have commenced much earlier. All quantitative estimates are partly guesswork;[b] but it is quite likely that the decadent sculptures were made considerably less than a million years ago, and that the actual desertion of the city was complete long before the conventional opening of the Pleistocene— 500,000[c] years ago—as reckoned in terms of the earth's whole surface.

In the decadent sculptures there were signs of thinner vegetation everywhere, and of a decreased country life on the part of the Old Ones. Heating devices were shewn[d] in the houses, and winter travellers[e] were represented as muffled in protective fabrics. Then we saw a series of cartouches (the continuous band arrangement being frequently interrupted in these late carvings)[f] depicting a constantly growing migration to the nearest refuges of greater warmth—some fleeing to cities under the sea off the far-away coast, and some clambering down through networks of limestone caverns in the hollow hills to the neighbouring[g] black abyss of subterrene[h] waters.

In the end[i] it seems to have been the neighbouring[j] abyss which received the greatest colonisation.[k] This was partly due, no doubt, to the traditional sacredness of this especial region;[l] but may have been more conclusively determined by the opportunities it gave for continuing the

---

[a] 500,000] five hundred thousand C, D

[b] guesswork;] guesswork, C, D

[c] 500,000] five hundred thousand C, D

[d] shewn] shown B, C, D

[e] travellers] travelers C, D

[f] (the . . . carvings)] —the . . . carvings— C, D

[g] neighbouring] neighboring C, D

[h] subterrene] subterrane C^c

[i] end] end, C^c

[j] neighbouring] neighboring C, D

[k] colonisation.] colonization. C, D

[l] especial region;] special region, C, D

use of the great temples on the honeycombed mountains, and for retaining the vast land city as a place of summer residence and base of communication with various mines.[a] The linkage of old and new abodes was made more effective by means of several gradings and improvements along the connecting routes, including the chiselling[b] of numerous direct tunnels from the ancient metropolis to the black abyss—sharply down-pointing tunnels whose mouths we carefully drew, according to our most thoughtful estimates, on the guide map we were compiling.[c] It was obvious that at least two of these tunnels lay within a reasonable exploring distance of where we were;[d] both being on the mountainward edge of the city, one less than a quarter-mile[e] toward the ancient rivercourse,[f] and the other perhaps twice that distance in the opposite direction.

The abyss, it seems, had shelving shores of dry land at certain places;[g] but the Old Ones built their new city under water—no doubt because of its greater certainty of uniform warmth. The depth of the hidden sea appears to have been very great, so that the earth's internal heat could ensure its habitability for an indefinite period.[h] The beings seem to have had no trouble in adapting themselves to part-time—and eventually, of course, whole-time—residence under water;[i] since they had never allowed their gill systems to atrophy.[j] There were many sculptures which shewed[k] how they had always frequently visited their submarine kinsfolk elsewhere, and how they had habitually bathed on the deep bottom of their great river. The darkness of inner earth could likewise have been no deterrent to a race accustomed to long antarctic nights.

[a] mines.] mines. ¶ C^c
[b] chiselling] chiseling C, D
[c] compiling.] compiling. ¶ C^c
[d] were;] were— C, D
[e] quarter-mile] quarter of a mile C, D
[f] rivercourse,] river course, D
[g] places;] places, C, D
[h] period.] period. ¶ C^c
[i] water;] water, C, D
[j] atrophy.] atrophy. ¶ C^c
[k] shewed] showed B, C, D

Decadent though their style undoubtedly was, these latest carvings had a truly epic quality where they told of the building of the new city in the cavern sea. The Old Ones had gone about it scientifically;[a] quarrying insoluble rocks from the heart of the honeycombed mountains, and employing expert workers from the nearest submarine city to perform the construction according to the best methods.[b] These workers brought with them all that was necessary to establish the new venture— shoggoth-tissue[c] from which to breed stone-lifters[d] and subsequent beasts of burden for the cavern city, and other protoplasmic matter to mould[e] into phosphorescent organisms for lighting purposes.

At last a mighty metropolis rose on the bottom of that Stygian sea;[f] its architecture much like that of the city above, and its workmanship displaying relatively little decadence because of the precise mathematical element inherent in building operations.[g] The newly bred shoggoths[h] grew to enormous size and singular intelligence, and were represented as taking and executing orders with marvellous[i] quickness. They seemed to converse with the Old Ones by mimicking their voices—a sort of musical piping over a wide range, if poor Lake's dissection had indicated aright—and to work more from spoken commands than from hypnotic suggestions as in earlier times.[j] They were, however, kept in admirable control. The phosphorescent organisms supplied light with vast effectiveness, and doubtless atoned for the loss of the familiar polar auroras of the outer-world night.

Art and decoration were pursued, though of course[k] with a certain decadence. The Old Ones seemed to realise[l] this falling off themselves;[m]

[a] scientifically;] scientifically— C, D
[b] methods.] methods. ¶ C[c]
[c] shoggoth-tissue] Shoggoth tissue C, D
[d] stone-lifters] stone lifters C, D
[e] mould] mold C, D
[f] sea;] sea, C, D
[g] operations.] operations. ¶ C[c]
[h] shoggoths] Shoggoths C, D
[i] marvellous] marvelous C, D
[j] times.] times. ¶ C[c]
[k] though of course] though, of course, C
[l] realise] realize C, D
[m] themselves;] themselves, C, D

and in many cases anticipated the policy of Constantine the Great by transplanting especially fine blocks of ancient carving from their land city, just as the emperor, in a similar age of decline, stripped Greece and Asia of their finest art to give his new Byzantine capital greater splendours[a] than its own people could create. That the transfer of sculptured blocks had not been more extensive,[b] was doubtless owing to the fact that the land city was not at first wholly abandoned.[c] By the time total abandonment did occur—and it surely must have occurred before the polar Pleistocene was far advanced—the Old Ones had perhaps become satisfied with their decadent art—or had ceased to recognise[d] the superior merit of the older carvings. At any rate, the aeon-silent ruins around us had certainly undergone no wholesale sculptural denudation;[e] though all the best separate statues, like other moveables,[f] had been taken away.

The decadent cartouches and dados[g] telling this story were, as I have said, the latest we could find in our limited search. They left us with a picture of the Old Ones shuttling back and forth betwixt the land city in summer and the sea-cavern city in winter, and sometimes trading with the sea-bottom cities off the antarctic coast.[h] By this time the ultimate doom of the land city must have been recognised,[i] for the sculptures shewed[j] many signs of the cold's malign encroachments. Vegetation was declining, and the terrible snows of the winter no longer melted completely even in midsummer.[k] The saurian livestock[l] were nearly all dead, and the mammals were standing it none too well. To keep on with the work of the upper world it had become necessary to

[a] splendours] splendors C, D
[b] extensive,] extensive D
[c] abandoned.] abandoned. ¶ C^c
[d] recognise] recognize C, D
[e] denudation;] denudation, C, D
[f] moveables,] movables, C, D
[g] dados] dadoes D
[h] coast.] coast. ¶ C^c
[i] recognised,] recognized, C, D
[j] shewed] showed B, C, D
[k] midsummer.] midsummer. ¶ C^c
[l] livestock] live stock C, D

adapt some of the amorphous and curiously cold-resistant shoggoths[a] to land life;[b] a thing the Old Ones had formerly been reluctant to do. The great river was now lifeless, and the upper sea had lost most of its denizens except the seals and whales. All the birds had flown away, save only the great, grotesque penguins.

What had happened afterward we could only guess. How long had the new sea-cavern city survived? Was it still down there, a stony corpse in eternal blackness? Had the subterranean waters frozen at last? To what fate had the ocean-bottom cities of the outer world been delivered? Had any of the Old Ones shifted north ahead of the creeping ice-cap?[c] Existing geology shews[d] no trace of their presence. Had the frightful Mi-Go been still a menace in the outer land world of the north? Could one be sure of what might or might not linger even to this day[e] in the lightless and unplumbed abysses of earth's deepest waters?[f] Those things had seemingly been able to withstand any amount of pressure—and men of the sea have fished up curious objects at times. And has the killer-whale theory really explained the savage and mysterious scars on antarctic seals noticed a generation ago by Borchgrevingk?

The specimens found by poor Lake did not enter into these guesses, for their geologic setting proved them to have lived at what must have been a very early date in the land city's history. They were, according to their location, certainly not less than thirty million years old;[g] and we reflected that in their day the sea-cavern city, and indeed the cavern itself, had had no existence.[h] They would have remembered an older scene, with lush Tertiary[i] vegetation everywhere, a younger land city of

[a] shoggoths] Shoggoths C, D
[b] life;] life— C, D
[c] ice-cap?] ice cap? C, D
[d] shews] shows B, C, D
[e] linger . . . day] linger, . . . day, C, D
[f] waters?] water? ¶ C[c]
[g] old;] old, C, D
[h] existence.] existence. ¶ C[c]
[i] Tertiary] tertiary A, B

flourishing arts around them, and a great river sweeping northward along the base of the mighty mountains toward a far-away[a] tropic ocean.

And yet we could not help thinking about these specimens— especially about the eight perfect ones that were missing from Lake's hideously ravaged camp. There was something abnormal about that whole business—the strange things we had tried so hard to lay to somebody's madness—those frightful graves—the amount *and nature*[b] of the missing material—Gedney—the unearthly toughness of those archaic monstrosities, and the queer vital freaks the sculptures now shewed[c] the race to have. . . . Danforth[d] and I had seen a good deal in the last few hours, and were prepared to believe and keep silent about many appalling and incredible secrets of primal Nature.[e]

IX.

I have said that our study of the decadent sculptures brought about a change in our immediate objective. This of course[f] had to do with the chiselled[g] avenues to the black inner world, of whose existence we had not known before, but which we were now eager to find and traverse.[h] From the evident scale of the carvings we deduced that a steeply descending walk of about a mile through either of the neighbouring[i] tunnels would bring us to the brink of the dizzy[j] sunless cliffs above[k] the great abyss;[l] down whose side adequate[m] paths, improved by the Old Ones, led to the rocky shore of the hidden and nighted ocean. To behold this fabulous gulf in stark reality was a lure which seemed

[a] far-away] far-/away C; faraway D
[b] *and nature*] and nature D
[c] shewed] showed B, C, D
[d] have. . . . Danforth] have— Danforth C; have—Danforth D
[e] Nature.] nature. A, B, C, D
[f] This of course] This, of course, C, D
[g] chiselled] chiseled C, D
[h] traverse.] traverse. ¶ C[c]
[i] neighbouring] neighboring C, D
[j] dizzy] dizzy, C, D
[k] above] about C, D
[l] abyss;] abyss, C[c]
[m] side adequate] side C; sides D

impossible of resistance once we knew of the thing—yet we realised[a] we must begin the quest at once if we expected to include it on our present flight.[b]

It[c] was now 8 p.m.,[d] and we had not[e] enough battery replacements to let our torches burn on for ever.[f] We had done so much of our[g] studying and copying below the glacial level that our battery supply had had at least five hours of nearly continuous use;[h] and despite the special dry cell formula would obviously be good for only about four more,[i] though by keeping one torch unused, except for especially interesting or difficult places, we might manage to eke out a safe margin beyond that.[j] It would not do to be without a light in these Cyclopean catacombs, hence in order to make the abyss trip we must give up all further mural deciphering. Of course we intended to revisit the place for days and perhaps weeks of intensive study and photography—curiosity having long ago got[k] the better of horror—but just now we must hasten.[l] Our supply of trail-blazing paper was far from unlimited, and we were reluctant to sacrifice spare notebooks or sketching paper to augment it;[m] but we did let one large notebook[n] go. If worst came to worst,[o] we could resort to rock-chipping[p]—and of course[q] it would be possible, even in case of really lost direction, to work up to full daylight by one channel or

[a] realised] realized C, D
[b] on . . . flight.] in . . . trip. C, D
[c] It] In C[c]
[d] 8 p.m.] eight p. m., C; 8 P.M., D
[e] had not] did not have D
[f] for ever.] forever. A, B, C, D
[g] of our] *om.* D
[h] use;] use, C, D
[i] more,] more; B; more— C, D
[j] that.] that. ¶ C[c]
[k] got] gotten C[c]
[l] hasten.] hasten. ¶ C[c], D
[m] it;] it, C, D
[n] notebook] note book D
[o] worst . . . worst,] worse . . . worst D
[p] rock-chipping] rock chipping A, B, C, D
[q] and of course] and, of course, C[c]

another if granted sufficient time for plentiful trial and error. So at last[a] we set off eagerly in the indicated direction of the nearest tunnel.

According to the carvings from which we had made our map, the desired tunnel-mouth[b] could not be much more than a quarter of a mile from where we stood; the intervening space shewing[c] solid-looking buildings quite likely to be penetrable still at a sub-glacial[d] level. The opening itself would be in the basement—on the angle nearest the foothills—of a vast five-pointed structure of evidently public and perhaps ceremonial nature, which we tried to identify from our aërial survey of the ruins.[e] No such structure came to our minds as we recalled our flight, hence we concluded that its upper parts had been greatly damaged, or that it had been totally shattered in an ice-rift[f] we had noticed. In the latter case the tunnel would probably turn out to be choked, so that we would have to try the next nearest one—the one less than a mile to the north.[g] The intervening rivercourse[h] prevented our trying any of the more southerly[i] tunnels on this trip; and indeed, if both of the neighbouring[j] ones were choked it was doubtful whether our batteries would warrant an attempt on the next northerly one—about a mile beyond our second choice.

As we threaded our dim way through the labyrinth with the aid of map and compass—traversing rooms and corridors in every stage of ruin or preservation, clambering up ramps,[k] crossing upper floors and bridges and clambering down again, encountering choked doorways and piles of debris,[l] hastening now and then along finely preserved and uncannily immaculate stretches, taking false leads and retracing our way

[a] So at last] So, at last, ¶ C[c]
[b] tunnel-mouth] tunnel mouth C, D
[c] shewing] showing B, C, D
[d] sub-glacial] subglacial C
[e] ruins.] ruins. ¶ C[c]
[f] ice-rift] ice rift C, D
[g] north.] north. ¶ C[c]
[h] rivercourse] river course C, D
[i] southerly] southern C, D
[j] neighbouring] neighboring C, D
[k] ramps,] ramps D
[l] debris,] débris, C

(in such cases removing the blind paper trail we had left), and once in a while striking the bottom of an open shaft through which daylight poured or trickled down—we were repeatedly tantalised[a] by the sculptured walls along our route. Many must have told tales of immense historical importance, and only the prospect of later visits reconciled us to the need of passing them by. As it was, we slowed down once in a while and turned on our second torch. If we had had more films we would certainly have paused briefly to photograph certain bas-reliefs, but time-consuming hand copying[b] was clearly out of the question.

I come now once more to a place where the temptation to hesitate, or to hint rather than state, is very strong. It is necessary, however, to reveal the rest in order to justify my course in discouraging further exploration.[c] We had wormed our way very close to the computed site of the tunnel's mouth—having crossed a second-story bridge to what seemed plainly the tip of a pointed wall, and descended to a ruinous corridor especially rich in decadently elaborate and apparently ritualistic sculptures of late workmanship—when, about[d] 8:30 p.m.,[e] Danforth's keen young nostrils gave us the first hint of something unusual.[f] If we had had a dog with us, I suppose we would have been warned before. At first we could not precisely say what was wrong with the formerly crystal-pure air, but after a few seconds our memories reacted[g] only too definitely. Let me try to state the thing without flinching. There was an odour—and that odour[h] was vaguely, subtly, and unmistakably akin to what had nauseated us upon opening the insane grave of the horror poor Lake had dissected.

Of course[i] the revelation was not as clearly cut at the time as it sounds now. There were several conceivable explanations, and we did a good deal of indecisive whispering. Most important of all, we did

---

[a] tantalised] tantalized C, D
[b] hand copying] *om.* C [*see below*]; hand-copying D
[c] route. Many . . . exploration.] route. ¶ C[c]
[d] about] shortly before D
[e] 8:30 p.m.,] eight thirty p. m., C; 8:30 P.M., D
[f] unusual.] unusual. ¶ C[c]
[g] reacted] reached C
[h] odour . . . odour] odor . . . odor C, D
[i] course] course, C[c]

not retreat without further investigation; for having come this far, we were loath to be balked by anything short of certain disaster.[a] Anyway, what we must have suspected was altogether too wild to believe. Such things did not happen in any normal world. It was probably sheer irrational instinct which made us dim our single torch—tempted no longer by the decadent and sinister sculptures that leered menacingly from the oppressive walls—and which softened our progress to a cautious tiptoeing and crawling over the increasingly littered floor and heaps of debris.[b]

Danforth's eyes as well as nose proved better than mine, for it was likewise he who first noticed the queer aspect of the debris[c] after we had passed many half-choked arches leading to chambers and corridors on the ground level. It did not look quite as it ought after countless thousands of years of desertion, and when we cautiously turned on more light we saw that a kind of swath seemed to have been lately tracked through it. The irregular nature of the litter[d] precluded any definite marks, but in the smoother places there were suggestions of the dragging of heavy objects. Once we thought there was a hint of parallel tracks,[e] as if of runners. This was what made us pause again.

It was during that pause that we caught—simultaneously this time— the other odour[f] ahead. Paradoxically, it was both a less frightful and a more frightful odour[g]—less frightful intrinsically, but infinitely appalling in this place under the known circumstances . . .[h] unless, of course, Gedney. . . . For[i] the odour[j] was the plain and familiar one of common petrol—every-day gasoline.

Our motivation after that is something I will leave to psychologists. We knew now that some terrible extension of the camp horrors must

---

[a] disaster.] disaster. ¶ C[c]
[b] debris.] débris. C
[c] debris] débris C
[d] litter] latter B, C[c]
[e] tracks,] tracks D
[f] odour] odor C, D
[g] odour] odor C, D
[h] circumstances . . .] circumstances— C, D
[i] Gedney. . . . For] Gedney— For C; Gedney—for D
[j] odour] odor C, D

have crawled into this nighted burial-place[a] of the aeons, hence could not doubt any longer the existence of nameless conditions—present or at least recent—[b]just ahead. Yet in the end we did let sheer burning curiosity—or anxiety—or auto-hypnotism[c]—or vague thoughts of responsibility toward Gedney—or[d] what not—drive us on.[e] Danforth whispered again of the print he thought he had seen at the alley-turning[f] in the ruins above; and of the faint musical piping— potentially of tremendous significance in the light of Lake's dissection report[g] despite its close resemblance to the cave-mouth echoes of the windy peaks—which he thought he had shortly afterward half heard[h] from unknown depths below.[i] I, in my turn, whispered of how the camp was left—of what had disappeared, and of how the madness of a lone survivor might have conceived the inconceivable—a wild trip across the monstrous mountains and a descent into the unknown[j] primal masonry—

But we could not convince each other, or even ourselves, of anything definite. We had turned off all light as we stood still, and vaguely noticed that a trace of deeply filtered upper day[k] kept the blackness from being absolute.[l] Having automatically begun to move ahead, we guided ourselves by occasional flashes from our torch. The disturbed debris[m] formed an impression we could not shake off, and the smell of gasoline grew stronger. More and more ruin met our eyes and hampered our feet, until very soon we saw that the forward way was about to cease. We had been all too correct in our pessimistic guess about that rift glimpsed from the air. Our tunnel quest was a

[a] burial-place] burial place C, D
[b] recent—] recent D
[c] auto-hypnotism] autohypnotism C, D
[d] or] of C
[e] on.] on. ¶ C[c]
[f] alley-turning] alley turning C, D
[g] report] report, C, D
[h] half heard] half-heard A, B
[i] below.] below. ¶ C[c]
[j] unknown] unknown, C, D
[k] day] daylight C[c]
[l] absolute.] absolute. ¶ C[c]
[m] debris] débris C

blind one, and we were not even going to be able to reach the basement out of which the abyssward aperture opened.

The torch, flashing over the grotesquely carven[a] walls of the blocked corridor in which we stood, shewed[b] several doorways in various states of obstruction; and from one of them the gasoline odour—quite submerging that other hint of odour[c]—came with especial distinctness. As we looked more steadily, we saw that beyond a doubt there had been a slight and recent clearing away of debris[d] from that particular opening. Whatever the lurking horror might be, we believed the direct avenue toward it was now plainly manifest. I do not think anyone[e] will wonder that we waited an appreciable time before making any further motion.

And yet, when we did venture inside that black arch, our first impression was one of anticlimax. For amidst the littered expanse of that sculptured crypt[f]—a perfect cube with sides of about twenty feet—there remained no recent object of instantly discernible size; so that we looked instinctively, though in vain, for a farther doorway.[g] In another moment, however,[h] Danforth's sharp vision had descried[i] a place where the floor debris[j] had been disturbed; and we[k] turned on both torches full strength. Though what we saw in that light was actually simple and trifling, I am none the less reluctant to tell of it because of what it implied.[l] It was a rough levelling[m] of the debris,[n] upon which several small objects lay carelessly scattered, and at one corner of which a considerable amount of gasoline must have been

---

[a] carven] carved C, D
[b] shewed] showed B, C, D
[c] odour . . . odour] odor . . . odor C, D
[d] debris] débris C
[e] anyone] any one C
[f] crypt] Crypt D
[g] doorway.] doorway. ¶ C[c]
[h] however,] however. D
[i] descried] discovered C[c]
[j] debris] débris C
[k] disturbed; and we] disturbed. We C[c]
[l] implied.] implied. ¶ C[c]
[m] levelling] leveling C, D
[n] debris,] débris, C

spilled lately enough to leave a strong odour[a] even at this extreme super-plateau[b] altitude. In other words, it could not be other than a sort of camp—a camp made by questing beings who like us[c] had been turned back by the unexpectedly choked way to the abyss.

Let me be plain. The scattered objects were, so far as substance was concerned, all from Lake's camp;[d] and consisted of[e] tin cans as queerly opened as those we had seen at that ravaged place, many spent matches, three illustrated books more or less curiously smudged, an empty ink bottle with its pictorial and instructional carton, a broken fountain pen, some oddly snipped fragments of fur and tent-cloth,[f] a used electric battery with circular of directions, a folder that came with our type of tent-heater,[g] and a sprinkling of crumpled papers.[h] It was all bad enough,[i] but when we smoothed out the papers and looked at what was on them we felt we had come to the worst. We had found certain inexplicably blotted papers at the camp which might have prepared us, yet the effect of the sight down there in the pre-human[j] vaults of a nightmare city[k] was almost too much to bear.

A mad Gedney might have made the groups of dots in imitation of those found on the greenish soapstones, just as the dots on those insane five-pointed grave-mounds[l] might have been made; and he might conceivably have prepared rough, hasty sketches—varying in their accuracy or[m] lack of it—which outlined the neighbouring[n] parts of the city and traced the way from a circularly represented place outside our previous route—a place we identified as a great cylindrical tower in the

---

[a] odour] odor C, D
[b] super-plateau] superplateau C, D
[c] who like us] who, like us, C, D
[d] camp;] camp, C^c
[e] of] of: C^c
[f] tent-cloth,] tent cloth, C, D
[g] tent-heater,] tent heater, C, D
[h] papers.] papers. ¶ C^c
[i] enough,] enough D
[j] pre-human] prehuman C, D
[k] sight . . . city] sight, . . . city, C^c
[l] grave-mounds] grave mounds C, D
[m] accuracy or] accuracy—or C^c
[n] neighbouring] neighboring C, D

carvings and as a vast circular gulf glimpsed[a] in our aërial survey—to the present five-pointed structure and the tunnel-mouth[b] therein.[c] He might, I repeat, have prepared such sketches; for those before us were quite obviously compiled as our own had been[d] from late sculptures somewhere in the glacial labyrinth, though not from the ones which we had seen and used. But what this[e] art-blind bungler could never have done was to execute those sketches in a strange and assured technique perhaps superior, despite haste and carelessness, to any of the decadent carvings from which they were taken—the characteristic and unmistakable technique of the Old Ones themselves in the dead city's heyday.

There are those who will say Danforth and I were utterly mad not to flee for our lives after that; since our conclusions were now—notwithstanding their wildness—completely fixed, and of a nature I need not even mention to those who have read my account as far as this. Perhaps we were mad—for have I not said those horrible peaks were mountains of madness? But I think I can detect something of the same spirit—albeit in a less extreme form—in the men who stalk deadly beasts through African jungles to photograph them or study their habits. Half-paralysed[f] with terror though we were, there was nevertheless fanned within us a blazing flame of awe and curiosity which triumphed in the end.

Of course[g] we did not mean to face that—or those—which we knew had been there, but we felt that they must be gone by now. They would by this time have found the other neighbouring[h] entrance to the abyss, and have passed within[i] to whatever night-black fragments of the past might await them in the ultimate gulf—the ultimate gulf they had never seen. Or if that entrance, too, was blocked, they would have

[a] glimpsed] glimpse C
[b] tunnel-mouth] tunnel mouth C, D
[c] therein.] therein. ¶ C[c], D
[d] compiled . . been] compiled, . . . been, C, D
[e] this] that D
[f] Half-paralysed] Half paralyzed C, D
[g] course] course, C[c]
[h] neighbouring] neighboring C, D
[i] within] within, C, D

gone on to the north seeking another. They were, we remembered, partly independent of light.

Looking back to that moment, I can scarcely recall just what precise form our new emotions took—just what change of immediate objective it was that so sharpened our sense of expectancy. We certainly did not mean to face what we feared—yet I will not deny that we may have had a lurking, unconscious wish to spy certain things from some hidden vantage-point.[a] Probably we had not given up our zeal to glimpse the abyss itself, though there was interposed a new goal in the form of that great circular place shewn[b] on the crumpled sketches we had found. We had at once recognised[c] it as a monstrous cylindrical tower figuring in the very earliest[d] carvings, but appearing only as a prodigious[e] round aperture from above.[f] Something about the impressiveness of its rendering, even in these hasty diagrams, made us think that its sub-glacial[g] levels must still form a feature of peculiar importance. Perhaps it embodied architectural marvels as yet unencountered by us. It was certainly of incredible age[h] according to the sculptures in which it figured—being indeed among the first things built in the city. Its carvings, if preserved, could not but be highly significant. Moreover, it might form a good present link with the upper world—a shorter route than the one we were so carefully blazing,[i] and probably that by which those others had descended.

At any rate, the thing we did was to study the terrible sketches—which quite perfectly confirmed our own—and start back over the indicated course to the circular place; the course which our nameless predecessors must have traversed twice before us. The other neighbouring[j] gate to the abyss would lie beyond that. I need not speak

---

[a] vantage-point.] vantage point. ¶ C [*paragraphing error corr. by HPL*]; vantage point. D
[b] shewn] shown B, C, D
[c] recognised] recognized C, D
[d] figuring . . . earliest] figuring in the A, B; in the C[c]
[e] prodigious] prodigious, C[c]
[f] above.] above. ¶ C[c]
[g] sub-glacial] sub-/glacial C; subglacial D
[h] age] age, C[c]
[i] blazing,] blazing C[c]
[j] neighbouring] neighboring C, D

of our journey—during which we continued to leave an economical trail of paper—for it was precisely the same in kind as that by which we had reached the cul-de-sac;[a] except that it tended to adhere more closely to the ground level and even descend to basement corridors.[b] Every now and then we could trace certain disturbing marks in the debris[c] or litter or detritus under foot;[d] and[e] after we had passed outside the radius of the gasoline scent[f] we were again faintly conscious—spasmodically—of that more hideous and more persistent scent. After the way had branched from our former course[g] we sometimes gave the rays of our single torch a furtive sweep along the walls; noting in almost every case the well-nigh omnipresent sculptures, which indeed seem to have formed a main aesthetic outlet for the Old Ones.

About 9:30 p.m.,[h] while traversing a[i] vaulted corridor whose increasingly glaciated floor seemed somewhat below the ground level and whose roof grew lower as we advanced, we began to see strong daylight ahead and were able to turn off our torch. It appeared that we were coming to the vast[j] circular place, and that our distance from the upper air could not be very great.[k] The corridor ended in an arch[l] surprisingly low for these megalithic ruins, but we could see much through it even before we emerged. Beyond there stretched a prodigious round space—fully 200[m] feet in diameter—strown[n] with debris[o] and containing many choked archways corresponding to the one we were about to cross. The walls were—in available spaces—boldly sculptured

---

[a] cul-de-sac;] cul-de-sac, C[c]
[b] corridors.] corridors. ¶ C[c]
[c] debris] débris C
[d] or detritus under foot;] underfoot; C, D
[e] and] and, C[c]
[f] scent] scent, C[c]
[g] course] course, C[c]
[h] 9:30 p.m.,] nine-thirty p. m., C; 9:30 P.M., D
[i] a] a long, D
[j] vast] vast, C[c]
[k] great.] great. ¶ C[c]
[l] arch] arch, C[c]
[m] 200] two hundred C, D
[n] strown] strewn D
[o] debris] débris C

into a spiral band of heroic proportions; and displayed, despite the destructive weathering caused by the openness of the spot, an artistic splendour[a] far beyond anything we had encountered before. The littered floor was quite heavily glaciated, and we fancied that the true bottom lay at a considerably lower depth.

But the salient object of the place was the titanic stone ramp which, eluding the archways by a sharp turn outward into the open floor, wound spirally up the stupendous cylindrical wall like an inside counterpart of those once climbing outside the monstrous towers or ziggurats[b] of antique Babylon. Only the rapidity of our flight, and the perspective which confounded the descent with the tower's inner wall, had prevented our noticing this feature from the air, and thus caused us to seek another avenue to the sub-glacial[c] level.[d] Pabodie might have been able to tell what sort of engineering held it in place, but Danforth and I could merely admire and marvel. We could see mighty stone corbels and pillars here and there, but what we saw seemed inadequate to the function performed. The thing was excellently preserved up to the present top of the tower—a highly remarkable circumstance[e] in view of its exposure—and its shelter had done much to protect the bizarre and disturbing cosmic sculptures on the walls.

As we stepped out into the awesome half-daylight[f] of this monstrous cylinder-bottom[g]—fifty million years old, and without doubt the most primally ancient structure ever to meet our eyes—we saw that the ramp-traversed sides stretched dizzily up to a height of fully sixty feet.[h] This, we recalled[i] from our[j] aërial survey, meant an outside glaciation of some forty feet; since the yawning gulf we had seen from the plane had been at the top of an approximately twenty-foot mound of crumbled masonry,

---

[a] splendour] splendor C, D
[b] ziggurats] zikkurats C
[c] sub-glacial] subglacial C, D
[d] level.] level. ¶ C^c
[e] circumstance] circumstances C^c
[f] half-daylight] half daylight C, D
[g] cylinder-bottom] cylinder bottom C, D
[h] feet.] feet. ¶ C^c
[i] recalled] recall D
[j] our] out C^c

somewhat sheltered for three-fourths[a] of its circumference by the massive curving walls of a line of higher ruins. According to the sculptures the original tower had stood in the centre[b] of an immense circular plaza;[c] and had been perhaps 500 or 600[d] feet high, with tiers of horizontal discs[e] near the top, and a row of needle-like[f] spires along the upper rim.[g] Most of the masonry had obviously toppled outward rather than inward—a fortunate happening, since otherwise the ramp might have been shattered and the whole interior choked. As it was, the ramp shewed[h] sad battering; whilst the choking was such that all the archways at the bottom[i] seemed to have been recently half-cleared.[j]

It took us only a moment to conclude that this was indeed the route by which those others had descended, and that this would be the logical route for our own ascent[k] despite the long trail of paper we had left elsewhere. The tower's mouth was no farther from the foothills and our waiting plane than was the great terraced building we had entered, and any further sub-glacial[l] exploration we might make on this trip would lie in this general region.[m] Oddly, we were still thinking about possible later trips—even after all we had seen and guessed. Then[n] as we picked our way cautiously over the debris[o] of the great floor, there came a sight which for the time excluded all other matters.

It was the neatly huddled array of three sledges in that farther angle of the ramp's lower and outward-projecting course which had

[a] three-fourths] three fourths C
[b] centre] center C, D
[c] plaza;] plaza, C, D
[d] 500 or 600] five hundred or six hundred C, D
[e] discs] disks C, D
[f] needle-like] needlelike C, D
[g] rim.] rim. ¶ C[c]
[h] shewed] showed B, C, D
[i] at the bottom] *om.* C[c]
[j] recently half-cleared.] B; recently cleared. A, D; cleared. C [*HPL has corrected to* recently cleared]
[k] ascent] ascent, C[c]
[l] sub-glacial] subglacial C, D
[m] region.] region. ¶ C[c]
[n] Then] Then, C, D
[o] debris] débris C

hitherto been screened from our view. There they were—the three sledges missing from Lake's camp—shaken by a hard usage which must have included forcible dragging along great reaches of snowless masonry and debris,[a] as well as much hand portage over utterly unnavigable places.[b] They were carefully and intelligently packed and strapped, and contained things memorably familiar enough—[c]the gasoline stove, fuel cans, instrument cases, provision tins, tarpaulins obviously bulging with books, and some bulging with less obvious contents—everything derived from Lake's equipment.[d] After what we had found in that other room, we were in a measure prepared for this encounter. The really great shock came when we stepped over and undid one tarpaulin[e] whose outlines had peculiarly disquieted us. It seems that others as well as Lake had been interested in collecting typical specimens; for there were two here, both stiffly frozen, perfectly preserved, patched with adhesive plaster where some wounds around the neck had occurred, and wrapped with patent[f] care to prevent further damage. They were the bodies of young Gedney and the missing dog.

X.

Many people will probably judge us callous as well as mad for thinking about the northward tunnel and the abyss so soon after our sombre[g] discovery, and I am not prepared to say that we would have immediately revived such thoughts but for a specific circumstance which broke in upon us and set up a whole new train of speculations.[h] We had replaced the tarpaulin over poor Gedney and were standing in a kind of mute bewilderment when the sounds finally reached our consciousness—the first sounds we had heard since descending out of

[a] debris,] débris, C
[b] places.] places. ¶ C[c]
[c] enough—] enough: C, D
[d] equipment.] equipment. ¶ C, D
[e] tarpaulin] tarpaulin, C[c]
[f] patent] obvious A; om. C, D
[g] sombre] somber C, D
[h] speculations.] speculations. ¶ C[c]

the open where the mountain wind whined faintly from its unearthly heights. Well known[a] and mundane though they were, their presence in this remote world of death was more unexpected and unnerving than any grotesque or fabulous tones could possibly have been—since they gave a fresh upsetting to all our notions of cosmic harmony.

Had it been some trace of that bizarre musical piping over a wide range[b] which Lake's dissection report had led us to expect in those others—and which, indeed, our overwrought fancies had been reading into every wind-howl[c] we had heard since coming on the camp horror—it would have had a kind of hellish congruity with the aeon-dead region around us. A voice from other epochs belongs in a graveyard of other epochs.[d] As it was, however, the noise shattered all our profoundly seated adjustments—all our[e] tacit acceptance of the inner antarctic as a waste as utterly and irrevocably void of every vestige of normal life as the sterile disc of the moon.[f] What we heard was not the fabulous note of any buried blasphemy of elder earth from whose supernal toughness an age-denied polar sun had evoked a monstrous response. Instead, it was a thing so mockingly normal and so unerringly familiarised[g] by our sea days off Victoria Land and our camp days at McMurdo Sound that we shuddered to think of it here, where such things ought not to be. To be brief—it was simply the raucous squawking of a penguin.

The muffled sound floated from sub-glacial[h] recesses nearly opposite to the corridor whence we had come—regions manifestly in the direction of that other tunnel to the vast abyss. The presence of a living water-bird[i] in such a direction—in a world whose surface was one of age-long and uniform lifelessness—could lead to only one conclusion;

[a] Well known] Well-known A, B, C, D
[b] range] range, C[c]
[c] wind-howl] wind howl C, D
[d] epochs.] epochs. ¶ C[c]
[e] our] out C[c]
[f] as utterly . . . moon.] utterly and irrevocably void of every vestige of normal life. C, D
[g] familiarised] familiarized C, D
[h] sub-glacial] sub-/glacial C; subglacial D
[i] water-bird] water bird C, D

hence our first thought was to verify the objective reality of the sound. It was, indeed, repeated;[a] and seemed at times to come from more than one throat.[b] Seeking its source, we entered an archway from which much debris[c] had been cleared; resuming our trail-blazing[d]—with an added paper-supply[e] taken with curious repugnance from one of the tarpaulin bundles on the sledges—when we left daylight behind.

As the glaciated floor gave place to a litter of detritus, we plainly discerned some curious[f] dragging tracks; and once Danforth found a distinct print of a sort whose description would be only too superfluous. The course indicated by the penguin cries was precisely what our map and compass prescribed as an approach to the more northerly tunnel-mouth,[g] and we were glad to find that a bridgeless thoroughfare on the ground and basement levels seemed open.[h] The tunnel, according to the chart, ought to start from the basement of a large pyramidal structure which we seemed vaguely to recall from our aërial survey as remarkably well preserved.[i] Along our path the single torch shewed[j] a customary profusion of carvings, but we did not pause to examine any of these.

Suddenly a bulky white shape loomed up ahead of us, and we flashed on the second torch. It is odd how wholly this new quest had turned our minds from earlier fears of what might lurk near. Those other ones, having left their supplies in the great circular place, must have planned to return after their scouting trip toward or into the abyss; yet we had now discarded all caution concerning them as completely as if they had never existed.[k] This white, waddling thing was fully six feet high, yet we seemed to realise[l] at once that it was not one of those others.

[a] repeated;] repeated, C, D
[b] throat.] throat. ¶ C[c]
[c] debris] débris C
[d] trail-blazing] trail blazing C, D
[e] paper-supply] paper supply C, D
[f] curious] curious, C, D
[g] tunnel-mouth,] tunnel mouth, C, D
[h] open.] open. ¶ C[c]
[i] well preserved.] well-preserved. A, B, C, D
[j] shewed] showed B, C, D
[k] existed.] existed. ¶ C[c]
[l] realise] realize C, D

They were larger and dark, and according to the sculptures[a] their motion over land surfaces was a swift, assured matter despite the queerness of their sea-born tentacle equipment. But to say that the white thing did not profoundly frighten us would be vain. We were indeed clutched for an instant by a[b] primitive dread almost sharper than the worst of our reasoned fears regarding those others.[c] Then came a flash of anticlimax as the white shape sidled into a lateral archway to our left[d] to join two others of its kind which had summoned it in raucous tones. For it was only a penguin—albeit of a huge, unknown species larger than the greatest of the known king penguins, and monstrous in its combined albinism and virtual eyelessness.

When we had followed the thing into the archway and turned both our torches on the indifferent and unheeding group of three[e] we saw that they were all eyeless albinos of the same unknown and gigantic species.[f] Their size reminded us of some of the archaic penguins depicted in the Old Ones' sculptures, and it did not take us long to conclude that they were descended from the same stock—undoubtedly surviving through a retreat to some warmer inner region whose perpetual blackness had destroyed their pigmentation and atrophied their eyes to mere useless slits.[g] That their present habitat was the vast abyss we sought, was not for a moment to be doubted; and this evidence of the gulf's continued warmth and habitability filled us with the most curious and subtly perturbing fancies.

We wondered, too, what had caused these three birds to venture out of their usual domain. The state and silence of the great dead city made it clear that it had at no time been an[h] habitual seasonal rookery, whilst the manifest indifference of the trio to our presence made it seem odd that any passing party of those others should have startled

---

[a] and . . . sculptures] and, . . . sculptures, C [*second comma removed by HPL*], D
[b] a] *om.* D
[c] others.] others. ¶ Cᶜ
[d] left] left, Cᶜ
[e] three] three, Cᶜ
[f] species.] species. ¶ Cᶜ
[g] slits.] slits. ¶ Cᶜ
[h] an] a Cᶜ

them.[a] Was it possible that those others had taken some aggressive action[b] or tried to increase their meat supply? We doubted whether that pungent odour[c] which the dogs had hated could cause an equal antipathy in these penguins;[d] since their ancestors had obviously lived on excellent terms with the Old Ones—an amicable relationship which must have survived in the abyss below as long as any of the Old Ones remained.[e] Regretting—in a flareup[f] of the old spirit of pure science— that we could not photograph these anomalous creatures, we shortly left them to their squawking and pushed on toward the abyss whose openness was now so positively proved to us, and whose exact direction occasional penguin tracks made clear.

Not long afterward a steep descent in a long, low, doorless, and peculiarly sculptureless corridor led us to believe that we were approaching the tunnel-mouth[g] at last. We had passed two more penguins, and heard others immediately ahead.[h] Then the corridor ended in a prodigious open space which made us gasp involuntarily—a perfect inverted hemisphere, obviously deep underground;[i] fully a hundred[j] feet in diameter and fifty feet high, with low archways opening around all parts of the circumference but one, and that one yawning cavernously with a black[k] arched aperture which broke the symmetry of the vault to a height of nearly fifteen feet. It was the entrance to the great abyss.

In this vast hemisphere, whose concave roof was impressively though decadently carved to a likeness of the primordial celestial dome, a few albino penguins waddled—aliens there, but indifferent and unseeing. The black tunnel yawned indefinitely off at a steep[l]

---

[a] them.] them. ¶ C^c
[b] action] notion B, C^c
[c] odour] odor C, D
[d] penguins;] penguins, D
[e] remained.] remained. ¶ C^c
[f] flareup] flare-up C, D
[g] tunnel-mouth] tunnel mouth C, D
[h] We . . . ahead.] We had passed two more penguins. C^c
[i] underground;] underground, C^c
[j] a hundred] 100 A
[k] black] black, C, D
[l] steep] steep, C, D

descending grade, its aperture adorned with grotesquely chiselled[a] jambs and lintel.[b] From that cryptical mouth we fancied a current of slightly warmer air and perhaps even a suspicion of vapour[c] proceeded; and we wondered what living entities other than penguins the limitless void below, and the contiguous honeycombings of the land and the titan mountains, might conceal.[d] We wondered, too, whether the trace of mountaintop smoke at first suspected by poor Lake, as well as the odd haze we had ourselves perceived around the rampart-crowned peak, might not be caused by the tortuous-channelled[e] rising of some such vapour[f] from the unfathomed regions of earth's core.

Entering the tunnel, we saw that its outline was—at least at the start—about fifteen feet each way;[g] sides, floor, and arched roof composed of the usual megalithic masonry. The sides were sparsely decorated with cartouches of conventional designs in a late,[h] decadent style; and all the construction and carving were marvellously well preserved.[i] The floor was quite clear, except for a slight detritus bearing outgoing penguin tracks and the inward tracks of those[j] others. The farther one advanced, the warmer it became; so that we were soon unbuttoning our heavy garments. We wondered whether there were any actually igneous manifestations below, and whether the waters of that sunless sea were hot.[k] After a short distance the masonry gave place to solid rock, though the tunnel kept the same proportions and presented the same aspect of carved regularity. Occasionally its varying grade became so steep that grooves were cut in the floor.[l] Several times we noted the mouths of small lateral galleries not recorded in

[a] chiselled] chiseled C, D
[b] lintel.] lintel. ¶ C[c]
[c] vapour] vapor C, D
[d] conceal.] conceal. ¶ C[c]
[e] tortuous-channelled] tortuous-channeled C, D
[f] vapour] vapor C, D
[g] way;] way— C, D
[h] late,] later, B, C[c]
[i] well preserved.] well-preserved. A, B, D; well-preserved. ¶ C [*paragraphing error corr. by HPL*]
[j] those] these D
[k] hot.] hot. ¶ C[c]
[l] floor.] floor. ¶ A, B, C[c]

our diagrams; none of them such as to complicate the problem of our return, and all of them welcome as possible refuges in case we met unwelcome entities on their way back from the abyss.[a] The nameless scent of such things was very distinct. Doubtless it was suicidally foolish to venture into that tunnel under the known conditions, but the lure of the unplumbed is stronger in certain persons than most suspect— indeed, it was just such a lure which had brought us to this unearthly polar waste in the first place.[b] We saw several penguins as we passed along, and speculated on the distance we would have to traverse. The carvings had led us to expect a steep downhill walk of about a mile to the abyss, but our previous wanderings had shewn[c] us that matters of scale were not wholly to be depended on.

After about a quarter of a mile that nameless scent became greatly accentuated, and we kept very careful track of the various lateral openings we passed. There was no visible vapour[d] as at the mouth, but this was doubtless due to the lack of contrasting cooler air. The temperature was rapidly ascending, and we were not surprised to come upon a careless heap of material shudderingly familiar to us. It was composed of furs and tent-cloths[e] taken from Lake's camp, and we did not pause to study the bizarre forms into which the fabrics had been slashed.[f] Slightly beyond this point we noticed a decided increase in the size and number of the side-galleries,[g] and concluded that the densely honeycombed region beneath the higher foothills must now have been reached.[h] The nameless scent was now curiously mixed with another and scarcely less offensive odour[i]—of what nature we could not guess, though we thought of decaying organisms and perhaps unknown subterrene fungi.[j] Then came a startling expansion of the tunnel for

---

[a] abyss.] abyss. ¶ C^c
[b] place.] place. ¶ C^c
[c] shewn] shown B, C, D
[d] vapour] vapor C, D
[e] tent-cloths] tent-cloth A; tent cloths C [s *removed by HPL*]; tent cloth D
[f] slashed.] slashed. ¶ C^c
[g] side-galleries,] side galleries, C, D
[h] reached.] reached. ¶ C^c
[i] odour] odor C, D
[j] subterrene fungi.] subterrane fungi. ¶ C^c; subterranean fungi. D

which the carvings had not prepared us—a broadening and rising into a lofty, natural-looking elliptical cavern with a level floor; some 75 feet long and 50[a] broad, and with many immense side-passages[b] leading away into cryptical darkness.

Though this cavern was natural in appearance, an inspection with both torches suggested that it had been formed by the artificial destruction of several walls between adjacent honeycombings. The walls were rough, and the high[c] vaulted roof was thick with stalactites; but the solid rock floor had been smoothed off, and was free from all debris,[d] detritus, or even dust to a positively abnormal extent.[e] Except for the avenue through which we had come, this was true of the floors of all the great galleries opening off from it; and the singularity of the condition was such as to set us vainly puzzling.[f] The curious new foetor[g] which had supplemented the nameless scent was excessively pungent here; so much so that it destroyed all trace of the other. Something about this whole place, with its polished and almost glistening floor, struck us as more vaguely baffling and horrible than any of the monstrous things we had[h] previously encountered.

The regularity of the passage immediately ahead, as well as the larger proportion of penguin-droppings there,[i] prevented all confusion as to the right course amidst this plethora of equally great cave-mouths.[j] Nevertheless we resolved to resume our paper trail-blazing[k] if any further complexity should develop; for dust tracks, of course, could no[l] longer be expected.[m] Upon resuming our direct progress we cast a beam of torchlight over the tunnel walls—and stopped short in amazement

[a] 75 . . . 50] seventy-five . . . fifty C, D
[b] side-passages] side passages A, B, C, D
[c] high] high, C, D
[d] debris,] débris, C
[e] extent.] extent. ¶ Cᶜ
[f] puzzling.] puzzling. ¶ Cᶜ
[g] foetor] fetor C, D
[h] had] have C
[i] as well . . . there,] *om.* ¶ Cᶜ
[j] cave-mouths.] cave mouths. C, D
[k] trail-blazing] trail blazing C; trailblazing D
[l] no] not D
[m] expected.] expected. ¶ Cᶜ

at the supremely radical change which had come over the carvings in this part of the passage. We realised,[a] of course, the great decadence of the Old Ones' sculpture at the time of the tunnelling;[b] and had indeed noticed the inferior workmanship of the arabesques in the stretches behind us.[c] But now, in this deeper section beyond the cavern, there was a sudden difference wholly transcending explanation—a difference in basic nature as well as in mere quality, and involving so profound and calamitous a degradation of skill that nothing in the hitherto observed rate of decline could have led one to expect it.

This new and degenerate work was coarse, bold, and wholly lacking in delicacy of detail. It was counter-sunk[d] with exaggerated depth in bands following the same general line as the sparse cartouches of the earlier sections, but the height of the reliefs did not reach the level of the general surface.[e] Danforth had the idea that it was a second carving—a sort of palimpsest formed after the obliteration of a previous design. In nature it was wholly decorative and conventional;[f] and consisted of crude spirals and angles roughly following the quintile mathematical tradition of the Old Ones, yet seeming[g] more like a parody than a perpetuation of that tradition. We could not get it out of our minds that some subtly but profoundly alien element had been added to the aesthetic feeling behind the technique—an alien element, Danforth guessed, that was responsible for the manifestly[h] laborious substitution. It was like, yet disturbingly unlike, what we had come to recognise[i] as the Old Ones' art; and I was persistently reminded of such hybrid things as the ungainly Palmyrene sculptures fashioned[j] in the Roman manner. That others had recently noticed this belt of

[a] realised,] realized, C, D
[b] tunnelling;] tunneling, C, D
[c] us.] us. ¶ C[c]
[d] counter-sunk] countersunk C, D
[e] surface.] surface. ¶ C[c]
[f] conventional;] conventional, C, D
[g] seeming] seemingly D
[h] manifestly] *om.* C[c] [*see below*], D
[i] recognise] *om.* C[c] [*see below*]; recognize D
[j] sculptures fashioned] sculptures, performed A, B; *om.* C[c] [*see below*]

carving was hinted by the presence of a used torch[a] battery on the floor in front of one of the most characteristic designs.[b] [c]

Since we could not afford to spend any considerable time in study, we resumed our advance after a cursory look; though frequently casting beams over the walls to see if any further decorative changes developed. Nothing of the sort was perceived, though the carvings were in places rather sparse because of the numerous mouths of smooth-floored lateral tunnels.[d] We saw and heard fewer penguins, but thought we caught a vague suspicion of an infinitely distant chorus of them somewhere deep within the earth. The new and inexplicable odour[e] was abominably strong, and we could detect scarcely a sign of that other nameless scent.[f] Puffs of visible vapour[g] ahead bespoke increasing contrasts in temperature, and the relative nearness of the sunless sea-cliffs[h] of the great abyss. Then, quite unexpectedly, we saw certain obstructions on the polished floor ahead—obstructions which were quite definitely not penguins—and turned on our second torch after making sure that the objects were quite stationary.

XI.

Still another time have I come to a place where it is very difficult to proceed. I ought to be hardened by this stage; but there are some experiences and intimations which scar too deeply to permit of healing, and leave only such an[i] added sensitiveness that memory reinspires[j] all the original horror.[k] We saw, as I have said, certain obstructions on the polished floor ahead; and I may add that our nostrils were assailed almost simultaneously by a very curious intensification of the strange

[a] torch] B; flashlight A, D; *om.* C [*corr. by HPL to* flashlight; *see below*]
[b] designs.] B; cartouches. A, D; *om.* C [*corr. by HPL to* cartouches; *see below*]
[c] We . . . designs.] *om.* C [*corr. by HPL as indicated above*]
[d] look; . . . tunnels.] look. ¶ C[c]
[e] odour] odor C, D
[f] scent.] scent. ¶ C[c]
[g] vapour] vapor C, D
[h] sea-cliffs] sea cliffs C, D
[i] an] *om.* B, C[c]
[j] reinspires] re-/inspired C[c]
[k] horror.] horror. ¶ C[c]

prevailing foetor,[a] now quite plainly mixed with the nameless stench of those others which had gone before us.[b] The light of the second torch left no doubt of what the obstructions were, and we dared approach them only because we could see, even from a distance, that they were quite as past all harming power as had been the six similar specimens unearthed from the monstrous star-mounded graves at poor Lake's camp.

They were, indeed, as lacking in completeness as most of those we had unearthed—though it grew plain from the thick, dark-green[c] pool gathering around them that their incompleteness was of infinitely greater recency. There seemed to be only four of them, whereas Lake's bulletins would have suggested no less than eight as forming the group which had preceded us. To find them in this state was wholly unexpected, and we wondered what sort of monstrous struggle had occurred down here in the dark.

Penguins, attacked in a body, retaliate savagely with their beaks;[d] and our ears now made certain the existence of a rookery far beyond. Had those others disturbed such a place and aroused murderous pursuit? The obstructions did not suggest it, for penguin[e] beaks against the tough tissues Lake had dissected could hardly account for the terrible damage our approaching glance was beginning to make out. Besides, the huge blind birds we had seen appeared to be singularly peaceful.

Had there, then, been a struggle among those others, and were the absent four responsible? If so, where were they? Were they close at hand and likely to form an immediate menace to us? We glanced anxiously at some of the smooth-floored lateral passages as we continued our slow and frankly reluctant approach.[f] Whatever the conflict was, it had clearly been that which had frightened the penguins into their unaccustomed wandering. It must, then, have arisen near that faintly heard rookery in the incalculable gulf beyond, since there were no signs that any birds had normally dwelt here.[g] Perhaps, we

[a] foetor,] fetor, C, D
[b] before us.] before. D
[c] dark-green] dark green D
[d] beaks;] beaks D
[e] penguin] penguins' D
[f] approach.] approach. ¶ C^c
[g] here.] here. ¶ C^c

reflected, there had been a hideous running fight, with the weaker party seeking to get back to the cached sledges when their pursuers finished them. One could picture the daemoniac[a] fray between namelessly monstrous entities as it surged out of the black abyss with great clouds of frantic penguins squawking and scurrying ahead.

I say that we approached those sprawling and incomplete obstructions slowly and reluctantly. Would to heaven[b] we had never approached them at all, but had run back at top speed out of that blasphemous tunnel with the greasily smooth floors and the degenerate murals aping and mocking the things they had superseded—run back, before we had seen what we did see, and before our minds were burned with something which will never let us breathe easily again!

Both of our torches were turned on the prostrate objects, so that we soon realised[c] the dominant factor in their incompleteness. Mauled, compressed, twisted, and ruptured as they were, their chief common injury was total decapitation.[d] From each one the tentacled starfish-head[e] had been removed; and as we drew near we saw that the manner of removal looked more like some hellish tearing or suction than like any ordinary form of cleavage.[f] Their noisome dark-green ichor formed a large, spreading pool; but its stench was half overshadowed[g] by that[h] newer and stranger stench, here more pungent than at any other point along our route.[i] Only when we had come very close to the sprawling obstructions could we trace that second, unexplainable foetor[j] to any immediate source—and the instant we did so Danforth, remembering certain very vivid sculptures of the Old Ones' history in the Permian age 150[k] million years ago, gave vent to a nerve-tortured

---

[a] daemoniac] demonic C [*corr. by HPL to* demoniac]; demoniac D
[b] heaven] Heaven B, C, D
[c] realised] realized C, D
[d] decapitation.] decapitation. ¶ C[c]
[e] starfish-head] starfish head C, D
[f] cleavage.] cleavage. ¶ C[c]
[g] half overshadowed] half-overshadowed A, B
[h] that] the D
[i] route.] route. ¶ C[c]
[j] foetor.] fetor. C, D
[k] age 150] Age one hundred and fifty C, D

cry which echoed hysterically through that vaulted and archaic passage with the evil[a] palimpsest carvings.

I came only just short of echoing his cry myself; for I had seen those primal sculptures, too, and had shudderingly admired the way the nameless artist had suggested that hideous slime-coating[b] found on certain incomplete and prostrate Old Ones—those whom the frightful shoggoths[c] had characteristically slain and sucked to a ghastly headlessness in the great war of re-subjugation.[d] They were infamous, nightmare sculptures even when telling of age-old, bygone things; for shoggoths[e] and their work ought not to be seen by human beings or portrayed by any beings.[f] The mad author of the "Necronomicon"[g] had nervously tried to swear that none had been bred on this planet, and that only drugged dreamers had ever[h] conceived them. Formless protoplasm able to mock and reflect all forms and organs and processes—viscous agglutinations of bubbling cells—rubbery fifteen-foot spheroids infinitely plastic and ductile—slaves of suggestion, builders of cities—more and more sullen, more and more intelligent, more and more amphibious, more and more imitative—[i]Great God![j] What madness made even those blasphemous Old Ones willing to use and to[k] carve such things?

And now, when Danforth and I saw the freshly glistening and reflectively iridescent black slime which clung thickly to those headless bodies and stank obscenely with that new unknown odour[l] whose cause only a diseased fancy could envisage—clung to those bodies and sparkled less voluminously on a smooth part of the accursedly re-

---

[a] evil] evil, C, D
[b] slime-coating] slime coating C, D
[c] shoggoths] Shoggoths C, D
[d] re-subjugation.] resubjugation. ¶ C [*paragraphing error corr. by HPL*]; resubjugation. D
[e] shoggoths] Shoggoths C, D
[f] beings.] beings. ¶ C[c]
[g] "Necronomicon"] *Necronomicon* A, B, C, D
[h] ever] even D
[i] imitative—] imitative! C, D
[j] God!] Heaven! C[c]
[k] to] *om.* D
[l] new . . . odour] new, . . . odor C, D

sculptured[a] wall *in a series of grouped dots* [b]—we understood the quality of cosmic fear to its uttermost depths.[c] It was not fear of those four missing others—for all too well did we suspect they would do no harm again. Poor devils! After all, they were not evil things of their kind. They were the men of another age and another order of being. Nature had played a hellish jest on them—as it will on any others that human madness, callousness, or cruelty may hereafter drag[d] up in that hideously dead or sleeping polar waste—and this was their tragic homecoming.[e]

They had not been even savages—for what indeed had they done? That awful awakening in the cold of an unknown epoch—perhaps an attack by the furry, frantically barking quadrupeds, and a dazed defence[f] against them and the equally frantic white simians with the queer wrappings and paraphernalia . . . poor Lake, poor Gedney . . . and[g] poor Old Ones! Scientists to the last—what had they done that we would not have done in their place? God,[h] what intelligence and persistence! What a facing of the incredible, just as those carven kinsmen and forbears had faced things only a little less incredible! Radiates, vegetables, monstrosities, star-spawn[i]—whatever they had been, they were men!

They had crossed the icy peaks on whose templed slopes they had once worshipped[j] and roamed among the tree-ferns.[k] They had found their dead city brooding under its curse, and had read its carven latter days as we had done. They had tried to reach their living fellows in fabled depths of blackness they had never seen—and what had they found?[l] All this flashed in unison through the thoughts of Danforth and me as we looked from those headless, slime-coated shapes to the loathsome

---

[a] re-sculptured] re-/sculptured C; resculptured D

[b] *in . . . dots*] in . . . dots C, D

[c] depths.] depths. ¶ C[c]

[d] drag] dig D

[e] homecoming. ¶] homecoming. D

[f] defence] defense C, D

[g] paraphernalia . . . and] paraphernalia. Poor Lake. Poor Godney. And C[c]

[h] God,] Lord, C[c]

[i] star-spawn] star spawn C, D

[j] worshipped] worshiped C

[k] tree-ferns.] tree ferns. C, D

[l] found?] found? ¶ C[c]

palimpsest sculptures and the diabolical dot-groups[a] of fresh slime on the wall beside them—looked and understood what must have triumphed and survived down there in the Cyclopean water-city[b] of that nighted, penguin-fringed abyss, whence even now a sinister curling mist had begun to belch pallidly as if in answer to Danforth's hysterical scream.

The shock of recognising[c] that monstrous slime and headlessness had frozen us into mute, motionless statues, and it is only through later conversations that we have learned of the complete identity of our thoughts at that moment.[d] It seemed aeons that we stood there, but actually it could not have been more than ten or fifteen seconds. That hateful, pallid mist curled forward as if veritably driven by some remoter advancing bulk—and then came a sound which upset much of what we had just decided, and in so doing broke the spell and enabled us to run like mad past squawking, confused penguins over our former trail back to the city, along ice-sunken megalithic corridors to the great open circle, and up that archaic spiral ramp in a frenzied[e] automatic plunge for the sane outer air and light of day.

The new sound, as I have intimated, upset much that we had decided; because it was what poor Lake's dissection had led us to attribute to those we had just[f] judged dead. It was, Danforth later told me, precisely what he had caught in infinitely muffled form when at that spot beyond the alley-corner[g] above the glacial level; and it certainly had a shocking resemblance to the wind-pipings[h] we had both heard around the lofty mountain caves.[i] At the risk of seeming puerile I will add another thing, too;[j] if only because of the surprising way Danforth's impression[k] chimed with mine. Of course[l] common

[a] dot-groups] dot groups C, D
[b] water-city] water city C, D
[c] recognising] recognizing C, D
[d] moment.] moment. ¶ C[c]
[e] frenzied] frenzied, C, D
[f] just] *om.* D
[g] alley-corner] alley corner C, D
[h] wind-pipings] wind pipings C, D
[i] caves.] caves. ¶ C[c]
[j] too;] too, C, D
[k] impression] impressions D
[l] course] course, C[c]

reading is what prepared us both to make the interpretation, though Danforth has hinted at queer notions about unsuspected and forbidden sources to which Poe may have had access when writing his "Arthur Gordon Pym"[a] a century ago.[b] It will be remembered that in that fantastic tale there is a word of unknown but terrible and prodigious significance connected with the antarctic and screamed eternally by the gigantic,[c] spectrally snowy birds of that malign region's core. *"Tekeli-li! Tekeli-li!"* That, I may admit, is exactly what we thought we heard conveyed by that sudden sound behind the advancing white mist—that insidious[d] musical piping over a singularly wide range.

We were in full flight before three notes or syllables had been uttered, though we knew that the swiftness of the Old Ones would enable any scream-roused and pursuing survivor of the slaughter to overtake us in a moment if it really wished to do so.[e] We had a vague hope, however, that non-aggressive[f] conduct and a display of kindred reason might cause such a being to spare us in case of capture;[g] if only from scientific curiosity.[h] After all, if such an[i] one had nothing to fear for itself it would have no motive in harming us. Concealment being futile at this juncture, we used our torch for a running glance behind, and perceived that the mist was thinning. Would we see,[j] at last, a complete and living specimen of those others? Again came that insidious musical piping—*"Tekeli-li! Tekeli-li!"*

Then, noting that we were actually gaining on our pursuer, it occurred to us that the entity might be wounded. We could take no chances, however, since it was very obviously approaching in answer to Danforth's scream[k] rather than in flight from any other entity. The

[a] "Arthur Gordon Pym"] *Arthur Gordon Pym* D
[b] ago.] ago. ¶ C^c
[c] gigantic,] gigantic D
[d] insidious] insidious, C^c
[e] so.] so. ¶ C^c
[f] non-aggressive] nonaggressive C, D
[g] capture;] capture, C, D
[h] curiosity.] curiosity. ¶ C^c
[i] an] a C^c
[j] see,] see C^c
[k] scream] scream, C, D

timing was too close to admit of doubt.[a] Of the whereabouts of that less conceivable and less mentionable nightmare—that foetid,[b] unglimpsed mountain of slime-spewing protoplasm whose race had conquered the abyss and sent land pioneers to re-carve[c] and squirm through the burrows of the hills—we could form no guess; and it cost us a genuine pang to leave this probably crippled Old One—perhaps a lone survivor—to the peril of recapture and a nameless fate.

Thank heaven[d] we did not slacken our run. The curling mist had thickened again, and was driving ahead with increased speed; whilst the straying penguins in our rear were squawking and screaming and displaying signs of a panic really surprising in view of their relatively minor confusion when we had passed them.[e] Once more came that sinister, wide-ranged piping—*"Tekeli-li! Tekeli-li!"* We had been wrong. The thing was not wounded, but had merely paused on encountering the bodies of its fallen kindred and the hellish slime inscription above them. We could never know what that daemon[f] message was—but those burials at Lake's camp had shewn[g] how much importance the beings attached to their dead.[h] Our recklessly used torch now revealed ahead of us the large open cavern where various ways converged, and we were glad to be leaving those morbid palimpsest sculptures— almost felt even when scarcely seen—behind.

Another thought which the advent of the cave inspired was the possibility of losing our pursuer at this bewildering focus of large galleries. There were several of the blind albino penguins in the open space, and it seemed clear that their fear of the oncoming entity was extreme to the point of unaccountability.[i] If at that point we dimmed our torch to the very lowest limit of travelling[j] need, keeping it strictly

---

[a] doubt.] doubt. ¶ C[c]
[b] foetid,] fetid, C, D
[c] re-carve] recarve C, D
[d] heaven] Heaven B, C, D
[e] them.] them. ¶ C[c]
[f] daemon] demon C, D
[g] shewn] shown B, C, D
[h] dead.] dead. ¶ C[c]
[i] unaccountability.] unaccountability. ¶ C[c]
[j] travelling] traveling C, D

in front of us, the frightened squawking motions of the huge birds in
the mist might muffle our footfalls, screen our true course, and
somehow set up a false lead.[a] Amidst the churning, spiralling fog[b] the
littered and unglistening floor of the main tunnel beyond this point, as
differing from the other morbidly polished burrows, could hardly form
a highly distinguishing feature; even, so far as we could conjecture, for
those indicated special senses which made the Old Ones partly though
imperfectly[c] independent of light in emergencies. In fact, we were
somewhat apprehensive lest we go astray ourselves in our haste. For we
had, of course, decided to keep straight on toward the dead city; since
the consequences of loss in those unknown foothill honeycombings
would be unthinkable.

The fact that we survived and emerged is sufficient proof that the
thing did take a wrong gallery whilst we providentially hit on the right
one. The penguins alone could not have saved us, but in conjunction
with the mist they seem to have done so. Only a benign fate kept the
curling vapours[d] thick enough at the right moment, for they were
constantly shifting and threatening to vanish.[e] Indeed, they did lift for
a second just before we emerged from the nauseously re-sculptured[f]
tunnel into the cave; so that we actually caught one first and only half-
glimpse[g] of the oncoming entity as we cast a final, desperately fearful
glance backward before dimming the torch and mixing with the
penguins in the hope of dodging pursuit. If the fate which screened us
was benign, that which gave us the half-glimpse[h] was infinitely the
opposite; for to that flash of semi-vision[i] can be traced a full half of
the horror which has ever since haunted us.

Our exact motive in looking back again was perhaps no more than
the immemorial instinct of the pursued to gauge the nature and course

---

[a] lead.] lead. ¶ C^c
[b] spiralling fog] spiraling fog, C [*comma removed by HPL*]; spiraling fog D
[c] partly . . . imperfectly] partly, . . . imperfectly, C, D
[d] vapours] vapors C, D
[e] vanish.] vanish. ¶ C^c
[f] re-sculptured] resculptured C, D
[g] half-glimpse] half glimpse C, D
[h] half-glimpse] half glimpse C, D
[i] semi-vision] semivision C, D

of its pursuer; or perhaps it was an automatic attempt to answer a subconscious question raised by one of our senses.[a] In the midst of our flight, with all our faculties centred[b] on the problem of escape, we were in no condition to observe and analyse[c] details; yet even so our latent brain-cells[d] must have wondered at the message brought them by our nostrils. Afterward[e] we realised[f] what it was—that our retreat from the foetid slime-coating[g] on those headless obstructions, and the coincident approach of the pursuing entity,[h] had not brought us the exchange of stenches which logic called for.[i] In the neighbourhood[j] of the prostrate things that new and lately unexplainable foetor[k] had been wholly dominant; but by this time it ought to have largely given place to the nameless stench associated with those others. This it had not done—for instead, the newer and less bearable smell was now virtually undiluted, and growing more and more poisonously insistent each second.

So we glanced back—[l]simultaneously, it would appear; though no doubt the incipient motion of one prompted the imitation of the other. As we did so we flashed both torches full strength at the momentarily thinned mist; either from sheer primitive anxiety to see all we could, or in a less primitive but equally unconscious effort to dazzle the entity before we dimmed our light and dodged among the penguins of the labyrinth-centre[m] ahead.[n] Unhappy act! Not Orpheus himself, or Lot's wife, paid much more dearly for a backward glance. And again came that shocking, wide-ranged piping— *"Tekeli-li! Tekeli-li!"*

I might as well be frank—even if I cannot bear to be quite

[a] senses.] senses. ¶ C[c]
[b] centred] centered C, D
[c] analyse] analyze C, D
[d] brain-cells] brain cells C, D
[e] Afterward] Afterward, C[c]
[f] realised] realized C, D
[g] foetid slime-coating] fetid slime coating C, D
[h] entity,] entity D
[i] for.] for. ¶ C[c]
[j] neighbourhood] neighborhood C, D
[k] foetor] fetor C, D
[l] back—] back D
[m] labyrinth-centre] labyrinth center C, D
[n] ahead.] ahead. ¶ C[c]

direct—in stating what we saw; though at the time we felt that it was not to be admitted even to each other. The words reaching the reader can never even suggest the awfulness of the sight itself. It crippled our consciousness so completely that I wonder we had the residual sense to dim our torches as planned, and to strike the right tunnel toward the dead city. Instinct alone must have carried us through—perhaps better than reason could have done; though if that was what saved us, we paid a high price. Of reason we certainly had little enough left.[a] Danforth was totally unstrung, and the first thing I remember of the rest of the journey was hearing him light-headedly chant an[b] hysterical formula in which I alone of mankind could have found anything but insane irrelevance. It reverberated in falsetto echoes among the squawks of the penguins; reverberated through the vaultings ahead, and—thank God[c]—through the now empty vaultings behind. He could not have begun it at once—else we would not have been alive and blindly racing. I shudder to think of what a shade of difference in his nervous reactions might have brought.

"South Station Under—Washington Under—Park Street Under—Kendall—Central—Harvard. . . ."[d] The poor fellow was chanting the familiar stations of the Boston-Cambridge tunnel that burrowed through our peaceful native soil thousands of miles away in New England, yet to me the ritual had neither irrelevance nor home-feeling.[e] It had only horror, because I knew unerringly the monstrous, nefandous analogy that had suggested it.[f] We had expected, upon looking back, to see a terrible and incredible moving entity if the mists were thin enough; but of that entity we had formed a clear idea. What we did see—for the mists were indeed all too malignly thinned—was something altogether different, and immeasurably more hideous and detestable. It was the utter, objective embodiment of the fantastic novelist's 'thing that

---

[a] I might . . . left.] *om.* C[c]; I might . . . left. ¶ D [*HPL had failed to indicate that omitted passage was meant to connect with passage that follows.*]

[b] an] a C

[c] God] Heaven C[c]

[d] Harvard. . . ." Harvard—" C, D

[e] home-feeling.] home feeling. C, D

[f] it.] it. ¶ C[c]

should not be';[a] and its nearest comprehensible analogue is a vast, onrushing subway train as one sees it from a station platform—the great black front looming colossally out of infinite subterraneous[b] distance, constellated with strangely coloured[c] lights and filling the prodigious burrow as a piston fills a cylinder.[d]

But we were not on a station platform. We were on the track ahead as the nightmare[e] plastic column of foetid[f] black iridescence oozed tightly onward through its fifteen-foot sinus;[g] gathering unholy speed and driving before it a spiral, re-thickening[h] cloud of the pallid abyss-vapour.[i] It was a terrible, indescribable thing[j] vaster than any subway train—a shapeless congeries of protoplasmic bubbles, faintly self-luminous, and with myriads of temporary eyes forming and unforming as pustules of greenish light all over the tunnel-filling front that bore down upon us, crushing the frantic penguins and slithering over the glistening floor that it and its kind had swept so evilly free of all litter. Still came that eldritch, mocking cry—*"Tekeli-li! Tekeli-li!"* And[k] at last we remembered that the daemoniac shoggoths[l]—given life, thought,[m] and plastic organ-patterns[n] solely by the Old Ones, and having no language save that which the dot-groups[o] expressed—*had likewise no voice save the imitated accents of their bygone masters.*[p]

[a] 'thing . . . be';] "thing . . . be"; D
[b] subterraneous] subterranean D
[c] coloured] colored C, D
[d] burrow . . . cylinder.] burrow. C[c]
[e] nightmare] nightmare, C, D
[f] foetid] fetid C, D
[g] sinus;] sinus, C, D
[h] re-thickening] rethickening C, D
[i] abyss-vapour.] abyss vapor. ¶ C [*paragraphing error corr. by HPL*]; abyss vapor. D
[j] thing] thing, C[c]
[k] And] and D
[l] daemoniac shoggoths] demonic Shoggoths C [demonic *corr. to* demoniac *by* HPL]; demoniac Shoggoths D
[m] thought,] though, C[c]
[n] organ-patterns] organ patterns C, D
[o] dot-groups] dot groups C, D
[p] *had . . . masters.*] had . . . masters. C, D

XII.

Danforth and I have recollections of emerging into the great sculptured hemisphere and of threading our back trail through the Cyclopean rooms and corridors of the dead city; yet these are purely dream-fragments[a] involving no memory of volition, details,[b] or physical exertion. It was as if we floated in a nebulous world or dimension without time, causation, or orientation. The grey[c] half-daylight of the vast circular space sobered us somewhat; but we did not go near those cached sledges or look again at poor Gedney and the dog. They have a strange and titanic mausoleum, and I hope the end of this planet will find them still undisturbed.

It was while struggling up the colossal spiral incline that we first felt the terrible fatigue and short breath which our race through the thin plateau air had produced; but not even the[d] fear of collapse could make us pause before reaching the normal outer realm of sun and sky.[e] There was something vaguely appropriate about our departure from those buried epochs; for as we wound our panting way up the sixty-foot cylinder of primal masonry we glimpsed beside us a continuous procession of heroic sculptures in the dead race's early and undecayed technique—a farewell from the Old Ones, written fifty million years ago.

Finally[f] scrambling out at the top, we found ourselves on a great mound of tumbled blocks;[g] with the curved walls of higher stonework rising westward, and the brooding peaks of the great mountains shewing[h] beyond the more crumbled structures toward the east. The low antarctic sun of midnight peered redly from the southern horizon through rifts in the jagged ruins, and the terrible age and deadness of the nightmare city seemed all the starker by contrast with such relatively known and accustomed things as the features of the polar landscape.[i]

[a] dream-fragments] dream fragments C, D
[b] details,] details D
[c] grey] *om.* C [*see below*]; gray D
[d] the] *om.* C [*see below*], D
[e] exertion. It was . . . sky.] exertion. ¶ C^c
[f] Finally] Finally, C^c
[g] blocks;] blocks, C, D
[h] shewing] showing B, C, D
[i] east. The low . . . landscape.] east. ¶ C^c

The sky above was a churning and opalescent mass of tenuous ice-vapours,[a] and the cold clutched at our vitals. Wearily resting the outfit-bags[b] to which we had instinctively clung throughout our desperate flight, we rebuttoned our heavy garments for the stumbling[c] climb down the mound and the walk through the aeon-old stone maze to the foothills where our aëroplane waited. Of what had set us fleeing from the[d] darkness of earth's secret and archaic gulfs we said nothing at all.[e]

In less than a quarter of an hour we had found the steep grade to the foothills—the probable ancient terrace—by which we had descended, and could see the dark bulk of our great plane amidst the sparse ruins on the rising slope ahead.[f] Half way[g] uphill toward our goal we paused for a momentary breathing-spell,[h] and turned to look again at the fantastic palaeogean[i] tangle of incredible stone shapes below us—once more outlined mystically against an unknown west. As we did so we saw that the sky beyond had lost its morning haziness; the restless ice-vapours[j] having moved up to the zenith, where their mocking outlines seemed on the point of settling into some bizarre pattern which they feared to make quite definite or conclusive.

There now lay revealed on the ultimate white horizon behind the grotesque city a dim, elfin line of pinnacled violet whose needle-pointed heights loomed dream-like[k] against the beckoning rose-colour[l] of the western sky. Up toward this shimmering rim sloped the ancient table-land,[m] the depressed course of the bygone river traversing it as an irregular ribbon of shadow.[n] For a second we gasped in admiration of

---

[a] ice-vapours,] ice vapors, C; ice-vapors, D

[b] outfit-bags] A, D; outfit bags B; *om.* C [*corr. by HPL to* outfit bags; *see below*]

[c] stumbling] A, D; scrambling B; *om.* C[c] [*see below*]

[d] the] *om.* C [*see below*]; that D

[e] Wearily . . . all.] *om.* C[c]

[f] ahead.] ahead. ¶ C[c]

[g] Half way] Halfway C, D

[h] breathing-spell,] breathing spell, C, D

[i] palaeogean] *om.* C, D

[j] ice-vapours] ice vapors C; ice-vapors D

[k] dream-like] dreamlike A, B, C, D

[l] rose-colour] rose color C, D

[m] table-land,] tableland, C; table-/land, D

[n] shadow.] shadow. ¶ C[c]

the scene's unearthly cosmic beauty, and then vague horror began to creep into our souls. For this far violet line could be nothing else than the terrible mountains of the forbidden land—highest of earth's peaks and focus of earth's evil; harbourers[a] of nameless horrors and archaean[b] secrets; shunned and prayed to by those who feared to carve their meaning; untrodden by any living thing of[c] earth, but visited by the sinister lightnings and sending strange beams across the plains in the polar night—beyond doubt the unknown archetype of that dreaded Kadath in the Cold Waste beyond abhorrent Leng, whereof unholy[d] primal legends hint evasively. We were the first human beings ever to see them—and I hope to God we may be the last.[e] [f]

If the sculptured maps and pictures in that pre-human[g] city had told truly, these cryptic violet mountains could not be much less than 300[h] miles away; yet none the less sharply did their dim elfin essence jut[i] above that remote and snowy rim, like the serrated edge of a monstrous alien planet about to rise into unaccustomed heavens. Their height, then, must have been tremendous beyond all known[j] comparison— carrying them up into tenuous atmospheric strata peopled[k] by such gaseous wraiths as rash flyers have barely lived to whisper of after unexplainable falls.[l] Looking at them, I thought nervously of certain sculptured hints of what the great bygone river had washed down into the city from their accursed slopes[m]—and wondered how much sense and how much folly had lain in the fears of those Old Ones who carved them so reticently.[n] I recalled how their northerly end must

[a] harbourers] harborers C, D
[b] archaean] Archaean D
[c] of] on D
[d] unholy] *om.* C [*see below*], D
[e] We were . . . last.] B; *om.* A, C, D
[f] night—. . . last.] night. C [*restored by HPL except for last sentence*]
[g] pre-human] prehuman C, D
[h] 300] three hundred A, B, C, D
[i] jut] appear D
[j] known] *om.* C [*see below*], D
[k] peopled] *om.* C [*see below*]; peopled only D
[l] heavens. Their height, . . . falls.] heavens. ¶ C[c]
[m] slopes] sloping C[c]
[n] reticently.] reticently. ¶ C[c]

come near the coast at Queen Mary Land, where even at that moment Sir Douglas Mawson's expedition was doubtless working less than a thousand miles away; and hoped that no evil fate would give Sir Douglas and his men a glimpse of what might lie beyond the protecting coastal range. Such thoughts formed[a] a measure of my overwrought condition at the time—and Danforth seemed to be even worse.

Yet long[b] before we had passed the great star-shaped ruin and reached our plane our fears had become transferred to the lesser but vast enough[c] range whose re-crossing[d] lay ahead of us.[e] From these foothills the black, ruin-crusted slopes reared up starkly and hideously against the east, again reminding us of those strange Asian paintings of Nicholas Roerich; and when we thought of the damnable honeycombs[f] inside them, and of the[g] frightful amorphous entities that might have pushed their foetidly[h] squirming way even to the topmost hollow pinnacles, we could not face without panic the prospect of again sailing by those suggestive skyward cave-mouths[i] where the wind made sounds like an evil musical piping over a wide range.[j] To make matters worse, we saw distinct traces of local mist around several of the summits—as poor Lake must have done when he made that early mistake about volcanism—and thought shiveringly of that kindred mist from which we had just escaped;[k] of that, and of the blasphemous, horror-fostering abyss whence all such vapours[l] came.

All was well with the plane, and we clumsily hauled on our heavy flying furs. Danforth got the engine started without trouble, and we made a very smooth takeoff[m] over the nightmare city. Below us the

[a] formed] form A, B

[b] long] *om.* B, C[c]

[c] lesser . . . vast enough] lesser, . . . vast enough C[c]; lesser . . . vast-enough D

[d] re-crossing] re-/crossing C; recrossing D

[e] us.] us. ¶ C[c]

[f] honeycombs] honeycombings C; *om.* D [*see below*]

[g] damnable . . . of the] *om.* D

[h] foetidly] fetidly C, D

[i] cave-mouths] cave mouths C, D

[j] range.] range. ¶ C[c]

[k] escaped;] escaped— C[c]

[l] vapours] vapors C, D

[m] takeoff] take-off C, D

primal Cyclopean masonry spread out as it had done when first we saw it—so short, yet infinitely long, a time ago—and[a] we began rising and turning to test the wind for our crossing through the pass.[b] At a very high level there must have been great disturbance, since the ice-dust clouds of the zenith were doing all sorts of fantastic things; but at 24,000[c] feet, the height we needed for the pass, we found navigation quite practicable.[d] As we drew close to the jutting peaks the wind's strange piping again became manifest, and I could see Danforth's hands trembling at the controls. Rank amateur though[e] I was, I thought at that moment that I might be a better navigator than he in effecting the dangerous crossing between pinnacles; and when I made motions to change seats and take over his duties he did not protest.[f] I tried to keep all my skill and self-possession about me, and stared at the sector of reddish farther sky betwixt the[g] walls of the pass—resolutely refusing to pay attention to the puffs of mountaintop vapour,[h] and wishing that I had wax-stopped ears like Ulysses' men off the Sirens'[i] coast to keep that disturbing wind-piping from my consciousness.

But[j] Danforth, released from his piloting and keyed up to a dangerous nervous pitch, could not keep quiet. I felt him turning and wriggling about as he looked back at the terrible receding city, ahead at the cave-riddled, cube-barnacled peaks, sidewise at the bleak sea of snowy, rampart-strown foothills, and upward at the seething, grotesquely clouded sky.[k] It was then, just as I was trying to steer safely through the pass, that his mad shrieking brought us so close to disaster[l] by shattering my tight hold on myself and causing me to fumble helplessly

---

[a] it—. . .—and] B; it, and A, D; *om.* C [*see below*]

[b] city. Below . . . pass.] city. ¶ C [*corr. by HPL except for the passage between em-dashes above*]

[c] 24,000] twenty-four thousand C, D

[d] practicable.] practicable. ¶ C[c]

[e] though] that D

[f] protest.] protest. ¶ C[c]

[g] the] The C

[h] mountaintop vapour,] *om.* C[c] [*see below*]; mountain-top vapor, D

[i] Sirens'] *om.* C[c] [*see below*]; Siren's D

[j] pass—. . . But] pass. ¶ But C[c]

[k] sky.] sky. ¶ C[c]

[l] disaster] disaster, C

with the controls for a moment. A second afterward my resolution triumphed and we made the crossing safely—yet[a] I am afraid that Danforth will never be the same again.

I have said that Danforth refused to tell me what final horror made him scream out so insanely—a horror which, I feel sadly sure, is mainly responsible for his present breakdown. We had snatches of shouted conversation above the wind's piping and the engine's buzzing as we reached the safe side of the range and swooped slowly down toward the camp, but that had mostly to do with the pledges of secrecy we had made as we prepared to leave the nightmare city. Certain things, we had agreed, were not for people to know and discuss lightly—and I would not speak of them now but for the need of heading off that Starkweather-Moore Expedition,[b] and others, at any cost. It is absolutely necessary, for the peace and safety of mankind, that some of earth's dark, dead corners and unplumbed depths be let alone; lest sleeping abnormalities wake to resurgent life, and blasphemously surviving nightmares squirm and splash out of their black lairs to newer and wider conquests.[c]

All that Danforth has ever hinted is that the final horror was a mirage. It was not, he declares, anything connected with the cubes and caves of echoing, vaporous, wormily honeycombed[d] mountains of madness which we crossed; but a single fantastic, daemoniac[e] glimpse, among the churning zenith-clouds,[f] of what lay back of those other violet westward mountains which the Old Ones had shunned and feared. It is very probable that the thing was a sheer delusion born of the previous stresses we had passed through, and of the actual though unrecognised[g] mirage of the dead transmontane city experienced near Lake's camp the day before; but it was so real to Danforth that he suffers from it still.[h]

[a] safely—yet] safely— Yet C^c
[b] Expedition,] *om.* C [*see below*]; expedition, D
[c] Certain . . . conquests.] *om.* C^c
[d] wormily honeycombed] wormily-honeycombed D
[e] daemoniac] demonic C [*corr. by HPL to* demoniac]; demoniac D
[f] zenith-clouds,] A; westward zenith-clouds, B; westward zenith clouds, C [westward *deleted by HPL*]; zenith clouds, D
[g] unrecognised] *om.* C [*see below*]; unrecognized D
[h] It is . . . still.] *om.* C^c

He has on rare occasions whispered disjointed and irresponsible things about "the[a] black pit", "the carven rim", "the proto-shoggoths", "the windowless solids with five dimensions",[b] "the nameless cylinder",[c] "the elder pharos",[d] "Yog-Sothoth", "the primal white jelly", "the colour out of space", "the wings", "the eyes in darkness", "the moon-ladder", "the original, the eternal, the undying",[e] and other bizarre conceptions; but when he is fully himself he repudiates all this and attributes it to his curious and macabre reading of earlier years. Danforth, indeed, is known to be among the few who have ever dared go completely through that worm-riddled copy of the "Necronomicon"[f] kept under lock and key in the college library.

The higher sky, as we crossed the range, was surely vaporous and disturbed enough; and although I did not see the zenith I can well imagine that its swirls of ice-dust[g] may have taken strange forms. Imagination, knowing how vividly distant scenes can sometimes be reflected, refracted, and magnified by such layers of restless cloud, might easily have supplied the rest—and of course[h] Danforth did not hint any of those[i] specific horrors till after his memory had had a chance to draw on his bygone reading. He could never have seen so much in one instantaneous glance.

At the time[j] his shrieks were confined to the repetition of a single[k] mad word of all too obvious source:[l]

"Tekeli-li! Tekeli-li!"

---

[a] "the] "The D

[b] pit", . . . rim", . . . proto-shoggoths", . . . dimensions",] pit," . . . rim," . . . proto-Shoggoths," . . . dimensions," C, D

[c] cylinder",] cylinders," C [*corr. by HPL to* cylinder,]; cylinder," D

[d] pharos",] pharos," C; Pharos," D

[e] "Yog-Sothoth", . . . jelly", . . . colour . . . space", . . . wings", . . . darkness", . . . moon-ladder", . . . undying",] "Yog-Sothoth," . . . jelly," . . . color . . . space," . . . wings," . . . darkness," . . . moon-ladder," . . . undying," C, D

[f] "Necronomicon"] *Necronomicon* A, B, C, D

[g] ice-dust] ice dust C, D

[h] and of course] and, of course, C [*second comma deleted by HPL*], D

[i] those] these C, D

[j] time] time, C, D

[k] single] single, C, D

[l] source: ¶] source: C, D

The Shadow over Innsmouth

I.

During the winter of 1927–28 officials of the Federal government made a strange and secret investigation of certain conditions in the ancient Massachusetts seaport of Innsmouth. The public first learned of it in February, when a vast series of raids and arrests occurred, followed by the deliberate burning and dynamiting—under suitable precautions—of an enormous number of crumbling, worm-eaten, and supposedly empty houses along the abandoned waterfront. Uninquiring souls let this occurrence[a] pass as one of the major clashes in a spasmodic war on liquor.

Keener news-followers, however, wondered at the prodigious number of arrests, the abnormally large force of men used in making

---

Editor's Note: HPL's original A.Ms. and T.Ms. (prepared by himself) survive. The story was twice rejected by *Weird Tales* and appeared in print only a few months before HPL's death in the Visionary Press edition of *The Shadow over Innsmouth*. For this edition, the publisher, William L. Crawford, used a carbon of HPL's typescript (this carbon later came into the hands of book dealer Roy A. Squires, who sold individual pages to collectors). HPL's correspondence is full of discussions of the difficulties he had in correcting the error-riddled proofs of the book; in the end, he forced Crawford to print an errata sheet, but this sheet still fails to correct a substantial number of errors in the printed text. August Derleth followed the Visionary Press edition for *The Outsider and Others* (1939). Whether he had access to the errata sheet is unclear; probably he did. This probably accounts for Arkham House's restoration of a dropped line from the Visionary Press edition (187.17–18), which Derleth could not otherwise have restored except by consultation with the T.Ms. or by having a copy of the Visionary Press edition corrected by HPL by hand. The 1963 reprint introduces a number of additional errors.

Texts: A = A.Ms. (JHL); B = T.Ms. (JHL); C = *The Shadow over Innsmouth* (Everett, PA: Visionary Press, 1936); C^c = HPL's errata sheet to the Visionary Press edition; D = *The Dunwich Horror and Others* (Arkham House, 1963), 308–69. Copy-text: B.

[a] occurrence] occurence C

them, and the secrecy surrounding the disposal of the prisoners. No trials, or even definite charges, were reported; nor were any of the captives seen thereafter in the regular gaols of the nation. There were vague statements about disease and concentration camps, and later about dispersal in various naval and military prisons, but nothing positive ever developed. Innsmouth itself was left almost depopulated, and[a] is even now only beginning to shew[b] signs of a sluggishly revived existence.

Complaints from many liberal organisations were met with long confidential discussions, and representatives were taken on trips to certain camps and prisons. As a result, these societies became surprisingly passive and reticent. Newspaper men were harder to manage, but seemed largely to coöperate[c] with the government in the end. Only one paper—a tabloid always discounted because of its wild policy—mentioned the deep-diving submarine that discharged torpedoes downward in the marine abyss just beyond Devil Reef. That item, gathered by chance in a haunt of sailors, seemed indeed rather far-fetched; since the low, black reef lies a full mile and a half out from Innsmouth Harbour.

People around the country and in the nearby towns muttered a great deal among themselves, but said very little to the outer world. They had talked about dying and half-deserted Innsmouth for nearly a century, and nothing new could be wilder or more hideous than what they had whispered and hinted years before. Many things had taught them secretiveness, and there was now[d] no need to exert pressure on them. Besides, they really knew very[e] little; for wide salt marshes, desolate and unpeopled, keep[f] neighbours off from Innsmouth on the landward side.

But at last I am going to defy the ban on speech about this thing. Results, I am certain, are so thorough that no public harm save a shock of repulsion could ever accrue from a hinting of what was found by those horrified raiders at Innsmouth. Besides, what was found might

[a] and] and it C, D
[b] shew] show C, D
[c] coöperate] cooperate C, D
[d] now] *om.* C, D
[e] very] *om.* D
[f] keep] kept C, D

possibly have more than one explanation. I do not know just how much of the whole tale has been told even to me, and I have many reasons for not wishing to probe deeper. For my contact with this affair has been closer than that of any other layman, and I have carried away impressions which are yet to drive me to drastic measures.

It was I who fled frantically out of Innsmouth in the early morning hours of July 16, 1927, and whose frightened appeals for government inquiry and action brought on the whole reported episode. I was willing enough to stay mute while the affair was fresh and uncertain; but now that it is an old story, with public interest and curiosity gone, I have an odd craving to whisper about those few frightful hours in that ill-rumoured and evilly shadowed[a] seaport of death and blasphemous abnormality. The mere telling helps me to restore confidence in my own faculties;[b] to reassure myself that I was not simply the first to succumb to a contagious[c] nightmare hallucination. It helps me, too, in making up my mind regarding a certain terrible step which lies ahead of me.

I never heard of Innsmouth till the day before I saw it for the first and—so far—last time. I was celebrating my coming of age by a tour of New England—sightseeing, antiquarian, and genealogical—and had planned to go directly from ancient Newburyport to Arkham, whence my mother's family was derived. I had no car, but was travelling by train, trolley,[d] and motor coach,[e] always seeking the cheapest possible route. In Newburyport they told me that the steam train was the thing to take to Arkham; and it was only at the station ticket-office, when I demurred at the high fare, that I learned about Innsmouth. The stout, shrewd-faced agent, whose speech shewed him to be no local man, seemed sympathetic toward my efforts at economy, and made a suggestion that none of my other informants had offered.

"You *could*[f] take that old bus, I suppose," he said with a certain hesitation, "but it ain't thought much of hereabouts. It goes through Innsmouth—you may have heard about that—and so the people don't

[a] evilly shadowed] evilly-shadowed A, B, C, D
[b] faculties;] faculties; C^c
[c] contagious] contagiouus C^c
[d] trolley,] trolley C, D
[e] motor coach,] motor-coach, A, B, C, D
[f] *could*] could D

like it. Run by an Innsmouth fellow—Joe Sargent—but never gets any custom from here, or Arkham either, I guess. Wonder it keeps running at all. I s'pose it's cheap enough, but I never see more'n[a] two or three people in it—nobody but those Innsmouth folks. Leaves the Square—front of Hammond's Drug Store—at 10 a.m. and 7 p.m.[b] unless they've changed lately. Looks like a terrible rattletrap—I've never ben on it."

That was the first I ever heard of shadowed Innsmouth. Any reference to a town not shewn[c] on common maps or listed in recent guide-books would have interested me, and the agent's odd manner of allusion roused something like real curiosity. A town able to inspire such dislike in its neighbours, I thought, must be at least rather unusual, and worthy of a tourist's attention. If it came before Arkham I would stop off there—and so I asked the agent to tell me something about it. He was very deliberate, and spoke with an air of feeling slightly superior to what he said.

"Innsmouth? Well, it's a queer kind of a town down at the mouth of the Manuxet. Used to be almost a city—quite a port before the War of 1812—but all gone to pieces in the last hundred years or so. No railroad now—B. &[d] M. never went through, and the branch line from Rowley was given up years ago.

"More empty houses than there are people, I guess, and no business to speak of except fishing and lobstering. Everybody trades mostly either here or in Arkham or Ipswich. Once they had quite a few mills, but nothing's left now except one[e] gold refinery running on the leanest kind of part time.

"That refinery, though, used to be a big thing, and Old Man[f] Marsh, who owns it, must be richer'n Croesus. Queer old duck, though, and sticks mighty close in his home. He's supposed to have developed some skin disease or deformity late in life that makes him keep out of sight. Grandson of Captain Obed Marsh, who founded the business. His mother seems to've ben some kind of foreigner—they

---

[a] more'n] mor'n C, D
[b] a.m. . . . p.m.] a. m. . . . . p. m. C
[c] shewn] shown C, D
[d] &] and C, D
[e] one] one old C
[f] Old Man] old man C, D

say a South Sea islander—so everybody raised Cain when he married an Ipswich girl fifty years ago. They always do that about Innsmouth people, and folks here and hereabouts always try to cover up any Innsmouth blood they have in 'em. But Marsh's children and grandchildren look just like anyone else so far's I can see. I've had 'em pointed out to me here—though, come to think of it, the elder children don't seem to be around lately. Never saw the old man.

"And why is everybody so down on Innsmouth? Well, young fellow, you mustn't take too much stock in what people around here say. They're hard to get started, but once they do get started they never let up. They've ben[a] telling things about Innsmouth—whispering 'em, mostly—for the last hundred years, I guess, and I gather they're more scared than anything else. Some of the stories would make you laugh—about old Captain Marsh driving bargains with the devil and bringing imps out of hell to live in Innsmouth, or about some kind of devil-worship and awful sacrifices in some place near the wharves that people stumbled on around 1845 or thereabouts—but I come from Panton, Vermont, and that kind of story don't go down with me.

"You ought to hear, though, what some of the old-timers tell about the black reef off the coast—Devil Reef, they call it. It's well above water a good part of the time, and never much below it, but at that you could hardly call it an island. The story is that there's a whole legion of devils seen sometimes on that reef—sprawled about, or darting in and out of some kind of caves near the top. It's a rugged, uneven thing, a good bit over a mile out, and toward the end of shipping days sailors used to make big detours just to avoid it.

"That is, sailors that didn't hail from Innsmouth. One of the things they had against old Captain Marsh was that he was supposed to land on it sometimes at night when the tide was right. Maybe he did, for I dare say the rock formation was interesting, and it's just barely possible he was looking for pirate loot and maybe finding it; but there was talk of his dealing with daemons[b] there. Fact is, I guess on the whole it[c] was really the Captain that gave the bad reputation to the reef.

[a] ben] been D
[b] daemons] demons C, D
[c] it] is Cc

"That was before the big epidemic of 1846, when over half the folks in Innsmouth was carried off. They never did quite figure out what the trouble was, but it was probably some foreign kind of disease brought from China or somewhere by the shipping. It surely was bad enough—there was riots over it, and all sorts of ghastly doings that I don't believe ever got outside of town—and it left the place in awful shape. Never came back—there can't be more'n 300 or 400 people living there now.

"But the real thing behind the way folks feel is simply race prejudice—and I don't say I'm blaming those that hold it. I hate those Innsmouth folks myself, and I wouldn't care to go to their town. I s'pose you know—though I can see you're a Westerner by your talk—what a lot our New England ships used to have to do with queer ports in Africa, Asia, the South Seas, and everywhere else, and what queer kinds of people they sometimes brought back with 'em. You've probably heard about the Salem man that came home with a Chinese wife, and maybe you know there's still a bunch of Fiji Islanders somewhere around Cape Cod.

"Well, there must be something like that back of the Innsmouth people. The place always was badly cut off from the rest of the country by marshes and creeks, and we can't be sure about the ins and outs of the matter; but it's pretty clear that old Captain Marsh must have brought home some odd specimens when he had all three of his ships in commission back in the 'twenties and 'thirties.[a] There certainly is a strange kind of streak in the Innsmouth folks today—I don't know how to explain it, but it sort of makes you crawl. You'll notice a little in Sargent if you take his bus. Some of 'em have queer narrow heads with flat noses and bulgy, stary eyes that never seem to shut, and their skin ain't quite right. Rough and scabby, and the sides of their necks are all shrivelled or creased up. Get bald, too, very young. The older fellows look the worst—fact is, I don't believe I've ever seen a very old chap of that kind. Guess they must die of looking in the glass! Animals hate 'em—they used to have lots of horse trouble before autos came in.

"Nobody around here or in Arkham or Ipswich will have anything to do with 'em, and they act kind of offish themselves when they come

---

[a] 'twenties and 'thirties.] twenties and thirties. A, B, C, D

to town or when anyone tries to fish on their grounds. Queer how fish are always thick off Innsmouth Harbour when there ain't any anywhere else around—but just try to fish there yourself and see how the folks chase you off! Those people used to come here on the railroad—walking and taking the train at Rowley after the branch was dropped—but now they use that bus.

"Yes, there's a hotel in Innsmouth—called the Gilman House—but I don't believe it can amount to much. I wouldn't advise you to try it. Better stay over here and take the ten o'clock bus tomorrow morning; then you can get an evening bus there for Arkham at eight o'clock. There was a factory inspector who stopped at the Gilman a couple of years ago,[a] and he had a lot of unpleasant hints about the place. Seems they get a queer crowd there, for this fellow heard voices in other rooms—though most of 'em was empty—that gave him the shivers. It was foreign talk, he thought, but he said the bad thing about it was the kind of voice that sometimes spoke. It sounded so unnatural—slopping-like, he said—that he didn't dare undress and go to sleep. Just waited up and lit out the first thing in the morning. The talk went on most all night.

"This fellow—Casey, his name was—had a lot to say about how the Innsmouth folks watched him and seemed kind of on guard. He found the Marsh refinery a queer place—it's in an old mill on the lower falls of the Manuxet. What he said tallied up with what I'd heard. Books in bad shape, and no clear account of any kind of dealings. You know it's always ben a kind of mystery where the Marshes get the gold they refine. They've never seemed to do much buying in that line, but years ago they shipped out an enormous lot of ingots.

"Used to be talk of a queer foreign kind of jewellery that the sailors and refinery men sometimes sold on the sly, or that was seen once or twice on some of the Marsh womenfolks.[b] People allowed maybe old Captain Obed traded for it in some heathen port, especially since he was always ordering[c] stacks of glass beads and trinkets such as seafaring men used to get for native trade. Others thought and still

---

[a] ago,] ago C, D
[b] womenfolks.] women-/folks. C; women-folks. D
[c] was always ordering] always ordered C, D

think he'd found an old pirate cache out on Devil Reef. But here's a funny thing. The old Captain's ben dead these sixty years, and there ain't ben a good-sized ship out of the place since the Civil War; but just the same the Marshes still keep on buying a few of those native trade things—mostly glass and rubber gewgaws, they tell me. Maybe the Innsmouth folks like 'em to look at themselves—Gawd knows they've gotten to be about as bad as South Sea cannibals and Guinea savages.

"That plague of '46 must have taken off the best blood in the place. Anyway, they're a doubtful lot now, and the Marshes and the other rich folks are as bad as any. As I told you, there probably ain't more'n 400 people in the whole town in spite of all the streets they say there are. I guess they're what they call 'white trash' down South—lawless and sly, and full of secret doings. They get a lot of fish and lobsters and do exporting by truck. Queer how the fish swarm right there and nowhere else.

"Nobody can ever keep track of these people, and state school officials and census men have a devil of a time. You can bet that prying strangers ain't welcome around Innsmouth. I've heard personally of more'n one business or government man that's disappeared there, and there's loose talk of one who went crazy and is out at Danvers now. They must have fixed up some awful scare for that fellow.

"That's why I wouldn't go at night if I was you. I've never ben there and have no wish to go, but I guess a daytime trip couldn't hurt you—even though the people hereabouts will advise you not to make it. If you're just sightseeing, and looking for old-time stuff, Innsmouth ought to be quite a place for you."

And so I spent part of that evening at the Newburyport Public Library looking up data about Innsmouth.[a] When I had tried to question the natives in the shops, the lunch room,[b] the garages, and the fire station, I had found them even harder to get started than the ticket-agent[c] had predicted; and realised that I could not spare the time to overcome their first instinctive reticences. They had a kind of obscure suspiciousness, as if there were something amiss with anyone

[a] Innsmouth.] Innsmouth, C
[b] lunch room,] lunchroom, C, D
[c] ticket-agent] ticket agent A, B, C, D

too much interested in Innsmouth. At the Y.M.C.A.,[a] where I was was stopping, the clerk merely discouraged my going to such a dismal, decadent place; and the people at the library shewed much the same attitude. Clearly, in the eyes of the educated, Innsmouth was merely an exaggerated case of civic degeneration.

The Essex County histories on the library shelves had very little to say, except that the town was founded in 1643, noted for shipbuilding before the Revolution, a seat of great marine prosperity in the early nineteenth[b] century, and later a minor factory centre using the Manuxet Manuxet as power. The epidemic and riots of 1846 were very sparsely treated, as if they formed a discredit to the county.

References to decline were few, though the significance of the later record was unmistakable. After the Civil War all industrial life was confined to the Marsh Refining Company, and the marketing of gold ingots formed the only remaining bit of major commerce aside from the eternal fishing. That fishing paid less and less as the price of the commodity fell and large-scale corporations offered competition, but there was never a dearth of fish around Innsmouth Harbour. Foreigners seldom settled there, and there was some discreetly veiled evidence that a number of Poles and Portuguese[c] who had tried it had been scattered in a peculiarly drastic fashion.

Most interesting of all was a glancing reference to the strange jewellery vaguely associated with Innsmouth. It had evidently impressed the whole countryside more than a little, for mention was made of specimens in the museum of Miskatonic University at Arkham, and in the display room of the Newburyport Historical Society. The fragmentary descriptions of these things were bald and prosaic, but they hinted to me an undercurrent of persistent strangeness. Something about them seemed so odd and provocative that I could not put them out of my mind, and despite the relative lateness of the hour I resolved to see the local sample—said to be a large, queerly proportioned[d] thing thing evidently meant for a tiara—if it could possibly be arranged.

---

[a] Y.M.C.A.,] Y. M. C. A., C, D
[b] nineteenth] 19th A, B, C, D
[c] Portuguese] Portugese A, B, C, D
[d] queerly proportioned] queerly-proportioned A, B, C, D

The librarian gave me a note of introduction to the curator of the Society, a Miss Anna Tilton, who lived nearby, and after a brief explanation that ancient gentlewoman was kind enough to pilot me into the closed building, since the hour was not outrageously late. The collection was a notable one indeed, but in my present mood I had eyes for nothing but the bizarre object which glistened in a corner cupboard under the electric lights.

It took no excessive sensitiveness to beauty to make me literally gasp at the strange, unearthly splendour of the alien, opulent phantasy that rested there on a purple velvet cushion. Even now I can hardly describe what I saw, though it was clearly enough a sort of tiara, as the description had said. It was tall in front, and with a very large and curiously irregular periphery, as if designed for a head of almost freakishly elliptical outline. The material seemed to be predominantly gold, though a weird[a] lighter lustrousness hinted at some strange alloy with an equally beautiful and scarcely[b] identifiable metal. Its condition was almost perfect, and one could have spent hours in studying the striking and puzzlingly untraditional designs—some simply geometrical, and some plainly marine—chased or moulded in high relief on its surface with a craftsmanship of incredible skill and grace.

The longer I looked, the more the thing fascinated me; and in this fascination there was a curiously disturbing element hardly to be classified or accounted for. At first I decided that it was the queer other-worldly quality of the art which made me uneasy. All other art objects I had ever seen either belonged to some known racial or national stream, or else were consciously modernistic defiances of every recognised stream. This tiara was neither. It clearly belonged to some settled technique of infinite maturity and perfection, yet that technique was utterly remote from any—Eastern or Western, ancient or modern—which I had ever heard of or seen exemplified. It was as if the workmanship were that of another planet.

However, I soon saw that my uneasiness had a second and perhaps equally potent source residing in the pictorial and mathematical

---

[a] weird] wierd C[c]
[b] scarcely] scaracely C[c]

suggestions[a] of the strange designs. The patterns all hinted of remote secrets and unimaginable abysses in time and space, and the monotonously aquatic nature of the reliefs became almost sinister. Among these reliefs were fabulous monsters of abhorrent grotesqueness and malignity—half ichthyic and half batrachian[b] in suggestion—which one could not dissociate from a certain haunting and uncomfortable sense of pseudo-memory, as if they called up some image from deep cells and tissues whose retentive functions are wholly primal and awesomely ancestral. At times I fancied that every contour of these blasphemous fish-frogs was overflowing with the ultimate quintessence of unknown and inhuman evil.

In odd contrast to the tiara's aspect was its brief and prosy history as related by Miss Tilton. It had been pawned for a ridiculous sum at a shop in State Street in 1873, by a drunken Innsmouth man shortly afterward killed in a brawl. The Society had acquired it directly from the pawnbroker, at once giving it a display worthy of its quality. It was labelled as of probable East-Indian or Indo-Chinese provenance, though the attribution was frankly tentative.

Miss Tilton, comparing all possible hypotheses regarding its origin and its presence in New England, was inclined to believe that it formed part of some exotic pirate hoard discovered by old Captain Obed Marsh. This view was surely not weakened by the insistent offers of purchase at a high price which the Marshes began to make as soon as they knew of its presence, and which they repeated to this day despite the Society's unvarying determination not to sell.

As the good lady shewed me out of the building she made it clear that the pirate theory of the Marsh fortune was a popular one among the intelligent people of the region. Her own attitude toward shadowed Innsmouth—which she had never seen—was one of disgust at a community slipping far down the cultural scale, and she assured me that the rumours of devil-worship were partly justified by a peculiar secret cult which had gained force there and engulfed all the orthodox churches.

It was called, she said, "The Esoteric Order of Dagon", and was

[a] suggestions] suggestion C, D
[b] batrachian] batrachain C[c]

undoubtedly a debased, quasi-pagan thing imported from the East a century before, at a time when the Innsmouth fisheries seemed to be going barren. Its persistence among a simple people was quite natural in view of the sudden and permanent return of abundantly fine fishing, and it soon came to be the greatest influence on[a] the town, replacing Freemasonry altogether and taking up headquarters in the old Masonic Hall on New Church Green.

All this, to the pious Miss Tilton, formed an excellent reason for shunning the ancient town of decay and desolation; but to me it was merely a fresh incentive. To my architectural and historical anticipations was now added an acute anthropological zeal, and I could scarcely sleep in my small room at the "Y" as the night wore away.

II.

Shortly before ten the next morning I stood with one small valise in front of Hammond's Drug Store in old Market Square waiting for the Innsmouth bus. As the hour for its arrival drew near I noticed a general drift of the loungers to other places up the street, or to the Ideal Lunch across the square. Evidently the ticket-agent had not exaggerated the dislike which local people bore toward[b] Innsmouth and its denizens. In a few moments a small motor coach[c] of extreme decrepitude and dirty grey colour rattled down State Street, made a turn, and drew up at the curb beside me. I felt immediately that it was the right one; a guess which the half-illegible[d] sign on the windshield—*"Arkham-Innsmouth-Newb'port"*[e]—soon verified.

There were only three passengers—dark, unkempt men of sullen visage and somewhat youthful cast—and when the vehicle stopped they clumsily shambled out and began walking up State Street in a silent, almost furtive fashion. The driver also alighted,[f] and I watched him as he went into the drug store to make some purchase. This, I

---

[a] on] in C, D
[b] toward] toword C
[c] motor coach] motor-coach A, B, C, D
[d] half-illegible] half-legible C, D
[e] *"Arkham . . . Newb'port"*] *"Arkham . . . Newb'port* C; *Arkham . . . Newb'port* D
[f] alighted,] alighted. C

reflected, must be the Joe Sargent mentioned by the ticket-agent; and even before I noticed any details there spread over me a wave of spontaneous aversion which could be neither checked nor explained.[a] It suddenly struck me as very natural that the local people should not wish to ride on a bus owned and driven by this man, or to visit any oftener than possible the habitat of such a man and his kinsfolk.

When the driver came out of the store I looked at him more carefully and tried to determine the source of my evil impression. He was a thin, stoop-shouldered man not much under six feet tall, dressed in shabby blue civilian clothes and wearing a frayed grey[b] golf cap. His age was perhaps thirty-five, but the odd, deep creases in the sides of his neck made him seem older when one did not study his dull, expressionless face. He had a narrow head, bulging, watery blue[c] eyes that seemed never to wink, a flat nose, a receding forehead and chin, and singularly undeveloped ears. His long,[d] thick lip and coarse-pored, greyish cheeks seemed almost beardless except for some sparse yellow hairs that straggled and curled in irregular patches; and in places the surface seemed queerly irregular, as if peeling from some cutaneous disease. His hands were large and heavily veined, and had a very unusual greyish-blue tinge. The fingers were strikingly short in proportion to the rest of the structure, and seemed to have a tendency to curl closely into the huge palm. As he walked toward the bus I observed his peculiarly shambling gait and saw that his feet were inordinately immense. The more I studied them the more I wondered how he could buy any shoes to fit them.

A certain greasiness about the fellow increased my dislike. He was evidently given to working or lounging around the fish docks, and carried with him much of their characteristic smell. Just what foreign blood was in him I could not even guess. His oddities certainly did not look Asiatic, Polynesian, Levantine,[e] or negroid, yet I could see why the people found him alien. I myself would have thought of biological degeneration rather than alienage.

---

[a] explained.] expained. C
[b] grey] *om.* C, D
[c] watery blue] watery-blue D
[d] long,] long C, D
[e] Levantine,] Levantine C, D

I was sorry when I saw that[a] there would be no other passengers on the bus. Somehow I did not like the idea of riding alone with this driver. But as leaving time obviously approached I conquered my qualms and followed the man aboard, extending him a dollar bill and murmuring the single word "Innsmouth".[b] He looked curiously at me for a second as he returned forty cents change without speaking. I took a seat far behind him, but on the same side of the bus, since I wished to watch the shore during the journey.

At length the decrepit vehicle started with a jerk, and rattled noisily past the old brick buildings of State Street amidst a cloud of vapour from the exhaust. Glancing at the people on the sidewalks, I thought I detected in them a curious wish to avoid looking at the bus—or at least a wish to avoid seeming to look at it. Then we turned to the left into High Street, where the going was smoother; flying by stately old mansions of the early republic and still older colonial farmhouses, passing the Lower Green and Parker River, and finally[c] emerging into a long, monotonous stretch of open shore country.

The day was warm and sunny, but the landscape of sand, sedge-grass, and stunted shrubbery became more and more desolate as we proceeded. Out the window I could see the blue water and the sandy line of Plum Island, and we presently drew very near the beach as our narrow road veered off from the main highway to Rowley and Ipswich. There were no visible houses, and I could tell by the state of the road that traffic was very light hereabouts. The small, weather-worn telephone poles carried only two wires. Now and then we crossed crude wooden bridges over tidal creeks that wound far inland and promoted the general isolation of the region.

Once in a while I noticed dead stumps and crumbling foundation-walls above the drifting sand, and recalled the old tradition quoted in one of the histories I had read, that this was once a fertile and thickly settled[d] countryside. The change, it was said, came simultaneously with

---

[a] that] *om.* C, D
[b] "Innsmouth".] "Innsmouth." C, D
[c] finally] fiinally C
[d] thickly settled] thickly-settled B, C, D

the Innsmouth epidemic of 1846, and was thought by[a] simple folk to have a dark connexion with hidden forces of evil. Actually, it was caused by the unwise cutting of woodlands near the shore, which robbed the soil of its best protection and opened the way for waves of wind-blown sand.

At last we lost sight of Plum Island and saw the vast expanse of the open Atlantic on our left. Our narrow course began to climb steeply, and I felt a singular sense of disquiet in looking at the lonely crest ahead where the rutted roadway met the sky. It was as if the bus were about to keep on in its ascent, leaving the sane earth altogether and merging with the unknown arcana of upper air and cryptical sky. The smell of the sea took on ominous implications, and the silent driver's bent, rigid back and narrow head became more and more hateful. As I looked at him I saw that the back of his head was almost as hairless as his face, having only a few straggling yellow strands upon a grey scabrous surface.

Then we reached the crest and beheld the outspread valley beyond, where the Manuxet joins the sea just north of the long line of cliffs that culminate in Kingsport Head and veer off toward Cape Ann. On the far,[b] misty horizon I could just make out the dizzy profile of the Head, topped by the queer ancient house of which so many legends are told; but for the moment all my attention was captured by the nearer panorama just below me. I had, I realised, come face to face with rumour-shadowed Innsmouth.

It was a town of wide extent and dense construction, yet one with a portentous dearth of visible life. From the tangle of chimney-pots scarcely a wisp of smoke came, and the three tall steeples loomed stark and unpainted against the seaward horizon. One of them was crumbling down at the top, and in that and another there were only black gaping holes where clock-dials should have been. The vast huddle of sagging gambrel roofs and peaked gables conveyed with offensive clearness the idea of wormy decay, and as we approached along the now descending road I could see that many roofs had wholly caved in. There were some

[a] by] by the C[c]
[b] far,] far C, D

large square Georgian houses,[a] too, with hipped roofs, cupolas, and railed "widow's walks".[b] These were mostly well back from the water, and one or two seemed to be in moderately sound condition. Stretching inland from among them I saw the rusted, grass-grown line of the abandoned railway, with leaning telegraph-poles now devoid of wires, and the half-obscured lines of the old carriage roads to Rowley and Ipswich.

The decay was worst close to the waterfront, though in its very midst I could spy the white belfry of a fairly well-preserved brick structure which looked like a small factory. The harbour, long clogged with sand, was enclosed by an ancient stone breakwater; on which I could begin to discern the minute forms of a few seated fishermen, and at whose end were what looked like the foundations of a bygone lighthouse. A sandy tongue had formed inside this barrier, and upon it I saw a few decrepit cabins, moored dories, and scattered lobster-pots. The only deep water seemed to be where the river poured out past the belfried structure and turned southward to join the ocean at the breakwater's end.

Here and there the ruins of wharves jutted out from the shore to end in indeterminate rottenness, those farthest south seeming the most decayed. And far out at sea, despite a high tide, I glimpsed a long, black line scarcely rising above the water yet carrying a suggestion of odd latent malignancy. This, I knew, must be Devil Reef. As I looked, a subtle, curious sense of beckoning seemed superadded to the grim repulsion; and oddly enough, I found this overtone more disturbing than the primary impression.

We met no one on the road, but presently began to pass deserted farms in varying stages of ruin. Then I noticed a few inhabited houses with rags stuffed in the broken windows and shells and dead fish lying about the littered yards. Once or twice I saw listless-looking people working in barren gardens or digging clams on the fishy-smelling beach below, and groups of dirty, simian-visaged children playing around weed-grown doorsteps. Somehow these people seemed more disquieting than the dismal buildings, for almost every one had certain peculiarities of face and motions which I instinctively disliked without

[a] houses,] house, C
[b] walks".] walks." C, D

being able to define or comprehend them. For a second I thought this typical physique suggested some picture I had seen, perhaps in a book, under circumstances of particular horror or melancholy; but this pseudo-recollection passed very quickly.

As the bus reached a lower level I began to catch the steady note of a waterfall through the unnatural stillness. The leaning, unpainted houses grew thicker, lined both sides of the road, and displayed more urban tendencies than did those we were leaving behind. The panorama ahead had contracted to a street scene, and in spots I could see where a cobblestone pavement and stretches of brick sidewalk had formerly existed. All the houses were apparently deserted, and there were occasional gaps where tumbledown chimneys and cellar walls told of buildings that had collapsed. Pervading everything was the most nauseous fishy odour imaginable.

Soon cross streets and junctions began to appear; those on the left leading to shoreward realms of unpaved squalor and decay, while those on the right shewed vistas of departed grandeur. So far I had seen no people in the town, but there now came signs of a sparse habitation— curtained windows here and there, and an occasional battered motor-car at the curb. Pavement and sidewalks were increasingly well defined,[a] and though most of the houses were quite old—wood and brick structures of the early nineteenth[b] century—they were obviously kept fit for habitation. As an amateur antiquarian I almost lost my olfactory disgust and my feeling of menace and repulsion amidst this rich, unaltered survival from the past.

But I was not to reach my destination without one very strong impression of poignantly disagreeable quality. The bus had come to a sort of open concourse or radial point with churches on two sides and the bedraggled remains of a circular green in the centre, and I was looking at a large pillared hall on the right-hand junction ahead. The structure's once white paint was now grey and peeling, and the black and gold sign on the pediment was so faded that I could only with difficulty make out the words "Esoteric Order of Dagon". This, then,[c]

[a] well defined,] well-defined, B, C, D
[b] nineteenth] 19th A, B, C, D
[c] then,] then D

was the former Masonic Hall now given over to a degraded cult. As I strained to decipher this inscription my notice was distracted by the raucous tones of a cracked bell across the street, and I quickly turned to look out the window on my side of the coach.

The sound came from a squat-towered stone church of manifestly later date than most of the houses, built in a clumsy Gothic fashion and having a disproportionately high basement with shuttered windows. Though the hands of its clock were missing on the side I glimpsed, I knew that those hoarse strokes were telling[a] the hour of eleven. Then suddenly all thoughts of time were blotted out by an onrushing image of sharp intensity and unaccountable horror which had seized me before I knew what it really was. The door of the church basement was open, revealing a rectangle of blackness inside. And as I looked, a certain object crossed or seemed to cross that dark rectangle; burning into my brain a momentary conception of nightmare which was all the more maddening because analysis could not shew a single nightmarish quality in it.

It was a living object—the first except the driver that I had seen since entering the compact part of the town—and had I been in a steadier mood I would have found nothing whatever of terror in it. Clearly, as I realised a moment later, it was the pastor; clad in some peculiar vestments doubtless introduced since the Order of Dagon had modified the ritual of the local churches. The thing which had probably caught my first subconscious glance and supplied the touch of bizarre horror was the tall tiara he wore; an almost exact duplicate of the one Miss Tilton had shewn[b] me the previous evening. This, acting on my imagination, had supplied namelessly sinister qualities to the indeterminate face and robed, shambling form beneath it. There was not, I soon decided, any reason why I should have felt that shuddering touch of evil pseudo-memory. Was it not natural that a local mystery cult should adopt among its regimentals an unique type of head-dress made familiar to the community in some strange way—perhaps as treasure-trove?

[a] telling] tolling D
[b] shewn] shown D

A very thin sprinkling of repellent-looking youngish people now became visible on the sidewalks—lone individuals, and silent knots of two or three. The lower floors of the crumbling houses sometimes harboured small shops with dingy signs, and I noticed a parked truck or two as we rattled along. The sound of waterfalls became more and more distinct, and presently I saw a fairly deep river-gorge ahead, spanned by a wide, iron-railed highway bridge beyond which a large square opened out. As we clanked over the bridge I looked out on both sides and observed some factory buildings on the edge of the grassy bluff or part way down. The water far below was very abundant, and I could see two vigorous sets of falls upstream on my right and at least one downstream on my left. From this point the noise was quite deafening. Then we rolled into the large semicircular square across the river and drew up on the right-hand side in front of a tall, cupola-crowned building with remnants of yellow paint and with a half-effaced sign proclaiming it to be the Gilman House.

I was glad to get out of that bus, and at once proceeded to check my valise in the shabby hotel lobby. There was only one person in sight—an elderly man without what I had come to call the "Innsmouth look"—and I decided not to ask him any of the questions which bothered me; remembering that odd things had been noticed in this hotel. Instead, I strolled out on the square, from which the bus had already gone, and studied the scene minutely and appraisingly.

One side of the cobblestoned open space was the straight line of the river; the other was a semicircle of slant-roofed brick buildings of about the 1800 period, from which several streets radiated away to the southeast, south, and southwest. Lamps were depressingly few and small—all low-powered incandescents—and I was glad that my plans called for departure before dark, even though I knew the moon would be bright. The buildings were all in fair condition, and included perhaps a dozen shops in current operation; of which one was a grocery of the First National chain, others a dismal restaurant, a drug store, and a wholesale fish-dealer's office, and still another, at the eastern[a] extremity of the square near the river,[b] an office of the town's only industry—the

---

[a] eastern] eastward C, D

[b] river,] river C, D

Marsh Refining Company. There were perhaps ten people visible, and four or five automobiles and motor trucks stood scattered about. I did not need to be told that this was the civic centre of Innsmouth. Eastward I could catch blue glimpses of the harbour, against which rose the decaying remains of three once beautiful Georgian steeples. And toward the shore on the opposite bank of the river I saw the white belfry surmounting what I took to be the Marsh refinery.

For some reason or other I chose to make my first inquiries at the chain grocery, whose personnel was not likely to be native to Innsmouth. I found a solitary boy of about seventeen in charge, and was pleased to note the brightness and affability which promised cheerful information. He seemed exceptionally eager to talk, and I soon gathered that he did not like the place, its fishy smell, or its furtive people. A word with any outsider was a relief to him. He hailed from Arkham, boarded with a family who came from Ipswich, and went back home[a] whenever he got a moment off. His family did not like him to work in Innsmouth, but the chain had transferred him there and he did not wish to give up his job.

There was, he said, no public library or chamber of commerce in Innsmouth, but I could probably find my way about. The street I had come down was Federal. West of that were the fine old residence streets—Broad, Washington, Lafayette, and Adams—and east of it were the shoreward slums. It was in these slums—along Main Street—that I would find the old Georgian churches, but they were all long abandoned. It would be well not to make oneself too conspicuous in such neighbourhoods—especially north of the river—since the people were sullen and hostile. Some strangers had even disappeared.

Certain spots were almost forbidden territory, as he had learned at considerable cost. One must not, for example, linger much around the Marsh refinery, or around any of the still used churches, or around the pillared Order of Dagon Hall at New Church Green. Those churches were very odd—all violently disavowed by their respective denominations elsewhere, and apparently using the queerest kind of ceremonials and clerical vestments. Their creeds were heterodox and mysterious, involving hints of certain marvellous transformations leading to bodily immortality—of a sort—on this earth. The youth's

---

[a] home] *om.* C, D

own pastor—Dr. Wallace of Asbury M. E. Church in Arkham—had gravely urged him not to join any church in Innsmouth.

As for the Innsmouth people—the youth hardly knew what to make of them. They were as furtive and seldom seen as animals that live in burrows, and one could hardly imagine how they passed the time apart from their desultory fishing. Perhaps—judging from the quantities of bootleg liquor they consumed—they lay for most of the daylight hours in an alcoholic stupor. They seemed sullenly banded together in some sort of fellowship and understanding—despising the world as if they had access to other and preferable spheres of entity. Their appearance—especially those staring, unwinking eyes which one never saw shut—was certainly shocking enough; and their voices were disgusting. It was awful to hear them chanting in their churches at night, and especially during their main festivals or revivals, which fell twice a year on April 30th and October 31st.

They were very fond of the water, and swam a great deal in both river and harbour. Swimming races out to Devil Reef were very common, and everyone in sight seemed well able to share in this arduous sport. When one came to think of it, it was generally only rather young people who were seen about in public, and of these the oldest were apt to be the most tainted-looking. When exceptions did occur, they were mostly persons with no trace of aberrancy, like the old clerk at the hotel. One wondered what became of the bulk of the older folk, and whether the "Innsmouth look" were not a strange and insidious disease-phenomenon which increased its hold as years advanced.

Only a very rare affliction, of course, could bring about such vast and radical anatomical changes in a single individual after maturity— changes involving osseous factors as basic as the shape of the skull— but then, even this aspect was no more baffling and unheard-of than the visible features of the malady as a whole. It would be hard, the youth implied, to form any real conclusions regarding such a matter; since one never came to know the natives personally no matter how long one might live in Innsmouth.

The youth was certain that many specimens even worse than the worst visible ones were kept locked indoors in some places. People sometimes heard the queerest kind of sounds. The tottering waterfront hovels north of the river were reputedly connected by hidden tunnels, being thus a veritable warren of unseen abnormalities. What kind of foreign blood—if any—these beings had, it was impossible to tell. They sometimes kept certain especially repulsive characters out of sight when government agents and others from the outside world came to town.

It would be of no use, my informant said, to ask the natives anything about the place. The only one who would talk was a very aged but normal-looking man who lived at the poorhouse on the north rim of the town and spent his time walking about or lounging around the fire station. This hoary character, Zadok Allen, was ninety-six[a] years old and somewhat touched in the head, besides being the town drunkard. He was a strange, furtive creature who constantly looked over his shoulder as if afraid of something, and when sober could not be persuaded to talk at all with strangers. He was, however, unable to resist any offer of his favourite poison; and once drunk would furnish the most astonishing fragments of whispered reminiscence.

After all, though, little useful data could be gained from him; since his stories were all insane, incomplete hints of impossible marvels and horrors which could have no source save in his own disordered fancy. Nobody ever believed him, but the natives did not like him to drink and talk with strangers; and it was not always safe to be seen questioning him. It was probably from him that some of the wildest popular whispers and delusions were derived.

Several non-native residents had reported monstrous glimpses from time to time, but between old Zadok's tales and the malformed denizens[b] it was no wonder such illusions were current. None of the non-natives ever stayed out late at night, there being a widespread impression that it was not wise to do so. Besides, the streets were loathsomely dark.

As for business—the abundance of fish was certainly almost uncanny, but the natives were taking less and less advantage of it. Moreover, prices were falling and competition was growing. Of course the town's real business was the refinery, whose commercial office was on the square only a few doors east of where we stood. Old Man Marsh was never seen, but sometimes went to the works in a closed, curtained car.

[a] ninety-six] 96 A, B, C, D
[b] denizens] inhabitants C, D

There were all sorts of rumours about how Marsh had come to look. He had once been a great dandy, and people said he still wore the frock-coated finery of the Edwardian age,[a] curiously adapted to certain deformities. His sons had formerly conducted the office in the square, but latterly they had been keeping out of sight a good deal and leaving the brunt of affairs to the younger generation. The sons and their sisters had come to look very queer, especially the elder ones; and it was said that their health was failing.

One of the Marsh daughters was a repellent, reptilian-looking woman who wore an excess of weird jewellery clearly of the same exotic tradition as that to which the strange tiara belonged. My informant had noticed it many times, and had heard it spoken of as coming from some secret hoard, either of pirates or of daemons.[b] The clergymen—or priests, or whatever they were called nowadays—also wore this kind of ornament as a head-dress; but one seldom caught glimpses of them. Other specimens the youth had not seen, though many were rumoured to exist around Innsmouth.

The Marshes, together with the other three gently bred families of the town—the Waites, the Gilmans, and the Eliots—were all very retiring. They lived in immense houses along Washington Street, and several were reputed to harbour in concealment certain living kinsfolk whose personal aspect forbade public view, and whose deaths had been reported and recorded.

Warning me that many of the street signs were down, the youth drew for my benefit a rough but ample and painstaking sketch map of the town's salient features. After a moment's study I felt sure that it would be of great help, and pocketed it with profuse thanks. Disliking the dinginess of the single restaurant I had seen, I bought a fair supply of cheese crackers and ginger wafers to serve as a lunch later on. My programme, I decided, would be to thread the principal streets, talk with any non-natives I might encounter, and catch the eight o'clock coach for Arkham. The town, I could see, formed a significant and

---

[a] age,] age D
[b] daemons.] demons. C, D

exaggerated example of communal decay; but being[a] no sociologist I would limit my serious observations to the field of architecture.

Thus I began my systematic though half-bewildered tour of Innsmouth's[b] narrow, shadow-blighted ways. Crossing the bridge and turning toward the roar of the lower falls, I passed close to the Marsh refinery, which seemed[c] oddly free from the noise of industry. This building stood on the steep river bluff near a bridge and an open confluence of streets which I took to be the earliest civic centre, displaced after the Revolution by the present Town Square.

Re-crossing the gorge on the Main Street bridge, I struck a region of utter desertion which somehow made me shudder. Collapsing huddles of gambrel roofs formed a jagged and fantastic skyline, above which rose the ghoulish, decapitated steeple of an ancient church. Some houses along Main Street were tenanted, but most were tightly boarded up. Down unpaved side streets I saw the black, gaping windows of deserted hovels, many of which leaned at perilous and incredible angles through the sinking of part of the foundations. Those windows stared so spectrally that it took courage to turn eastward toward the waterfront. Certainly, the terror of a deserted house swells in geometrical rather than arithmetical progression as houses mutiply to form a city of stark desolation. The sight of such endless avenues of fishy-eyed vacancy and death, and the thought of such linked infinities of black, brooding compartments given over to cobwebs and memories and the conqueror worm, start up vestigial fears and aversions that not even the stoutest philosophy can disperse.

Fish Street was as deserted as Main, though it differed in having many brick and stone warehouses still in excellent shape. Water Street was almost its duplicate, save that there were great seaward gaps where wharves had been. Not a living thing did I see,[d] except for the scattered fishermen on the distant breakwater,[e] and not a sound did I hear save the lapping of the harbour tides and the roar of the falls in

---

[a] being] benig D
[b] Innsmouth's] Innsmouth''s C
[c] seemed] seemed to be C, D
[d] see,] see C, D
[e] breakwater,] break-/water, C; break-water, D

the Manuxet. The town was getting more and more on my nerves, and I looked behind me furtively as I picked my way back over the tottering Water Street bridge. The Fish Street bridge, according to the sketch, was in ruins.

North of the river there were traces of squalid life—active fish-packing houses in Water Street, smoking chimneys and patched roofs here and there, occasional sounds from indeterminate sources, and infrequent shambling forms in the dismal streets and unpaved lanes—but I seemed to find this even more oppressive than the southerly desertion. For one thing, the people were more hideous and abnormal than those near the centre of the town; so that I was several times evilly reminded of something utterly fantastic which I could not quite place. Undoubtedly the alien strain in the Innsmouth folk was stronger here than farther inland—unless, indeed, the "Innsmouth look" were a disease rather than a blood strain, in which case this district might be held to harbour the more advanced cases.

One detail that annoyed me was the *distribution*[a] of the few faint sounds I heard. They ought naturally to have come wholly from the visibly inhabited houses, yet in reality were often strongest inside the most rigidly boarded-up facades. There were creakings, scurryings, and hoarse doubtful noises; and I thought uncomfortably about the hidden tunnels suggested by the grocery boy. Suddenly I found myself wondering what the voices of those denizens would be like. I had heard no speech so far in this quarter, and was unaccountably anxious not to do so.

Pausing only long enough to look at two fine but ruinous old churches at Main and Church Streets, I hastened out of that vile waterfront slum. My next logical goal was New Church Green, but somehow or other I could not bear to re-pass[b] the church in whose basement I had glimpsed the inexplicably frightening form of that strangely diademmed priest or pastor. Besides, the grocery youth had told me that the[c] churches, as well as the Order of Dagon Hall, were not advisable neighbourhoods for strangers.

[a] *distribution*] distribution D
[b] re-pass] repass A, B, C, D
[c] the] *om.* C, D

Accordingly I kept north along Main to Martin, then turning inland, crossing Federal Street safely north of the Green, and entering the decayed patrician neighbourhood of northern Broad, Washington, Lafayette, and Adams Streets. Though these stately old avenues were ill-surfaced and unkempt, their elm-shaded dignity had not entirely departed. Mansion after mansion claimed my gaze, most of them decrepit and boarded up amidst neglected grounds, but one or two in each street shewing signs of occupancy. In Washington Street there was a row of four or five in excellent repair and with finely tended[a] lawns and gardens. The most sumptuous of these—with wide terraced parterres extending back the whole way to Lafayette Street—I took to be the home of Old Man Marsh, the afflicted refinery owner.

In all these streets no living thing was visible, and I wondered at the complete absence of cats and dogs from Innsmouth. Another thing which puzzled and disturbed me, even in some of the best-preserved mansions, was the tightly shuttered condition of many third-story[b] and attic windows. Furtiveness and secretiveness seemed universal in this hushed city of alienage and death, and I could not escape the sensation of being watched from ambush on every hand by sly, staring eyes that never shut.

I shivered as the cracked stroke of three sounded from a belfry on my left. Too well did I recall the squat church from which those notes came. Following Washington Street toward the river, I now faced a new zone of former industry and commerce; noting the ruins of a factory ahead, and seeing others, with the traces of an old railway station and covered railway bridge beyond,[c] up the gorge on my right.

The uncertain bridge now before me was posted with a warning sign, but I took the risk and crossed again to the south bank where traces of life reappeared. Furtive, shambling creatures stared cryptically in my direction, and more normal faces eyed me coldly and curiously. Innsmouth was rapidly becoming intolerable, and I turned down Paine Street toward the Square in the hope of getting some vehicle to take me to Arkham before the still-distant starting-time of that sinister bus.

[a] finely tended] finely-tended B, C, D
[b] third-story] third story A; third-storey B, C, D
[c] beyond,] beyond B, C

It was then that I saw the tumbledown fire station on my left, and noticed the red-faced, bushy-bearded, watery-eyed old man in nondescript rags who sat on a bench in front of it talking with a pair of unkempt but not abnormal-looking firemen. This, of course, must be Zadok Allen, the half-crazed, liquorish nonagenarian whose tales of old Innsmouth and its shadow were so hideous and incredible.

III.

[a]It must have been some imp of the perverse—or some sardonic pull from dark, hidden sources—which made me change my plans as I did. I had long before resolved to limit my observations to architecture alone, and I was even then hurrying toward the Square in an effort to get quick transportation out of this festering city of death and decay; but the sight of old Zadok Allen set up new currents in my mind and made me slacken my pace uncertainly.

I had been assured that the old man could do nothing but hint at wild, disjointed, and incredible legends, and I had been warned that the natives made it unsafe to be seen talking with him; yet the thought of this aged witness to the town's decay, with memories going back to the early days of ships and factories, was a lure that no amount of reason could make me resist. After all, the strangest and maddest of myths are often merely symbols or allegories based upon truth—and old Zadok must have seen everything which went on around Innsmouth for the last ninety years. Curiosity flared up beyond sense and caution, and in my youthful egotism I fancied I might be able to sift a nucleus of real history from the confused, extravagant outpouring I would probably extract with the aid of raw whiskey.

I knew that I could not accost him then and there, for the firemen would surely notice and object. Instead, I reflected, I would prepare by getting some bootleg liquor at a place where the grocery boy had told me it was plentiful. Then I would loaf near the fire station in apparent

---

[a] An imp of the perverse made me stop and speak to the old man, calling him "Uncle Zadok" as the grocery youth had said his friends usually did. He looked up with a nervous start, and when I saw the hunted look in his bloodshot, watery blue eyes I felt a new thrill of mystery—and of some deep-seated bond amounting to kinship. For this ancient being, I knew instinctively, was not a part of A [excised]

casualness, and fall in with old Zadok after he had started on one of his frequent rambles. The youth said that he was very restless, seldom sitting around the station for more than an hour or two at a time.

A quart bottle of whiskey was easily, though not cheaply, obtained in the rear of a dingy variety-store just off the Square in Eliot Street. The dirty-looking fellow who waited on me had a touch of the staring "Innsmouth look", but was quite civil in his way; being perhaps used to the custom of such convivial strangers—truckmen, gold-buyers, and the like—as were occasionally in town.

Reëntering[a] the Square I saw that luck was with me; for—shuffling out of Paine Street around the corner of the Gilman House—I glimpsed nothing less than the tall, lean, tattered form of old Zadok Allen himself. In accordance with my plan, I attracted his attention by brandishing my newly purchased[b] bottle;[c] and soon realised that he had begun to shuffle wistfully after me as I turned into Waite Street on my way to the most deserted region I could think of.

I was steering my course by the map the grocery boy had prepared, and was aiming for the wholly abandoned stretch of southern waterfront which I had previously visited. The only people in sight there had been the fishermen on the distant breakwater; and by going a few squares south I could get beyond the range of these, finding a pair of seats on some abandoned wharf and being free to question old Zadok unobserved for an indefinite time. Before I reached Main Street I could hear a faint and wheezy "Hey, Mister!" behind me, and I presently allowed the old man to catch up and take copious pulls from the quart bottle.

I began putting out feelers as we walked along to Water Street and turned southward[d] amidst[e] the omnipresent desolation and crazily tilted ruins, but found that the aged tongue did not loosen as quickly as I had expected. At length I saw a grass-grown opening toward the sea between crumbling brick walls, with the weedy length of an earth-and-masonry wharf projecting beyond. Piles of moss-covered stones near

[a] Reëntering] Reentering C, D
[b] newly purchased] newly-purchased A, B, C, D
[c] bottle;] bottle: D
[d] along . . . southward] *om.* C, D
[e] amidst] amist C[c]

the water promised tolerable seats, and the scene was sheltered from all possible view by a ruined warehouse on the north. Here, I thought, was the ideal place for a long secret colloquy; so I guided my companion down the lane and picked out spots to sit in among the mossy stones. The air of death and desertion was ghoulish, and the smell of fish almost insufferable; but I was resolved to let nothing deter me.

About four hours remained for conversation if I were to catch the eight o'clock coach for Arkham, and I began to dole out more liquor to the ancient tippler; meanwhile eating my own frugal lunch. In my donations I was careful not to overshoot the mark, for I did not wish Zadok's vinous garrulousness to pass into a stupor. After an hour his furtive taciturnity shewed signs of disappearing, but much to my disappointment he still sidetracked my questions about Innsmouth and its shadow-haunted past. He would babble of current topics, revealing a wide acquaintance with newspapers and a great tendency to philosophise in a sententious village fashion.

Toward the end of the second hour I feared my quart of whiskey would not be enough to produce results, and was wondering whether I had better leave old Zadok and go back for more. Just then, however, chance made the opening which my questions had been unable to make; and the wheezing ancient's rambling took a turn that caused me to lean forward and listen alertly. My back was toward the fishy-smelling sea, but he was facing it, and something or other had caused his wandering gaze to light on the low, distant line of Devil Reef, then shewing plainly and almost fascinatingly above the waves. The sight seemed to displease him, for he began a series of weak curses which ended in a confidential whisper and a knowing leer. He bent toward me, took hold of my coat lapel, and hissed out some hints that could not be mistaken.

"Thar's whar it all begun—that cursed place of all wickedness whar the deep water starts. Gate o' hell—sheer drop daown to a bottom no saoundin'-line kin tech. Ol' Cap'n Obed done it—him that faound aout more'n was good fer him in the Saouth Sea islands.

"Everybody was in a bad way them days. Trade fallin' off, mills losin' business—even the new ones—an' the best of our menfolks kilt a-privateerin'[a] in the War of 1812 or lost with the *Elizy* brig an' the *Ranger* snow[b]—both on 'em Gilman venters. Obed Marsh he had three ships afloat—brigantine *Columby*, brig *Hetty*, an' barque *Sumatry Queen*. He was the only one as kep' on with the East-Injy an' Pacific trade, though Esdras Martin's barkentine *Malay Pride*[c] made a venter as late as 'twenty-eight.[d]

"Never was nobody like Cap'n Obed—old limb o' Satan! Heh, heh! I kin mind him a-tellin' abaout furren parts, an' callin' all the folks stupid fer goin' to Christian meetin' an' bearin' their burdens meek an' lowly. Says they'd orter git better gods like some o' the folks in the Injies—gods as ud bring 'em good fishin' in return for their sacrifices, an' ud reely answer folks's prayers.

"Matt Eliot, his fust mate, talked a lot,[e] too, only he was agin' folks's doin' any heathen things. Told abaout an island east of Otaheité[f] whar they was a lot o' stone ruins older'n anybody knew anything abaout, kind o' like them on Ponape, in the Carolines, but with carvin's of faces that looked like the big statues on Easter Island. They[g] was a little volcanic island[h] near thar, too, whar they was other ruins with diff'rent carvin's—ruins all wore away like they'd ben under the sea onct, an' with picters of awful monsters all over 'em.

"Wal, Sir, Matt he says the natives araound thar had all the fish they cud ketch, an' sported bracelets an' armlets an' head rigs made aout of[i] a queer kind o' gold an' covered with picters o' monsters jest like the ones carved over the ruins on the little island—sorter fish-like[j] frogs or frog-like[k] fishes that was drawed in all kinds o' positions like

---

[a] kilt a-privateerin'] kilt / on Easter Island. They was a little volcanic / a-privateerin' C[c] [*see 187.17–18*]

[b] snow] scow D

[c] *Pride*] A; *Bride* B, C[c], D

[d] 'twenty-eight.] twenty-eight. D

[e] lot,] lot C, D

[f] Otaheité] Otaheit' C; Othaheite D

[g] They] *om.* C [*see below*]; Thar D

[h] statues . . . island] statues / island C[c] [*see note a above*]

[i] of] o' C, D

[j] fish-like] fishlike A, B

[k] frog-like] froglike A, B, C, D

they was human bein's. Nobody cud git aout o' them whar[a] they got all the stuff, an' all the other natives wondered haow they managed to find fish in plenty even when the very next islands had lean pickin's. Matt he got to wonderin' too,[b] an' so did Cap'n Obed. Obed he notices, besides, that lots of the han'some young folks ud drop aout o' sight fer good from year to year, an' that they wa'n't many old folks araound. Also, he thinks some of the folks looks[c] durned queer even fer[d] Kanakys.

"It took Obed to git the truth aout o' them heathen. I dun't know haow he done it, but he begun by tradin' fer the gold-like things they wore. Ast 'em whar they come from, an' ef they cud git more, an' finally wormed the story aout o' the old chief—Walakea, they called him. Nobody but Obed ud ever a believed the old yeller devil, but the Cap'n cud read folks like they was books. Heh, heh![e] Nobody never believes me naow when I tell 'em, an' I dun't s'pose you will, young feller—though come to look at ye, ye hev kind o' got them sharp-readin' eyes like Obed had."

The old man's whisper grew fainter, and I found myself shuddering at the terrible and sincere portentousness of his intonation, even though I knew his tale could be nothing but drunken phantasy.

"Wal, Sir, Obed he larnt that they's things on this arth as most folks never heerd abaout[f]—an' wouldn't believe ef they did hear. It seems these Kanakys was sacrificin' heaps o' their young men an' maidens to some kind o' god-things that lived under the sea, an' gittin' all kinds o' favour in return. They met the things on the little islet with the queer ruins, an' it seems them awful picters o' frog-fish monsters was supposed to be picters o' these things. Mebbe they was the kind o' critters as got all the mermaid stories an' sech started. They had all kinds o' cities on the sea-bottom, an' this island was heaved up from thar. Seems they was some of the things alive in the stone buildin's when the island come up sudden to the surface. That's haow the Kanakys got wind they was daown thar. Made sign-talk as soon as they

[a] whar] what B
[b] too,] too C, D
[c] looks] looked C, D
[d] fer] for C, D
[e] heh!] heh,! D
[f] abaout] about C, D

got over bein' skeert, an' pieced up a bargain afore long.

"Them things liked human sacrifices. Had had 'em ages afore, but lost track o' the upper world arter a time. What they done to the victims it ain't fer me to say, an' I guess Obed wa'n't none too sharp abaout askin'. But it was all right with the heathens, because they'd ben havin' a hard time an' was desp'rate abaout everything. They give a sarten number o' young folks to the sea-things twict[a] every year—May-Eve an' Hallowe'en—reg'lar as cud be. Also give some o' the carved knick-knacks they made. What the things agreed to give in return was plenty o' fish—they druv 'em in from all over the sea—an' a few gold-like things naow an' then.

"Wal, as I says, the natives met the things on the little volcanic islet—goin' thar in canoes with the sacrifices et cet'ry, and bringin' back any of the gold-like jools as was comin' to 'em. At fust the things didn't never go onto the main island, but arter a time they come to want to. Seems they hankered arter mixin' with the folks, an' havin' j'int ceremonies on the big days—May-Eve an' Hallowe'en. Ye see, they was able to live both in an' aout o' water—what they call amphibians, I guess. The Kanakys told 'em as haow folks from the other islands might wanta wipe 'em aout ef they got wind o' their bein' thar, but they says they dun't keer much, because they cud wipe aout the hull brood o' humans ef they was willin' to bother—that is, any as didn't hev sarten signs sech as was used onct by the lost Old Ones, whoever they was. But not wantin' to bother, they'd lay low when anybody visited the island.

"When it come to matin' with them toad-lookin' fishes, the Kanakys kind o' balked, but finally they larnt something as put a new face on the matter. Seems that human folks has got a kind o' relation to sech water-beasts—that everything alive come aout o' the water onct, an' only needs a little change to go back agin. Them things told the Kanakys that ef they mixed bloods there'd be children as ud look human at fust, but later turn more'n more like the things, till finally they'd take to the water an' jine the main lot o' things daown thar.[b] An' this is the important part, young feller—them as turned into fish things

[a] twict] twice D
[b] thar.] har. D

an' went into the water *wouldn't never die*.[a] Them things never died excep' they was kilt violent.

"Wal, Sir, it seems by the time Obed knowed them islanders they was all[b] full o' fish blood from them deep-water[c] things. When they got old an'[d] begun to shew it, they was kep' hid until they felt like takin' to the water an'[e] quittin' the place. Some was more teched than others, an' some never did change quite enough to take to the water; but mostly they turned aout[f] jest the way them things said. Them as was born more like the things changed arly, but them as was nearly human sometimes stayed on the island till they was past seventy, though they'd usually go daown under fer[g] trial trips afore that. Folks as had took to the water gen'rally come back a good deal to visit, so's a man ud often be a-talkin' to his own five-times-great-grandfather,[h] who'd left the dry land a couple o' hundred years or so afore.

"Everybody[i] got aout o' the idee o' dyin'—excep' in canoe wars with the other islanders, or as sacrifices to the sea-gods daown below, or from snake-bite or plague or sharp gallopin' ailments or somethin' afore they cud take to the water—but simply looked forrad to a kind o' change that wa'n't a bit horrible arter a while. They thought what they'd got was well wuth all they'd had to give up—an' I guess Obed kind o' come to think the same hisself when he'd chewed over old Walakea's story a bit. Walakea, though, was one of the few as hadn't got none of the fish blood—bein' of a royal line that intermarried with royal lines on other islands.

"Walakea he shewed Obed a lot o' rites an' incantations as had to do with the sea-things,[j] an' let him see some o' the folks in the village as had changed a lot from human shape. Somehaow or other, though,

---

[a] *wouldn't never die.*] wouldn't never die. D
[b] all] al B
[c] deep-water] deep water C, D
[d] an'] an C, D
[e] an;] an C, D
[f] aout] out D
[g] fer] for C, D
[h] -grandfather,] -grandfather C, D
[i] "Everybody] Everybody C
[j] sea-things,] sea things, A, B, C, D

he never would let him see one of the reg'lar things from right aout o' the water. In the end he give him a funny kind o' thingumajig made aout o' lead or something, that he said ud bring up the fish things from any place in the water whar they might be a nest of[a] 'em. The idee was to drop it daown with the right kind o' prayers an' sech. Walakea allaowed as the things was scattered all over the world, so's anybody that looked abaout cud find a nest an' bring 'em up ef they was wanted.

"Matt he didn't like this business at all, an' wanted Obed shud keep away from the island; but the Cap'n was sharp fer gain, an' faound he cud git them gold-like things so cheap it ud pay him to make a specialty of 'em. Things went on that way fer[b] years, an' Obed got enough o' that gold-like stuff to make him start the refinery in Waite's old run-daown fullin'[c] mill. He didn't dass sell the pieces like they was, fer[d] folks ud be all the time askin' questions. All the same his crews ud git a piece an' dispose of it naow and then, even though they was swore to keep quiet; an' he let his womenfolks wear some o' the pieces as was more human-like than most.

"Wal, come abaout 'thutty-eight—when I was seven year' old—Obed he faound the island people all wiped aout between v'yages. Seems the other islanders had got wind o' what was goin' on, an'[e] had took matters into their own hands. S'pose they musta[f] had, arter[g] all, them old magic signs as the sea-things says was the only things they was afeard of. No tellin' what any o' them Kanakys will chance to git a holt of when the sea-bottom throws up some island with ruins older'n the deluge. Pious cusses, these was—they didn't leave nothin' standin' on either the main island or the little volcanic islet excep' what parts of the ruins was too big to knock daown. In some places they was little stones strewed abaout—like charms—with somethin' on 'em like what ye call a swastika naowadays.[h] Prob'ly them was the Old Ones' signs.

[a] of] o' C, D
[b] fer] for C, D
[c] fullin'] fullin C
[d] fer] for C, D
[e] an;] and C, D
[f] musta] must a D
[g] arter] after C, D
[h] naowadays.] naowadays C

Folks all wiped aout, no trace o' no gold-like things, an' none o' the nearby Kanakys ud breathe a word abaout the matter. Wouldn't even admit they'd ever ben any people on that island.

"That naturally hit Obed pretty hard, seein' as his normal trade was doin' very poor. It hit the whole of Innsmouth, too, because in seafarin' days what profited the master of a ship gen'lly profited the crew proportionate. Most o'[a] the folks araound the taown took the hard times kind o' sheep-like[b] an' resigned, but they was in bad shape because the fishin' was peterin' aout an' the mills wa'n't[c] doin' none too well.

"Then's[d] the time Obed he begun a-cursin' at the folks fer bein' dull sheep an' prayin' to a Christian heaven as didn't help 'em none. He told 'em he'd knowed of[e] folks as prayed to gods that give somethin' ye reely need, an' says ef a good bunch o' men ud stand by him, he cud mebbe git a holt o' sarten paowers as ud bring plenty o' fish an' quite a bit o' gold. O' course them as sarved on the *Sumatry Queen*[f] an' seed the island knowed what he meant, an' wa'n't none too anxious to git clost to sea-things[g] like they'd heerd tell on, but them as didn't know what 'twas all abaout got kind o' swayed by what Obed had to say, an'[h] begun to ast him what he cud do to set 'em on the way to the faith as ud bring 'em results."

Here the old man faltered, mumbled, and lapsed into a moody and apprehensive silence; glancing nervously over his shoulder and then turning back to stare fascinatedly at the distant black reef. When I spoke to him he did not answer, so I knew I would have to let him finish the bottle. The insane yarn I was hearing interested me profoundly, for I fancied there was contained within it a sort of crude allegory based upon the strangenesses[i] of Innsmouth and elaborated by an imagination at once creative and full of scraps of exotic legend. Not for a moment did I

[a] o'] of C, D
[b] sheep-like] sheeplike A, B, C, D
[c] wa'n't] wan't A, B, C, D
[d] "Then's] Then's C
[e] of] o' C, D
[f] *Sumatry Queen*] Sumatry Queen C; *Sumatry Queen*, D
[g] sea-things] sea things A, B
[h] an'] and C, D
[i] strangenesses] strangeness C, D

believe that the tale had any really substantial foundation; but none the less the account held a hint of genuine terror,[a] if only because it brought in references to strange jewels clearly akin to the malign tiara I had seen at Newburyport. Perhaps the ornaments had, after all, come from some strange island; and possibly the wild stories were lies of the bygone Obed himself rather than of this antique toper.

I handed Zadok the bottle, and he drained it to the last drop. It was curious how he could stand so much whiskey, for not even a trace of thickness had come into his high, wheezy voice. He licked the nose of the bottle and slipped it into his pocket, then beginning to nod and whisper softly to himself. I bent close to catch any articulate words he might utter, and thought I saw a sardonic smile behind the stained,[b] bushy whiskers. Yes—he was really forming words, and I could grasp a fair proportion of them.

"Poor Matt—Matt he allus was agin[c] it—tried to line up the folks on his side, an' had long talks with the preachers—no use—they run the Congregational parson aout o' taown, an' the Methodist feller quit—never did see Resolved Babcock, the Baptist parson, agin— Wrath o' Jehovy—I was a mighty little critter, but I heerd what I heerd an' seen what I seen—Dagon an' Ashtoreth—Belial an' Beëlzebub[d]— Golden Caff an' the idols o' Canaan an' the Philistines—Babylonish abominations—*Mene, mene, tekel, upharsin*—"[e]

He stopped again, and from the look in his watery blue eyes I feared he was close to a stupor after all. But when I gently shook his shoulder he turned on me with astonishing alertness and snapped out some more obscure phrases.

"Dun't believe me, hey? Heh, heh, heh—then jest tell me, young feller, why Cap'n Obed an' twenty odd other folks used to row aout to Devil Reef in the dead o' night an' chant things so laoud ye cud hear 'em all over taown when the wind was right? Tell me that, hey? An' tell me why Obed was allus droppin' heavy things daown into the deep

---

[a] terror,] terror C, D
[b] stained,] stained C, D
[c] agin'] agin A, B, C, D
[d] Beëlzebub] Beelzebub C, D
[e] *upharsin*—"] *upharsin*—." D

water t'other side o' the reef whar the bottom shoots daown like a cliff lower'n ye kin saound? Tell me what he done with that funny-shaped lead thingumajig as Walakea give him? Hey, boy? An' what did they all haowl on May-Eve, an' agin the next Hallowe'en? An' why'd the new church parsons—fellers as used to be sailors—wear them queer robes an' cover theirselves with them gold-like things Obed brung? Hey?"

The watery blue eyes were almost savage and maniacal now, and the dirty white beard bristled electrically. Old Zadok probably saw me shrink back, for he began to cackle evilly.

"Heh, heh, heh, heh! Beginnin' to see,[a] hey? Mebbe ye'd like to a ben me in them days, when I seed things at night aout to sea from the cupalo top o' my haouse. Oh, I kin tell ye,[b] little pitchers hev big ears, an' I wa'n't missin' nothin' o' what was gossiped abaout Cap'n Obed an' the folks aout to the reef! Heh, heh, heh! Haow abaout the night I took my pa's ship's glass up to the cupalo an' seed the reef a-bristlin' thick with shapes that dove off quick soon's the moon riz? Obed an'[c] the folks was in a dory, but them shapes dove off the far side into the deep water an' never come up. . . . Haow'd ye like to be a little shaver alone up in a cupalo[d] a-watchin' shapes *as wa'n't human shapes?*[e] . . . Hey? . . . Heh, heh,[f] heh, heh. . . ."

The old man was getting hysterical, and I began to shiver with a nameless alarm. He laid a gnarled claw on my shoulder, and it seemed to me that its shaking was not altogether that of mirth.

"S'pose one night ye seed somethin' heavy heaved offen Obed's dory beyond the reef, an' then larned[g] nex' day a young feller was missin' from home? Hey?[h] Did anybody ever see hide or hair o' Hiram Gilman agin?[i] Did they? An' Nick Pierce, an' Luelly Waite, an' Adoniram

[a] see,] see A, B, D

[b] ye,] ye' C, D

[c] an'] an C, D

[d] cupalo] cupola C, D

[e] shapes . . . *shapes?*] shapes a*s wa'n't human* shapes? C; *shapes as wa'n't human shapes?* D

[f] heh,] *om.* C, D

[g] an' . . . larned] and . . . learned C, D

[h] home? Hey?] home. Hey! D

[i] agin?] agin. D

Saouthwick, an' Henry Garrison?[a] Hey? Heh, heh, heh, heh. . . . Shapes talkin' sign language with their hands . . . them as had reel hands. . . .

"Wal,[b] Sir, that was the time Obed begun to git on his feet agin. Folks see his three darters a-wearin' gold-like things as nobody'd never see on 'em afore, an' smoke started comin' aout o' the refin'ry chimbly. Other folks was prosp'rin',[c] too—fish begun to swarm into the harbour fit to kill, an' heaven knows what sized cargoes we begun to ship aout to Newb'ryport, Arkham, an' Boston. 'Twas then Obed got the ol' branch railrud put through. Some Kingsport fishermen heerd abaout the ketch an' come up in sloops, but they was all lost. Nobody never see 'em agin. An' jest then our folks organised the Esoteric Order o' Dagon, an' bought Masonic Hall offen Calvary Commandery for it . . . heh, heh, heh! Matt Eliot was a Mason an' agin' the sellin', but he dropped aout o' sight jest then.

"Remember, I ain't sayin' Obed was set on hevin' things jest like they was on that Kanaky isle. I dun't think he aimed at fust to do no mixin', nor raise no younguns to take to the water an' turn into fishes with eternal life. He wanted them gold things, an' was willin' to pay heavy, an' I guess the *others*[d] was satisfied fer a while. . . .

"Come in 'forty-six[e] the taown done some lookin' an' thinkin' fer itself. Too many folks missin'—too much wild preachin' at meetin' of[f] a Sunday—too much talk abaout that reef. I guess I done a bit by tellin' Selectman Mowry what I see from the cupalo. They was a party one night as follered Obed's craowd aout to the reef, an' I heerd shots betwixt the dories. Nex' day Obed an'[g] thutty-two others was in gaol, with everbody a-wonderin' jest what was afoot an'[h] jest what charge agin'[i] 'em cud be got to holt. God, ef anybody'd look'd ahead . . . a

[a] Garrison?] Garrison. D
[b] "Wal,] Wal, C
[c] prosp'rin',] prosp'rin, C, D
[d] *others*] others D
[e] in 'forty-six] in'forty-six D
[f] lookin' . . . of] missin'—too much wild preachin' at meetin' of / lookin' an' thinkin' fer itself. Too many folks C[c]
[g] an'] and C, D
[h] an'] and C, D
[i] agin'] agin C, D

couple o' weeks later, when nothin' had ben throwed into the sea fer that[a] long. . . ."

Zadok was shewing signs of fright and exhaustion, and I let him keep silence for a while, though glancing apprehensively at my watch. The tide had turned and was coming in now, and the sound of the waves seemed to arouse him. I was glad of that tide, for at high water the fishy smell might not be so bad. Again I strained to catch his whispers.

"That awful night . . . I seed 'em . . .[b] I was up in the cupalo . . . hordes of 'em . . . swarms of 'em . . . all over the reef an' swimmin' up the harbour into the Manuxet. . . . God, what happened in the streets of Innsmouth that night . . . they rattled our door, but pa wouldn't open . . . then he clumb aout the kitchen winder with his musket to find Selectman[c] Mowry an' see what he cud[d] do. . . . Maounds o' the dead an' the dyin' . . . shots an'[e] screams . . . shaoutin' in Ol' Squar an' Taown Squar an' New Church Green . . .[f] gaol throwed open . . .[g] proclamation . . . treason . . . called it the plague when folks come in an' faound haff our people missin' . . . nobody left but them as ud jine in with Obed an' them things or else keep quiet . . . never heerd o' my pa no more. . . ."

The old man was panting, and perspiring profusely. His grip on my shoulder tightened.

"Everything cleaned up in the mornin'—but they was *traces*.[h] . . . Obed he kinder takes charge an' says things is goin' to be changed . . . *others'll* worship with us at meetin'-time, an' sarten haouses hez got to entertain *guests* . . . *they*[i] wanted to mix like they done with the Kanakys, an' he fer one didn't feel baound to stop 'em. Far gone, was Obed . . . jest like a crazy man on the subjeck. He says they brung us fish an' treasure, an' shud hev what they hankered arter.[j] . . .

[a] that] thet C, D
[b] 'em . . .] 'em. D
[c] Selectman] Selecman D
[d] cud] cud; D
[e] an'] and C, D
[f] Green . . .] Green— D
[g] open . . .] open . . . . . · C; open . . .— D
[h] *traces*.] traces. C
[i] *they*] they C, D
[j] arter.] after. C, D

"Nothin' was to be diff'runt on the aoutside, only we was to keep shy o' strangers ef we knowed what was good fer us. We all hed to take the Oath o' Dagon, an' later on they was secon' an' third Oaths that some on us took. Them as ud help special, ud git special rewards— gold an' sech— No use balkin', fer they was millions of 'em daown thar. They'd ruther not start risin' an' wipin' aout humankind,[a] but ef they was gave away an' forced to, they cud do a lot toward jest that. We didn't hev them old charms to cut 'em off like folks in the Saouth Sea did, an' them Kanakys wudn't never give away their secrets.

"Yield up enough sacrifices an' savage knick-knacks an' harbourage in the taown when they wanted it, an' they'd let well enough alone. Wudn't bother no strangers as might bear tales aoutside—that is, withaout they got pryin'. All in the band of the faithful—Order o' Dagon—an' the children shud never die, but go back to the Mother Hydra an' Father Dagon what we all come from onct—[b]*Iä! Iä!*[c] *Cthulhu fhtagn! Ph'nglui mglw'nafh Cthulhu R'lyeh wgah-nagl fhtagn—*"[d]

Old Zadok was fast lapsing into stark raving, and I held my breath. Poor old soul—to what pitiful depths of hallucination had his liquor,[e] plus his hatred of the decay, alienage, and disease around him, brought that fertile, imaginative brain! He began to moan now, and tears were coursing down his channelled cheeks into the depths of his beard.

"God, what I seen senct I was fifteen year' old—*Mene, mene, tekel, upharsin!*—the folks as was missin', an' them as kilt theirselves—them as told things in Arkham or Ipswich or sech places was all called crazy, like you're a-callin'[f] me right naow—but God, what I seen— They'd a kilt me long ago fer what I know, only I'd took the fust an' secon' Oaths o' Dagon offen Obed, so was pertected unlessen a jury of 'em proved I told things knowin' an' delib'rit . . . but I wudn't take the third Oath—I'd a died ruther'n take that—

---

[a] humankind,] human-kind, C, D
[b] onct—] onct. . . . C, D
[c] *Iä! Iä!*] *Ia! Ia!* C
[d] *fhtagn—*"] *fhtaga—*" D
[e] liquor,] liquor. D
[f] a-callin'] a callin' D

"It got wuss araound Civil War time, *when children born senct 'forty-six begun to grow up*—some of 'em, that is. I was afeard[a]—never did no pryin' arter that awful night, an' never see one of—*them*—clost to in all my life. That is, never no full-blooded one. I went to the war, an' ef I'd a had any guts or sense I'd a never come back, but settled away from here. But folks wrote me things wa'n't so bad. That, I s'pose, was because gov'munt draft men was in taown arter 'sixty-three. Arter the war it was jest as bad agin. People begun to fall off—mills an' shops shet daown—shippin' stopped an' the harbour choked up—railrud give up—but *they* . . . they never stopped swimmin' in an' aout o' the river from that cursed reef o' Satan—an' more an' more attic winders got a-boarded up, an' more an' more noises was heerd in haouses as wa'n't s'posed to hev nobody in 'em. . . .

"Folks aoutside hev their stories abaout us—s'pose you've heerd a plenty on 'em, seein' what questions ye ast—stories abaout things they've seed naow an' then, an' abaout that queer joolry as still comes in from somewhars an' ain't quite all melted up—but nothin' never gits def'nite. Nobody'll believe nothin'.[b] They call them gold-like things pirate loot, an' allaow the Innsmouth folks hez furren blood or is distempered or somethin'. Besides, them that lives here shoo off as many strangers as they kin, an' encourage the rest not to git very cur'ous, specially raound night time. Beasts balk at the critters—hosses wuss'n mules—but when they got autos that was all right.

"In 'forty-six[c] Cap'n Obed took a second wife *that nobody in the taown never see*—some says he didn't want to, but was made to by them as he'd called in—had three children by her—two as disappeared young, but one gal as looked like anybody else an' was eddicated in Europe. Obed finally got her married off by a trick to an Arkham feller as didn't suspect nothin'. But nobody aoutside'll hev nothin' to do with Innsmouth folks naow. Barnabas Marsh that runs the refin'ry naow is Obed's grandson by his fust wife—son of Onesiphorus, his eldest son, *but his mother was another o' them as wa'n't never seed aoutdoors*.

"Right naow Barnabas is abaout changed. Can't shet his eyes no

---

[a] afeard] afeared D
[b] nothin'.] nothin' C[c]
[c] 'forty-six] forty-six C, D

more, an' is all aout o' shape. They say he still wears clothes, but he'll take to the water soon. Mebbe he's tried it already—they do sometimes go daown fer little spells afore they go fer[a] good. Ain't ben seed abaout in public fer nigh[b] on ten year'. Dun't know haow his poor wife kin feel—she come from Ipswich, an' they nigh lynched Barnabas when he courted her fifty odd year' ago. Obed he died in 'seventy-eight, an' all the next gen'ration is gone naow—the fust[c] wife's children dead, an' the rest . . . God knows. . . ."

The sound of the incoming tide was now very insistent, and little by little it seemed to change the old man's mood from maudlin tearfulness to watchful fear. He would pause now and then to renew those nervous glances over his shoulder or out toward the reef, and despite the wild absurdity of his tale, I could not help beginning to share his vague apprehensiveness. Zadok now grew shriller, and seemed to be trying to whip up his courage with louder speech.

"Hey, yew, why dun't ye say somethin'? Haow'd ye like to be livin' in a taown like this, with everything a-rottin' an' a-dyin', an' boarded-up monsters crawlin' an' bleatin' an' barkin' an' hoppin' araoun' black cellars an' attics every way ye turn? Hey? Haow'd ye like to hear the haowlin' night arter night from the churches an' Order o' Dagon Hall,[d] *an'[e] know what's doin' part o' the haowlin'?* Haow'd ye like to hear what comes from that awful reef every May-Eve an' Hallowmass? Hey? Think the old man's crazy, eh? Wal, Sir, *let me tell ye that ain't the wust!*"

Zadok was really screaming now, and the mad frenzy of his voice disturbed me more than I care to own.

"Curse ye, dun't set thar a-starin' at me with them eyes—I tell Obed Marsh he's in hell, an' hez got to stay thar! Heh, heh . . . in hell, I says! Can't git me—I hain't done nothin' nor told nobody nothin'—

"Oh, you, young feller? Wal, even ef I hain't told nobody nothin' yet, I'm a-goin' to naow! You[f] jest set still an' listen to me, boy—this is

[a] go fer] go daown for C, D
[b] nigh] night D
[c] fust] *fust* D
[d] Hall,] hall, A, B
[e] *an*'] *an* C
[f] You] Yew D

what I ain't never told nobody. . . . I says I didn't[a] do no pryin' arter that night—*but I faound things aout jest the same!*

"Yew want to know what the reel horror is, hey? Wal, it's this—it ain't what them fish devils *hez done, but what they're a-goin' to do!* They're a-bringin' things up aout o' whar they come from into the taown—ben doin' it fer years, an' slackenin' up lately. Them haouses north o' the river betwixt Water an' Main Streets is full of 'em—them devils *an' what they brung*—an' when they git ready. . . . I say, *when they git ready* . . . ever hear tell of a *shoggoth? . . .*

"Hey, d'ye hear me? I tell ye[b] *I know what them things be—I seen 'em one night when*[c] . . . EH—AHHHH—AH! E'YAAHHHH.[d] . . ."

The hideous suddenness and inhuman frightfulness of the old man's shriek almost made me faint. His eyes, looking past me toward the malodorous sea, were positively starting from his head; while his face was a mask of fear worthy of Greek tragedy. His bony claw dug monstrously into my shoulder, and he made no motion as I turned my head to look at whatever he had glimpsed.

There was nothing that I could see. Only the incoming tide, with perhaps one set of ripples more local than the long-flung line of breakers. But now Zadok was shaking me, and I turned back to watch the melting of that fear-frozen face into a chaos of twitching eyelids and mumbling gums. Presently his voice came back—albeit as a trembling whisper.

"*Git aout o' here!* Git aout o' here! *They seen us*—git aout fer your life! Dun't wait fer nothin'—*they know naow*—[e] [f]Run fer it—quick—*aout o' this taown—*"

Another heavy wave dashed against the loosening masonry of the bygone wharf, and changed the mad ancient's whisper to another inhuman and blood-curdling scream.

[a] didn't] didn't get to D
[b] I tell ye] *I tell ye* C
[c] *when*] when C
[d] EH-AHHHH-AH! E'YAAHHHH.] eh-ahhhh-ah! e'yahhh. C; *eh-ahhh-ah! e-yahhh.* D
[e] *they know naow*—] they know naow— C
[f] [*two illegible lines*] one o' the local folks. Any delivery wagon that ye know's from outa taown. *It's curious strangers like you be that they dun't never let go!* ¶ "Hustle up, thar—I'm goin' back past the farm—think I know whar to hide A [*excised*]

"E—YAAHHHH! . . . YHAAAAAAA! . . ."[a]

Before I could recover my scattered wits he had relaxed his clutch on my shoulder and dashed wildly inland toward the street, reeling northward around the ruined warehouse wall.

I glanced back at the sea, but there was nothing there. And when I reached Water Street and looked along it toward the north there was no remaining trace of Zadok Allen.

IV.

I can hardly describe the mood in which I was left by this harrowing episode—an episode at once mad and pitiful, grotesque and terrifying. The grocery boy had prepared me for it, yet the reality left me none the less bewildered and disturbed. Puerile though the story was, old Zadok's insane earnestness and horror had communicated to me a mounting unrest which joined with my earlier sense of loathing for the town and its blight of intangible shadow.

Later I might sift the tale and extract some nucleus of historic allegory; just now I wished to put it out of my head. The hour had grown perilously late—my watch said 7:15, and the Arkham bus left Town Square at eight—so I tried to give my thoughts as neutral and practical a cast as possible, meanwhile walking rapidly through the deserted streets of gaping roofs and leaning houses toward the hotel where I had checked my valise and would find my bus.

Though the golden light of late afternoon gave the ancient roofs and decrepit chimneys an air of mystic loveliness and peace, I could not help glancing over my shoulder now and then. I would surely be very glad to get out of malodorous and fear-shadowed Innsmouth, and wished there were some other vehicle than the bus driven by that sinister-looking fellow Sargent. Yet I did not hurry too precipitately, for there were architectural details worth viewing at every silent corner; and I could easily, I calculated, cover the necessary distance in a half-hour.

Studying the grocery youth's map and seeking a route I had not traversed before, I chose Marsh Street instead of State for my

---

[a] scream. ¶ "E—YAAHHHH! . . . YHAAAAAAA! . . ."] scream. "E'yaahhhh! . . . *yhaaaaaaa!* . . ." C; scream. *"E-yaahhhh! . . . yhaaaaaaa! . . ."* D

approach to Town Square. Near the corner of Fall Street I began to see scattered groups of furtive whisperers, and when I finally reached the Square I saw that almost all the loiterers were congregated around the door of the Gilman House. It seemed as if many bulging, watery, unwinking eyes looked oddly at me as I claimed my valise in the lobby, and I hoped that none of these unpleasant creatures would be my fellow-passengers on the coach.

The bus, rather early, rattled in with three passengers somewhat before eight, and an evil-looking fellow on the sidewalk muttered a few indistinguishable words to the driver. Sargent threw out a mail-bag and a roll of newspapers, and entered the hotel; while the passengers—the same men whom I had seen arriving in Newburyport that morning—shambled to the sidewalk and exchanged some faint guttural words with a loafer in a language I could have sworn was not English. I boarded the empty coach and took the same seat I had taken before, but was hardly settled before Sargent reappeared and began mumbling in a throaty voice of peculiar repulsiveness.

I was, it appeared, in very bad luck. There had been something wrong with the engine, despite the excellent time made from Newburyport, and the bus could not complete the journey to Arkham. No, it could not possibly be repaired that night, nor was there any other way of getting transportation out of Innsmouth,[a] either to Arkham or elsewhere. Sargent was sorry, but I would have to stop over at the Gilman. Probably the clerk would make the price easy for me, but there was nothing else to do. Almost dazed by this sudden obstacle, and violently dreading the fall of night in this decaying and half-unlighted town, I left the bus and reëntered[b] the hotel lobby; where the sullen,[c] queer-looking night clerk told[d] me I could have Room 428 on next the top floor—large, but without running water—for a dollar.

Despite what I had heard of this hotel in Newburyport, I signed the register, paid my dollar, let the clerk take my valise, and followed that sour, solitary attendant up three creaking flights of stairs past dusty

[a] Innsmouth,] Innsmouh C[c]; Innsmouth D
[b] reëntered] reentered C, D
[c] sullen,] sullen D
[d] told] tolk D

corridors which seemed wholly devoid of life. My room, a dismal rear one with two windows and bare, cheap furnishings, overlooked a dingy courtyard[a] otherwise hemmed in by low, deserted brick blocks, and commanded a view of decrepit westward-stretching roofs with a marshy countryside beyond. At the end of the corridor was a bathroom—a discouraging relique with ancient marble bowl, tin tub, faint electric light, and musty wooden panelling around all the plumbing fixtures.

It being still daylight, I descended to the Square and looked around for a dinner of some sort; noticing as I did so the strange glances I received from the unwholesome loafers. Since the grocery was closed, I was forced to patronise the restaurant I had shunned before; a stooped, narrow-headed man with staring, unwinking eyes, and a flat-nosed wench with unbelievably thick, clumsy hands being in attendance. The service was all of the counter type, and it relieved me to find that much was evidently served from cans and packages. A bowl of vegetable soup with crackers was enough for me, and I soon headed back for my cheerless room at the Gilman; getting an evening paper and a flyspecked magazine from the evil-visaged clerk at the rickety stand beside his desk.

As twilight deepened I turned on the one feeble electric bulb over the cheap, iron-framed bed, and tried as best I could to continue the reading I had begun. I felt it advisable to keep my mind wholesomely occupied, for it would not do to brood over the abnormalities of this ancient, blight-shadowed town while I was still within its borders. The insane yarn I had heard from the aged drunkard did not promise very pleasant dreams, and I felt I must keep the image of his wild, watery eyes as far as possible from my imagination.

Also, I must not dwell on what that factory inspector had told the Newburyport ticket-agent about the Gilman House and the voices of its nocturnal tenants[b]—not on that, nor on the face beneath the tiara in the black church doorway; the face for whose horror my conscious mind could not account. It would perhaps have been easier to keep my thoughts from disturbing topics had the room not been so gruesomely

---

[a] courtyard] court-/yard C; court-yard D
[b] tenants] tenents C

musty. As it was, the lethal mustiness blended hideously with the town's general fishy odour and persistently focussed one's fancy on death and decay.

Another thing that disturbed me was the absence of a bolt on the door of my room. One had been there, as marks clearly shewed, but there were signs of recent removal. No doubt it had become out of order, like so many other things in this decrepit edifice. In my nervousness I looked around and discovered a bolt on the clothespress which seemed to be of the same size, judging from the marks, as the one formerly on the door. To gain a partial relief from the general tension I busied myself by transferring this hardware to the vacant place with the aid of a handy three-in-one device including a screw-driver which I kept on my key-ring. The bolt fitted perfectly, and I was somewhat relieved when I knew that I could shoot it firmly upon retiring. Not that I had any real apprehension of its need, but that any symbol of security was welcome in an environment of this kind. There were adequate bolts on the two lateral doors to connecting rooms, and these I proceeded to fasten.

I did not undress, but decided to read till I was sleepy and then lie down with only my coat, collar, and shoes off. Taking a pocket flashlight[a] from my valise, I placed it in my trousers, so that I could read my watch if I woke up later in the dark. Drowsiness, however, did not come; and when I stopped to analyse my thoughts I found to my disquiet that I was really unconsciously listening for something—listening for something which I dreaded but could not name. That inspector's story must have worked on my imagination more deeply than I had suspected. Again I tried to read, but found that I made no progress.

After a time I seemed to hear the stairs and corridors creak at intervals as if with footsteps, and wondered if the other rooms were beginning to fill up. There were no voices, however, and it struck me that there was something subtly furtive about the creaking. I did not like it, and debated whether I had better try to sleep at all. This town had some queer people, and there had undoubtedly been several disappearances. Was this one of those inns where travellers[b] were slain

---

[a] flashlight] flash light C, D
[b] travellers] travelers D

for their money? Surely I had no look of excessive prosperity. Or were the townsfolk really so resentful about curious visitors? Had my obvious sightseeing, with its frequent map-consultations, aroused unfavourable notice? It occurred to me that I must be in a highly nervous state to let a few random creakings set me off speculating in this fashion—but I regretted none the less that I was unarmed.

At length, feeling a fatigue which had nothing of drowsiness in it, I bolted the newly outfitted hall door, turned off the light, and threw myself down on the hard, uneven bed—coat, collar, shoes, and all. In the darkness every faint noise of the night seemed magnified, and a flood of doubly unpleasant thoughts swept over me. I was sorry I had put out the light, yet was too tired to rise and turn it on again. Then, after a long, dreary interval, and prefaced by a fresh creaking of stairs and corridor, there came that soft, damnably unmistakable sound which seemed like a malign fulfilment of all my apprehensions. Without the least shadow of a doubt, the lock on my hall[a] door was being tried—cautiously, furtively, tentatively—with a key.

My sensations upon recognising this sign of actual peril were perhaps less rather than more tumultuous because of my previous vague fears. I had been, albeit without definite reason, instinctively on my guard—and that was to my advantage in the new and real crisis, whatever it might turn out to be. Nevertheless the change in the menace from vague premonition to immediate reality was a profound shock, and fell upon me with the force of a genuine blow. It never once occurred to me that the fumbling might be a mere mistake. Malign purpose was all I could think of, and I kept deathly quiet, awaiting the would-be intruder's next move.

After a time the cautious rattling ceased, and I heard the room to the north entered with a pass-key.[b] Then the lock of the connecting door to my room was softly tried. The bolt held, of course, and I heard the floor creak as the prowler left the room. After a moment there came another soft rattling, and I knew that the room to the south of me was being entered. Again a furtive trying of a bolted connecting door, and again a receding creaking. This time the creaking went along

---

[a] on my hall] on my C; of my D
[b] pass-key.] pass key. A, B, C, D

the hall and down the stairs, so I knew that the prowler had realised the bolted condition of my doors and was giving up his attempt for a greater or lesser time, as the future would shew.

The readiness with which I fell into a plan of action proves that I must have been subconsciously fearing some menace and considering possible avenues of escape for hours. From the first I felt that the unseen fumbler meant a danger not to be met or dealt with, but only to be fled from as precipitately as possible. The one thing to do was to get out of that hotel alive as quickly as I could, and through some channel other than the front stairs and lobby.

Rising softly and throwing my flashlight on the switch, I sought to light the bulb over my bed in order to choose and pocket some belongings for a swift, valiseless flight. Nothing, however, happened; and I saw that the power had been cut off. Clearly, some cryptic, evil movement was afoot on a large scale—just what, I could not say. As I stood pondering with my hand on the now useless switch I heard a muffled creaking on the floor below, and thought I could barely distinguish voices in conversation. A moment later I felt less sure that the deeper sounds were voices, since the apparent hoarse barkings and loose-syllabled croakings bore so little resemblance to recognised human speech. Then I thought with renewed force of what the factory inspector had heard in the night in this mouldering and pestilential building.

Having filled my pockets with the flashlight's aid, I put on my hat and tiptoed to the windows to consider chances of descent. Despite the state's safety regulations there was no fire escape on this side of the hotel, and I saw that my windows commanded only a sheer three-story[a] drop to the cobbled courtyard. On the right and left, however, some ancient brick business blocks abutted on the hotel; their slant roofs coming up to a reasonable jumping distance from my fourth-story[b] level. To reach either of these lines of buildings I would have to be in a room two doors from my own—in one case on the north and in the other case on the south—and my mind instantly set to work calculating what chances I had of making the transfer.

[a] three-story] three-storey A, B, C, D
[b] fourth-story] fourth-storey A, B, C, D

I could not, I decided, risk an emergence into the corridor; where my footsteps would surely be heard, and where the difficulties of entering the desired room would be insuperable. My progress, if it was to be made at all, would have to be through the less solidly built[a] connecting doors of the rooms; the locks and bolts of which I would have to force violently, using my shoulder as a battering-ram whenever they were set against me. This, I thought, would be possible owing to the rickety nature of the house and its fixtures; but I realised I could not do it noiselessly. I would have to count on sheer speed, and the chance of getting to a window before any hostile forces became coördinated[b] enough to open the right door toward me with a pass-key. My own outer door I reinforced by pushing the bureau against it—little by little, in order to make a minimum of sound.

I perceived that my chances were very slender, and was fully prepared for any calamity.[c] Even getting to another roof would not solve the problem, for there would then remain the task of reaching the ground and escaping from the town. One thing in my favour was the deserted and ruinous state of the abutting buildings, and the number of skylights gaping blackly open in each row.

Gathering from the grocery boy's map that the best route out of town was southward, I glanced first at the connecting door on the south side of the room. It was designed to open in my direction, hence I saw—after drawing the bolt and finding other fastenings in place—it was not a favourable[d] one for forcing. Accordingly abandoning it as a route, I cautiously moved the bedstead against it to hamper any attack which might be made on it later from the next room. The door on the north was hung to open away from me, and this—though a test proved it to be locked or bolted from the other side—I knew must be my route. If I could gain the roofs of the buildings in Paine Street and descend successfully to the ground level, I might perhaps dart through the courtyard and the adjacent or opposite buildings to Washington or Bates—or else emerge in Paine and edge around southward into

---

[a] solidly built] solidly-built A, B, C, D
[b] coördinated] coordinated C, D
[c] calamity.] calamity C[c]
[d] favourable] favorable C, D

Washington. In any case, I would aim to strike Washington somehow and get quickly out of the Town Square region. My preference would be to avoid Paine, since the fire station there might be open all night.

As I thought of these things I looked out over the squalid sea of decaying roofs below me, now brightened by the beams of a moon not much past full. On the right the black gash of the river-gorge clove the panorama; abandoned factories and railway station clinging barnacle-like to its sides. Beyond it the rusted railway and the Rowley road led off through a flat, marshy terrain dotted with islets of higher and dryer scrub-grown land. On the left the creek-threaded countryside was nearer, the narrow road to Ipswich gleaming white in the moonlight. I could not see from my side of the hotel the southward route toward[a] Arkham which I had determined to take.

I was irresolutely speculating on when I had better attack the northward door, and on how I could least audibly manage it, when I noticed that the vague noises underfoot had given place to a fresh and heavier creaking of the stairs. A wavering flicker of light shewed through my transom, and the boards of the corridor began to groan with a ponderous load. Muffled sounds of possible vocal origin approached, and at length a firm knock came at my outer door.

For a moment I simply held my breath and waited. Eternities seemed to elapse, and the nauseous fishy odour of my environment seemed to mount suddenly and spectacularly. Then the knocking was repeated—continuously, and with growing insistence. I knew that the time for action had come, and forthwith drew the bolt of the northward connecting door, bracing myself for the task of battering it open. The knocking waxed louder, and I hoped that its volume would cover the sound of my efforts. At last beginning my attempt, I lunged again and again at the thin panelling with my left shoulder, heedless of shock or pain. The door resisted even more than I had expected, but I did not give in. And all the while the clamour at the outer door increased.

Finally the connecting door gave, but with such a crash that I knew those outside must have heard. Instantly the outside knocking became a violent battering, while keys sounded ominously in the hall

---

[a] toward] to ward C[c]

doors of the rooms[a] on both sides of me. Rushing through the newly opened connexion, I succeeded in bolting the northerly hall door before the lock could be turned; but even as I did so I heard the hall door of the third room—the one from whose window I had hoped to reach the roof below—being tried with a pass-key.[b]

For an instant I felt absolute despair, since my trapping in a chamber with no window egress seemed complete. A wave of almost abnormal horror swept over me, and invested with a terrible but unexplainable singularity the flashlight-glimpsed dust prints made by the intruder who had lately tried my door from this room. Then, with a dazed automatism which persisted despite hopelessness, I made for the next connecting door and performed the blind motion of pushing at it in an effort to get through and—granting that fastenings might be as providentially intact as in this second room—bolt the hall door beyond before the lock could be turned from outside.

Sheer fortunate chance gave me my reprieve—for the connecting door before me was not only unlocked but actually ajar. In a second I was through, and had my right knee and shoulder against a hall door which was visibly opening inward. My pressure took the opener off guard, for the thing shut as I pushed, so that I could slip the well-conditioned bolt as I had done with the other door. As I gained this respite I heard the battering at the two other doors abate, while a confused clatter came from the connecting door I had shielded with the bedstead. Evidently the bulk of my assailants had entered the southerly room and were massing in a lateral attack. But at the same moment a pass-key[c] sounded in the next door to the north, and I knew that a nearer peril was at hand.

The northward connecting door was wide open, but there was no time to think about checking the already turning lock in the hall. All I could do was to shut and bolt the open connecting door, as well as its mate on the opposite side—pushing a bedstead against the one and a bureau against the other, and moving a washstand in front of the hall door. I must, I saw, trust to such makeshift barriers to shield me till I

---

[a] rooms] roms C[c]
[b] pass-key.] pass key. B, C, D
[c] pass-key] pass key A, B, C, D

could get out the window and on the roof of the Paine Street block. But even in this acute moment my chief horror was something apart from the immediate weakness of my defences. I was shuddering because not one of my pursuers, despite some hideous pantings, gruntings, and subdued barkings at odd intervals, was uttering an unmuffled or intelligible vocal sound.

As I moved the furniture and rushed toward the windows I heard a frightful scurrying along the corridor toward the room north of me, and perceived that the southward battering had ceased. Plainly, most of my opponents were about to concentrate against the feeble connecting door which they knew must open directly on me. Outside, the moon played on the ridgepole of the block below, and I saw that the jump would be desperately hazardous because of the steep surface on which I must land.

Surveying the conditions, I chose the more southerly of the two windows as my avenue of escape; planning to land on the inner slope of the roof and make for the nearest skylight. Once inside one of the decrepit brick structures I would have to reckon with pursuit; but I hoped to descend and dodge in and out of yawning doorways along the shadowed courtyard, eventually getting to Washington Street and slipping out of town toward the south.

The clatter at the northerly connecting door was now terrific, and I saw that the weak panelling was beginning to splinter. Obviously, the besiegers had brought some ponderous object into play as a battering-ram. The bedstead, however, still held firm; so that I had at least a faint chance of making good my escape. As I opened the window I noticed that it was flanked by heavy velour draperies suspended from a pole by brass rings, and also that there was a large projecting catch for the shutters on the exterior. Seeing a possible means of avoiding the dangerous jump, I yanked at the hangings and brought them down, pole and all; then quickly hooking two of the rings in the shutter catch and flinging the drapery outside. The heavy folds reached fully to the abutting roof, and I saw that the rings and catch would be likely to bear my weight. So, climbing out of the window and down the improvised rope ladder, I left behind me for ever the morbid and horror-infested fabric of the Gilman House.

I landed safely on the loose slates of the steep roof, and succeeded in gaining the gaping black skylight without a slip. Glancing up at the window I had left, I observed it was still dark, though far across the crumbling chimneys to the north I could see lights ominously blazing in the Order of Dagon Hall,[a] the Baptist church, and the Congregational church which I recalled so shiveringly. There had seemed to be no one in the courtyard below, and I hoped there would be a chance to get away before the spreading of a general alarm. Flashing my pocket lamp into the skylight, I saw that there were no steps down. The distance was slight, however, so I clambered over the brink and dropped; striking a dusty floor littered with crumbling boxes and barrels.

The place was ghoulish-looking, but I was past minding such impressions and made at once for the staircase revealed by my flashlight—after a hasty glance at my watch, which shewed the hour to be 2 a.m.[b] The steps creaked, but seemed tolerably sound; and I raced down past a barn-like second story[c] to the ground floor. The desolation was complete, and only echoes answered my footfalls. At length I reached the lower hall,[d] at one end of which I saw a faint luminous rectangle marking the ruined Paine Street doorway. Heading the other way, I found the back door also open; and darted out and down five stone steps to the grass-grown cobblestones of the courtyard.

The moonbeams did not reach down here, but I could just see my way about without using the flashlight. Some of the windows on the Gilman House side were faintly glowing, and I thought I heard confused sounds within. Walking softly over to the Washington Street side I perceived several open doorways, and chose the nearest as my route out. The hallway inside was black, and when I reached the opposite end I saw that the street door was wedged immovably shut. Resolved to try another building, I groped my way back toward the courtyard, but stopped short when close to the doorway.

For out of an opened door in the Gilman House a large crowd of doubtful shapes was pouring—lanterns bobbing in the darkness, and horrible croaking voices exchanging low cries in what was certainly not English. The figures moved uncertainly, and I realised to my relief that

---

[a] Hall,] hall, A

[b] a.m.] a. m. C, D

[c] barn-like . . . story] barnlike . . . storey A, B, C, D

[d] hall,] hall D

they did not know where I had gone; but for all that they sent a shiver of horror through my frame. Their features were indistinguishable, but their crouching, shambling gait was abominably repellent. And worst of all, I perceived that one figure was strangely robed, and unmistakably surmounted by a tall tiara of a design altogether too familiar. As the figures spread throughout the courtyard, I felt my fears increase. Suppose I could find no egress from this building on the street side? The fishy odour was detestable, and I wondered I could stand it without fainting. Again groping toward the street, I opened a door off the hall and came upon an empty room with closely shuttered but sashless windows. Fumbling in the rays of my flashlight, I found I could open the shutters; and in another moment had climbed outside and was carefully closing the aperture in its original manner.

I was now in Washington Street, and for the moment saw no living thing nor any light save that of the moon. From several directions in the distance, however, I could hear the sound of hoarse voices, of footsteps, and of a curious kind of pattering which did not sound quite like footsteps. Plainly I had no time to lose. The points of the compass were clear to me, and I was glad that all the street-lights[a] were turned off, as is often the custom on strongly moonlit nights in unprosperous rural regions. Some of the sounds came from the south, yet I retained my design of escaping in that direction. There would, I knew, be plenty of deserted doorways to shelter me in case I met any person or group who looked like pursuers.

I walked rapidly, softly, and close to the ruined houses. While hatless and dishevelled after my arduous climb, I did not look especially noticeable; and stood a good chance of passing unheeded if forced to encounter any casual wayfarer. At Bates Street I drew into a yawning vestibule while two shambling figures crossed in front of me, but was soon on my way again and approaching the open space where Eliot Street obliquely crosses Washington at the intersection of South. Though I had never seen this space, it had looked dangerous to me on the grocery youth's map; since the moonlight would have free play there. There was no use trying to evade it, for any alternative course would involve detours of possibly disastrous visibility and delaying

[a] street-lights] street lights A, B, C, D

effect. The only thing to do was to cross it boldly and openly; imitating the typical shamble of the Innsmouth folk as best I could, and trusting that no one—or at least no pursuer of mine—would be there.

Just how fully the pursuit was organised—and indeed, just what its purpose might be—I could form no idea. There seemed to be unusual activity in the town, but I judged that the news of my escape from the Gilman had not yet spread. I would, of course, soon have to shift from Washington to some other southward street; for that party from the hotel would doubtless be after me. I must have left dust prints in that last old building, revealing how I had gained the street.

The open space was, as I had expected, strongly moonlit; and I saw the remains of a park-like,[a] iron-railed green in its centre. Fortunately no one was about, though a curious sort of buzz or roar seemed to be increasing in the direction of Town Square. South Street was very wide, leading directly down a slight declivity to the waterfront and commanding a long view out at sea; and I hoped that no one would be glancing up it from afar as I crossed in the bright moonlight.

My progress was unimpeded, and no fresh sound arose to hint that I had been spied. Glancing about me, I involuntarily let my pace slacken for a second to take in the sight of the sea, gorgeous in the burning moonlight at the street's end. Far out beyond the breakwater was the dim, dark line of Devil Reef, and as I glimpsed it I could not help thinking of all the hideous legends I had heard in the last thirty-four hours—legends which portrayed this ragged rock as a veritable gateway to realms of unfathomed horror and inconceivable abnormality.

Then, without warning, I saw the intermittent flashes of light on the distant reef. They were definite and unmistakable, and awaked in my mind a blind horror beyond all rational proportion. My muscles tightened for panic flight, held in only by a certain unconscious caution and half-hypnotic fascination. And to make matters worse, there now flashed forth from the lofty cupola of the Gilman House, which loomed up to the northeast behind me, a series of analogous though differently spaced gleams which could be nothing less than an answering signal.

Controlling my muscles, and realising afresh how plainly visible I was, I resumed my brisker and feignedly shambling pace; though

[a] park-like,] parklike, A, B, C, D

keeping my eyes on that hellish and ominous reef as long as the opening of South Street gave me a seaward view. What the whole proceeding[a] meant, I could not imagine; unless it involved some strange rite connected with Devil Reef, or unless some party had landed from a ship on that sinister rock. I now bent to the left around the ruinous green; still gazing toward the ocean as it blazed in the spectral summer moonlight, and watching the cryptical flashing of those nameless, unexplainable beacons.

It was then that the most horrible impression of all was borne in upon me—the impression which destroyed my last vestige of self-control and set[b] me running frantically southward past the yawning black doorways and fishily staring windows of that deserted nightmare street. For at a closer glance I saw that the moonlit waters between the reef and the shore were far from empty. They were alive with a teeming horde of shapes swimming inward toward the town; and even at my vast distance and in my single moment of perception I could tell that the bobbing heads and flailing arms were alien and aberrant in a way scarcely to be expressed or consciously formulated.

My frantic running ceased before I had covered a block, for at my left I began to hear something like the hue and cry of organised pursuit. There were footsteps and guttural sounds, and a rattling motor wheezed south along Federal Street. In a second all my plans were utterly changed—for if the southward highway were blocked ahead of me, I must clearly[c] find another egress from Innsmouth. I paused and drew into a gaping doorway, reflecting how lucky I was to have left the moonlit open space before these pursuers came down the parallel street.

A second reflection was less comforting. Since the pursuit was down another street, it was plain that the party was not following me directly. It had not seen me, but was simply obeying a general plan of cutting off my escape. This, however, implied that all roads leading out of Innsmouth were similarly patrolled; for the denizens[d] could not have known what route I intended to take. If this were so, I would have

---

[a] proceeding] preceeding C[c]
[b] set] sent D
[c] clearly] clearly / ly C[c]
[d] denizens] people C, D

to make my retreat across country away from any road; but how could I do that in view of the marshy and creek-riddled nature of all the surrounding region? For a moment my brain reeled—both from sheer hopelessness and from a rapid increase in the omnipresent fishy odour.

Then I thought of the abandoned railway to Rowley, whose solid line of ballasted, weed-grown earth still stretched off to the northwest from the crumbling station on the edge of the river-gorge. There was just a chance that the townsfolk would not think of that; since its brier-choked[a] desertion made it half-impassable, and the unlikeliest of all avenues for a fugitive to choose. I had seen it clearly from my hotel window, and knew about how it lay. Most of its earlier length was uncomfortably visible from the Rowley road, and from high places in the town itself; but one could perhaps crawl inconspicuously through the undergrowth. At any rate, it would form my only chance of deliverance, and there was nothing to do but try it.

Drawing inside the hall of my deserted shelter, I once more consulted the grocery boy's map with the aid of the flashlight. The immediate problem was how to reach the ancient railway; and I now saw that the safest course was ahead to Babson Street, then west to Lafayette—there edging around but not crossing an open space homologous to the one I had traversed—and subsequently back northward and westward in a zigzagging line through Lafayette, Bates, Adams, and Bank Streets—the latter skirting the river-gorge[b]—to the abandoned and dilapidated station I had seen from my window. My reason for going ahead to Babson was that I wished neither to re-cross the earlier open space nor to begin my westward course along a cross street as broad as South.

Starting once more, I crossed the street to the right-hand[c] side in order to edge around into Babson as inconspicuously as possible. Noises still continued in Federal Street, and as I glanced behind me I thought I saw a gleam of light near the building through which I had escaped. Anxious to leave Washington Street, I broke into a quiet dog-trot, trusting to luck not to encounter any observing eye. Next the corner of

[a] brier-choked] briar-choked C, D
[b] river-gorge] river gorge A, B, C, D
[c] right-hand] right, hand C[c]

Babson Street I saw to my alarm that one of the houses was still inhabited, as attested by curtains at the window; but there were no lights within, and I passed it without disaster.

In Babson Street, which crossed Federal and might thus reveal me to the searchers, I clung as closely as possible to the sagging, uneven buildings; twice pausing in a doorway as the noises behind me momentarily increased. The open space ahead shone wide and desolate under the moon, but my route would not force me to cross it. During my second pause I began to detect a fresh distribution of the[a] vague sounds; and upon looking cautiously out from cover beheld a motor-car[b] darting across the open space, bound outward along Eliot Street, which there intersects both Babson and Lafayette.

As I watched—choked by a sudden rise in the fishy odour after a short abatement—I saw a band of uncouth, crouching shapes loping and shambling in the same direction; and knew that this must be the party guarding the Ipswich road, since that highway forms an extension of Eliot Street. Two of the figures I glimpsed were in voluminous robes, and one wore a peaked diadem which glistened whitely in the moonlight. The gait of this figure was so odd that it sent a chill through me—for it seemed to me the creature was almost *hopping*.[c]

When the last of the band was out of sight I resumed my progress; darting around the corner into Lafayette Street, and crossing Eliot very hurriedly lest stragglers of the party be still advancing along that thoroughfare. I did hear some croaking and clattering[d] sounds far off toward Town Square,[e] but accomplished the passage without disaster. My greatest dread was in re-crossing broad and moonlit South Street— with its seaward view—and I had to nerve myself for the ordeal. Someone might easily be looking, and possible Eliot Street stragglers could not fail to glimpse me from either of two points. At the last moment I decided I had better slacken my trot and make the crossing as before in the shambling gait of an average Innsmouth native.

[a] the] *om.* C, D
[b] motor-car] motor car A, B, C, D
[c] *hopping.*] hopping. D
[d] croaking and clattering] croaakng and clatterng C[c]
[e] Square,] Square C[c]

When the view of the water again opened out—this time on my right—I was half-determined not to look at it at all. I could not, however, resist; but cast a sidelong glance as I carefully and imitatively shambled[a] toward the protecting shadows ahead. There was no ship visible, as I had half expected[b] there would be. Instead, the first thing which caught my eye was a small rowboat pulling in toward the abandoned wharves and laden with some bulky, tarpaulin-covered[c] object. Its rowers, though distantly and indistinctly seen, were of an especially repellent aspect. Several swimmers were still discernible; while on the far black reef I could see a faint, steady glow unlike the winking beacon visible before, and of a curious colour which I could not precisely identify. Above the slant roofs ahead and to the right there loomed the tall cupola of the Gilman House, but it was completely dark. The fishy odour, dispelled for a moment by some merciful breeze, now closed in again with maddening intensity.

I had not quite crossed the street when I heard a muttering band advancing along Washington from the north. As they reached the broad open space where I had had my first disquieting glimpse of the moonlit water I could see them plainly only a block away—and was horrified by the[d] bestial abnormality of their faces and the dog-like[e] sub-humanness of their crouching gait. One man moved in a positively simian way, with long arms frequently touching the ground; while another figure—robed and tiaraed[f]—seemed to progress in an almost hopping fashion. I judged this party to be the one I had seen in the Gilman's courtyard—the one, therefore, most closely on my trail. As some of the figures turned to look in my direction I was transfixed with fright,[g] yet managed to preserve the casual, shambling gait I had assumed. To this day I do not know whether they saw me or not. If they did, my stratagem must have deceived them, for they passed on across

---

[a] shambled] shamble C[c]
[b] half expected] half-expected A, B, C, D
[c] tarpaulin-covered] tarpaulin-coverd D
[d] the] he C
[e] dog-like] doglike A, B, C, D
[f] tiaraed] tiarared B, C
[g] fright,] freight, C[c]

the moonlit space without varying their course—meanwhile croaking and jabbering in some hateful guttural patois I could not identify.

Once more in shadow, I resumed my former dog-trot past the leaning and decrepit houses that stared blankly into the night. Having crossed to the western sidewalk I rounded the nearest corner into Bates Street, where I kept close to the buildings on the southern side. I passed two houses shewing signs of habitation, one of which had faint lights in upper rooms, yet met with no obstacle. As I turned into Adams Street I felt measurably safer, but received a shock when a man reeled out of a black doorway directly in front of me. He proved, however, too hopelessly drunk to be a menace; so that I reached the dismal ruins of the Bank Street warehouses in safety.

No one was stirring in that dead street beside the river-gorge, and the roar of the waterfalls quite drowned my footsteps. It was a long dog-trot to the ruined station, and the great brick warehouse walls around me seemed somehow more terrifying than the fronts of private houses. At last I saw the ancient arcaded station—or what was left of it—and made directly for the tracks that started from its farther end.

The rails were rusty but mainly intact, and not more than half the ties had rotted away. Walking or running on such a surface was very difficult; but I did my best, and on the whole made very fair time. For some distance the line kept on along the gorge's brink, but at length I reached the long covered bridge where it crossed the chasm at a dizzy height. The condition of this bridge would determine my next step. If humanly possible, I would use it; if not, I would have to risk more street wandering and take the nearest intact highway bridge.

The vast, barn-like[a] length of the old bridge gleamed spectrally in the moonlight, and I saw that the ties were safe for at least a few feet within. Entering, I began to use my flashlight, and was almost knocked down by the cloud of bats that flapped past me. About half way[b] across there was a perilous gap in the ties which I feared for a moment would halt me; but in the end I risked a desperate jump which fortunately succeeded.

I was glad to see the moonlight again when I emerged from that

[a] barn-like] barnlike A, B, C, D
[b] half way] half-way B, C, D

macabre tunnel. The old tracks crossed River Street at grade, and at once veered off into a region increasingly rural and with less and less of Innsmouth's abhorrent fishy odour. Here the dense growth of weeds and briers hindered me and cruelly tore my clothes, but I was none the less glad that they were there to give me concealment in case of peril. I knew that much of my route must be visible from the Rowley road.

The marshy region began very shortly, with the single track on a low, grassy embankment where the weedy growth was somewhat thinner. Then came a sort of island of higher ground, where the line passed through a shallow open cut choked with bushes and brambles. I was very glad of this partial shelter, since at this point the Rowley road was uncomfortably near according to my window view. At the end of the cut it would cross the track and swerve off to a safer distance; but meanwhile I must be exceedingly careful. I was by this time thankfully certain that the railway itself was not patrolled.

Just before entering the cut I glanced behind me, but saw no pursuer. The ancient spires and roofs of decaying Innsmouth gleamed lovely and ethereal in the magic yellow moonlight, and I thought of how they must have looked in the old days before the shadow fell. Then, as my gaze circled inland from the town, something less tranquil arrested my notice and held me immobile for a second.

What I saw—or fancied I saw—was a disturbing suggestion of undulant motion far to the south; a suggestion which made me conclude that a very large horde must be pouring out of the city along the level Ipswich road. The distance was great, and I could distinguish nothing in detail; but I did not at all like the look of that moving column. It undulated too much, and glistened too brightly in the rays of the now westering moon. There was a suggestion of sound, too, though the wind was blowing the other way—a suggestion of bestial scraping and bellowing even worse than the muttering of the parties I had lately overheard.

All sorts of unpleasant conjectures crossed my mind. I thought of those very extreme Innsmouth types said to be hidden in crumbling, centuried warrens near the waterfront. I thought, too, of those nameless swimmers I had seen. Counting the parties so far glimpsed, as well as those presumably covering other roads, the number of my pursuers must be strangely large for a town as depopulated as Innsmouth.

Whence could come the dense personnel of such a column as I now beheld? Did those ancient, unplumbed warrens teem with a twisted, uncatalogued, and unsuspected life? Or had some unseen ship indeed landed a legion of unknown outsiders on that hellish reef? Who were they? Why were they here? And if such a column of them was scouring the Ipswich road, would the patrols on the other roads be likewise augmented?

I had entered the brush-grown cut and was struggling along at a very slow pace when that damnable fishy odour again waxed dominant. Had the wind suddenly changed eastward, so that it blew in from the sea and over the town? It must have, I concluded, since I now began to hear shocking guttural murmurs from that hitherto[a] silent direction. There was another sound, too—a kind of wholesale, colossal flopping or pattering which somehow called up images of the most detestable sort. It made me think illogically of that unpleasantly undulating column on the far-off Ipswich road.

And then both stench and sounds grew stronger, so that I paused shivering and grateful for the cut's protection. It was here, I recalled, that the Rowley road drew so close to the old railway before crossing westward and diverging. Something was coming along that road, and I must lie low till its passage and vanishment in the distance. Thank heaven these creatures employed no dogs for tracking—though perhaps that would have been impossible amidst the omnipresent regional odour. Crouched in the bushes of that sandy cleft I felt reasonably safe, even though I knew the searchers would have to cross the track in front of me not much more than a hundred yards away. I would be able to see them, but they could not, except by a malign miracle, see me.

All at once I began dreading to look at them as they passed. I saw the close moonlit space where they would surge by, and had curious thoughts about the irredeemable pollution of that space. They would perhaps be the worst of all Innsmouth types—something one would not care to remember.

The stench waxed overpowering, and the noises swelled to a bestial babel of croaking, baying,[b] and barking without the least suggestion of

[a] hitherto] hithero C[c]
[b] baying,] baying C, D

human speech. Were these indeed the voices of my pursuers? Did they have dogs after all? So far I had seen none of the lower animals in Innsmouth. That flopping or pattering was monstrous—I could not look upon the degenerate creatures responsible for it. I would keep my eyes shut till the sounds[a] receded toward the west. The horde was very close now—the air foul with their hoarse snarlings, and the ground almost shaking with their alien-rhythmed footfalls. My breath nearly ceased to come, and I put every ounce of will power[b] into the task of holding my eyelids down.

I am not even yet willing to say whether what followed was a hideous actuality or only a nightmare hallucination. The later action of the government, after my frantic appeals, would tend to confirm it as a monstrous truth; but could not an hallucination have been repeated under the quasi-hypnotic spell of that ancient, haunted, and shadowed town? Such places have strange properties, and the legacy of insane legend might well have acted on more than one human imagination amidst those dead, stench-cursed streets and huddles of rotting roofs and crumbling steeples. Is it not possible that the germ of an actual contagious madness lurks in the depths of that shadow over Innsmouth? Who can be sure of reality after hearing things like the tale of old Zadok Allen? The government men never found poor Zadok, and have no conjectures to make as to what became of him. Where does madness leave off and reality begin? Is it possible that even my latest fear is sheer delusion?[c]

But I must try to tell what I thought I saw that night under the mocking yellow moon—saw surging and hopping down the Rowley road in plain sight in front of me as I crouched among the wild brambles of that desolate railway cut. Of course my resolution to keep my eyes shut had failed. It was foredoomed to failure—for who could crouch blindly while a legion of croaking, baying entities[d] of unknown[e] source flopped noisomely past, scarcely more than a hundred yards[f] away?

[a] sounds] sound D
[b] will power] will-power A, B, C, D
[c] delusion?] dilusion? C
[d] entities] entitles C[c]
[e] unknown] unkwown D
[f] yards] years D

I thought I was prepared for the worst, and I really ought to have been prepared considering what I had seen before. My other pursuers had been accursedly abnormal—so should I not have been ready to face a *strengthening*[a] of the abnormal element; to look upon forms in which there was no mixture of the normal at all? I did not open my eyes until the raucous clamour came loudly from a point obviously straight ahead. Then I knew that a long section of them must be plainly in sight where the sides of the cut flattened out and the road crossed the track—and I could no longer keep myself from sampling whatever horror that leering yellow moon might have to shew.

It was the end, for whatever remains to me of life on the surface of this earth, of every vestige of mental peace and confidence in the integrity of Nature[b] and of the human mind. Nothing that I could have imagined—nothing, even, that I could have gathered had I credited old Zadok's crazy tale in the most literal way—would be in any way comparable to the daemoniac,[c] blasphemous reality that I saw—or believe I saw. I have tried to hint what it was in order to postpone the horror[d] of writing it down baldly. Can it be possible that this planet has actually spawned such things; that human eyes have truly seen, as objective flesh, what man has hitherto known only in febrile phantasy and tenuous legend?

And yet I saw them in a limitless stream—flopping, hopping, croaking, bleating—surging inhumanly through the spectral moonlight in a grotesque, malignant saraband of fantastic nightmare. And some of them had tall tiaras of that nameless whitish-gold metal . . . and some were strangely robed . . . and one, who led the way, was clad in a ghoulishly humped black coat and striped trousers, and had a man's felt hat perched on the shapeless thing that answered for a head. . . .[e]

I think their predominant colour was a greyish-green, though they had white bellies. They were mostly shiny and slippery, but the ridges of their backs were scaly. Their forms vaguely suggested the anthropoid,

---

[a] *strengthening*] strengthening D
[b] Nature] nature A, B, C, D
[c] daemoniac,] demoniac, B, C, D
[d] horror] horrr C[c]
[e] head. . . .] head. C, D

while their heads were the heads of fish, with prodigious bulging eyes that never closed. At the sides of their necks were palpitating gills, and their long paws were webbed. They hopped irregularly, sometimes on two legs and sometimes on four. I was somehow glad that they had no more than four limbs. Their croaking, baying voices, clearly used for articulate speech, held all the dark shades of expression which their staring faces lacked.

But for all of their monstrousness they were not unfamiliar to me. I knew too well what they must be—for was not the memory of that[a] evil tiara at Newburyport still fresh? They were the blasphemous fish-frogs of the nameless design—living and horrible—and as I saw them I knew also of what that humped, tiaraed[b] priest in the black church basement had so[c] fearsomely reminded me. Their number was past guessing. It seemed to me that there were limitless swarms of them—and certainly my momentary glimpse could have shewn only the least fraction. In another instant everything was blotted out by a merciful fit of fainting; the first I had ever had.

V.

[d]It was a gentle daylight rain that awaked me from my stupor in the brush-grown railway cut, and when I staggered out to the roadway ahead I saw no trace of any prints in the fresh mud. The fishy odour, too, was gone.[e] Innsmouth's ruined roofs and toppling steeples loomed up greyly toward the southeast, but not a living creature did I spy in all the desolate salt marshes around. My watch was still going, and told me that the hour was past noon.

The reality of what I had been through was highly uncertain in my mind, but I felt that something hideous lay in the background. I must get away from evil-shadowed Innsmouth—and accordingly I began to

[a] that] the D
[b] tiaraed] tiarared B, C
[c] so] *om.* C, D
[d] I wish there were nothing more to [*erasure*] fortunate I would be if there were not! Perhaps it is madness that is overtaking me—yet perhaps a greater horror is reaching out. Who can tell A [*excised*]
[e] gone.] gone, D

test my cramped, wearied powers of locomotion. Despite weakness, hunger, horror, and bewilderment I found myself after a time able to walk; so started slowly along the muddy road to Rowley. Before evening I was in the village, getting a meal and providing myself with presentable clothes. I caught the night train to Arkham, and the next day talked long and earnestly with government officials there; a process I later repeated in Boston. With the main result of these colloquies the public is now familiar—and I wish, for normality's sake, there were nothing more to tell. Perhaps it is madness that is overtaking me—yet perhaps a greater horror—or a greater marvel—is reaching out.

As may well be imagined, I gave up most of the foreplanned features of the rest of my tour—the scenic, architectural, and antiquarian diversions on which I had counted so heavily. Nor did I dare look for that piece of strange jewellery said to be in the Miskatonic University Museum. I did, however, improve my stay in Arkham by collecting some genealogical notes I had long wished to possess; very rough and hasty data, it is true, but capable of good use later on when I might have time to collate and codify them. The curator of the historical society there—Mr. E. Lapham Peabody—was very courteous about assisting me, and expressed unusual interest when I told him I was a grandson of Eliza Orne of Arkham, who was born in 1867 and had married James Williamson of Ohio at the age of seventeen.

It seemed that a maternal uncle of mine had been there many years before on a quest much like my own; and that my grandmother's family was a topic of some local curiosity. There had, Mr. Peabody said, been considerable discussion about the marriage of her father, Benjamin Orne, just after the Civil War; since the ancestry of the bride was peculiarly puzzling. That bride was understood to have been an orphaned Marsh of New Hampshire—a cousin of the Essex County Marshes—but her education had been in France and she knew very little of her family. A guardian had deposited funds in a Boston bank to maintain her and her French governess; but that guardian's name was unfamiliar to Arkham people, and in time he dropped out of sight, so that the governess assumed his role by court appointment. The Frenchwoman—now long dead—was very taciturn, and there were those who said she could have told more than she did.

But the most baffling thing was the inability of anyone to place the recorded parents of the young woman—Enoch and Lydia (Meserve) Marsh—among the known families of New Hampshire. Possibly, many suggested, she was the natural daughter of some Marsh of prominence— she certainly had the true Marsh eyes. Most of the puzzling was done after her early death, which took place at the birth of my grandmother— her only child. Having formed some disagreeable impressions connected with the name of Marsh, I did not welcome the news that it belonged on my own ancestral tree; nor was I pleased by Mr. Peabody's suggestion that I had the true Marsh eyes myself. However, I was grateful for data which I knew would prove valuable; and took copious notes and lists of book references regarding the well-documented Orne family.

I went directly home to Toledo from Boston, and later spent a month at Maumee recuperating from my ordeal. In September I entered Oberlin for my final year, and from then till the next June was busy with studies and other wholesome activities—reminded of the bygone terror only by occasional official visits from government men in connexion with the campaign which my pleas and evidence had started. Around the middle of July—just a year after the Innsmouth experience—I spent a week with my late mother's family in Cleveland; checking some of my new genealogical data with the various notes, traditions, and bits of heirloom material in existence there, and seeing what kind of a connected chart I could construct.

I did not exactly relish this task, for the atmosphere of the Williamson home had always depressed me. There was a strain of morbidity there, and my mother had never encouraged my visiting her parents as a child, although she always welcomed her father when he came to Toledo. My Arkham-born grandmother had seemed strange and almost terrifying to me, and I do not think I grieved when she disappeared. I was eight years old then, and it was said that she had wandered off in grief after the suicide of my uncle Douglas, her eldest son. He had shot himself after a trip to New England—the same trip, no doubt, which had caused him to be recalled at the Arkham Historical Society.

This uncle had resembled her, and I had never liked him either. Something about the staring, unwinking expression of both of them had given me a vague, unaccountable uneasiness. My mother and uncle Walter had not looked like that. They were like their father, though poor little cousin Lawrence—Walter's son—had been an almost perfect duplicate of his grandmother before his condition took him to the permanent seclusion of a sanitarium at Canton. I had not seen him in four years, but my uncle once implied that his state, both mental and physical, was very bad. This worry had probably been a major cause of his mother's death two years before.

My grandfather and his widowed son Walter now comprised the Cleveland household, but the memory of older times hung thickly over it. I still disliked the place, and tried to get my researches done as quickly as possible. Williamson records and traditions were supplied in abundance by my grandfather; though for Orne material I had to depend on my uncle Walter, who put at my disposal the contents of all his files, including notes,[a] letters, cuttings, heirlooms, photographs, and miniatures.

It was in going over the letters and pictures on the Orne side that I began to acquire a kind of terror of my own ancestry. As I have said, my grandmother and uncle Douglas had always disturbed me. Now, years after their passing, I gazed at their pictured faces with a measurably heightened feeling of repulsion and alienation. I could not at first understand the change, but gradually a horrible sort of *comparison*[b] began to obtrude itself on my unconscious mind despite the steady refusal of my consciousness to admit even the least suspicion of it. It was clear that the typical expression of these faces now suggested something it had not suggested before—something which would bring stark panic if too openly thought of.[c]

---

[a] notes,] notes Cᶜ

[b] *comparison*] comparison D

[c] of.] of. And when I read the grim note my self-slain uncle had left behind, that panic was close to breaking loose within me. He was shooting himself, he wrote, because he had found out something he dared not tell. He wanted to be dead before some expected disaster overtook him. His mother would understand, for she had lived in Arkham and heard stray stories of a certain kind. He advised his brother to remain unmarried as he had done, and urged my mother to tell me I had better do so when I grew up. No need of explaining, he said, but [*excised; new passage begun:*] The archives told of many family matters, and even brought in my long-dead great-grandmother, whose origin was still so great a puzzle in Arkham. She had had many costly and singular belongings, some of which I knew about, but others of which I had never seen. There were, in particular, some jewels which her French governess had told her never to wear in New England though

But the worst shock came when my uncle shewed me the Orne jewellery in a downtown safe-deposit vault. Some of the items were delicate and inspiring enough, but there was one box of strange old pieces descended[a] from my mysterious great-grandmother which my uncle was almost reluctant to produce. They were, he said, of very grotesque and almost repulsive design, and had never to his knowledge been publicly worn; though my grandmother used to enjoy looking at them. Vague legends of bad luck clustered around them, and my great-grandmother's French governess had said they ought not to be worn in New England, though it would be quite safe to wear them in Europe.

As my uncle began slowly and grudgingly to unwrap the things he urged me not to be shocked by the strangeness and frequent hideousness of the designs. Artists and archaeologists who had seen them pronounced the workmanship superlatively and exotically exquisite, though no one seemed able to define their exact material or assign them to any specific art tradition. There were two armlets, a tiara, and a kind of pectoral; the latter having in high relief certain figures of almost unbearable extravagance.

During this description I had kept a tight rein on my emotions, but my face must have betrayed my mounting fears. My uncle looked concerned, and paused in his unwrapping to study my countenance. I motioned to him to continue, which he did with renewed signs of reluctance. He seemed to expect some demonstration when the first piece—the tiara—became visible, but I doubt if he expected quite what actually happened. I did not expect it, either, for I thought I was thoroughly forewarned regarding what the jewellery would turn out to be. What I did was to faint silently away, just as I had done in that brier-choked[b] railway cut a year before.

From that day on my life has been a nightmare of brooding and apprehension, nor do I know how much is hideous truth and how much madness. My great-grandmother had been a Marsh of unknown source whose husband lived in Arkham—and did not old Zadok say

---

she might wear them freely in Europe. My grandmother had taken over this precept and applied it to herself A [*excised*]

[a] descended] detrended C[c]

[b] brier-choked] brier choked D

that the daughter of Obed Marsh by a monstrous mother was married to an Arkham man through a trick? What was it the ancient toper had muttered about the likeness of my eyes to Captain Obed's? In Arkham, too, the curator had told me I had the true Marsh eyes. Was Obed Marsh my own great-great-grandfather? Who—or *what*[a]—then, was my great-great-grandmother? But perhaps this was all madness. Those whitish-gold ornaments might easily have been bought from some Innsmouth sailor by the father of my great-grandmother, whoever he was. And that look in the staring-eyed faces of my grandmother and self-slain uncle might be sheer fancy on my part—sheer fancy, bolstered up by the Innsmouth shadow which had so darkly coloured my imagination. But why had my uncle killed himself after an ancestral quest in New England?

For more than two years I fought off these reflections with partial success. My father secured me a place in an insurance office, and I buried myself[b] in routine as deeply as possible. In the winter of 1930–31, however, the dreams began. They were very sparse and insidious at first, but increased in frequency and vividness as the weeks went by. Great watery spaces opened out before me, and I seemed to wander through titanic sunken porticos and labyrinths of weedy Cyclopean[c] walls with grotesque fishes as my companions. Then the *other shapes*[d] began to appear, filling me with nameless horror the moment I awoke. But during the dreams they did not horrify me at all—I was one with them; wearing their unhuman trappings, treading their aqueous ways, and praying monstrously at their evil sea-bottom temples.

There was much more than I could remember, but even what I did remember each morning would be enough to stamp me as a madman or a genius if ever I dared write it down. Some frightful influence, I felt, was seeking gradually to drag me out of the sane world of wholesome life into unnamable abysses of blackness and alienage; and the process told heavily on me. My health and appearance grew steadily worse, till finally I was forced to give up my position and adopt the static,

---

[a] *what*] what D
[b] myself] my self C
[c] Cyclopean] cyclopean A, B, C, D
[d] *other shapes*] other shapes D

secluded life of an invalid. Some odd nervous affliction had me in its grip, and I found myself at times almost unable to shut my eyes.

It was then that I began to study the mirror with mounting alarm. The slow ravages of disease are not pleasant to watch, but in my case there was something subtler and more puzzling in the background. My father seemed to notice it, too, for he began looking at me curiously and almost affrightedly. What was taking place in me? Could it be that I was coming to resemble my grandmother[a] and uncle Douglas?

One night I had a frightful dream in which I met my grandmother under the sea. She lived in a phosphorescent palace of many terraces, with gardens of strange leprous corals and grotesque brachiate efflorescences, and welcomed me with a warmth that may have been sardonic. She had changed—as those who take to the water change—and told me she had never died. Instead, she had gone to a spot her dead son had learned about, and had leaped to a realm whose wonders—destined for him as well—he had spurned with a smoking pistol. This was to be my realm, too—I could not escape it. I would never die, but would live with those who had lived since before man ever walked the earth.

I met also that which had been her grandmother. For eighty thousand years Pth'thya-l'yi had lived in Y'ha-nthlei, and thither she had gone back after Obed Marsh was dead. Y'ha-nthlei was not destroyed when the upper-earth men shot death into the sea. It was hurt, but not destroyed. The Deep Ones could never be destroyed, even though the palaeogean magic of the forgotten Old Ones might sometimes check them. For the present they would rest; but some day, if they remembered, they would rise again for the tribute Great Cthulhu craved. It would be a city greater than Innsmouth next time. They had planned to spread, and had brought up that which would help them, but now they must wait once more. For bringing the upper-earth men's death I must do a penance, but that would not be heavy. This was the dream in which I saw a *shoggoth* for the first time, and the sight set me awake in a frenzy of screaming. That morning the mirror definitely told me I had acquired *the*[b] *Innsmouth look.*

[a] grandmother] grann-/mother C[c]
[b] *the*] the C

So far I have not shot myself as my uncle Douglas did. I bought an automatic and almost took the step, but certain dreams deterred me. The tense extremes of horror are lessening, and I feel queerly drawn toward the unknown sea-deeps instead of fearing them. I hear and do strange things in sleep, and awake with a kind of exaltation instead of terror. I do not believe I need to wait for the full change as most have waited. If I did, my father would probably shut me up in a sanitarium as my poor little cousin is shut up. Stupendous and unheard-of splendours await me below, and I shall seek them soon. *Iä-R'lyeh!* [a] *Cthulhu fhtagn! Iä! Iä!* [b] No, I shall not shoot myself—I cannot be made to shoot myself!

I shall plan my cousin's escape from that Canton madhouse, and together we shall go to marvel-shadowed Innsmouth. We shall swim out to that brooding reef in the sea and dive down through black abysses to Cyclopean[c] and many-columned Y'ha-nthlei, and in that lair of the Deep Ones we shall dwell amidst wonder and glory for ever.

[a] *Iä-R'lyeh!*] *Ia-R'lyeh!* C
[b] *Iä! Iä!*] *Ia! Ia!* C
[c] Cyclopean] cyclopean A, B

The Dreams in the Witch House

Whether the dreams brought on the fever or the fever brought on the dreams Walter Gilman did not know. Behind everything crouched the brooding, festering horror of the ancient town, and of the mouldy,[a] unhallowed garret gable where he wrote and studied and wrestled with figures and formulae when he was not tossing on the meagre[b] iron bed. His ears were growing sensitive to a preternatural and intolerable degree, and he had long ago stopped the cheap mantel clock whose ticking had come to seem like a thunder of artillery. At night the subtle stirring of the black city outside, the sinister scurrying of rats in the wormy partitions, and the creaking of

---

Editor's Note: HPL's A.Ms. is an extensively revised pencil draft and presumably represents his final wishes for the story. He was too discouraged by recent setbacks to type the story, but August Derleth did so without HPL's knowledge (see *SL* 4.146); it is on the whole reasonably accurate, although it makes several errors and omissions as well as introducing an erroneous hyphen in the title. Derleth sent this T.Ms. on his own initiative to *Weird Tales* (see *SL* 4.154), where it appeared—with the usual editorial alterations—in the issue for July 1933. The *Weird Tales* text made some celebrated blunders that HPL pointed out when he read the galleys (see *SL* 4.213), but which were not corrected before publication. HPL's copy of the issue (JHL) contains only one correction in pencil ("known" for "human"). The first Arkham House edition (*The Outsider and Others*, 1939) wisely followed the T.Ms., hence its text is fairly sound; but in the 1964 reprint Derleth committed the incredible folly of following the *Weird Tales* appearance, with the result that its text is very poor. One is at a loss to understand why Derleth did not use his own earlier text to prepare the later one.

Texts: A = A.Ms. (JHL); B = T.Ms. (JHL) (as "The Dreams in the Witch-House"); C = *Weird Tales* 22, No. 1 (July 1933): 86–111 (as "The Dreams in the Witch-House"); D = *The Outsider and Others* (Arkham House, 1939), 194–216 (as "The Dreams in the Witch-House"); E = *At the Mountains of Madness and Other Novels* (Arkham House, 1964), 248–83 (as "The Dreams in the Witch-House"). Copy-text: A.

[a] mouldy,] moldy, C, E
[b] meagre] meager C, E

hidden timbers in the centuried house, were enough to give him a sense of strident pandemonium. The darkness always teemed with unexplained sound—and yet he sometimes shook with fear lest the noises he heard should subside and allow him to hear certain other, fainter[a] noises which he suspected were lurking behind them.

He was in the changeless, legend-haunted city of Arkham, with its clustering gambrel roofs that sway and sag over attics where witches hid from the King's men in the dark, olden days of the Province. Nor was any spot in that city more steeped in macabre memory than the gable room which harboured[b] him—for it was this house and this room which had likewise harboured[c] old Keziah Mason, whose flight from Salem Gaol[d] at the last no one was ever able to explain. That was in 1692—the gaoler[e] had gone mad and babbled of a small,[f] white-fanged furry thing which scuttled out of Keziah's cell, and not even Cotton Mather could explain the curves and angles smeared on the grey[g] stone walls with some red, sticky fluid.

Possibly Gilman ought not to have studied so hard. Non-Euclidean calculus and quantum physics are enough to stretch any brain; and when one mixes them with folklore, and tries to trace a strange background of multi-dimensional reality behind the ghoulish hints of the Gothic tales and the wild whispers of the chimney-corner, one can hardly expect to be wholly free from mental tension. Gilman came from Haverhill, but it was only after he had entered college in Arkham that he began to connect his mathematics with the fantastic legends of elder magic. Something in the air of the hoary town worked obscurely on his imagination. The professors at Miskatonic had urged him to slacken up, and had voluntarily cut down his course at several points. Moreover, they had stopped him from consulting the dubious old books on forbidden secrets that were kept under lock and key in a vault at the university library. But all these precautions came late in the day, so that

[a] other, fainter] other, fainter, A, B, D; other fainter E
[b] harboured] harbored C, E
[c] harboured] harbored C, E
[d] Gaol] jail C
[e] gaoler] jailer C
[f] small,] small B, C, D, E
[g] grey] gray C, E

Gilman had some terrible hints from the dreaded "Necronomicon"[a] of Abdul Alhazred, the fragmentary "Book of Eibon",[b] and the suppressed "Unaussprechlichen Kulten"[c] of von Junzt to correlate with his abstract formulae on the properties of space and the linkage of dimensions known and unknown.

He knew his room was in the old Witch House[d]—that, indeed,[e] was why he had taken it. There was much in the Essex County records about Keziah Mason's trial, and what she had admitted under pressure to the Court of Oyer and Terminer had fascinated Gilman beyond all reason. She had told Judge Hathorne of lines and curves that could be made to point out directions leading through the[f] walls of space to other spaces beyond, and had implied that such lines and curves were frequently used at certain midnight meetings in the dark valley of the white stone beyond Meadow Hill and on the unpeopled island in the river. She had spoken also of the Black Man, of her oath, and of her new secret name of Nahab. Then she had drawn those devices on the walls of her cell and vanished.

Gilman believed strange things about Keziah, and had felt a queer thrill on learning that her dwelling was still standing after more than 235[g] years. When he heard the hushed Arkham whispers about Keziah's persistent presence in the old house and the narrow streets, about the irregular human tooth-marks left on certain sleepers in that and other houses, about the childish cries heard near May-Eve[h] and Hallowmass, about the stench often noted in the old house's attic just after those dreaded seasons, and about the small, furry, sharp-toothed thing which haunted the mouldering[i] structure and the town and nuzzled people curiously in the black hours before dawn, he resolved

[a] "Necronomicon"] *Necronomicon* A, B, C, D, E
[b] "Book of Eibon",] *Book of Eibon,* C, E
[c] "Unaussprechlichen Kulten"] *Unaussprechlichen Kulten* A, B; *Unaussprechlichen Kulten* C, D, E
[d] Witch House] Witch-House C, E
[e] indeed,] indeed D
[f] the] *om.* D
[g] 235] two hundred thirty-five E
[h] May-Eve] May-/eve, D; May-Eve, E
[i] mouldering] moldering C, E

to live in the place at any cost. A room was easy to secure; for the house was unpopular, hard to rent, and long given over to cheap lodgings. Gilman could not have told what he expected to find there, but he knew he wanted to be in the building where some circumstance had more or less suddenly given a mediocre old woman of the seventeenth century[a] an insight into mathematical depths perhaps beyond the utmost modern delvings of Planck, Heisenberg, Einstein, and de Sitter.

He studied the timber and plaster walls for traces of cryptic designs at every accessible spot where the paper had peeled, and within a week managed to get the eastern attic room where Keziah was held to have practiced[b] her spells. It had been vacant from the first—for no one had ever been willing to stay there long—but the Polish landlord had grown wary about renting it. Yet nothing whatever happened to Gilman till about the time of the fever. No ghostly Keziah flitted through the sombre[c] halls and chambers, no small furry thing crept into his dismal eyrie to nuzzle him, and no record of the witch's incantations rewarded his constant search. Sometimes he would take walks through shadowy tangles of unpaved musty-smelling lanes where eldritch brown houses of unknown age leaned and tottered and leered mockingly through narrow, small-paned windows. Here he knew strange things had happened once, and there was a faint suggestion behind the surface that everything of that monstrous past might not—at least in the darkest, narrowest, and most intricately crooked alleys—have utterly perished. He also rowed out twice to the ill-regarded island in the river, and made a sketch of the singular angles described by the moss-grown rows of grey[d] standing stones whose origin was so obscure and immemorial.

Gilman's room was of good size but queerly irregular shape; the north wall slanting perceptibly inward from the outer to the inner end, while the low ceiling slanted gently downward in the same direction. Aside from an obvious rat-hole and the signs of other stopped-up ones, there was no access—nor any appearance of a former avenue of access—to the space which must have existed between the slanting

[a] seventeenth century] Seventeenth Century C, E
[b] practiced] practised B, C, D, E
[c] sombre] somber C, E
[d] grey] gray C, E

wall and the straight outer wall on the house's north side, though a view from the exterior shewed[a] where a window had been boarded up at a very remote date. The loft above the ceiling—which must have had a slanting floor—was likewise inaccessible. When Gilman climbed up a ladder to the cobwebbed[b] level loft above the rest of the attic he found vestiges of a bygone aperture tightly and heavily covered with ancient planking and secured by the stout wooden pegs common in colonial[c] carpentry. No amount of persuasion, however, could induce the stolid landlord to let him investigate either of these two closed spaces.

As time wore along, his absorption in the irregular wall and ceiling of his room increased; for he began to read into the odd angles a mathematical significance which seemed to offer vague clues regarding their purpose. Old Keziah, he reflected, might have had excellent reasons for living in a room with peculiar angles; for was it not through certain angles that she claimed to have gone outside the boundaries of the world of space we know? His interest gradually veered away from the unplumbed voids beyond the slanting surfaces, since it now appeared that the purpose of those surfaces concerned the side he was already[d] on.

The touch of brain-fever and the dreams began early in February. For some time, apparently, the curious angles of Gilman's room had been having a strange, almost hypnotic effect on him; and as the bleak winter advanced he had found himself staring more and more intently at the corner where the down-slanting ceiling met the inward-slanting[e] wall. About this period his inability to concentrate on his formal studies worried him considerably, his apprehensions about the mid-year examinations being very acute. But the exaggerated sense of hearing was scarcely less annoying. Life had become an insistent and almost unendurable cacophony, and there was that constant, terrifying impression of *other* sounds[f]—perhaps from regions beyond life—trembling on the very brink of audibility. So far as concrete noises went, the rats in the ancient partitions were the worst. Sometimes their

[a] shewed] showed B, C, D, E
[b] cobwebbed] cob-/webbed C; cob-webbed E
[c] colonial] Colonial C
[d] already] *om.* E
[e] inward-slanting] inward slanting D
[f] *other* sounds] other *sounds* D

scratching seemed not only furtive but deliberate. When it came from beyond the slanting north wall it was mixed with a sort of dry rattling—[a]and when it came from the century-closed loft above the slanting ceiling Gilman always braced himself as if expecting some horror which only bided its time before descending to engulf him utterly.

The dreams were wholly beyond the pale of sanity, and Gilman felt that they must be a result, jointly, of his studies in mathematics and in folklore. He had been thinking too much about the vague regions which his formulae told him must lie beyond the three dimensions we know, and about the possibility that old Keziah Mason—guided by some influence past all conjecture—had actually found the gate to those regions. The yellowed county[b] records containing her testimony and that of her accusers were so damnably suggestive of things beyond human experience—and the descriptions of the darting little furry object which served as her familiar were so painfully realistic despite their incredible details.

That object—no larger than a good-sized rat and quaintly called by the townspeople "Brown Jenkin"—seemed to have been the fruit of a remarkable case of sympathetic herd-delusion, for in 1692 no less than eleven persons had testified to glimpsing it. There were recent rumours,[c] too, with a baffling and disconcerting amount of agreement. Witnesses said it had long hair and the shape of a rat, but that its sharp-toothed, bearded face was evilly human while its paws were like tiny human hands. It took messages betwixt old Keziah and the devil, and was nursed on the witch's blood—[d]which it sucked like a vampire. Its voice was a kind of loathsome titter, and it could speak all languages. Of all the bizarre monstrosities in Gilman's dreams, nothing filled him with greater panic and nausea than this blasphemous and diminutive hybrid, whose image flitted across his vision in a form a thousandfold more hateful than anything his waking mind had deduced from the ancient records and the modern whispers.

Gilman's dreams consisted largely in plunges though limitless abysses

[a] rattling—] rattling; C, E
[b] county] country E
[c] rumours,] rumors, C, E
[d] blood—] blood, C, E

of inexplicably coloured[a] twilight and bafflingly disordered sound; abysses whose material and gravitational properties, and whose relation to his own entity, he could not even begin to explain. He did not walk or climb, fly or swim, crawl or wriggle; yet always experienced a mode of motion partly voluntary and[b] partly involuntary. Of his own condition he could not well judge, for sight of his arms, legs, and torso seemed always cut off by some odd disarrangement of perspective; but he felt that his physical organisation[c] and faculties were somehow marvellously[d] transmuted and obliquely projected—though not without a certain grotesque relationship to his normal proportions and properties.

The abysses were by no means vacant, being crowded with indescribably angled masses of alien-hued substance, some of which appeared to be organic while others seemed inorganic. A few of the organic objects tended to awake vague memories in the back of his mind, though he could form no conscious idea of what they mockingly resembled or suggested.[e] In the later dreams he began to distinguish separate categories into which the organic objects appeared to be divided, and which seemed to involve in each case a radically different species of conduct-pattern and basic motivation. Of these categories one seemed to him to include objects slightly less illogical and irrelevant in their motions than the members of the other categories.

All the objects—organic and inorganic alike—were totally beyond description or even comprehension. Gilman sometimes compared the inorganic masses[f] to prisms, labyrinths, clusters of cubes and planes, and Cyclopean[g] buildings; and the organic things struck him variously as groups of bubbles, octopi, centipedes, living Hindoo idols, and intricate Arabesques[h] roused into a kind of ophidian animation. Everything he saw was unspeakably menacing and horrible; and whenever one of the organic entities appeared by its motions to be noticing him, he felt a

[a] coloured] colored C, E
[b] partly voluntary and] *om.* D
[c] organisation] organization B, C, D, E
[d] marvellously] marvelously B, C, E
[e] suggested.] suggestd. E
[f] masses] matter C, E
[g] Cyclopean] cyclopean A, B, C, D, E
[h] Arabesques] arabesques C, E

stark, hideous fright which generally jolted him awake. Of how the organic entities moved, he could tell no more than of how he moved himself. In time he observed a further mystery—the tendency of certain entities to appear suddenly out of empty space, or to disappear totally with equal suddenness. The shrieking, roaring confusion of sound which permeated the abysses was past all analysis as to pitch, timbre,[a] or rhythm; but seemed to be synchronous with vague visual changes in all the indefinite objects, organic and inorganic alike. Gilman had a constant sense of dread that it might rise to some unbearable degree of intensity during one or another of its obscure, relentlessly inevitable fluctuations.

But it was not in these vortices of complete alienage that he saw Brown Jenkin. That shocking little horror was reserved for certain lighter, sharper dreams which assailed him just before he dropped into the fullest depths of sleep. He would be lying in the dark fighting to keep awake when a faint lambent glow would seem to shimmer around the centuried room, shewing[b] in a violet mist the convergence of angled planes which had seized his brain so insidiously. The horror would appear to pop out of the rat-hole in the corner and patter toward him over the sagging,[c] wide-planked floor with evil expectancy in its tiny, bearded human face—[d]but mercifully, this dream always melted away before the object got close enough to nuzzle him. It had hellishly long, sharp, canine teeth. Gilman tried to stop up the rat-hole every day, but each night the real tenants of the partitions would gnaw away the obstruction, whatever it might be. Once he had the landlord nail tin over it, but the next night the rats gnawed a fresh hole—[e]in making which they pushed or dragged out into the room a curious little fragment of bone.

Gilman did not report his fever to the doctor, for he knew he could not pass the examinations if ordered to the college infirmary when every moment was needed for cramming. As it was, he failed in Calculus D and Advanced General Psychology, though not without hope of making

---

[a] timbre,] timbre B, C, E; timber D
[b] shewing] showing B, C, D, E
[c] sagging,] sagging D
[d] face—] face; C, E
[e] hole—] hole, B, C, D, E

up lost ground before the end of the term.[a] It was in March when the fresh element entered his lighter preliminary dreaming, and the nightmare shape of Brown Jenkin began to be companioned by the nebulous blur which grew more and more to resemble a bent old woman. This addition disturbed him more than he could account for, but finally he decided that it was like an ancient crone whom he had twice actually encountered in the dark tangle of lanes near the abandoned wharves. On those[b] occasions the evil, sardonic, and seemingly unmotivated stare of the beldame had set him almost shivering—especially the first time,[c] when an overgrown rat darting across the shadowed mouth of a neighbouring[d] alley had made him think irrationally of Brown Jenkin. Now, he reflected, those nervous fears were being mirrored in his disordered dreams.

That the influence of the old house was unwholesome,[e] he could not deny;[f] but traces of his early morbid interest still held him there. He argued that the fever alone was responsible for his nightly phantasies,[g] and that when the touch abated he would be free from the monstrous visions.[h] Those visions, however, were of abhorrent[i] vividness and convincingness, and whenever he awaked he retained a vague sense of having undergone much more than he remembered. He was hideously sure that in unrecalled dreams he had talked with both Brown Jenkin and the old woman, and that they had been urging him to go somewhere with them and to meet a third being of greater potency.

[a] term.] term. ¶ C, E
[b] those] these D
[c] time,] time E
[d] neighbouring] neighboring C, D, E
[e] unwholesome,] unwholesome C, E
[f] deny;] deny, B, C, D, E
[g] phantasies,] fantasies, C, E
[h] visions.] visions. But even at their worst those visions had a redeeming feature, for they were free from the exaggeration of sound which hounded all his waking hours. The pattering of the furry object and the tread of the slowly solidifying old woman were never above normal intensity, while there were no aural impressions at all in the alien abysses. Gradually he came to develop a fear lest he grow sensitive to sounds within the abysses, for he felt that A [*excised*]
[i] abhorrent] absorbing C, E

Toward the end of March he began to pick up in his mathematics, though other studies bothered him increasingly. He was getting an intuitive knack for solving Riemannian equations, and astonished Professor Upham by his comprehension of fourth-dimensional[a] and other problems which had floored all the rest of the class. One afternoon there was a discussion of possible freakish curvatures in space, and of theoretical points of approach or even contact between our part of the cosmos and various other regions as distant as the farthest stars or the trans-galactic[b] gulfs themselves—or even as fabulously remote as the tentatively conceivable cosmic units beyond the whole Einsteinian space-time continuum. Gilman's handling of this theme filled everyone[c] with admiration, even though some of his hypothetical illustrations caused an increase in the always plentiful gossip about his nervous and solitary eccentricity. What made the students shake their heads was his sober theory that a man might—given mathematical knowledge admittedly beyond all likelihood of human acquirement—step deliberately from the earth to any other celestial body which might lie at one of an infinity of specific points in the cosmic pattern.

Such a step, he said, would require only two stages; first, a passage out of the three-dimensional sphere we know, and second, a passage back to the three-dimensional sphere at another point, perhaps one of infinite remoteness. That this could be accomplished without loss of life was in many cases conceivable. Any being from any part of three-dimensional space could probably survive in the fourth dimension; and its survival of the second stage would depend upon what alien part of three-dimensional space it might select for its re-entry. Denizens of some planets might be able to live on certain others—even planets belonging to other galaxies, or to similar-dimensional[d] phases of other space-time continua—though of course there must be vast numbers of mutually uninhabitable even though mathematically juxtaposed bodies or zones of space.

It was also possible that the inhabitants of a given dimensional realm

---

[a] fourth-dimensional] fourth dimensional D
[b] trans-galactic] transgalactic E
[c] everyone] every one C
[d] similar-dimensional] similar dimensional B, C, D, E

could survive entry to many unknown and incomprehensible realms of additional or indefinitely multiplied dimensions—be they within or outside the given space-time continuum—and that the converse would be likewise true. This was a matter for speculation, though one could be fairly certain that the type of mutation involved in a passage from any given dimensional plane to the next higher plane would not be destructive of biological integrity as we understand it. Gilman could not be very clear about his reasons for this last assumption, but his haziness here was more than overbalanced by his clearness on other[a] complex points. Professor Upham especially liked his demonstration of the kinship of higher mathematics to certain phases of magical lore[b] transmitted down the ages from an ineffable antiquity—human or pre-human—whose knowledge of the cosmos and its laws was greater than ours.[c]

Around the first of April Gilman worried considerably because his slow fever did not abate. He was also troubled by what some of his fellow-lodgers said about his sleep-walking. It seemed that he was often absent from his bed, and that the creaking of his floor at certain hours of the night was remarked by the man in the room below. This fellow also spoke of hearing the tread of shod feet in the night; but Gilman was sure he must have been mistaken in this, since shoes as well as other apparel were always precisely in place in the morning. One could develop all sorts of aural delusions[d] in this morbid old house—for did not Gilman himself, even in daylight, now feel certain that noises other than rat-scratchings[e] came from the black voids beyond the slanting wall and above the slanting ceiling? His pathologically sensitive ears began to listen for faint footfalls in the immemorially sealed loft overhead, and sometimes the illusion of such things was agonisingly[f] realistic.

---

[a] other] *om.* D

[b] lore] love C

[c] ours.] ours. Upham had himself undertaken some odd researches and was prepared to weigh certain problems with a mind free from hard-boiled conventionality. A [*excised*]

[d] delusions] delutions E

[e] rat-scratchings] rat-scratching C, E

[f] agonisingly] agonizingly C, E

However, he knew that he had actually become a somnambulist; for twice at night his room had been found vacant, though with all his clothing in place. Of this he had been assured by Frank Elwood, the one fellow-student whose poverty forced him to room in this squalid and unpopular house. Elwood had been studying in the small hours and had come up for help on a differential equation, only to find Gilman absent. It had been rather presumptuous of him to open the unlocked door after knocking had failed to rouse a response, but he had needed the help very badly and thought that his host would not mind a gentle prodding awake. On neither occasion,[a] though, had Gilman been there—[b] and when told of the matter he wondered where he could have been wandering, barefoot and with only his night-clothes[c] on. He resolved to investigate the matter if reports of his sleep-walking continued, and thought of sprinkling flour on the floor of the corridor to see where his footsteps might lead. The door was the only conceivable egress, for there was no possible foothold outside the narrow window.

As April advanced[d] Gilman's fever-sharpened ears were disturbed by the whining prayers of a superstitious loomfixer[e] named Joe Mazurewicz,[f] who had a room on the ground floor. Mazurewicz[g] had told long, rambling stories about the ghost of old Keziah and the furry,[h] sharp-fanged, nuzzling thing, and had said he was so badly haunted at times that only his silver crucifix—given him for the purpose by Father Iwanicki of St. Stanislaus' Church—could bring him relief. Now he was praying because the Witches' Sabbath[i] was drawing near. May-Eve[j] was Walpurgis-Night,[k] when hell's blackest evil roamed the earth and all the slaves of Satan gathered for nameless rites and

[a] occasion,] occasion B, D
[b] there—] there; C, E
[c] night-clothes] nightclothes B, C, D
[d] advanced] advanced, C, E
[e] loomfixer] loom-fixer C, E
[f] Mazurewicz,] Mazurewiez, D
[g] Mazurewicz] Mazurewiez D
[h] furry,] furry E
[i] Sabbath] Sabbat D
[j] May-Eve] May Eve C, E
[k] Walpurgis-Night,] Walpurgis-night, B, D; Walpurgis Night, C

deeds. It was always a very bad time in Arkham, even though the fine folks up in Miskatonic Avenue and High and Saltonstall Streets pretended to know nothing about it. There would be bad doings—[a] and a child or two would probably be missing. Joe knew about such things, for his grandmother in the old country had heard tales from her grandmother. It was wise to pray and count one's beads at this season. For three months Keziah and Brown Jenkin had not been near Joe's room, nor near Paul Choynski's room, nor anywhere else—and it meant no good when they held off like that. They must be up to something.

Gilman dropped in at a[b] doctor's office on the sixteenth[c] of the month, and was surprised to find his temperature was not as high as he had feared. The physician questioned him sharply, and advised him to see a nerve specialist. On reflection, he was glad he had not consulted the still more inquisitive college doctor. Old Waldron, who had curtailed his activities before, would have made him take a rest—an impossible thing now that he was so close to great results in his equations. He was certainly near the boundary between the known universe and the fourth dimension, and who could say how much farther he might go?

But even as these thoughts came to him he wondered at the source of his strange confidence. Did all of this perilous sense of imminence come from the formulae on the sheets he covered day by day? The soft, stealthy, imaginary footsteps in the sealed loft above were unnerving. And now, too, there was a growing feeling that somebody was constantly persuading him to do something terrible which he could not do. How about the somnambulism? Where did he go sometimes in the night? And what was that faint suggestion of sound which once in a while seemed to trickle through the maddening[d] confusion of identifiable sounds even in broad daylight and full wakefulness? Its rhythm did not correspond to anything on earth, unless perhaps to the cadence of one or two unmentionable Sabbat-chants, and sometimes he feared it corresponded to certain attributes of the vague shrieking or roaring in those wholly alien abysses of dream.

[a] doings—] doings; C, E
[b] a] the C, E
[c] sixteenth] 16th A, B, C, D
[d] maddening] *om.* B, C, D, E

The dreams were meanwhile getting to be atrocious. In the lighter preliminary phase the evil old woman was now of fiendish distinctness, and Gilman knew she was the one who had frightened him in the slums. Her bent back, long nose, and shrivelled chin were unmistakable, and her shapeless brown garments were like those he remembered. The expression on her face was one of hideous malevolence and exultation, and when he awaked he could recall a croaking voice that persuaded and threatened. He must meet the Black Man,[a] and go with them all to the throne of Azathoth at the centre[b] of ultimate Chaos.[c] That was what she said. He must sign in his own blood the book of Azathoth[d] and take a new secret name now that his independent delvings had gone so far. What kept him from going with her and Brown Jenkin and the other to the throne of Chaos where the thin flutes pipe mindlessly was the fact that he had seen the name "Azathoth" in the "Necronomicon",[e] and knew it stood for a primal evil too horrible for description.

The old woman always appeared out of thin air near the corner where the downward slant met the inward slant. She seemed to crystallise[f] at a point closer to the ceiling than to the floor, and every night she was a little nearer and more distinct before the dream shifted. Brown Jenkin, too, was always a little nearer at the last, and its[g] yellowish-white fangs glistened shockingly in that unearthly violet phosphorescence. Its shrill loathsome tittering stuck more and more in Gilman's head, and he could remember in the morning how it had pronounced the words "Azathoth" and "Nyarlathotep".[h]

In the deeper dreams everything was likewise more distinct, and Gilman felt that the twilight abysses around him were those of the fourth dimension. Those organic entities whose motions seemed least flagrantly irrelevant and unmotivated were probably projections of life-forms from our own planet, including human beings. What the others

[a] Man,] Man E
[b] centre] center C, E
[c] Chaos.] chaos. B, C, D, E
[d] sign . . . Azathoth] sign the book of Azathoth in his own blood B, C, D, E
[e] "Necronomicon",] *Necronomicon,* A, B, C, D, E
[f] crystallise] crystallize B, C, D, E
[g] its] his B, C
[h] "Nyarlathotep".] "Nyarlathotep." C, D, E

were in their own dimensional sphere or spheres he dared not try to think. Two of the less irrelevantly moving things—a rather large congeries of iridescent, prolately spheroidal bubbles and a very much smaller polyhedron of unknown colours[a] and rapidly shifting surface angles—seemed to take notice of him and follow him about or float ahead as he changed position among the titan prisms, labyrinths, cube-and-plane clusters,[b] and quasi-buildings; and all the while the vague shrieking and roaring waxed louder and louder, as if approaching some monstrous climax of utterly unendurable intensity.

During the night of April 19–20th[c] the new development occurred. Gilman was half-involuntarily[d] moving about in the twilight abysses with the bubble-mass and the small polyhedron floating ahead, when he noticed the peculiarly regular angles formed by the edges of some gigantic neighbouring[e] prism-clusters. In another second he was out of the abyss and standing tremulously on a rocky hillside bathed in intense, diffused green light. He was barefooted and in his night-clothes,[f] and when he tried to walk discovered that he could scarcely lift his feet. A swirling vapour[g] hid everything but the immediate sloping terrain from sight, and he shrank from the thought of the sounds that might surge out of that vapour.[h]

Then he saw the two shapes laboriously crawling toward him—the old woman and the little furry thing.[i] The crone strained up to her knees and managed to cross her arms in a singular fashion, while Brown Jenkin pointed in a certain direction with a horribly anthropoid fore-paw[j] which it raised with evident difficulty. Spurred by an impulse he did not originate, Gilman dragged himself forward along a course determined by the angle of the old woman's arms and the direction of

---

[a] colours] colors C, E
[b] clusters,] clusters B, C, D, E
[c] 19–20th] 19–20 D, E
[d] half-involuntarily] half involuntarily B, C, D, E
[e] neighbouring] neighboring C, E
[f] night-clothes,] nightclothes, B, D, E; night-/clothes, C
[g] vapour] vapor C, E
[h] vapour.] vapor. C, E
[i] thing.] think. D
[j] fore-paw] fore paw A

the small monstrosity's paw, and before he had shuffled three steps he was back in the twilight abysses. Geometrical shapes seethed around him, and he fell dizzily and interminably. At last he woke in his bed in the crazily angled garret of the eldritch old house.

He was good for nothing that morning, and stayed away from all his classes. Some unknown attraction was pulling his eyes in a seemingly irrelevant direction, for he could not help staring at a certain vacant spot on the floor. As the day advanced[a] the focus of his unseeing eyes changed position, and by noon he had conquered the impulse to stare at vacancy. About two[b] o'clock he went out for lunch,[c] and as he threaded the narrow lanes of the city he found himself turning always to the southeast. Only an effort halted him at a cafeteria in Church Street, and after the meal he felt the unknown pull still more strongly.

He would have to consult a nerve specialist after all—perhaps there was a connexion[d] with his somnambulism—but meanwhile he might at least try to break the morbid spell himself. Undoubtedly he could still manage to walk away from the pull; so with great resolution he headed against it and dragged himself deliberately north along Garrison Street. By the time he had reached the bridge over the Miskatonic he was in a cold perspiration, and he clutched at the iron railing as he gazed upstream at the ill-regarded[e] island whose regular lines of ancient standing stones brooded sullenly in the afternoon sunlight.

Then he gave a start. For there was a clearly visible living figure on that desolate island, and a second glance told him it was certainly the strange old woman whose sinister aspect had worked itself so disastrously into his dreams. The tall grass near her was moving, too, as if some other living thing were crawling close to the ground. When the old woman began to turn toward him he fled precipitately off the bridge and into the shelter of the town's labyrinthine[f] waterfront alleys. Distant though the island was, he felt that a monstrous and invincible evil could flow from the sardonic stare of that bent, ancient figure in brown.

[a] advanced] advanced, C, E
[b] two] 2 A
[c] lunch,] lunch E
[d] connexion] connection C, D, E
[e] ill-regarded] ill regarded B, D
[f] labyrinthine] labyrinthin C

The southeastward pull still held, and only with tremendous resolution could Gilman drag himself into the old house and up the rickety stairs. For hours he sat silent and aimless, with his eyes shifting gradually westward. About six o'clock his sharpened ears caught the whining prayers of Joe Mazurewicz[a] two floors below, and in desperation he seized his hat and walked out into the sunset-golden streets, letting the now directly southward pull carry him where it might. An hour later darkness found him in the open fields beyond Hangman's Brook, with the glimmering spring stars shining ahead. The urge to walk was gradually changing to an urge to leap mystically into space, and suddenly he realised[b] just where the source of the pull lay.

It was in the sky. A definite point among the stars had a claim on him and was calling him. Apparently it was a point somewhere between Hydra and Argo Navis, and he knew that he had been urged toward it ever since he had awaked soon after dawn. In the morning it had been underfoot; afternoon found it rising in the southeast,[c] and now it was roughly south but wheeling[d] toward the west. What was the meaning of this new thing? Was he going mad? How long would it last? Again mustering his resolution, Gilman turned and dragged himself back to the sinister old house.

Mazurewicz[e] was waiting for him at the door, and seemed both anxious and reluctant to whisper some fresh bit of superstition. It was about the witch light.[f] Joe had been out celebrating the night before—it was Patriots'[g] Day in Massachusetts—and had come home after midnight. Looking up at the house from outside, he had thought at first that Gilman's window was dark;[h] but then he had seen the faint violet glow within. He wanted to warn the gentleman about that glow, for everybody in Arkham knew it was Keziah's witch light[i] which

---

[a] Mazurewicz] Mazurewiez D
[b] realised] realized B, C, D, E
[c] underfoot; . . . southeast,] underfoot, and B, C, D, E
[d] wheeling] stealing B, C, D, E
[e] Mazurewicz] Mazurewiez D
[f] witch light.] witch-light. C, E
[g] Patriots'] Patriot's D
[h] dark;] dark, B, C, D, E
[i] witch light] witch-light C, E

played near Brown Jenkin and the ghost of the old crone herself. He had not mentioned this before, but now he must tell about it because it meant that Keziah and her long-toothed familiar were haunting the young gentleman. Sometimes he and Paul Choynski and Landlord Dombrowski thought they saw that light seeping out of cracks in the sealed loft above the young gentleman's room, but they had all agreed not to talk about that. However, it would be better for the gentleman to take another room and get a crucifix from some good priest like Father Iwanicki.

As the man rambled on[a] Gilman felt a nameless panic clutch at his throat. He knew that Joe must have been half drunk when he came home the night before,[b] yet this[c] mention of a violet light in the garret window was of frightful import. It was a lambent glow of this sort which always played about the old woman and the small furry thing in those lighter, sharper dreams which prefaced his plunge into unknown abysses, and the thought that a wakeful second person could see the dream-luminance was utterly beyond sane harbourage.[d] Yet where[e] had the fellow got such an odd notion? Had he himself talked as well as walked around the house in his sleep? No, Joe said, he had not—but he must check up on this. Perhaps Frank Elwood could tell him something, though he hated to ask.

Fever—wild dreams—somnambulism—illusions of sounds—a pull toward a point in the sky—and now a suspicion of insane sleep-talking![f] He must stop studying, see a nerve specialist, and take himself in hand. When he climbed to the second story[g] he paused at Elwood's door but saw that the other youth was out. Reluctantly he continued up to his garret room and sat down in the dark. His gaze was still pulled to the southwest,[h] but he also found himself listening intently for some

---

[a] on] on, C, E
[b] before,] before; C, E
[c] this] the B, C, D, E
[d] harbourage.] harborage. C, E
[e] where] were E
[f] sleep-talking!] sleep-walking! D
[g] story] storey A
[h] southwest,] southward, B, C, D, E

sound in the closed loft above, and half imagining[a] that an evil violet light seeped down through an infinitesimal crack in the low, slanting ceiling.

That night as Gilman slept[b] the violet light broke upon him with heightened intensity, and the old witch and small furry thing—getting closer than ever before—[c]mocked him with inhuman squeals and devilish gestures. He was glad to sink into the vaguely roaring twilight abysses, though the pursuit of that iridescent[d] bubble-congeries and that kaleidoscopic little polyhedron was menacing and irritating. Then came the shift as vast converging planes of a slippery-looking substance loomed above and below him—a shift which ended in a flash of delirium and a blaze of unknown, alien light in which yellow, carmine, and indigo were madly and inextricably blended.

He was half lying[e] on a high, fantastically balustraded terrace above a boundless jungle of outlandish, incredible peaks, balanced planes, domes, minarets, horizontal discs[f] poised on pinnacles, and numberless forms of still greater wildness—some of stone and some of metal— which glittered gorgeously in the mixed, almost blistering glare from a polychromatic sky. Looking upward he saw three stupendous discs[g] of flame, each of a different hue, and at a different height above an infinitely distant curving horizon of low mountains. Behind him tiers of higher terraces towered aloft as far as he could see. The city below stretched away to the limits of vision, and he hoped that no sound would well up from it.

The pavement from which he easily raised himself was of[h] a veined, polished stone beyond his power to identify, and the tiles were cut in bizarre-angled shapes which struck him as less asymmetrical than based on some unearthly symmetry whose laws he could not comprehend. The balustrade was chest-high, delicate, and fantastically

[a] half imagining] half-imagining A, B, D
[b] slept] slept, C, E
[c] thing— . . . before—] thing, . . . before, C, E
[d] iridescent] irridescent D
[e] half lying] half-lying A, B, D
[f] discs] disks C, E
[g] discs] disks C, E
[h] of] *om.* E

wrought, while along the rail were ranged at short intervals little figures of grotesque design and exquisite workmanship. They, like the whole balustrade, seemed to be made of some sort of shining metal whose colour[a] could not be guessed in this[b] chaos of mixed effulgences;[c] and their nature utterly defied conjecture. They represented some ridged,[d] barrel-shaped object with thin horizontal arms radiating spoke-like[e] from a central ring,[f] and with vertical knobs or bulbs projecting from the head and base of the barrel. Each of these knobs was the hub of a system of five long, flat, triangularly tapering arms arranged around it like the arms of a starfish—nearly horizontal, but curving slightly away from the central barrel. The base of the bottom knob was fused to the long railing with so delicate a point of contact that several figures had been broken off and were missing. The figures were about four and a half inches in height, while the spiky arms gave them a maximum diameter of about two and a half inches.

When Gilman stood up[g] the tiles felt hot to his bare feet. He was wholly alone, and his first act was to walk to the balustrade and look dizzily down at the endless, Cyclopean[h] city almost two thousand feet below. As he listened he thought a rhythmic confusion of faint musical pipings covering a wide tonal range welled up from the narrow streets beneath, and he wished he might discern the denizens of the place. The sight turned him giddy after a while, so that he would have fallen to the pavement had he not clutched instinctively at the lustrous balustrade. His right hand fell on one of the projecting figures, the touch seeming to steady him slightly. It was too much, however, for the exotic delicacy of the metal-work, and the spiky figure snapped off under his grasp. Still half-dazed,[i] he continued to clutch it as his other hand seized a vacant space on the smooth railing.

---

[a] colour] color C, E
[b] this] the B, C, D, E
[c] effulgences;] effulgences, B, C, D, E
[d] ridged,] ridged B, C, D, E
[e] spoke-like] spokelike B, D; spoke-/like E
[f] ring,] ring B, C, D, E
[g] up] up, C, E
[h] Cyclopean] cyclopean A, B, C, E
[i] half-dazed,] half dazed, A, B, C, D, E

But now his oversensitive[a] ears caught something behind him, and he looked back across the level terrace. Approaching him softly though without apparent furtiveness were five figures, two of which were the sinister old woman and the fanged, furry little animal. The other three were what sent him unconscious—[b]for they were living entities about eight feet high, shaped precisely like the spiky images on the balustrade,[c] and propelling themselves by a spider-like wriggling of their lower set of starfish-arms.[d]

Gilman awaked[e] in his bed, drenched by a cold perspiration and with a smarting sensation in his face, hands,[f] and feet. Springing to the floor, he washed and dressed in frantic haste, as if it were necessary for him to get out of the house as quickly as possible. He did not know where he wished to go, but felt that once more he would have to sacrifice his classes. The odd pull toward that spot in the sky between Hydra and Argo had abated, but another of even greater strength had taken its place. Now he felt that he must go north—infinitely north. He dreaded to cross the bridge that gave a view of the desolate island in the Miskatonic, so went over the Peabody Avenue bridge.[g] Very often he stumbled, for his eyes and ears were chained to an extremely lofty point in the blank blue sky.

After about an hour he got himself under better control, and saw that he was far from the city. All around him stretched the bleak emptiness of salt marshes, while the narrow road ahead led to Innsmouth—that ancient, half-deserted town which Arkham people were so curiously unwilling to visit. Though the northward pull had not diminished,[h] he resisted it as he had resisted the other pull, and finally found that he could almost balance the one against the other. Plodding back to town and getting some coffee at a soda fountain, he dragged himself into the public library and browsed aimlessly among

[a] oversensitive] over-sensitive A, B, C, D, E
[b] unconscious—] unconscious; C, E
[c] balustrade,] balustrade B, D
[d] starfish-arms.] starfish arms. D
[e] awaked] awoke E
[f] hands,] hands C, E
[g] bridge.] Bridge. D
[h] diminished,] diminished B, D

the lighter magazines. Once he met some friends who remarked how oddly sunburned he looked, but he did not tell them of his walk. At three[a] o'clock he took some lunch at a restaurant, noting meanwhile that the pull had either lessened or divided itself. After that he killed the time at a cheap cinema show, seeing the inane performance over and over again without paying any attention to it.

About nine at night he drifted homeward and stumbled[b] into the ancient house. Joe Mazurewicz[c] was whining unintelligible prayers, and Gilman hastened up to his own garret chamber without pausing to see if Elwood was in. It was when he turned on the feeble electric light that the shock came. At once he saw there was something on the table which did not belong there, and a second look left no room for doubt. Lying on its side—for it could not stand up alone—was the exotic spiky figure which in his monstrous dream he had broken off the fantastic balustrade. No detail was missing. The ridged, barrel-shaped centre,[d] the thin,[e] radiating arms, the knobs at each end, and the flat, slightly outward-curving starfish-arms spreading from those knobs— all were there. In the electric light the colour[f] seemed to be a kind of iridescent grey[g] veined with green,[h] and Gilman could see amidst his horror and bewilderment that one of the knobs ended in a jagged break[i] corresponding to its former point of attachment to the dream-railing.

Only his tendency toward a dazed stupor prevented him from screaming aloud. This fusion of dream and reality was too much to bear. Still dazed, he clutched at the spiky thing and staggered downstairs to Landlord Dombrowski's quarters. The whining prayers of the superstitious loomfixer[j] were still sounding through the mouldy[k] halls,

---

[a] three] 3 A
[b] stumbled] shuffled B, C, D, E
[c] Mazurewicz] Mazurewiez D
[d] centre,] center, C, E
[e] thin,] thin B, C, D, E
[f] colour] color C, E
[g] iridescent grey] iridescent gray B, C, E; irridescent gray D
[h] green,] green; B, C, D, E
[i] break] break, B, C, D, E
[j] loomfixer] loom-/fixer C; loom-fixer E
[k] mouldy] moldy C, E

but Gilman did not mind them now. The landlord was in, and greeted him pleasantly. No, he had not seen that thing before and did not know anything about it. But his wife had said she found a funny tin thing in one of the beds when she fixed the rooms at noon, and maybe that was it. Dombrowski called her, and she waddled in. Yes, that was the thing. She had found it in the young gentleman's bed—on the side next the wall. It had looked very queer to her, but of course the young gentleman had lots of queer things in his room—books and curios and pictures and markings on paper. She certainly knew nothing about it.

So Gilman climbed upstairs again in a[a] mental turmoil, convinced that he was either still dreaming or that his somnambulism had run to incredible extremes and led him to depredations in unknown places. Where had he got this outré thing? He did not recall seeing it in any museum in Arkham. It must have been somewhere, though; and the sight of it as he snatched it in his sleep must have caused the odd dream-picture of the balustraded terrace. Next day he would make some very guarded inquiries—and perhaps see the nerve specialist.

Meanwhile he would try to keep track of his somnambulism. As he went upstairs and across the garret hall he sprinkled about some flour which he had borrowed—with a frank admission as to its purpose— from the landlord. He had stopped at Elwood's door on the way, but had found all dark within. Entering his room, he placed the spiky thing on the table, and lay down in complete mental and physical exhaustion without pausing to undress. From the closed loft above the slanting ceiling he thought he heard a faint scratching and padding, but he was too disorganised[b] even to mind it. That cryptical pull from the north was getting very strong again, though it seemed now to come from a lower place in the sky.

In the dazzling violet light of dream the old woman and the fanged, furry thing came again and with a greater distinctness than on any former[c] occasion. This time they actually reached him, and he felt the crone's withered claws clutching at him. He was pulled out of bed and into empty space, and for a moment he heard a rhythmic roaring

[a] a] *om.* B, C, D, E
[b] disorganised] disorganized B, C, D, E
[c] former] other D

and saw the twilight amorphousness of the vague abysses seething around him. But that moment was very brief, for presently he was in a crude, windowless little space with rough beams and planks rising to a peak just above his head, and with a curious slanting floor underfoot. Propped level on that floor were low cases full of books of every degree of antiquity and disintegration, and in the centre[a] were a table and bench, both apparently fastened in place. Small objects of unknown shape and nature were ranged on the tops of the cases, and in the flaming violet light Gilman thought he saw a counterpart[b] of the spiky image which had puzzled him so horribly. On the left the floor fell abruptly away, leaving a black triangular gulf out of which, after a second's dry rattling, there presently climbed the hateful little furry thing with the yellow fangs and bearded human face.

The evilly grinning beldame still clutched him, and beyond the table stood a figure he had never seen before—a tall, lean man of dead black colouration[c] but without the slightest sign of negroid features; wholly devoid of either hair or beard, and wearing as his only garment a shapeless robe of some heavy black fabric. His feet were indistinguishable because of the table and bench, but he must have been shod, since there was a clicking whenever he changed position. The man did not speak, and bore no trace of expression on his small, regular features. He merely pointed to a book of prodigious size which lay open on the table, while the beldame thrust a huge grey[d] quill into Gilman's right hand. Over everything was a pall of intensely maddening fear, and the climax was reached when the furry thing ran up the dreamer's clothing to his shoulders and then down his left arm, finally biting him sharply in the wrist just below his cuff. As the blood spurted from this wound Gilman lapsed into a faint.

He awaked on the morning of the 22nd[e] with a pain in his left wrist, and saw that his cuff was brown with dried blood. His recollections were very confused, but the scene with the black man in

---

[a] centre] center C, E

[b] counterpart] counter-/part B; counter-part D

[c] colouration] coloration C, E

[d] grey] gray B, C, D, E

[e] 22nd] twenty-second E

the unknown space stood out vividly. The rats must have bitten him as he slept, giving rise to the climax of that frightful dream. Opening the door, he saw that the flour on the corridor floor was undisturbed except for the huge prints of the loutish fellow who roomed at the other end of the garret. So he had not been sleep-walking this time. But something would have to be done about those rats. He would speak to the landlord about them. Again he tried to stop up the hole at the base of the slanting wall, wedging in a candlestick which seemed of about the right size. His ears were ringing horribly, as if with the residual echoes of some horrible noise heard in dreams.

As he bathed and changed clothes he tried to recall what he had dreamed after the scene in the violet-litten space, but nothing definite would crystallise[a] in his mind. That scene itself must have corresponded to the sealed loft overhead, which had begun to attack his imagination so violently, but later impressions were faint and hazy. There were suggestions of the vague, twilight abysses, and of still vaster, blacker abysses beyond them—abysses in which all fixed suggestions of form[b] were absent. He had been taken there by the bubble-congeries and the little polyhedron which always dogged him; but they, like himself, had changed to wisps of milky, barely luminous[c] mist in this farther void of ultimate blackness. Something else had gone on ahead—a larger wisp which now and then condensed into nameless approximations of form— and he thought that their progress had not been in a straight line, but rather along the alien curves and spirals of some ethereal vortex which obeyed laws unknown to the physics and mathematics of any conceivable cosmos. Eventually there had been a hint of vast, leaping shadows, of a monstrous, half-acoustic pulsing, and of the thin, monotonous piping of an unseen flute—but that was all. Gilman decided he had picked up that last conception from what he had read in the "Necronomicon"[d] about the mindless entity Azathoth, which rules all time and space from a curiously environed[e] black throne at the centre[f] of Chaos.

[a] crystallise] crystallize B, C, D, E
[b] of form] *om.* B, C, D, E
[c] milky, barely luminous] *om.* B, C, D, E
[d] "Necronomicon"] *Necronomicon* A, B, C, D, E
[e] curiously environed] *om.* E
[f] centre] center C, E

When the blood was washed away the wrist wound proved very slight, and Gilman puzzled over the location of the two tiny punctures. It occurred to him that there was no blood on the bedspread where he had lain—which was very curious in view of the amount on his skin and cuff. Had he been sleep-walking within his room, and had the rat bitten him as he sat in some chair or paused in some less rational position? He looked in every corner for brownish drops or stains, but did not find any. He had better, he thought, sprinkle flour within the room as well as outside the door—though after all no further proof of his sleep-walking[a] was needed. He knew he did walk—and the thing to do now was to stop it. He must ask Frank Elwood for help. This morning the strange pulls from space seemed lessened, though they were replaced by another sensation even more inexplicable. It was a vague, insistent impulse to fly away from his present situation, but held not a hint of the specific direction in which he wished to fly. As he picked up the strange spiky image on the table he thought the older northward pull grew a trifle stronger;[b] but even so, it was wholly overruled by the newer and more bewildering urge.

He took the spiky image down to Elwood's room, steeling himself against the whines of the loomfixer[c] which welled up from the ground floor. Elwood was in, thank heaven,[d] and appeared to be stirring about. There was time for a little conversation before leaving for breakfast and college,[e] so Gilman hurriedly poured forth an account of his recent dreams and fears. His host was very sympathetic, and agreed that something ought to be done. He was shocked by his guest's drawn, haggard aspect, and noticed the queer, abnormal-looking sunburn which others had remarked during the past week. There was not much, though, that he could say. He had not seen Gilman on any sleep-walking expedition, and had no idea what the curious image could be. He had, though, heard the French-Canadian who lodged just under Gilman talking to Mazurewicz[f] one evening. They were telling each

---

[a] sleep-walking] sleep-/walking D; sleepwalking E

[b] stronger;] stronger, E

[c] loomfixer] loom-fixer C, E

[d] heaven,] Heaven, A, B, D

[e] college,] college; C, E

[f] Mazurewicz] Mazurewiez D

other how badly they dreaded the coming of Walpurgis-Night,[a] now only a few days off; and were exchanging pitying comments about the poor, doomed young gentleman. Desrochers, the fellow under Gilman's room, had spoken of nocturnal footsteps both[b] shod and unshod, and of the violet light he saw one night when he had stolen fearfully up to peer through Gilman's keyhole. He had not dared to peer, he told Mazurewicz,[c] after he had glimpsed that light through the cracks around the door. There had been soft talking, too—and as he began to describe it his voice had sunk to an inaudible whisper.

Elwood could not imagine what had set these superstitious creatures gossiping, but supposed their imaginations had been roused by Gilman's late hours and somnolent walking and talking on the one hand, and by the nearness of traditionally feared[d] May-Eve[e] on the other hand. That Gilman talked in his sleep was plain, and it was obviously from Desrochers'[f] keyhole-listenings that the delusive notion of the violet dream-light[g] had got abroad. These simple people were quick to imagine they had seen any odd thing they had heard about. As for a plan of action—Gilman had better move down to Elwood's room and avoid sleeping alone. Elwood would, if awake, rouse him whenever he began to talk or rise in his sleep. Very soon, too, he must see the specialist. Meanwhile they would take the spiky image around to the various museums and to certain professors; seeking identification and stating that it had been found in a public rubbish-can. Also, Dombrowski must attend to the poisoning of those rats in the walls.

Braced up by Elwood's companionship, Gilman attended classes that day. Strange urges still tugged at him, but he could sidetrack[h] them with considerable success. During a free period he shewed[i] the queer

---

[a] Walpurgis-Night,] Walpurgis Night, A, C, E; Walpurgis night, B, D

[b] both] *om.* B, C, D, E

[c] Mazurewicz,] Mazurewiez, D

[d] traditionally feared] traditionally-feared A, B, C, D, E

[e] May-Eve] May Eve E

[f] Desrochers'] Desrocher's C

[g] dream-light] dream-/light B; dreamlight D

[h] sidetrack] side-track D

[i] shewed] showed B, C, D, E

image to several professors, all of whom were intensely interested, though none of them could shed any light upon its nature or origin. That night he slept on a couch which Elwood had had the landlord bring to the second-story room, and for the first time in weeks was wholly free from disquieting dreams. But the feverishness still hung on, and the whines of the loomfixer[a] were an unnerving influence.

During the next few days Gilman enjoyed an almost perfect immunity from morbid manifestations. He had, Elwood said, shewed[b] no tendency to talk or rise in his sleep; and meanwhile the landlord was putting rat-poison everywhere. The only disturbing element was the talk among the superstitious foreigners, whose imaginations had become highly excited. Mazurewicz[c] was always trying to make him get a crucifix, and finally forced one upon him which he said had been blessed by the good Father Iwanicki. Desrochers, too, had something to say—[d]in fact, he insisted that cautious steps had sounded in the now vacant room above him on the first and second nights of Gilman's absence from it. Paul Choynski thought he heard sounds in the halls and on the stairs at night, and claimed that his door had been softly tried, while Mrs. Dombrowski vowed she had seen Brown Jenkin for the first time since All-Hallows. But such naive[e] reports could mean very little, and Gilman let the cheap metal crucifix hang idly from a knob on his host's dresser.

For three days Gilman and Elwood canvassed the local museums in an effort to identify the strange spiky image, but always without success. In every quarter, however, interest was intense; for the utter alienage of the thing was a tremendous challenge to scientific curiosity. One of the small radiating arms was broken off and subjected to chemical analysis, and the result is still talked about in college circles.[f] Professor Ellery found platinum, iron,[g] and tellurium in the strange alloy; but mixed with these were at least three other apparent elements of high

[a] loomfixer] loom-fixer C, E
[b] shewed] showed B, C, D, E
[c] Mazurewicz] Mazurewiez D
[d] say—] say; C, E
[e] naive] naïve C, D, E
[f] analysis . . . circles.] analysis. B, C, D, E
[g] iron,] iron C, E

atomic weight which chemistry was absolutely powerless to classify. Not only did they fail to correspond with any known[a] element, but they did not even fit the vacant places reserved for probable elements in the periodic system. The mystery remains unsolved to this day, though the image is on exhibition at the museum of Miskatonic University.

On the morning of April 27th[b] a fresh rat-hole appeared in the room where Gilman was a guest, but Dombrowski tinned it up during the day. The poison was not having much effect, for scratchings and scurryings in the walls were virtually undiminished.[c] Elwood was out late that night, and Gilman waited up for him. He did not wish to go to sleep in a room alone—especially since he thought he had glimpsed in the evening twilight the repellent old woman whose image had become so horribly transferred to his dreams. He wondered who she was, and what had been near her rattling the tin cans[d] in a rubbish-heap at the mouth of a squalid courtyard. The crone had seemed to notice him and leer evilly at him—though perhaps this was merely his imagination.

The next day both youths felt very tired, and knew they would sleep like logs when night came. In the evening they drowsily discussed the mathematical studies which had so completely and perhaps harmfully engrossed Gilman, and speculated about the linkage with ancient magic and folklore which seemed so darkly probable. They spoke of old Keziah Mason, and Elwood agreed that Gilman had good scientific grounds for thinking she might have stumbled on strange and significant information. The hidden cults to which these witches belonged often guarded and handed down surprising[e] secrets from elder, forgotten aeons;[f] and it was by no means impossible that Keziah had actually mastered the art of passing through dimensional gates. Tradition emphasises[g] the uselessness of material barriers in halting a

---

[a] known] human C
[b] 27th] 27 A; twenty-seventh E
[c] undiminished.] undiminished. ¶ C, E
[d] cans] can E
[e] surprising] surprizing C
[f] aeons;] eons; C, E
[g] emphasises] emphasizes C, E

witch's motions;[a] and who can say what underlies the old tales of broomstick rides through the night?

Whether a modern student could ever gain similar powers from mathematical research alone, was still to be seen. Success, Gilman added, might lead to dangerous and unthinkable situations; for who could foretell the conditions pervading an adjacent but normally inaccessible dimension? On the other hand, the picturesque possibilities were enormous. Time could not exist in certain belts of space, and by entering and remaining in such a belt one might preserve one's life and age indefinitely; never suffering organic metabolism or deterioration except for slight amounts incurred during visits to one's own or similar planes. One might, for example, pass into a timeless dimension and emerge at some remote period of the earth's history as young as before.

Whether anybody had ever managed to do this, one could hardly conjecture with any degree of authority. Old legends are hazy and ambiguous, and in historic times all attempts at crossing forbidden gaps seem complicated by strange and terrible alliances with beings and messengers from outside. There was the immemorial figure of the deputy or messenger of hidden and terrible powers—the "Black Man" of the witch-cult, and the "Nyarlathotep" of the "Necronomicon".[b] There was, too, the baffling problem of the lesser messengers or intermediaries—the quasi-animals and queer hybrids which legend depicts as witches' familiars. As Gilman and Elwood retired, too sleepy to argue further, they heard Joe Mazurewicz[c] reel into the house half-drunk,[d] and shuddered at the desperate wildness of his whining prayers.

That night Gilman saw the violet light again. In his dream he had heard a scratching and gnawing in the partitions, and thought that someone[e] fumbled clumsily at the latch. Then he saw the old woman and the small furry thing advancing toward him over the carpeted floor. The beldame's face was alight with inhuman exultation, and the little yellow-toothed morbidity tittered mockingly as it pointed at the heavily

---

[a] motions;] motions, B, C, D, E
[b] "Necronomicon".] *Necronomicon.* A, B, C, D, E
[c] Mazurewicz] Mazurewiez D
[d] half-drunk,] half drunk C, E
[e] someone] some one C, E

sleeping[a] form of Elwood on the other couch across the room. A paralysis of fear stifled all attempts to cry out. As once before, the hideous crone seized Gilman by the shoulders, yanking him out of bed and into empty space. Again the infinitude of the shrieking twilight[b] abysses flashed past him, but in another second he thought he was in a dark, muddy, unknown alley of foetid odours,[c] with the rotting walls of ancient houses towering up on every hand.

Ahead was the robed black man he had seen in the peaked space in the other dream, while from a lesser distance the old woman was beckoning and grimacing imperiously. Brown Jenkin was rubbing itself with a kind of affectionate playfulness around the ankles of the black man, which the deep mud largely concealed. There was a dark open doorway on the right, to which the black man silently pointed. Into this the grimacing[d] crone started, dragging Gilman after her by his pajama sleeve.[e] There were evil-smelling staircases which creaked ominously, and on which the old woman seemed to radiate a faint violet light; and finally a door leading off a landing. The crone fumbled with the latch and pushed the door open, motioning to Gilman to wait[f] and disappearing inside the black aperture.

The youth's oversensitive[g] ears caught a hideous strangled cry, and presently the beldame came out of the room bearing a small, senseless form which she thrust at the dreamer as if ordering him to carry it. The sight of this form, and the expression on its face, broke the spell. Still too dazed to cry out, he plunged recklessly down the noisome staircase and into the mud outside; halting only when seized and choked by the waiting black man. As consciousness departed he heard the faint, shrill tittering of the fanged, rat-like[h] abnormality.

[a] heavily sleeping] heavily-sleeping A, D; hearty-sleeping B, C, E
[b] twilight] *om.* B, C, D, E
[c] foetid odours,] foetid odours B; fetid odors C, E; fetid odours D
[d] grimacing] grinning B, C, D, E
[e] sleeve.] sleeves. B, C, D, E
[f] wait] wait, B, C, D, E
[g] oversensitive] over-sensitive A, B, C, D, E
[h] rat-like] ratlike A, B, D; rat-/like C

On the morning of the 29th[a] Gilman awaked into a maelstrom of horror. The instant he opened his eyes he knew something was terribly wrong, for he was back in his old garret room with the slanting wall and ceiling, sprawled on the now unmade bed. His throat was aching inexplicably, and as he struggled to a sitting posture he saw with growing fright that his feet and pajama-bottoms[b] were brown with caked mud. For the moment his recollections were hopelessly hazy, but he knew at least that he must have been sleep-walking. Elwood had been lost too deeply in slumber to hear and stop him. On the floor were confused muddy prints, but oddly enough they did not extend all the way to the door. The more Gilman looked at them, the more peculiar they seemed; for in addition to those he could recognise[c] as his there were some smaller, almost round markings—such as the legs of a large chair or[d] table might make, except that most of them tended to be divided into halves. There were also some curious muddy rat-tracks leading out of a fresh hole and back into it again. Utter bewilderment and the fear of madness racked Gilman as he staggered to the door and saw that there were no muddy prints outside. The more he remembered of his hideous dream the more terrified he felt, and it added to his desperation to hear Joe Mazurewicz[e] chanting mournfully two floors below.

Descending to Elwood's room he roused his still-sleeping host and began telling of how he had found himself, but Elwood could form no idea of what might really have happened. Where Gilman could have been, how he got back to his room without making tracks in the hall, and how the muddy, furniture-like prints came to be mixed with his in the garret chamber, were wholly beyond conjecture. Then there were those dark, livid marks on his throat, as if he had tried to strangle himself. He put his hands up to them, but found that they did not even approximately fit. While they were talking[f] Desrochers dropped in to say that he had heard a terrific clattering overhead in the dark small

[a] 29th] twenty-ninth E
[b] pajama-bottoms] pajama bottoms B, C, D, E
[c] recognise] recognize B, C, D, E
[d] or] or a B, C, D, E
[e] Mazurewicz] Mazurewiez D
[f] talking] talking, C, E

hours. No, there had been no one on the stairs after midnight—[a] though just before midnight he had heard faint footfalls in the garret, and cautiously descending steps he did not like. It was, he added, a very bad time of year for Arkham. The young gentleman had better be sure to wear the crucifix Joe Mazurewicz[b] had given him. Even the daytime was not safe, for after dawn there had been strange sounds in the house—especially a thin, childish wail hastily choked off.

Gilman mechanically attended classes that morning, but was wholly unable to fix his mind on his studies. A mood of hideous apprehension and expectancy had seized him, and he seemed to be awaiting the fall of some annihilating blow. At noon he lunched at the University Spa, picking up a paper from the next seat as he waited for dessert. But he never ate that dessert; for an item on the paper's first page left him limp, wild-eyed, and able only to pay his check and stagger back to Elwood's room.

There had been a strange kidnapping the night before in Orne's Gangway, and the two-year-old child of a clod-like laundry worker named Anastasia Wolejko had completely vanished from sight. The mother, it appeared, had feared the event for some time; but the reasons she assigned for her fear were so grotesque that no one took them seriously. She had, she said, seen Brown Jenkin about the place now and then ever since early in March, and knew from its grimaces and titterings that little Ladislas must be marked for sacrifice at the awful Sabbat on Walpurgis-Night.[c] She had asked her neighbour[d] Mary Czanek to sleep in the room and try to protect the child, but Mary had not dared. She could not tell the police, for they never believed such things. Children had been taken that way every year ever since she could remember. And her friend Pete Stowacki would not help because he wanted the child out of the way anyhow.[e]

But what threw Gilman into a cold perspiration was the report of a pair of revellers who had been walking past the mouth of the gangway

---

[a] midnight—] midnight, C, E
[b] Mazurewicz] Mazurewiez D
[c] Walpurgis-Night.] Walpurgis Night. A, B, C, D, E
[d] neighbour] neighbor B, C, D, E
[e] way anyhow.] way. C, E

just after midnight. They admitted they had been drunk, but both vowed they had seen a crazily dressed trio furtively entering the dark passageway. There had, they said, been a huge robed negro, a little old woman in rags, and a young white man in his night-clothes.[a] The old woman had been dragging the youth, while around the feet of the negro a tame rat was rubbing and weaving in the brown mud.

Gilman sat in a daze all the afternoon, and Elwood—who had meanwhile seen the papers and formed terrible conjectures from them—found him thus when he came home. This time neither could doubt but that something hideously serious was closing in around them. Between the phantasms[b] of nightmare and the realities of the objective world a monstrous and unthinkable relationship was crystallising,[c] and only stupendous vigilance could avert still more direful developments. Gilman must see a specialist sooner or later, but not just now, when all the papers were full of this kidnapping business.

Just what had really happened was maddeningly obscure, and for a moment both Gilman and Elwood exchanged whispered theories of the wildest kind. Had Gilman unconsciously succeeded better than he knew in his studies of space and its dimensions? Had he actually slipped outside our sphere to points unguessed and unimaginable? Where—if anywhere—had he been on those nights of daemoniac[d] alienage? The roaring twilight abysses—the green hillside—the blistering terrace—the pulls from the stars—the ultimate black vortex—the black man—the muddy alley and the stairs—the old witch and the fanged, furry horror— the bubble-congeries and the little polyhedron—the strange sunburn— the wrist wound[e]—the unexplained image—the muddy feet—the throat-marks—the tales and fears of the superstitious foreigners—what did all this mean? To what extent could the laws of sanity apply to such a case?

There was no sleep for either of them that night, but next day they both cut classes and drowsed. This was April 30th,[f] and with the dusk would come the hellish Sabbat-time which all the foreigners and the

[a] night-clothes.] nightclothes. C
[b] phantasms] fantasms C
[c] crystallising,] crystallizing, B, C, D, E
[d] daemoniac] demoniac C, E
[e] wrist wound] wrist-wound E
[f] 30th,] thirtieth, E

superstitious old folk feared. Mazurewicz[a] came home at six o'clock and said people at the mill were whispering that the Walpurgis-revels would be held in the dark ravine beyond Meadow Hill where the old white stone stands in a place queerly void[b] of all plant-life.[c] Some of them had even told the police and advised them to look there for the missing Wolejko child, but they did not believe anything would be done. Joe insisted that the poor young gentleman wear his nickel-chained crucifix, and Gilman put it on and dropped it inside his shirt to humour[d] the fellow.

Late at night the two youths sat drowsing in their chairs, lulled by the rhythmical[e] praying of the loomfixer[f] on the floor below. Gilman listened as he nodded, his preternaturally sharpened hearing seeming to strain for some subtle, dreaded murmur beyond the noises in the ancient house. Unwholesome recollections of things in the "Necronomicon"[g] and the Black Book[h] welled up, and he found himself swaying to infandous rhythms said to pertain to the blackest ceremonies of the Sabbat and to have an origin outside the time and space we comprehend.

Presently he realised[i] what he was listening for—the hellish chant of the celebrants in the distant black valley. How did he know so much about what they expected? How did he know the time when Nahab and her acolyte were due to bear the brimming bowl which would follow the black cock and the black goat? He saw that Elwood had dropped asleep, and tried to call out and waken him. Something, however, closed his throat. He was not his own master. Had he signed the black man's book after all?

Then his fevered, abnormal hearing caught the distant, wind-borne[j] notes. Over miles of hill and field and alley they came, but he

---

[a] Mazurewicz] Mazurewiez D
[b] void] devoid B, C, D, E
[c] plant-life.] plant life. C, E
[d] humour] humor C, E
[e] rhythmical] *om.* B, C, D, E
[f] loomfixer] loom-fixer C, E
[g] "Necronomicon"] *Necronomicon* A, B, C, D, E
[h] Black Book] "Black Book" B, D; *Black Book* C, E
[i] realised] realized B, C, D, E
[j] wind-borne] wind-/borne A; windborne E

recognised[a] them none the less. The fires must be lit, and the dancers must be starting in. How could he keep himself from going? What was it that had enmeshed him? Mathematics—folklore—the house—old Keziah—Brown Jenkin . . . and now he saw that there was a fresh rat-hole[b] in the wall near his couch. Above the distant chanting and the nearer praying of Joe Mazurewicz[c] came another sound—a stealthy, determined scratching in the partitions. He hoped the electric lights would not go out. Then he saw the fanged, bearded little face in the rat-hole—the accursed little face which he at last realised[d] bore such a shocking, mocking resemblance to old Keziah's—and heard the faint fumbling at the door.

The screaming twilight abysses flashed before him, and he felt himself helpless in the formless grasp of the iridescent bubble-congeries. Ahead raced the small, kaleidoscopic polyhedron,[e] and all through the churning void there was a heightening and acceleration of the vague tonal pattern which seemed to foreshadow some unutterable and unendurable climax. He seemed to know what was coming—the monstrous burst of Walpurgis-rhythm in whose cosmic timbre would be concentrated all the primal, ultimate space-time seethings which lie behind[f] the massed spheres of matter and sometimes break forth in measured reverberations that penetrate[g] faintly to every layer of entity and give hideous significance throughout the worlds to certain dreaded periods.

But all this vanished in a second. He was again in the cramped, violet-litten peaked space with the slanting floor, the low cases of ancient books, the bench and table, the queer objects, and the triangular gulf at one side. On the table lay a small white figure—an infant boy, unclothed and unconscious—while on the other side stood the monstrous, leering old woman with a gleaming, grotesque-hafted knife in her right hand, and a queerly proportioned[h] pale metal bowl covered with

---

[a] recognised] recognized B, C, D, E
[b] rat-hole] rat hole B, D
[c] Mazurewicz] Mazurewiez D
[d] realised] realized B, C, D, E
[e] polyhedron,] polyhedron E
[f] behind] beyond D [*In B*, behind *is typed over* beyond]
[g] penetrate] penetate E
[h] queerly proportioned] queerly-proportioned A, B, D

curiously chased designs and having delicate lateral handles in her left. She was intoning some croaking ritual in a language which Gilman could not understand, but which seemed like something guardedly quoted in the "Necronomicon".[a]

As the scene grew clear[b] he saw the ancient crone bend forward and extend the empty bowl across the table—and unable to control his own motions,[c] he reached far forward and took it in both hands, noticing as he did so its comparative lightness. At the same moment the disgusting form of Brown Jenkin scrambled up over the brink of the triangular black gulf on his left. The crone now motioned him to hold the bowl in a certain position while she raised the huge, grotesque knife above the small white victim as high as her right hand could reach. The fanged, furry thing began tittering a continuation of the unknown ritual, while the witch croaked loathsome responses. Gilman felt a gnawing,[d] poignant abhorrence shoot through his mental and emotional paralysis, and the light metal bowl shook in his grasp. A second later the downward motion of the knife broke the spell completely, and he dropped the bowl with a resounding bell-like clangour[e] while his hands darted out frantically to stop the monstrous deed.

In an instant he had edged up the slanting floor around the end of the table and wrenched the knife from the old woman's claws; sending it clattering over the brink of the narrow triangular gulf. In another instant, however, matters were reversed; for those murderous claws had locked themselves tightly around his own throat, while the wrinkled face was twisted with insane fury. He felt the chain of the cheap crucifix grinding into his neck, and in his peril wondered how the sight of the object itself would affect the evil creature. Her strength was altogether superhuman, but as she continued her choking he reached feebly in his shirt and drew out the metal symbol, snapping the chain and pulling it free.

At sight of the device the witch seemed struck with panic, and her grip relaxed long enough to give Gilman a chance to break it entirely.

[a] "Necronomicon".] *Necronomicon.* A, B, C, D, E
[b] clear] clearer E
[c] motions,] emotions, E
[d] gnawing,] gnawing E
[e] clangour] clangor C, E

He pulled the steel-like claws from his neck, and would have dragged the beldame over the edge of the gulf had not the claws received a fresh access of strength and closed in again. This time he resolved to reply in kind, and his own hands reached out for the creature's throat. Before she saw what he was doing he had the chain of the crucifix twisted about her neck, and a moment later he had tightened it enough to cut off her breath. During her last struggle he felt something bite at his ankle, and saw that Brown Jenkin had come to her aid. With one savage kick he sent the morbidity over the edge of the gulf and heard it whimper on some level far below.

Whether he had killed the ancient crone he did not know, but he let her rest on the floor where she had fallen. Then, as he turned away, he saw on the table a sight which nearly snapped the last thread of his reason. Brown Jenkin, tough of sinew and with four tiny hands of daemoniac[a] dexterity,[b] had been busy while the witch was throttling him, and his efforts had been in vain. What he had prevented the knife from doing to the victim's chest, the yellow fangs of the furry blasphemy had done to a wrist—and the bowl so lately on the floor stood full beside the small lifeless body.

In his dream-delirium[c] Gilman heard the hellish,[d] alien-rhythmed chant of the Sabbat coming from an infinite distance, and knew the black man must be there. Confused memories mixed themselves with his mathematics, and he believed his subconscious mind held the *angles* which he needed to guide him back to the normal world—[e]alone and unaided for the first time. He felt sure he was in the immemorially sealed loft above his own room, but whether he could ever escape through the slanting floor or the long-stopped[f] egress he doubted greatly. Besides, would not an escape from a dream-loft bring him merely into a dream-house—an abnormal projection of the actual place he sought? He was wholly bewildered as to the relation betwixt dream and reality in all his experiences.

[a] daemoniac] demoniac C, E
[b] dexterity,] dexterity D
[c] dream-delirium] dream delirium D
[d] hellish,] hellish B, C, D, E
[e] world—] world B, C, D, E
[f] long-stopped] long-stooped E

The passage through the vague abysses would be frightful, for the Walpurgis-rhythm would be vibrating, and at last he would have to hear that hitherto veiled[a] cosmic pulsing which he so mortally dreaded. Even now he could detect a low, monstrous shaking whose tempo he suspected all too well. At Sabbat-time it always mounted and reached through to the worlds to summon the initiate to nameless rites. Half the chants of the Sabbat were patterned on this faintly overheard pulsing which no earthly ear could endure in its unveiled spatial fulness.[b] Gilman wondered, too, whether he could trust his instinct[c] to take him back to the right part of space. How could he be sure he would not land on that green-litten hillside of a far planet, on the tessellated[d] terrace above the city of tentacled monsters somewhere beyond the galaxy,[e] or in the spiral black vortices of that ultimate void of Chaos wherein[f] reigns the mindless daemon-sultan[g] Azathoth?

Just before he made the plunge the violet light went out and left him in utter blackness. The witch—old Keziah—Nahab—that must have meant her death. And mixed with the distant chant of the Sabbat and the whimpers of Brown Jenkin in the gulf below he thought he heard another and wilder whine from unknown depths. Joe Mazurewicz[h]—the prayers against the Crawling Chaos now turning to an inexplicably triumphant shriek—worlds of sardonic actuality impinging on vortices of febrile dream—Iä! Shub-Niggurath! The Goat with a Thousand Young. . . .

They found Gilman on the floor of his queerly angled[i] old garret room long before dawn, for the terrible cry had brought Desrochers and Choynski and Dombrowski and Mazurewicz[j] at once, and had even wakened the soundly sleeping Elwood in his chair. He was alive,

---

[a] hitherto veiled] hitherto-veiled A, B, C, D, E
[b] fulness.] fullness. C, E
[c] instinct] instincts C, E
[d] tessellated] tesselated D
[e] galaxy,] galaxy E
[f] wherein] where B, C, D, E
[g] daemon-sultan] demon-sultan C, E
[h] Mazurewicz] Mazurewiez D
[i] queerly angled] queerly-angled A, B, C, D, E
[j] Mazurewicz] Mazurewiez D

and with open, staring eyes, but seemed largely unconscious. On his throat were the marks of murderous hands, and on his left ankle was a distressing rat-bite. His clothing was badly rumpled, and Joe's crucifix was missing. Elwood trembled, afraid even to speculate on[a] what new form his friend's sleep-walking had taken. Mazurewicz[b] seemed half-dazed[c] because of a "sign" he said he had had in response to his prayers, and he crossed himself frantically when the squealing and whimpering of a rat sounded from beyond the slanting partition.

When the dreamer was settled on his couch in Elwood's room they sent for Dr.[d] Malkowski—a local practitioner who would repeat no tales where they might prove embarrassing—and he gave Gilman two hypodermic injections which caused him to relax in something like natural drowsiness. During the day the patient regained consciousness at times and whispered his newest dream disjointedly to Elwood. It was a painful process, and at its very start brought out a fresh and disconcerting fact.

Gilman—whose ears had so lately possessed an abnormal sensitiveness—was now stone deaf.[e] Dr.[f] Malkowski, summoned again in haste, told Elwood that both ear-drums were ruptured, as if by the impact of some stupendous sound intense beyond all human conception or endurance. How such a sound could have been heard in the last few hours without arousing all the Miskatonic Valley was more than the honest physician could say.

Elwood wrote his part of the colloquy on paper, so that a fairly easy communication was maintained. Neither knew what to make of the whole chaotic business, and decided it would be better if they thought as little as possible about it. Both, though, agreed that they must leave this ancient and accursed house as soon as it could be arranged. Evening papers spoke of a police raid on some curious revellers in a ravine beyond Meadow Hill just before dawn, and mentioned that the white stone there was an object of age-long

[a] on] *om.* E
[b] Mazurewicz] Mazurewiez D
[c] half-dazed] half dazed C, E
[d] Dr.] Doctor C, E
[e] stone deaf.] stone-deaf. C, E
[f] Dr.] Doctor C, E

superstitious regard. Nobody had been caught, but among the scattering fugitives had been glimpsed a huge negro. In another column it was stated that no trace of the missing Ladislas Wolejko had been found.

The crowning horror came that very night. Elwood will never forget it, and was forced to stay out of college the rest of the term because of the resulting nervous breakdown. He had thought he heard rats in the partitions[a] all the evening, but paid little attention to them. Then, long after both he and Gilman had retired, the atrocious shrieking began. Elwood jumped up, turned on the lights,[b] and rushed over to his guest's couch. The occupant was emitting sounds of veritably inhuman nature, as if racked by some torment beyond description. He was writhing under the bedclothes, and a great red stain was beginning to appear on the blankets.

Elwood scarcely dared to touch him, but gradually the screaming and writhing subsided. By this time Dombrowski, Choynski, Desrochers, Mazurewicz,[c] and the top-floor lodger were all crowding into the doorway, and the landlord had sent his wife back to telephone for Dr.[d] Malkowski. Everybody shrieked when a large rat-like[e] form suddenly jumped out from beneath the ensanguined bedclothes and scuttled across the floor to a fresh, open hole close by. When the doctor arrived and began to pull down those frightful covers Walter Gilman was dead.

It would be barbarous to do more than suggest what had killed Gilman. There had been virtually a tunnel through his body—something had eaten his heart out. Dombrowski, frantic at the failure of his constant[f] rat-poisoning efforts, cast aside all thought of his lease and within a week had moved with all his older lodgers to a dingy but less ancient house in[g] Walnut Street. The worst thing for a while was keeping Joe Mazurewicz[h] quiet; for the brooding loomfixer[i] would

[a] partitions] partition E
[b] lights,] lights E
[c] Mazurewicz,] Mazurewiez, D
[d] Dr.] Doctor C, E
[e] rat-like] ratlike A, B, D
[f] constant] *om.* B, C, D, E
[g] in] on D
[h] Mazurewicz] Mazurewiez D
[i] loomfixer] loom-/fixer C; loom-fixer E

never stay sober, and was constantly whining and muttering about spectral and terrible things.

It seems that on that last hideous night Joe had stooped to look at the crimson rat-tracks which led from Gilman's couch to the nearby[a] hole. On the carpet they were very indistinct, but a piece of open flooring intervened between the carpet's edge and the base-board.[b] There Mazurewicz[c] had found something monstrous—or thought he had, for no one else could quite agree with him despite the undeniable queerness of the prints. The tracks on the flooring were certainly vastly unlike the average prints of a rat,[d] but even Choynski and Desrochers would not admit that they were like the prints of four tiny human hands.

The house was never rented again. As soon as Dombrowski left it the pall of its final desolation began to descend, for people shunned it both on account of its old reputation and because of the new foetid odour.[e] Perhaps the ex-landlord's rat-poison had worked after all, for not long after his departure the place became a neighbourhood[f] nuisance. Health officials traced the smell to the closed spaces above and beside the eastern garret room, and agreed that the number of dead rats must be enormous. They decided, however, that it was not worth their while to hew open and disinfect the long-sealed spaces; for the foetor[g] would soon be over, and the locality was not one which encouraged fastidious standards. Indeed, there were always vague local tales of unexplained stenches upstairs in the Witch House[h] just after May-Eve and Hallowmass. The neighbours grumblingly[i] acquiesced in the inertia—but the foetor[j] none the less formed an additional count against the place. Toward the last the house was condemned as a habitation by the building inspector.

---

[a] nearby] near-by C, E
[b] base-board.] baseboard. B, C, D, E
[c] Mazurewicz] Mazurewiez D
[d] rat,] rat E
[e] foetid odour.] fetid odor. C, E
[f] neighbourhood] neighborhood C, E
[g] foetor] fetor C, E
[h] Witch House] Witch-House B, C, D, E
[i] neighbours grumblingly] neighbours B, D; neighbors C, E
[j] foetor] fetor C, E

Gilman's dreams and their attendant circumstances have never been explained. Elwood, whose thoughts on the entire episode are sometimes almost maddening, came back to college the next autumn and[a] graduated in the following June. He found the spectral gossip of the town much diminished, and it is indeed a fact that—notwithstanding certain reports of a ghostly tittering in the deserted house which lasted almost as long as that edifice itself—no fresh appearances either of old[b] Keziah or of Brown Jenkin have been muttered of since Gilman's death. It is rather fortunate that Elwood was not in Arkham in that later year when certain events abruptly renewed the local whispers about elder horrors. Of course he heard about the matter afterward and suffered untold torments of black and bewildered speculation; but even that was not as bad as actual nearness and several possible sights would have been.

In March, 1931, a gale wrecked the roof and great chimney of the vacant Witch House,[c] so that a chaos of crumbling bricks, blackened, moss-grown shingles, and rotting planks and timbers crashed down into the loft and broke through the floor beneath. The whole attic story[d] was choked with debris from above, but no one took the trouble to touch the mess before the inevitable razing of the decrepit structure. That ultimate step came in the following December, and it was when Gilman's old room was cleared out by reluctant, apprehensive workmen that the gossip began.

Among the rubbish which had crashed through the ancient slanting ceiling were several things which made the workmen pause and call in the police. Later the police in turn called in the coroner and several professors from the university. There were bones—badly[e] crushed and splintered, but clearly recognisable[f] as human—whose manifestly modern date conflicted puzzlingly with the remote period at which their only possible lurking-place,[g] the low, slant-floored loft

[a] and] and was E
[b] old] A?, D; Old C, E [Old *apparently changed to* old *in* B]
[c] Witch House,] Witch-House, B, C, D, E
[d] story] storey A
[e] bones—badly] bones-/badly B; bones badly D
[f] recognisable] recognizable B, C, D, E
[g] lurking-place,] lurking place, C, E

overhead, had supposedly been sealed from all human access. The coroner's physician decided that some belonged to a small child, while certain others—found mixed with shreds of rotten brownish cloth—belonged to a rather undersized, bent female of advanced years. Careful sifting of debris also disclosed many tiny bones of rats caught in the collapse, as well as older rat-bones gnawed by small fangs in a fashion now and then highly productive of controversy and reflection.

Other objects found included the mingled fragments of many books and papers, together with a yellowish dust left from the total disintegration of still older books and papers. All, without exception, appeared to deal with black magic in its most advanced and horrible forms; and the evidently recent date of certain items is still a mystery as unsolved as that of the modern human bones. An even greater mystery is the absolute homogeneity of the crabbed, archaic writing found on a wide range of papers whose conditions and watermarks suggest age differences of at least 150 to 200[a] years. To some, though, the greatest mystery of all is the variety of utterly inexplicable objects—objects whose shapes, materials, types of workmanship, and purposes baffle all conjecture—found scattered amidst the wreckage in evidently diverse states of injury. One of these things—which excited several Miskatonic professors profoundly—is a badly damaged monstrosity plainly resembling the strange image which Gilman gave to the college museum, save that it is larger,[b] wrought of some peculiar bluish stone instead of metal, and possessed of a singularly angled pedestal with undecipherable hieroglyphics.

Archaeologists[c] and anthropologists are still trying to explain the bizarre designs chased on a crushed bowl of light metal whose inner side bore ominous brownish stains when found. Foreigners and credulous grandmothers are equally garrulous about the modern nickel crucifix with broken chain mixed in the rubbish and shiveringly identified by Joe Mazurewicz[d] as that which he had given poor Gilman many years before. Some believe this crucifix was dragged up to the sealed loft by rats, while others think it must have been on the floor in

---

[a] 150 to 200] one hundred fifty to two hundred E
[b] larger,] large, E
[c] Archaeologists] Archeologists C, E
[d] Mazurewicz] Mazurewiez D

some corner of Gilman's old room all[a] the time. Still others, including Joe himself, have theories too wild and fantastic for sober credence.

When the slanting wall of Gilman's room was torn out, the once sealed triangular space between that partition and the house's north wall was found to contain much less structural debris, even in proportion to its size, than the room itself; though it had a ghastly layer of older materials which paralysed[b] the wreckers with horror. In brief, the floor was a veritable ossuary of the bones of small children—some fairly modern, but others extending back in infinite gradations to a period so remote that crumbling was almost complete. On this deep bony layer rested a knife of great size, obvious antiquity, and grotesque, ornate, and exotic design—above which the debris was piled.

In the midst of this debris, wedged between a fallen plank and a cluster of cemented bricks from the ruined chimney, was an object destined to cause more bafflement, veiled fright, and openly superstitious talk in Arkham than anything else discovered in the haunted and accursed building. This object was the partly crushed skeleton of a huge,[c] diseased rat, whose abnormalities of form are still a topic of debate and source of singular reticence among the members of Miskatonic's department of comparative anatomy. Very little concerning this skeleton has leaked out, but the workmen who found it whisper in shocked tones about the long, brownish hairs with which it was associated.

The bones of the tiny paws, it is rumoured,[d] imply prehensile characteristics more typical of a diminutive monkey than of a rat;[e] while the small skull with its savage yellow fangs is of the utmost anomalousness, appearing from certain angles like a miniature, monstrously degraded parody of a human skull. The workmen crossed themselves in fright when they came upon this blasphemy, but later burned candles of gratitude in St. Stanislaus' Church because of the shrill, ghostly tittering they felt they would never hear again.

[a] all] at E
[b] paralysed] paralyzed B, C, D, E
[c] huge,] huge C, E
[d] rumoured,] rumored, C, E
[e] rat;] rat, B, C, D, E

Through the Gates of the Silver Key

(with E. Hoffmann Price)

I.

In a vast room hung with strangely figured arras and carpeted with Bokhara[a] rugs of impressive age and workmanship[b] four men were sitting around a document-strown[c] table. From the far corners, where odd tripods of wrought-iron[d] were now and then replenished by an incredibly aged negro[e] in sombre livery,[f] came the hypnotic fumes

Editor's Note: HPL's A.Ms., a pencil draft, survives. He presumably sent this to his collaborator, E. Hoffmann Price, who prepared a T.Ms that is quite inaccurate, containing all kinds of stenographic errors. Price sent the T.Ms. to HPL with marginal comments, recommending that he change some phrases (most related to theosophical terms HPL had cited in the text). HPL has done so, although he has failed to correct the many errors in Price's T.Ms. (it appears that Price did not immediately return HPL's A.Ms., so that HPL did not have it at hand when checking the T.Ms.). Price must have prepared a new T.Ms. and sent it to *Weird Tales,* where—after being initially rejected—it was accepted and published in the July 1934 issue. A case could be made that it was Price's prerogative as collaborator to make the deliberate changes that he made in HPL's text; but I feel it more relevant for the purposes of this edition to present HPL's text as he himself initially wrote it, incorporating the revisions HPL made based on Price's marginal comments. I have also restored the manuscript reading of "Dholes" (which I had previously corrected to "bholes"), as I now believe these are not the same as the entities cited in *The Dream-Quest of Unknown Kadath.*

Texts: A = A.Ms. (JHL); B = T.Ms. (by E. Hoffmann Price) (JHL); B[c] = HPL's corrections to T.Ms.; C = *Weird Tales* 24, No. 1 (July 1934): 60–85; D = *At the Mountains of Madness and Other Novels* (Arkham House, 1964), 398–432. Copy-text: A (with a few readings from B[c]).

[a] Bokhara] Boukhara B, C, D
[b] workmanship] workmanship, B, C, D
[c] document-strown] document-strewn D
[d] wrought-iron] wrought iron C, D
[e] negro] Negro D
[f] sombre livery,] robe and turban, A B[c]; somber livery, C, D

of olibanum; while in a deep niche on one side there ticked a curious[a] coffin-shaped clock whose dial bore baffling hieroglyphs and whose four hands did not move in consonance with any time system known on this planet. It was a singular and disturbing room, but well fitted to the business now[b] at hand. For here,[c] in the New Orleans home of this continent's greatest mystic, mathematician,[d] and orientalist, there was being settled at last the estate of a scarcely less great mystic, scholar, author,[e] and dreamer who had vanished from the face of the earth four years before.

Randolph Carter, who had all his life sought to escape from the tedium and limitations of waking reality in the beckoning vistas of dreams and fabled avenues of other dimensions, disappeared from the sight of man on the seventh[f] of October, 1928, at the age of fifty-four.[g] His career had been a strange and lonely one, and there were those who inferred from his curious novels many episodes more bizarre than any in his recorded history. His association with Harley Warren, the South Carolina mystic whose studies in the primal Naacal language of the Himalayan priests had led to such outrageous conclusions, had been close. Indeed, it was he who—one mist-clad,[h] terrible night in an ancient graveyard—had seen Warren descend into a dank and nitrous vault, never to emerge. Carter lived in Boston, but it was from the wild, haunted hills behind hoary and witch-accursed Arkham that all his forbears[i] had come. And it was amid those[j] ancient, cryptically brooding hills that he had ultimately vanished.

His old servant[k] Parks—who died early in 1930—had spoken of the strangely aromatic and hideously carven box he had found in the

[a] curious] curious, B, C, D
[b] now] then B, C, D
[c] here,] there, B, C, D
[d] mathematician,] mathematician B, C, D
[e] author,] author B, C, D
[f] seventh] 7th A, B
[g] fifty-four.] 54. A, B
[h] mist-clad,] mist-mad, B, C, D
[i] forbears] forebears C, D
[j] those] these C, D
[k] servant] servant, B, C, D

attic, and of the undecipherable parchments and queerly figured silver key which that box had contained;[a] matters of which Carter had also written to others. Carter, he said, had told him that this key had come down from his ancestors, and that it would help him to unlock the gate[b] to his lost boyhood, and to strange dimensions and fantastic realms which he had hitherto visited only in vague, brief,[c] and elusive dreams. Then one day Carter took the box and its contents and rode away in his car, never to return.

Later on[d] people found the car at the side of an old, grass-grown road in the hills behind crumbling Arkham—the hills where Carter's forbears[e] had once dwelt, and where the ruined cellar of the great Carter homestead still gaped to the sky. It was in a grove of tall elms nearby[f] that another of the Carters had mysteriously vanished in 1781, and not far away was the half-rotted cottage where Goody Fowler the witch[g] had brewed her ominous potions still earlier. The region had been settled in 1692 by fugitives from the witchcraft trials in Salem, and even now it bore a name for vaguely ominous things scarcely to be envisaged. Edmund Carter had fled from the shadow of Gallows Hill just in time, and the tales of his sorceries were many. Now, it seemed, his lone descendant had gone somewhere to join him.[h]

In the car they found the hideously carved box of fragrant wood, and the parchment which no man could read. The Silver Key[i] was gone— presumably with Carter. Further than that there was no certain clue. Detectives from Boston said that the fallen timbers of the old Carter place seemed oddly disturbed, and somebody found a handkerchief on the rock-ridged, sinisterly wooded slope behind the ruins near the dreaded cave called the "Snake-Den".[j] It was then that the country legends about the

---

[a] contained;] contained: B, C, D
[b] gate] gates B, C, D
[c] brief,] brief C
[d] on] on, B, C, D
[e] forbears] forebears C, D
[f] nearby] near by C, D
[g] Fowler the witch] Fowler, the witch, B, C, D
[h] him.] him! B, C, D
[i] Silver Key] silver key C, D
[j] "Snake-Den".] "Snake Den". B; Snake Den. ¶ C, D

Snake-Den[a] gained a new vitality. Farmers whispered of the blasphemous uses to which old Edmund Carter the wizard had put that horrible grotto, and added later tales about the fondness which Randolph Carter himself had had for it when a boy. In Carter's boyhood the venerable gambrel-roofed homestead was still standing and tenanted by his great-uncle Christopher. He had visited there often, and had talked singularly about the Snake-Den.[b] People remembered what he had said about a deep fissure and an unknown inner cave beyond, and speculated on the change he had shewn[c] after spending one whole memorable day in the cavern when he was nine. That was in October, too—and ever after that he had seemed to have an uncanny knack at prophesying future events.

It had rained late in the night that Carter vanished, and no one was quite able to trace his footprints from the car. Inside the Snake-Den[d] all was amorphous liquid mud[e] owing to[f] copious seepage. Only the ignorant rustics whispered about the prints they thought they spied where the great elms overhang the road, and on the sinister hillside near the Snake-Den,[g] where the handkerchief was found. Who could pay attention to whispers that spoke of stubby little tracks like those which Randolph Carter's square-toed boots made when he was a small boy? It was as crazy a notion as that other whisper—that the tracks of old Benijah Corey's peculiar heel-less[h] boots had met the stubby little tracks in the road. Old Benijah had been the Carters' hired man when Randolph was young—[i]but he had died thirty years ago.

It must have been these whispers—plus Carter's own statement to Parks and others that the queerly arabesqued Silver Key[j] would help

---

[a] Snake-Den] Snake Den B, C, D
[b] Snake-Den.] Snake Den. B, C, D
[c] shewn] shown B, C, D
[d] Snake-Den] Snake Den B, C, D
[e] mud] mud, C, D
[f] to] to the B, C, D
[g] Snake-Den,] Snake Den, B, C, D
[h] heel-less] heelless C, D
[i] young—] young; B, C, D
[j] Silver Key] silver key C, D

him unlock the gate[a] of his lost boyhood—which caused a number of mystical students to declare that the missing man had actually doubled back on the trail of time and returned through forty-five[b] years to that other October day in 1883 when he had stayed in the Snake-Den[c] as a small boy. When he came out that night, they argued, he had somehow made the whole trip to 1928 and back—[d]for did he not thereafter know of things which were to happen later? And yet he had never spoken of anything to happen after 1928.

One student—an elderly eccentric of Providence, Rhode Island, who had enjoyed a long and close correspondence with Carter—had a still more elaborate theory, and believed that Carter had not only returned to boyhood, but achieved a further liberation, roving at will through the prismatic vistas of boyhood dream. After a strange vision this man published a tale of Carter's vanishing,[e] in which he hinted that the lost one now reigned as king on the opal throne of Ilek-Vad, that fabulous town of turrets atop the hollow cliffs of glass overlooking the twilight sea wherein the bearded and finny Gnorri build their singular labyrinths.

It was this old man, Ward Phillips, who pleaded most loudly against the apportionment of Carter's estate to his heirs—all distant cousins—on the ground that he was still alive in another time-dimension and might well return some day. Against him was arrayed the legal talent of one of the cousins, Ernest B.[f] Aspinwall of Chicago, a man ten years Carter's senior, but keen as a youth in forensic battles. For four years the contest had raged, but now the time for apportionment had come, and this vast, strange room in New Orleans was to be the scene of the arrangements.

It was the home of Carter's literary and financial executor—the distinguished Creole student of mysteries and Eastern antiquities, Etienne-Laurent de Marigny. Carter had met de Marigny during the war, when they both served in the French Foreign Legion, and had at

---

[a] gate] gates A, B, C, D
[b] forty-five] 45 A
[c] Snake-Den] Snake Den B, C, D
[d] back—] back; B, C, D
[e] vanishing,] vanishing B, C, D
[f] B.] K. A, B, C, D

once cleaved to him because of their similar tastes and outlook. When, on a memorable joint furlough, the learned young Creole had taken the wistful Boston dreamer to Bayonne, in the south of France, and had shewn[a] him certain terrible secrets in the nighted and immemorial crypts that burrow beneath that brooding, aeon-weighted[b] city, the friendship was for ever[c] sealed. Carter's will had named de Marigny as executor, and now that vivid[d] scholar was reluctantly presiding over the settlement of the estate. It was sad work for him, for like the old Rhode-Islander[e] he did not believe that Carter was dead. But what weight have[f] the dreams of mystics against the harsh wisdom of the world?

Around the table in that strange room in the old French quarter[g] sat the men who claimed an interest in the proceedings. There had been the usual legal advertisements of the conference in papers wherever Carter[h] heirs were thought to live,[i] yet only four now sat listening to the abnormal ticking of that coffin-shaped clock which told no earthly time, and to the bubbling of the courtyard fountain beyond half-curtained, fanlighted[j] windows. As the hours wore on[k] the faces of the four were half-shrouded[l] in the curling fumes from the tripods, which, piled recklessly with fuel, seemed to need less and less attention from the[m] silently gliding and increasingly nervous old negro.[n]

There was Etienne de Marigny himself—slim, dark, handsome, moustached,[o] and still young. Aspinwall, representing the heirs, was white-haired, apoplectic-faced, side-whiskered, and portly. Phillips, the

---

[a] shewn] shown C, D
[b] aeon-weighted] eon-weighted C, D
[c] for ever] forever A, B; for-/ever D
[d] vivid] avid B, C, D
[e] Rhode-Islander] Rhode Islander B, C, D
[f] have] had D
[g] quarter] Quarter B, C, D
[h] Carter] Carter's B, C, D
[i] live,] live; C; live: D
[j] fanlighted] fan-lighted C, D
[k] on] on, B, C, D
[l] half-shrouded] half shrouded B, C, D
[m] the] the turbaned, A, B^c
[n] negro.] Negro. D
[o] moustached,] mustached, C, D

Providence mystic, was lean, grey,[a] long-nosed, clean-shaven, and stoop-shouldered. The fourth man was non-committal in age—lean, and[b] with a dark, bearded, singularly immobile face of very regular contour, bound with the turban of a high-caste Brahmin[c] and having night-black, burning, almost irisless eyes which seemed to gaze out from a vast distance behind the features. He had announced himself as the Swami Chandraputra, an adept from Benares[d] with important information to give; and both de Marigny and Phillips—who had corresponded with him—had been quick to recognise[e] the genuineness of his mystical pretensions. His speech had an oddly forced, hollow, metallic quality, as if the use of English taxed his vocal apparatus; yet his language was as easy, correct,[f] and idiomatic as any native Anglo-Saxon's. In general attire he was the normal European civilian, but his loose clothes sat peculiarly badly on him, while his bushy black beard, Eastern turban, and large[g] white mittens gave him an air of exotic eccentricity.

De Marigny, fingering the parchment found in Carter's car, was speaking.

"No, I have not been able to make anything of the parchment. Mr. Phillips, here, also gives it up. Col.[h] Churchward declares it is not Naacal, and it looks nothing at all like the hieroglyphs[i] on that Easter Island wooden club.[j] The carvings on that box, though, do strongly suggest Easter Island images. The nearest thing I can recall to these parchment characters—notice how all the letters seem to hang down from horizontal word-bars—is the writing in a book poor Harley Warren once had. It came from India while Carter and I were visiting him in 1919, and he never would tell us anything about it. Said[k] it would

---

[a] grey,] gray, B, C, D
[b] and] *om.* B, C, D
[c] Brahmin] Brahman C, D
[d] Benares] Benares, B, C, D
[e] recognise] recognize B, C, D
[f] correct,] correct A, B, C, D
[g] large] large, B, C, D
[h] Col.] Colonel B, C, D
[i] hieroglyphs] hieroglyphics C, D
[j] wooden club.] war-club. B, C, D
[k] it. Said] it—said C, D

be better if we didn't know, and hinted that it might have come originally from some place other than the earth.[a] He took it with him in December[b] when he went down into the vault in that old graveyard— but neither he nor the book ever came to the surface again. Some time ago I sent our friend here—the Swami Chandraputra—a memory-sketch of some of those letters, and also a photostatic copy of the Carter parchment. He believes he may be able to shed light on them after certain references and consultations.

"But the key—Carter sent me a photograph of that. Its curious arabesques were not letters, but seem to have belonged to the same culture-tradition as the hieroglyphs on[c] the parchment. Carter always spoke of being on the point of solving the mystery, though he never gave details. Once he grew almost poetic about the whole business. That antique Silver Key,[d] he said, would unlock the successive doors that bar our free march down the mighty corridors of space and time to the very Border which no man has crossed since Shaddad with his terrific genius built and concealed in the sands of Arabia Petraea the prodigious domes and uncounted minarets of thousand-pillared Irem. Half-starved dervishes[e]—wrote Carter—and thirst-crazed nomads have returned to tell of that monumental portal, and of the Hand[f] that is sculptured above the keystone of the arch, but no man has passed and returned[g] to say that his footprints on the garnet-strown[h] sands within bear witness to his visit. The key, he surmised, was that for which the Cyclopean[i] sculptured Hand[j] vainly grasps.

"Why Carter didn't take the parchment as well as the key, we cannot[k] say. Perhaps he forgot it—or perhaps he forbore to take it through

[a] earth.] Earth. B, C, D
[b] December] December, B, C, D
[c] the hieroglyphs on] *om.* B, C, D
[d] Silver Key,] silver key, C, D
[e] dervishes] darvishes B, C
[f] Hand] hand C, D
[g] returned] retraced his steps B, C, D
[h] garnet-strown] garnet-strewn D
[i] Cyclopean] cyclopean A, B, C, D
[j] Hand] hand C, D
[k] cannot] can not B, C, D

recollection of one who had taken a book of like characters into a vault and never returned. Or perhaps it was really immaterial to what he wished to do."

As de Marigny paused, old Mr. Phillips spoke in a harsh, shrill voice.

"We can know of Randolph Carter's wandering only what we dream. I have been to many strange places in dreams, and have heard many strange and significant things in Ulthar, beyond the river[a] Skai. It does not appear that the parchment was needed, for certainly Carter reëntered[b] the world of his boyhood dreams, and is now a king in Ilek-Vad."

Mr. Aspinwall grew doubly apoplectic-looking as he sputtered.[c]

"Can't somebody shut that old fool up? We've had enough of these moonings. The problem is to divide the property, and it's about time we got to it."

For the first time Swami Chandraputra spoke in his queerly alien voice.

"Gentlemen, there is more to this matter than you think. Mr. Aspinwall does not do well to laugh at the evidence of dreams. Mr. Phillips has taken an incomplete view—perhaps because he has not dreamed enough. I, myself, have done much dreaming—we[d] in India have always done that, just as all the Carters seem to have done it. You, Mr. Aspinwall, as a maternal cousin, are naturally not a Carter. My own dreams, and certain other sources of information, have told me a great deal which you still find obscure. For example, Randolph Carter forgot that parchment—which[e] he couldn't then decipher—[f]yet it would have been well for him had he remembered to take it. You see, I have really learned pretty much what happened to Carter after he left his car with the Silver Key[g] at sunset on that seventh[h] of October[i] four years ago."

[a] river] River A, B, C, D
[b] reëntered] reentered B, D; re-/entered C
[c] sputtered. ¶] sputtered: B, C, D
[d] dreaming—we] dreaming. We B, C, D
[e] parchment—] parchment C, D
[f] then decipher—] decipher— B, C, D
[g] Slver Key] silver key C, D
[h] seventh] 7th A, B
[i] October] October, B, C, D

Aspinwall audibly sneered, but the others sat up with heightened interest. The smoke from the tripods increased, and the crazy ticking of that coffin-shaped clock seemed to fall into bizarre patterns like the dots and dashes of some alien and insoluble telegraph message from outer space. The Hindoo leaned back, half closed his eyes, and continued in that oddly laboured[a] yet idiomatic voice,[b] while before his audience there began to float a picture of what had happened to Randolph Carter.

II.

The hills behind[c] Arkham are full of a strange magic—something, perhaps, which the old wizard Edmund Carter called down from the stars and up from the crypts of nether earth when he fled there from Salem in 1692. As soon as Randolph Carter was back among them he knew that he was close to one of the gates which a few audacious, abhorred,[d] and alien-souled men have blasted through titan walls betwixt the world and the outside absolute. Here, he felt, and on this day of the year, he could carry out with success the message he had deciphered months before from the arabesques of that tarnished and incredibly ancient Silver Key.[e] He knew now how it must be rotated,[f] how it must be held up to the setting sun, and what syllables of ceremony must be intoned into the void at the ninth and last turning. In a spot as close to a dark polarity and induced gate as this, it could not fail in its primary function.[g] Certainly, he would rest that night in the lost boyhood for which he had never ceased to mourn.

He got out of the car with the key in his pocket, walking uphill[h] deeper and deeper into the shadowy core of that brooding, haunted countryside of winding road, vine-grown stone wall, black woodland,

[a] laboured] labored C, D
[b] voice,] speech, B, C, D
[c] behind] beyond B, C, D
[d] abhorred,] abhorred A, B, C, D
[e] Silver Key.] silver key. C, D
[f] rotated,] rotated, and B, C, D
[g] function.] functions. B, C, D
[h] uphill] up-hill C, D

gnarled, neglected orchard, gaping-windowed, deserted farmhouse, and nameless ruin. At the sunset hour, when the distant spires of Kingsport gleamed in the ruddy blaze, he took out the key and made the needed turnings and intonations. Only later did he realise[a] how soon the ritual had taken effect.

Then in the deepening twilight he had heard a voice out of the past.[b] Old Benijah Corey, his great-uncle's hired man. Had not old Benijah been dead for thirty years? Thirty years before when?[c] What was time? Where had he been? Why was it strange that Benijah should be calling him on this seventh[d] of October, 1883? Was he not out later than Aunt Martha had told him to stay? What was this key in his blouse pocket, where his little telescope—given him by his father on his ninth birthday[e] two months before—ought to be? Had he found it in the attic at home? Would it unlock the mystic pylon which his sharp eye had traced amidst the jagged rocks at the back of that inner cave behind the Snake-Den[f] on the hill? That was the place they always coupled with old Edmund Carter the wizard. People wouldn't go there, and nobody but him had ever noticed or squirmed through the root-choked fissure to that great black inner chamber with the pylon. Whose hands had carved that hint of a pylon out of the living rock? Old Wizard Edmund's—or *others* that he had conjured up and commanded?[g] That evening little Randolph ate supper with Uncle Chris and Aunt Martha in the old gambrel-roofed farmhouse.

Next morning he was up early,[h] and out through the twisted-boughed apple orchard to the upper timber-lot where the mouth of the Snake-Den[i] lurked black and forbidding amongst grotesque, overnourished[j] oaks. A nameless expectancy was upon him, and he did

[a] realise] realize B, C, D
[b] past.] past: C, D
[c] when?] *when?* B, C; *when.* D
[d] seventh] 7th A, B
[e] birthday] birthday, B, C, D
[f] Snake-Den] Snake Den C, D
[g] commanded?] commanded? ¶ B, C, D
[h] early,] early B, C, D
[i] Snake-Den] Snake Den C, D
[j] overnourished] over-nourished B; over-/nourished C

not even notice the loss of his handkerchief as he fumbled in his blouse pocket to see if the queer Silver Key[a] was safe. He crawled through the dark orifice with tense, adventurous assurance, lighting his way with matches taken from the sitting-room. In another moment he had wriggled through the root-choked fissure at the farther end, and was in the vast, unknown inner grotto whose ultimate rock wall seemed half like a monstrous and consciously shapen pylon. Before that dank, dripping wall he stood silent and awestruck, lighting one match after another as he gazed. Was that stony bulge above the keystone of the imagined arch really a gigantic sculptured hand? Then he drew forth the Silver Key,[b] and made motions and intonations whose source he could only dimly remember. Was anything forgotten? He knew only that he wished to cross the barrier to the untrammelled land of his dreams and the gulfs where all dimensions dissolve[c] in the absolute.

III.

What happened then is scarcely to be described in words. It is full of those paradoxes, contradictions,[d] and anomalies which have no place in waking life, but which fill our more fantastic dreams,[e] and are taken as matters of course till we return to our narrow, rigid, objective world of limited causation and tri-dimensional logic. As the Hindoo continued his tale, he had difficulty in avoiding what seemed—even more than the notion of a man transferred through the years to boyhood—an air of trivial, puerile extravagance. Mr. Aspinwall, in disgust, gave an apoplectic snort and virtually stopped listening.

For the rite of the Silver Key,[f] as practiced[g] by Randolph Carter in that black, haunted cave within a cave, did not prove unavailing. From the first gesture and syllable an aura of strange, awesome mutation was apparent—a sense of incalculable disturbance and confusion in time

[a] Silver Key] silver key C, D
[b] Silver Key,] silver key, C; silver key D
[c] dissolve] dissolved B, C, D
[d] contradictions,] contradictions C, D
[e] dreams,] dreams B, C, D
[f] Silver Key,] silver key, C, D
[g] practiced] practised C

and space, yet one which held no hint of what we recognise[a] as motion and duration. Imperceptibly, such things as age and location ceased to have any significance whatever. The day before, Randolph Carter had miraculously leaped a gulf of years. Now there was no distinction between boy and man. There was only the entity Randolph Carter, with a certain store of images which had lost all connexion[b] with terrestrial scenes and circumstances of acquisition. A moment before, there had been an inner cave with vague suggestions of a monstrous arch and gigantic sculptured hand on the farther wall. Now there was neither cave nor absence of cave; neither wall nor absence of wall. There was only a flux of impressions not so much visual as cerebral, amidst which the entity that was Randolph Carter experienced perceptions or registrations of all that his mind revolved on, yet without any clear consciousness of the way in which he received them.

By the time the rite was over[c] Carter knew that he was in no region whose place could be told by earth's[d] geographers, and in no age whose date history could fix. For[e] the nature of what was happening was not wholly unfamiliar to him. There were hints of it in the cryptical Pnakotic fragments, and a whole chapter in the forbidden "Necronomicon"[f] of the mad Arab Abdul Alhazred[g] had taken on significance when he had deciphered the designs graven on the Silver Key.[h] A gate had been unlocked—not indeed[i] the Ultimate Gate, but one leading from earth and time to that extension of earth[j] which is outside time, and from which in turn the Ultimate Gate leads fearsomely and perilously to the Last Void which is outside all earths, all universes, and all matter.

There would be a Guide—and a very terrible one; a Guide who

[a] recognise] recognize B, C, D
[b] connexion] connection B, C, D
[c] over] over, B, C, D
[d] earth's] Earth's B, C, D
[e] fix. For] fix; for C, D
[f] "Necronomicon"] *Necronomicon* A, B, C, D
[g] Arab . . . Alhazred] Arab, . . . Alhazred, C, D
[h] Silver Key.] silver key. C, D
[i] not indeed] not, indeed, B, C, D
[j] earth . . . earth] Earth . . . Earth B, C, D

had been an entity of earth[a] millions of years before, when man was undreamed of, and when forgotten shapes moved on a steaming planet building strange cities among whose last, crumbling ruins the earliest[b] mammals were to play. Carter remembered what the monstrous "Necronomicon"[c] had vaguely and disconcertingly adumbrated concerning that Guide.[d]

"And while there are those," the mad Arab had written, "who have dared to seek glimpses beyond the Veil, and to accept HIM as a Guide,[e] they would have been more prudent had they avoided commerce with HIM; for it is written in the Book of Thoth how terrific is the price of a single glimpse. Nor may those who pass ever return, for in the Vastnesses[f] transcending our world are Shapes[g] of darkness that seize and bind. The Affair that shambleth about in the night, the Evil[h] that defieth the Elder Sign, the Herd that stand watch at the secret portal each tomb is known to have,[i] and that thrive on that which groweth out of the tenants within—[j]all these Blacknesses are lesser than HE Who[k] guardeth the Gateway; HE Who[l] will guide the rash one beyond all the worlds into the Abyss of unnamable Devourers.[m] For HE[n] is 'UMR AT-TAWIL, the Most Ancient One, which the scribe rendereth as THE PROLONGED OF LIFE."[o]

Memory and imagination shaped dim half-pictures with uncertain outlines amidst the seething chaos, but Carter knew that they were of memory and imagination only. Yet he felt that it was not chance which

[a] earth] Earth B, C, D
[b] earliest] first B, C, D
[c] "Necronomicon"] *Necronomicon* A, B, C, D
[d] Guide.] Guide: B, C, D
[e] as a Guide,] *as guide,* B, C, D
[f] Vastnesses] *vastnesses* B, C, D
[g] Shapes] *shapes* B, C, D
[h] Evil] *evil* B, C, D
[i] have,] *have* D
[j] within—] *thereof:*— B, C, D
[k] Who] *WHO* B, C, D
[l] Gateway; . . . Who] *Gateway:* . . . *WHO* B, C, D
[m] Devourers.] *devourers.* B, C, D
[n] HE] *He* D
[o] "And . . . LIFE."] *"And . . . LIFE."* B, C, D

built these things in his consciousness, but rather some vast reality, ineffable and undimensioned, which surrounded him and strove to translate itself into the only symbols he was capable of grasping. For no mind of earth[a] may grasp the extensions of shape which interweave in the oblique gulfs outside time and the dimensions we know.

There floated before Carter a cloudy pageantry of shapes and scenes which he somehow linked with earth's[b] primal, aeon-forgotten[c] past. Monstrous living things moved deliberately through vistas of fantastic handiwork that no sane dream ever held, and landscapes bore incredible vegetation and cliffs and mountains and masonry of no human pattern. There were cities under the sea, and denizens thereof; and towers in great deserts where globes and cylinders and nameless winged entities shot off into space[d] or hurtled down out of space. All this Carter grasped, though the images bore no fixed relation to one another or to him. He himself had no stable form or position, but only such shifting hints of form and position as his whirling fancy supplied.

He had wished to find the enchanted regions of his boyhood dreams, where galleys sail up the river Oukranos past the gilded spires of Thran, and elephant caravans tramp through perfumed jungles in Kled[e] beyond forgotten palaces with veined ivory columns that sleep lovely and unbroken under the moon. Now, intoxicated with wider visions, he scarcely knew what he sought. Thoughts of infinite and blasphemous daring rose in his mind, and he knew he would face the dreaded Guide without fear, asking monstrous and terrible things of him.

All at once the pageant of impressions seemed to achieve a vague kind of stabilisation.[f] There were great masses of towering stone, carven into alien and incomprehensible designs and disposed according to the laws of some unknown, inverse geometry. Light filtered down from a sky of no assignable colour[g] in baffling, contradictory directions, and played almost sentiently over what seemed to be a curved line of

[a] earth] Earth B, C, D
[b] earth's] Earth's B, C, D
[c] aeon-forgotten] eon-forgotten C, D
[d] space] space, B, C, D
[e] Kled] Kled, B, C, D
[f] stabilisation.] stabilization. B, C, D
[g] colour] color C, D

gigantic hieroglyphed pedestals more hexagonal than otherwise[a] and surmounted by cloaked, ill-defined Shapes.[b]

There was another Shape,[c] too, which occupied no pedestal, but which seemed to glide or float over the cloudy, floor-like lower level. It was not exactly permanent in outline, but held transient suggestions of something remotely preceding or paralleling the human form, though half as large again as an ordinary man. It seemed to be heavily cloaked, like the Shapes[d] on the pedestals, with some neutral-coloured[e] fabric; and Carter could not detect any eye-holes through which it might gaze. Probably it did not need to gaze, for it seemed to belong to an order of being[f] far outside the merely physical in organisation[g] and faculties.

A moment later Carter knew that this was so, for the Shape had spoken to his mind without sound or language. And though the name it uttered was a dreaded and terrible one, Randolph Carter did not flinch in fear. Instead, he spoke back, equally without sound or language, and made those obeisances which the hideous "Necronomicon"[h] had taught him to make. For this Shape[i] was nothing less than that which all the world has feared since Lomar[j] rose out of the sea[k] and the Winged Ones[l] came to earth[m] to teach the Elder Lore to man. It was indeed the frightful Guide and Guardian of the Gate—'Umr at-Tawil,[n] the ancient one, which the scribe rendereth the Prolonged of Life.[o]

The Guide knew, as he knew all things, of Carter's quest and coming, and that this seeker of dreams and secrets stood before him

[a] otherwise] otherwise, B, C, D
[b] Shapes.] shapes. B, C, D
[c] Shape,] shape, B, C, D
[d] Shapes] shapes B, C, D
[e] neutral-coloured] neutral-colored C, D
[f] being] beings B, C, D
[g] organisation] organization B, C, D
[h] "Necronomicon"] *Necronomicon* A, B, C, D
[i] Shape] shape B, C, D
[j] Lomar] Shalmali A, B[c]
[k] sea] sea, B, C, D
[l] Winged Ones] Lords of Venus A; Children of the Fire Mist B[c], C, D
[m] earth] Earth B, C, D
[n] 'Umr at-Tawil,] 'Umr-at-Tawil, A; 'UMR AT TAWIL, B; 'UMR AT-TAWIL, C, D
[o] Prolonged of Life.] PROLONGED OF LIFE. B, C, D

unafraid. There was no horror or malignity in what he radiated, and Carter wondered for a moment whether the mad Arab's terrific blasphemous hints, and extracts from the Book of Thoth, might not have come[a] from envy and a baffled wish to do what was now about to be done. Or perhaps the Guide reserved his horror and malignity for those who feared. As the radiations continued, Carter mentally[b] interpreted them in the form of words.

"I am indeed that Most Ancient One," said the Guide, "of whom you know. We have awaited you—the Ancient Ones and I. You are welcome, even though long delayed. You have the Key,[c] and have unlocked the First Gate. Now the Ultimate Gate is ready for your trial. If you fear, you need not advance. You may still go back unharmed[d] the way you came. But if you choose to advance . . ."[e]

The pause was ominous, but the radiations continued to be friendly. Carter hesitated not a moment, for a burning curiosity drove him on.

"I will advance," he radiated back, "and I accept you as my Guide."

At this reply the Guide seemed to make a sign by certain motions of his robe which may or may not have involved the lifting of an arm or some homologous member. A second sign followed, and from his well-learnt[f] lore Carter knew that he was at last very close to the Ultimate Gate. The light now changed to another inexplicable colour,[g] and the Shapes[h] on the quasi-hexagonal pedestals became more clearly defined. As they sat more erect, their outlines became more like those of men, though Carter knew that they could not be men. Upon their cloaked heads there now seemed to rest tall, uncertainly coloured mitres,[i] strangely suggestive of those on certain nameless figures chiselled by a forgotten sculptor

[a] hints, . . . come] hints came B, C, D
[b] mentally] eventually B, C, D
[c] Key,] key, C, D
[d] unharmed] unharmed, B, C, D
[e] advance . . ."] advance—" C, D
[f] well-learnt] well-learned B, C, D
[g] colour,] color, C, D
[h] Shapes] shapes B, C, D
[i] coloured mitres,] colored miters, C, D

along the living cliffs of a high, forbidden mountain in Tartary; while grasped in certain folds of their swathings were long sceptres[a] whose carven heads bodied forth a grotesque and archaic mystery.

Carter guessed what they were,[b] whence they came, and Whom they served; and guessed, too, the price of their service. But he was still content, for at one mighty venture he was to learn all. Damnation, he reflected, is but a word bandied about by those whose blindness leads them to condemn all who can see, even with a single eye. He wondered at the vast conceit of those who had babbled of the *malignant* Ancient Ones, as if They could pause from their everlasting dreams to wreak a wrath upon[c] mankind. As well, he thought, might a mammoth pause to visit frantic vengeance on an angleworm. Now the whole assemblage on the vaguely hexagonal pillars was greeting him with a gesture of those oddly carven sceptres,[d] and[e] radiating a message which he understood:

"We salute you, Most Ancient One, and you, Randolph Carter, whose daring has made you one of us."

Carter saw now that one of the pedestals was vacant, and a gesture of the Most Ancient One told him it was reserved for him. He saw also another pedestal, taller than the rest, and at the centre[f] of the oddly curved line (neither semicircle nor ellipse, parabola nor hyperbola)[g] which they formed. This, he guessed, was the Guide's own throne. Moving and rising in a manner hardly definable, Carter took his seat; and as he did so he saw that the Guide had likewise[h] seated himself.

Gradually and mistily it became apparent that the Most Ancient One was holding something—some object clutched in the outflung folds of his robe as if for the sight, or what answered for sight, of the cloaked Companions. It was a large sphere or apparent sphere[i] of some obscurely iridescent metal, and as the Guide put it forward a low,

[a] sceptres] scepters C, D
[b] were,] were and B, C, D
[c] upon] on B, C, D
[d] sceptres,] scepters C, D
[e] and] and a D
[f] centre] center B, C, D
[g] line (. . .)] line—. . .— B, C, D
[h] likewise] *om.* C, D
[i] sphere . . . sphere] sphere, . . . sphere, B, C, D

pervasive half-impression of *sound* began to rise and fall in intervals which seemed to be rhythmic even though they followed no rhythm of earth.[a] There was a suggestion of chanting—or what human imagination might interpret as chanting. Presently the quasi-sphere began to grow luminous, and as it gleamed up into a cold, pulsating light of unassignable colour[b] Carter saw that its flickerings conformed to the alien rhythm of the chant. Then all the mitred, sceptre-bearing[c] Shapes on the pedestals commenced a slight, curious swaying in the same inexplicable rhythm, while nimbuses of unclassifiable light—resembling that of the quasi-sphere—played round[d] their shrouded heads.

The Hindoo paused in his tale and looked curiously at the tall, coffin-shaped clock with the four hands and hieroglyphed dial, whose crazy ticking followed no known rhythm of earth.[e]

"You, Mr. de Marigny," he suddenly said to his learned host, "do not need to be told the particular[f] alien rhythm to which those cowled Shapes on the hexagonal pillars chanted and nodded. You are the only one else—in America—who has had a taste of the Outer Extension. That clock—I suppose it was sent you by the Yogi poor Harley Warren used to talk about—the seer who said that he alone of living men had been to Yian-Ho, the hidden legacy of sinister, aeon-old Leng,[g] and had borne certain things away from that dreadful and forbidden city. I wonder how many of its subtler properties you know? If my dreams and readings be correct, it was made by those who knew much of the First Gateway. But let me go on with my tale."

At last, continued the Swami, the swaying and the suggestion of chanting ceased, the lambent nimbuses around the now drooping and motionless heads faded away, while the[h] cloaked Shapes[i] slumped

[a] earth.] Earth. B, C, D
[b] colour] colour, B; color, C, D
[c] mitred, sceptre-bearing] mitered, scepter-bearing C, D
[d] round] around C, D
[e] earth.] Earth. B, C, D
[f] particular] particularly B, C, D
[g] Yian-Ho, . . . sinister, aeon-old Leng,] Holy Shamballah, . . . aeon-old Lemuria, A, Bᶜ; Yian-Ho, . . . eon-old Leng, C, D
[h] faded, while the] faded, and the A; faded. The Bᶜ
[i] Shapes] shapes B, C, D

curiously on their pedestals. The quasi-sphere, however, continued to pulsate with inexplicable light. Carter felt that the Ancient Ones were sleeping as they had been when he first saw them, and he wondered out of what cosmic dreams his coming had wakened[a] them. Slowly there filtered into his mind the truth that this strange chanting ritual had been one of instruction, and that the Companions had been chanted by the Most Ancient One into a new and peculiar kind of sleep,[b] in order that their dreams might open the Ultimate Gate to which the Silver Key[c] was a passport. He knew that in the profundity of this deep sleep they were contemplating unplumbed vastnesses of utter and absolute Outsideness with which the earth[d] had nothing to do,[e] and that they were to accomplish that which his presence had demanded.

The Guide did not share this sleep, but seemed still to be giving instructions in some subtle, soundless way. Evidently he was implanting images of those things which he wished the Companions to dream;[f] and Carter knew that as each of the Ancient Ones pictured the prescribed thought, there would be born the nucleus of a manifestation visible to his own[g] earthly eyes. When the dreams of all the Shapes had achieved a oneness, that manifestation would occur, and[h] everything he required be materialised,[i] through concentration. He had seen such things on earth[j]—in India, where the combined, projected will of a circle of adepts can make a thought take tangible substance, and in hoary Atlaanât, of which few men[k] dare speak.

Just what the Ultimate Gate was, and how it was to be passed, Carter could not be certain; but a feeling of tense expectancy surged over him. He was conscious of having a kind of body, and of holding

[a] wakened] aroused B, C, D
[b] sleep,] sleep B, C, D
[c] Silver Key] silver key C, D
[d] earth] Earth B; *om.* C, D (see below)
[e] Outsideness . . . do,] outsideness, C, D
[f] dream;] dream: B, C, D
[g] own] *om.* B, C, D
[h] occur, and] occur— A, B[c]
[i] materialised,] materialized, B, C, D
[j] earth] Earth C, D
[k] men] even B, C, D

the fateful Silver Key[a] in his hand. The masses of towering stone opposite him seemed to possess the evenness of a wall, toward the centre[b] of which his eyes were irresistibly drawn. And then suddenly he felt the mental currents of the Most Ancient One cease to flow forth.

For the first time Carter realised[c] how terrific utter silence, mental and physical, may be. The earlier moments had never failed to contain some perceptible rhythm, if only the faint, cryptical pulse of the earth's[d] dimensional extension, but now the hush of the abyss seemed to fall upon everything. Despite his intimations of body, he had no audible breath;[e] and the glow of 'Umr at-Tawil's[f] quasi-sphere had grown petrifiedly fixed and unpulsating. A potent nimbus, brighter than those which had played round the heads of the Shapes, blazed frozenly over the shrouded skull of the terrible Guide.

A dizziness assailed Carter, and his sense of lost orientation waxed a thousandfold. The strange lights seemed to hold the quality of the most impenetrable blacknesses heaped upon blacknesses,[g] while about the Ancient Ones, so close on their pseudo-hexagonal thrones, there hovered an air of the most stupefying remoteness. Then he felt himself wafted into immeasurable depths, with waves of perfumed warmth lapping against his face. It was as if he floated in a torrid, rose-tinctured sea; a sea of drugged wine whose waves broke foaming against shores of brazen fire. A great fear clutched him as he half saw[h] that vast expanse of surging sea lapping against its far-off coast. But the moment of silence was broken—the surgings were speaking to him in a language that was not of physical sound or articulate words.

"The man[i] of Truth is beyond good and evil," intoned a voice that was not a voice. "The man[j] of Truth has ridden to All-Is-One. The

[a] Silver Key] silver key C, D
[b] centre] center C, D
[c] realised] realized B, C, D
[d] earth's] Earth's B, C, D
[e] breath;] breath, D
[f] 'Umr at-Tawil's] 'Umr-at-Tawil's A
[g] blacknesses,] blacknesses D
[h] half saw] half-saw A, B
[i] man] *Man* B, C, D
[j] man] *Man* B, C, D

man[a] of Truth has learnt[b] that Illusion is the only reality,[c] and that substance is an impostor."[d] [e]

And now, in that rise of masonry to which his eyes had been so irresistibly drawn, there appeared the outline of a titanic arch not unlike that which he thought he had glimpsed so long ago in that cave within a cave, on the far, unreal surface of the three-dimensioned earth.[f] He realised[g] that he had been using the Silver Key[h]—moving it in accord with an unlearnt[i] and instinctive ritual closely akin to that which had opened the Inner Gate. That rose-drunken sea which lapped his cheeks was, he realised,[j] no more or less than the adamantine mass of the solid wall yielding before his spell, and the vortex of thought with which the Ancient Ones had aided his spell. Still guided by instinct and blind determination, he floated forward—and through the Ultimate Gate.

IV.

Randolph Carter's advance through that Cyclopean[k] bulk of abnormal[l] masonry was like a dizzy precipitation through the measureless gulfs between the stars. From a great distance he felt triumphant, godlike surges of deadly sweetness, and after that the rustling of great wings, and impressions of sound like the chirpings and murmurings of objects unknown on earth[m] or in the solar system. Glancing backward, he saw not one gate alone,[n] but a multiplicity of gates, at some of

[a] man] *Man* B, C, D
[b] learnt] *learned* B, C, D
[c] only reality,] *One Reality,* B, C, D
[d] substance is an impostor."] *Substance is the Great Impostor."* B, C, D
[e] "The . . . impostor."] *"The . . . Impostor."* B, C, D
[f] earth.] Earth. B, C, D
[g] realised] realized B, C, D
[h] Silver Key] silver key C, D
[i] unlearnt] unlearned B, C, D
[j] realised,] realized, B, C, D
[k] Cyclopean] cyclopean C, D
[l] abnormal] *om.* B, C, D
[m] earth] Earth B, C, D
[n] alone,] alone D

which clamoured[a] Forms he strove not to remember.

And then, suddenly, he felt a greater terror than that which any of the Forms could give—a terror from which he could not flee because it was connected with himself. Even the First Gateway had taken something of stability from him, leaving him uncertain about his bodily form and about his relationship to the mistily defined objects around him, but it had not disturbed his sense of unity. He had still been Randolph Carter, a fixed point in the dimensional seething. Now, beyond the Ultimate Gateway, he realised[b] in a moment of consuming fright that he was not one person, but many persons.

He was in many places at the same time. On earth,[c] on October 7, 1883, a little boy named Randolph Carter was leaving the Snake-Den[d] in the hushed evening light and running down the rocky slope[e] and through the twisted-boughed orchard toward his Uncle Christopher's house in the hills beyond Arkham—[f]yet at that same moment, which was also somehow in the earthly year of 1928, a vague shadow not less Randolph Carter was sitting on a pedestal among the Ancient Ones in earth's[g] trans-dimensional[h] extension. Here, too, was a third Randolph Carter[i] in the unknown and formless cosmic abyss beyond the Ultimate Gate. And elsewhere, in a chaos of scenes whose infinite multiplicity and monstrous diversity brought him close to the brink of madness, were a limitless confusion of beings which he knew were as much himself as the local manifestation now beyond the Ultimate Gate.

There were "Carters"[j] in settings belonging to every known and suspected age of earth's[k] history, and to remoter ages of earthly entity

---

[a] clamoured] clamored C, D
[b] realised] realized B, C, D
[c] earth,] Earth, B, C, D
[d] Snake-Den] Snake Den A, C, D
[e] slope] slope, B, C, D
[f] Arkham—] Arkham; C, D
[g] earth's] Earth's B, C, D
[h] trans-dimensional] transdimensional C, D
[i] Carter] Carter, C, D
[j] credibility. "Carters"] credibility; *"Carters"* B; credibility; Carters C, D
[k] earth's] Earth's C, D

transcending knowledge, suspicion, and credibility. "Carters"[a] of forms both human and non-human, vertebrate and invertebrate, conscious and mindless, animal and vegetable. And more, there were "Carters"[b] having nothing in common with earthly life, but moving outrageously amidst backgrounds of other planets and systems and galaxies and cosmic continua. Spores[c] of eternal life drifting from world to world, universe to universe, yet all equally himself. Some of the glimpses recalled dreams—both faint and vivid, single and persistent—which he had had through the long years since he first began to dream,[d] and a few possessed a haunting, fascinating,[e] and almost horrible familiarity which no earthly logic could explain.

Faced with this realisation,[f] Randolph Carter reeled in the clutch of supreme horror—horror such as had not been hinted even at the climax of that hideous night when two had ventured into an ancient and abhorred necropolis under a waning moon and only one had emerged. No death, no doom, no anguish can arouse the surpassing despair which flows from a loss of *identity*. Merging with nothingness is peaceful oblivion; but to be aware of existence and yet to know that one is no longer a definite being distinguished from other beings—that one no longer has a *self*—that is the nameless summit of agony and dread.

He knew that there had been a Randolph Carter of Boston, yet could not be sure whether he—the fragment or facet of an earthly[g] entity beyond the Ultimate Gate—had been that one or some other. His *self* had been annihilated; and yet he—if indeed there could, in view of that utter nullity of individual existence, be such a thing as *he*—was equally aware of being in some inconceivable way a legion of selves. It was as though his body had been suddenly transformed into one of those many-limbed and many-headed effigies sculptured in Indian temples, and he contemplated the aggregation in a bewildered attempt to discern which was the original and which the additions—if indeed

[a] "Carters"] *"Carters"* B; Carters C, D
[b] "Carters"] *"Carters"* B; Carters C, D
[c] continua. Spores] continua; spores C, D
[d] dream,] dream; C, D
[e] fascinating,] fascinating A, B, C, D
[f] realisation,] realization, C, D
[g] earthly] *om.* B, C, D

(supremely monstrous thought)[a] there *were* any original as distinguished from other embodiments.

Then, in the midst of these devastating reflections, Carter's beyond-the-gate fragment was hurled from what had seemed the nadir of horror to black, clutching pits of a horror still more profound. This time it was largely external—a force or[b] personality which at once confronted and surrounded and pervaded him, and which in addition to its local presence, seemed also to be a part of himself, and likewise to be coexistent with all time and coterminous[c] with all space. There was no visual image, yet the sense of entity and the awful concept of combined localism, identity,[d] and infinity lent a paralysing[e] terror beyond anything which any Carter-fragment had hitherto deemed capable of existing.

In the face of that awful wonder, the quasi-Carter forgot the horror of destroyed individuality. It was an All-in-One and One-in-All of limitless being and self—not merely a thing of one Space-Time[f] continuum, but allied to the ultimate animating essence of existence's whole unbounded sweep—the last, utter sweep which has no confines and which outreaches fancy and mathematics alike. It was perhaps that which certain secret cults of earth have[g] whispered of as YOG-SOTHOTH,[h] and which has been a deity under other names; that which the crustaceans of Yuggoth worship as the Beyond-One, and which the vaporous brains of the spiral nebulae know by an untranslatable Sign[i]—yet in a flash the Carter-facet realised[j] how slight and fractional all these conceptions are.

And now the BEING[k] was addressing the Carter-facet in prodigious waves that smote and burned and thundered—a concentration of

---

[a] thought)] thought!) B, C, D
[b] or] of D
[c] coexistent . . . coterminous] co-existent . . . conterminous C, D
[d] localism, identity,] localism and identity B, C, D
[e] paralysing] paralyzing C, D
[f] Space-Time] space-time B, C, D
[g] earth have] Earth had C, D
[h] YOG-SOTHOTH,] *YOG-SOTHOTH,* B; *Yog-Sothoth,* C, D
[i] Sign] sign B, C, D
[j] realised] realized C, D
[k] BEING] *BEING* B; Being C, D

energy that blasted its recipient with well-nigh unendurable violence, and that followed, with certain definite variations, the singular unearthly rhythm which had marked the chanting and swaying[a] of the Ancient Ones, and the flickering of the monstrous lights, in that baffling region beyond the First Gate. It was as though suns and worlds and universes had converged upon one point whose very position in space they had conspired to annihilate with an impact of resistless fury. But amidst the greater terror one lesser terror was diminished; for the searing waves appeared somehow to isolate the beyond-the-gate[b] Carter from his infinity of duplicates—to restore, as it were, a certain amount of the illusion of identity. After a time the hearer began to translate the waves into speech-forms known to him, and his sense of horror and oppression waned. Fright became pure awe, and what had seemed blasphemously abnormal seemed now only ineffably majestic.

"Randolph Carter," IT seemed to say, "MY[c] manifestations on your planet's extension, the Ancient Ones, have sent you as one who would lately have returned to small lands of dream which he had lost, yet who with greater freedom has risen to greater and nobler desires and curiosities. You wished to sail up golden Oukranos, to search out forgotten ivory cities in orchid-heavy Kled, and to reign on the opal throne of Ilek-Vad, whose fabulous towers and numberless domes rise mighty toward a single red star in a firmament alien to your earth[d] and to all matter. Now, with the passing of two Gates, you wish loftier things. You would not flee like a child from a scene disliked to a dream beloved, but would plunge like a man into that last and inmost of secrets which lies behind all scenes and dreams.

"What you wish, I have found good; and I am ready to grant that which I have granted eleven times only to beings of your planet—five times only to those you call men, or those resembling them. I am ready to shew[e] you the Ultimate Mystery, to look on which is to blast a

---

[a] that followed, . . . swaying] that followed, with certain definite swaying B
[*erroneously corr. by* HPL *to* that parallelled [*sic*] in an unearthly rhythm the curious swaying]; that paralleled in an unearthly rhythm the curious [curios D] swaying C, D
[b] beyond-the-gate] Beyond-the-Gate C, D
[c] IT . . . "MY] it . . . "my C, D
[d] earth] Earth B, C, D
[e] shew] show C, D

feeble spirit. Yet before you gaze full at that last and first of secrets you may still wield a free choice, and return if you will through the two Gates with the Veil still unrent before your eyes."

V.

A sudden shutting-off of the waves left Carter in a chilling and awesome silence full of the spirit of desolation. On every hand pressed the illimitable vastness of the void,[a] yet the seeker knew that the BEING[b] was still there. After a moment he thought of words whose mental substance he flung into the abyss:[c]

"I accept. I will not retreat."

The waves surged forth again, and Carter knew that the BEING[d] had heard. And now there poured from that limitless MIND[e] a flood of knowledge and explanation which opened new vistas to the seeker, and prepared him for such a grasp of the cosmos as he had never hoped to possess. He was told how childish and limited is the notion of a tri-dimensional world, and what an infinity of directions there are besides the known directions of up-down, forward-backward, right-left. He was shewn[f] the smallness and tinsel emptiness of the little gods of earth,[g] with their petty, human interests and connexions[h]—their hatreds, rages, loves,[i] and vanities; their craving for praise and sacrifice, and their demands for faiths contrary to reason and Nature.[j]

While most of the impressions translated themselves to Carter as words, there were others to which other senses gave interpretation. Perhaps with eyes and perhaps with imagination he perceived that he was in a region of dimensions beyond those conceivable to the eye and

[a] void,] void; C, D
[b] BEING] Being C, D
[c] abyss: ¶] abyss: B, C, D
[d] BEING] Being C, D
[e] MIND] Mind C, D
[f] shewn] shown C, D
[g] gods of earth,] earth gods, B; Earth gods, C, D
[h] connexions] connections B, C, D
[i] loves,] loves A, B, C, D
[j] Nature.] nature. A, B, C, D

brain of man. He saw now, in the brooding shadows of that which had been first a vortex of power and then an illimitable void, a sweep of creation that dizzied his senses. From some inconceivable vantage-point he looked upon prodigious forms whose multiple extensions transcended any conception of being, size,[a] and boundaries which his mind had hitherto been able to hold, despite a lifetime of cryptical study. He began to understand dimly why there could exist at the same time the little boy Randolph Carter in the Arkham farmhouse in 1883, the misty form on the vaguely hexagonal pillar beyond the First Gate, the fragment now facing the PRESENCE[b] in the limitless abyss, and all the other "Carters"[c] his fancy or perception envisaged.

Then the waves increased in strength,[d] and sought to improve his understanding, reconciling him to the multiform entity of which his present fragment was an infinitesimal part. They told him that every figure of space is but the result of the intersection by a plane of some corresponding figure of one more dimension—as a square is cut from a cube[e] or a circle from a sphere. The cube and sphere, of three dimensions, are thus cut from corresponding forms of four dimensions that[f] men know only through guesses and dreams; and these in turn are cut from forms of five dimensions, and so on up to the dizzy and reachless heights of archetypal infinity. The world of men and of the gods of men is merely an infinitesimal phase of an infinitesimal thing—the three-dimensional phase of that small wholeness reached by the First Gate, where 'Umr at-Tawil[g] dictates dreams to the Ancient Ones. Though men hail it as reality[h] and brand thoughts of its many-dimensioned original as unreality, it is in truth the very opposite. That which we call substance and reality is shadow and illusion, and that which we call shadow and illusion is substance and reality.

Time, the waves went on, is motionless, and without beginning or

[a] size,] size A, B, C, D
[b] PRESENCE] Presence C, D
[c] "Carters"] Carters C, D
[d] strength,] strength C, D
[e] cube] cube, B, C, D
[f] dimensions that] dimensions, that B; dimensions which C, D
[g] 'Umr at-Tawil] 'Umr-at-Tawil A
[h] reality] reality, B, C, D

end. That it has motion, and is the cause of change,[a] is an illusion. Indeed, it is itself really an illusion, for except to the narrow sight of beings in limited dimensions there are no such things as past, present,[b] and future. Men think of time only because of what they call change, yet that too is illusion. All that was, and is, and is to be, exists simultaneously.

These revelations came with a godlike[c] solemnity which left Carter unable to doubt. Even though they lay almost beyond his comprehension, he felt that they must be true in the light of that final cosmic reality which belies all local perspectives and narrow partial views; and he was familiar enough with profound speculations to be free from the bondage of local and partial conceptions. Had his whole quest not been based upon a faith in the unreality of the local and partial?

After an impressive pause the waves continued, saying that what the denizens of few-dimensioned zones call change is merely a function of their consciousness, which views the external world from various cosmic angles. As the shapes[d] produced by the cutting of a cone seem to vary with the angles of cutting—being circle, ellipse, parabola,[e] or hyperbola according to that angle, yet without any change in the cone itself—so do the local aspects of an unchanged and endless reality seem to change with the cosmic angle of regarding. To this variety of angles of consciousness the feeble beings of the inner worlds are slaves, since with rare exceptions they cannot[f] learn to control them. Only a few students of forbidden things have gained inklings of this control, and have thereby conquered time and change. But the entities outside the Gates command all angles, and view the myriad parts of the cosmos in terms of fragmentary,[g] change-involving perspective, or of the changeless totality beyond perspective, in accordance with their will.

As the waves paused again, Carter began to comprehend, vaguely and terrifiedly, the ultimate background of that riddle of lost individuality which had at first so horrified him. His intuition pieced together the

[a] motion, . . . change,] motion . . . change B, C, D
[b] present,] present C, D
[c] godlike] god-like C, D
[d] shapes] Shapes B, C, D
[e] parabola,] parabola C, D
[f] cannot] can not B, C, D
[g] fragmentary,] fragmentary B, C, D

fragments of revelation, and brought him closer and closer to a grasp of the secret. He understood that much of the frightful revelation would have come upon him—splitting up his ego amongst myriads of earthly counterparts—inside the First Gate, had not the magic of 'Umr at-Tawil[a] kept it from him in order that he might use the Silver Key[b] with precision for the Ultimate Gate's opening. Anxious for clearer knowledge, he sent out waves of thought, asking more of the exact relationship between his various facets—the fragment now beyond the Ultimate Gate, the fragment still on the quasi-hexagonal pedestal beyond the First Gate, the boy of 1883, the man of 1928, the various ancestral beings who had formed his heritage and the bulwark of his ego, and the nameless denizens of the other aeons[c] and other worlds which that first hideous flash of ultimate perception had identified with him. Slowly the waves of the BEING[d] surged out in reply, trying to make plain what was almost beyond the reach of an earthly mind.

All descended lines of beings of the finite dimensions, continued the waves, and all stages of growth in each one of these beings, are merely manifestations of one archetypal and eternal being in the space outside dimensions. Each local being—son, father, grandfather, and so on—and each stage of individual being—infant, child, boy, young man, old[e] man—is merely one of the infinite phases of that same archetypal and eternal being, caused by a variation in the angle of the consciousness-plane which cuts it. Randolph Carter at all ages; Randolph Carter and all his ancestors[f] both human and pre-human, terrestrial and pre-terrestrial; all these were only phases of one ultimate, eternal "Carter" outside space and time—phantom projections differentiated only by the angle at which the plane of consciousness happened to cut the eternal archetype in each case.

A slight change of angle could turn the student of today into the child of yesterday; could turn Randolph Carter into that wizard[g]

---

[a] 'Umr at-Tawil] 'Umr-at-Tawil A
[b] Silver Key] silver key C, D
[c] aeons] eons C, D
[d] BEING] Being C, D
[e] young man, old] *om.* B, C, D
[f] ancestors] ancestors, B, C, D
[g] wizard] wizard, C, D

Edmund Carter who fled from Salem to the hills behind Arkham in 1692, or that Pickman Carter who in the year 2169 would use strange means in repelling the Mongol hordes from Australia; could turn a human Carter into one of those earlier entities which had dwelt in primal Hyperborea and worshipped black, plastic Tsathoggua after flying down from Kythanil,[a] the double planet that once revolved around Arcturus; could turn a terrestrial Carter to a remotely ancestral and doubtfully shaped dweller on Kythanil[b] itself, or a still remoter creature of trans-galactic Shonhi,[c] or a four-dimensioned gaseous consciousness in an older space-time continuum, or a vegetable brain of the future on a dark, radio-active comet of inconceivable orbit—and so on, in the endless cosmic circle.[d]

The archetypes, throbbed the waves, are the people of the ultimate abyss[e]—formless, ineffable, and guessed at only by rare dreamers on the low-dimensioned worlds. Chief among such was this informing BEING[f] itself . . . *which indeed was Carter's own archetype.* The glutless zeal of Carter and all his forbears[g] for forbidden cosmic secrets was a natural result of derivation from the SUPREME ARCHETYPE.[h] On every world all great wizards, all great thinkers, all great artists, are facets of IT.[i]

Almost stunned with awe, and with a kind of terrifying delight, Randolph Carter's consciousness did homage to that transcendent ENTITY[j] from which it was derived. As the waves paused again he pondered in the mighty silence, thinking of strange tributes, stranger questions, and still stranger requests. Curious concepts flowed conflictingly through a brain dazed with unaccustomed vistas and unforeseen disclosures. It occurred to him that, if those[k] disclosures

[a] Kythanil,] Kythamil, B, C, D
[b] Kythanil] Kythamil B, C, D
[c] Shonhi,] Stronti, B, C, D
[d] in the . . . circle.] in . . . cycle. B, C, D
[e] ultimate abyss] Ultimate Abyss B, C, D
[f] BEING] Being C, D
[g] forbears] forebears C, D
[h] SUPREME ARCHETYPE.] Supreme Archetype. C, D
[i] IT.] It. C, D
[j] ENTITY] Entiy C, D
[k] those] these B, C, D

were literally true, he might *bodily*[a] visit all those infinitely distant ages and parts of the universe which he had hitherto known only in dreams, could he but command the magic to change the angle of his consciousness-plane. And did not the Silver Key[b] supply that magic? Had it not first changed him from a man in 1928 to a boy in 1883, and then to something quite outside time? Oddly, despite his present apparent absence of body, he knew that the Key[c] was still with him.

While the silence still lasted, Randolph Carter radiated forth the thoughts and questions which assailed him. He knew that in this ultimate abyss he was equidistant from every facet of his archetype— human or non-human, earthly or extra-earthly,[d] galactic or trans-galactic; and his curiosity regarding the other phases of his being— especially those phases which were farthest from an earthly 1928 in time and space, or which had most persistently haunted his dreams throughout life—was at fever heat. He felt that his archetypal ENTITY[e] could at will send him bodily to any of these phases of bygone and distant life by changing his consciousness-plane, and despite the marvels he had undergone he burned for the further marvel of walking in the flesh through those grotesque and incredible scenes which visions of the night had fragmentarily brought him.

Without definite intention he was asking the PRESENCE[f] for access to a dim, fantastic world whose five multi-coloured[g] suns, alien constellations, dizzy[h] black crags, clawed, tapir-snouted denizens, bizarre metal towers, unexplained tunnels, and cryptical floating cylinders had intruded again and again upon his slumbers. That world, he felt vaguely, was in all the conceivable cosmos the one most freely in touch with others; and he longed to explore the vistas whose beginnings he had glimpsed, and to embark through space to those still remoter

[a] *bodily*] bodily B, C, D
[b] Silver Key] silver key C, D
[c] Key] key C, D
[d] earthly or extra-earthly,] earthly or extra-terrestrial, B [*erroneously corr. by HPL to* terrestrial or extra-terrestrial,]; terrestrial or extra-terrestrial, C, D
[e] ENTITY] Entity C, D
[f] PRESENCE] Presence C, D
[g] multi-coloured] multicoloured A; multicolored C, D
[h] dizzy] dizzily B [*changed to* dizzy *by Price*], C, D

worlds with which the clawed, snouted denizens trafficked. There was no time for fear. As at all crises of his strange life, sheer cosmic curiosity triumphed over everything else.

When the waves resumed their awesome pulsing[a] Carter knew that his terrible request was granted. The BEING[b] was telling him of the nighted gulfs through which he would have to pass, of the unknown quintuple star in an unsuspected galaxy around which the alien world revolved, and of the burrowing inner horrors against which the clawed, snouted race of that world perpetually fought. IT[c] told him, too, of how the angle of his personal consciousness-plane, and the angle of his consciousness-plane regarding the space-time elements of the sought-for world, would have to be tilted simultaneously in order to restore to that world the Carter-facet which had dwelt there.

The PRESENCE[d] warned him to be sure of his symbols if he wished ever to return from the remote and alien world he had chosen, and he radiated back an impatient affirmation; confident that the Silver Key,[e] which he felt was with him and which he knew had tilted both world and personal planes in throwing him back to 1883, contained those symbols which were meant. And now the BEING,[f] grasping his impatience, signified Its[g] readiness to accomplish the monstrous precipitation. The waves abruptly ceased, and there supervened a momentary stillness tense with nameless and dreadful expectancy.

Then, without warning, came a whirring and drumming that swelled to a terrific thundering. Once again Carter felt himself the focal point of an intense concentration of energy which smote and hammered and seared unbearably in the now-familiar alien[h] rhythm of outer space, and which he could not classify as either the blasting heat of a blazing star[i] or the all-petrifying cold of the ultimate abyss. Bands

[a] pulsing] pulsing, B, C, D
[b] BEING] Being C, D
[c] IT] It C, D
[d] PRESENCE] Presence C, D
[e] Silver Key,] silver key, C, D
[f] BEING,] Being, C, D
[g] Its] ITS B; its C, D
[h] alien] *om.* B, C, D
[i] star] star, B, C, D

and rays of colour[a] utterly foreign to any spectrum of our universe played and wove and interlaced before him, and he was conscious of a frightful velocity of motion. He caught one fleeting glimpse of a figure sitting *alone* upon a cloudy throne more hexagonal than otherwise. . . .

VI.

As the Hindoo paused in his story he saw that de Marigny and Phillips were watching him absorbedly. Aspinwall pretended to ignore the narrative,[b] and kept his eyes ostentatiously on the papers before him. The alien-rhythmed ticking of the coffin-shaped clock took on a new and portentous meaning, while the fumes from the choked, neglected tripods wove themselves into fantastic and inexplicable shapes, and formed disturbing combinations with the grotesque figures of the draught-swayed[c] tapestries. The old negro[d] who had tended them was gone—perhaps some growing tension had frightened him out of the house. An almost apologetic hesitancy hampered the speaker as he resumed in his oddly laboured[e] yet idiomatic voice.

"You have found these things of the abyss hard to believe," he said, "but you will find the tangible and material things ahead still harder. That is the way of our minds. Marvels are doubly incredible when brought into three dimensions from the vague regions of possible dream. I shall not try to tell you much—that would be another and very different story. I will tell only what you absolutely have to know."

Carter, after that final vortex of alien and polychromatic rhythm, had found himself in what for a moment he thought was his old insistent dream. He was, as many a night before, walking amidst throngs of clawed, snouted beings through the streets of a labyrinth of inexplicably fashioned metal under a blaze of diverse solar colour;[f] and as he looked down he saw that his body was like those of the others—rugose, partly squamous, and curiously articulated in a fashion mainly insect-like yet

[a] colour] color C, D
[b] narrative,] narrative B, C, D
[c] draught-swayed] draft-swayed C, D
[d] negro] Negro D
[e] laboured] labored C, D
[f] colour;] color, C, D

not without a caricaturish resemblance to the human outline. The Silver Key[a] was still in his grasp—[b]though held by a noxious-looking claw.

In another moment the dream-sense vanished, and he felt rather as one just awaked[c] from a dream. The ultimate abyss—the BEING—an[d] entity of absurd, outlandish race called "Randolph Carter"[e] on a world of the future not yet born—some of these things were parts of the persistent,[f] recurrent dreams of the wizard Zkauba on the planet Yaddith. They were too persistent—they interfered with his duties in weaving spells to keep the frightful Dholes in their burrows, and became mixed up with his recollections of the myriad real worlds he had visited in his light-beam envelope.[g] And now they had become quasi-real as never before. This heavy, material Silver Key[h] in his right upper claw, exact image of one he had dreamt about, meant no good. He must rest and reflect, and consult the Tablets of Nhing[i] for advice on what to do. Climbing a metal wall in a lane off the main concourse, he entered his apartment and approached the rack of tablets.

Seven day-fractions later Zkauba squatted on his prism in awe and half-despair,[j] for the truth had opened up a new and conflicting set of memories. Nevermore could he know the peace of being one entity. For all time and space he was two: Zkauba the Wizard[k] of Yaddith, disgusted with the thought of the repellent earth-mammal Carter that he was to be and had been, and Randolph Carter, of Boston on the earth,[l] shivering with fright at the clawed, snouted thing which he had once been, and had become again.

[a] Silver Key] silver key C, D

[b] grasp—] grasp, C, D

[c] awaked] awakened C, D

[d] BEING—an] BEING—and A; BEING—the B[c]; Being—the C, D

[e] "Randolph Carter"] Randoph Carter B, C, D

[f] persistent,] persistent B, C, D

[g] his light-beam envelope.] light-beam envelope [*changed to* envelopes *by Price*] B; light-beam envelopes. C, D

[h] Silver Key] silver key C, D

[i] Tablets of Nhing] Tablets of Dzyan A; tablets of Dzyan B[c]; tablets of Nhing C, D

[j] half-despair,] half despair, B, C, D

[k] Wizard] wizard B, C, D

[l] earth,] Earth, B, C, D

The time-units[a] spent on Yaddith, croaked the Swami—whose laboured[b] voice was beginning to shew[c] signs of fatigue—made a tale in themselves which could not be related in brief compass. There were trips to Shonhi[d] and Mthura and Kath, and other worlds in the twenty-eight[e] galaxies accessible to the light-beam envelopes of the creatures of Yaddith, and trips back and forth through aeons[f] of time with the aid of the Silver Key[g] and various other symbols known to Yaddith's wizards. There were hideous struggles with the bleached,[h] viscous Dholes in the primal tunnels that honeycombed the planet. There were awed sessions in libraries amongst the massed lore of ten thousand worlds living and dead. There were tense conferences with other minds of Yaddith, including that of the Arch-Ancient Buo. Zkauba told no one of what had befallen his personality, but when the Randolph Carter facet was uppermost he would study furiously every possible means of returning to the earth[i] and to human form, and would desperately practice[j] human speech with the buzzing,[k] alien throat-organs so ill adapted to it.

The Carter-facet had soon learned with horror that the Silver Key[l] was unable to effect his return to human form. It was, as he deduced too late from things he remembered, things he dreamed, and things he inferred from the lore of Yaddith, a product of Hyperborea on earth;[m] with power over the personal consciousness-angles of human beings alone. It could, however, change the planetary angle and send the user at will through time in an unchanged body. There had been an added spell which gave it limitless powers it otherwise lacked; but this, too, was a human discovery—peculiar to a spatially unreachable region, and

[a] time-units] time units B, C, D
[b] laboured] labored C, D
[c] shew] show B, C, D
[d] Shonhi] Stronti B, C, D
[e] twenty-eight] 28 A; twenty eight B
[f] aeons] eons C, D
[g] Silver Key] silver key C, D
[h] bleached,] bleached B, C, D
[i] earth] Earth C, D
[j] practice] practise C, D
[k] buzzing,] *om.* C, D
[l] Silver Key] silver key C, D
[m] earth;] Earth; C, D

not to be duplicated by the wizards of Yaddith. It had been written on the undecipherable parchment in the hideously carven box with the Silver Key,[a] and Carter bitterly lamented that he had left it behind. The now inaccessible BEING[b] of the abyss had warned him to be sure of his symbols, and had doubtless thought he lacked nothing.

As time wore on he strove harder and harder to utilise[c] the monstrous lore of Yaddith in finding a way back to the abyss and the omnipotent ENTITY.[d] With his new knowledge he could have done much toward reading the cryptic parchment; but that power, under present conditions, was merely ironic. There were times, however, when the Zkauba-facet was uppermost,[e] and when he strove to erase the conflicting Carter-memories which troubled him.

Thus long spaces of time wore on—ages longer than the brain of man could grasp, since the beings of Yaddith die only after prolonged cycles. After many hundred[f] revolutions the Carter-facet seemed to gain on the Zkauba-facet, and would spend vast periods calculating the distance of Yaddith in space and time from the human earth[g] that was to be. The figures were staggering—aeons[h] of light-years beyond counting—but the immemorial lore of Yaddith fitted Carter to grasp such things. He cultivated the power of dreaming himself momentarily earthward,[i] and learned many things about our planet that he had never known before. But he could not dream the needed formula on the missing parchment.

Then at last he conceived a wild plan of escape from Yaddith—which began when he found a drug that would keep his Zkauba-facet always dormant, yet without dissolution of the knowledge and memories of Zkauba. He thought that his calculations would let him perform a voyage with a light-wave envelope such as no being of Yaddith had

---

[a] Silver Key,] silver key, C, D
[b] BEING] Being C, D
[c] utilise] utilize B, C, D
[d] ENTITY.] Entity. C, D
[e] uppermost,] uppermost D
[f] hundred] hundreds of B, C, D
[g] earth] Earth B, C, D
[h] aeons] eons C, D
[i] earthward,] Earthward, C, D

ever performed—a *bodily* voyage through nameless aeons[a] and across incredible[b] galactic reaches to the solar system and the earth[c] itself. Once on earth,[d] though in the body of a clawed, snouted thing, he might be able somehow to find—and finish deciphering—the strangely hieroglyphed parchment he had left in the car at Arkham; and with its aid—and the Key's[e]—resume his normal terrestrial semblance.

He was not blind to the perils of the attempt. He knew that when he had brought the planet-angle to the right aeon[f] (a thing impossible to do while hurtling through space), Yaddith would be a dead world dominated by triumphant Dholes, and that his escape in the light-wave envelope would be a matter of grave doubt. Likewise was he aware of how he must achieve suspended animation, in the manner of an adept, to endure the aeon-long[g] flight through fathomless abysses. He knew, too, that—assuming his voyage succeeded—he must immunise[h] himself to the bacterial and other earthly conditions hostile to a body from Yaddith. Furthermore, he must provide a way of feigning human shape on earth[i] until he might recover and decipher the parchment and resume that shape in truth. Otherwise he would probably be discovered and destroyed by the people in horror as a thing that should not be. And there must be some gold—luckily obtainable on Yaddith—to tide him over that period of quest.

Slowly Carter's plans went forward. He provided a light-wave envelope of abnormal toughness, able to stand both the prodigious time-transition and the unexampled flight through space. He tested all his calculations, and sent forth his earthward[j] dreams again and again, bringing them as close as possible to 1928. He practiced[k] suspended

[a] aeons] eons C, D
[b] across incredible] *om.* A; across B[c]
[c] earth] Earth C, D
[d] earth,] Earth, C, D
[e] Key's] key's C, D
[f] aeon] eon C, D
[g] aeon-long] eon-long C, D
[h] immunise] immunize B, C, D
[i] earth] Earth B, C, D
[j] earthward] Earthward C, D
[k] practiced] practised C, D

animation with marvellous[a] success. He discovered just the bacterial agent he needed, and worked out the varying gravity-stress to which he must become used. He artfully fashioned a waxen mask and loose costume enabling him to pass among men as a human being of a sort, and devised a doubly potent spell with which to hold back the Dholes at the moment of his starting from the black, dead[b] Yaddith of the inconceivable future. He took care, too, to assemble a large supply of the drugs—unobtainable on earth[c]—which would keep his Zkauba-facet in abeyance till he might shed the Yaddith body, nor did he neglect a small store of gold for earthly use.

The starting-day was a time of doubt and apprehension. Carter climbed up to his envelope-platform, on the pretext of sailing for the triple star Nython, and crawled into the sheath of shining metal. He had just room to perform the ritual of the Silver Key,[d] and as he did so he slowly started the levitation of his envelope. There was an appalling seething and darkening of the day, and a hideous racking of pain. The cosmos seemed to reel irresponsibly, and the other constellations danced in a black sky.

All at once Carter felt a new equilibrium. The cold of interstellar gulfs gnawed at the outside of his envelope, and he could see that he floated free in space—the metal building from which he had started having decayed ages[e] before. Below him the ground was festering with gigantic Dholes; and even as he looked, one reared up several hundred feet and levelled a bleached, viscous end at him. But his spells were effective, and in another moment he was falling away from Yaddith[f] unharmed.

VII.

In that bizarre room in New Orleans, from which the old black servant had instinctively fled, the odd voice of Swami Chandraputra grew hoarser still.

[a] marvellous] marvelous C, D
[b] black, dead] dead, black B, C, D
[c] earth] Earth C, D
[d] Silver Key,] silver key, C, D
[e] ages] years B, C, D
[f] Yaddith] Yaddith, C, D

"Gentlemen," he continued, "I will not ask you to believe these things until I have shewn[a] you special proof. Accept it, then, as a myth, when I tell you of the *thousands of light-years—thousands of years of time, and uncounted billions of miles* [b]—that Randolph Carter hurtled through space as a nameless, alien entity in a thin envelope of electron-activated metal. He timed his period of suspended animation with utmost care, planning to have it end only a few years before the time of landing on the earth[c] in or near 1928.

"He will never forget that awakening. Remember, gentlemen, that before that aeon-long[d] sleep *he had lived consciously for thousands of terrestrial years amidst the alien and horrible wonders of Yaddith.* There was a hideous gnawing of cold, a cessation of menacing dreams, and a glance through the eye-plates of the envelope. Stars, clusters, nebulae, on every hand— *and at last their outlines bore some kinship to the constellations of earth[e] that he knew.*

"Some day his descent into the solar system may be told. He saw Kynarth and Yuggoth on the rim, passed close to Neptune and glimpsed the hellish white fungi that spot it, learned an untellable secret from the close-glimpsed mists of Jupiter[f] and saw the horror on one of the satellites, and gazed at the Cyclopean[g] ruins that sprawl over Mars' ruddy disc.[h] When the earth[i] drew near he saw it as a thin crescent which swelled alarmingly in size. He slackened speed, though his sensations of homecoming made him wish to lose not a moment. I will not try to tell you of those[j] sensations as I learned them from Carter.

"Well, toward the last Carter hovered about in the earth's[k] upper air waiting till daylight came over the western hemisphere.[l] He wanted

---

[a] shewn] shown C, D
[b] *thousands of years . . . miles—*] *uncounted* billions of earthly years— A, B[c]; *thousands of years . . . miles* C, D
[c] earth] Earth B, C, D
[d] aeon-long] eon-long C, D
[e] *earth*] *Earth* C, D
[f] Jupiter] Jupiter, B, C, D
[g] Cyclopean] cyclopean C, D
[h] disc.] disk. C, D
[i] earth] Earth B, C, D
[j] those] these D
[k] earth's] Earth's C, D
[l] western hemisphere.] Western Hemisphere. C, D

to land where he had left—near the Snake-Den[a] in the hills behind Arkham. If any of you have been away from home long—and I know one of you has—I leave it to you how the sight of New England's rolling hills and great elms and gnarled orchards and ancient stone walls must have affected him.

"He came down at dawn in the lower meadow of the old Carter place, and was thankful for the silence and solitude. It was autumn, as when he had left, and the smell of the hills was balm to his soul. He managed to drag the metal envelope up the slope of the timber-lot[b] into the Snake-Den,[c] though it would not go through the weed-choked fissure to the inner cave. It was there also that he covered his alien body with the human clothing and waxen mask which would be necessary. He kept the envelope here for over a year, till certain circumstances made a new hiding-place necessary.

"He walked to Arkham—incidentally practicing[d] the management of his body in human posture and against terrestrial gravity—and got his gold changed to money at a bank. He also made some inquiries— posing as a foreigner ignorant of much English—and found that the year was 1930, only two years after the goal he had aimed at.

"Of course, his position was horrible. Unable to assert his identity, forced to live on guard every moment, with certain difficulties regarding food, and with a need to conserve the alien drug which kept his Zkauba-facet dormant, he felt that he must act as quickly as possible. Going to Boston and taking a room in the decaying West End, where he could live cheaply and inconspicuously, he at once established inquiries concerning Randolph Carter's estate and effects. It was then that he learned how anxious Mr. Aspinwall, here, was to have the estate divided, and how valiantly Mr. de Marigny and Mr. Phillips strove to keep it intact."

The Hindoo bowed, though no expression crossed his dark, tranquil, and thickly bearded face.

---

[a] Snake-Den] Snake Den A, B, C, D
[b] timber-lot] timber lot A, B, C, D
[c] Snake-Den,] Snake Den, A, B, C, D
[d] practicing] practising C, D

"Indirectly," he continued, "Carter secured a good copy of the missing parchment and began work[a] on its deciphering. I am glad to say that I was able to help in all this—for he appealed to me quite early, and through me came in touch with other mystics throughout the world. I went to live with him in Boston—a wretched place in Chambers St.[b] As for the parchment—I am pleased to help Mr. de Marigny in his perplexity. To him let me say that the language of those hieroglyphics is not Naacal[c] but R'lyehian,[d] which was brought to earth[e] by the spawn of Cthulhu countless cycles ago.[f] It is, of course, a translation—there was an Hyperborean original millions of years earlier in the primal tongue of Tsath-yo.

"There was more to decipher than Carter had looked for, but at no time did he give up hope. Early this year he made great strides through a book he imported from Nepal, and there is no question but that he will win before long. Unfortunately, however, one handicap has developed—the exhaustion of the alien drug which keeps the Zkauba-facet dormant. This is not, however, as great a calamity as was feared. Carter's personality is gaining in the body, and when Zkauba comes uppermost—for shorter and shorter periods, and now only when evoked by some unusual excitement—he is generally too dazed to undo any of Carter's work. He cannot[g] find the metal envelope that would take him back to Yaddith, for although he almost did, once, Carter hid it anew at a time when the Zkauba-facet was wholly latent. All the harm he has done is to frighten a few people and create certain nightmare rumours[h] among the Poles and Lithuanians of Boston's West End. So far, he has never injured the careful disguise prepared by the Carter-facet, though he sometimes throws it off so that parts have to be replaced. I have seen what lies beneath—and it is not good to see.

[a] work] working C, D

[b] St.] Street. B, C, D

[c] Naacal] Naacal, B, C, D

[d] R'lyehian,] Senzar, A, B[c]

[e] earth] Earth C, D

[f] earth . . . ago.] earth 18,000 years ago by the Lords of Venus. A, B[c]; Earth by the spawn of Cthulhu countless ages ago. C, D

[g] cannot] can not B, C, D

[h] rumours] rumors B, C, D

"A month ago Carter saw the advertisement of this meeting, and knew that he must act quickly to save his estate. He could not wait to decipher the parchment and resume his human form. Consequently he deputed me to act for him, and in that capacity I am here.[a]

"Gentlemen, I say to you that Randolph Carter is not dead; that he is temporarily in an anomalous condition, but that within two or three months at the outside[b] he will be able to appear in proper form and demand the custody of his estate. I am prepared to offer proof if necessary. Therefore I beg that you will adjourn this meeting for an indefinite period."

VIII.

De Marigny and Phillips stared at the Hindoo as if hypnotised,[c] while Aspinwall emitted a series of snorts and bellows. The old attorney's disgust had by now surged into open rage, and he pounded the table with an apoplectically veined fist. When he spoke, it was in a kind of bark.

"How long is this foolery to be borne? I've listened an hour to this madman—this faker—and now he has the damned effrontery to say that Randolph Carter is alive—to ask us to postpone the settlement for no good reason! Why don't you throw the scoundrel out, de Marigny? Do you mean to make us all the butts of a charlatan or idiot?"

De Marigny quietly raised his hands and spoke softly.

"Let us think slowly and clearly. This has been a very singular tale, and there are things in it which I, as a mystic not altogether ignorant, recognise[d] as far from impossible. Furthermore—since 1930 I have received letters from the Swami which tally with his account."

As he paused, old Mr. Phillips ventured a word.

"Swami Chandraputra spoke of proofs. I, too, recognise[e] much that is significant in this story, and I have myself had many oddly corroborative letters from the Swami during the last two years; but

---

[a] him, . . . here.] him. C, D
[b] outside] outset B
[c] hypnotised,] hypnotized, B, C, D
[d] recognise] recognize B, C, D
[e] recognise] recognize B, C, D

some of these statements are very extreme. Is there not something tangible which can be shewn?"[a]

At last the impassive-faced Swami replied, slowly and hoarsely, and drawing an object from the pocket of his loose coat as he spoke.

"While none of you here has ever *seen* the Silver Key[b] itself, Messrs. de Marigny and Phillips have seen photographs of it. *Does this look familiar to you?*"

He fumblingly laid on the table, with his large, white-mittened hand, a heavy key of tarnished silver—nearly five inches long, of unknown and utterly exotic workmanship, and covered from end to end with hieroglyphs of the most bizarre description. De Marigny and Phillips gasped.

"That's it!" cried de Marigny. "The camera doesn't lie. I couldn't be mistaken!"

But Aspinwall had already launched a reply.

"Fools! What does it prove? If that's really the key that belonged to my cousin, it's up to this foreigner—this damned nigger—to explain how he got it! Randolph Carter vanished with the key four years ago. How do we know he wasn't robbed and murdered? He was half-crazy[c] himself, and in touch with still crazier people.

"Look here, you nigger—where did you get that key? Did you kill Randolph Carter?"

The Swami's features, abnormally placid, did not change; but the remote, irisless black eyes behind them blazed dangerously. He spoke with great difficulty.

"Please control yourself, Mr. Aspinwall. There is another form of proof that I *could* give, but its effect upon everybody would not be pleasant. Let us be reasonable. Here are some papers obviously written since 1930, and in the unmistakable style of Randolph Carter."

He clumsily drew a long envelope from inside his loose coat and handed it to the sputtering attorney as de Marigny and Phillips watched with chaotic thoughts and a dawning feeling of supernal wonder.

[a] shewn?"] shown?" C, D
[b] Silver Key] silver key C, D
[c] half-crazy] half crazy B, C, D

"Of course the handwriting is almost illegible—but remember that Randolph Carter now has no hands well adapted to forming human script."

Aspinwall looked through the papers hurriedly, and was visibly perplexed, but he did not change his demeanour.[a] The room was tense with excitement and nameless dread, and the alien rhythm of the coffin-shaped clock had an utterly diabolic sound to de Marigny and Phillips—[b]though the lawyer seemed affected not at all. Aspinwall spoke again.[c]

"These look like clever forgeries. If they aren't, they may mean that Randolph Carter has been brought under the control of people with no good purpose. There's only one thing to do—have this faker arrested. De Marigny, will you telephone for the police?"

"Let us wait," answered their host. "I do not think this case calls for the police. I have a certain idea. Mr. Aspinwall, this gentleman is a mystic of real attainments. He says he is in the confidence of Randolph Carter. Will it satisfy you if he can answer certain questions which could be answered only by one in such confidence? I know Carter, and can ask such questions. Let me get a book which I think will make a good test."

He turned toward the door to the library, Phillips dazedly following in a kind of automatic way. Aspinwall remained where he was, studying closely the Hindoo who confronted him with abnormally impassive face. Suddenly, as Chandraputra clumsily restored the Silver Key[d] to his pocket, the lawyer emitted a guttural shout which stopped de Marigny and Phillips in their tracks.[e]

"Hey, by God,[f] I've got it! This rascal is in disguise. I don't believe he's an East Indian at all. That face—it isn't a face, but a *mask!* I guess his story put that into my head, but it's true. It never moves, and that turban and beard hide the edges. This fellow's a common crook! He isn't even a foreigner—I've been watching his language. He's a Yankee of some sort. And look at those mittens—he knows his fingerprints could be spotted. Damn you, I'll pull that thing off—"

---

[a] demeanour.] demeanor. C, D
[b] Phillips—] Phillips, C, D
[c] all. . . . again. ¶] all. ¶ . . . again. C, D
[d] Silver Key] silver key C, D
[e] shout . . . tracks.] shout. C, D
[f] God,] God! B; Heaven! C; Heaven D

"Stop!" The hoarse, oddly alien voice of the Swami held a tone beyond all mere earthly fright. "I told you there was *another form of proof which I could give if necessary,* and I warned you not to provoke me to it. This red-faced old meddler is right—I'm not really an East Indian. *This face is a mask, and what it covers is not human.* You others have guessed—I felt that minutes ago. It wouldn't be pleasant if I took that mask off—let it alone, Ernest. I may as well tell you that *I am Randolph Carter.*"

No one moved. Aspinwall snorted and made vague motions. De Marigny and Phillips, across the room, watched the workings of his[a] red face and studied the back of the turbaned figure that confronted him. The clock's abnormal ticking was hideous, and the tripod fumes and swaying arras danced a dance of death. The half-choking lawyer broke the silence.

"No you don't, you crook—you can't scare me! You've reasons of your own for not wanting that mask off. Maybe we'd know who you are. Off with it—"

As he reached forward, the Swami seized his hand with one of his own clumsily mittened members, evoking a curious cry of mixed pain and surprise.[b] De Marigny started toward the two, but paused confused as the pseudo-Hindoo's shout of protest changed to a wholly inexplicable rattling and buzzing sound. Aspinwall's red face was furious, and with his free hand he made another lunge at his opponent's bushy beard. This time he succeeded in getting a hold, and at his frantic tug the whole waxen visage came loose from the turban and clung to the lawyer's apoplectic fist.

As it did so, Aspinwall uttered a frightful gurgling cry, and Phillips and de Marigny saw his face convulsed with a wilder, deeper,[c] and more hideous epilepsy of stark panic than ever they had seen on human countenance before. The pseudo-Swami had meanwhile released his other hand and was standing as if dazed, making buzzing noises of a most abnormal quality. Then the turbaned figure slumped oddly into a posture scarcely human, and began a curious, fascinated

[a] his] the B, C, D
[b] surprise.] surprize. C, D
[c] deeper,] deeper A, B, C, D

sort of shuffle toward the coffin-shaped[a] clock that ticked out its cosmic and abnormal rhythm. His now uncovered face was turned away, and de Marigny and Phillips could not see what the lawyer's act had disclosed. Then their attention was turned to Aspinwall, who was sinking ponderously to the floor. The spell was broken—but when they reached the old man he was dead.

Turning quickly to the shuffling Swami's receding back, de Marigny saw one of the great white mittens drop listlessly off a dangling arm. The fumes of the olibanum were thick, and all that could be glimpsed of the revealed hand was something long and black. Before the Creole could reach the retreating figure, old Mr. Phillips laid a restraining hand on his shoulder.

"Don't!" he whispered. "We don't know what we're up against—that[b] other facet, you know—Zkauba, the wizard of Yaddith. . . ."

The turbaned figure had now reached the abnormal clock, and the watchers saw through the dense fumes a blurred black claw fumbling with the tall, hieroglyphed door. The fumbling made a queer[c] clicking sound. Then the figure entered the coffin-shaped case and pulled the door shut after it.

De Marigny could no longer be restrained, but when he reached and opened the clock it was empty. The abnormal ticking went on, beating out the dark[d] cosmic rhythm which underlies all mystical gate-openings. On the floor the great white mitten, and the dead man with a bearded mask clutched in his hand, had nothing further to reveal.

A year has[e] passed, and nothing has been heard of Randolph Carter. His estate is still unsettled. The Boston address from which one "Swami Chandraputra" sent inquiries to various mystics in 1930–31–32 was indeed tenanted by a strange Hindoo, but he left shortly before the date of the New Orleans conference and has never been seen since.

---

[a] coffin-shaped] coffin shaped A
[b] against—that] against. That B, C, D
[c] queer] queer, B, C, D
[d] dark] dark, B, C, D
[e] has] *om.* B[c], C, D

He was said to be dark, expressionless, and bearded, and his landlord thinks the swarthy mask—which was duly exhibited—looks very much like him. He was never, however, suspected of any connexion[a] with the nightmare apparitions whispered of by local Slavs. The hills behind Arkham were searched for the "metal envelope",[b] but nothing of the sort was ever found. However, a clerk in Arkham's First National Bank does recall a queer turbaned man who cashed an odd bit of gold bullion in October, 1930.

De Marigny and Phillips scarcely know what to make of the business. After all, what was proved? There was a story. There was a key which might have been forged from one of the pictures Carter had freely distributed in 1928. There were papers—all indecisive. There was a masked stranger, but who now living saw behind the mask? Amidst the strain and the olibanum fumes that act of vanishing in the clock might easily have been a dual hallucination. Hindoos know much of hypnotism. Reason proclaims the "Swami" a criminal with designs on Randolph Carter's estate. But the autopsy said that Aspinwall had died of shock. Was it rage *alone* which caused it? And some things in that story . . .

In a vast room hung with strangely figured arras and filled with olibanum fumes, Etienne-Laurent de Marigny often sits listening with vague sensations to the abnormal rhythm of that hieroglyphed, coffin-shaped clock.

[a] connexion] connection B, C, D
[b] envelope",] envelope," C, D

The Thing on the Doorstep

I.^a

It is true that I have sent six bullets through the head of my best friend, and yet I hope to shew^b by this statement that I am not his murderer. At first I shall be called a madman—madder than the man I shot in his cell at the Arkham Sanitarium. Later some of my readers will weigh each statement, correlate it with the known facts, and ask themselves how I could have believed otherwise than as^c I did after facing the evidence of that horror—that thing on the doorstep.^d

Until then I also saw nothing but madness in the wild tales I have acted on. Even now I ask myself whether I was misled—or whether I am not mad after all. I do not know—but others have strange things

---

Editor's Note: The surviving A.Ms. is HPL's original draft, written in pencil. The T.Ms. (by an unknown hand: HPL remarked that he had a "delinquent [revision] client [Hazel Heald?]" [*SL* 4.310] type the text) is none too accurate, and HPL failed to proofread the text adequately (he has made only a single correction in the text). Among the errors in the T.Ms. are extensive alterations of HPL's punctuation (especially as regards ellipses), the omission of words and phrases, and an erroneous rendering of HPL's chapter divisions of the story. The typist has left out section breaks and numbers for chapters 5 and 6. The *Weird Tales* appearance (January 1937) luckily hit upon the correct division for chapter 5 but chose an erroneous one for section 6. The Arkham House texts, deriving from the T.Ms., simply renumber chapter 7 as chapter 5. The Arkham House editions make numerous errors of their own beyond those in the T.Ms.

Texts: A = A.Ms. (JHL); B = T.Ms. (JHL); B^c = HPL's correction in T.Ms.; C = *Weird Tales* 29, No. 1 (January 1937): 52–70 (as "The Thing on the Door-Step"); D = *The Dunwich Horror and Others* (Arkham House, 1963), 281–307. Copy-text: A.

^a I.] *om.* A, B, C, D
^b shew] show B, C, D
^c as] *om.* D
^d doorstep.] door-step. C

to tell of Edward and Asenath Derby, and even the stolid police are at their wits' ends to account for that last terrible visit. They have tried weakly to concoct a theory of a ghastly jest or warning by discharged servants,[a] yet they know in their hearts that the truth is something infinitely more terrible and incredible.

So I say that I have not murdered Edward Derby. Rather have I avenged him, and in so doing purged the earth of a horror whose survival might have loosed untold terrors on all mankind. There are black zones of shadow close to our daily paths, and now and then some evil soul breaks a passage through. When that happens, the man who knows must strike before reckoning the consequences.

I have known Edward Pickman Derby all his life. Eight years my junior, he was so precocious that we had much in common from the time he was eight and I[b] sixteen. He was the most phenomenal child scholar I have ever known, and at seven was writing verse of a sombre,[c] fantastic, almost morbid cast which astonished the tutors surrounding him. Perhaps his private education and coddled seclusion had something to do with his premature flowering. An only child, he had organic weaknesses which startled his doting parents and caused them to keep him closely chained to their side. He was never allowed out without his nurse, and seldom had a chance to play unconstrainedly with other children. All this doubtless fostered a strange,[d] secretive inner life in the boy, with imagination as his one avenue of freedom.

At any rate, his juvenile learning was prodigious and bizarre; and his facile writings such as to captivate me despite my greater age. About that time I had leanings toward art of a somewhat grotesque cast, and I found in this younger child a rare kindred spirit. What lay behind our joint love of shadows and marvels was, no doubt, the ancient, mouldering,[e] and subtly fearsome town in which we lived—witch-cursed, legend-haunted Arkham, whose huddled, sagging gambrel

---

[a] servants,] servants; C
[b] I] I was D
[c] sombre,] somber, C
[d] strange,] strange B, C, D
[e] mouldering,] moldering, C

roofs and crumbling Georgian balustrades brood out the centuries beside the darkly muttering Miskatonic.

As time went by I turned to architecture and gave up my design of illustrating a book of Edward's daemoniac[a] poems, yet our comradeship suffered no lessening. Young Derby's odd genius developed remarkably, and in his eighteenth year his collected nightmare-lyrics made a real sensation when issued under the title "Azathoth and Other Horrors".[b] He was a close correspondent of the notorious Baudelairean poet Justin Geoffrey, who wrote "The People of the Monolith"[c] and died screaming in a madhouse in 1926 after a visit to a sinister, ill-regarded village in Hungary.

In self-reliance and practical affairs, however, Derby was greatly retarded because of his coddled existence. His health had improved, but his habits of childish dependence were fostered by overcareful[d] parents;[e] so that he never travelled[f] alone, made independent decisions, or assumed responsibilities. It was early seen that he would not be equal to a struggle in the business or professional arena, but the family fortune was so ample that this formed no tragedy. As he grew to years of manhood he retained a deceptive aspect of boyishness. Blond and blue-eyed, he had the fresh complexion of a child;[g] and his attempts to raise a moustache[h] were discernible only with difficulty. His voice was soft and light, and his pampered,[i] unexercised life gave him a juvenile chubbiness rather than the paunchiness of premature middle age. He was of good height, and his handsome face would have made him a notable gallant had not his shyness held him to seclusion and bookishness.[j]

[a] daemoniac] demoniac A, B, C, D
[b] "Azathoth . . . Horrors".] *Azathoth . . . Horrors.* A, B, C, D
[c] "The . . . Monolith"] *The . . . Monolith* A, B, C, D
[d] overcareful] over-careful A, B, C, D
[e] parents;] parents, B, C, D
[f] travelled] traveled C
[g] child;] child, C
[h] moustache] mustache C
[i] pampered,] *om.* B, C, D
[j] bookishness.] bookishness. By the time he was 25 Derby was a fairly well-known minor poet and fantaisiste, though his lack of contacts & experience had slowed down his literary growth by making his products derivative & over-bookish. I was perhaps his closest friend, seeing him A [*excised*]

Derby's parents took him abroad every summer, and he was quick to seize on the surface aspects of European thought and expression. His Poe-like talents turned more and more toward the decadent, and other artistic sensitivenesses and yearnings were half-aroused[a] in him.[b] We had great discussions in those days. I had been through Harvard, had studied in a Boston architect's office, had married, and had finally returned to Arkham to practice[c] my profession—settling in the family homestead in Saltonstall St.,[d] since my father had moved to Florida for his health. Edward used to call almost every evening, till I came to regard him as one of the household. He had a characteristic way of ringing the doorbell[e] or sounding the knocker that grew to be a veritable code signal, so that after dinner I always listened for the familiar three brisk strokes followed by two more after a pause. Less frequently I would visit at his house and note with envy the obscure volumes in his constantly growing library.

Derby went through Miskatonic University in Arkham,[f] since his parents would not let him board away from them. He entered at sixteen and completed his course in three years, majoring in English and French literature and receiving high marks in everything but mathematics and the sciences. He mingled very little with the other students, though looking enviously at the "daring" or "Bohemian" set—whose superficially "smart" language and meaninglessly[g] ironic pose he aped, and whose dubious conduct he wished he dared adopt.

What he did do was to become an almost fanatical devotee of subterranean magical lore, for which Miskatonic's library was and is famous. Always a dweller on the surface of phantasy and strangeness, he now delved deep into the actual runes and riddles left by a fabulous past for the guidance or puzzlement of posterity. He read things like the

---

[a] half-aroused] half aroused C
[b] him.] him. ¶ C
[c] practice] practise B, C, D
[d] St.,] St. A; Street B, D; Street, C
[e] doorbell] door-bell C
[f] Arkham,] Arkham A, B, D
[g] meaninglessly] meaningless D

frightful "Book of Eibon",[a] the "Unaussprechlichen Kulten"[b] of von Junzt, and the forbidden "Necronomicon"[c] of the mad Arab Adbul Alhazred, though he did not tell his parents he had seen them. Edward was twenty[d] when my son and only child was born, and seemed pleased when I named the newcomer Edward Derby Upton, after him.

By the time he was twenty-five Edward Derby was a prodigiously learned man and a fairly well-known poet and fantaisiste,[e] though his lack of contacts and responsibilities had slowed down his literary growth by making his products derivative and overbookish.[f] I was perhaps his closest friend—finding him an inexhaustible mine of vital theoretical topics, while he relied on me for advice in whatever matters he did not wish to refer to his parents. He remained single—more through shyness, inertia,[g] and parental protectiveness than through inclination—and moved in society only to the slightest and most perfunctory extent. When the war came both health and ingrained timidity kept him at home. I went to Plattsburg for a commission, but never got overseas.

So the years wore on. Edward's mother died when he was thirty-four, and for months he was incapacitated by some odd psychological malady. His father took him to Europe, however, and he managed to pull out of his trouble without visible effects. Afterward he seemed to feel a sort of grotesque exhilaration, as if of partial escape from some unseen bondage. He began to mingle in the more "advanced" college set despite his middle age, and was present at some extremely wild doings—on one occasion paying heavy blackmail (which he borrowed of me) to keep his presence at a certain affair from his father's notice. Some of the whispered rumours[h] about the wild Miskatonic set were extremely singular. There was even talk of black magic and of happenings utterly beyond credibility.

[a] "Book of Eibon",] Book of Eibon, A, B [*revised by HPL to* Book of Eibon,], *Book of Eibon,* C, D
[b] "Unaussprechlichen Kulten"] *Unaussprechlichen Kulten* A, B, C, D
[c] "Necronomicon"] *Necronomicon* A, B, C, D
[d] twenty] 20 A
[e] fantaisiste,] *fantaisiste,* C
[f] overbookish.] over-bookish. A, B, C, D
[g] inertia,] inertia C
[h] rumours] rumors C, D

II.

Edward was thirty-eight when he met Asenath Waite. She was, I judge, about twenty-three[a] at the time; and was taking a special course in mediaeval metaphysics at Miskatonic. The daughter of a friend of mine had met her before—in the Hall School at Kingsport—and had been inclined to shun her because of her odd reputation. She was dark, smallish, and very good-looking except for overprotuberant[b] eyes; but something in her expression alienated extremely sensitive people. It was, however, largely her origin and conversation which caused average folk to avoid her. She was one of the Innsmouth Waites, and dark legends have clustered for generations about crumbling, half-deserted Innsmouth and its people. There are tales of horrible bargains about the year 1850, and of a strange element "not quite human" in the ancient families of the run-down fishing port[c]—tales such as only old-time Yankees can devise and repeat with proper awesomeness.

Asenath's case was aggravated by the fact that she was Ephraim Waite's daughter—the child of his old age by an unknown wife who always went veiled. Ephraim lived in a half-decayed mansion in Washington Street, Innsmouth, and those who had seen the place (Arkham folk avoid going to Innsmouth whenever they can) declared that the attic windows were always boarded, and that strange sounds sometimes floated from within as evening drew on. The old man was known to have been a prodigious magical student in his day, and legend averred that he could raise or quell storms at sea according to his whim. I had seen him one or twice in my youth as he came to Arkham to consult forbidden tomes at the college library, and had hated his wolfish, saturnine face with its tangle of iron-grey[d] beard. He had died insane—under rather queer circumstances—just before his daughter (by his will made a nominal ward of the principal) entered the Hall School, but she had been his morbidly avid pupil and looked fiendishly like him at times.

The friend whose daughter had gone to school with Asenath Waite repeated many curious things when the news of Edward's acquaintance

[a] thirty-eight . . . twenty-three] 38 . . . 23 A
[b] overprotuberant] over-/protuberant A; over-protuberant B, C, D
[c] fishing port] fishing-port C
[d] iron-grey] iron-gray C

with her began to spread about. Asenath, it seemed, had posed as a kind
of magician at school; and had really seemed able to accomplish some
highly baffling marvels. She professed to be able to raise thunderstorms,
though her seeming success was generally laid to some uncanny knack
at prediction. All animals markedly disliked her, and she could make
any dog howl by certain motions of her right hand. There were times
when she displayed snatches of knowledge and language very singular—
and very shocking—for a young girl; when she would frighten her
schoolmates with leers and winks of an inexplicable kind, and would
seem to extract an obscene and[a] zestful irony from her present situation.

Most unusual, though, were the well-attested cases of her influence
over other persons. She was, beyond question, a genuine hypnotist. By
gazing peculiarly at a fellow-student she would often give the latter a
distinct feeling of *exchanged personality*—as if the subject were placed
momentarily in the magician's body and able to stare half across the
room at her real body, whose eyes blazed and protruded with an alien
expression. Asenath often made wild claims about the nature of
consciousness and about its independence of the physical frame—or at
least from the life-processes of the physical frame. Her crowning rage,
however, was that she was not a man; since she believed a male brain
had certain unique and far-reaching cosmic powers. Given a man's brain,
she declared, she could not only equal but surpass her father in mastery
of unknown forces.

Edward met Asenath at a gathering of "intelligentsia" held in one
of the students' rooms, and could talk of nothing else when he came to
see me the next day. He had found her full of the interests and erudition
which engrossed him most, and was in addition wildly taken with her
appearance. I had never seen the young woman, and recalled casual
references only faintly, but I knew who she was. It seemed rather
regrettable that Derby should become so upheaved about her; but I said
nothing to discourage him, since infatuation thrives on opposition. He
was not, he said, mentioning her to his father.

In the next few weeks I heard of very little but Asenath from
young Derby. Others now remarked Edward's autumnal gallantry,
though they agreed that he did not look even nearly his actual age, or

[a] and] *om.* D

seem at all inappropriate as an escort for his bizarre divinity. He was only a trifle paunchy despite his indolence and self-indulgence, and his face was absolutely without lines. Asenath, on the other hand, had the premature crow's feet[a] which come from the exercise[b] of an intense will.

About this time Edward brought the girl to call on me, and I at once saw that his interest was by no means one-sided. She eyed him continually with an almost predatory air, and I perceived that their intimacy was beyond untangling.[c] Soon afterward I had a visit from old Mr. Derby, whom I had always admired and respected. He had heard the tales of his son's new friendship,[d] and had wormed the whole truth out of "the boy".[e] Edward meant to marry Asenath, and had even been looking at houses in the suburbs. Knowing my usually great influence with his son, the father wondered if I could help to break the ill-advised affair off; but I regretfully expressed my doubts. This time it was not a question of Edward's weak will but of the woman's strong will. The perennial child had transferred his dependence from the parental image to a new and stronger image, and nothing could be done about it.

The wedding was performed a month later—by a justice of the peace,[f] according to the bride's request. Mr. Derby, at my advice, offered no opposition;[g] and he, my wife, my son,[h] and I attended the brief ceremony—the other guests being wild young people from the college. Asenath had bought the old Crowninshield place in the country at the end of High Street, and they proposed to settle there after a short trip to Innsmouth, whence three servants and some books and household goods were to be brought. It was probably not so much

---

[a] crow's feet] crow's-feet C
[b] exercise] exercises D
[c] untangling.] untangling. This rather disturbed me, for the Derbys are old Essex County stock & I did not wish to see any incongruous element enter in. Not only did my daughter's recollections influence me, but I had heard from others that Asenath was in every way an "uninhibited young modern" of the sort that good old families cannot well assimilate. A [*excised*]
[d] friendship,] friendship C
[e] boy".] boy." D
[f] later—by . . . peace,] later by . . . peace A, B[c], C
[g] opposition;] opposition, B, C, D
[h] son,] son C

consideration for Edward and his father as a personal wish to be near the college, its library, and its crowd of "sophisticates",[a] that made Asenath settle in Arkham instead of returning permanently home.

When Edward called on me after the honeymoon I thought he looked slightly changed. Asenath had made him get rid of the undeveloped moustache,[b] but there was more than that. He looked soberer and more thoughtful, his habitual pout of childish rebelliousness being exchanged for a look almost of genuine sadness. I was puzzled to decide whether I liked or disliked the change. Certainly,[c] he seemed for the moment more normally adult than ever before. Perhaps the marriage was a good thing—might not the *change* of dependence form a start toward actual *neutralisation,*[d] leading ultimately to responsible independence? He came alone, for Asenath was very busy. She had brought a vast store of books and apparatus from Innsmouth (Derby shuddered as he spoke the name), and was finishing the restoration of the Crowninshield house and grounds.

Her home in—that[e] town—was a rather disquieting[f] place, but certain objects in it had taught him some surprising[g] things. He was progressing fast in esoteric lore now that he had Asenath's guidance. Some of the experiments she proposed were very daring and radical— he did not feel at liberty to describe them—but he had confidence in her powers and intentions. The three servents were very queer—an incredibly aged couple who had been with old Ephraim and referred occasionally to him and to Asenath's dead mother in a cryptic way, and a swarthy young wench who had marked anomalies of feature and seemed to exude a perpetual odour[h] of fish.[i]

---

[a] "sophisticates",] "sophisticates," D
[b] moustache,] mustache, C
[c] Certainly,] Certainly B, C, D
[d] *neutralisation,*] *neutralization,* C
[e] in—that] —in that D
[f] disquieting] disgusting B, C, D
[g] surprising] surprizing C
[h] odour] odor C
[i] fish.] fish. ¶ My first call at Derby's new home was by no means unpleasant. The servants—especially the flat-nosed wench who opened the door—distinctly repelled me; and my wife, who was with me, thought Asenath's expression was vaguely

III.

For the next two years I saw less and less of Derby. A fortnight would sometimes slip by without the familiar three-and-two strokes at the front door; and when he did call—or when, as happened with increasing infrequency, I called on him—he was very little disposed to converse on vital topics. He had become secretive about those occult studies which he used to describe and discuss so minutely, and preferred not to talk of his wife. She had aged tremendously since her marriage, till now—oddly enough—she seemed the elder of the two. Her face held the most concentratedly determined expression I had ever seen, and her whole aspect seemed to gain a vague, unplaceable repulsiveness. My wife and son noticed it as much as I, and we all ceased gradually to call on her—for which, Edward admitted in one of his boyishly tactless moments, she was unmitigatedly grateful. Occasionally the Derbys would go on long trips—ostensibly to Europe, though Edward sometimes hinted at obscurer destinations.[a]

It was after the first year that people began talking about the change in Edward Derby. It was very casual talk, for the change was purely psychological; but it brought up some interesting points. Now

sardonic. Of the conversation I recall only a queer outburst from our hostess, who repeated vehemently that wish to be a man which had so impressed my daughter at school. This was fixed in my mind because of an even queerer and surprisingly tasteless rejoinder of Edward's—a rejoinder which had the aspect of a sly "dig", and which was cut off by a crushing glance from Asenath. He had murmured 'that some people would give a good deal to be wholly human'—no doubt referring to the anile whispers of grandams about Innsmouth folk. A [*excised*]

[a] destinations.] destinations. [*Three lines erased and written over with the following:*] which professional ethics ought to have held back. He had been summoned one Candlemas to the lonely Crowninshield place; and could not feel easy after what he had seen. Fortunately, it was dead. He had known monstrous births before— but when monstrosity takes certain directions, there are questions one has to ask oneself . . . questions about people, and about the universe itself. Candlemas is nine months after the Witches' Sabbat, and country legend has much to say about it. Were not Innsmouth folk said to keep the Sabbat? Where were the Derbys last May-Eve? Dr. Hathorne allowed that if he were Edward Derby he would leave Asenath while the leaving was good. He was never quite specific, though, until that night at the last when the horror came to my doorstep. Now he will back me up in trying to do what must be done. A [*excised*]

and then, it seemed,[a] Edward was observed to wear an expression and to do things wholly incompatible with his usual flabby nature. For example—although in the old days he could not drive a car, he was now seen occasionally to dash into or out of the old Crowninshield driveway with Asenath's powerful Packard, handling it like a master, and meeting traffic entanglements with a skill and determination utterly alien to his accustomed nature. In such cases he seemed always to be just back from some trip or just starting on one—what sort of trip, no one could guess, although he mostly favoured[b] the Innsmouth road.

Oddly, the metamorphosis did not seem altogether pleasing. People said he looked too much like his wife, or like old Ephraim Waite himself, in these moments—or perhaps these moments seemed unnatural because they were so rare. Sometimes, hours after starting out in this way, he would return listlessly sprawled on the rear seat of his car while an obviously hired chauffeur or mechanic drove. Also, his preponderant aspect on the streets during his decreasing round of social contacts (including, I may say, his calls on me) was the old-time indecisive one—its irresponsible childishness even more marked than in the past. While Asenath's face aged, Edward's—aside from those exceptional occasions—actually relaxed into a kind of exaggerated immaturity, save when a trace of the new sadness or understanding would flash across it. It was really very puzzling. Meanwhile the Derbys almost dropped out of the gay college circle—not through their own disgust, we heard, but because something about their present studies shocked even the most callous of the other decadents.

It was in the third year of the marriage that Edward began to hint openly to me of a certain fear and dissatisfaction. He would let fall remarks about things 'going too far',[c] and would talk darkly about the need of 'saving his identity'.[d] At first I ignored such references, but in time I began to question him guardedly, remembering what my friend's daughter had said about Asenath's hypnotic influence over the other

[a] seemed,] seemed D
[b] favoured] favored C
[c] 'going too far',] "going too far", C; "going too far," D
[d] 'saving his identity'.] 'gaining his identity'. B; "gaining his identity". C; "gaining his identity." D

girls at school—the cases where students had thought they were in her body looking across the room at themselves. This questioning seemed to make him at once alarmed and grateful, and once he mumbled something about having a serious talk with me later.

About this time old Mr. Derby died, for which I was afterward very thankful. Edward was badly upset, though by no means disorganised.[a] He had seen astonishingly little of his parent since his marriage, for Asenath had concentrated in herself all his vital sense of family linkage. Some called him callous in his loss—especially since those jaunty and confident moods in[b] the car began to increase. He now wished to move back into the old Derby[c] mansion, but Asenath insisted on staying in the Crowninshield house,[d] to which she had become well adjusted.

Not long afterward my wife heard a curious thing from a friend— one of the few who had not dropped the Derbys. She had been out to the end of High St.[e] to call on the couple, and had seen a car shoot briskly out of the drive with Edward's oddly confident and almost sneering face above the wheel. Ringing the bell, she had been told by the repulsive wench that Asenath was also out; but had chanced to look up[f] at the house in leaving. There, at one of Edward's library windows, she had glimpsed a hastily withdrawn face—a face whose expression of pain, defeat, and wistful hopelessness was poignant beyond description. It was—incredibly enough in view of its usual domineering cast—Asenath's; yet the caller had vowed that in that instant the sad, muddled eyes of poor Edward were gazing out from it.

Edward's calls now grew a trifle more frequent, and his hints occasionally became concrete. What he said was not to be believed, even in centuried and legend-haunted Arkham; but he threw out his dark lore with a sincerity and convincingness which made one fear for his sanity. He talked about terrible meetings in lonely places, of Cyclopean[g] ruins

[a] disorganised.] disorganized. B, C, D
[b] in] with C
[c] Derby] family B, C, D
[d] house,] house B, D
[e] St.] Street B, C, D
[f] up] *om.* D
[g] Cyclopean] cyclopean A, B, C, D

in the heart of the Maine woods beneath which vast staircases lead down to abysses of nighted secrets, of complex angles that lead[a] through invisible walls to other regions of space and time, and of hideous exchanges of personality that permitted explorations in remote and forbidden places, on other worlds, and in different space-time continua.

He would now and then back up certain crazy hints by exhibiting objects which utterly nonplussed me—elusively coloured[b] and bafflingly textured objects like nothing ever heard of on earth, whose insane curves and surfaces answered no conceivable purpose and followed no conceivable geometry. These things, he said, came 'from outside';[c] and his wife knew how to get them. Sometimes—but always in frightened and ambiguous whispers—he would suggest things about old Ephraim Waite, whom he had seen occasionally at the college library in the old days. These adumbrations were never specific, but seemed to revolve around some especially horrible doubt as to whether the old wizard were really dead—in a spiritual as well as corporeal sense.[d]

At times Derby would halt abruptly in his revelations, and I wondered whether Asenath could possibly have divined his speech at a distance and cut him off through some unknown sort of telepathic mesmerism—some power of the kind she had displayed at school. Certainly, she suspected that he told me things, for as the weeks passed she tried to stop his visits with words and glances of a most inexplicable potency. Only with difficulty could he get to see me, for although he would pretend to be going somewhere else, some invisible force would

[a] lead . . . lead] led . . . led C, D
[b] coloured] colored C
[c] 'from outside';] "from outside"; A, B, C, D
[d] sense.] sense. [*Some erasures, then the following:*] upstairs—but sometimes she couldn't hold on, and he would find himself suddenly in his own body again in some far off, horrible, and perhaps unknown place. Sometimes she would get hold of him again and sometimes she couldn't. Often he had to find his way home from frightful distances, getting somebody to drive the car after he found it. The worst thing was that she was holding on to him longer and longer at a time. She wanted to be a man—to be fully human—that's why she got hold of him. Some day she would crowd him out and disappear with his body—disappear to become a great magician like her father and leave him stranded in that female shell that wasn't even quite human. Yes, he knew about the Innsmouth blood now. There had been traffick with things from the sea—it was horrible. . . . A [*excised*]

generally clog his motions or make him forget his destination for the time being. His visits usually came when Asenath was away—'away in her own body',[a] as he once oddly put it. She always found out later— the servants watched his goings and comings—but evidently she thought it inexpedient to do anything drastic.

IV.

Derby had been married more than three years on that August day when I got the[b] telegram from Maine. I had not seen him for two months, but had heard he was away "on business".[c] Asenath was supposed to be with him, though watchful gossips[d] declared there was someone upstairs in the house behind the doubly curtained windows. They had watched the purchases made by the servants. And now the town marshal of Chesuncook had wired of the draggled madman who stumbled out of the woods with delirious ravings and screamed to me for protection. It was Edward—and he had been just able to recall his own name and my name[e] and address.

Chesuncook is close to the wildest, deepest, and least explored forest belt in Maine, and it took a whole day of feverish jolting through fantastic and forbidding scenery to get there in a car. I found Derby in a cell at the town farm, vacillating between frenzy and apathy. He knew me at once, and began pouring out a meaningless, half-incoherent torrent of words in my direction.

"Dan—for God's sake! The pit of the shoggoths![f] Down the six thousand steps . . . the abomination of abominations . . . I never would let her take me, and then I found myself there. . . .[g] Iä! Shub-Niggurath! . . .[h] The shape rose up from the altar, and there were 500[i] that

---

[a] 'away . . . body',] "away . . . body," C, D
[b] the] that B, C, D
[c] business".] business." D
[d] gossips] gossip B, C, D
[e] and my name] *om.* B, C, D
[f] shoggoths!] shaggoths! D
[g] there. . . .] there— B, C, D
[h] Shub-Niggurath! . . .] Shub-Niggurath!— B, C, D
[i] 500] five hundred B, C, D

howled. . . . The[a] Hooded Thing bleated 'Kamog! Kamog!'—that was old Ephraim's secret name in the coven. . . .[b] I was there, where she promised she wouldn't take me. . . .[c] A minute before I was locked in the library, and then I was there where she had gone with my body—in the place of utter blasphemy, the unholy pit where the black realm begins and the watcher guards the gate. . . .[d] I saw a shoggoth[e]—it changed shape. . . .[f] I can't stand it. . . .[g] I won't stand it. . . .[h] I'll kill her if she ever sends me there again. . . .[i] I'll kill that entity . . .[j] her, him, it . . .[k] I'll kill it! I'll kill it with my own hands!"

It took me an hour to quiet him, but he subsided at last. The next day I got him decent clothes in the village, and set out with him for Arkham. His fury of hysteria was spent, and he was inclined to be silent;[l] though he began muttering darkly to himself when the car passed through Augusta—as if the sight of a city aroused unpleasant memories. It was clear that he did not wish to go home; and considering the fantastic delusions he seemed to have about his wife—delusions undoubtedly springing from some actual hypnotic ordeal to which he had been subjected—I thought it would be better if he did not. I would, I resolved, put him up myself for a time;[m] no matter what unpleasantness it would make with Asenath. Later I would help him get a divorce, for most assuredly there were mental factors which made this marriage suicidal for him. When we struck open country again Derby's muttering faded away, and I let him nod and drowse on the seat beside me as I drove.

During our sunset dash through Portland the muttering commenced

---

[a] howled. . . . The] howled—The B, D; howled—the C
[b] coven. . . .] coven— B, C, D
[c] me. . . .] me— B, C, D
[d] gate. . . .] gate— B, C, D
[e] shoggoth] shaggoth D
[f] shape. . . .] shape— B, C, D
[g] it. . . .] it— B, C, D
[h] I won't stand it. . . .] om. B, C, D
[i] again. . . .] again— B, C, D
[j] entity . . .] entity— B, C, D
[k] it . . .] it— B, C, D
[l] silent;] silent, B, C, D
[m] time;] time, C

again, more distinctly than before, and as I listened I caught a stream of utterly insane drivel about Asenath. The extent to which she had preyed on Edward's nerves was plain, for he had woven a whole set of hallucinations around her. His present predicament, he mumbled furtively, was only one of a long series. She was getting hold of him, and he knew that some day she would never let go. Even now she probably let him go only when she had to, because she couldn't hold on long at a time. She constantly took his body and went to nameless places for nameless rites, leaving him in her body and locking him upstairs—but sometimes she couldn't hold on, and he would find himself suddenly in his own body again in some far-off, horrible,[a] and perhaps unknown place. Sometimes she'd get hold of him again and sometimes she couldn't. Often he was left stranded somewhere as I had found him . . .[b] time and again he had to find his way home from frightful distances, getting somebody to drive the car after he found it.

The worst thing was that she was holding on to him longer and longer at a time. She wanted to be a man—to be fully human—that was why she got hold of him. She had sensed the mixture of fine-wrought brain and weak will in him. Some day she would crowd him out and disappear with his body—disappear to become a great magician like her father and leave him marooned in that female shell that wasn't even quite human. Yes, he knew about the Innsmouth blood now. There had been traffick[c] with things from the sea—it was horrible. . . . And old Ephraim—he had known the secret, and when he grew old did a hideous thing to keep alive . . .[d] he wanted to live for ever . . .[e] Asenath would succeed—one successful demonstration had taken place already.

As Derby muttered on I turned to look at him closely, verifying the impression of change which an earlier scrutiny had given me. Paradoxically, he seemed in better shape than usual—harder, more normally developed, and without the trace of sickly flabbiness caused by his indolent habits. It was as if he had been really active and

[a] horrible,] horrible C
[b] him . . .] him— B, D; him; C
[c] traffick] traffic C
[d] alive . . .] alive— B, C, D
[e] for ever . . .] forever . . . A; forever— B, D; for ever— C

properly exercised for the first time in his coddled life, and I judged that Asenath's force must have pushed him into unwonted channels of motion and alertness. But just now his mind was in a pitiable state; for he was mumbling wild extravagances about his wife, about black magic, about old Ephraim, and about some revelation which would convince even me. He repeated names which I recognised[a] from bygone browsings in forbidden volumes, and at times made me shudder with a certain thread of mythological consistency—of[b] convincing coherence— which ran through his maundering. Again and again he would pause, as if to gather courage for some final and terrible disclosure.

"Dan, Dan, don't you remember him—the[c] wild eyes and the unkempt beard that never turned white? He glared at me once, and I never forgot it. Now *she* glares that way. *And I know why!* He found it in the 'Necronomicon'[d]—the formula. I don't dare tell you the page yet, but when I do you can read and understand. Then you will know what has engulfed me. On, on, on, on—body to body to body—he means never to die. The life-glow—he knows how to break the link . . . it can flicker on a while even when the body is dead. I'll give you hints,[e] and maybe you'll guess. Listen, Dan—do you know why my wife always takes such pains with that silly backhand writing? Have you ever seen a manuscript of old Ephraim's? Do you want to know why I shivered when I saw some hasty notes Asenath had jotted down?

"Asenath . . .[f] *is there such a person?* Why did they half think[g] there was poison in old Ephraim's stomach? Why do the Gilmans whisper about the way he shrieked—like a frightened child—when he went mad and Asenath locked him up in the padded attic room where—the other—had been? *Was it old Ephraim's soul that was locked in? Who locked in whom?* Why had he been looking for months for someone with a fine mind and a weak will?[h] Why did he curse that his daughter wasn't a

---

[a] recognised] recognized B, C, D
[b] of] or D
[c] the] *om.* D
[d] 'Necronomicon'] *Necronomicon* A, B, C, D
[e] hints,] hints B, C, D
[f] "Asenath . . .] "Asenath— B, C, D
[g] half think] half-think A, B, D
[h] will?] will?— B, D

son? Tell me, Daniel Upton—*what devilish exchange was perpetrated in the house of horror where that blasphemous monster had his trusting, weak-willed,*[a] *half-human child at his mercy?* Didn't he make it permanent—as she'll do in the end with me? Tell me why that thing that calls itself Asenath writes differently when[b] off guard, *so that you can't tell its script from . . ."*[c]

Then the thing happened. Derby's voice was rising to a thin treble scream as he raved, when suddenly it was shut off with an almost mechanical click. I thought of those other occasions at my home when his confidences had abruptly ceased—when I had half fancied[d] that some obscure telepathic wave of Asenath's mental force was intervening to keep him silent. This, though, was something altogether different—and, I felt, infinitely more horrible. The face beside me was twisted almost unrecognisably[e] for a moment, while through the whole body there passed a shivering motion—as if all the bones, organs, muscles, nerves, and glands were readjusting themselves to a radically different posture, set of stresses, and general personality.

Just where the supreme horror lay, I could not for my life tell; yet there swept over me such a swamping wave of sickness and repulsion—such a freezing, petrifying sense of utter alienage and abnormality—that my grasp of the wheel grew feeble and uncertain. The figure beside me seemed less like a lifelong[f] friend than like some monstrous intrusion from outer space—some damnable, utterly accursed focus of unknown and malign cosmic forces.

I had faltered only a moment, but before another moment was over my companion had seized the wheel and forced me to change places with him. The dusk was now very thick, and the lights of Portland far behind,[g] so I could not see much of his face. The blaze of his eyes, though, was phenomenal; and I knew that he must now be in that queerly energised[h] state—so unlike his usual self—which so many

[a] *weak-willed,*] *weak-willed* B, D
[b] when] *om.* B, C, D
[c] *from . . .'*] *from—*" B, C, D
[d] half fancied] half-fancied A, B, D
[e] unrecognisably] unrecognizably B, C, D
[f] lifelong] life-/long C; life-long D
[g] behind,] behind; C
[h] energised] energized B, C, D

people had noticed. It seemed odd and incredible that listless Edward Derby—he who could never assert himself, and who had never learned to drive—should be ordering me about and taking the wheel of my own car,[a] yet that was precisely what had happened. He did not speak for some time, and in my inexplicable horror I was glad he did not.

In the lights of Biddeford and Saco I saw his firmly set mouth, and shivered at the blaze of his eyes. The people were right—he did look damnably like his wife and like old Ephraim when in these moods. I did not wonder that the moods were disliked—there was certainly something unnatural and diabolic[b] in them, and I felt the sinister element all the more because of the wild ravings I had been hearing. This man, for all my lifelong knowledge of Edward Pickman Derby, was a stranger—an intrusion of some sort from the black abyss.

He did not speak until we were on a dark stretch of road, and when he did his voice seemed utterly unfamiliar. It was deeper, firmer, and more decisive than I had ever known it to be; while its accent and pronunciation were altogether changed—though vaguely, remotely, and rather disturbingly recalling something I could not quite place. There was, I thought, a trace of very profound and very genuine irony in the timbre—not the flashy, meaninglessly jaunty pseudo-irony of the callow "sophisticate",[c] which Derby had habitually affected, but something grim, basic, pervasive, and potentially evil. I marvelled[d] at the self-possession so soon following the spell of panic-struck muttering.

"I hope you'll forget my attack back there, Upton," he was saying. "You know what my nerves are, and I guess you can excuse such things. I'm enormously grateful, of course, for this lift home.

"And you must forget, too, any crazy things I may have been saying about my wife—and about things in general. That's what comes from overstudy in a field like mine. My philosophy is full of bizarre concepts, and when the mind gets worn out it cooks up all sorts of imaginary concrete applications. I shall take a rest from now on—you probably

---

[a] car,] car; C
[b] and diabolic] *om.* B, C, D
[c] "sophisticate",] "sophisticate," D
[d] marvelled] marveled C

won't see me for some time, and you needn't blame Asenath for it.[a]

"This trip was a bit queer, but it's really very simple. There are certain Indian relics in the north woods—standing stones, and all that—which mean a good deal in folklore, and Asenath and I are following that stuff up. It was a hard search, so I seem to have gone off my head. I must send somebody for the car when I get home. A month's relaxation will put me back[b] on my feet."

I do not recall just what my own part of the conversation was, for the baffling alienage of my seatmate filled all my consciousness. With every moment my feeling of elusive cosmic horror increased, till at length I was in a virtual delirium of longing for the end of the drive. Derby did not offer to relinquish the wheel, and I was glad of the speed with which Portsmouth and Newburyport flashed by.

At the junction where the main highway runs inland and avoids Innsmouth[c] I was half-afraid[d] my driver would take the bleak shore road that goes through that damnable place. He did not, however, but darted rapidly past Rowley and Ipswich toward our destination. We reached Arkham before midnight, and found the lights still on at the old Crowninshield house. Derby left the car with a hasty repetition of his thanks, and I drove home alone with a curious feeling of relief. It had been a terrible drive—all the more terrible because I could not quite tell why— and I did not regret Derby's forecast of a long absence from my company.

V.[e]

The next two[f] months were full of rumours.[g] People spoke of seeing Derby more and more in his new energised[h] state, and Asenath was

[a] it.] it. ¶ "Don't be frightened on her account, either—in case I've been unloading any savage nonsense. *She is better protected than you can realise.* I'd be a fool to harm her, for it would all come back on me sooner or later. And of course I don't wish to harm her. Those spells of mine are just overwrought nerves. A [*excised*]
[b] back] *om.* B, C, D
[c] Innsmouth] Innsmouth, B, C, D
[d] half-afraid] half afraid C
[e] V.] *om.* B, D
[f] two] 2 A
[g] rumours.] rumors. C
[h] energised] energized B, C, D

scarcely ever in to her few[a] callers. I had only one visit from Edward, when he called briefly in Asenath's car—duly reclaimed from wherever he had left it in Maine—to get some books he had lent me. He was in his new state, and paused only long enough for some evasively polite remarks. It was plain that he had nothing to discuss with me when in this condition—and I noticed that he did not even trouble to give the old three-and-two signal when ringing the doorbell.[b] As on that evening in the car, I felt a faint, infinitely deep horror which I could not explain; so that his swift departure was a prodigious relief.

In mid-September Derby was away for a week, and some of the decadent college set talked knowingly of the matter—hinting at a meeting with a notorious cult-leader, lately expelled from England, who had established headquarters in New York. For my part I could not get that strange ride from Maine out of my head. The transformation I had witnessed had affected me profoundly, and I caught myself again and again trying to account for the thing—and for the extreme horror it had inspired in me.

But the oddest rumours[c] were those about the sobbing in the old Crowninshield house. The voice seemed to be a woman's, and some of the younger people thought it sounded like Asenath's. It was heard only at rare intervals, and would sometimes be choked off as if by force. There was talk of an investigation, but this was dispelled one day when Asenath appeared in the streets and chatted in a sprightly way with a large number of acquaintances—apologising[d] for her recent absences[e] and speaking incidentally about the nervous breakdown and hysteria of a guest from Boston. The guest was never seen, but Asenath's appearance left nothing to be said. And then someone complicated matters by whispering that the sobs had once or twice been in a man's voice.[f]

---

[a] few] *om.* B, C, D

[b] doorbell.] door-bell. C

[c] rumours] rumors C

[d] apologising] apologizing B, C, D

[e] absences] absence B, C, D

[f] voice.] voice. ¶ The tragic culmination came in mid-October. It was Thursday, the night when the three Derby servants went out—always together, and always heading for the same unknown haven in their native Innsmouth. I was waked about three in the morning by a frantic ringing and pounding of the knocker at the front

One evening in mid-October[a] I heard the familiar three-and-two ring at the front door. Answering it myself, I found Edward on the steps, and saw in a moment that his personality was the old one which I had not encountered since the day of his ravings on that terrible ride from Chesuncook. His face was twitching with a mixture of odd emotions in which fear and triumph seemed to share dominion, and he looked furtively over his shoulder as I closed the door behind him.

Following me clumsily to the study, he asked for some whiskey[b] to steady his nerves. I forbore to question him, but waited till he felt like beginning whatever he wanted to say. At length he ventured some information in a choking voice.

"Asenath has gone, Dan. We had a long talk last night while the servants were out, and I made her promise to stop preying on me. Of course I had certain—certain occult defences[c] I never told you about. She had to give in, but got frightfully angry. Just packed up and started for New York—walked right out to catch the 8:20[d] in to Boston. I suppose people will talk, but I can't help that. You needn't mention that there was any trouble—just say she's gone on a long research trip.

"She's probably going to stay with one of her horrible groups of devotees. I hope she'll go west and get a divorce—anyhow, I've made her promise to keep away and let me alone. It was horrible, Dan—she was stealing my body—crowding me out—making a prisoner of me. I laid[e] low and pretended to let her do it, but I had to be on the watch. I could plan if I was careful, for she can't read my mind literally, or in detail. All she could read of my planning was a sort of general mood of rebellion—and she always thought I was helpless. Never thought I could get the best of her . . . but I had a spell or two that worked."

door, and when I slipped on a dressing gown and went down I found Edward [*erasure*]. It was Edward, and I saw in a flash that his personality was the old one which I had not encountered since the day of his ravings on that terrible ride from Chesuncook. His face was distorted by a mixture of wild emotions in which fright and triumph seemed incongruously to have dominance. I could see A [*excised*]
[a] mid-October] mid-October, D
[b] whiskey] whisky C
[c] defences] defenses C
[d] 8:20] eight-/twenty D
[e] laid] lay B, C, D

Derby looked over his shoulder and took some more whiskey.[a]

"I paid off those damned servants this morning when they got back. They were ugly about it, and asked questions, but they went. They're her kind—Innsmouth people—and were hand and glove with her. I hope they'll let me alone—I didn't like the way they laughed when they walked away. I must get as many of Dad's old servants again as I can. I'll move back home now.

"I suppose you think I'm crazy, Dan—but Arkham history ought to hint at things that back up what I've told you—and what I'm going to tell you. You've seen one of the changes, too—in your car after I told you about Asenath that day coming home from Maine. That was when she got me—drove me out of my body. The last thing of the ride[b] I remember was when I was all worked up trying to tell you *what that she-devil is.* Then she got me, and in a flash I was back at the house—in the library where those damned servants had me locked up—and in that cursed fiend's body . . . that isn't even human. . . . You know,[c] it was she you must have ridden home with . . .[d] that preying wolf in my body. . . . You[e] ought to have known the difference!"

I shuddered as Derby paused. Surely, I *had* known the difference—yet could I accept an explanation as insane as this? But my distracted caller was growing even wilder.

"I had to save myself—I had to, Dan! She'd have got me for good at Hallowmass—they hold a Sabbat up there beyond Chesuncook, and the sacrifice would have clinched things. She'd have got me for good . . .[f] she'd have been I, and I'd have been she . . .[g] for ever . . .[h] too late. . . .[i] My body'd have been hers for good. . . .[j] She'd have been a man, and

[a] whiskey.] whisky. C
[b] of the ride] *om.* B, C, D
[c] know,] know B, C, D
[d] with . . .] with— B, C, D
[e] body. . . . You] body—You B, D; body—you C
[f] good . . .] good— B, C, D
[g] she . . .] she— B, C, D
[h] for ever . . .] forever . . . A; forever— B, D; for ever— C
[i] late. . . .] late— B, C, D
[j] good. . . .] good— B, C, D

fully human, just as she wanted to be. . . .[a] I suppose she'd have put me out of the way—killed her own ex-body with me in it, damn her, *just as she did before*—just as she, he, or it did before. . . ."[b]

Edward's face was now atrociously distorted, and he bent it uncomfortably close to mine as his voice fell to a whisper.

"You must know what I hinted in the car—*that she isn't Asenath at all, but really old Ephraim himself*. I suspected it a year and a half ago, and I know it now. Her handwriting shews[c] it when she's[d] off guard—sometimes she jots down a note in writing that's just like her father's manuscripts, stroke for stroke—and sometimes she says things that nobody but an old man like Ephraim could say. He changed forms with her when he felt death coming—she was the only one he could find with the right kind of brain and a weak enough will—he got her body permanently, just as she almost got mine, and then poisoned the old body he'd put her into. Haven't you seen old Ephraim's soul glaring out of that she-devil's eyes dozens of times . . .[e] and out of mine when she had control of my body?"

The whisperer was panting, and paused for breath. I said nothing,[f] and when he resumed[g] his voice was nearer normal. This, I reflected, was a case for the asylum, but I would not be the one to send him there. Perhaps time and freedom from Asenath would do its work. I could see that he would never wish to dabble in morbid occultism again.

"I'll tell you more later—I must have a long rest now. I'll tell you something of the forbidden horrors she led me into—something of the age-old horrors that even now are festering in out-of-the-way corners with a few monstrous priests to keep them alive. Some people know things about the universe that nobody ought to know, and can do things that nobody ought to be able to do. I've been in it up to my

[a] be. . . .] be— B, C, D

[b] before. . . ." ¶] before—" B, C, D

[c] shews] shows B, C, D

[d] she's] she goes B, C, D

[e] times . . .] times— B, C, D

[f] nothing,] nothing; D

[g] resumed] resumed, C

neck, but that's the end. Today I'd burn that damned 'Necronomicon'[a] and all the rest if I were librarian at Miskatonic.

"But she can't get me now. I must get out of that accursed house as soon as I can, and settle down at home. You'll help me, I know, if I need help. Those devilish servants, you know . . .[b] and if people should get too inquisitive about Asenath. You see, I can't give them her address. . . . Then there are certain groups of searchers—certain cults, you know—that might misunderstand our breaking up . . . some of them have damnably curious ideas and methods. I know you'll stand by me if anything happens—even if I have to tell you a lot that will shock you. . . ."

I had Edward stay and sleep in one of the guest-chambers that night, and in the morning he seemed calmer. We discussed certain possible arrangements for his moving back into the Derby mansion, and I hoped he would lose no time in making the change.[c] He did not call the next evening, but I saw him frequently during the ensuing weeks. We talked as little as possible about strange and unpleasant things, but discussed the renovation of the old Derby house, and the travels which Edward promised to take with my son and me the following summer.

Of Asenath we said almost nothing, for I saw that the subject was a peculiarly disturbing one. Gossip, of course, was rife; but that was no novelty in connexion[d] with the strange menage at the old Crowninshield house. One thing I did not like was what Derby's banker let fall in an overexpansive[e] mood at the Miskatonic Club—about the cheques[f] Edward was sending regularly to a Moses and Abigail Sargent and a Eunice Babson in Innsmouth. That looked as if those evil-faced servants were extorting some kind of tribute from him—yet he had not mentioned the matter to me.

I wished that the summer—and my son's Harvard vacation— would come, so that we could get Edward to Europe. He was not, I soon saw, mending as rapidly as I had hoped he would; for there was

---

[a] 'Necronomicon'] *Necronomicon* A, B, C, D
[b] know . . .] know— B, C, D
[c] change.] change. ¶ C
[d] connexion] connection C, D
[e] overexpansive] over-expansive A, B, C, D
[f] cheques] checks C

something a bit hysterical in his occasional exhilaration, while his moods of fright and depression were altogether too frequent. The old Derby house was ready by December, yet Edward constantly put off moving. Though he hated and seemed to fear the Crowninshield place, he was at the same time queerly enslaved by it. He could not seem to begin dismantling things, and invented every kind of excuse to postpone action. When I pointed this out to him he appeared unaccountably frightened. His father's old butler—who was there with other reacquired family[a] servants—told me one day that Edward's occasional prowlings about the house, and especially down cellar, looked odd and unwholesome to him. I wondered if Asenath had been writing disturbing letters, but the butler said there was no mail which could have come from her.

VI.[b]

It was about Christmas that Derby broke down one evening while calling on me. I was steering the conversation toward next summer's travels when he suddenly shrieked and leaped up from his chair with a look of shocking, uncontrollable fright—a cosmic panic and loathing such as only the nether gulfs of nightmare could bring to any sane mind.

"My brain! My brain! God, Dan—it's tugging—from beyond—knocking—clawing—that she-devil—even now—Ephraim—Kamog! Kamog!—The pit of the shoggoths[c]—Iä! Shub-Niggurath! The Goat with a Thousand Young! . . .

"The flame—the flame . . .[d] beyond body, beyond life . . .[e] in the earth . . .[f] oh, God! . . ."

I pulled him back to his chair and poured some wine down his throat as his frenzy sank to a dull apathy. He did not resist, but kept his

---

[a] reacquired family] reacquired B, D; re-acquired C
[b] VI.] *om.* B, C, D
[c] shoggoths] shaggoths D
[d] flame . . .] flame— B, C, D
[e] life . . .] life— B, C, D
[f] earth . . .] earth— B, C, D

lips moving as if talking to himself. Presently I realised[a] that he was trying to talk to me, and bent my ear to his mouth to catch the feeble words.

"... again, again ...[b] she's trying ...[c] I might have known ...[d] nothing can stop that force; not distance,[e] nor magic, nor death ...[f] it comes and comes, mostly in the night ...[g] I can't leave ...[h] it's horrible ...[i] oh, God, Dan, *if you only knew as I do just how horrible it is.* ..."[j]

When he had slumped down into a stupor I propped him with pillows and let normal sleep overtake him. I did not call a doctor, for I knew what would be said of his sanity, and wished to give nature a chance if I possibly could. He waked at midnight, and I put him to bed upstairs, but he was gone by morning. He had let himself quietly out of the house—and his butler, when called on the wire, said he was at home pacing restlessly[k] about the library.[l]

Edward went to pieces rapidly after that. He did not call again, but I went daily to see him. He would always be sitting in his library, staring at nothing and having an air of abnormal *listening*. Sometimes he talked rationally, but always on trivial topics. Any mention of his trouble, of future plans, or of Asenath would send him into a frenzy. His butler said he had frightful seizures at night, during which he might eventually do himself harm.

I had a long talk with his doctor, banker, and lawyer, and finally took the physician with two specialist colleagues to visit him. The spasms that resulted from the first questions were violent and pitiable—and that evening a closed car took his poor struggling body to the Arkham

---

[a] realised] realized B, C, D

[b] "... again, again ...] "—again, again— B, C; "—Again, again— D

[c] trying ...] trying— B, C, D

[d] known ...] known— B, C, D

[e] distance,] distance B, D

[f] death ...] death— B, C, D

[g] night ...] night— B, C, D

[h] leave ...] leave— B, C, D

[i] horrible ...] horrible— B, C, D

[j] *is.* ...'] *is!* ..."C

[k] restlessly] *om.* D

[l] library.] library. / [*Section divison:* 6] C

Sanitarium. I was made his guardian and called on him twice weekly—almost weeping to hear his wild shrieks, awesome whispers, and dreadful, droning repetitions of such phrases as "I had to do it—I had to do it . . .^{a} it'll get me . . .^{b} it'll get me . . .^{c} down there . . .^{d} down there in the dark. . . .^{e} Mother, mother!^{f} Dan! Save me . . .^{g} save me. . . ."^{h}

How much hope of recovery there was, no one could say;^{i} but I tried my best to be optimistic. Edward must have a home if he emerged, so I transferred his servants to the Derby mansion, which would surely be his sane choice. What to do about the Crowninshield place with its complex arrangements and collections of utterly inexplicable objects I could not decide, so left it momentarily untouched—telling the Derby housemaid^j to go over and dust the chief rooms once a week, and ordering the furnace man to have a fire on those days.

The final nightmare came before Candlemas—heralded, in cruel irony, by a false gleam of hope. One morning late in January the sanitarium telephoned to report that Edward's reason had suddenly come back. His continuous memory, they said, was badly impaired; but sanity itself was certain. Of course he must remain some time for observation, but there could be little doubt of the outcome. All going well, he would surely be free in a week.

I hastened over in a flood of delight, but stood bewildered when a nurse took me to Edward's room. The patient rose to greet me, extending his hand with a polite smile; but I saw in an instant that he bore the strangely energised^k personality which had seemed so foreign to his own nature—the competent personality I had found so vaguely horrible, and which Edward himself had once vowed was the intruding soul of

---

^{a} it . . .] it— B, C, D
^{b} me . . .] me— B, C, D
^{c} me . . .] me— B, C, D
^{d} there . . .] there— B, C, D
^{e} dark. . . .] dark— B, C, D
^{f} Mother, mother!] Mother! Mother! B, C, D
^{g} me . . .] me— B, C, D
^{h} me. . . ."] me—" B, C, D
^{i} say;] say, B, C, D
^{j} housemaid] household B, C, D
^{k} energised] energized B, C, D

his wife. There was the same blazing vision—so like Asenath's and old Ephraim's—and the same firm mouth;[a] and when he spoke I could sense the same grim, pervasive irony in his voice—the deep irony so redolent of potential evil. This was the person who had driven my car through the night five months before—the person I had not seen since that brief call when he had forgotten the old-time doorbell[b] signal and stirred such nebulous fears in me—and now he filled me with the same dim feeling of blasphemous alienage and ineffable cosmic hideousness.

He spoke affably of arrangements for release—and there was nothing for me to do but assent, despite some remarkable gaps in his recent memories. Yet I felt that something was terribly, inexplicably wrong and abnormal. There were horrors in this thing that I could not reach. This was a sane person—but was it indeed the Edward Derby I had known? If not, who or what was it—*and where was Edward?*[c] Ought it to be free or confined . . .[d] or ought it to be extirpated from the face of the earth? There was a hint of the abysmally sardonic in everything the creature said—the Asenath-like eyes lent a special and baffling mockery to certain words about the 'early liberty earned by an *especially close confinement*'.[e] I must have behaved very awkwardly, and was glad to beat a retreat.

All that day and the next I racked my brain over the problem. What had happened? What sort of mind looked out through those alien eyes in Edward's face? I could think of nothing but this dimly terrible enigma, and gave up all efforts to perform my usual work. The second morning the hospital called up to say that the recovered patient was unchanged, and by evening I was close to a nervous collapse—a state I admit, though others will vow it coloured[f] my subsequent vision. I have nothing to say on this point except that no madness of mine could account for *all* the evidence.

---

[a] mouth;] mouth! C
[b] old-time doorbell] old-time door-bell C; oldtime doorbell D
[c] *and . . . Edward?*] and . . . Edward? B, C, D
[d] confined . . .] confined— B, C, D
[e] 'early . . . *confinement*'.] 'early . . . *confinement.* ' A; early . . . *confinement!* B, C, D
[f] coloured] colored C

VII.[a]

It was in the night—after that second evening—that stark, utter horror burst over me and weighted my spirit with a black, clutching panic from which it can never shake free. It began with a telephone call just before midnight. I was the only one up, and sleepily took down the receiver in the library. No one seemed to be on the wire, and I was about to hang up and go to bed when my ear caught a very faint suspicion of sound at the other end. Was someone trying under great difficulties to talk? As I listened I thought I heard a sort of half-liquid bubbling noise—*"glub . . . glub . . . glub"*[b]—which had an odd suggestion of inarticulate, unintelligible word and syllable divisions. I called,[c] "Who is it?" But the only answer was *"glub-glub . . . glub-glub"*.[d] I could only assume that the noise was mechanical; but fancying that it might be a case of a broken instrument able to receive but not to send, I added, "I can't hear you. Better hang up and try Information."[e] Immediately I heard the receiver go on the hook at the other end.

This, I say, was just before[f] midnight. When that[g] call was traced afterward it was found to come from the old Crowninshield house, though it was fully half a week from the housemaid's day to be there. I shall only hint what was found at that house—the upheaval in a remote cellar storeroom, the tracks, the dirt, the hastily rifled wardrobe, the baffling marks on the telephone, the clumsily used stationery, and the detestable stench lingering over everything. The police, poor fools, have their smug little theories, and are still searching for those sinister discharged servants—who have dropped out of sight amidst the present furore.[h] They speak of a ghoulish revenge for things that were done, and say I was included because I was Edward's best friend and adviser.

[a] VII.] 7 C; V. D
[b] *"glub . . . glub . . . glub"*] "glub . . . glub . . . glub" D
[c] called] called, C
[d] *"glub-glub . . . glub-glub".*] *"glub-glub . . . glub-glub."* B, C; "glub . . . glub . . . glub-glub." D
[e] Information."] Information". A
[f] before] about D
[g] that] the D
[h] furore.] furor. C

Idiots!—do[a] they fancy those brutish clowns could have forged that handwriting? Do they fancy they could have brought what later came? Are they blind to the changes in that body that was Edward's? As for me, *I now believe all that Edward Derby ever told me.* There are horrors beyond life's edge that we do not suspect, and once in a while man's evil prying calls them just within our range. Ephraim—Asenath—that devil called them in, and they engulfed Edward as they are engulfing me.

Can I be sure that I am safe? Those powers survive the life of the physical form. The next day—in the afternoon, when I pulled out of my prostration and was able to walk and talk coherently—I went to the madhouse[b] and shot him dead for Edward's and the world's sake, but can I be sure till he is cremated? They are keeping the body for some silly autopsies by different doctors—but I say he must be cremated. *He must be cremated—he who was not Edward Derby when I shot him.* I shall go mad if he is not, for I may be the next. But my will is not weak—and I shall not let it be undermined by the terrors I know are seething around it. One life—Ephraim, Asenath, and Edward—who now? I *will not* be driven out of my body . . . I *will not* change souls with that bullet-ridden lich in the madhouse!

But let me try to tell coherently of that final horror. I will not speak of what the police persistently ignored—the tales of that dwarfed, grotesque, malodorous thing met by at least three wayfarers in High St.[c] just before two o'clock, and the nature of the single footprints in certain places. I will say only that just about two the doorbell and knocker waked me—doorbell[d] and knocker both, plied alternately and uncertainly in a kind of weak desperation, *and each trying to keep to Edward's old signal of three-and-two strokes.*

Roused from sound sleep, my mind leaped into a turmoil. Derby at the door—and remembering the old code! That new personality had not remembered it . . . was Edward suddenly back in his rightful state? Why was he here in such evident stress and haste? Had he been released ahead of time, or had he escaped? Perhaps, I thought as I

---

[a] Idiots!—do] Idiots! do B, C; Idiots! Do D
[b] madhouse] madhouse next day A
[c] St.] Street B, C, D
[d] doorbell . . . doorbell] door-bell . . . door-bell C

flung on a robe and bounded downstairs, his return to his own self had brought raving and violence, revoking his discharge and driving him to a desperate dash for freedom. Whatever had happened, he was good old Edward again, and I would help him!

When I opened the door into the elm-arched blackness a gust of insufferably foetid[a] wind almost flung me prostrate. I choked in nausea, and for a second scarcely saw the dwarfed, humped figure on the steps. The summons had been Edward's, but who was this foul, stunted parody? Where had Edward had time to go? His ring had sounded only a second before the door opened.

The caller had on one of Edward's overcoats—its bottom almost touching the ground, and its sleeves rolled back yet still covering the hands. On the head was a slouch hat pulled low, while a black silk muffler concealed the face. As I stepped unsteadily forward, the figure made a semi-liquid sound like that I had heard over the telephone— "*glub . . . glub . . .*"[b]—and thrust at me a large, closely written paper impaled on the end of a long pencil. Still reeling from the morbid and unaccountable foetor,[c] I seized this[d] paper and tried to read it in the light from the doorway.

Beyond question, it was in Edward's script. But why had he written when he was close enough to ring—and why was the script so awkward, coarse,[e] and shaky? I could make out nothing in the dim half light,[f] so edged back into the hall, the dwarf figure clumping mechanically after but pausing on the inner door's threshold. The odour[g] of this singular messenger was really appalling, and I hoped (not in vain, thank God!) that my wife would not wake and confront it.

Then, as I read the paper, I felt my knees give under me and my vision go black. I was lying on the floor when I came to, that accursed sheet still clutched in my fear-rigid hand. This is what it said.[h]

[a] foetid] fetid C
[b] "*glub . . . glub . . .*"] "glub . . . glub . . ." D
[c] foetor,] fetor, C
[d] this] the B, C, D
[e] coarse,] coarse B, C, D
[f] half light] half-light, C
[g] odour] odor C
[h] said.] said: C

"Dan—go to the sanitarium and kill it. Exterminate it. It isn't Edward Derby any more. She got me—it's Asenath—*and she has been dead three months and a half.* I lied when I said she had gone away. I killed her. I had to. It was sudden, but we were alone and I was in my right body. I saw a candlestick and smashed her head in. She would have got me for good at Hallowmass.

"I buried her in the farther cellar storeroom under some old boxes and cleaned up all the traces. The servants suspected next morning, but they have such secrets that they dare not tell the police. I sent them off, but God knows what they—and others of the cult—will do.

"I thought for a while I was all right, and then I felt the tugging at my brain. I knew what it was—I ought to have remembered. A soul like hers—or Ephraim's—is half detached, and keeps right on after death as long as the body lasts. She was getting me—making me change bodies with her—*seizing my body and putting me in that corpse of hers buried in the cellar.*

"I knew what was coming—that's why I snapped and had to go to[a] the asylum. Then it came—I found myself choked in the dark—in Asenath's rotting carcass down there in the cellar under the boxes where I put it. And I knew she must be in my body at the sanitarium—*permanently,*[b] for it was after Hallowmass, and the sacrifice would work even without her being there—sane, and ready for release as a menace to the world. I was desperate, *and in spite of everything I clawed my way out.*

"I'm too far gone to talk—I couldn't manage to telephone—but I can still write. I'll get fixed up somehow and bring you[c] this last word and warning. *Kill that fiend* if you value the peace and comfort of the world. *See that it is cremated.* If you don't, it will live on and on, body to body for ever,[d] and I can't tell you what it will do. Keep clear of black magic, Dan,[e] it's the devil's business. Goodbye[f]—you've been a great friend. Tell the police whatever they'll believe—and I'm damnably sorry to drag all this on you. I'll be at peace before long—this thing won't hold together much more. Hope you can read this. *And kill that thing—kill it.*

Yours—Ed."[g]

---

[a] to] *om.* A
[b] *permanently,*] permanently, B, C, D
[c] you] *om.* B, C, D
[d] for ever,] forever, A, B, D
[e] Dan,] Dan— C
[f] Goodbye] Good-bye C
[g] Ed."] ED." C

It was only afterward that I read the last half of this paper, for I had fainted at the end of the third paragraph. I fainted again when I saw and smelled what cluttered up the threshold where the warm air had struck it. The messenger would not move or have consciousness any more.

The butler, tougher-fibred[a] than I, did not faint at what met him in the hall in the morning. Instead, he telephoned the police. When they came I had been taken upstairs to bed, but the—other mass—lay where it had collapsed in the night. The men put handkerchiefs to their noses.

What they finally found inside Edward's oddly assorted[b] clothes was mostly liquescent horror. There were bones, too—and a crushed-in skull. Some dental work positively identified the skull as Asenath's.

[a] tougher-fibred] tougher-fibered C
[b] oddly assorted] oddly-assorted A, B, C, D

The Book

My memories are very confused. There is even much doubt as to where they begin; for at times I feel appalling vistas of years stretching behind me, while at other times it seems as if the present moment were an isolated point in a grey, formless infinity. I am not even certain how I am communicating this message. While I know I am speaking, I have a vague impression that some strange and perhaps terrible mediation will be needed to bear what I say to the points where I wish to be heard. My identity, too, is bewilderingly cloudy. I seem to have suffered a great shock—perhaps from some utterly monstrous outgrowth of my cycles of unique, incredible experience.

These cycles of experience, of course, all stem from that worm-riddled book. I remember when I found it—in a dimly lighted place near the black, oily river where the mists always swirl. That place was very old, and the ceiling-high shelves full of rotting volumes reached back endlessly through windowless inner rooms and alcoves. There were, besides, great formless heaps of books on the floor and in crude bins; and it was in one of these heaps that I found the thing. I never learned its title, for the early pages were missing; but it fell open toward the end and gave me a glimpse of something which sent my senses reeling.

There was a formula—a sort of list of things to say and do—which I recognised as something black and forbidden; something which I had read of before in furtive paragraphs of mixed abhorrence and fascination penned by those strange ancient delvers into the universe's guarded secrets whose decaying texts[a] I loved to absorb. It was a key—a guide—

Editor's Note: The A.Ms. is HPL's original draft, somewhat revised and interlined. The title was supplied by R. H. Barlow and written on the A.Ms. in pencil. All texts derive from the first publication, in Barlow's *Leaves,* which presented the text accurately enough.

Texts: A = A.Ms. (untitled) (JHL); B = *Leaves* 2 (1938): 110–12; C = *Dagon and Other Macabre Tales* (Arkham House, 1965), 340–42. Copy-text: A.

to certain gateways and transitions of which mystics have dreamed and whispered since the race was young, and which lead to freedoms and discoveries beyond the three dimensions and realms of life and matter that we know. Not for centuries had any man recalled its vital substance or known where to find it, but this book was very old indeed. No printing-press, but the hand of some half-crazed monk, had traced these ominous Latin phrases in uncials of awesome[a] antiquity.

I remember how the old man leered and tittered, and made a curious sign with his hand when I bore it away. He had refused to take pay for it, and only long afterward did I guess why. As I hurried home through those narrow, winding, mist-choked[b] waterfront streets I had a frightful impression of being stealthily followed by softly padding feet. The centuried, tottering houses on both sides seemed alive with a fresh and morbid malignity—as if some hitherto closed channel of evil understanding had abruptly been opened. I felt that those walls and overhanging gables of mildewed brick and fungous[c] plaster and timber— with fishy, eye-like,[d] diamond-paned windows that leered—could hardly desist from advancing and crushing me . . . yet I had read only the least fragment of that blasphemous rune before closing the book and bringing it away.

I remember how I read the book at last—white-faced, and locked in the attic room that I had long devoted to strange searchings. The great house was very still, for I had not gone up till after midnight. I think I had a family then—though the details are very uncertain—and I know there were many servants. Just what the year was, I cannot say; for since then I have known many ages and dimensions, and have had all my notions of time dissolved and refashioned. It was by the light of candles that I read—I recall the relentless dripping of the wax—and there were chimes that came every now and then from distant belfries. I seemed to keep track of those chimes with a peculiar intentness, as if I feared to hear some very remote, intruding note among them.

[a] texts] textx B
[a] of awesome] ofawesome B
[b] mist-choked] mist-cloaked B, C
[c] fungous] fungoid B, C
[d] fishy, eye-like,] eye-like, B; eyelike, C

Then came the first scratching and fumbling at the dormer window that looked out high above the other roofs of the city. It came as I droned aloud the ninth verse of that primal lay, and I knew amidst my shudders what it meant. For he who passes the gateways always wins a shadow, and never again can he be alone. I had evoked—and the book was indeed all I had suspected. That night I passed the gateway to a vortex of twisted time and vision, and when morning found me in the attic room I saw in the walls and shelves and fittings that which I had never seen before.

Nor could I ever after see the world as I had known it. Mixed with the present scene was always a little of the past and a little of the future, and every once-familiar object loomed alien in the new perspective brought by my widened sight. From then on I walked in a fantastic dream of unknown and half-known shapes; and with each new gateway crossed, the less plainly could I recognise the things of the narrow sphere to which I had so long been bound. What I saw about me[a] none else saw; and I grew doubly silent and aloof lest I be thought mad. Dogs had a fear of me, for they felt the outside shadow which never left my side. But still I read more—in hidden, forgotten books and scrolls to which my new vision led me—and pushed through fresh gateways of space and being and life-patterns toward the core of the unknown cosmos.

I remember the night I made the five concentric circles of fire on the floor, and stood in the innermost one chanting that monstrous litany the messenger from Tartary had brought. The walls melted away, and I was swept by a black wind through gulfs of fathomless grey with the needle-like pinnacles of unknown mountains miles below me. After a while there was utter blackness, and then the light of myriad stars forming strange, alien constellations. Finally I saw a green-litten plain far below me, and discerned on it the twisted towers of a city built in no fashion I had ever known or read of or dreamed of. As I floated closer to that city I saw a great square building of stone in an open space, and felt a hideous fear clutching at me. I screamed and struggled, and after a blankness was again in my attic room,[b] sprawled flat over the five phosphorescent

[a] me] me, B, C
[b] room,] room B, C

circles on the floor. In that night's wandering there was no more of strangeness than in many a former night's wandering; but there was more of terror because I knew I was closer to those outside gulfs and worlds than I had ever been before. Thereafter I was more cautious with my incantations, for I had no wish to be cut off from my body and from the earth in unknown abysses whence I could never return.

The Shadow out of Time

I.

After twenty-two[a] years of nightmare and terror, saved only by a desperate conviction of the mythical source of certain impressions, I am unwilling to vouch for the truth of that which I think I found in Western Australia on the night of July 17–18,

Editor's Note: The restoration of the text of this story became considerably easier with the unexpected discovery of HPL's original A.Ms. in 1994. I prepared the first corrected edition (Hippocampus Press, 2001), and that edition contains an essay by John H. Stanley recounting the discovery of the A.Ms. The story was surreptitiously typed by R. H. Barlow during HPL's visit with him in Florida in the summer of 1935. (A fragmentary A.Ms., long held by JHL, appears to be a fair copy of one page of the original A.Ms., perhaps because Barlow was unable to read this page adequately.) Barlow's T.Ms. (non-extant) was probably quite inaccurate in spots, and HPL does not seem to have corrected it very carefully, if at all, before it was submitted (by Donald Wandrei) to *Astounding Stories,* where it appeared in the June 1936 issue.

HPL inexplicably declared to many correspondents that the text was not tampered with in the same manner as was *At the Mountains of Madness,* but it is clear that the same kind of editorial alterations—changes in punctuation and especially the breaking up of HPL's long paragraphs into shorter ones—have occurred here, although no actual cuts were made. HPL did prepare a hand-corrected copy of the *Astounding* issue containing the story, but he corrected only a few obvious errors and none of the paragraphing changes (he clearly did not have the A.Ms. at hand while doing so, since he had presented it as a gift to Barlow). There will always be uncertainty whether a given variant between the A.Ms. and the *Astounding* appearance is a result of Barlow's error in the T.Ms. or a change by the *Astounding* editors, but the matter is largely academic. The Arkham House text appears to have been based on HPL's corrected copy of *Astounding,* since it restores a phrase at one point in the text (429.7) where *Astounding* erroneously printed a line of text from another passage.

Texts: A = A.Ms. (JHL); A2 = fragmentary A.Ms. (JHL); B = *Astounding Stories* 17, No. 4 (June 1936): 110–54; B[c] = HPL's corrected copy of *Astounding* issue (JHL); C = *The Dunwich Horror and Others* (Arkham House, 1963), 370–431. Copy-text: A.

[a] twenty-two] 22 A

1935. There is reason to hope that my experience was wholly or partly an hallucination—for which, indeed, abundant causes existed. And yet, its realism was so hideous that I sometimes find hope impossible.[a] If the thing did happen, then man must be prepared to accept notions of the cosmos, and of his own place in the seething vortex of time, whose merest mention is paralysing.[b] He must, too, be placed on guard against a specific[c] lurking peril which, though it will never engulf the whole race, may impose monstrous and unguessable horrors upon certain venturesome members of it.[d] It is for this latter reason that I urge, with all the force of my being, a final abandonment of all[e] attempts at unearthing those fragments of unknown, primordial masonry which my expedition set out to investigate.

Assuming that I was sane and awake, my experience on that night was such as has befallen no man before. It was, moreover, a frightful confirmation of all I had sought to dismiss as myth and dream. Mercifully there is no proof, for in my fright I lost the awesome object which would—if real and brought out of that noxious abyss—have formed irrefutable evidence.[f] When I came upon the horror I was alone—and I have up to now told no one about it. I could not stop the others from digging in its direction, but chance and the shifting sand have so far saved them from finding it. Now I must formulate some definitive[g] statement—not only for the sake of my own mental balance, but to warn such others as may read it seriously.

These pages—much in whose earlier parts will be familiar to close readers of the general and scientific press—are written in the cabin of the ship that is bringing me home. I shall give them to my son, Prof.[h] Wingate Peaslee of Miskatonic University—the only member of my family who stuck to me after my queer amnesia of long ago, and the man best informed on the inner facts of my case. Of all living persons,

---

[a] impossible.] impossible. ¶ B, C
[b] paralysing.] paralyzing. B, C
[c] specific] specific, B, C
[d] it.] it. ¶ B, C
[e] all] all the B, C
[f] evidence.] evidence. ¶ B, C
[g] definitive] definite C
[h] Prof.] Professor B, C

he is least likely to ridicule what I shall tell of that fateful night.[a] I did not enlighten him orally before sailing, because I think he had better have the revelation in written form. Reading and re-reading[b] at leisure will leave with him a more convincing picture than my confused tongue could hope to convey.[c] He can do as[d] he thinks best with this account—shewing[e] it, with suitable comment, to[f] any quarters where it will be likely to accomplish good. It is for the sake of such readers as are unfamiliar with the earlier phases of my case that I am prefacing the revelation itself with a fairly ample summary of its background.

My name is Nathaniel Wingate Peaslee, and those who recall the newspaper tales of a generation back—or the letters and articles in psychological journals six or seven years ago—will know who and what I am. The press was filled with the details of my strange amnesia in 1908–13, and much was made of the traditions of horror, madness, and witchcraft which lurk[g] behind the ancient Massachusetts town then and now forming my place of residence. Yet I would have it known that there is nothing whatever of the mad or sinister in my heredity and early life. This is a highly important fact in view of the shadow which fell so suddenly upon me from *outside* sources.[h] It may be that centuries of dark brooding had given to crumbling, whisper-haunted Arkham a peculiar vulnerability as regards such shadows—though even this seems doubtful in the light of those other cases which I later came to study. But the chief point is that my own ancestry and background are altogether normal. What came, came from *somewhere else*—where, I even now hesitate to assert in plain words.

I am the son of Jonathan and Hannah (Wingate) Peaslee, both of wholesome old Haverhill stock. I was born and reared in Haverhill—at the old homestead in Boardman Street near Golden Hill—and did not go to Arkham till I entered Miskatonic University at the age of

[a] night.] night. ¶ B, C
[b] re-reading] rereading B, C
[c] convey.] convey. ¶ B, C
[d] as] anything that B, C
[e] shewing] showing B, C
[f] to] in B, C
[g] lurk] lurked B, C
[h] sources.] sources. ¶ B, C

eighteen. That was in 1889. After my graduation I studied economics at Harvard, and came back to Miskatonic[a] as Instructor of Political Economy[b] in 1895.[c] For thirteen years more my life ran smoothly and happily. I married Alice Keezar of Haverhill in 1896, and my three children, Robert K.,[d] Wingate,[e] and Hannah,[f] were born in 1898, 1900, and 1903, respectively. In 1898 I became an associate professor, and in 1902 a full professor. At no time had I the least interest in either occultism or abnormal psychology.

It was on Thursday, May 14, 1908, that the queer amnesia came. The thing was quite sudden, though later I realised[g] that certain brief, glimmering visions of several hours previous—chaotic visions which disturbed me greatly because they were so unprecedented—must have formed premonitory symptoms. My head was aching, and I had a singular feeling—altogether new to me—that someone[h] else was trying to get possession of my thoughts.

The collapse occurred about 10:20 a.m.,[i] while I was conducting a class in Political Economy VI—history and present tendencies of economics—for juniors and a few sophomores. I began to see strange shapes before my eyes, and to feel that I was in a grotesque room other than the classroom.[j] My thoughts and speech wandered from my subject, and the students saw that something was gravely amiss. Then I slumped down, unconscious[k] in my chair, in a stupor from which no one could arouse me. Nor did my rightful faculties again look out upon the daylight of our normal world for five years, four months, and thirteen days.

---

[a] at the age . . . Miskatonic] *om.* B, C
[b] Instructor . . . Economy] instructor of political economy C
[c] 1895.] 1895. ¶ B, C
[d] K.] *om.* B, C
[e] Wingate,] Wingate B, C
[f] Hannah,] Hannah B, C
[g] realised] realized B, C
[h] someone] some one B, C
[i] a.m.,] a. m., B, C
[j] classroom.] classroom. ¶ B, C
[k] unconscious] unconscious, B, C

It is, of course, from others that I have learned what followed. I shewed[a] no sign of consciousness for sixteen and a half hours, though removed to my home at 27 Crane Street[b] and given the best of medical attention.[c] At 3 a.m.[d] May 15[e] my eyes opened and I began to speak, but before long the doctors[f] and my family were thoroughly frightened by the trend of my expression and language. It was clear that I had no remembrance of my identity or of[g] my past, though for some reason I seemed anxious to conceal this lack of knowledge. My eyes gazed strangely at the persons around me, and the flexions[h] of my facial muscles were altogether unfamiliar.

Even my speech seemed awkward and foreign. I used my vocal organs clumsily and gropingly, and my diction had a curiously stilted quality, as if I had laboriously learned the English language from books. The pronunciation was barbarously alien, whilst the idiom seemed to include both scraps of curious archaism[i] and expressions of a wholly incomprehensible cast.[j] Of the latter[k] one in particular was very potently—even terrifiedly—recalled by the youngest of the physicians twenty years afterward. For at that late period such a phrase began to have an actual currency—first in England and then in the United States—and though of much complexity and indisputable newness, it reproduced in every least particular the mystifying words of the strange Arkham patient of 1908.

Physical strength returned at once, although I required an odd amount of re-education[l] in the use of my hands, legs, and bodily apparatus in general. Because of this and other handicaps inherent in

[a] shewed] showed B, C
[b] Street] St. A; Street, B, C
[c] attention.] attention. ¶ B, C
[d] a.m.] a. m. B, C
[e] 15] 15th B, C
[f] doctors] doctor C
[g] or of] and B, C
[h] flexions] flections B[c], C
[i] archaism] Archaism B[c]
[j] cast.] cast. ¶ B, C
[k] latter] latter, B, C
[l] re-education] re-/education B; reeducation C

the mnemonic lapse, I was for some time kept under strict medical care.[a] When I saw that my attempts to conceal the lapse had failed, I admitted it openly, and became eager for information of all sorts. Indeed, it seemed to the doctors that I lost interest in my proper personality as soon as I found the case of amnesia accepted as a natural thing.[b] They noticed that my chief efforts were to master certain points in history, science, art, language, and folklore—some of them tremendously abstruse, and some childishly simple—which remained, very oddly in many cases, outside my consciousness.

At the same time they noticed that I had an inexplicable command of many almost unknown sorts of knowledge—a command which I seemed to wish to hide rather than display. I would inadvertently refer, with casual assurance, to specific events in dim ages outside[c] the range of accepted history—passing off such references as a jest when I saw the surprise they created. And I had a way of speaking of the future which two or three times caused actual fright.[d] These uncanny flashes soon ceased to appear, though some observers laid their vanishment more to a certain furtive caution on my part than to any waning of the strange knowledge behind them. Indeed, I seemed anomalously avid to absorb the speech, customs, and perspectives of the age around me; as if I were a studious traveller[e] from a far, foreign land.

As soon as permitted, I haunted the college library at all hours; and shortly began to arrange for those odd travels, and special courses at American and European universities,[f] which evoked so much comment during the next few years.[g] I did not at any time suffer from a lack of learned contacts, for my case had a mild celebrity among the psychologists of the period. I was lectured upon as a typical example of secondary personality—even though I seemed to puzzle the

---

[a] care.] care. ¶ B, C
[b] thing.] thing. ¶ B, C
[c] outside] outside of C
[d] fright.] fright. ¶ B, C
[e] traveller] traveler B, C
[f] universities,] Universities, B[c], C
[g] years.] years. ¶ B, C

lecturers now and then with some bizarre symptom[a] or some queer trace of carefully veiled mockery.

Of real friendliness, however, I encountered little. Something in my aspect and speech seemed to excite vague fears and aversions in everyone[b] I met, as if I were a being infinitely removed from all that is normal and healthful. This idea of a black, hidden horror connected with incalculable gulfs of some sort of *distance* was oddly widespread and persistent.[c] My own family formed no exception. From the moment of my strange waking my wife had regarded me with extreme horror and loathing, vowing that I was some utter alien usurping the body of her husband. In 1910 she obtained a legal divorce, nor would she ever consent to see me[d] even after my return to normalcy[e] in 1913. These feelings were shared by my elder son and my small daughter, neither of whom I have ever seen since.

Only my second son Wingate[f] seemed able to conquer the terror and repulsion which my change aroused. He indeed felt that I was a stranger, but though only eight years old held fast to a faith that my proper self would return. When it did return he sought me out, and the courts gave me his custody. In succeeding years he helped me with the studies to which I was driven, and today[g] at thirty-five[h] he is a professor of psychology at Miskatonic.[i] But I do not wonder at the horror I caused—for certainly, the mind, voice, and facial expression of the being that awaked[j] on May 15, 1908[k] were not those of Nathaniel Wingate Peaslee.

I will not attempt to tell much of my life from 1908 to 1913, since readers may glean all the outward essentials—as I largely had to do—

[a] symptom] symptoms C
[b] everyone] every one B, C
[c] persistent.] persistent. ¶ B, C
[d] me] me, B[c]
[e] normalcy] normality B, C
[f] son Wingate] son, Wingate, B, C
[g] today] to-day, B; today, C
[h] thirty-five] 35 A; thirty-five, B, C
[i] Miskatonic.] Miskatonic. ¶ B, C
[j] awaked] awakened C
[k] 1908] 1908, B, C

from files of old newspapers and scientific journals.[a] I was given charge of my funds, and spent them slowly[b] and on the whole wisely, in travel and in study at various centres[c] of learning. My travels, however, were singular in the extreme;[d] involving long visits to remote and desolate places.[e] In 1909 I spent a month in the Himalayas, and in 1911 aroused much attention through a camel trip into the unknown deserts of Arabia. What happened on those journeys I have never been able to learn.[f] During the summer of 1912 I chartered a ship and sailed in the arctic[g] north of Spitzbergen, afterward shewing[h] signs of disappointment.[i] Later in that year I spent weeks alone beyond the limits of previous or subsequent exploration in the vast limestone cavern systems[j] of western Virginia—black labyrinths so complex that no retracing of my steps could even be considered.

My sojourns at the universities were marked by abnormally rapid assimilation, as if the secondary personality had an intelligence enormously superior to my own. I have found, also, that my rate of reading and solitary study was phenomenal. I could master every detail of a book merely by glancing over it as fast as I could turn the leaves; while my skill at interpreting complex figures in an instant was veritably awesome.[k] At times there appeared almost ugly reports of my power to influence the thoughts and acts of others, though I seemed to have taken care to minimise[l] displays of this faculty.

Other ugly reports concerned my intimacy with leaders of occultist groups, and scholars suspected of connexion[m] with nameless bands of

[a] journals.] journals. ¶ B, C
[b] slowly] slowly, C
[c] centres] centers B, C
[d] the extreme;] the extreme, B; extreme, C
[e] places.] places. ¶ B, C
[f] learn.] learn. ¶ B, C
[g] arctic] Arctic A; arctic, B; Arctic, C
[h] shewing] showing A, B, C
[i] disappointment.] disappointment. ¶ B, C
[j] cavern systems] caverns system B[c]
[k] awesome.] awesome. ¶ B, C
[l] minimise] minimize B, C
[m] connexion] connection B, C

abhorrent elder-world hierophants. These rumours,[a] though never proved at the time, were doubtless stimulated by the known tenor of some of my reading—for the consultation of rare books at libraries cannot be effected secretly.[b] There is tangible proof—in the form of marginal notes—that I went minutely through such things as the Comte d'Erlette's "Cultes des Goules",[c] Ludvig Prinn's "De Vermis Mysteriis",[d] the "Unaussprechlichen Kulten"[e] of von Junzt, the surviving fragments of the puzzling "Book of Eibon",[f] and the dreaded "Necronomicon"[g] of the mad Arab Abdul Alhazred. Then, too, it is undeniable that a fresh and evil wave of underground cult activity set in about the time of my odd mutation.

In the summer of 1913 I began to display signs of ennui and flagging interest, and to hint to various associates that a change might soon be expected in me. I spoke of returning memories of my earlier life—though most auditors judged me insincere, since all the recollections I gave were casual, and such as might have been learned from my old private papers.[h] About the middle of August I returned to Arkham and reopened my long-closed house in Crane Street.[i] Here I installed a mechanism of the most curious aspect, constructed piecemeal by different makers of scientific apparatus in Europe and America, and guarded carefully from the sight of anyone[j] intelligent enough to analyse it.[k] Those who did see it—a workman, a servant, and the new housekeeper—say that it was a queer mixture of rods, wheels, and mirrors, though only about two feet tall, one foot wide, and one foot thick. The central mirror was circular and convex. All this is borne out by such makers of parts as can be located.

---

[a] rumours,] rumors, B, C

[b] secretly.] secretly. ¶ B, C

[c] "Cultes des Goules",] *Cultes des Goules*, A, B, C

[d] "De Vermis Mysteriis",] *De Vermis Mysteriis*, A, B, C

[e] "Unaussprechlichen Kulten"] *Unaussprechlichen Kulten* A, B, C

[f] "Book of Eibon",] *Book of Eibon*, A, B, C

[g] "Necronomicon"] *Necronomicon* A, B, C

[h] papers.] papers. ¶ B, C

[i] Street] St. A

[j] anyone] any one B, C

[k] analyse it.] analyze it. ¶ B, C

On the evening of Friday, September[a] 26, I dismissed the housekeeper and the maid till[b] noon of the next day. Lights burned in the house till late, and a lean, dark, curiously foreign-looking man called in an automobile.[c] It was about 1 a.m.[d] that the lights were last seen. At 2:15 a.m.[e] a policeman observed the place in darkness, but with[f] the stranger's motor still at the curb. By four[g] o'clock the motor was certainly gone.[h] It was at six[i] that a hesitant, foreign voice on the telephone asked Dr. Wilson to call at my house and bring me out of a peculiar faint. This call—a long-distance one—was later traced to a public booth in the North Station in Boston, but no sign of the lean foreigner was ever unearthed.

When the doctor reached my house he found me unconscious in the sitting-room[j]—in an easy-chair with a table drawn up before it. On the polished table-top[k] were scratches shewing[l] where some heavy object had rested. The queer machine was gone, nor was anything afterward heard of it. Undoubtedly the dark, lean foreigner had taken it away.[m] In the library grate were abundant ashes[n] evidently left from the burning of every remaining scrap of paper on which I had written since the advent of the amnesia. Dr. Wilson found my breathing very peculiar, but after an[o] hypodermic injection it became more regular.

At 11:15 a.m.,[p] September 27,[q] I stirred vigorously, and my

[a] September] Sept. A
[b] till] until B, C
[c] automobile.] automobile. ¶ B, C
[d] 1 a.m.] one a. m. B, C
[e] a.m.] a. m. B, C
[f] with] *om.* C
[g] four] 4 A, B, C
[h] gone.] gone. ¶ B, C
[i] six] 6 o'clock B, C
[j] sitting-room] sitting room B, C
[k] table-top] table top B; top C
[l] shewing] showing A, B, C
[m] away.] away. ¶ B, C
[n] ashes] ashes, B, C
[o] an] A, B [*changed to* a *by HPL*]; a C
[p] a.m.,] a. m., B, C
[q] September 27,] Sept. 27, A; September 27th, B, C

hitherto mask-like[a] face began to shew[b] signs of expression. Dr. Wilson remarked that the expression was not that of my secondary personality, but seemed much like[c] that of my normal self. About 11:30 I muttered some very curious syllables—syllables which seemed unrelated to any human speech. I appeared, too, to struggle against something. Then, just after noon—the housekeeper and the maid having meanwhile returned—I began to mutter in English.[d]

"... of[e] the orthodox economists of that period, Jevons typifies the prevailing trend toward scientific correlation. His attempt to link the commercial cycle of prosperity and depression with the physical cycle of the solar spots forms perhaps the apex of . . ."[f]

Nathaniel Wingate Peaslee had come back—a spirit in whose time-scale[g] it was still that[h] Thursday morning in 1908, with the economics class gazing up at the battered desk on the platform.

II.

My reabsorption into normal life was a painful and difficult process. The loss of over five years creates more complications than can be imagined, and in my case there were countless matters to be adjusted.[i] What I heard of my actions since 1908 astonished and disturbed me, but I tried to view the matter as philosophically as I could. At last[j] regaining custody of my second son[k] Wingate, I settled down with him in the Crane Street house and endeavoured[l] to resume[m] teaching—my old professorship having been kindly offered me by the college.

[a] mask-like] masklike A, B, C
[b] shew] show A, B, C
[c] like] ike B
[d] English.] English: B
[e] "... of] "—of B, C
[f] of . . ."] of—" B, C
[g] time-scale] time scale B, C
[h] that] om. C
[i] adjusted.] adjusted. ¶ B, C
[j] last] last, B, C
[k] son] son, B, C
[l] endeavoured] endeavored B, C
[m] resume] resume my B, C

I began work with the February, 1914,[a] term, and kept at it just a year. By that time I realised[b] how badly my experience had shaken me. Though perfectly sane—I hoped—and with no flaw in my original personality, I had not the nervous energy of the old days. Vague dreams and queer ideas continually haunted me, and when the outbreak of the world war[c] turned my mind to history I found myself thinking of periods and events in the oddest possible fashion.[d] My conception of *time*—my ability to distinguish between consecutiveness and simultaneousness—seemed subtly disordered; so that I formed chimerical notions about living in one age and casting one's mind all over eternity for knowledge of past and future ages.

The war[e] gave me strange impressions of *remembering*[f] some of its far-off *consequences*[g]—as if I knew how it was coming out and could look *back* upon it in the light of future information. All such quasi-memories[h] were attended with much pain, and with a feeling that some artificial psychological barrier was set against them.[i] When I diffidently hinted to others about my impressions[j] I met with varied responses. Some persons looked uncomfortably at me, but men in the mathematics department spoke of new developments in those theories of relativity—then discussed only in learned circles—which were later to become so famous. Dr. Albert Einstein, they said, was rapidly reducing *time*[k] to the status of a mere dimension.

But the dreams and disturbed feelings gained on me, so that I had to drop my regular work in 1915. Certain of the impressions were taking an annoying shape—giving me the persistent notion that my

---

[a] February, 1914,] February 1914 B
[b] realised] realized B, C
[c] world war] World War B, C
[d] fashion.] fashion. ¶ B, C
[e] war] War B[c], C
[f] *remembering*] remembering B, C
[g] *consequences*] consequences B, C
[h] quasi-memories] quasi memories B
[i] them.] them. ¶ B
[j] impressions] impressions, B, C
[k] *time*] time B, C

amnesia had formed some unholy sort of *exchange;*[a] that the secondary personality had indeed been an intruding force from unknown regions, and that my own personality had suffered displacement.[b] Thus I was driven to vague and frightful speculations concerning the whereabouts of my true self during the years that another had held my body. The curious knowledge and strange conduct of my body's late tenant troubled me more and more as I learned further details from persons, papers, and magazines.[c] Queernesses that had baffled others seemed to harmonise[d] terribly with some background of black knowledge which festered in the chasms of my subconscious. I began to search feverishly for every scrap of information bearing on the studies and travels of *that other one*[e] during the dark years.

Not all of my troubles were as semi-abstract as this. There were the dreams—and these seemed to grow in vividness and concreteness. Knowing how most would regard them, I seldom mentioned them to anyone[f] but my son or certain trusted psychologists, but eventually I commenced a scientific study of other cases in order to see how typical or non-typical[g] such visions might be among amnesia victims.[h] My results, aided by psychologists, historians, anthropologists, and mental specialists of wide experience, and by a study that included all records of split personalities from the days of daemoniac-possession[i] legends to the medically realistic present, at first bothered me more than they consoled me.

I soon found that my dreams had indeed[j] no counterpart in the overwhelming bulk of true amnesia cases. There remained, however, a tiny residue of accounts which for years baffled and shocked me with their parallelism to my own experience. Some of them were bits of

---

[a] *exchange;*] exchange; B, C
[b] displacement.] displacement. ¶ B, C
[c] magazines.] magazines. ¶ B, C
[d] harmonise] harmonize B, C
[e] *that other one*] that other one B, C
[f] anyone] any one B, C
[g] non-typical] nontypical B, C
[h] victims.] victims. ¶ B, C
[i] daemoniac-possession] demoniac-possession A, B, C
[j] had indeed] had, indeed, B, C

ancient folklore; others were case-histories[a] in the annals of medicine; one or two were anecdotes obscurely buried in standard histories.[b] It thus appeared that, while my special kind of affliction was prodigiously rare, instances of it had occurred at long intervals ever since the beginning of man's[c] annals. Some centuries might contain one, two, or three cases;[d] others none—or at least none whose record survived.

The essence was always the same—a person of keen thoughtfulness seized with a strange secondary life and leading for a greater or lesser period an utterly alien existence typified at first by vocal and bodily awkwardness, and later by a wholesale acquisition of scientific, historic, artistic, and anthropological knowledge; an acquisition carried on with feverish zest and with a wholly abnormal absorptive power. Then a sudden return of the rightful consciousness, intermittently plagued ever after with vague unplaceable dreams suggesting fragments of some hideous memory elaborately blotted out.[e] And the close resemblance of those nightmares to my own— even in some of the smallest particulars—left no doubt in my mind of their significantly typical nature. One or two of the cases had an added ring of faint, blasphemous familiarity, as if I had heard of them before through some cosmic channel too morbid and frightful to contemplate. In three instances there was specific mention of such an unknown machine as had been in my house before the second change.

Another thing that cloudily[f] worried me during my investigation was the somewhat greater frequency of cases where a brief, elusive glimpse of the typical nightmares was afforded to persons not visited with well-defined amnesia.[g] These persons were largely of mediocre mind or less—some so primitive that they could scarcely be thought of as vehicles for abnormal scholarship and preternatural mental acquisitions.

---

[a] case-histories] case histories B, C
[b] histories.] histories. ¶ B, C
[c] man's] men's B, C
[d] cases;] cases, B, C
[e] out.] out. ¶ B, C
[f] cloudily] *om.* B, C
[g] amnesia.] amnesia. ¶ B, C

For a second they would be fired with alien force—then a backward lapse[a] and a thin, swift-fading memory of unhuman[b] horrors.

There had been at least three such cases during the past half century—one only fifteen[c] years before. Had something been *groping blindly through time*[d] from some unsuspected abyss in Nature?[e] Were these faint cases monstrous, sinister *experiments*[f] of a kind and authorship utterly beyond sane belief?[g] Such were a few of the formless speculations of my weaker hours—fancies abetted by myths which my studies uncovered. For I could not doubt but that certain persistent legends of immemorial antiquity,[h] apparently unknown to the victims and physicians connected with recent amnesia cases, formed a striking and awesome elaboration of memory lapses such as mine.

Of the nature of the dreams and impressions which were growing so clamorous I still almost fear to speak. They seemed to savour[i] of madness, and at times I believed I was indeed going mad. Was there a special type of delusion afflicting those who had suffered lapses of memory? Conceivably, the efforts of the subconscious mind to fill up a perplexing blank with pseudo-memories[j] might give rise to strange imaginative vagaries.[k] This, indeed (though an alternative folklore theory finally seemed to me more plausible),[l] was the belief of many of the alienists who helped me in my search for parallel cases, and who shared my puzzlement at the exact resemblances sometimes discovered.[m] They did not call the condition true[n] insanity, but classed it rather among neurotic disorders. My course in trying to track it

[a] lapse] lapse, B, C
[b] unhuman] un-human A
[c] fifteen] 15 A
[d] *groping . . . time*] groping . . . time B, C
[e] Nature?] nature? A, B, C
[f] *experiments*] experiments B, C
[g] belief?] belief? ¶ B, C
[h] antiquity,] antiquity C
[i] savour] savor B, C
[j] pseudo-memories] pseudomemories B, C
[k] vagaries.] vagaries. ¶ B, C
[l] indeed (. . .),] indeed, (. . .) A; indeed—. . .— B, C
[m] discovered.] discovered. ¶ B, C
[n] true] pure C

down and analyse[a] it, instead of vainly seeking to dismiss or forget it, they heartily endorsed as correct according to the best psychological principles. I especially valued the advice of such physicians as had studied me during my possession by the other personality.

My first disturbances were not visual at all, but concerned the more abstract matters which I have mentioned. There was, too, a feeling of profound and inexplicable horror concerning *myself.*[b] I developed a queer fear of seeing my own form, as if my eyes would find it something utterly alien and inconceivably abhorrent.[c] When I did glance down and behold the familiar human shape in quiet grey[d] or blue clothing[e] I always felt a curious relief, though in order to gain this relief I had to conquer an infinite dread. I shunned mirrors as much as possible, and was always shaved at the barber's.

It was a long time before I correlated any of these disappointed feelings with the fleeting visual impressions which began to develop. The first such correlation had to do with the odd sensation of an external, artificial restraint on my memory.[f] I felt that the snatches of sight I experienced had a profound and terrible meaning, and a frightful connexion[g] with myself, but that some purposeful influence held me from grasping that meaning and that connexion.[h] Then came that queerness about the element of *time,*[i] and with it desperate efforts to place the fragmentary dream-glimpses[j] in the chronological and spatial pattern.

The glimpses themselves were at first merely strange rather than horrible. I would seem to be in an enormous vaulted chamber whose lofty stone groinings were well-nigh[k] lost in the shadows overhead. In

---

[a] analyse] analyze B, C
[b] *myself.*] myself. B, C
[c] abhorrent.] abhorrent. ¶ B, C
[d] grey] gray B, C
[e] clothing] clothing, B, C
[f] memory.] memory. ¶ B, C
[g] connexion] connection B, C
[h] connexion.] connection. B, C
[i] *time,*] time, B, C
[j] dream-glimpses] dream glimpses B, C
[k] well-nigh] well nigh B, C

whatever time or place the scene might be, the principle of the arch was known as fully and used as extensively as by the Romans.[a] There were colossal[b] round windows and high[c] arched doors, and pedestals or tables each as tall as the height of an ordinary room. Vast shelves of dark wood lined the walls, holding what seemed to be volumes of immense size with strange hieroglyphs on their backs.[d] The exposed stonework held curious carvings, always in curvilinear mathematical designs, and there were chiselled[e] inscriptions in the same characters that the huge books bore. The dark granite masonry was of a monstrous megalithic type, with lines of convex-topped blocks fitting the concave-bottomed courses which rested upon them.[f] There were no chairs, but the tops of the vast pedestals were littered with books, papers, and what seemed to be writing materials—oddly figured jars of a purplish metal, and rods with stained tips. Tall as the pedestals were, I seemed at times able to view them from above. On some of them were great globes of luminous crystal serving as lamps, and inexplicable machines formed of vitreous tubes and metal rods.[g] The windows were glazed, and latticed with stout-looking bars. Though I dared not approach and peer out them, I could see from where I was the waving tops of singular fern-like[h] growths. The floor was of massive octagonal flagstones, while rugs and hangings were entirely lacking.

Later[i] I had visions of sweeping through Cyclopean[j] corridors of stone, and up and down gigantic[k] inclined planes of the same monstrous masonry. There were no stairs anywhere, nor was any passageway less than thirty feet wide. Some of the structures through

[a] Romans.] Romans. ¶ B, C
[b] colossal] colossal, B, C
[c] high] high, B, C
[d] backs.] backs. ¶ B, C
[e] chiselled] chiseled B, C
[f] them.] them. ¶ B, C
[g] rods.] rods. ¶ B, C
[h] fern-like] fernlike A, B, C
[i] Later] Later, B[c], C
[j] Cyclopean] cyclopean A, C
[k] gigantic] gigantic, B[c]

which I floated must have towered into[a] the sky for thousands of feet.[b] There were multiple levels of black vaults below, and never-opened trap-doors,[c] sealed down with metal bands and holding dim suggestions of some special peril.[d] I seemed to be a prisoner, and horror hung broodingly over everything I saw. I felt that the mocking curvilinear hieroglyphs on the walls would blast my soul with their message were I not guarded by a merciful ignorance.

Still later my dreams included vistas from the great round windows, and from the titanic flat roof, with its curious gardens, wide barren area, and high, scalloped parapet of stone, to which the topmost of the inclined planes led.[e] There were almost endless leagues of giant buildings, each in its garden, and ranged along paved roads fully 200 feet wide. They differed greatly in aspect, but few were less than 500[f] feet square or a thousand feet high. Many seemed so limitless that they must have had a frontage of several thousand feet, while some shot up to mountainous altitudes in the grey,[g] steamy heavens.[h] They seemed to be mainly of stone or concrete, and most of them embodied the oddly curvilinear type of masonry noticeable in the building that held me. Roofs were flat and garden-covered, and tended to have scalloped parapets. Sometimes there were terraces and higher levels, and wide[i] cleared spaces amidst the gardens. The great roads held hints of motion, but in the earlier visions I could not resolve this impression into details.

In certain places I beheld enormous dark cylindrical towers which climbed far above any of the other structures. These appeared to be of a totally unique nature,[j] and shewed[k] signs of prodigious age and

[a] into] in B, C
[b] feet.] feet. ¶ B, C
[c] trap-doors,] trapdoors, A; trap-/doors, B
[d] peril.] peril. ¶ B, C
[e] led.] led. ¶ B, C
[f] 200 . . . 500] two hundred . . . five hundred A, B, C
[g] grey,] gray, B, C
[h] heavens.] heavens. ¶ B, C
[i] wide] wide, B, C
[j] nature,] nature B, C
[k] shewed] showed B, C

dilapidation. They were built of a bizarre type of square-cut basalt masonry, and tapered slightly toward their rounded tops. Nowhere in any of them could the least traces of windows or other apertures save huge doors be found. I noticed also some lower buildings—all crumbling with the weathering of aeons—which resembled these dark[a] cylindrical towers in basic architecture. Around all these aberrant piles of square-cut masonry there hovered an inexplicable aura of menace and concentrated fear, like that bred by the sealed trap-doors.[b]

The omnipresent gardens were almost terrifying in their strangeness, with bizarre and unfamiliar forms of vegetation nodding over broad paths lined with curiously carven monoliths. Abnormally vast fern-like[c] growths predominated;[d] some green, and some of a ghastly, fungoid pallor.[e] Among them rose great spectral things resembling calamites,[f] whose bamboo-like trunks towered to fabulous heights. Then there were tufted forms like fabulous cycads,[g] and grotesque dark-green shrubs and trees of coniferous aspect.[h] Flowers were small, colourless, and unrecognisable,[i] blooming in geometrical beds and at large among the greenery.[j] In a few of the terrace and roof-top gardens were larger and more vivid[k] blossoms of almost offensive contours and seeming to suggest artificial breeding. Fungi of inconceivable size, outlines, and colours[l] speckled the scene in patterns bespeaking some unknown but well-established horticultural tradition. In the larger gardens on the ground there seemed to be some attempt to preserve the irregularities of Nature,[m] but on the roofs there was more selectiveness, and more evidences of the topiary art.

---

[a] dark] dark, B, C
[b] trap-doors.] trap doors. A; trapdoors. B, C
[c] fern-like] fernlike A, B, C
[d] predominated;] predominated— B, C
[e] pallor.] pallor. ¶ B, C
[f] calamites,] Calamites, B[c]
[g] cycads,] cycades, C
[h] aspect.] aspect. ¶ B, C
[i] colourless, and unrecognisable,] colorless, and unrecognizable, B, C
[j] greenery.] greenery. ¶ B, C
[k] more vivid] more-vivid B
[l] colours] colors B, C
[m] Nature,] nature, A, B, C

The skies were almost always moist and cloudy, and sometimes I would seem to witness tremendous rains. Once in a while, though, there would be glimpses of the sun[a]—which looked abnormally large—and of the moon,[b] whose markings held a touch of difference from the normal that I could never quite fathom. When—very rarely—the night sky was clear to any extent, I beheld constellations which were nearly beyond recognition. Known outlines were sometimes approximated, but seldom duplicated; and from the position of the few groups I could recognise,[c] I felt I must be in the earth's[d] southern hemisphere, near the Tropic of Capricorn.[e] The far horizon was always steamy and indistinct, but I could see that great jungles of unknown tree-ferns,[f] calamites, lepidodendra, and sigillaria[g] lay outside the city, their fantastic frondage[h] waving mockingly in the shifting vapours.[i] Now and then there would be suggestions of motion in the sky, but these my early visions never resolved.

By the autumn of 1914 I began to have infrequent dreams of strange floatings over the city and and through the regions around it. I saw interminable roads through forests of fearsome growths with mottled, fluted, and banded trunks, and past other cities as strange as the one which persistently haunted me.[j] I saw monstrous constructions of black or iridescent stone in glades and clearings where perpetual twilight reigned, and traversed long causeways over swamps so dark that I could tell but little of their moist, towering vegetation.[k] Once I saw an area of countless miles strown[l] with age-blasted basaltic ruins whose architecture had been like that of the few windowless, round-

[a] sun] Sun B
[b] moon,] Moon, B
[c] recognise,] recognize, B, C
[d] earth's] Earth's B
[e] Capricorn.] Capricorn. ¶ B, C
[f] tree-ferns,] tree ferns, B, C
[g] calamites, lepidodendra, and sigillaria] Calamites, Lepidodendron, and sigillaria B[c]; Calamites, Lepidodendro, and Sigillaria C
[h] frondage] frontage B[c]
[i] vapours.] vapors. B, C
[j] me.] me. ¶ B, C
[k] vegetation.] vegetation. ¶ B, C
[l] strown] strewn B, C

topped towers in the haunting city.[a] And once I saw the sea—a
boundless[b] steamy expanse beyond the colossal stone piers of an
enormous town of domes and arches. Great shapeless suggestions of
shadow moved over it, and here and there its surface was vexed with
anomalous spoutings.

III.

As I have said, it was not immediately that these wild visions began to
hold their terrifying quality. Certainly, many persons have dreamed
intrinsically stranger things—things compounded of unrelated scraps
of daily life, pictures, and reading, and arranged in fantastically novel
forms by the unchecked caprices of sleep.[c] For some time I accepted
the visions as natural, even though I had never before been an
extravagant dreamer. Many of the vague anomalies, I argued, must
have come from trivial sources too numerous to track down; while
others seemed to reflect a common text-book[d] knowledge of the
plants and other conditions of the primitive world of a hundred and
fifty million years ago—the world of the Permian or Triassic[e] age.[f] In
the course of some months, however, the element of terror did figure
with accumulating force. This was when the dreams began so
unfailingly to have the aspect of *memories,*[g] and when my mind began to
link them with my growing abstract disturbances—the feeling of
mnemonic restraint, the curious impressions regarding *time,*[h] the sense
of a loathsome exchange with my secondary personality of 1908–13,
and, considerably later, the inexplicable loathing of my own person.

   As certain definite details began to enter the dreams, their horror
increased a thousandfold—until by October, 1915, I felt I must do
something. It was then that I began an intensive study of other cases

[a] city.] city. ¶ B, C
[b] boundless] boundless, B, C
[c] sleep.] sleep. ¶ B, C
[d] text-book] text-/book B; textbook C
[e] Permian or Triassic] permian or triassic A
[f] age.] Age. ¶ B, C
[g] *memories,*] memories, B, C
[h] *time,*] time, B, C

of amnesia and visions, feeling that I might thereby objectivise[a] my trouble and shake clear of its emotional grip.[b] However, as before mentioned, the result was at first almost exactly opposite. It disturbed me vastly to find that my dreams had been so closely duplicated; especially since some of the accounts were too early to admit of any geological knowledge—and therefore of any idea of primitive landscapes—on the subjects' part.[c] What is more, many of these accounts supplied very horrible details and explanations in connexion[d] with the visions of great buildings and jungle gardens—and other things. The actual sights and vague impressions were bad enough, but what was hinted or asserted by some of the other dreamers savoured[e] of madness and blasphemy. Worst of all, my own pseudo-memory[f] was aroused to wilder dreams and hints of coming revelations. And yet most doctors deemed my course, on the whole, an advisable one.

I studied psychology systematically,[g] and under the prevailing stimulus my son Wingate did the same—his studies leading eventually to his present professorship. In 1917 and 1918 I took special courses at Miskatonic. Meanwhile[h] my examination of medical, historical, and anthropological records became indefatigable;[i] involving travels to distant libraries, and finally including even a reading of the hideous books of forbidden elder[j] lore in which my secondary personality had been so disturbingly interested.[k] Some of the latter were the actual copies I had consulted in my altered state, and I was greatly disturbed by certain marginal notations and ostensible *corrections* of the hideous text in a script and idiom which somehow seemed oddly unhuman.[l]

[a] objectivise] objectivize B, C
[b] grip.] grip. ¶ B, C
[c] part.] part. ¶ B, C
[d] connexion] connection B, C
[e] savoured] savored B, C
[f] pseudo-memory] pseudomemory B, C
[g] systematically,] systematically B
[h] Meanwhile] Meanwhile, B, C
[i] indefatigable;] indefatigable, B, C
[j] elder] *om.* C
[k] interested.] interested. ¶ B, C
[l] unhuman.] un-human. A

These markings were mostly in the respective languages of the various books, all of which the writer seemed to know with equal though obviously[a] academic facility. One note appended to von Junzt's "Unaussprechlichen Kulten",[b] however, was alarmingly otherwise. It consisted of certain curvilinear hieroglyphs in the same ink as that of the German corrections, but following no recognised[c] human pattern. And these hieroglyphs were closely and unmistakably akin to the characters constantly met with in my dreams—characters whose meaning I would sometimes momentarily fancy I knew[d] or was just on the brink of recalling.[e] To complete my black confusion, many librarians assured me that, in view of previous examinations and records of consultation of the volumes in question, all of these notations must have been made by myself in my secondary state. This despite the fact that I was and still am ignorant of three of the languages involved.[f]

Piecing together the scattered records, ancient and modern, anthropological and medical, I found a fairly consistent mixture of myth and hallucination whose scope and wildness left me utterly dazed. Only one thing consoled me—[g]the fact that the myths were of such early existence. What lost knowledge could have brought pictures of the Palaeozoic or Mesozoic[h] landscape into these primitive fables, I could not even guess,[i] but the pictures had been there. Thus, a basis existed for the formation of a fixed type of delusion.[j] Cases of amnesia no doubt created the general myth-pattern[k]—but afterward the fanciful accretions of the myths must have reacted on amnesia

---

[a] equal . . . obviously] equal, . . . obviously, B, C
[b] "Unaussprechlichen Kulten",] *Unaussprechlichen Kulten,* A, B, C
[c] recognised] recognized B, C
[d] knew] knew, B, C
[e] recalling.] recalling. ¶ B, C
[f] involved. ¶] involved. C
[g] me—] me: C
[h] Palaeozoic or Mesozoic] palaeozoic or mesozoic A; Paleozoic or Mesozoic B, C
[i] guess,] guess; B, C
[j] delusion.] delusion. ¶ B, C
[k] myth-pattern] myth pattern B, C

sufferers and coloured their pseudo-memories.[a] I myself had read and heard all the early tales during my memory lapse—my quest had amply proved that. Was it not natural, then, for my subsequent dreams and emotional impressions to become coloured and moulded[b] by what my memory subtly held over from my secondary state?[c] A few of the myths had significant connexions[d] with other cloudy legends of the pre-human[e] world, especially those Hindoo[f] tales involving stupefying gulfs of time and forming part of the lore of modern theosophists.

Primal myth and modern delusion joined in their assumption that mankind is only one—perhaps the least—of the highly evolved[g] and dominant races of this planet's long and largely unknown career. Things of inconceivable shape, they implied, had reared great towers to the sky and delved into every secret of Nature[h] before the first amphibian forbear of man had crawled out of the hot sea three hundred million years ago.[i] Some had come down from the stars; a few were as old as the cosmos itself; others had arisen[j] swiftly from terrene[k] germs as far behind the first germs of our life-cycle[l] as those germs are behind ourselves. Spans of thousands of millions of years, and linkages with[m] other galaxies and universes, were freely[n] spoken of. Indeed, there was no such thing as time in its humanly accepted sense.

But most of the tales and impressions concerned a relatively late race, of a queer and intricate shape[o] resembling no life-form[p] known to

[a] coloured their pseudo-memories.] colored their pseudomemories. B, C
[b] coloured and moulded] colored and molded B, C
[c] state?] state? ¶ B, C
[d] connexions] connections B, C
[e] pre-human] prehuman B, C
[f] Hindoo] Hindu B, C
[g] highly evolved] highly-evolved A
[h] Nature] nature A, B, C
[i] ago.] ago. ¶ B, C
[j] arisen] risen B
[k] terrene] terrane B[c], C
[l] life-cycle] life cycle B, C
[m] with] of B, C
[n] freely] *om.* C
[o] shape] shape, B, C
[p] life-form] life form B, C

science, which had lived till only fifty million years before the advent of man. This, they indicated, was the greatest race of all;[a] because it alone had conquered the secret of time.[b] It had learned all things that ever were known *or ever would be known*[c] on the earth,[d] through the power of its keener minds to project themselves into the past and future, even through gulfs of millions of years, and study the lore of every age. From the accomplishments of this race arose all legends of *prophets,*[e] including those in human mythology.

In its vast libraries were volumes of texts and pictures holding the whole of earth's[f] annals—histories and descriptions of every species that had ever been or that ever would be, with full records of their arts, their achievements, their languages, and their psychologies.[g] With this aeon-embracing knowledge, the Great Race chose from every era and life-form[h] such thoughts, arts, and processes as might suit its own nature and situation. Knowledge of the past, secured through a kind of mind-casting[i] outside the recognised[j] senses, was harder to glean than knowledge of the future.

In the latter case the course was easier and more material. With suitable mechanical aid a mind would project itself forward in time, feeling its dim, extra-sensory way till it approached the desired period. Then, after preliminary trials, it would seize on the best discoverable representative of the highest of that period's life-forms; entering[k] the organism's brain and setting[l] up therein its own vibrations[m] while the displaced mind would strike back to the period of the displacer,

[a] all;] all B, C
[b] time.] time. ¶ B, C
[c] *or . . . known*] or . . . known B, C
[d] earth,] Earth, B, C
[e] *prophets,*] prophets, B, C
[f] earth's] Earth's B, C
[g] psychologies.] psychologies. ¶ B, C
[h] life-form] life form B, C
[i] mind-casting] mind casting B; mindcasting C
[j] recognised] recognized B, C
[k] life-forms; entering] life forms. It would enter B, C
[l] setting] set B, C
[m] vibrations] vibrations, B, C

remaining in the latter's body till a reverse process was set up.[a] The projected mind, in the body of the organism of the future, would then pose as a member of the race whose outward form it wore;[b] learning as quickly as possible all that could be learned of the chosen age and its massed information and techniques.

Meanwhile the displaced mind, thrown back to the displacer's age and body, would be carefully guarded. It would be kept from harming the body it occupied, and would be drained of all its knowledge by trained questioners. Often it could be questioned in its own language, when previous quests into the future had brought back records of that language.[c] If the mind came from a body whose language the Great Race could not physically reproduce, clever machines would be made, on which the alien speech could be played as on a musical instrument.[d] The Great Race's members were immense rugose cones ten feet high, and with head and other organs attached to foot-thick,[e] distensible limbs spreading from the apexes. They spoke by the clicking or scraping of huge paws or claws attached to the end of two of their four limbs, and walked by the expansion and contraction of a viscous layer attached to their vast[f] ten-foot bases.

When the captive mind's amazement and resentment had worn off, and when (assuming that it came from a body vastly different from the Great Race's)[g] it had lost its horror at its unfamiliar[h] temporary form, it was permitted to study its new environment and experience a wonder and wisdom approximating that of its displacer.[i] With suitable precautions, and in exchange for suitable services, it was allowed to rove all over the habitable world in titan airships or on the huge boat-like[j] atomic-engined vehicles which traversed the great roads, and to

[a] up.] up. ¶ B, C
[b] wore;] wore, B, C
[c] language.] language. ¶ B, C
[d] instrument.] instrument. ¶ B, C
[e] foot-thick,] foot-thick C
[f] vast] vast, B, C
[g] when (. . .)] when—. . .— B, C
[h] unfamiliar] unfamiliar, B, C
[i] displacer.] displacer. ¶ B, C
[j] boat-like] boatlike A; boatlike, B

delve freely into the libraries containing the records of the planet's past and future.[a] This reconciled many captive minds to their lot; since none were other than keen, and to such minds the unveiling of hidden mysteries of earth[b]—closed chapters of inconceivable pasts and dizzying vortices of future time which include the years ahead of their own natural ages—forms always, despite the abysmal horrors often unveiled, the supreme experience of life.

Now and then certain captives were permitted to meet other captive minds seized from the future—to exchange thoughts with consciousnesses[c] living a hundred or a thousand or a million years before or after their own ages. And all were urged to write copiously in their own languages of themselves and their respective periods;[d] such documents to be filed in the great central archives.

It may be added that there was one sad[e] special type of captive whose privileges were far greater than those of the majority. These were the dying *permanent* exiles, whose bodies in the future had been seized by keen-minded members of the Great Race who, faced with death, sought to escape mental extinction.[f] Such melancholy exiles were not as common as might be expected, since the longevity of the Great Race lessened its love of life—especially among those superior minds capable of projection. From cases of the permanent projection of elder minds arose many of those lasting changes of personality noticed in later history—including mankind's.

As for the ordinary cases of exploration—when the displacing mind had learned what it wished in the future, it would build an apparatus like that which had started its flight and reverse the process of projection. Once more it would be in its own body in its own age,[g] while the lately captive mind would return to that body of the future to which it properly belonged.[h] Only when one or the other of the bodies

[a] future.] future. ¶ B, C
[b] earth] Earth B, C
[c] consciousnesses] consciousness B[c]
[d] periods;] periods, B; periods C
[e] sad] *om.* B, C
[f] extinction.] extinction. ¶ B, C
[g] age,] age C
[h] belonged.] belonged. ¶ B, C

had died during the exchange was this restoration impossible. In such cases, of course, the exploring mind had—like those of the death-escapers[a]—to live out an alien-bodied life in the future; or else the captive mind—like the dying permanent exiles—had to end its days in the form and past age of the Great Race.

This fate was least[b] horrible when the captive mind was also of the Great Race—a not infrequent occurrence, since in all its periods that race was intensely concerned with its own future. The number of dying permanent exiles of the Great Race was very slight—largely because of the tremendous penalties attached to displacements of future Great Race minds by the moribund.[c] Through projection, arrangements were made to inflict these penalties on the offending minds in their new future bodies—and sometimes forced re-exchanges[d] were effected.[e] Complex cases of the displacement of exploring or already captive minds by minds in various regions of the past had been known and carefully rectified. In every age since the discovery of mind-projection,[f] a minute but well-recognised[g] element of the population consisted of Great Race minds from past ages, sojourning for a longer or shorter while.

When a captive mind of alien origin was returned to its own body in the future, it was purged by an intricate mechanical hypnosis of all it had learned in the Great Race's age[h]—this because of certain troublesome consequences inherent in the general carrying forward of knowledge in large quantities.[i] The few existing instances of clear transmission had caused, and would cause at known future times, great disasters. And it was largely in consequence of two cases of the kind (said the old myths)[j] that mankind had learned what it had concerning

[a] death-escapers] death escapers B, C
[b] least] less C
[c] moribund.] moribund. ¶ B, C
[d] re-exchanges] reëxchanges B, C
[e] effected.] effected. ¶ B, C
[f] mind-projection,] mind projection, B, C
[g] well-recognised] well-recognized B, C
[h] Race's age] Race Age B[c]; Race's Age C
[i] quantities.] quantities. ¶ B, C
[j] kind (. . .)] kind—. . .— B, C

the Great Race.[a] Of all things surviving *physically and directly*[b] from that aeon-distant world, there remained only certain ruins of great stones in far places and under the sea, and parts of the text of the frightful Pnakotic Manuscripts.

Thus[c] the returning mind reached its own age with only the faintest and most fragmentary visions[d] of what it had undergone since its seizure. All memories that could be eradicated were eradicated, so that in most cases only a dream-shadowed blank stretched back to the time of the first exchange. Some minds recalled more than others, and the chance joining of memories had at rare times brought hints of the forbidden past to future ages.[e] There probably never was a time when groups or cults did not secretly cherish certain of these hints. In the "Necronomicon"[f] the presence of such a cult among human beings was suggested—a cult that sometimes gave aid to minds voyaging down the aeons from the days of the Great Race.

And meanwhile[g] the Great Race itself waxed well-nigh omniscient, and turned to the task of setting up exchanges with the minds of other planets, and of exploring their pasts and futures. It sought likewise to fathom the past years and origin of that black, aeon-dead orb in far space whence its own mental heritage had come—for the mind of the Great Race was older than its bodily form.[h] The beings of a dying elder world, wise with the ultimate secrets, had looked ahead for a new world and species wherein they might have long life;[i] and had sent their minds en masse[j] into that future race best adapted to house them—the cone-shaped things that peopled our earth[k] a billion years

---

[a] Race.] Race. ¶ B, C

[b] *physically and directly*] physically and directly B, C

[c] Thus]Thus, B[c]

[d] visions] vision C

[e] ages.] ages. ¶ B, C

[f] "Necronomicon"] *Necronomicon* A, B, C

[g] And meanwhile] And, meanwhile, B, C

[h] form.] form. ¶ B, C

[i] life;] life, B, C

[j] en masse] *en masse* B, C

[k] earth] Earth B

ago.[a] Thus the Great Race came to be, while the myriad minds sent backward were left to die in the horror of strange shapes. Later the race would again face death, yet would live through another forward migration of its best minds into the bodies of others who had a longer physical span ahead of them.

Such was the background of intertwined legend and hallucination. When, around 1920, I had my researches in coherent shape, I felt a slight lessening of the tension which their earlier stages had increased. After all, and in spite of the fancies prompted by blind emotions, were not most of my phenomena readily explainable? Any chance might have turned my mind to dark studies during the amnesia—and then I read the forbidden legends and met the members of ancient and ill-regarded cults. That, plainly, supplied the material for the dreams and disturbed feelings which came after the return of memory.[b] As for the marginal notes in dream-hieroglyphs[c] and languages unknown to me, but laid at my door by librarians—I might easily have picked up a smattering of the tongues during my secondary state, while the hieroglyphs were doubtless coined by my fancy from descriptions in old legends, and *afterward* [d] woven into my dreams. I tried to verify certain points through conversation with known cult-leaders,[e] but never succeeded in establishing the right connexions.[f]

At times the parallelism of so many cases in so many distant ages continued to worry me as it had at first, but on the other hand I reflected that the excitant folklore was undoubtedly more universal in the past than in the present.[g] Probably all the other victims whose cases were like mine had had a long and familiar knowledge of the tales I had learned only when in my secondary state. When these victims had lost their memory, they had associated themselves with the creatures of their household myths—the fabulous invaders supposed to displace men's minds—and had thus embarked upon quests for

[a] ago.] ago. ¶ B, C
[b] memory.] memory. ¶ B, C
[c] dream-hieroglyphs] dream hieroglyphs B, C
[d] *afterward*] afterward B, C
[e] cult-leaders,] cult leaders, B, C
[f] connexions.] connections. B, C
[g] present.] present. ¶ B, C

knowledge which they thought they could take back to a fancied, non-human past.[a] Then[b] when their memory returned, they reversed the associative process and thought of themselves as the former captive minds instead of as the displacers. Hence the dreams and pseudo-memories[c] following the conventional myth-pattern.[d]

Despite the seeming cumbrousness[e] of these explanations, they came finally to supersede all others in my mind—largely because of the greater weakness of any rival theory. And a substantial number of eminent psychologists and anthropologists gradually agreed with me.[f] The more I reflected, the more convincing did my reasoning seem; till in the end I had a really effective bulwark against the visions and impressions which still assailed me. Suppose I did see strange things at night? These were only what I had heard and read of. Suppose I did have odd loathings and perspectives and pseudo-memories?[g] These, too, were only echoes of myths absorbed in my secondary state. Nothing that I might dream, nothing that I might feel, could be of any actual significance.

Fortified by this philosophy, I greatly improved in nervous equilibrium, even though the visions (rather than the abstract impressions)[h] steadily became more frequent and more disturbingly detailed. In 1922 I felt able to undertake regular work again, and put my newly gained[i] knowledge to practical use by accepting an instructorship in psychology at the university.[j] My old chair of political economy had long been adequately filled—besides which, methods of teaching economics had changed greatly since my heyday. My son was at this time just entering on the post-graduate studies leading to his present professorship, and we worked together a great deal.

[a] non-human past.] nonhuman past. ¶ B, C
[b] Then] Then, B, C
[c] pseudo-memories] pseudo-/memories B; pseudomemories C
[d] myth-pattern.] myth pattern. B, C
[e] cumbrousness] cumberousness B[c]
[f] me.] me. ¶ B, C
[g] pseudo-memories?] pseudomemories? B, C
[h] visions (. . .)] visions—. . .— B, C
[i] newly gained] newly-gained A
[j] university.] university. ¶ B, C

IV.

I continued, however, to keep a careful record of the outré[a] dreams which crowded upon me so thickly and vividly. Such a record, I argued, was of genuine value as a psychological document. The glimpses still seemed damnably like *memories*,[b] though I fought off this impression with a goodly measure of success.[c] In writing, I treated the phantasmata as things seen; but at all other times I brushed them aside like any gossamer illusions of the night. I had never mentioned such matters in common conversation; though reports of them, filtering out as such things will, had aroused sundry rumours[d] regarding my mental health. It is amusing to reflect that these rumours[e] were confined wholly to laymen, without a single champion among physicians or psychologists.

Of my visions after 1914 I will here mention only a few, since fuller accounts and records are at the disposal of the serious student. It is evident that with time the curious inhibitions somewhat waned, for the scope of my visions vastly increased. They have never, though, become other than disjointed fragments seemingly without clear motivation.[f] Within the dreams I seemed gradually to acquire a greater and greater freedom of wandering. I floated through many strange buildings of stone, going from one to the other along mammoth underground passages which seemed to form the common avenues of transit. Sometimes I encountered those gigantic sealed trap-doors[g] in the lowest level, around which such an aura of fear and forbiddenness clung.[h] I saw tremendous tessellated[i] pools, and rooms of curious and inexplicable utensils of myriad sorts. Then there were colossal caverns of intricate machinery whose outlines and purpose were wholly strange

[a] outré] *outré* B; *outre* C
[b] *memories*,] memories, B, C
[c] success.] success. ¶ B, C
[d] rumours] rumors B, C
[e] rumours] rumors B, C
[f] motivation.] motivation. ¶ B, C
[g] trap-doors] trap doors A; trapdoors B, C
[h] clung.] clung. ¶ B, C
[i] tessellated] tesselated A

to me, and whose *sound* [a] manifested itself only after many years of dreaming. I may here remark that sight and sound are the only senses I have ever exercised in the visionary world.

The real horror began in May, 1915, when I first saw the *living things*.[b] This was before my studies had taught me what, in view of the myths and case histories, to expect. As mental barriers wore down, I beheld great masses of thin vapour[c] in various parts of the building and in the streets below.[d] These steadily grew more solid and distinct, till at last I could trace their monstrous outlines with uncomfortable ease. They seemed to be enormous[e] iridescent cones, about ten feet high and ten feet wide at the base, and made up of some ridgy, scaly, semi-elastic[f] matter. From their apexes projected four flexible, cylindrical members, each a foot thick, and of a ridgy substance like that of the cones themselves.[g] These members were sometimes contracted almost to nothing, and sometimes extended to any distance up to about ten feet. Terminating two of them were enormous claws or nippers. At the end of a third were four red, trumpet-like[h] appendages. The fourth terminated in an irregular yellowish globe some two feet in diameter and having three great dark eyes ranged along its central circumference.[i] Surmounting this head were four slender grey[j] stalks bearing flower-like[k] appendages, whilst from its nether side dangled eight greenish antennae or tentacles. The great base of the central cone was fringed with a rubbery, grey[l] substance which moved the whole entity through expansion and contraction.

---

[a] *sound*] sound B, C
[b] *living things*.] living things. B, C
[c] vapour] vapor B, C
[d] below.] below. ¶ B, C
[e] enormous] enormous, B, C
[f] semi-elastic] semielastic B
[g] themselves.] themselves. ¶ B, C
[h] trumpet-like] trumpetlike B, C
[i] circumference.] circumference. ¶ B, C
[j] grey] gray B, C
[k] flower-like] flowerlike B; flower-/like C
[l] grey] gray B, C

Their actions, though harmless, horrified me even more than their appearance—for it is not wholesome to watch monstrous objects doing what one has[a] known only human beings to do. These objects moved intelligently around[b] the great rooms, getting books from the shelves and taking them to the great tables, or vice versa,[c] and sometimes writing diligently with a peculiar rod gripped in the greenish head-tentacles.[d] The huge nippers were used in carrying books and in conversation—speech consisting of a kind of clicking and scraping.[e] The objects had no clothing, but wore satchels or knapsacks suspended from the top of the conical trunk. They commonly carried their head and its supporting member at the level of the cone top, although it was frequently raised or lowered.[f] The other three great members tended to rest downward on[g] the sides of the cone, contracted to about[h] five[i] feet each, when not in use. From their rate of reading, writing, and operating their machines (those on the tables seemed somehow connected with thought)[j] I concluded that their intelligence was enormously greater than man's.

Afterward I saw them everywhere; swarming in all the great chambers and corridors, tending monstrous machines in vaulted crypts, and racing along the vast roads in gigantic[k] boat-shaped cars. I ceased to be afraid of them, for they seemed to form supremely natural parts of their environment.[l] Individual differences amongst them began to be manifest, and a few appeared to be under some kind of restraint. These latter, though shewing[m] no physical variation, had a diversity of gestures and habits which marked them off not only from

[a] has] had B, C
[b] around] about B, C
[c] vice versa,] *vice versa,* B, C
[d] head-tentacles.] head tentacles. B, C
[e] clicking and scraping.] clicking and scraping. ¶ B; clicking. ¶ C
[f] lowered.] lowered. ¶ B, C
[g] on] at B, C
[h] about] above C
[i] five] 5 A
[j] machines (. . .)] machines—. . .— B, C
[k] gigantic] gigantic, B, C
[l] environment.] environment. ¶ B, C
[m] shewing] showing B, C

the majority, but very largely from one another.[a] They wrote a great deal in what seemed to my cloudy vision a vast variety of characters— never the typical curvilinear hieroglyphs of the majority. A few, I fancied, used our own familiar alphabet. Most of them worked much more slowly than the general mass of the entities.

All this time *my own part* [b] in the dreams seemed to be that of a disembodied consciousness with a range of vision wider than the normal;[c] floating freely about, yet confined to the ordinary avenues and speeds of travel. Not until August, 1915, did any suggestions of bodily existence begin to harass me. I say *harass,*[d] because the first phase was a purely abstract though infinitely terrible[e] association of my previously noted body-loathing[f] with the scenes of my visions.[g] For a while my chief concern during dreams was to avoid looking down at myself, and I recall how grateful I was for the total absence of large mirrors in the strange rooms. I was mightily troubled by the fact that I always saw the great tables—whose height could not be under ten feet—from a level not below that of their surfaces.

And then the morbid temptation to look down at myself became greater and greater, till one night I could not resist it. At first my downward glance revealed nothing whatever. A moment later I perceived that this was because my head lay at the end of a flexible neck of enormous length. Retracting this neck and gazing down very sharply, I saw the scaly,[h] rugose, iridescent bulk of a vast cone ten feet tall and ten feet wide at the base. That was when I waked half of Arkham with my screaming as I plunged madly up from the abyss of sleep.

Only after weeks of hideous repetition did I grow half-reconciled[i] to these visions of myself in monstrous form. In the dreams I now moved bodily among the other unknown entities, reading terrible

[a] another.] another. ¶ B, C
[b] *my own part*] my own part B, C
[c] normal;] normal, B, C
[d] *harass,*] harass, B, C
[e] abstract . . . terrible] abstract, . . . terrible, B, C
[f] body-loathing] body loathing B
[g] visions.] visions. ¶ B, C
[h] scaly,] scaley, C
[i] half-reconciled] half reconciled B, C

books from the endless shelves and writing for hours at the great tables with a stylus managed by the green tentacles that hung down from my head.[a] Snatches of what I read and wrote would linger in my memory. There were horrible annals of other worlds and other universes, and of stirrings of formless life outside of all universes. There were records of strange orders of beings which had peopled the world in forgotten pasts,[b] and frightful chronicles of grotesque-bodied intelligences which would people it millions of years after the death of the last human being. And I[c] learned of chapters in human history whose existence no scholar of today[d] has ever suspected. Most of these writings were in the language of the hieroglyphs; which I studied in a queer way with the aid of droning machines, and which was evidently an agglutinative speech with root systems utterly unlike any found in human languages.[e] Other volumes were in other unknown tongues learned in the same queer way. A very few were in languages I knew. Extremely clever pictures, both inserted in the records and forming separate collections, aided me immensely. And all the time I seemed to be setting down a history of my own age in English. On waking, I could recall only minute and meaningless scraps of the unknown tongues which my dream-self[f] had mastered, though whole phrases[g] of the history stayed with me.

I learned—even before my waking self had studied the parallel cases or the old myths from which the dreams doubtless sprang—that the entities around me were of the world's greatest race, which had conquered time and had sent exploring minds into every age. I knew, too, that I had been snatched from my age[h] while *another*[i] used my body in that age, and that a few of the other strange forms housed similarly captured minds. I seemed to talk, in some odd language of

[a] head.] head. ¶ B, C
[b] pasts,] parts, Bc
[c] being. And I] being. ¶ I B, C
[d] today] to-day B
[e] languages.] languages. ¶ B, C
[f] dream-self] dream self B, C
[g] phrases] phases Bc
[h] age] age, C
[i] *another*] another B, C

claw-clickings,[a] with exiled intellects from every corner of the solar system.

There was a mind from the planet we know as Venus, which would live incalculable epochs to come, and one from an outer moon of Jupiter six million years in the past. Of earthly[b] minds there were some from the winged, star-headed, half-vegetable race of palaeogean[c] Antarctica; one from the reptile people of fabled Valusia; three from the furry pre-human[d] Hyperborean worshippers of Tsathoggua; one from the wholly abominable Tcho-Tchos;[e] two from the arachnid[f] denizens of earth's[g] last age; five from the hardy coleopterous[h] species immediately following mankind, to which the Great Race[i] was some day to transfer its keenest minds en masse[j] in the face of horrible peril; and several from different branches of humanity.

I talked with the mind of Yiang-Li, a philosopher from the cruel empire of Tsan-Chan, which is to come in A.D. 5000;[k] with that of a general of the great-headed brown people who held South Africa in B.C. 50,000;[l] with that of a twelfth-century[m] Florentine monk named Bartolomeo Corsi; with that of a king of Lomar who had ruled that terrible polar land 100,000[n] years before the squat, yellow Inutos came from the west to engulf it; with that[o] of Nug-Soth, a magician of the dark conquerors of A.D. 16,000;[p] with that of a Roman named Titus Sempronius Blaesus, who had been a quaestor in Sulla's time; with that

[a] claw-clickings,] claw clickings, B; claw clicking, C
[b] earthly] Earthly B
[c] palaeogean] Paleogean B [changed by HPL to paleogean]; paleogean C
[d] pre-human] prehuman B, C
[e] Tcho-Tchos;] Tcho-Tchos, A
[f] arachnid] Arachnida B [changed by HPL to Arachnid]; Arachnid C
[g] earth's] Earth's B
[h] coleopterous] Coleopterous B[c], C
[i] Great Race] great race A
[j] en masse] en masse B, C
[k] A.D. 5000;] 5,000 A. D.; B, C
[l] B.C. 50,000;] 50,000 B. C.; B, C
[m] twelfth-century] 12th century A
[n] 100,000] one hundred thousand B, C
[o] it; with that] it. ¶ I talked with the mind B, C
[p] A.D. 16,000;] 16,000 A. D.; B, C

of Khephnes, an Egyptian of the 14th Dynasty[a] who told me the hideous secret of Nyarlathotep; with that of a priest of Atlantis' middle kingdom; with that of a Suffolk gentleman of Cromwell's day, James Woodville;[b] with that of a court astronomer of pre-Inca Peru; with that of the Australian physicist Nevil Kingston-Brown, who will die in A.D. 2518;[c] with that of an[d] archimage of vanished Yhe in the Pacific; with that of Theodotides, a Graeco-Bactrian official of B.C. 200;[e] with that of an aged Frenchman of Louis XIII's time named Pierre-Louis Montmagny;[f] with that of Crom-Ya, a Cimmerian chieftain of B.C. 15,000;[g] and with so many others that my brain cannot[h] hold the shocking secrets and dizzying marvels I learned from them.

　　I awaked[i] each morning in a fever, sometimes frantically trying to verify or discredit such information as fell within the range of modern human knowledge. Traditional facts took on new and doubtful aspects, and I marvelled[j] at the dream-fancy[k] which could invent such surprising addenda to history and science.[l] I shivered at the mysteries the past may conceal, and trembled at the menaces the future may bring forth. What was hinted in the speech of post-human entities of the fate of mankind produced such an effect on me that I will not set it down here.[m] After man there would be the mighty beetle civilisation,[n] the bodies of whose members the cream of the Great Race would seize when the monstrous doom overtook the elder world. Later, as the earth's[o] span closed, the transferred minds would again migrate

[a] Dynasty] Dynasty, B, C
[b] Woodville;] Woodville. Also, B[c]
[c] A.D. 2518;] 2,518 A. D.; B, C
[d] an] the A, B[c]
[e] B.C. 200;] 200 B. C.; B, C
[f] Montmagny;] Montagny; B, C
[g] B.C. 15,000;] 15,000 B. C.; B, C
[h] cannot] can not B, C
[i] awaked] awakened B, C
[j] marvelled] marveled B, C
[k] dream-fancy] dream fancy B, C
[l] science.] science. ¶ B, C
[m] here.] here. ¶ B, C
[n] civilisation,] civilization, B, C
[o] earth's] Earth's B

through time and space—to another stopping-place[a] in the bodies of the bulbous vegetable entities of Mercury. But there would be races after them, clinging pathetically to the cold planet and burrowing to its horror-filled core, before the utter end.

Meanwhile, in my dreams, I wrote endlessly in that history of my own age which I was preparing—half voluntarily and half through promises of increased library and travel opportunities—for the Great Race's central archives. The archives were in a colossal subterranean structure near the city's centre,[b] which I came to know well through frequent labours[c] and consultations. Meant to last as long as the race, and to withstand the fiercest of earth's[d] convulsions, this titan repository surpassed all other buildings in the massive, mountain-like[e] firmness of its construction.

The records, written or printed on great sheets of a curiously tenacious cellulose fabric, were bound into books that opened from the top, and were kept in individual cases of a strange, extremely light rustless metal of greyish[f] hue, decorated with mathematical designs and bearing the title in the Great Race's curvilinear hieroglyphs.[g] These cases were stored in tiers of rectangular vaults—like closed, locked shelves—wrought of the same rustless metal and fastened by knobs with intricate turnings. My own history was assigned a specific place in the vaults of the lowest or vertebrate level—the section devoted to the cultures of mankind and of the furry and[h] reptilian races immediately preceding it in terrestrial[i] dominance.

But none of the dreams ever gave me a full picture of daily life. All were the merest misty, disconnected fragments, and it is certain that these fragments were not unfolded in their rightful sequence. I have, for example, a very imperfect idea of my own living arrangements in the

[a] stopping-place] stopping place B, C
[b] centre,] center, B, C
[c] labours] labors B, C
[d] earth's] Earth's B
[e] mountain-like] mountainlike B, C
[f] greyish] grayish B, C
[g] hieroglyphs.] hieroglyphs. ¶ B, C
[h] furry and] furry, B[c]
[i] terrestrial] Terrestrial B

dream-world;[a] though I seem to have possessed a great stone room of my own. My restrictions as a prisoner gradually disappeared, so that some of the visions included vivid travels over the mighty jungle roads, sojourns in strange cities, and explorations of some of the vast dark[b] windowless ruins from which the Great Race shrank in curious fear. There were also long sea-voyages[c] in enormous, many-decked boats of incredible swiftness, and trips over wild regions in closed, projectile-like[d] airships lifted and moved by electrical repulsion.[e] Beyond the wide, warm ocean were other cities of the Great Race, and on one far continent I saw the crude villages of the black-snouted, winged creatures who would evolve as a dominant stock after the Great Race had sent its foremost minds into the future to escape the creeping horror. Flatness and exuberant green life were always the keynote of the scene. Hills were low and sparse, and usually displayed signs of volcanic forces.

Of the animals I saw, I could write volumes. All were wild; for the Great Race's mechanised[f] culture had long since done away with domestic beasts, while food was wholly vegetable or synthetic. Clumsy reptiles of great bulk floundered in steaming morasses, fluttered in the heavy air, or spouted in the seas and lakes; and among these I fancied I could vaguely recognise[g] lesser, archaic prototypes of many forms—dinosaurs,[h] pterodactyls,[i] ichthyosaurs,[j] labyrinthodonts,[k] rhamphorhynci,[l] plesiosaurs,[m]

[a] dream-world;] dream world; B, C
[b] vast dark] vast, dark, B, C
[c] sea-voyages] sea voyages B, C
[d] projectile-like] projectilelike B; projectile-/like C
[e] repulsion.] repulsion. ¶ B, C
[f] mechanised] mechanized B, C
[g] recognise] recognize B, C
[h] dinosaurs,] Dinosauria, B [*changed by HPL to* Dinosaurs]; Dinosaurs, C
[i] pterodactyls,] Pterodactyls, B
[j] ichthyosaurs,] Ichthyosauria, B [*changed by HPL to* Ichthyosaurs]
[k] labyrinthodonts,] labyrinthodons, A; Labyrinthodonta, B [*changed by HPL to* Labyrinthodonts]
[l] rhamphorhynci,] ramphorhynci, A; *om.* B, C
[m] plesiosaurs,] Plesiosauri, B [*changed by HPL to* Plesiosaurs]

and the like—made familiar through palaeontology.[a] Of birds or mammals there were none that I could discern.[b]

The ground and swamps were constantly alive with snakes, lizards, and crocodiles, while insects buzzed incessantly amidst[c] the lush vegetation. And far out at sea[d] unspied and unknown monsters spouted mountainous columns of foam into the vaporous sky. Once I was taken under the ocean in a gigantic submarine vessel with searchlights, and glimpsed some living horrors of awesome magnitude. I saw also the ruins of incredible sunken cities, and the wealth of crinoid,[e] brachiopod, coral, and ichthyic life which everywhere abounded.

Of the physiology, psychology, folkways, and detailed history of the Great Race my visions preserved but little information, and many of the scattered points I here set down were gleaned from my study of old legends and other cases rather than from my own dreaming.[f] For in time, of course, my reading and research caught up with and passed the dreams in many phases;[g] so that certain dream-fragments[h] were explained in advance,[i] and formed verifications of what I had learned. This consolingly established my belief that similar reading and research, accomplished by my secondary self, had formed the source of the whole terrible fabric of pseudo-memories.[j]

The period of my dreams, apparently, was one somewhat less than 150,000,000 years ago, when the Palaeozoic age[k] was giving place to the Mesozoic.[l] The bodies occupied by the Great Race represented no surviving—or even scientifically known—line of terrestrial[m] evolution,

[a] palaeontology.] paleontology. B, C
[b] discern.] discover. B, C
[c] amidst] among B, C
[d] sea] sea, B, C
[e] crinoid,] orinoid, Bᶜ
[f] dreaming.] dreaming. ¶ B, C
[g] phases;] phases, B, C
[h] dream-fragments] dream fragments B, C
[i] advance,] advance B, C
[j] pseudo-memories.] pseudo-/memories. B; pseudomemories. C
[k] Palaeozoic age] palaeozoic age A; Paleozoic Age B, C
[l] Mesozoic.] mesozoic. A; Mesozoic Age. Bᶜ
[m] terrestrial] Terrestrial B

but were of a peculiar, closely homogeneous, and highly specialised[a] organic type inclining as much to the vegetable as to the animal state.[b] Cell-action[c] was of an unique sort almost precluding fatigue, and wholly eliminating the need of sleep. Nourishment, assimilated through the red trumpet-like[d] appendages on one of the great flexible limbs, was always semi-fluid[e] and in many aspects wholly unlike the food of existing animals.[f] The beings had but two of the senses which we recognise[g]—sight and hearing, the latter accomplished through the flower-like[h] appendages on the grey[i] stalks above their heads—but of[j] other and incomprehensible senses (not, however, well utilisable[k] by alien captive minds inhabiting their bodies)[l] they possessed many. Their three eyes were so situated as to give them a range of vision wider than the normal. Their blood was a sort of deep-greenish ichor of great thickness.[m] They had no sex, but reproduced through seeds or spores which clustered on their bases and could be developed only under water. Great, shallow tanks were used for the growth of their young—which were, however, reared only in small numbers on account of the longevity of individuals;[n] four or five thousand years being the common life span.

Markedly defective individuals were quietly[o] disposed of as soon as their defects were noticed. Disease and the approach of death were, in the absence of a sense of touch or of physical pain, recognised[p] by

[a] specialised] specialized B, C
[b] state.] state. ¶ B, C
[c] Cell-action] Cell action B, C
[d] trumpet-like] trumpetlike B, C
[e] semi-fluid] semi-/fluid B; semifluid C
[f] animals.] animals. ¶ B, C
[g] recognise] recognize B, C
[h] flower-like] flowerlike A, B, C
[i] grey] gray B, C
[j] heads—but of] heads. Of B, C
[k] utilisable] utilizable B, C
[l] senses (. . .)] senses—. . .— B, C
[m] thickness.] thickness. ¶ B, C
[n] individuals;] individuals— B, C
[o] quietly] quickly B, C
[p] recognised] recognized B, C

purely visual symptoms.[a] The dead were incinerated with dignified ceremonies. Once in a while, as before mentioned, a keen mind would escape death by forward projection in time; but such cases were not numerous. When one did occur, the exiled mind from the future was treated with the utmost kindness till the dissolution of its unfamiliar tenement.

The Great Race seemed to form a single[b] loosely knit[c] nation or league, with major institutions in common, though there were four definite divisions. The political and economic[d] system of each unit was a sort of fascistic socialism, with major resources rationally distributed, and power delegated to a small governing board elected by the votes of all able to pass certain educational and psychological tests. Family organisation[e] was not overstressed, though ties among persons of common descent were recognised,[f] and the young were generally reared by their parents.

Resemblances to human attitudes and institutions were, of course, most marked in those fields where on the one hand highly abstract elements were concerned, or[g] where on the other hand there was a dominance of the basic, unspecialised[h] urges common to all organic life. A few added likenesses came through conscious adoption as the Great Race probed the future and copied what it liked.[i] Industry, highly mechanised,[j] demanded but little time from each citizen; and the abundant leisure was filled with intellectual and aesthetic activities of various sorts.[k] The sciences were carried to an unbelievable height of development, and art was a vital part of life, though at the period of my dreams it had passed its crest and meridian. Technology was

[a] symptoms.] symptoms. ¶ B, C
[b] single] single, B, C
[c] loosely knit] loosely-knit A
[d] economic] economical B[c]
[e] organisation] organization B, C
[f] recognised,] recognized, B, C
[g] or] or, B, C
[h] unspecialised] unspecialized B
[i] liked.] liked. ¶ B, C
[j] mechanised,] mechanized, B, C
[k] sorts.] sorts. ¶ B, C

enormously stimulated through the constant struggle to survive, and to keep in existence the physical fabric of great cities, imposed by the prodigious geologic upheavals of those primal days.

Crime was surprisingly scanty,[a] and was dealt with through highly efficient policing. Punishments ranged from privilege-deprivation[b] and imprisonment to death or major emotion-wrenching,[c] and were never administered without a careful study of the criminal's motivations.[d] Warfare, largely civil for the last few millennia though sometimes waged against reptilian and octopodic invaders, or against[e] the winged, star-headed Old Ones[f] who centred[g] in the antarctic,[h] was infrequent though infinitely devastating. An enormous army, using camera-like[i] weapons which produced tremendous electrical effects, was kept on hand for purposes seldom mentioned, but obviously connected with the ceaseless fear of the dark, windowless elder ruins and of the great sealed trap-doors[j] in the lowest subterrene[k] levels.

This fear of the basalt ruins and trap-doors[l] was largely a matter of unspoken suggestion—or, at most, of furtive quasi-whispers.[m] Everything specific which bore on it was significantly absent from such books as were on the common shelves. It was the one subject lying altogether under a taboo among the Great Race, and seemed to be connected alike with horrible bygone struggles, and with that future peril which would some day force the race to send its keener minds ahead en masse[n] in time.[o] Imperfect and fragmentary as were the other things

[a] scanty,] scant, B, C
[b] privilege-deprivation] privilege deprivation B, C
[c] emotion-wrenching,] emotion wrenching, B, C
[d] motivations.] motivations. ¶ B, C
[e] reptilian . . . against] *om.* C
[f] Old Ones] old ones B
[g] centred] centered B, C
[h] antarctic,] Antarctic, A
[i] camera-like] camera-/like B; cameralike C
[j] trap-doors] trapdoors A, B, C
[k] subterrene] subterranean B, C
[l] trap-doors] trap doors A; trapdoors B, C
[m] furtive quasi-whispers.] furtive, quasi whispers. B [*comma removed by HPL*]
[n] en masse] *en masse* B, C
[o] time.] time. ¶ B, C

presented by dreams and legends, this matter was still more bafflingly shrouded. The vague old myths avoided it—or perhaps all allusions had for some reason been excised. And in the dreams of myself and others, the hints were peculiarly few. Members of the Great Race never intentionally referred to the matter, and what could be gleaned came only from some of the more sharply observant captive minds.

According to these scraps of information, the basis of the fear was a horrible elder race of half-polypous,[a] utterly alien entities which had come through space from immeasurably distant universes and had dominated the earth[b] and three other solar planets about six hundred million years ago. They were only partly material—as we understand matter—and their type of consciousness and media of perception differed wholly[c] from those of terrestrial[d] organisms. For example, their senses did not include that of sight; their mental world being a strange, non-visual[e] pattern of impressions.[f] They were, however, sufficiently material to use implements of normal matter when in cosmic areas containing it; and they required housing—albeit of a peculiar kind. Though their *senses* could penetrate all material barriers, their *substance*[g] could not; and certain forms of electrical energy could wholly destroy them. They had the power of aërial motion[h] despite the absence of wings or any other visible means of levitation. Their minds were of such texture that no exchange with them could be effected by the Great Race.

When these things had come to the earth[i] they had built mighty basalt cities of windowless towers, and had preyed horribly upon the beings they found. Thus it was when the minds of the Great Race sped across the void from that obscure trans-galactic[j] world known in the

[a] half-polypous,] half polypous, B, C
[b] earth] Earth B
[c] wholly] widely B, C
[d] terrestrial] Terrestrial B
[e] non-visual] nonvisual B, C
[f] impressions.] impressions. ¶ B, C
[g] *senses . . . substance*] senses . . . substance B, C
[h] motion] motion, B, C
[i] earth] Earth B, C
[j] obscure trans-galactic] obscure, transgalactic B, C

disturbing and debatable Eltdown Shards as Yith.[a] The newcomers, with the instruments they created, had found it easy to subdue the predatory entities and drive them down to those caverns of inner earth which they had already joined to their abodes and begun to inhabit.[b] Then they had sealed the entrances and left them to their fate, afterward occupying most of their great cities and preserving certain important buildings for reasons connected more with superstition than with indifference, boldness, or scientific and historical zeal.

But as the aeons passed, there came vague, evil signs that the Elder Things[c] were growing strong and numerous in the inner world. There were sporadic irruptions of a particularly hideous character in certain small and remote cities of the Great Race, and in some of the deserted elder cities which the Great Race had not peopled—places where the paths to the gulfs below had not been properly sealed or guarded.[d] After that greater precautions were taken, and many of the paths were closed for ever[e]—though a few were left with sealed trap-doors[f] for strategic use in fighting the Elder Things[g] if ever they broke forth in unexpected places; fresh rifts caused by that selfsame geologic change which had choked some of the paths and had slowly lessened the number of outer-world structures and ruins surviving from the conquered entities.[h]

The irruptions of the Elder Things[i] must have been shocking beyond all description, since they had permanently coloured[j] the psychology of the Great Race. Such was the fixed mood of horror that the very *aspect*[k] of the creatures was left unmentioned—at[l] no time was

[a] Yith.] Yith. ¶ B, C
[b] inhabit.] inhabit. ¶ B, C
[c] Elder Things] elder things B, C
[d] guarded.] guarded. ¶ B, C
[e] for ever] forever B, C
[f] trap-doors] trap doors A; trapdoors B, C
[g] Elder Things] elder things B, C
[h] places; fresh . . . entities.] places. B, C
[i] Elder Things] elder things B, C
[j] coloured] colored B, C
[k] *aspect*] aspect B, C
[l] unmentioned—at] unmentioned. At B, C

I able to gain a clear hint of what they looked like.[a] There were veiled suggestions of a monstrous *plasticity,* and of temporary *lapses of visibility,* while other fragmentary whispers referred to their control and military use of *great winds.* Singular *whistling*[b] noises, and colossal footprints made up of five circular toe-marks,[c] seemed also to be associated with them.

It was evident that the coming doom so desperately feared by the Great Race—the doom that was one day to send millions of keen minds across the chasm of time to strange bodies in the safer future—had to do with a final successful irruption of the Elder Beings.[d] Mental projections down the ages had clearly foretold such a horror, and the Great Race had resolved that none who could escape should face it. That the foray would be a matter of vengeance, rather than an attempt to reoccupy the outer world, they knew from the planet's later history—for their projections shewed[e] the coming and going of subsequent races untroubled by the monstrous entities.[f] Perhaps these entities had come to prefer earth's[g] inner abysses to the variable, storm-ravaged surface,[h] since light meant nothing to them. Perhaps, too, they were slowly weakening with the aeons. Indeed, it was known that they would be quite dead in the time of the post-human beetle race which the fleeing minds would tenant.[i] Meanwhile[j] the Great Race maintained its cautious vigilance, with potent weapons ceaselessly ready despite the horrified banishing of the subject from common speech and visible records. And always the shadow of nameless fear hung about the sealed trap-doors[k] and the dark, windowless elder towers.

[a] like.] like. ¶ B, C
[b] *plasticity, . . . lapses of visibility, . . . great winds. . . . whistling*] plasticity, . . . lapses of visibility, . . . great winds. . . . whistling B, C
[c] toe-marks,] toe marks, B, C
[d] Elder Beings.] elder beings. ¶ B, C
[e] shewed] showed B, C
[f] entities.] entities. ¶ B, C
[g] earth's] Earth's B, C
[h] surface,] surfaces, Bᶜ
[i] tenant.] tenant. ¶ B, C
[j] Meanwhile] Meanwhile, B, C
[k] trap-doors] trapdoors A, B, C

V.

That is the world of which my dreams brought me dim, scattered echoes every night. I cannot hope to give any true idea of the horror and dread contained in such echoes, for it was upon a wholly intangible quality—the sharp sense of *pseudo-memory*[a]—that such feelings mainly depended.[b] As I have said, my studies gradually gave me a defence[c] against these feelings,[d] in the form of rational psychological explanations; and this saving influence was augmented by the subtle touch of accustomedness which comes with the passage of time. Yet in spite of everything[e] the vague, creeping terror would return momentarily now and then. It did not, however, engulf me as it had before; and after 1922 I lived a very normal life of work and recreation.

In the course of years I began to feel that my experience—together with the kindred cases and the related folklore—ought to be definitely summarised[f] and published for the benefit of serious students; hence[g] I prepared a series of articles briefly covering the whole ground and illustrated with crude sketches of some of the shapes, scenes, decorative motifs, and hieroglyphs remembered from the dreams.[h] These appeared at various times during 1928 and 1929 in the *Journal of the American Psychological Society*, but did not attract much attention. Meanwhile[i] I continued to record my dreams with the minutest care, even though the growing stack of reports attained troublesomely vast proportions.

On July 10, 1934, there was forwarded to me by the Psychological Society the letter which opened the culminating and most horrible phase of the whole mad ordeal. It was postmarked Pilbarra, Western Australia, and bore the signature of one whom I found, upon inquiry,

[a] *pseudo-memory*] pseudomemory B, C
[b] depended.] depended. ¶ B, C
[c] defence] defense B, C
[d] feelings,] feelings B, C
[e] Yet . . . everything] Yet, . . . everything, Bᶜ
[f] summarised] summarized B, C
[g] hence] hence, Bᶜ, C
[h] dreams.] dreams. ¶ B, C
[i] Meanwhile] Meanwhile, Bᶜ, C

to be a mining engineer of considerable prominence. Enclosed[a] were some very curious snapshots. I will reproduce the text in its entirety, and no reader can fail to understand how tremendous an effect it and the photographs had upon me.

I was, for a time, almost stunned and incredulous; for[b] although I had often thought that some basis of fact must underlie certain phases of the legends which had coloured[c] my dreams, I was none the less unprepared for anything like a tangible survival from a lost world remote beyond all imagination. Most devastating of all were the photographs—for here, in cold, incontrovertible realism, there stood out against a background of sand certain worn-down, water-ridged, storm-weathered blocks of stone whose slightly convex tops and slightly concave bottoms told their own story.[d] And when I studied them with a magnifying glass I could see all too plainly, amidst the batterings and pittings, the traces of those vast curvilinear designs and occasional hieroglyphs whose significance had become so hideous to me. But here is the letter, which speaks for itself:

49, Dampier Str.,[e]
Pilbarra, W. Australia,
18 May,[f] 1934.

Prof. N. W. Peaslee,
c/o Am. Psychological Society,
30, E. 41st Str.,[g]
N. Y.[h] City, U.S.A.[i]

My dear Sir:—[j]
A recent conversation with Dr. E. M. Boyle of Perth, and some papers

[a] Enclosed] Inclosed B, C
[b] for] for, B[c], C
[c] coloured] colored B, C
[d] story.] story. ¶ B, C
[e] 49, . . . Str.,] 49, . . . St., B; 49 . . . St., C
[f] 18 May,] May 18, B, C
[g] 30, . . . Str.,] 30 . . . St., B, C
[h] N. Y.] New York B, C
[i] c/o . . . U.S.A.] c/o Am. Psychological Society, 30, E. 41st Str., N. Y. City, U.S.A. A; c/o . . . U. S. A. B
[j] My dear Sir:—] MY DEAR SIR: B; My Dear Sir: C

with your articles which he has just sent me, make it advisable for me to tell you about certain things I have seen in the Great Sandy Desert east of our gold field here. It would seem, in view of the peculiar legends about old cities with huge stonework and strange designs and hieroglyphs which you describe, that I have come upon something very important.

The blackfellows have always been full of talk about "great stones with marks on them",[a] and seem to have a terrible fear of such things. They connect them in some way with their common racial legends about Buddai, the gigantic old man who lies asleep for ages underground with his head on his arm, and who will some day awake and eat up the world.[b] There are some very old and half-forgotten tales of enormous underground huts of great stones, where passages lead down and down, and where horrible things have happened. The blackfellows claim that once some warriors, fleeing in battle, went down into one and never came back, but that frightful winds began to blow from the place soon after they went down. However, there usually isn't much in what these natives say.

But what I have to tell is more than this. Two years ago, when I was prospecting about 500[c] miles east in the desert, I came on a lot of queer pieces of dressed stone perhaps 3 × 2 × 2 feet in size, and weathered and pitted to the very limit.[d] At first I couldn't find any of the marks the blackfellows told about, but when I looked close enough I could make out some deeply carved lines in spite of the weathering. They[e] were peculiar curves, just like what the blacks[f] had tried to describe. I imagine there must have been 30 or 40[g] blocks, some nearly buried in the sand, and all within a circle[h] perhaps a quarter of a mile's[i] diameter.

When I saw some, I looked around closely for more, and made a careful reckoning of the place with my instruments. I also took pictures of 10 or 12[j] of the most typical blocks, and will enclose[k] the prints for you to

[a] them",] them," B, C
[b] world.] world. ¶ B, C
[c] 500] five hundred B, C
[d] limit.] limit. ¶ B, C
[e] They] There B, C
[f] blacks] blackfellows B, C
[g] 30 or 40] thirty or forty B, C
[h] circle] circle of B[c]
[i] mile's] mile in B, C
[j] 10 or 12] ten or twelve B, C
[k] enclose] inclose B, C

see.[a] I turned my information and pictures over to[b] the government at Perth, but they have done nothing with them.[c] Then I met Dr. Boyle, who had read your articles in the *Journal of the American Psychological Society,* and in time[d] happened to mention the stones. He was enormously interested,[e] and became quite excited when I shewed[f] him my snapshots, saying that the stones and[g] markings were just like those of the masonry you had dreamed about and seen described in legends.[h] He meant to write you, but was delayed. Meanwhile[i] he sent me most of the magazines with your articles,[j] and I saw at once from your drawings and descriptions[k] that my stones are certainly the kind you mean. You can appreciate this from the enclosed[l] prints. Later on you will hear directly from Dr. Boyle.

Now I can understand how important all this will be to you. Without question we are faced with the remains of an unknown civilisation[m] older than any dreamed of before, and forming a basis for your legends.[n] As a mining engineer,[o] I have some knowledge of geology, and can tell you that these blocks are so ancient they frighten me. They are mostly sandstone and granite, though one is almost certainly made of a queer sort of *cement* or *concrete.*[p] They bear evidence of water action, as if this part of the world had been submerged and come up again after long ages—all since these[q] blocks were made and used. It is a matter of hundreds of thousands of years—or heaven[r] knows how much more. I don't like to think about it.

In view of your previous diligent work in tracking down the legends and everything connected with them, I cannot doubt but that you will

[a] see.] see. ¶ B, C
[b] over to] into B[c]
[c] them.] them. ¶ B, C
[d] and in time] and, in time, B, C
[e] interested,] interested B, C
[f] shewed] showed B, C
[g] and] and the B, C
[h] legends.] legends. ¶ B, C
[i] Meanwhile] Meanwhile, B, C
[j] articles,] articles B, C
[k] once . . . descriptions] once, . . . descriptions, B, C
[l] enclosed] inclosed B, C
[m] civilisation] civilization B, C
[n] legends.] legends. ¶ B, C
[o] engineer,] engineer C
[p] *cement* or *concrete.*] cement or concrete. ¶ B, C
[q] these] those B, C
[r] heaven] Heaven B, C

want to lead an expedition to the desert and make some archaeological excavations. Both Dr. Boyle and I are prepared to coöperate in such work if you—or organisations[a] known to you—can furnish the funds.[b] I can get together a dozen miners for the heavy digging—the blacks[c] would be of no use, for I've found that they have an almost maniacal fear of this particular spot. Boyle and I are saying nothing to others, for you very obviously ought to have precedence in any discoveries or credit.

The place can be reached from Pilbarra in about 4[d] days by motor tractor—which we'd need for our apparatus. It is somewhat west and south of Warburton's path of 1873, and 100[e] miles southeast of Joanna Spring. We could float things up the De Grey River instead of starting from Pilbarra—but all that can be talked over later. Roughly,[f] the stones lie at a point about 22° 3' 14" South Latitude, 125° 0' 39" East Longitude. The climate is tropical, and the desert conditions are trying. Any expedition had better be made in winter—June or July or August.[g] I shall welcome further correspondence upon this subject, and am indeed keenly eager to assist in any plan you may devise. After studying your articles I am deeply impressed with the profound significance of the whole matter. Dr. Boyle will write later. When rapid communication is needed, a cable to Perth can be relayed by wireless.

Hoping profoundly for an early message,

Believe me,

Most faithfully yours,

Robert B. F. Mackenzie.[h]

Of the immediate aftermath of this letter, much can be learned from the press. My good fortune in securing the backing of Miskatonic University was great, and both Mr. Mackenzie and Dr. Boyle proved invaluable in arranging matters at the Australian end. We were not too specific with the public about our objects, since the whole matter would have lent itself unpleasantly to sensational and jocose treatment

---

[a] organisations] organizations B, C

[b] funds.] funds. ¶ B, C

[c] blacks] blackfellows B, C

[d] 4] four B, C

[e] 100] one hundred B, C

[f] later. Roughly,] later. ¶ Roughly B, C

[g] trying. Any . . . August.] trying. ¶ B, C

[h] Robert B. F. Mackenzie.] ROBERT B. F. MACKENZIE. B; ROBERT B. F. MACKENZIE C

by the cheaper newspapers. As a result, printed reports were sparing; but enough appeared to tell of our quest for reported Australian ruins and to chronicle our various preparatory steps.

Professors[a] William Dyer of the college's geology department (leader of the Miskatonic Antarctic Expedition of 1930–31),[b] Ferdinand[c] C. Ashley of the department of ancient history, and Tyler M. Freeborn of the department of anthropology—together with my son Wingate—accompanied me.[d] My correspondent Mackenzie[e] came to Arkham early in 1935 and assisted in our final preparations. He proved to be a tremendously competent and affable man of about fifty, admirably well-read, and deeply familiar with all the conditions of Australian travel.[f] He had tractors waiting at Pilbarra, and we chartered a tramp steamer of sufficiently light draught[g] to get up the river to that point. We were prepared to excavate in the most careful and scientific fashion, sifting every particle of sand, and disturbing nothing which might seem to be in or near its original situation.

Sailing from Boston aboard the wheezy *Lexington* on March 28, 1935, we had a leisurely trip across the Atlantic and Mediterranean, through the Suez Canal, down the Red Sea, and across the Indian Ocean to our goal. I need not tell how the sight of the low, sandy West Australian coast depressed me, and how I detested the crude mining town and dreary gold fields where the tractors were given their last loads.[h] Dr. Boyle, who met us, proved to be elderly, pleasant,[i] and intelligent—and his knowledge of psychology led him into many long discussions with my son and me.

Discomfort and expectancy were oddly mingled in most of us when at length our party of eighteen[j] rattled forth over the arid leagues

[a] Professors] Professor B, C
[b] department (. . .),] department—. . .— B, C
[c] Ferdinand] Ferndinand C
[d] me.] me. ¶ B, C
[e] correspondent Mackenzie] correspondent, Mackenzie, B, C
[f] travel.] travel. ¶ B, C
[g] of . . . draught] *om.* B [*changed by HPL to* sufficiently small]; sufficiently small C
[h] loads.] loads. ¶ B, C
[i] pleasant,] pleasant B, C
[j] eighteen] 18 A

of sand and rock. On Friday, May 31st,[a] we forded a branch of the De Grey and entered the realm of utter desolation. A certain positive terror grew on me as we advanced to this actual site of the elder world behind the legends—a terror of course[b] abetted by the fact that my disturbing dreams and pseudo-memories[c] still beset me with unabated force.

It was on Monday, June 3,[d] that we saw the first of the half-buried blocks. I cannot describe the emotions with which I actually touched—in objective reality—a fragment of Cyclopean[e] masonry in every respect like the blocks in the walls of my dream-buildings.[f] There was a distinct trace of carving—and my hands trembled as I recognised[g] part of a curvilinear decorative scheme made hellish to me through years of tormenting nightmare and baffling research.

A month of digging brought a total of some 1250 blocks in varying stages of wear and disintegration. Most of these were carven megaliths with curved tops and bottoms. A minority were smaller, flatter, plain-surfaced, and square or octagonally cut—like those of the floors and pavements in my dreams—while a few were singularly massive and curved or slanted in such a manner as to suggest use in vaulting or groining, or as parts of arches or round window casings.[h] The deeper—and the farther north and east—we dug, the more blocks we found;[i] though we still failed to discover any trace of arrangement among them. Professor Dyer was appalled at the measureless age of the fragments, and Freeborn found traces of symbols which fitted darkly into certain Papuan and Polynesian legends of infinite antiquity. The condition and scattering of the blocks told mutely[j] of vertiginous cycles of time and geologic upheavals of cosmic savagery.

[a] 31st,] 31, C

[b] terror of course] terror, of course, B, C

[c] pseudo-memories] pseudomemories B, C

[d] 3,] 3rd, B

[e] Cyclopean] cyclopean A, C

[f] dream-buildings.] dream buildings. B, C

[g] recognised] recognized B, C

[h] casings.] casings. ¶ B, C

[i] found;] found— C

[j] mutely] minutely B[c]

We had an aëroplane[a] with us, and my son Wingate would often go up to different heights and scan the sand-and-rock waste for signs of dim, large-scale outlines—either differences of level or trails of scattered blocks. His results were virtually negative; for whenever he would one day think he had glimpsed some significant trend, he would on his next trip find the impression replaced by another equally insubstantial—a result of the shifting, wind-blown sand.[b] One or two of these ephemeral suggestions, though, affected me queerly and disagreeably. They seemed, after a fashion, to dovetail horribly with something which[c] I had dreamed or read, but which I could no longer remember. There was a terrible *pseudo-familiarity*[d] about them—which somehow made me look furtively and apprehensively over the abominable, sterile terrain toward the north and northeast.[e]

Around the first week in July I developed an unaccountable set of mixed emotions about that general northeasterly region. There was horror, and there was curiosity—but more than that, there was a persistent and perplexing illusion of *memory*.[f] I tried all sorts of psychological expedients to get these notions out of my head, but met with no success. Sleeplessness also gained upon me, but I almost welcomed this because of the resultant shortening of my dream-periods.[g] I acquired the habit of taking long, lone walks in the desert late at night—usually to the north or northeast, whither the sum of my strange new impulses seemed subtly to pull me.

Sometimes, on these walks, I would stumble over nearly buried[h] fragments of the ancient masonry. Though there were fewer visible blocks here than where we had started, I felt sure that there must be a vast abundance beneath the surface. The ground was less level than at our camp, and the prevailing high winds now and then piled the sand

---

[a] aëroplane] aeroplane A, C; airplane B [*changed by HPL to* aeroplane]
[b] sand.] sand. ¶ B, C
[c] which] *om.* B, C
[d] *pseudo-familiarity*] familiarity B, C
[e] terrain . . . northeast.] terrain. C
[f] *memory.*] memory. ¶ B, C
[g] dream-periods.] dream periods. B, C
[h] nearly buried] nearly-buried A

into fantastic temporary hillocks—exposing some[a] traces of the elder stones while it covered other traces.[b] I was queerly anxious to have the excavations extend to this territory, yet at the same time dreaded what might be revealed. Obviously, I was getting into a rather bad state—all the worse because I could not account for it.

An indication of my poor nervous health can be gained from my response to an odd discovery which I made on one of my nocturnal rambles. It was on the evening of July 11th,[c] when a gibbous moon[d] flooded the mysterious hillocks with a curious pallor.[e] Wandering somewhat beyond my usual limits, I came upon a great stone which seemed to differ markedly from any we had yet encountered. It was almost wholly covered, but I stooped and cleared away the sand with my hands, later studying the object carefully and supplementing the moonlight[f] with my electric torch.[g] Unlike the other very large rocks, this one was perfectly square-cut, with no convex or concave surface. It seemed, too, to be of a dark basaltic substance[h] wholly dissimilar to the granite and sandstone and occasional concrete of the now familiar fragments.

Suddenly I rose, turned, and ran for the camp at top speed. It was a wholly unconscious and irrational flight, and only when I was close to my tent did I fully realise[i] why I had run. Then it came to me. The queer dark stone was something which[j] I had dreamed and read about, and which was linked with the uttermost horrors of the aeon-old legendry.[k] It was one of the blocks of that basaltic elder masonry which the fabled Great Race held in such fear—the tall, windowless

---

[a] some] low B, C
[b] traces.] traces. ¶ B, C
[c] 11th,] 11ᵗʰ, A; 11, B, C
[d] a gibbous moon] the Moon B [*changed by HPL to* the moon]; the moon C
[e] pallor.] pallor. ¶ B, C
[f] moonlight] Moonlight Bᶜ
[g] torch.] torch. ¶ B, C
[h] substance] substance, B, C
[i] realise] realize B, C
[j] which] *om.* Bᶜ
[k] legendry.] legendry. ¶ B, C

ruins left by those brooding, half-material, alien Things[a] that festered in earth's[b] nether abysses and against whose wind-like,[c] invisible forces the trap-doors[d] were sealed and the sleepless sentinels posted.

I remained awake all that[e] night, but by dawn realised[f] how silly I had been to let the shadow of a myth upset me. Instead of being frightened, I should have had a discoverer's enthusiasm.[g] The next forenoon I told the others about my find, and Dyer, Freeborn, Boyle, my son, and I set out to view the anomalous block. Failure, however, confronted us. I had formed no clear idea of the stone's location, and a late wind had wholly altered the hillocks of shifting sand.

VI.

I come now to the crucial and[h] most difficult part of my narrative—all the more difficult because I cannot be quite certain of its reality. At times I feel uncomfortably sure that I was not dreaming or deluded; and it is this feeling—in view of the stupendous implications which the objective truth of my experience would raise—which impels me to make this record.[i] My son—a trained psychologist with the fullest and most sympathetic knowledge of my whole case—shall be the primary judge of what I have to tell.

First let me outline the externals of the matter, as those at the camp know them.[j] On the night of July 17–18, after a windy day, I retired early but could not sleep. Rising shortly before eleven,[k] and afflicted as usual with that strange feeling regarding the northeastward terrain, I set out on one of my typical nocturnal walks;[l] seeing and

[a] Things] things B, C
[b] earth's] Earth's B
[c] wind-like,] windlike, B, C
[d] trap-doors] trapdoors A; trap-/doors B, C
[e] that] om. B, C
[f] realised] realized B, C
[g] enthusiasm.] enthusiasm. ¶ B, C
[h] and] and the B[c]
[i] record.] record. ¶ B, C
[j] them.] them: B, C
[k] eleven,] eleven C
[l] walks;] walks, B, C

greeting only one person—an Australian miner named Tupper—as I left our precincts.[a] The moon,[b] slightly past full, shone from a clear sky[c] and drenched the ancient sands with a white, leprous radiance which seemed to me somehow infinitely evil. There was no longer any wind, nor did any return for nearly five hours, as amply attested by Tupper and others who did not sleep through the night. The Australian last[d] saw me walking rapidly across the pallid, secret-guarding hillocks toward the northeast.

About 3:30 a.m.[e] a violent wind blew up, waking everyone[f] in camp and felling three of the tents. The sky was unclouded, and the desert still blazed with that leprous moonlight.[g] As the party saw to the tents my absence was noted, but in view of my previous walks this circumstance gave no one alarm. And yet[h] as many as three men—all Australians—seemed to feel something sinister in the air.[i] Mackenzie explained to Prof.[j] Freeborn that this was a fear picked up from blackfellow folklore—the natives having woven a curious fabric of malignant myth about the high winds which at long intervals sweep across the sands under a clear sky. Such winds, it is whispered, blow out of the great stone huts under the ground[k] where terrible things have happened—and are never felt except near places where the big marked stones are scattered. Close to four the gale subsided as suddenly as it had begun, leaving the sand hills in new and unfamiliar shapes.

It was just past five, with the bloated, fungoid moon[l] sinking in the[m] west, when I staggered into camp—hatless, tattered, features scratched and ensanguined, and without my electric torch. Most of the men had

[a] precincts.] precincts. ¶ B, C
[b] moon,] Moon, B
[c] sky] sky, B, C
[d] did not . . . last] *om.* B, C
[e] a.m.] a. m., B, C
[f] everyone] every one B, C
[g] moonlight.] Moonlight. B^c
[h] yet] yet, B, C
[i] air.] air. ¶ B, C
[j] Prof.] Professor B, C
[k] ground] ground, B, C
[l] moon] Moon B
[m] the] *beginning of A2*

returned to bed, but Prof.[a] Dyer was smoking a pipe in front of his tent. Seeing my winded and almost frenzied state, he called Dr. Boyle, and the two of them got me on my cot and made me comfortable. My son, roused by the stir, soon joined them, and they all tried to force me to lie still and attempt sleep.

But there was no sleep for me. My psychological state was very extraordinary—different from anything I had previously suffered. After a time I insisted upon talking—nervously and elaborately explaining my condition.[b] I told them I had become fatigued, and had lain down in the sand for a nap. There had, I said, been dreams even more frightful than usual—and when I was awaked by the sudden high wind my overwrought nerves had snapped. I had fled in panic, frequently falling over half-buried stones and thus gaining my tattered and bedraggled aspect. I must have slept long—hence the hours of my absence.

Of anything strange either seen or experienced I hinted absolutely nothing—exercising the greatest self-control in that respect. But I spoke of a change of mind regarding the whole work of the expedition, and earnestly urged a halt in all digging toward the northeast.[c] My reasoning was patently weak—for I mentioned a dearth of blocks, a wish not to offend the superstitious miners, a possible shortage of funds from the college, and other things either untrue or irrelevant. Naturally, no one paid the least attention to my new wishes—not even my son, whose concern for my health was very obvious.[d]

The next day I was up and around the camp, but took no part in the excavations. Seeing that I could not stop the work,[e] I decided to return home as soon as possible for the sake of my nerves, and made my son promise[f] to fly me in the plane to Perth—a thousand miles to the southwest—as soon as he had surveyed the region I wished let alone.[g] If, I reflected, the thing I had seen was still visible, I might decide to attempt a specific warning even at the cost of ridicule. It was

[a] Prof.] Professor A2, B, C
[b] condition.] condition. ¶ B, C
[c] northeast.] northeast. ¶ B, C
[d] obvious.] *end of A2*
[e] Seeing . . . work,] *om.* C
[f] made my son promise] my son promised C
[g] alone.] alone. ¶ B, C

just conceivable that the miners who knew the local folklore might back me up. Humouring[a] me, my son made the survey that very afternoon;[b] flying over all the terrain my walk could possibly have covered. Yet nothing of what I had found remained in sight.[c] It was the case of the anomalous basalt block all over again—the shifting sand had wiped out every trace. For an instant I half regretted[d] having lost a certain awesome object in my stark fright—but now I know that the loss was merciful. I can still believe my whole experience an illusion—especially if, as I devoutly hope, that hellish abyss is never found.

Wingate took me to Perth July 20,[e] though declining to abandon the expedition and return home. He stayed with me until the 25th,[f] when the steamer for Liverpool sailed. Now, in the cabin of the *Empress,* I am pondering long and frantically on[g] the entire matter, and have decided that my son at least[h] must be informed. It shall rest with him whether to diffuse the matter more widely.[i] In order to meet any eventuality I have prepared this summary of my background—as already known in a scattered way to others—and will now tell as briefly as possible what seemed to happen during my absence from the camp that hideous night.

Nerves on edge, and whipped into a kind of perverse eagerness by that inexplicable, dread-mingled, pseudo-mnemonic[j] urge toward the northeast, I plodded on beneath the evil, burning moon.[k] Here and there I saw, half-shrouded[l] by the sand, those primal Cyclopean[m] blocks left from nameless and forgotten aeons.[n] The incalculable age

[a] Humouring] Humoring B
[b] afternoon;] afternoon, B, C
[c] sight.] sight. ¶ B
[d] half regretted] half-regretted A
[e] Perth July 20,] Perth on July 20th, B; Perth on July 20, C
[f] 25th,] 25ᵗʰ, A
[g] on] upon B, C
[h] son at least] son, at least, B, C
[i] widely.] widely. ¶ B, C
[j] pseudo-mnemonic] mnemonic B, C
[k] moon.] Moon. B
[l] half-shrouded] half shrouded B, C
[m] Cyclopean] cyclopean A, C
[n] aeons.] aeons. ¶ B, C

and brooding horror of this monstrous waste began to oppress me as never before, and I could not keep from thinking of my maddening dreams, of the frightful legends which lay behind them, and of the present fears of natives and miners concerning the desert and its carven stones.

And yet I plodded on as if to some eldritch rendezvous—more and more assailed by bewildering fancies, compulsions, and pseudo-memories.[a] I thought of some of the possible contours of the lines of stones as seen by my son from the air, and wondered why they seemed at once so ominous and so familiar. Something was fumbling and rattling at the latch of my recollection, while another unknown force sought to keep the portal barred.

The night was windless, and the pallid sand curved upward and downward like frozen waves of the sea. I had no goal, but somehow ploughed[b] along as if with fate-bound assurance. My dreams welled up into the waking world, so that each sand-embedded megalith seemed part of endless rooms and corridors of pre-human[c] masonry, carved and hieroglyphed with symbols that I knew too well from years of custom as a captive mind of the Great Race.[d] At moments I fancied I saw those omniscient[e] conical horrors moving about at their accustomed tasks, and I feared to look down lest I find myself one with them in aspect. Yet all the while I saw the sand-covered blocks as well as the rooms and corridors; the[f] evil, burning moon[g] as well as the lamps of luminous crystal; the endless desert as well as the waving ferns and cycads[h] beyond the windows. I was awake and dreaming at the same time.

I do not know how long or how far—or indeed, in just what direction—I had walked when I first spied the heap of blocks bared by the day's wind. It was the largest group in one place that I had so far

[a] pseudo-memories.] pseudomemories. B, C
[b] ploughed] plowed B, C
[c] pre-human] prehuman B, C
[d] Race.] Race. ¶ B, C
[e] omniscient] omniscient, B, C
[f] the] *om.* C
[g] moon] Moon B
[h] and cycads] *om.* B, C

seen,[a] and so sharply did it impress me that the visions of fabulous aeons faded suddenly away.[b] Again there were only the desert and the evil moon[c] and the shards of an unguessed past. I drew close and paused, and cast the added light of my electric torch over the tumbled pile. A hillock had blown away, leaving a low, irregularly round mass of megaliths and smaller fragments some forty feet across and from two to eight feet high.

From the very outset I realised[d] that there was some utterly unprecedented quality about these[e] stones. Not only was the mere number of them quite without parallel, but something in the sand-worn[f] traces of design arrested me as I scanned them under the mingled beams of the moon[g] and my torch.[h] Not that any one differed essentially from the earlier specimens we had found. It was something subtler than that. The impression did not come when I looked at one block alone, but only when I ran my eye over several almost simultaneously.[i] Then, at last, the truth dawned upon me. The curvilinear patterns on many of these[j] blocks were *closely related*[k]—parts of one vast decorative conception.[l] For the first time in this aeon-shaken[m] waste I had come upon a mass of masonry in its old position—tumbled and fragmentary, it is true, but none the less existing in a very definite sense.

Mounting at a low place, I clambered laboriously over the heap; here and there clearing away the sand with my fingers, and constantly striving to interpret varieties of size, shape, and style, and relationships of design.[n] After a while I could vaguely guess at the nature of the

[a] so far seen,] seen so far, B, C
[b] away.] away. ¶ B, C
[c] moon] Moon B
[d] realised] realized B, C
[e] these] those B, C
[f] sand-worn] sandworn C
[g] moon] Moon B
[h] torch.] torch. ¶ B, C
[i] simultaneously.] simultaneously. ¶ B, C
[j] these] those B, C
[k] *closely related*] closely related B, C
[l] conception.] conception B[c]
[m] aeon-shaken] aeon-shaking C
[n] design.] design. ¶ B, C

bygone structure, and at the designs which had once stretched over the vast surfaces of the primal masonry. The perfect identity of the whole with some of my dream-glimpses[a] appalled and unnerved me.[b] This was once a Cyclopean[c] corridor thirty feet tall, paved with octagonal blocks and solidly vaulted overhead. There would have been rooms opening off on the right, and at the farther end one of those strange inclined planes would have wound down to still lower depths.

I started violently as these conceptions occurred to me, for there was more in them than the blocks themselves had supplied. How did I know that this level should have been far underground? How did I know that the plane leading upward should have been behind me? How did I know that the long subterrene[d] passage to the Square of Pillars[e] ought to lie on the left one level above me?[f] How did I know that the room of machines, and the rightward-leading tunnel to the central archives,[g] ought to lie two levels below? How did I know that there would be one of those horrible, metal-banded trap-doors[h] at the very bottom,[i] four levels down? Bewildered by this intrusion from the dream-world,[j] I found myself shaking and bathed in a cold perspiration.

Then, as a last, intolerable touch, I felt that faint, insidious stream of cool air trickling upward from a depressed place near the centre[k] of the huge heap. Instantly, as once before, my visions faded, and I saw again only the evil moonlight,[l] the brooding desert, and the spreading tumulus of palaeogean[m] masonry. Something real and tangible, yet fraught with infinite suggestions of nighted mystery, now confronted

[a] dream-glimpses] dream glimpses B, C

[b] me.] me. ¶ B, C

[c] Cyclopean] cyclopean A, C

[d] subterrene] subterrane B[c], C

[e] Square of Pillars] square of pillars A, B[c]

[f] me?] me? ¶ B, C

[g] machines, . . . archives,] machines . . . archives B, C

[h] trap-doors] trap doors A; trapdoors B, C

[i] bottom,] bottom B, C

[j] dream-world,] dream world, B, C

[k] centre] center B, C

[l] moonlight,] Moonlight, B[c]

[m] palaeogean] A; Paleogean B [*changed by HPL to* paleogean]; paleogean C

me. For that stream of air could argue but one thing—a hidden gulf of great size beneath the disordered blocks on the surface.

My first thought was of the sinister blackfellow legends of vast underground huts among the megaliths where horrors happen and great winds are born. Then thoughts of my own dreams came back, and I felt dim pseudo-memories[a] tugging at my mind. What manner of place lay below me? What primal, inconceivable source of age-old myth-cycles[b] and haunting nightmares might I be on the brink of uncovering?[c] It was only for a moment that I hesitated, for more than curiosity and scientific zeal was driving me on and working against my growing fear.

I seemed to move almost automatically, as if in the clutch of some compelling fate. Pocketing my torch, and struggling with a strength that I had not thought I possessed, I wrenched aside first one titan fragment of stone and then another, till there welled up a strong draught[d] whose dampness contrasted oddly with the desert's dry air. A black rift began to yawn, and at length—when I had pushed away every fragment small enough to budge—the leprous moonlight[e] blazed on an aperture of ample width to admit me.

I drew out my torch and cast a brilliant beam into the opening. Below me was a chaos of tumbled masonry, sloping roughly down toward the north at an angle of about forty-five degrees, and evidently the result of some bygone collapse from above.[f] Between its surface and the ground level was a gulf of impenetrable blackness at whose upper edge were signs of gigantic, stress-heaved vaulting. At this point, it appeared, the desert's sands lay directly upon a floor of some titan structure of earth's[g] youth—how preserved through aeons of geologic convulsion I could not then and cannot now even attempt to guess.

---

[a] pseudo-memories] pseudomemories B, C

[b] myth-cycles] myth cycles B, C

[c] uncovering?] uncovering? ¶ B, C

[d] draught] draft B, C

[e] moonlight] Moonlight B[c]

[f] above.] above. ¶ B, C

[g] earth's] Earth's B, C

In retrospect, the barest idea of a sudden,[a] lone descent into such a doubtful abyss—and at a time when one's whereabouts were unknown to any living soul—seems like the utter apex of insanity. Perhaps it was—yet that night I embarked without hesitancy upon such a descent.[b] Again there was manifest that lure and driving of fatality which had all along seemed to direct my course. With torch flashing intermittently to save the battery, I commenced a mad scramble down the sinister, Cyclopean[c] incline below the opening—sometimes facing forward as I found good hand and foot holds, and at other times turning to face the heap of megaliths as I clung and fumbled more precariously.[d] In two directions beside me, distant walls of carven, crumbling masonry loomed dimly under the direct beams of my torch. Ahead, however, was only unbroken blackness.[e]

I kept no track of time during my downward scramble. So seething with baffling hints and images was my mind,[f] that all objective matters seemed withdrawn into incalculable distances. Physical sensation was dead, and even fear remained as a wraith-like,[g] inactive gargoyle leering impotently at me.[h] Eventually I reached a level floor strown[i] with fallen blocks, shapeless fragments[j] of stone, and sand and detritus of every kind. On either side—perhaps thirty feet apart—rose massive walls culminating in huge groinings. That they were carved I could just discern, but the nature of the carvings was beyond my perception.[k] What held me the most was the vaulting overhead. The beam from my torch could not reach the roof, but the lower parts of the monstrous arches stood out distinctly. And so perfect was their identity with what

[a] sudden,] sudden C
[b] descent.] descent. ¶ B, C
[c] Cyclopean] cyclopean A, C
[d] precariously.] precariously. ¶ B, C
[e] only unbroken blackness.] darkness. C
[f] mind,] mind B, C
[g] wraith-like,] wraithlike, A, B, C
[h] me.] me. ¶ B, C
[i] strown] strewn B, C
[j] fragments] fragments, B[c]
[k] perception.] perception. ¶ B, C

I had seen in countless dreams of the elder world, that I trembled actively for the first time.

Behind and high above, a faint luminous blur told of the distant moonlit[a] world outside. Some vague shred of caution warned me that I should not let it out of my sight, lest I have no guide for my return.[b] I now advanced toward the wall on[c] my left, where the traces of carving were plainest. The littered floor was nearly[d] as hard to traverse as the downward heap had been, but I managed to pick my difficult way.[e] At one place I heaved aside some blocks and kicked away the detritus to see what the pavement was like, and shuddered at the utter, fateful familiarity of the great octagonal stones whose buckled surface still held roughly together.

Reaching a convenient distance from the wall, I cast the torchlight[f] slowly and carefully over its worn remnants of carving. Some bygone influx of water seemed to have acted on the sandstone surface, while there were curious incrustations which I could not explain.[g] In places the masonry was very loose and distorted, and I wondered how many aeons more this primal, hidden edifice could keep its remaining traces of form amidst earth's[h] heavings.

But it was the carvings themselves that excited me most. Despite their time-crumbled state, they were relatively easy to trace at close range; and the complete, intimate familiarity of every detail almost stunned my imagination. That the major attributes of this hoary masonry should be familiar, was not beyond normal credibility.[i] Powerfully impressing the weavers of certain myths, they had become embodied in a stream of cryptic lore which, somehow[j] coming to my notice during the amnesic period, had evoked vivid images in my

---

[a] moonlit] Moonlighted B[c]; moonlight C
[b] return.] return. ¶ B, C
[c] on] at B, C
[d] carving . . . nearly] carving / seemed to have acted on the sandstone / nearly B[c]
[e] way.] way. ¶ B, C
[f] torchlight] searchlight B, C
[g] explain.] explain. ¶ B, C
[h] earth's] Earth's B
[i] credibility.] credibility. ¶ B, C
[j] somehow] somehow, B, C

subconscious mind.[a] But how could I explain the exact and minute fashion in which each line and spiral of these strange designs tallied with what I had dreamt[b] for more than a score of years? What obscure, forgotten iconography could have reproduced each subtle shading and nuance[c] which so persistently, exactly, and unvaryingly besieged my sleeping vision night after night?

For this was no chance or remote resemblance. Definitely and absolutely, the millennially ancient, aeon-hidden corridor in which I stood was the original of something I knew in sleep as intimately as I knew my own house in Crane Street, Arkham. True, my dreams shewed[d] the place in its undecayed prime; but the identity was no less real on that account. I was wholly and horribly oriented.[e] The particular structure I was in was known to me. Known, too, was its place in that terrible elder city of dreams. That I could visit unerringly any point in that structure or in that city which had escaped the changes and devastations of uncounted ages, I realised[f] with hideous and instinctive certainty. What in God's[g] name could all this mean? How had I come to know what I knew? And what awful reality could lie behind those antique tales of the beings who had dwelt in this labyrinth of primordial stone?

Words can convey only fractionally the welter of dread and bewilderment which ate at my spirit. I knew this place. I knew what lay before me, and what had lain overhead before the myriad towering stories had fallen to dust and debris[h] and the desert. No need now, I thought with a shudder, to keep that faint blur of moonlight[i] in view.[j] I was torn betwixt a longing to flee and a feverish mixture of burning curiosity and driving fatality. What had happened to this monstrous

---

[a] mind.] mind. ¶ B, C
[b] dreamt] dreamed B, C
[c] nuance] *nuance* B, C
[d] shewed] showed B, C
[e] oriented.] oriented. ¶ B, C
[f] realised] realized B, C
[g] God's] Heaven's B, C
[h] debris] débris B
[i] moonlight] Moonlight B
[j] view.] view. ¶ B, C

megalopolis of eld[a] in the millions of years since the time of my dreams? Of the subterrene[b] mazes which had underlain the city and linked all its[c] titan towers, how much had still survived the writhings of earth's[d] crust?

Had I come upon a whole buried world of unholy archaism? Could I still find the house of the writing-master,[e] and the tower where S'gg'ha, a[f] captive mind from the star-headed vegetable carnivores of Antarctica, had chiselled[g] certain pictures on the blank spaces of the walls?[h] Would the passage at the second level down,[i] to the hall of the alien minds, be still unchoked and traversable? In that hall the captive mind of an incredible entity—a half-plastic denizen of the hollow interior of an unknown trans-Plutonian planet eighteen million years in the future—had kept a certain thing which it had modelled[j] from clay.

I shut my eyes and put my hand to my head in a vain, pitiful effort to drive these insane dream-fragments[k] from my consciousness. Then, for the first time,[l] I felt acutely the coolness, motion, and dampness of the surrounding air. Shuddering, I realised[m] that a vast chain of aeon-dead black gulfs must indeed be yawning somewhere beyond and below me.[n] I thought of the frightful chambers and corridors and inclines as I recalled them from my dreams. Would the way to the central archives still be open? Again that driving fatality tugged insistently at my brain as I recalled the awesome records that once lay cased in those rectangular vaults of rustless metal.

[a] eld] old B, C
[b] subterrene] subterrane B[c]
[c] its] the B, C
[d] earth's] Earth's B
[e] writing-master,] writing master, B, C
[f] a] the B, C
[g] Antarctica, had chiselled] antarctica, had chiseled B; Antarctica, had chiseled C
[h] walls?] walls? ¶ B, C
[i] down,] down C
[j] modelled] modeled B, C
[k] dream-fragments] dream fragments B, C
[l] time,] time B, C
[m] realised] realized B, C
[n] me.] me. ¶ B, C

There, said the dreams and legends, had reposed the whole history, past and future, of the cosmic space-time continuum—written by captive minds from every orb and every age in the solar system. Madness, of course—but had I not now stumbled into a nighted world as mad as I?[a] I thought of the locked metal shelves, and of the curious knob-twistings[b] needed to open each one. My own came vividly into my consciousness. How often had I gone through that intricate routine of varied turns and pressures in the terrestrial[c] vertebrate section on the lowest level! Every detail was fresh and familiar.[d] If there were such a vault as I had dreamed of, I could open it in a moment. It was then that madness took me utterly. An instant later, and I was leaping and stumbling over the rocky debris[e] toward the well-remembered incline to the depths below.

VII.

From that point forward my impressions are scarcely to be relied on—indeed, I still possess a final, desperate hope that they all form parts of some daemoniac[f] dream—[g]or illusion born of delirium. A fever raged in my brain, and everything came to me through a kind of haze—sometimes only intermittently.[h] The rays of my torch shot feebly into the engulfing blackness, bringing phantasmal flashes of hideously familiar walls and carvings, all blighted with the decay of ages. In one place a tremendous mass of vaulting had fallen, so that I had to clamber over a mighty mound of stones reaching almost to the ragged, grotesquely stalactited roof.[i] It was all the ultimate apex of nightmare, made worse by the blasphemous tug of pseudo-memory.[j] One thing

[a] I?] I? ¶ B, C
[b] knob-twistings] knob twistings B, C
[c] terrestrial] Terrestrial B
[d] familiar.] familiar. ¶ B, C
[e] debris] débris B
[f] daemoniac] demoniac A, B, C
[g] dream—] dream B, C
[h] intermittently.] intermittently. ¶ B, C
[i] roof.] roof. ¶ B, C
[j] pseudo-memory.] pseudomemory. B, C

only was unfamiliar, and that was my own size in relation to the monstrous masonry. I felt oppressed by a sense of unwonted smallness, as if the sight of these towering walls from a mere human body was something wholly new and abnormal. Again and again I looked nervously down at myself, vaguely disturbed by the human form I possessed.

Onward through the blackness of the abyss I leaped, plunged,[a] and staggered—often falling and bruising myself, and once nearly shattering my torch. Every stone and corner of that daemoniac[b] gulf was known to me, and at many points I stopped to cast beams of light through choked and crumbling yet familiar archways.[c] Some rooms had totally collapsed; others were bare or debris-filled.[d] In a few I saw masses of metal—some fairly intact, some broken, and some crushed or battered—which I recognised[e] as the colossal pedestals or tables of my dreams. What they could in truth have been, I dared not guess.

I found the downward incline and began its descent—though after a time halted by a gaping, ragged chasm whose narrowest point could not be much less than four feet across. Here the stonework[f] had fallen through, revealing incalculable inky depths beneath.[g] I knew there were two more cellar levels in this titan edifice, and trembled with fresh panic as I recalled the metal-clamped trap-door[h] on the lowest one. There could be no guards now—for what had lurked beneath had long since done its hideous work and sunk into its long decline. By the time of the post-human[i] beetle race it would be quite dead. And yet, as I thought of the native legends, I trembled anew.

It cost me a terrible effort to vault that yawning chasm, since the littered floor prevented a running start—but madness drove me on. I chose a place close to the left-hand wall—where the rift was least wide

[a] plunged,] plunged B, C
[b] daemoniac] demoniac A, B, C
[c] crumbling yet familiar archways.] crumbling, yet familiar, archways. ¶ B, C
[d] bare or debris-filled.] bare, or débris-filled. B; bare, or debris-filled. C
[e] recognised] recognized B, C
[f] stonework] stone-/work B; stone-work C
[g] beneath.] beneath. ¶ B, C
[h] trap-door] trapdoor B, C
[i] post-human] post-/human B; posthuman C

and the landing-spot[a] reasonably clear of dangerous debris[b]—and after one frantic moment reached the other side in safety.[c] At last[d] gaining the lower level, I stumbled on past the archway of the room of machines, within which were fantastic ruins of metal half-buried[e] beneath fallen vaulting. Everything was where I knew it would be, and I climbed confidently over the heaps which barred the entrance of a vast transverse corridor. This, I realised,[f] would take me under the city to the central archives.

Endless ages seemed to unroll as I stumbled, leaped, and crawled along that debris-cluttered[g] corridor. Now and then I could make out carvings on the age-stained walls—some familiar, others seemingly added since the period of my dreams. Since this was a subterrene[h] house-connecting highway, there were no archways save when the route led through the lower levels of various buildings.[i] At some of these intersections I turned aside long enough to look down well-remembered corridors and into well-remembered[j] rooms. Twice only did I find any radical changes from what I had dreamed of—and in one of these cases I could trace the sealed-up outlines of the archway I remembered.

I shook violently, and felt a curious surge of retarding weakness,[k] as I steered a hurried and reluctant course through the crypt of one of those great windowless ruined towers whose alien[l] basalt masonry bespoke a whispered and horrible origin.[m] This primal vault was round and fully 200[n] feet across, with nothing carved upon the dark-hued

[a] landing-spot] landing spot B, C
[b] debris] débris B
[c] safety.] safety. ¶ B, C
[d] last] last, B, C
[e] metal half-buried] metal, half buried B, C
[f] realised,] realized, B, C
[g] debris-cluttered] débris-cluttered B
[h] subterrene] subterrane B[c]
[i] buildings.] buildings. ¶ B, C
[j] corridors . . . well-remembered] om. C
[k] weakness,] weakness B, C
[l] windowless . . . alien] windowless, . . . alien, B, C
[m] origin.] origin. ¶ B, C
[n] 200] two hundred B, C

stonework. The floor was here free from anything save dust and sand, and I could see the apertures leading upward and downward. There were no stairs or inclines—indeed, my dreams had pictured those elder towers as wholly untouched by the fabulous Great Race. Those who had built them had not needed stairs or inclines.[a] In the dreams, the downward aperture had been tightly sealed and nervously guarded. Now it lay open—black and yawning, and giving forth a current of cool, damp air. Of what limitless caverns of eternal night might brood below, I would not permit myself to think.

Later, clawing my way along a badly heaped section of the corridor, I reached a place where the roof had wholly caved in. The debris[b] rose like a mountain, and I climbed up over it, passing through a vast[c] empty space where my torchlight could reveal neither walls nor vaulting. This, I reflected, must be the cellar of the house of the metal-purveyors,[d] fronting on the third square not far from the archives. What had happened to it I could not conjecture.

I found the corridor again beyond the mountain of detritus and stones,[e] but after a short distance encountered a wholly choked place where the fallen vaulting almost touched the perilously sagging ceiling. How I managed to wrench and tear aside enough blocks to afford a passage, and how I dared disturb the tightly packed fragments when the least shift of equilibrium might have brought down all the tons of superincumbent masonry to crush me to nothingness, I do not know.[f] It was sheer madness that impelled and guided me—if, indeed, my whole underground adventure was not—as I hope—a hellish delusion or phase of dreaming. But I did make—or dream that I made—a passage that I could squirm through. As I wriggled over the mound of debris[g]—my torch, switched continuously on, thrust deeply within[h] my

---

[a] inclines.] inclines. ¶ B, C
[b] debris] débris B
[c] vast] vast, B, C
[d] metal-purveyors,] metal purveyors, B, C
[e] stones,] stone, B, C
[f] know.] know. ¶ B, C
[g] debris] débris B
[h] within] in B, C

mouth—I felt myself torn by the fantastic stalactites of the jagged floor above me.

I was now close to the great underground archival structure which seemed to form my goal. Sliding and clambering down the farther side of the barrier, and picking my way along the remaining stretch of corridor with hand-held,[a] intermittently flashing torch, I came at last to a low, circular crypt with arches—still in a marvellous[b] state of preservation—opening off on every side.[c] The walls, or such parts of them as lay within reach of my torchlight, were densely hieroglyphed and chiselled[d] with typical curvilinear symbols—some added since the period of my dreams.

This, I realised,[e] was my fated destination, and I turned at once through a familiar archway on my left. That I could find a clear passage up and down the incline to all the surviving levels, I had oddly[f] little doubt. This vast, earth-protected[g] pile, housing the annals of all the solar system, had been built with supernal skill and strength to last as long as that system itself.[h] Blocks of stupendous size,[i] poised with mathematical genius and bound with cements of incredible toughness,[j] had combined to form a mass as firm as the planet's rocky core. Here, after ages more prodigious than I could sanely grasp, its buried bulk stood in all its essential contours;[k] the vast, dust-drifted floors scarce sprinkled with the litter elsewhere so dominant.

The relatively easy walking from this point onward went curiously to my head. All the frantic eagerness hitherto frustrated by obstacles now took itself out in a kind of febrile speed, and I literally raced along the low-roofed, monstrously well-remembered aisles beyond the

---

[a] hand-held,] hand-/held, B; handheld, C
[b] marvellous] marvelous B, C
[c] side.] side. ¶ B, C
[d] chiselled] chiseled B, C
[e] realised,] realized, B, C
[f] had oddly] had, oddly, B, C
[g] earth-protected] Earth-protected B
[h] itself.] itself. ¶ B, C
[i] size,] size B, C
[j] toughness,] toughness C
[k] contours;] contours, B, C

archway.[a] I was past being astonished by the familiarity of what I saw. On every hand the great hieroglyphed metal shelf-doors[b] loomed monstrously; some yet in place, others sprung open, and still others bent and buckled under bygone geological stresses not quite strong enough to shatter the titan masonry.[c] Here and there a dust-covered[d] heap below a gaping[e] empty shelf seemed to indicate where cases had been shaken down by earth-tremors.[f] On occasional pillars were great symbols or[g] letters proclaiming classes and sub-classes[h] of volumes.

Once I paused before an open vault where I saw some of the accustomed metal cases still in position amidst the omnipresent gritty dust. Reaching up, I dislodged one of the thinner specimens with some difficulty, and rested it on the floor for inspection. It was titled in the prevailing curvilinear hieroglyphs, though something in the arrangement of the characters[i] seemed subtly unusual.[j] The odd mechanism of the hooked fastener was perfectly well known to me, and I snapped up the still rustless and workable lid and drew out the book within. The latter, as expected, was some 20×15[k] inches in area, and two inches thick; the thin metal covers opening at the top.[l] Its tough cellulose pages seemed unaffected by the myriad cycles of time they had lived through, and I studied the queerly pigmented,[m] brush-drawn letters of the text—symbols utterly[n] unlike either the usual curved hieroglyphs or any alphabet known to human scholarship—with a haunting, half-aroused memory.[o] It came to me that this was the

[a] archway.] archway. ¶ B, C
[b] shelf-doors] shelf doors B, C
[c] masonry.] masonry. ¶ B, C
[d] dust-covered] dust covered A
[e] below a gaping] beneath a gaping, B, C
[f] earth-tremors.] Earth tremors. B; earth termors. C
[g] or] and B, C
[h] sub-classes] subclasses B, C
[i] characters] character B[c]
[j] unusual.] unusual. ¶ B, C
[k] 20 × 15] twenty by fifteen A, B, C
[l] top.] top. ¶ B, C
[m] queerly pigmented,] queerly-pigmented, A
[n] utterly] *om.* B, C
[o] memory.] memory. ¶ B, C

language used by a captive mind I had known slightly[a] in my dreams—
a mind from a large asteroid on which had survived much of the
archaic life and lore of the primal planet whereof it formed a
fragment.[b] At the same time I recalled that this level of the archives
was devoted to volumes dealing with the non-terrestrial[c] planets.

As I ceased poring over this incredible document[d] I saw that the
light of my torch was beginning to fail, hence quickly inserted the extra
battery I always had with me. Then, armed with the stronger radiance,
I resumed my feverish racing through unending tangles of aisles and
corridors—recognising[e] now and then some familiar shelf, and vaguely
annoyed by the acoustic conditions which made my footfalls[f] echo
incongruously in these catacombs of aeon-long death and silence.[g] The
very prints of my shoes behind me in the millennially untrodden dust
made me shudder. Never before, if my mad dreams held anything of
truth, had human feet pressed upon those immemorial pavements.[h] Of
the particular goal of my insane racing, my conscious mind held no
hint. There was, however, some force of evil potency pulling at my
dazed will and buried recollections,[i] so that I vaguely felt I was not
running at random.

I came to a downward incline and followed it to profounder[j]
depths. Floors flashed by me as I raced, but I did not pause to explore
them. In my whirling brain there had begun to beat a certain rhythm
which set my right hand twitching in unison. I wanted to unlock
something, and felt that I knew all the intricate twists and pressures
needed to do it. It would be like a modern safe with a combination lock.[k]
Dream or not, I had once known and still knew. How any dream—or

[a] slightly] slightly, B[c]
[b] fragment.] fragrant. B[c]
[c] non-terrestrial] non-/Terrestrial B
[d] document] document, C
[e] recognising] recognizing B, C
[f] footfalls] foot-falls C
[g] catacombs . . . silence.] catacombs. ¶ B, C
[h] pavements.] pavements. ¶ B, C
[i] recollections,] recollection, B, C
[j] profounder] profound C
[k] lock.] lock. ¶ B, C

scrap of unconsciously absorbed legend—could have taught me a detail so minute, so intricate, and so complex, I did not attempt to explain to myself. I was beyond all coherent thought. For was not this whole experience—this shocking familiarity with a set of unknown ruins, and this monstrously exact identity of everything before me with what only dreams and scraps of myth could have suggested—a horror beyond all reason?[a] Probably it was my basic conviction then—as it is now during my saner moments—that I was not awake at all, and that the entire buried city was a fragment of febrile hallucination.

Eventually[b] I reached the lowest level and struck off to the right of the incline. For some shadowy reason I tried to soften my steps, even though I lost speed thereby. There was a space I was afraid to cross on this last, deeply buried[c] floor, and as[d] I drew near it I recalled what thing in that space I feared. It was merely one of the metal-barred and closely guarded trap-doors.[e] There would be no guards now, and on that account I trembled and tiptoed as I had done in passing through that black basalt vault where a similar trap-door[f] had yawned.[g] I felt a current of cool,[h] damp air,[i] as I had felt there, and wished that my course led in another direction. Why I had to take the particular course I was taking, I did not know.

When I came to the space I saw that the trap-door[j] yawned widely open. Ahead[k] the shelves began again, and I glimpsed on the floor before one of them a heap very thinly covered with dust, where a number of cases had recently fallen. At the same moment a fresh wave of panic clutched me, though for some time I could not discover why.[l]

---

[a] reason?] reason? ¶ B, C
[b] Eventually] Eventually, B, C
[c] deeply buried] deeply-buried A
[d] floor, and as] floor. ¶ As B, C
[e] trap-doors.] trapdoors. B, C
[f] trap-door] trapdoor B, C
[g] yawned.] yawned. ¶ B, C
[h] cool,] cold, C
[i] air,] air B, C
[j] trap-door] trapdoor A, B, C
[k] Ahead] Ahead, B, C
[l] why.] why. ¶ B, C

Heaps of fallen cases were not uncommon, for all through the aeons this lightless labyrinth had been racked by the heavings of earth[a] and had echoed at intervals to the deafening clatter of toppling objects. It was only when I was nearly across the space that I realised[b] why I shook so violently.

Not the heap, but something about the dust of the level floor[c] was troubling me. In the light of my torch it seemed as if that dust were not as even as it ought to be—there were places where it looked thinner, as if it had been disturbed not many months before. I could not be sure, for even the apparently thinner places were dusty enough; yet a certain suspicion of regularity in the fancied unevenness was highly disquieting.[d] When I brought the torchlight close to one of the queer places I did not like what I saw—for the illusion of regularity became very great. It was as if there were regular lines of composite impressions—impressions that went in threes, each slightly over a foot square, and consisting of five nearly circular three-inch prints, one in advance of the other four.

These possible lines of foot-square impressions appeared to lead in two directions, as if something had gone somewhere and returned. They were of course[e] very faint, and may have been illusions or accidents; but there was an element of dim, fumbling terror about the way I thought they ran. For at one end of them was the heap of cases which must have clattered down not long before, while at the other end was the ominous trap-door[f] with the cool, damp wind, yawning unguarded down to abysses past imagination.

VIII.

That my strange sense of compulsion was deep and overwhelming is shewn[g] by its conquest of my fear. No rational motive could have

[a] Earth] earth B
[b] realised] realized B, C
[c] floor] floor, B, C
[d] disquieting.] disquieting. ¶ B, C
[e] were of course] were, of course, B, C
[f] trap-door] trapdoor A, B, C
[g] shewn] shown B, C

drawn me on after that hideous suspicion of prints and the creeping dream-memories[a] it excited. Yet my right hand, even as it shook with fright, still twitched rhythmically in its eagerness to turn a lock it hoped to find. Before I knew it I was past the heap of lately fallen cases and running on tiptoe through aisles of utterly unbroken dust toward a point which I seemed to know morbidly, horribly well.[b] My mind was asking itself questions whose origin and relevancy I was only beginning to guess. Would the shelf be reachable by a human body? Could my human hand master all the aeon-remembered motions of the lock? Would the lock be undamaged and workable? And what would I do— what dare I do—with what (as I now commenced to realise)[c] I both hoped and feared to find? Would it prove the awesome, brain-shattering truth of something past normal conception, or shew[d] only that I was dreaming?

The next I knew I had ceased my tiptoe[e] racing and was standing still, staring at a row of maddeningly familiar hieroglyphed shelves. They were in a state of almost perfect preservation, and only three of the doors in this vicinity had sprung open.[f] My feelings toward these shelves cannot be described—so utter and insistent was the sense of old acquaintance. I was looking high up,[g] at a row near the top and wholly out of my reach, and wondering how I could climb to best advantage. An open door four rows from the bottom would help, and the locks of the closed doors formed possible holds for hands and feet. I would grip the torch between my teeth[h] as I had in other places where both hands were needed.[i] Above all,[j] I must make no noise.[k]

---

[a] dream-memories] dream memories B, C
[b] well.] well. ¶ B, C
[c] what (. . . realise)] what—. . . realize— B, C
[d] shew] show B, C
[e] tiptoe] tiptoed B, C
[f] open.] open. ¶ B, C
[g] up,] up B, C
[h] teeth] teeth, B, C
[i] needed.] needed C
[j] all,] all B, C
[k] noise.] noise. ¶ B, C

How to get down what I wished to remove would be difficult, but[a] I could probably hook its movable fastener in my coat collar and carry it like a knapsack. Again I wondered whether the lock would be undamaged. That I could repeat each familiar motion I had not the least doubt. But I hoped the thing would not scrape or creak—and that my hand could work it properly.

Even as I thought these things I had taken the torch in my mouth and begun[b] to climb. The projecting locks were poor supports; but as I had expected, the opened shelf helped greatly. I used both the difficultly[c] swinging door and the edge of the aperture itself in my ascent, and managed to avoid any loud creaking.[d] Balanced on the upper edge of the door, and leaning far to my right, I could just reach the lock I sought. My fingers, half-numb[e] from climbing, were very clumsy at first; but I soon saw that they were anatomically adequate. And the memory-rhythm[f] was strong in them.[g] Out of unknown gulfs of time the intricate[h] secret motions had somehow reached my brain correctly in every detail—for after less than five minutes of trying there came a click whose familiarity was all the more startling because I had not consciously anticipated it. In another instant the metal door was slowly swinging open with only the faintest grating sound.

Dazedly I looked over the row of greyish case-ends[i] thus exposed, and felt a tremendous surge of some wholly inexplicable emotion. Just within reach of my right hand was a case whose curving hieroglyphs made me shake with a pang infinitely more complex than one of mere fright. Still shaking, I managed to dislodge it amidst a shower of gritty flakes, and ease it over toward myself without any violent noise.[j] Like

---

[a] but] but, B
[b] begun] began C
[c] difficultly] *om.* B, C
[d] creaking.] creaking. ¶ B, C
[e] half-numb] half numb B, C
[f] memory-rhythm] memory rhythm B, C
[g] them.] them. ¶ B, C
[h] intricate] intricate, B, C
[i] greyish case-ends] grayish case ends B, C
[j] noise.] noise. ¶ B, C

the other case I had handled, it was slightly more than 20×15^a inches in size, with curved mathematical designs in low relief. In thickness it just exceeded three inches.[b] Crudely wedging it between myself and the surface I was climbing, I fumbled with the fastener and finally got the hook free. Lifting the cover, I shifted the heavy object to my back, and let the hook catch hold of my collar. Hands now free, I awkwardly clambered down to the dusty floor,[c] and prepared to inspect my prize.

Kneeling in the gritty dust, I swung the case around and rested it in front of me. My hands shook, and I dreaded to draw out the book within almost as much as I longed—and felt compelled—to do so. It had very gradually become clear to me what I ought to find, and this realisation nearly paralysed my faculties.[d] If the thing were there—and if I were not dreaming—the implications would be quite beyond the power of the human spirit to bear. What tormented me most was my momentary inability to feel that my surroundings were a dream. The sense of reality was hideous—and again becomes so as I recall the scene.

At length I tremblingly pulled the book from its container and stared fascinatedly at the well-known hieroglyphs on the cover. It seemed to be in prime condition, and the curvilinear letters of the title held me in almost as hypnotised[e] a state as if I could read them. Indeed, I cannot swear that I did not actually read them in some transient and terrible access of abnormal memory.[f] I do not know how long it was before I dared to lift that thin metal cover. I temporised[g] and made excuses to myself. I took the torch from my mouth and shut it off to save the battery. Then, in the dark, I screwed up[h] my courage— finally lifting the cover without turning on the light. Last of all[i] I did indeed flash the torch upon the exposed page—steeling myself in advance to suppress any sound no matter what I should find.

---

[a] 20 × 15] twenty by fifteen B, C

[b] inches.] inches. ¶ B, C

[c] floor,] floor B, C

[d] realisation . . . paralysed my faculties.] realization . . . paralyzed my faculties. ¶ B, C

[e] hypnotised] hypnotized B, C

[f] memory.] memory. ¶ B, C

[g] temporised] temporized B, C

[h] screwed up] collected B, C

[i] all] all, B, C

I looked for an instant, then almost[a] collapsed. Clenching my teeth, however, I kept silence.[b] I sank wholly to the floor and put a hand to my forehead amidst the engulfing blackness. What I dreaded and expected was there. Either I was dreaming, or time and space had become a mockery.[c] I must be dreaming—but I would test the horror by carrying this thing back and shewing[d] it to my son if it were indeed a reality. My head swam frightfully, even though there were no visible objects in the unbroken gloom to swirl around[e] me. Ideas and images of the starkest terror—excited by vistas which my glimpse had opened up—began to throng in upon me and cloud my senses.

I thought of those possible prints in the dust, and trembled at the sound of my own breathing as I did so. Once again I flashed on the light and looked at the page as a serpent's victim may look at his destroyer's eyes and fangs.[f] Then, with clumsy fingers[g] in the dark, I closed the book, put it in its container, and snapped the lid and the curious[h] hooked fastener. This was what I must carry back to the outer world if it truly existed—if the whole abyss truly existed—if I, and the world itself, truly existed.

Just when I tottered to my feet and commenced my return I cannot be certain. It comes[i] to me oddly—as a measure of my sense of separation from the normal world—that I did not even once look at my watch during those hideous hours underground.[j] Torch in hand, and with the ominous case under one arm, I eventually found myself tiptoeing in a kind of silent panic past the draught-giving[k] abyss and those lurking suggestions of prints. I lessened my precautions as I climbed up the endless inclines, but could not shake off a shadow of

[a] almost] *om.* C
[b] silence.] silent. B, C
[c] mockery.] mockery. ¶ B, C
[d] shewing] showing B, C
[e] around] about B, C
[f] fangs.] fangs. ¶ B, C
[g] fingers] fingers, B, C
[h] curious] curious, B, C
[i] comes] came B[c]
[j] underground.] underground. ¶ B, C
[k] draught-giving] draft-giving B, C

apprehension which I had not felt on the downward journey.

I dreaded having to re-pass[a] through that black basalt crypt that was older than the city itself, where cold draughts[b] welled up from unguarded depths. I thought of that which the Great Race had feared, and of what might still be lurking—be it ever so weak and dying—down there. I thought of those possible[c] five-circle prints and of what my dreams had told me of such prints—and of strange winds and whistling noises associated with them. And I thought of the tales of the modern blacks,[d] wherein the horror of great winds and nameless subterrene[e] ruins was dwelt upon.

I knew from a carven wall symbol the right floor to enter, and came at last—after passing that other book I had examined—to the great circular space with the branching archways. On my right, and at once recognisable,[f] was the arch through which I had arrived. This I now entered, conscious that the rest of my course would be harder because of the tumbled state of the masonry outside the archive building. My new metal-cased burden weighed upon me, and I found it harder and harder to be quiet as I stumbled among debris[g] and fragments of every sort.

Then I came to the ceiling-high mound of debris[h] through which I had wrenched a scanty passage. My dread at wriggling through again was infinite;[i] for my first passage had made some noise, and I now—after seeing those possible prints—dreaded sound above all things. The case, too, doubled the problem of traversing the narrow crevice.[j] But I clambered up the barrier as best I could, and pushed the case through the aperture ahead of me. Then, torch in mouth, I scrambled

---

[a] re-pass] repass B, C
[b] draughts] drafts B, C
[c] possible] *om.* B, C
[d] blacks,] blackfellows, B, C
[e] subterrene] subterrane B[c] *om.* C
[f] recognisable,] recognizable, B, C
[g] debris] débris B
[h] debris] débris B
[i] infinite;] infinite, B, C
[j] crevice.] crevice. ¶ B, C

through myself—my back torn as before by stalactites.[a] As I tried to grasp the case again, it fell some distance ahead of me down the slope of the debris,[b] making a disturbing clatter and arousing echoes which sent me into a cold perspiration. I lunged for it at once, and regained it without further noise—but a moment afterward the slipping of blocks under my feet raised a sudden and unprecedented din.

That din was my undoing. For, falsely or not, I thought I heard it answered in a terrible way from spaces far behind me. I thought I heard a shrill, whistling sound, like nothing else on earth,[c] and beyond any adequate verbal description. It may have been only my imagination.[d] If so, what followed has a certain[e] grim irony—since,[f] save for the panic of this thing, the second thing might never have happened.

As it was, my frenzy was absolute and unrelieved. Taking my torch in my hand and clutching feebly at the case, I leaped and bounded wildly ahead with no idea in my brain beyond a mad desire to race out of these nightmare ruins to the waking world of desert and moonlight[g] which lay so far above.[h] I hardly knew it when I reached the mountain of debris[i] which towered into the vast blackness beyond the caved-in roof, and bruised and cut myself repeatedly in scrambling up its steep slope of jagged blocks and fragments.[j] Then came the great disaster. Just as I blindly crossed the summit, unprepared for the sudden dip ahead, my feet slipped utterly and I found myself involved in a mangling avalanche of sliding masonry whose cannon-loud uproar split the black[k] cavern air in a deafening series of earth-shaking[l] reverberations.

[a] stalactites.] stalactites. ¶ B, C
[b] debris,] débris, B
[c] earth,] Earth, B, C
[d] It may . . . imagination.] *om.* B, C
[e] certain] *om.* C
[f] since,] *om.* C
[g] moonlight] Moonlight B[c]
[h] above.] above. ¶ B, C
[i] debris] débris B
[j] fragments.] fragments. ¶ B, C
[k] black] black, B, C
[l] earth-shaking] Earth-shaking B

I have no recollection of emerging from this chaos, but a momentary fragment of consciousness shews[a] me as plunging and tripping and scrambling along the corridor amidst the clangour[b]—case and torch still with me.[c] Then, just as I approached that primal basalt crypt I had so dreaded, utter madness came. For as the echoes of the avalanche died down, there became audible a repetition of that frightful,[d] alien whistling I thought I had heard before. This time there was no doubt about it—and what was worse, it came from a point not behind but *ahead of me.*

Probably I shrieked aloud then. I have a dim picture of myself as flying through the[e] hellish basalt vault of the Elder Things,[f] and hearing that damnable alien sound piping up from the open, unguarded door of limitless nether blacknesses. There was a wind, too—not merely a cool, damp draught,[g] but a violent, purposeful blast belching savagely and frigidly from that abominable gulf whence the obscene whistling came.

There are memories of leaping and lurching over obstacles of every sort, with that torrent of wind and shrieking sound growing moment by moment, and seeming to curl and twist purposefully around me as it struck out wickedly from the spaces behind and beneath.[h] Though in my rear, that wind had the odd effect of hindering instead of aiding my progress; as if it acted like a noose or lasso thrown around me. Heedless of the noise I made, I clattered over a great barrier of blocks and was again in the structure that led to the surface.[i] I recall glimpsing the archway to the room of machines and almost crying out as I saw the incline leading down to where one of those blasphemous trap-doors[j] must be yawning two levels below. But

[a] shews] shows B, C
[b] clangour] clangor B, C
[c] me.] me. ¶ B, C
[d] frightful,] frightful B, C
[e] the] A, B [*changed by HPL to* that, *then erased?*], C
[f] Elder Things,] elder things, B, C
[g] draught,] draft, B, C
[h] beneath.] beneath. ¶ B, C
[i] surface.] surface. ¶ B, C
[j] trap-doors] trap-/doors B; trapdoors C

instead of crying out I muttered over and over to myself that this was all a dream from which I must soon awake.[a] Perhaps I was in camp—perhaps I was at home in Arkham. As these hopes bolstered up my sanity I began to mount the incline to the higher level.

I knew, of course, that I had the four-foot cleft to re-cross,[b] yet was too racked by other fears to realise[c] the full horror until I came almost upon it. On my descent, the leap across had been easy—but could I clear the gap as readily when going uphill, and hampered by fright, exhaustion, the weight of the metal case, and the anomalous backward tug of that daemon[d] wind? I thought of these things at the last moment, and thought also of the nameless entities which might be lurking in the black abysses below the chasm.

My wavering torch was growing feeble, but I could tell by some obscure memory when I neared the cleft. The chill blasts of wind and the nauseous whistling shrieks behind me were for the moment like a merciful opiate, dulling my imagination to the horror of the yawning gulf ahead. And then I became aware of the added blasts and whistling *in front of me*[e]—tides of abomination surging up through the cleft itself from depths unimagined and unimaginable.

Now, indeed, the essence of pure nightmare was upon me. Sanity departed—and[f] ignoring everything except the animal impulse of flight, I merely struggled and plunged upward over the incline's debris[g] as if no gulf had existed. Then I saw the chasm's edge, leaped frenziedly with every ounce of strength I possessed, and was instantly engulfed in a pandaemoniac[h] vortex of loathsome sound and utter, materially tangible blackness.

That is the end of my experience, so far as I can recall. Any further impressions belong wholly to the domain of phantasmagoric delirium. Dream, madness, and memory merged wildly together in a series of

[a] awake.] wake. B
[b] re-cross,] recross, B, C
[c] realise] realize B, C
[d] daemon] demon B, C
[e] *in front of me*] in front of me B, C
[f] and] and, B, C
[g] debris] débris B
[h] pandaemoniac] pandemoniac A, B, C

fantastic, fragmentary delusions which can have no relation to anything real.[a] There was a hideous fall through incalculable leagues of viscous, sentient darkness, and a babel of noises utterly alien to all that we know of the earth[b] and its organic life. Dormant, rudimentary senses seemed to start into vitality within me, telling of pits and voids peopled by floating horrors and leading to sunless crags and oceans and teeming cities of windowless[c] basalt towers upon which no light ever shone.

Secrets of the primal planet and its immemorial aeons flashed through my brain without the aid of sight or sound, and there were known to me things which not even the wildest of my[d] former dreams had ever suggested. And all the while cold fingers of damp vapour[e] clutched and picked at me, and that eldritch, damnable whistling shrieked fiendishly above all the alternations of babel and silence in the whirlpools of darkness around.

Afterward there were visions of the Cyclopean[f] city of my dreams— not in ruins, but just as I had dreamed of it. I was in my conical, non-human[g] body again, and mingled with crowds of the Great Race and the captive minds who carried books up and down the lofty corridors and vast inclines.[h] Then, superimposed upon these pictures, were frightful[i] momentary flashes of a non-visual[j] consciousness involving desperate struggles, a writhing free from clutching tentacles of whistling wind, an insane, bat-like[k] flight through half-solid air, a feverish burrowing through the cyclone-whipped dark, and a wild stumbling and scrambling over fallen masonry.

[a] real.] real. ¶ B, C
[b] earth] Earth B, C
[c] windowless] windowless, B, C
[d] my] *om.* C
[e] vapour] vapor B, C
[f] Cyclopean] cyclopean C
[g] non-human] nonhuman B; non-/human C
[h] inclines.] inclines. ¶ B, C
[i] frightful] frightful, B, C
[j] non-visual] nonvisual B, C
[k] bat-like] batlike B, C

Once there was a curious, intrusive flash of half-sight[a]—a faint, diffuse suspicion of bluish radiance far overhead. Then there came a dream of wind-pursued climbing and crawling—of wriggling into a blaze of sardonic moonlight[b] through a jumble of debris[c] which slid and collapsed after me amidst[d] a morbid hurricane. It was the evil, monotonous beating of that maddening moonlight[e] which at last told me of the return of what I had once known as the objective, waking world.

I was clawing prone through the sands of the Australian desert, and around me shrieked such a tumult of wind as I had never before known on our planet's surface. My clothing was in rags, and my whole body was a mass of bruises and scratches.[f] Full consciousness returned very slowly, and at no time could I tell just where true memory left off and delirious dream[g] began. There had seemed to be a mound of titan blocks, an abyss beneath it, a monstrous revelation from the past, and a nightmare horror at the end—but how much of this was real?[h] My flashlight was gone, and likewise any[i] metal case I may have discovered. Had there been such a case—or any abyss—or any mound? Raising my head, I looked behind me, and saw only the sterile, undulant sands of the waste.[j]

The daemon[k] wind died down, and the bloated, fungoid moon[l] sank reddeningly in the west. I lurched to my feet and began to stagger southwestward toward the camp. What in truth had happened to me? Had I merely collapsed in the desert and dragged a dream-racked body over miles of sand and buried blocks? If not, how could I bear to live

[a] half-sight] half sight B, C
[b] moonlight] Moonlight B[c]
[c] debris] débris B
[d] amidst] admist B[c]
[e] moonlight] Moonlight B[c]
[f] scratches.] scratches. ¶ B, C
[g] true . . . dream] delirious dream left and true memory B [*HPL has only restored the omitted word* off]; delirious dream left off and true memory C
[h] real?] real? ¶ B, C
[i] any] my C
[j] waste.] desert. B, C
[k] daemon] demon B, C
[l] moon] Moon B

any longer? For in this new doubt[a] all my faith in the myth-born
unreality of my visions dissolved once more into the hellish older
doubting. If that abyss was real, then the Great Race was real—and its
blasphemous reachings and seizures in the cosmos-wide vortex of time
were no myths or nightmares, but a terrible, soul-shattering actuality.

Had I, in full[b] hideous fact, been drawn back to a pre-human[c]
world of a hundred and fifty million years ago in those dark, baffling
days of the amnesia? Had my present body been the vehicle of a
frightful alien consciousness from palaeogean[d] gulfs of time?[e] Had I, as
the captive mind of those shambling horrors, indeed known that
accursed city of stone in its primordial heyday, and wriggled down
those familiar corridors in the loathsome shape of my captor? Were
those tormenting dreams of more than twenty years the offspring of
stark, monstrous *memories?*[f] Had I once veritably talked with minds
from reachless corners of time and space, learned the universe's
secrets[g] past and to come, and written the annals of my own world for
the metal cases of those titan archives? And were those others—those
shocking Elder Things[h] of the mad winds and daemon[i] pipings—in
truth a lingering, lurking menace, waiting and slowly weakening in
black abysses while varied shapes of life drag out their multimillennial
courses on the planet's age-racked surface?

I do not know. If that abyss and what it held were real, there is no
hope. Then, all too truly, there lies upon this world of man a mocking
and incredible shadow out of time. But[j] mercifully, there is no proof
that these things are other than fresh phases of my myth-born dreams.
I did not bring back the metal case that would have been a proof, and

---

[a] longer? For . . . doubt] longer? ¶ For, . . . doubt, B, C
[b] full] full, B, C
[c] pre-human] prehuman B, C
[d] palaeogean] Paleogean B [*changed by HPL to* paleogean]; paleogean C
[e] time?] time? ¶ B, C
[f] *memories?*] memories? ¶ B, C
[g] secrets] secrets, B, C
[h] Elder Things] elder things B, C
[i] daemon] demon B, C
[j] But] But, B, C

so far those subterrene[a] corridors have not been found.[b] If the laws of the universe are kind, they will never be found. But I must tell my son what I saw or thought I saw, and let him use his judgment as a psychologist in gauging the reality of my experience, and communicating this account to others.

I have said that the awful truth behind my tortured years of dreaming hinges absolutely upon the actuality of what I thought I saw in those Cyclopean[c] buried ruins. It has been hard for me literally[d] to set down the[e] crucial revelation, though no reader can have failed to guess it. Of course[f] it lay in that book within the metal case—the case which I pried out of its forgotten lair amidst the undisturbed dust of a million centuries.[g] No eye had seen, no hand had touched that book since the advent of man to this planet. And yet, when I flashed my torch upon it in that frightful megalithic[h] abyss, I saw that the queerly pigmented[i] letters on the brittle, aeon-browned cellulose pages were not indeed any nameless hieroglyphs of earth's[j] youth. They were, instead, the letters of our familiar alphabet, spelling out the words of the English language[k] in my own handwriting.

---

[a] subterrene] subterrane B[c], C
[b] found.] found. ¶ B, C
[c] Cyclopean] cyclopean A; Cyclopean, B; cyclopean, C
[d] me literally] me, literally, B, C
[e] the] that B, C
[f] course] course, B, C
[g] centuries.] centuries. ¶ B, C
[h] megalithic] om. B, C
[i] queerly pigmented] queerly-pigmented A
[j] earth's] Earth's B
[k] language] language, B[c]

The Haunter of the Dark

(Dedicated to Robert Bloch)

I have seen the dark universe yawning
Where the black planets roll without aim—
Where they roll in their horror unheeded,
Without knowledge or lustre[a] or name.[b]
—*Nemesis.*[c]

C autious investigators will hesitate to challenge the common belief that Robert Blake was killed by lightning, or by some profound nervous shock derived from an electrical discharge. It is true that the window he faced was unbroken, but Nature has shewn[d] herself capable of many freakish performances. The expression on his face may easily have arisen from some obscure muscular source

Editor's Note: HPL gave the A.Ms. of this story to Donald A. Wollheim. Many years later, Wollheim apparently sold it to an Australian collector, Ron Graham. His collection was later deposited at the Fisher Library of Sydney, and among the effects was a card entry for an item in the collection that clearly refers to the A.Ms. of "The Haunter of the Dark"; but the ms. itself appears to have been sold earlier, or at any rate did not end up in the Fisher library. (For further information, see Leigh Blackmore's article "H. P. Lovecraft: The Mystery of the Missing Manuscript," http://www.scribd.com/doc/23003535/H-P-Lovecraft-the-Mystery-of-the-Missing-Manuscript.) As a result, the A.Ms. must be considered lost.

In its absence, we are forced to rely on the only appearance in HPL's lifetime—*Weird Tales* (December 1936). So far as can be ascertained, the text appears to have been printed accurately, with the usual editorial alterations. The Arkham House texts follow the *Weird Tales* text somewhat mechanically, and with some additional errors.

Texts: A = *Weird Tales* 28, No. 5 (December 1936): 538–53; B = *The Dunwich Horror and Others* (Arkham House, 1963), 98-120. Copy-text: A.

[a] lustre] luster A, B
[b] I have . . . name.] *I have . . . name.* B
[c] —*Nemesis.*] —NEMESIS. B
[d] Nature has shewn] nature has shown A, B

unrelated to anything he saw, while the entries in his diary are clearly the result of a fantastic imagination aroused by certain local superstitions and by certain old matters he had uncovered. As for the anomalous conditions at the deserted church on[a] Federal Hill—the shrewd analyst is not slow in attributing them to some charlatanry, conscious or unconscious, with at least some of which Blake was secretly connected.

For after all, the victim was a writer and painter wholly devoted to the field of myth, dream, terror, and superstition, and avid in his quest for scenes and effects of a bizarre, spectral sort. His earlier stay in the city—a visit to a strange old man as deeply given to occult and forbidden lore as he—had ended amidst death and flame, and it must have been some morbid instinct which drew him back from his home in Milwaukee. He may have known of the old stories despite his statements to the contrary in the diary, and his death may have nipped in the bud some stupendous hoax destined to have a literary reflection.

Among those, however, who have examined and correlated all this evidence, there remain several who cling to less rational and commonplace theories. They are inclined to take much of Blake's diary at its face value, and point significantly to certain facts such as the undoubted genuineness of the old church record, the verified existence of the disliked and unorthodox Starry Wisdom sect prior to 1877, the recorded disappearance of an inquisitive reporter named Edwin M. Lillibridge in 1893, and—above all—the look of monstrous, transfiguring fear on the face of the young writer when he died. It was one of these believers who, moved to fanatical extremes, threw into the bay the curiously angled stone and its strangely adorned metal box found in the old church steeple—the black windowless steeple, and not the tower where Blake's diary said those things originally were. Though widely censured both officially and unofficially, this man—a reputable physician with a taste for odd folklore—averred that he had rid the earth of something too dangerous to rest upon it.

Between these two schools of opinion the reader must judge for himself. The papers have given the tangible details from a sceptical[b] angle, leaving for others the drawing of the picture as Robert Blake saw

---

[a] on] of B
[b] sceptical] skeptical A, B

it—or thought he saw it—or pretended to see it. Now, studying the diary closely, dispassionately, and at leisure, let us summarise[a] the dark chain of events from the expressed point of view of their chief actor.

Young Blake returned to Providence in the winter of 1934–5, taking the upper floor of a venerable dwelling in a grassy court off College Street—on the crest of the great eastward hill near the Brown University campus and behind the marble John Hay Library. It was a cosy and fascinating place, in a little garden oasis of village-like antiquity where huge, friendly cats sunned themselves atop a convenient shed. The square Georgian house had a monitor roof, classic doorway with fan carving, small-paned windows, and all the other earmarks of early nineteenth-century[b] workmanship. Inside were six-panelled[c] doors, wide floor-boards, a curving colonial staircase, white Adam-period[d] mantels, and a rear set of rooms three steps below the general level.

Blake's study, a large southwest chamber, overlooked the front garden on one side, while its west windows—before one of which he had his desk—faced off from the brow of the hill and commanded a splendid view of the lower town's outspread roofs and of the mystical sunsets that flamed behind them. On the far horizon were the open countryside's purple slopes. Against these, some two miles away, rose the spectral hump of Federal Hill, bristling with huddled roofs and steeples whose remote outlines wavered mysteriously, taking fantastic forms as the smoke of the city swirled up and enmeshed them. Blake had a curious sense that he was looking upon some unknown, ethereal world which might or might not vanish in dream if ever he tried to seek it out and enter it in person.

Having sent home for most of his books, Blake bought some antique furniture suitable to his quarters and settled down to write and paint—living alone, and attending to the simple housework himself. His studio was in a north attic room, where the panes of the monitor roof furnished admirable lighting. During that first winter he produced

---

[a] summarise] summarize A, B
[b] nineteenth-century] Nineteenth Century A, B
[c] six-panelled] six-paneled A, B
[d] Adam-period] Aram-period B

five of his best-known short stories—"The Burrower Beneath", "The Stairs in the Crypt", "Shaggai", "In the Vale of Pnath", and "The Feaster from the Stars"[a]—and painted seven canvases; studies of nameless, unhuman monsters, and profoundly alien, non-terrestrial landscapes.

At sunset he would often sit at his desk and gaze dreamily off at the outspread west—the dark towers of Memorial Hall just below, the Georgian court-house[b] belfry, the lofty pinnacles of the downtown section, and that shimmering, spire-crowned mound in the distance whose unknown streets and labyrinthine gables so potently provoked his fancy. From his few local acquaintances he learned that the far-off slope was a vast Italian quarter, though most of the houses were remnants of older Yankee and Irish days. Now and then he would train his field-glasses on that spectral, unreachable world beyond the curling smoke; picking out individual roofs and chimneys and steeples, and speculating upon the bizarre and curious mysteries they might house. Even with optical aid Federal Hill seemed somehow alien, half fabulous, and linked to the unreal, intangible marvels of Blake's own tales and pictures. The feeling would persist long after the hill had faded into the violet, lamp-starred twilight, and the court-house floodlights and the red Industrial Trust beacon had blazed up to make the night grotesque.

Of all the distant objects on Federal Hill, a certain huge, dark church most fascinated Blake. It stood out with especial distinctness at certain hours of the day, and at sunset the great tower and tapering steeple loomed blackly against the flaming sky. It seemed to rest on especially high ground; for the grimy facade,[c] and the obliquely seen north side with sloping roof and the tops of great pointed windows, rose boldly above the tangle of surrounding ridgepoles and chimney-pots. Peculiarly grim and austere, it appeared to be built of stone, stained and weathered with the smoke and storms of a century and more. The style, so far as the glass could shew, was that earliest

---

[a] "The Burrower . . . Stars"] *The Burrower Beneath, The Stairs in the Crypt, Shaggai, In the Vale of Pnath,* and *The Feaster from the Stars* A, B

[b] court-house] courthouse B

[c] facade] façade A, B

experimental form of Gothic revival which preceded the stately Upjohn period and held over some of the outlines and proportions of the Georgian age. Perhaps it was reared around 1810 or 1815.

As months passed, Blake watched the far-off, forbidding structure with an oddly mounting interest. Since the vast windows were never lighted, he knew that it must be vacant. The longer he watched, the more his imagination worked, till at length he began to fancy curious things. He believed that a vague, singular aura of desolation hovered over the place, so that even the pigeons and swallows shunned its smoky eaves. Around other towers and belfries his glass would reveal great flocks of birds, but here they never rested. At least, that is what he thought and set down in his diary. He pointed the place out to several friends, but none of them had even been on Federal Hill or possessed the faintest notion of what the church was or had been.

In the spring a deep restlessness gripped Blake. He had begun his long-planned novel—based on a supposed survival of the witch-cult in Maine—but was strangely unable to make progress with it. More and more he would sit at his westward window and gaze at the distant hill and the black, frowning steeple shunned by the birds. When the delicate leaves came out on the garden boughs the world was filled with a new beauty, but Blake's restlessness was merely increased. It was then that he first thought of crossing the city and climbing bodily up that fabulous slope into the smoke-wreathed world of dream.

Late in April, just before the aeon-shadowed[a] Walpurgis time, Blake made his first trip into the unknown. Plodding through the endless downtown streets and the bleak, decayed squares beyond, he came finally upon the ascending avenue of century-worn steps, sagging Doric porches, and blear-paned cupolas which he felt must lead up to the long-known, unreachable world beyond the mists. There were dingy blue-and-white street signs which meant nothing to him, and presently he noted the strange, dark faces of the drifting crowds, and the foreign signs over curious shops in brown, decade-weathered buildings. Nowhere could he find any of the objects he had seen from afar; so that once more he half fancied that the Federal Hill of that distant view was a dream-world never to be trod by living human feet.

---

[a] aeon-shadowed] eon-shadowed A, B

Now and then a battered church facade[a] or crumbling spire came in sight, but never the blackened pile that he sought. When he asked a shopkeeper about a great stone church the man smiled and shook his head, though he spoke English freely. As Blake climbed higher, the region seemed stranger and stranger, with bewildering mazes of brooding brown alleys leading eternally off to the south. He crossed two or three broad avenues, and once thought he glimpsed a familiar tower. Again he asked a merchant about the massive church of stone, and this time he could have sworn that the plea of ignorance was feigned. The dark man's face had a look of fear which he tried to hide, and Blake saw him make a curious sign with his right hand.

Then suddenly a black spire stood out against the cloudy sky on his left, above the tiers of brown roofs lining the tangled southerly alleys. Blake knew at once what it was, and plunged toward it through the squalid, unpaved lanes that climbed from the avenue. Twice he lost his way, but he somehow dared not ask any of the patriarchs or housewives who sat on their doorsteps,[b] or any of the children who shouted and played in the mud of the shadowy lanes.

At last he saw the tower plain against the southwest, and a huge stone bulk rose darkly at the end of an alley. Presently he stood in a windswept[c] open square, quaintly cobblestoned, with a high bank wall on the farther side. This was the end of his quest; for upon the wide, iron-railed, weed-grown plateau which the wall supported—a separate, lesser world raised fully six feet above the surrounding streets—there stood a grim, titan bulk whose identity, despite Blake's new perspective, was beyond dispute.

The vacant church was in a state of great decrepitude. Some of the high stone buttresses had fallen, and several delicate finials lay half lost among the brown, neglected weeds and grasses. The sooty Gothic windows were largely unbroken, though many of the stone mullions were missing. Blake wondered how the obscurely painted panes could have survived so well, in view of the known habits of small boys the world over. The massive doors were intact and tightly closed. Around

[a] facade] façade A, B
[b] doorsteps,] door-steps, A, B
[c] windswept] wind-swept A, B

the top of the bank wall, fully enclosing the grounds, was a rusty iron fence whose gate—at the head of a flight of steps from the square—was visibly padlocked. The path from the gate to the building was completely overgrown. Desolation and decay hung like a pall above the place, and in the birdless eaves and black, ivyless walls Blake felt a touch of the dimly sinister beyond his power to define.

There were very few people in the square, but Blake saw a policeman at the northerly end and approached him with questions about the church. He was a great wholesome Irishman, and it seemed odd that he would do little more than make the sign of the cross and mutter that people never spoke of that building. When Blake pressed him he said very hurriedly that the Italian priests warned everybody against it, vowing that a monstrous evil had once dwelt there and left its mark. He himself had heard dark whispers of it from his father, who recalled certain sounds and rumours[a] from his boyhood.

There had been a bad sect there in the ould[b] days—an outlaw sect that called up awful things from some unknown gulf of night. It had taken a good priest to exorcise what had come, though there did be those who said that merely the light could do it. If Father O'Malley were alive there would be many the thing he could tell. But now there was nothing to do but let it alone. It hurt nobody now, and those that owned it were dead or far away. They had run away like rats after the threatening talk in '77, when people began to mind the way folks vanished now and then in the neighbourhood.[c] Some day the city would step in and take the property for lack of heirs, but little good would come of anybody's touching it. Better it be left alone for the years to topple, lest things be stirred that ought to rest for ever in their black abyss.

After the policeman had gone Blake stood staring at the sullen steepled pile. It excited him to find that the structure seemed as sinister to others as to him, and he wondered what grain of truth might lie behind the old tales the bluecoat had repeated. Probably they were mere legends evoked by the evil look of the place, but even so, they

[a] rumours] rumors A, B
[b] ould] old B
[c] neighbourhood.] neighborhood. A

were like a strange coming to life of one of his own stories.

The afternoon sun came out from behind dispersing clouds, but seemed unable to light up the stained, sooty walls of the old temple that towered on its high plateau. It was odd that the green of spring had not touched the brown, withered growths in the raised, iron-fenced yard. Blake found himself edging nearer the raised area and examining the bank wall and rusted fence for possible avenues of ingress. There was a terrible lure about the blackened fane which was not to be resisted. The fence had no opening near the steps, but around on the north side were some missing bars. He could go up the steps and walk around on the narrow coping outside the fence till he came to the gap. If the people feared the place so wildly, he would encounter no interference.

He was on the embankment and almost inside the fence before anyone noticed him. Then, looking down, he saw the few people in the square edging away and making the same sign with their right hands that the shopkeeper in the avenue had made. Several windows were slammed down, and a fat woman darted into the street and pulled some small children inside a rickety, unpainted house. The gap in the fence was very easy to pass through, and before long Blake found himself wading amidst the rotting, tangled growths of the deserted yard. Here and there the worn stump of a headstone told him that there had once been burials in this field; but that, he saw, must have been very long ago. The sheer bulk of the church was oppressive now that he was close to it, but he conquered his mood and approached to try the three great doors in the facade.[a] All were securely locked, so he began a circuit of the Cyclopean building in quest of some minor and more penetrable opening. Even then he could not be sure that he wished to enter that haunt of desertion and shadow, yet the pull of its strangeness dragged him on automatically.

A yawning and unprotected cellar window in the rear furnished the needed aperture. Peering in, Blake saw a subterrene gulf of cobwebs and dust faintly litten by the western sun's filtered rays. Debris, old barrels, and ruined boxes and furniture of numerous sorts met his eye, though over everything lay a shroud of dust which softened all sharp

[a] facade.] façade. A, B

outlines. The rusted remains of a hot-air furnace shewed[a] that the building had been used and kept in shape as late as mid-Victorian[b] times.

Acting almost without conscious initiative, Blake crawled through the window and let himself down to the dust-carpeted and debris-strown[c] concrete floor. The vaulted cellar was a vast one, without partitions; and in a corner far to the right, amid dense shadows, he saw a black archway evidently leading upstairs. He felt a peculiar sense of oppression at being actually within the great spectral building, but kept it in check as he cautiously scouted about—finding a still-intact barrel amid the dust, and rolling it over to the open window to provide for his exit. Then, bracing himself, he crossed the wide, cobweb-festooned space toward the arch. Half choked with the omnipresent dust, and covered with ghostly gossamer fibres,[d] he reached and began to climb the worn stone steps which rose into the darkness. He had no light, but groped carefully with his hands. After a sharp turn he felt a closed door ahead, and a little fumbling revealed its ancient latch. It opened inward, and beyond it he saw a dimly illumined corridor lined with worm-eaten panelling.[e]

Once on the ground floor, Blake began exploring in a rapid fashion. All the inner doors were unlocked, so that he freely passed from room to room. The colossal nave was an almost eldritch place with its drifts and mountains of dust over box pews, altar, hour-glass pulpit, and sounding-board, and its titanic ropes of cobweb stretching among the pointed arches of the gallery and entwining the clustered Gothic columns. Over all this hushed desolation played a hideous leaden light as the declining afternoon sun sent its rays through the strange, half-blackened panes of the great apsidal windows.

The paintings on those windows were so obscured by soot that Blake could scarcely decipher what they had represented, but from the little he could make out he did not like them. The designs were largely conventional, and his knowledge of obscure symbolism told him much

[a] shewed] showed A, B
[b] mid-Victorian] Mid-Victorian B
[c] debris-strown] debris-strewn A, B
[d] fibres,] fibers, A, B
[e] panelling.] paneling. A, B

concerning some of the ancient patterns. The few saints depicted bore expressions distinctly open to criticism, while one of the windows seemed to shew[a] merely a dark space with spirals of curious luminosity scattered about in it. Turning away from the windows, Blake noticed that the cobwebbed cross above the altar was not of the ordinary kind, but resembled the primordial ankh or crux ansata of shadowy Egypt.

In a rear vestry room beside the apse Blake found a rotting desk and ceiling-high shelves of mildewed, disintegrating books. Here for the first time he received a positive shock of objective horror, for the titles of those books told him much. They were the black, forbidden things which most sane people have never even heard of, or have heard of only in furtive, timorous whispers; the banned and dreaded repositories of equivocal secrets and immemorial formulae which have trickled down the stream of time from the days of man's youth, and the dim, fabulous days before man was. He had himself read many of them—a Latin version of the abhorred "Necronomicon",[b] the sinister "Liber Ivonis",[c] the infamous "Cultes des Goules"[d] of Comte d'Erlette, the "Unaussprechlichen Kulten"[e] of von Junzt, and old Ludvig Prinn's hellish "De Vermis Mysteriis".[f] But there were others he had known merely by reputation or not at all—the Pnakotic Manuscripts,[g] the "Book of Dzyan",[h] and a crumbling volume in wholly unidentifiable characters yet with certain symbols and diagrams shudderingly recognisable[i] to the occult student. Clearly, the lingering local rumours[j] had not lied. This place had once been the seat of an evil older than mankind and wider than the known universe.

In the ruined desk was a small leather-bound[k] record-book filled with

---

[a] shew] show A, B
[b] "Necronomicon",] *Necronomicon,* A, B
[c] "Liber Ivonis",] *Liber Ivonis,* A, B
[d] "Cultes des Goules"] *Cultes des Goules* A, B
[e] "Unaussprechlichen Kulten"] *Unaussprechlichen Kulten* A, B
[f] "De Vermis Mysteriis".] *De Vermis Mysteriis.* A, B
[g] Pnakotic Manuscripts,] *Pnakotic Manuscripts,* A, B
[h] "Book of Dzyan",] *Book of Dzyan,* A, B
[i] recognisable] recognizable A, B
[j] rumours] rumors A, B
[k] leather-bound] leather-/bound A; leatherbound B

entries in some odd cryptographic medium. The manuscript writing consisted of the common traditional symbols used today in astronomy and anciently in alchemy, astrology, and other dubious arts—the devices of the sun, moon, planets, aspects, and zodiacal signs—here massed in solid pages of text, with divisions and paragraphings suggesting that each symbol answered to some alphabetical letter.

In the hope of later solving the cryptogram, Blake bore off this volume in his coat pocket. Many of the great tomes on the shelves fascinated him unutterably, and he felt tempted to borrow them at some later time. He wondered how they could have remained undisturbed so long. Was he the first to conquer the clutching, pervasive fear which had for nearly sixty years protected this deserted place from visitors?

Having now thoroughly explored the ground floor, Blake ploughed[a] again through the dust of the spectral nave to the front vestibule, where he had seen a door and staircase presumably leading up to the blackened tower and steeple—objects so long familiar to him at a distance. The ascent was a choking experience, for dust lay thick, while the spiders had done their worst in this constricted place. The staircase was a spiral with high, narrow wooden treads, and now and then Blake passed a clouded window looking dizzily out over the city. Though he had seen no ropes below, he expected to find a bell or peal of bells in the tower whose narrow, louver-boarded lancet windows his field-glass had studied so often. Here he was doomed to disappointment; for when he attained the top of the stairs he found the tower chamber vacant of chimes, and clearly devoted to vastly different purposes.

The room, about fifteen feet square, was faintly lighted by four lancet windows, one on each side, which were glazed within their screening of decayed louver-boards. These had been further fitted with tight, opaque screens, but the latter were now largely rotted away. In the centre[b] of the dust-laden floor rose a curiously angled stone pillar some four feet in height and two in average diameter, covered on each side

[a] ploughed] plowed A, B
[b] centre] center A, B

with bizarre, crudely incised,[a] and wholly unrecognisable[b] hieroglyphs. On this pillar rested a metal box of peculiarly asymmetrical form; its hinged lid thrown back, and its interior holding what looked beneath the decade-deep dust to be an egg-shaped or irregularly spherical object some four inches through. Around the pillar in a rough circle were seven high-backed Gothic chairs still largely intact, while behind them, ranging along the dark-panelled[c] walls, were seven colossal images of crumbling, black-painted plaster, resembling more than anything else the cryptic carven megaliths of mysterious Easter[d] Island. In one corner of the cobwebbed chamber a ladder was built into the wall, leading up to the closed trap-door[e] of the windowless steeple above.

As Blake grew accustomed to the feeble light he noticed odd bas-reliefs on the strange open box of yellowish metal. Approaching, he tried to clear the dust away with his hands and handkerchief, and saw that the figurings were of a monstrous and utterly alien kind; depicting entities which, though seemingly alive, resembled no known life-form ever evolved on this planet. The four-inch seeming sphere turned out to be a nearly black, red-striated polyhedron with many irregular flat surfaces; either a very remarkable crystal of some sort, or an artificial object of carved and highly polished mineral matter. It did not touch the bottom of the box, but was held suspended by means of a metal band around its centre,[f] with seven queerly designed[g] supports extending horizontally to angles of the box's inner wall near the top. This stone, once exposed, exerted upon Blake an almost alarming fascination. He could scarcely tear his eyes from it, and as he looked at its glistening surfaces he almost fancied it was transparent, with half-formed worlds of wonder within. Into his mind floated pictures of alien orbs with great stone towers, and other orbs with titan mountains and no mark of life, and still remoter spaces where only a stirring in vague blacknesses told of the presence of consciousness and will.

[a] incised,] incised A, B
[b] unrecognisable] unrecognizable A, B
[c] dark-panelled] dark-paneled A, B
[d] Easter] Eastern B
[e] trap-door] trap door B
[f] centre,] center, A, B
[g] queerly designed] queerly-designed A, B

When he did look away, it was to notice a somewhat singular mound of dust in the far corner near the ladder to the steeple. Just why it took his attention he could not tell, but something in its contours carried a message to his unconscious mind. Ploughing[a] toward it, and brushing aside the hanging cobwebs as he went, he began to discern something grim about it. Hand and handkerchief soon revealed the truth, and Blake gasped with a baffling mixture of emotions. It was a human skeleton, and it must have been there for a very long time. The clothing was in shreds, but some buttons and fragments of cloth bespoke a man's grey[b] suit. There were other bits of evidence—shoes, metal clasps, huge buttons for round cuffs, a stickpin of bygone pattern, a reporter's badge with the name of the old *Providence Telegram,* and a crumbling leather pocketbook.[c] Blake examined the latter with care, finding within it several bills of antiquated issue, a celluloid advertising calendar for 1893, some cards with the name "Edwin M. Lillibridge",[d] and a paper covered with pencilled[e] memoranda.

This paper held much of a puzzling nature, and Blake read it carefully at the dim westward window. Its disjointed text included such phrases as the following:

"Prof. Enoch Bowen home from Egypt May 1844—buys old Free-Will Church in July—his archaeological work & studies in occult well known."

"Dr. Drowne of 4th Baptist warns against Starry Wisdom in sermon Dec. 29, 1844."

"Congregation 97 by end of '45."

"1846—3 disappearances—first mention of Shining Trapezohedron."

"7 disappearances 1848—stories of blood sacrifice begin."

"Investigation 1853 comes to nothing—stories of sounds."

"Fr. O'Malley tells of devil-worship with box found in great Egyptian ruins—says they call up something that can't exist in light. Flees a little light, and banished by strong light. Then has to be summoned again. Probably got this from deathbed confession of Francis X. Feeney, who

---

[a] Ploughing] Plowing A, B
[b] grey] gray A, B
[c] pocketbook.] pocket-book. A, B
[d] Lillibridge",] Lillibridge," A, B
[e] pencilled] penciled A, B

had joined Starry Wisdom in '49. These people say the Shining Trapezohedron shews[a] them heaven & other worlds, & that the Haunter of the Dark tells them secrets in some way."

"Story of Orrin B. Eddy 1857. They call it up by gazing at the crystal, & have a secret language of their own."

"200 or more in cong. 1863, exclusive of men at front."

"Irish boys mob church in 1869 after Patrick Regan's disappearance."

"Veiled article in J. March 14, '72, but people don't talk about it."

"6 disappearances 1876—secret committee calls on Mayor Doyle."

"Action promised Feb. 1877—church closes in April."

"Gang—Federal Hill Boys—threaten Dr. ――――― and vestrymen in May."

"181 persons leave city before end of '77—mention no names."

"Ghost stories begin around 1880—try to ascertain truth of report that no human being has entered church since 1877."

"Ask Lanigan for photograph of place taken 1851." . . .

Restoring the paper to the pocketbook[b] and placing the latter in his coat, Blake turned to look down at the skeleton in the dust. The implications of the notes were clear, and there could be no doubt but that this man had come to the deserted edifice forty-two years before in quest of a newspaper sensation which no one else had been bold enough to attempt. Perhaps no one else had known of his plan—who could tell? But he had never returned to his paper. Had some bravely suppressed[c] fear risen to overcome him and bring on sudden heart-failure? Blake stooped over the gleaming bones and noted their peculiar state. Some of them were badly scattered, and a few seemed oddly *dissolved* at the ends. Others were strangely yellowed, with vague suggestions of charring. This charring extended to some of the fragments of clothing. The skull was in a very peculiar state—stained yellow, and with a charred aperture in the top as if some powerful acid had eaten through the solid bone. What had happened to the skeleton during its four decades of silent entombment here Blake could not imagine.

Before he realised[d] it, he was looking at the stone again, and letting its curious influence call up a nebulous pageantry in his mind. He saw

[a] shews] shows A, B
[b] pocketbook] pocket-/book A
[c] bravely suppressed] bravely-suppressed A, B
[d] realised] realized A, B

processions of robed, hooded figures whose outlines were not human, and looked on endless leagues of desert lined with carved, sky-reaching monoliths. He saw towers and walls in nighted depths under the sea, and vortices of space where wisps of black mist floated before thin shimmerings of cold purple haze. And beyond all else he glimpsed an infinite gulf of sheer[a] darkness, where solid and semi-solid forms were known only by their windy stirrings, and cloudy patterns of force seemed to superimpose order on chaos and hold forth a key to all the paradoxes and arcana of the worlds we know.

Then all at once the spell was broken by an access of gnawing, indeterminate panic fear. Blake choked and turned away from the stone, conscious of some formless alien presence close to him and watching him with horrible intentness. He felt entangled with something—something which was not in the stone, but which had looked through it at him—something which would ceaselessly follow him with a cognition that was not physical sight. Plainly, the place was getting on his nerves—as well it might in view of his gruesome find. The light was waning, too, and since he had no illuminant with him he knew he would have to be leaving soon.

It was then, in the gathering twilight, that he thought he saw a faint trace of luminosity in the crazily angled stone. He had tried to look away from it, but some obscure compulsion drew his eyes back. Was there a subtle phosphorescence of radio-activity about the thing? What was it that the dead man's notes had said concerning a *Shining Trapezohedron?* What, anyway, was this[b] abandoned lair of cosmic evil? What had been done here, and what might still be lurking in the bird-shunned shadows? It seemed now as if an elusive touch of foetor[c] had arisen somewhere close by, though its source was not apparent. Blake seized the cover of the long-open box and snapped it down. It moved easily on its alien hinges, and closed completely over the unmistakably glowing stone.

At the sharp click of that closing a soft stirring sound seemed to come from the steeple's eternal blackness overhead, beyond the trap-

[a] sheer] *om.* B
[b] this] his B
[c] foetor] fetor A, B

door. Rats, without question—the only living things to reveal their presence in this accursed pile since he had entered it. And yet that stirring in the steeple frightened him horribly, so that he plunged almost wildly down the spiral stairs, across the ghoulish nave, into the vaulted basement, out amidst the gathering dusk of the deserted square, and down through the teeming, fear-haunted alleys and avenues of Federal Hill toward the sane central streets and the home-like brick sidewalks of the college district.

During the days which followed, Blake told no one of his expedition. Instead, he read much in certain books, examined long years of newspaper files downtown, and worked feverishly at the cryptogram in that leather volume from the cobwebbed vestry room. The cipher, he soon saw, was no simple one; and after a long period of endeavour[a] he felt sure that its language could not be English, Latin, Greek, French, Spanish, Italian, or German. Evidently he would have to draw upon the deepest wells of his strange erudition.

Every evening the old impulse to gaze westward returned, and he saw the black steeple as of yore amongst the bristling roofs of a distant and half-fabulous world. But now it held a fresh note of terror for him. He knew the heritage of evil lore it masked, and with the knowledge his vision ran riot in queer new ways. The birds of spring were returning, and as he watched their sunset flights he fancied they avoided the gaunt, lone spire as never before. When a flock of them approached it, he thought, they would wheel and scatter in panic confusion—and he could guess at the wild twitterings which failed to reach him across the intervening miles.

It was in June that Blake's diary told of his victory over the cryptogram. The text was, he found, in the dark Aklo language used by certain cults of evil antiquity, and known to him in a halting way through previous researches. The diary is strangely reticent about what Blake deciphered, but he was patently awed and disconcerted by his results. There are references to a Haunter of the Dark awaked by gazing into the Shining Trapezohedron, and insane conjectures about the black gulfs of chaos from which it was called. The being is spoken of as holding all knowledge, and demanding monstrous sacrifices.

[a] endeavour] endeavor A, B

Some of Blake's entries shew fear lest the thing, which he seemed to regard as summoned, stalk abroad; though he adds that the street-lights[a] form a bulwark which cannot be crossed.

Of the Shining Trapezohedron he speaks often, calling it a window on all time and space, and tracing its history from the days it was fashioned on dark Yuggoth, before ever the Old Ones brought it to earth. It was treasured and placed in its curious box by the crinoid things of Antarctica, salvaged from their ruins by the serpent-men of Valusia, and peered at aeons[b] later in Lemuria by the first human beings. It crossed strange lands and stranger seas, and sank with Atlantis before a Minoan fisher meshed it in his net and sold it to swarthy merchants from nighted Khem. The Pharaoh Nephren-Ka built around it a temple with a windowless crypt, and did that which caused his name to be stricken from all monuments and records. Then it slept in the ruins of that evil fane which the priests and the new Pharaoh destroyed, till the delver's spade once more brought it forth to curse mankind.

Early in July the newspapers oddly supplement Blake's entries, though in so brief and casual a way that only the diary has called general attention to their contribution. It appears that a new fear had been growing on Federal Hill since a stranger had entered the dreaded church. The Italians whispered of unaccustomed stirrings and bumpings and scrapings in the dark windowless steeple, and called on their priests to banish an entity which haunted their dreams. Something, they said, was constantly watching at a door to see if it were dark enough to venture forth. Press items mentioned the long-standing[c] local superstitions, but failed to shed much light on the earlier background of the horror. It was obvious that the young reporters of today are no antiquarians. In writing of these things in his diary, Blake expresses a curious kind of remorse, and talks of the duty of burying the Shining Trapezohedron and of banishing what he had evoked by letting daylight into the hideous jutting spire. At the same time, however, he displays the dangerous extent of his fascination, and admits a morbid

[a] street-lights] street-/lights A; streetlights B
[b] aeons] eons A, B
[c] long-standing] long-/standing A; longstanding B

longing—pervading even his dreams—to visit the accursed tower and gaze again into the cosmic secrets of the glowing stone.

Then something in the *Journal* on the morning of July 17 threw the diarist into a veritable fever of horror. It was only a variant of the other half-humorous items about the Federal Hill restlessness, but to Blake it was somehow very terrible indeed. In the night a thunderstorm had put the city's lighting-system out of commission for a full hour, and in that black interval the Italians had nearly gone mad with fright. Those living near the dreaded church had sworn that the thing in the steeple had taken advantage of the street-lamps'[a] absence and gone down into the body of the church, flopping and bumping around in a viscous, altogether dreadful way. Toward the last it had bumped up to the tower, where there were sounds of the shattering of glass. It could go wherever the darkness reached, but light would always send it fleeing.

When the current blazed on again there had been a shocking commotion in the tower, for even the feeble light trickling through the grime-blackened, louver-boarded windows was too much for the thing. It had bumped and slithered up into its tenebrous steeple just in time—for a long dose of light would have sent it back into the abyss whence the crazy stranger had called it. During the dark hour praying crowds had clustered round the church in the rain with lighted candles and lamps somehow shielded with folded papers[b] and umbrellas—a guard of light to save the city from the nightmare that stalks in darkness. Once, those nearest the church declared, the outer door had rattled hideously.

But even this was not the worst. That evening in the *Bulletin* Blake read of what the reporters had found. Aroused at last to the whimsical news value of the scare, a pair of them had defied the frantic crowds of Italians and crawled into the church through the cellar window after trying the doors in vain. They found the dust of the vestibule and of the spectral nave ploughed[c] up in a singular way, with bits[d] of rotted cushions and satin pew-linings scattered curiously around. There was a

[a] street-lamps'] street lamps' A, B
[b] papers] paper B
[c] ploughed] plowed A, B
[d] bits] pits A, B

bad odour[a] everywhere, and here and there were bits of yellow stain and patches of what looked like charring. Opening the door to the tower, and pausing a moment at the suspicion of a scraping sound above, they found the narrow spiral stairs wiped roughly clean.

In the tower itself a similarly half-swept condition existed. They spoke of the heptagonal stone pillar, the overturned Gothic chairs, and the bizarre plaster images; though strangely enough the metal box and the old mutilated skeleton were not mentioned. What disturbed Blake the most—except for the hints of stains and charring and bad odours[b]—was the final detail that explained the crashing glass. Every one of the tower's lancet windows was broken, and two of them had been darkened in a crude and hurried way by the stuffing of satin pew-linings and cushion-horsehair into the spaces between the slanting exterior louver-boards. More satin fragments and bunches of horsehair lay scattered around the newly swept floor, as if someone had been interrupted in the act of restoring the tower to the absolute blackness of its tightly curtained days.

Yellowish stains and charred patches were found on the ladder to the windowless spire, but when a reporter climbed up, opened the horizontally sliding[c] trap-door,[d] and shot a feeble flashlight beam into the black and strangely foetid[e] space, he saw nothing but darkness, and an heterogeneous litter of shapeless fragments near the aperture. The verdict, of course, was charlatanry. Somebody had played a joke on the superstitious hill-dwellers, or else some fanatic had striven to bolster up their fears for their own supposed good. Or perhaps some of the younger and more sophisticated dwellers had staged an elaborate hoax on the outside world. There was an amusing aftermath when the police sent an officer to verify the reports. Three men in succession found ways of evading the assignment, and the fourth went very reluctantly and returned very soon without adding to the account given by the reporters.

[a] odour] odor A, B
[b] odours] odors A, B
[c] horizontally sliding] horizontally-sliding A, B
[d] trap-door,] trap-/door A; trapdoor B
[e] foetid] fetid A, B

From this point onward Blake's diary shews[a] a mounting tide of insidious horror and nervous apprehension. He upbraids himself for not doing something, and speculates wildly on the consequences of another electrical breakdown. It has been verified that on three occasions—during thunderstorms—he telephoned the electric light company in a frantic vein and asked that desperate precautions against a lapse of power be taken. Now and then his entries shew[b] concern over the failure of the reporters to find the metal box and stone, and the strangely marred old skeleton, when they explored the shadowy tower room. He assumed that these things had been removed—whither, and by whom or what, he could only guess. But his worst fears concerned himself, and the kind of unholy rapport he felt to exist between his mind and that lurking horror in the distant steeple—that monstrous thing of night which his rashness had called out of the ultimate black spaces. He seemed to feel a constant tugging at his will, and callers of that period remember how he would sit abstractedly at his desk and stare out of the west window at that far-off,[c] spire-bristling mound beyond the swirling smoke of the city. His entries dwell monotonously on certain terrible dreams, and of a strengthening of the unholy rapport in his sleep. There is mention of a night when he awaked[d] to find himself fully dressed, outdoors, and headed automatically down College Hill toward the west. Again and again he dwells on the fact that the thing in the steeple knows where to find him.

The week following July 30 is recalled as the time of Blake's partial breakdown. He did not dress, and ordered all his food by telephone. Visitors remarked the cords he kept near his bed, and he said that sleep-walking had forced him to bind his ankles every night with knots which would probably hold or else waken him with the labour[e] of untying.

In his diary he told of the hideous experience which had brought the collapse. After retiring on the night of the 30th he had suddenly

[a] shews] shows A, B
[b] shew] show A, B
[c] far-off,] far-off B
[d] awaked] awakened B
[e] labour] labor A, B

found himself groping about in an almost black space. All he could see were short, faint, horizontal streaks of bluish light, but he could smell an overpowering foetor[a] and hear a curious jumble of soft, furtive sounds above him. Whenever he moved he stumbled over something, and at each noise there would come a sort of answering sound from above— a vague stirring, mixed with the cautious sliding of wood on wood.

Once his groping hands encountered a pillar of stone with a vacant top, whilst later he found himself clutching the rungs of a ladder built into the wall, and fumbling his uncertain way upward toward some region of intenser stench where a hot, searing blast beat down against him. Before his eyes a kaleidoscopic range of phantasmal[b] images played, all of them dissolving at intervals into the picture of a vast, unplumbed abyss of night wherein whirled suns and worlds of an even profounder blackness. He thought of the ancient legends of Ultimate Chaos, at whose centre[c] sprawls the blind idiot god Azathoth, Lord of All Things, encircled by his flopping horde of mindless and amorphous dancers, and lulled by the thin monotonous piping of a daemoniac[d] flute held in nameless paws.

Then a sharp report from the outer world broke through his stupor and roused him to the unutterable horror of his position. What it was, he never knew—perhaps it was some belated peal from the fireworks heard all summer on Federal Hill as the dwellers hail their various patron saints, or the saints of their native villages in Italy. In any event he shrieked aloud, dropped frantically from the ladder, and stumbled blindly across the obstructed floor of the almost lightless chamber that encompassed him.

He knew instantly where he was, and plunged recklessly down the narrow spiral staircase, tripping and bruising himself at every turn. There was a nightmare flight through a vast cobwebbed nave whose ghostly arches reached up to realms of leering shadow, a sightless scramble through a littered basement, a climb to regions of air and

[a] foetor] fetor A, B
[b] phantasmal] fantasmal A, B
[c] centre] center A, B
[d] daemoniac] demoniac A, B

street-lights[a] outside, and a mad racing down a spectral hill of gibbering gables, across a grim, silent city of tall black towers, and up the steep eastward precipice to his own ancient door.

On regaining consciousness in the morning he found himself lying on his study floor fully dressed. Dirt and cobwebs covered him, and every inch of his body seemed sore and bruised. When he faced the mirror he saw that his hair was badly scorched, while a trace of strange, evil odour[b] seemed to cling to his upper outer clothing. It was then that his nerves broke down. Thereafter, lounging exhaustedly about in a dressing-gown, he did little but stare from his west window, shiver at the threat of thunder, and make wild entries in his diary.

The great storm broke just before midnight on August 8th. Lightning struck repeatedly in all parts of the city, and two remarkable fireballs were reported. The rain was torrential, while a constant fusillade of thunder brought sleeplessness to thousands. Blake was utterly frantic in his fear for the lighting system, and tried to telephone the company around 1 a.m.,[c] though by that time service had been temporarily cut off in the interest of safety. He recorded everything in his diary—the large, nervous, and often undecipherable hieroglyphs telling their own story of growing frenzy and despair, and of entries scrawled blindly in the dark.

He had to keep the house dark in order to see out the window, and it appears that most of his time was spent at his desk, peering anxiously through the rain across the glistening miles of downtown roofs at the constellation of distant lights marking Federal Hill. Now and then he would fumblingly make an entry in his diary, so that detached phrases such as "The lights must not go"; "It knows where I am"; "I must destroy it"; and "It is calling to me, but perhaps it means no injury this time"[d] are found scattered down two of the pages.

Then the lights went out all over the city. It happened at 2:12 a.m.[e] according to power-house records, but Blake's diary gives no indication

---

[a] street-lights] street lights A, B

[b] odour] odor A, B

[c] 1 a.m.,] one a.m., A; one A.M., B

[d] time"] time"; A, B

[e] a.m.] A.M. B

of the time. The entry is merely, "Lights out—God help me." On Federal Hill there were watchers as anxious as he, and rain-soaked knots of men paraded the square and alleys around the evil church with umbrella-shaded candles, electric flashlights, oil lanterns, crucifixes, and obscure charms of the many sorts common to southern Italy. They blessed each flash of lightning, and made cryptical signs of fear with their right hands when a turn in the storm caused the flashes to lessen and finally to cease altogether. A rising wind blew out most of the candles, so that the scene grew threateningly[a] dark. Someone roused Father Merluzzo of Spirito Santo Church, and he hastened to the dismal square to pronounce whatever helpful syllables he could. Of the restless and curious sounds in the blackened tower, there could be no doubt whatever.

For what happened at 2:35 we have the testimony of the priest, a young, intelligent, and well-educated person; of Patrolman William J. Monahan[b] of the Central Station, an officer of the highest reliability who had paused at that part of his beat to inspect the crowd; and of most of the seventy-eight men who had gathered around the church's high bank wall—especially those in the square where the eastward facade[c] was visible. Of course there was nothing which can be proved as being outside the order of Nature.[d] The possible causes of such an event are many. No one can speak with certainty of the obscure chemical processes arising in a vast, ancient, ill-aired, and long-deserted building of heterogeneous contents. Mephitic vapours[e]—spontaneous combustion—pressure of gases born of long decay—any one of numberless phenomena might be responsible. And then, of course, the factor of conscious charlatanry can by no means be excluded. The thing was really quite simple in itself, and covered less than three minutes of actual time. Father Merluzzo, always a precise man, looked at his watch repeatedly.

[a] threateningly] threatening B
[b] Monahan] Monohan B
[c] facade] façade A, B
[d] Nature.] nature. A, B
[e] vapours] vapors A, B

It started with a definite swelling of the dull fumbling sounds inside the black tower. There had for some time been a vague exhalation of strange, evil odours[a] from the church, and this had now become emphatic and offensive. Then at last there was a sound of splintering wood, and a large, heavy object crashed down in the yard beneath the frowning easterly facade.[b] The tower was invisible now that the candles would not burn, but as the object neared the ground the people knew that it was the smoke-grimed louver-boarding of that tower's east window.

Immediately afterward an utterly unbearable foetor[c] welled forth from the unseen heights, choking and sickening the trembling watchers, and almost prostrating those in the square. At the same time the air trembled with a vibration as of flapping wings, and a sudden east-blowing wind more violent than any previous blast snatched off the hats and wrenched the dripping umbrellas of the crowd. Nothing definite could be seen in the candleless night, though some upward-looking spectators thought they glimpsed a great spreading blur of denser blackness against the inky sky—something like a formless cloud of smoke that shot with meteor-like speed toward the east.

That was all. The watchers were half numbed with fright, awe, and discomfort, and scarcely knew what to do, or whether to do anything at all. Not knowing what had happened, they did not relax their vigil; and a moment later they sent up a prayer as a sharp flash of belated lightning, followed by an earsplitting crash of sound, rent the flooded heavens. Half an hour later the rain stopped, and in fifteen minutes more the street-lights[d] sprang on again, sending the weary, bedraggled watchers relievedly back to their homes.

The next day's papers gave these matters minor mention in connexion[e] with the general storm reports. It seems that the great lightning flash and deafening explosion which followed the Federal Hill occurrence were even more tremendous farther east, where a burst

[a] odours] odors A, B
[b] facade.] façade. A, B
[c] foetor] fetor A, B
[d] street-lights] street lights A, B
[e] connexion] connection A, B

of the singular foetor[a] was likewise noticed. The phenomenon was most marked over College Hill, where the crash awaked all the sleeping inhabitants and led to a bewildered round of speculations. Of those who were already awake only a few saw the anomalous blaze of light near the top of the hill, or noticed the inexplicable upward rush of air which almost stripped the leaves from the trees and blasted the plants in the gardens. It was agreed that the lone, sudden lightning-bolt must have struck somewhere in this neighbourhood,[b] though no trace of its striking could afterward be found. A youth in the Tau Omega fraternity house thought he saw a grotesque and hideous mass of smoke in the air just as the preliminary flash burst, but his observation has not been verified. All of the few observers, however, agree as to the violent gust from the west and the flood of intolerable stench which preceded the belated stroke; whilst evidence concerning the momentary burned odour[c] after the stroke is equally general.

These points were discussed very carefully because of their probable connexion[d] with the death of Robert Blake. Students in the Psi Delta house, whose upper rear windows looked into Blake's study, noticed the blurred white face at the westward window on the morning of the 9th,[e] and wondered what was wrong with the expression. When they saw the same face in the same position that evening, they felt worried, and watched for the lights to come up in his apartment. Later they rang the bell of the darkened flat, and finally had a policeman force the door.

The rigid body sat bolt upright at the desk by the window, and when the intruders saw the glassy, bulging eyes, and the marks of stark, convulsive fright on the twisted features, they turned away in sickened dismay. Shortly afterward the coroner's physician made an examination, and despite the unbroken window reported electrical shock, or nervous tension induced by electrical discharge, as the cause of death. The hideous expression he ignored altogether, deeming it a

[a] foetor] fetor A, B
[b] neighbourhood,] neighborhood, A, B
[c] odour] odor A, B
[d] connexion] connection A, B
[e] 9th,] ninth, B

not improbable result of the profound shock as experienced by a person of such abnormal imagination and unbalanced emotions. He deduced these latter qualities from the books, paintings, and manuscripts found in the apartment, and from the blindly scrawled entries in the diary on the desk. Blake had prolonged his frenzied jottings to the last, and the broken-pointed pencil was found clutched in his spasmodically contracted right hand.

The entries after the failure of the lights were highly disjointed, and legible only in part. From them certain investigators have drawn conclusions differing greatly from the materialistic official verdict, but such speculations have little chance for belief among the conservative. The case of these imaginative theorists has not been helped by the action of superstitious Dr.[a] Dexter, who threw the curious box and angled stone—an object certainly self-luminous as seen in the black windowless steeple where it was found—into the deepest channel of Narragansett Bay. Excessive imagination and neurotic unbalance on Blake's part, aggravated by knowledge of the evil bygone cult whose startling traces he had uncovered, form the dominant interpretation given those final frenzied jottings. These are the entries—or all that can be made of them.

> "Lights still out—must be five minutes now. Everything depends on lightning. Yaddith grant it will keep up! . . . Some influence seems beating through it. . . . Rain and thunder and wind deafen. . . . The thing is taking hold of my mind. . . .
>
> "Trouble with memory. I see things I never knew before. Other worlds and other galaxies . . . Dark . . . The lightning seems dark and the darkness seems light. . . .
>
> "It cannot be the real hill and church that I see in the pitch-darkness. Must be retinal impression left by flashes. Heaven grant the Italians are out with their candles if the lightning stops!
>
> "What am I afraid of? Is it not an avatar of Nyarlathotep, who in antique and shadowy Khem even took the form of man? I remember Yuggoth, and more distant Shaggai, and the ultimate void of the black planets. . . .

---

[a] Dr.] Doctor A, B

"The long, winging flight through the void . . . cannot cross the universe of light . . . re-created by the thoughts caught in the Shining Trapezohedron . . . send it through the horrible abysses of radiance. . . .

"My name is Blake—Robert Harrison Blake of 620 East Knapp Street, Milwaukee, Wisconsin. . . . I am on this planet. . . .

"Azathoth have mercy!—the lightning no longer flashes—horrible—I can see everything with a monstrous sense that is not sight—light is dark and dark is light . . . those people on the hill . . . guard . . . candles and charms . . . their priests . . .

"Sense of distance gone—far is near and near is far. No light—no glass—see that steeple—that tower—window—can hear—Roderick Usher—am mad or going mad—the thing is stirring and fumbling in the tower—I am it and it is I—I want to get out . . . must get out and unify the forces. . . . It knows where I am. . . .

"I am Robert Blake, but I see the tower in the dark. There is a monstrous odour[a] . . . senses transfigured . . . boarding at that tower window cracking and giving way. . . . Iä . . . ngai . . . ygg. . . .

"I see it—coming here—hell-wind—titan blur—black wings—Yog-Sothoth save me—the three-lobed burning eye. . . ."

[a] odour] odor A, B

Appendix

[Juvenilia]

THE LITTLE GLASS BOTTLE

"Heave to, there's something floating to the leeward" the speaker was a short stockily built man whose name was William Jones. he was the captain of a small cat boat in which he & a party of men were sailing at the time the story opens.

"Aye aye sir" answered John Towers & the boat was brought to a stand still Captain Jones reached out his hand for the object which he now discerned to be a glass bottle "Nothing but a rum flask that the men on a passing boat threw over" he said but from an impulse of curiosity he reached out for it. it was a rum flask & he was about to throw it away when he noticed a piece of paper in it. He pulled it out & on it read the following

> Jan 1 1864
> I am John Jones who writes this letter my ship is fast sinking with a treasure on board I am where it is marked * on the enclosed chart

Captain Jones turned the sheet over & the other side was a chart

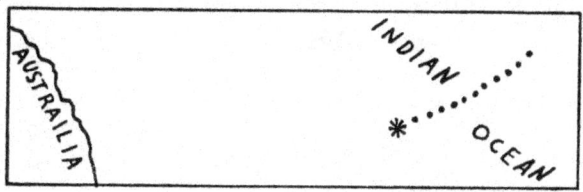

Editor's Note: "The Little Glass Bottle," "The Secret Cave," "The Mystery of the Grave-Yard," and "The Mysterious Ship" (short version), all written in the period 1897–1902, exist in A.Mss. at JHL. These stories were first published in *The Shuttered Room and Other Pieces* (Arkham House, 1959); a corrected text was printed in my edition of *Juvenilia: 1895–1905* (West Warwick, RI: Necronomicon Press, 1984). The long version of "The Mysterious Ship" exists only in a typed transcript in the Arkham House Transcripts; the original is presumably lost. It was first published in *H. P. Lovecraft: The Complete Fiction* (New York: Barnes & Noble, 2008). It does not seem profitable to present textual variants for these texts.

on the edge were written these words

dotted lines represent course we took

"Towers" Said Capt. Jones excitedly "read this" Towers did as he was directed "I think it would pay to go" said Capt. Jones "do you"? "Just as you say" replied Towers. "We'll charter a schooner this very day" said the exited captain "All right" said Towers so they hired a boat and started off govnd by the dotted lines of they chart in 4 weeks the reached the place where directed & the divers went down and came up with an iron bottle they found in it the following lines scribbled on a piece of brown paper

> Dec 3 1880
> Dear Searcher excuse me for the practical joke I have played on you but it serves you right to find nothing for your foolish act—

"Well it does" said Capt Jones "go on"

> However I will defray your expenses to & from the place you found your bottle I think it will be $25.0.00 so that amount you will find in an Iron box I know where you found the bottle because I put this bottle here & the iron box & then found a good place to put the second bottle hoping the enclosed money will defray your expenses some I close—Anonymus"

"I'd like to kick his head off" said Capt Jones "Here diver go & get the $25.0.00 in a minute the diver came up bearing an iron box inside it was found $25.0.00 It defrayed their expenses but I hardly think that they will ever go to a mysterious place as directed by a mysterious bottle

THE SECRET CAVE

OR JOHN LEES ADVENTURE

"Now be good children" Said Mrs. Lee "While I am away & dont get into mischief". Mr. & Mrs. Lee were going off for the day & To leave The Two children John 10 yrs old & Alice 2 yrs old "Yes" replied John

As Soon as The Elder Lees were away the younger Lees went down cellar & began to rummage among the rubbish little alice leaned against the wall watching John. As John was making a boat of barrel staves the Little girl gave a piercing cry as the bricks behind her crumbled away he rushed up to her & Lifted her out screaming loudly as soon as her screams subsided she said "the wall went away" John went up & saw that there was a passage he said to the little girl "lets come & see what this is" "Yes" she said the entered the place they could stand up it the passage was farther than they could see they John went back upstairs & went to the kitchen drawer & got 2 candles & some matches & then they went back to the cellar passage. the two once more entered there was plastering on the walls ceiling & floor nothing was visible but a box this was for a seat nevertheless they examined it & found it to contain nothing the walked on farther & pretty soon the plastering left off & they were in a cave Little alice was frightened at first but at her brothers assurance that it was "all right" she allayed her fears. soon they came to a small box which John took up & carried within pretty soon they came on a *boat* in it were two oars he dragged it with difficulty along with him soon they found the passage came to an abrupt stop he pulled the obstacle away & to his dismay water rushed in in torrents John was an expert swimmer & long breathed he had Just taken a breath so he tried to rise but with the box & his sister he found it quite impossible then he caught sight of the boat rising he grasped it————

The next he knew he was on the surface clinging tightly to the body of his sister & the mysterious box he could not imagine how the water got in but a new peril menaced them if the water continued rising it would rise to the top suddenly a thought presented itself. he could shut off the water he speedily did this & lifting the now lifeless body of his sister into the boat he himself climed in & sailed down the passage it was gruesome & uncanny absolutely dark his candle being put out by the flood & a dead body lying near he did not gaze about him but rowed for his life when he did look up he was floating in his own cellar he quickly rushed up stairs with the body, to find his parents had come home He told them the story

*   *   *   *   *   *

The funeral of alice occupied so much time that John quite forgot about the box—but when they *did* open it they found it to be a *solid gold* chunk worth about $10,000 enough to pay for any thing but the death of his sister.

End

THE MYSTERY OF THE GRAVE-YARD

OR "A DEAD MAN'S REVENGE"

A Detective Story
by H. P. Lovecraft.

Chapter I
The Burns's Tomb.

It was noon in the Little village of Mainville, and a sorrowful group of people were standing around the Burns's Tomb. Joseph Burns was dead. (when dying, he had given the following strange orders:— "Before you put my body in the tomb, drop this ball onto the floor, at a spot marked "A"." he then handed a small golden ball to the rector.) The people greatly regretted his death. After The funeral services were finished, Mr Dobson (the rector) said, "My friends, I will now gratify the last wishes of the deceased. So saying, he descended into the tomb. (to lay the ball on the spot marked "A") Soon the funeral party Began to be impatient, and after a time Mr. Cha's. Greene (the Lawyer) descended to make a search. Soon he came up with a frightened face, and said, "Mr Dobson is *not there*"!

Chapter II
Mysterious Mr. Bell.

It was 3.10 o'clock in yᵉ afternoone whenne The door bell of the Dobson mansion rang loudly, and the servant on going to the door, found an elderly man, with black hair, and side whiskers. He asked to see Miss Dobson. Upon arriving in her presence he said, "Miss Dobson, I know where your father is, and for £10,000 I will restore him. My name is Mr. Bell." "Mr. Bell," said Miss Dobson, "will you excuse me from the room a moment?" "Certainly". replied Mr Bell. In a short time she returned, and said, "Mr. Bell, I understand you. You have abducted my father, and hold him for a ransom"

Chapter III
At The Police Station.

It was 3.20 o'clock in the afternoon when the telephone bell at the North End Police Station rang furiously, and Gibson, (the telephone Man) Inquired what was the matter,

"Have found out about fathers dissapearance"! a womans voice said. "Im Miss Dobson, and father has been abducted, "Send King John"! King John was a famous western detective. Just then a man rushed in, and shouted, "Oh! Terrors! Come To the Graveyard!"

Chapter IV
The West Window.

Now let us return to the Dobson Mansion. Mr Bell was rather taken aback by Miss Dobson's plain speaking, but when he recovered his speech he said, "Don't put it quite so plain, Miss Dobson, for I—" He was interrupted by the entrance of King John, who with a brace of revolvers in his hands, barred all egress by the doorway. But quicker than thought Bell sprang to a west window,—and jumped.

Chapter V
The Secret of The grave.

Now let us return to the station house. After the exited visitor had calmed somewhat, he could tell his story straighter. He had seen three men in the graveyard shouting "Bell! Bell! where are you old man!?" and acting very suspiciously. He then followed them, and *they entered The Burns's Tomb!* He then followed them in and they touched a spring at a

point marked "A" and then Dissapeared". "I wish king John were here",
Said Gibson, "What's your name,"? "John Spratt". replied the visitor.

Chapter VI
The chase for Bell.

Now let us return To the Dobson Mansion again:—King John was
utterly confounded at the Sudden movement of Bell, but when he
recovered from his surprise, his first thought was of chase. Accordingly,
he started in pursuit of the abductor. He tracked him down to the R. R.
Station and found to his dismay that he had taken the train for Kent, a
large city toward the south, and between which and Mainville there
existed no telegraph or telephone. The train had Just Started!

Chapter VII
The Negro Hackman.

The Kent train started at 10.35, and about 10.36 an exited, dusty, and
tired man* rushed into the Mainville hack. office and said to a negro
hackman who was standing by the door—"If you can take me to Kent
in 15 minutes I will give you a dollar". "I doan' see how I'm ter git
there", said the negro "I hab'n't got a decent pair of hosses an' I hab—"
"Two Dollars"! Shouted The Traveller, "all right" said the Hackman.

Chapter VIII   (Long.)
Bells Surprise.

It was 11 o'clock at Kent, all of the stores were closed but one, a
dingy, dirty, little shop, down at the west end. It lay between Kent
Harbour, & the Kent & Mainville R. R. In the Front room a shabbily
dressed person of doubtful age was conversing with a middle aged
woman with gray haire, "I have agreed to do the job, Lindy," he said,
"Bell will arrive at 11.30 and the carraige is ready to take him down to
the wharf, where a ship for Africa sails to-nighte."

---

*King John.

"But If King John were to come?" queried "Lindy"

"Then we'd get nabbed, an' Bell would be hung" Replied The man.

Just then a rap sounded at the door "Are you Bell"? inquired Lindy "Yes" was the response, "And I caught the 10.35 and King John got Left, so we are all right". At 11.40 the party reached The Landing, and saw a ship Loom up in the darkness. "The Kehdive" "of Africa" was painted on the hull, and Just as they were to step on board, a man stepped forward in the darkness and said "John Bell, I arrest you in the Queen's name"!

It was King John.

Chapter IX
The Trial.

The daye of The Trial had arrived, and a crowd of people had gathered around the Little grove, (which served for a court house in summer) To hear the trial of John Bell on the charge of kid-napping. "Mr. Bell," said the judge "what is the secret of the Burns's tomb"

"I well tell you this much" said Bell, "If you go into the tomb and touch a certain spot marked "A" you will find out"

"Now where is Mr Dobson"? queried the judge, "Here"! said a voice behind them, and The *figure of Mr Dobson HIMSELF* loomed up in the doorway.

"How did you get here"! &c was chorused. "'Tis a long story," said Dobson.

Chapter X
Dobson's Story.

"When I went down into the tomb," Said Dobson, "Everything was darkness, I could see nothing. but Finally I discerned the letter "A" printed in white on the onyx floor, I dropped the ball on the Letter, and immediately a trap-door opened and a man sprang up. It was this man, here," (he said (pointing at Bell, who stood Trembling on the prisoner's docke) "and he pulled me down into a brilliantly lighted, and palatial apartment where I have Lived until to-day. One day a young man rushed in and exclaimed "The secret Is revealed!" and was gone. He did not see me. Once Bell left his key behind, and I took the impression in wax, and the next day was spent in filing keys to fit the Lock. The next day my key fitted. and the next day (which is to-day) I escaped."

Chapter XI
The Mystery unveiled.

"Why did the late J. Burns, ask you to put the ball there"? (at "A"?) queried the Judge? "To get me into trouble" replied Dobson "He, and Francis Burns, (his brother) have plotted against me for years, and I knew not, in what way they would harm me". "Sieze Francis Burns"! yelled the Judge.

Chapter XII
Conclusion.

Francis Burns, and John Bell, were sent to prison for life. Mr Dobson was cordially welcomed by his daughter, who, by the way had become Mrs King John. "Lindy" and her accomplice were sent to Newgate for 30 days as aidors and abbettors of a criminal escape.

The End.

Price 25¢

THE MYSTERIOVS SHIP [SHORT VERSION]

BY
HOWARD PHILLIPS LOVECRAFT.

THE ROYAL PRESS.
1902.

Chapter 1.

In the spring of 1847, the little village of Ruralville was thrown into a state of exitement by the arrival of a strange brig in the harbour. It carried no flag, & everything about it was such as would exite suspicion. It had no name. Its captain was named Manuel Ruello. The exitement increased however when John Griggs dissapeared from his home. This was Oct. 4. on Oct. 5 the brig was gone.

Chapter 2.

The brig, in leaving, was met by a U. S. Frigate and a sharp fight ensued. When over, they* missed a man named Henry Johns.

Chapter 3.

The brig continued its course in the direction of Madagascar, upon its arrival, The natives fled in all directions. When they came together on the other side of the island, one was missing. His name was Dahabea.

Chapter 4.

At length it was decided that something must be done. A reward of £5,000 was offered for the capture of Manuel Ruello, When startling news came, a nameless brig was wrecked on the Florida Keys.

Chapter 5.

A ship was sent to Florida, and the mystery was solved. In the exitement of the fight they would launch a sub-marine boat and take what they wanted. there it lay, tranquilly rocking on the waters of the Atlantic when someone called out "John Brown has dissapeared." And sure enough John Brown was gone.

Chapter 6.

The finding of the sub-marine boat, and the dissapearance of John Brown, cause renewed exitement amongst the people, when a new

*(The Frigate.)

discovery was made. In transcribing this discovery it is necessary to relate a geographical fact. At the N. Pole there exists a vast continent composed of volcanic soil, a portion of which is open to explorers. It is called "No-Mans Land."

Chapter 7.

In the extreme southern part of No-Mans Land, there was found a hvt, and several other signs of human habitation. they promptly entered, and, chained to the floor, lay Griggs, Johns, & Dahabea. They, upon arriving in London, separated, Griggs going to Ruralville, Johns to the Frigate, & Dahabea to Madagascar.

Chapter 8.

But the mystery of John Brown was still unsolved, so they kept strict watch over the port at No-Mans Land, and when the sub-marine boat arrived, and the pirates, one by one, and headed by Manuel Ruello, left the ship, they were met by a rapid fire. After the fight brown was recovered.

Chapter 9.

Griggs was royally received at Ruralville, & a dinner was given in honour of Henry Johns, Dahabea was made King of Madagascar, & Brown was made Captain of his ship.

THE END.

THE MYSTERIOUS SHIP [LONG VERSION]

by Anonymus

In the Spring of 1847, the little village of Ruralville was thrown into a state of excitement by the landing of a strange Brig in the harbour. It carried no flag, and no name was painted on its side, and everything about it was such as would excite suspicion. It was from Tripoli, Africa, and the captain was named Manuel Ruello. The Excitement increased, however; when John Griggs, (The magnate of the villiage) suddenly disappeared from his home. This was the night of October 4th—on October 5th the Brig left.

Chapter II

It was 8 bells on the U.S. Frigate "Constitution" when Commander Farragut sighted a strange brig to the westward. It carried no flag, and no name was painted on its side, and everything about it was such as would excite suspicion. On hailing it put up the Pirates Flag. Farragut ordered a gun fired and no sooner did he fire, than the pirate ship gave them a broadside when the Fight was over Commander Farragut Missed one man named Henry F. Johns.

Chapter III

It was Summer on the Island of Madagascar. And Natives were picking corn, when one cried "Companions! I sight a ship! with no flag and with no name printed on the side and with eveything about it such as would excite Suspicion!" And The Natives fled in all directions when They came together on The other side of The Island one was missing his name was Dahabea.

Chapter IV

At length it was Decided Something must be done, Notes were compared. Three abductions were found to have taken place Dissapearance of John Griggs, Henry John, & Dahabea, were recalled. Finally Advertisements were issued offering £5000 reward for the capture of Manuel Ruello, Ship, Prisoners, & crew. When exciting News reached London! An unknown Brig with no name was wrecked of The Florida Keys in America!

Chapter V

The People Hurried to Florida and Beheld————. A steel spindle shaped object Lay placidly on the water Beside the shattered wreck of The brig. "A Submarine Boat"! shouted one "Yes!" shouted another "The mystery is cleared" said a wise looking man. "In the excitement of the fight they launch the submarine boat and take as many as they wish, unseen. And————." "John Brown has dissapeared"! shouted a voice from the deck. Sure enough John Brown was gone!

Chapter VI

The Finding of The Submarine boat and the dissapearance of John Brown caused renewed excitement among the People. and a new discovery was made. In relating this discovery It is necessary to relate a geographical Fact:—At the North Pole there is supposed to exist a vast continent composed of volcanic soil, a portion is open to travellers and explorers but it is barren and unfruitful. and thus absolutely Impassable. It is called "No-Mans Land".

Chapter VII

In the Extreme southern part of No-Mans Land There was found a wharf and a hut &c and every sign of former human habitation. A rusty door-plate was nailed to the hut inscribed in old English "M. Ruello". This, then, was the home of Manuel Ruello. the house brought to light a note book belonging to John Griggs, and The Log of the "Constitution" taken from Henry Johns, and the Madagascar Reaper belong To Dahabea.

Chapter VIII

When about to leave, they Observed a spring on the side of the hut. They pressed it.—A hole appeared in the side of the hut which they promptly entered. They were in a subterranean cavern. the beach ran down to the edge of a black, murky, sea. on the sea lay a dark oblong object—viz another Submarine boat which they entered. There bound to the cabin Floor Lay Griggs, Johns, and Dahabea, all alive and well. They, when arriving in London, separated, Griggs going to Ruralville, Johns, To the Constitution and Dahabea to Madagascar.

Chapter IX

But The mystery of John Brown lay still unsolved. So They Kept strict watch over the port at no-mans Land, Hoping The Submarine Boat would arrive. At length, however, it did arrive bearing with it John Brown. They Fixed upon the 5th of October For the Attack. They ranged along the shore and Formed Bodies. Finally one by one and Headed by Manuel Ruello The Pirates left the Boat. They were (to their astonishment) Met By a Rapid Fire.

Chapter X Conclusion

The Pirates were at Length defeated and a search was made for Brown. At Length he (the aforesaid Brown) was found. John Gregg was royally received at Ruralville and a dinner was

Dahabea was made King of Madagascar, and Manuel Ruello was Executed at Newgate Prison.

The End

The Very Old Folk

I have myself been carried back to Roman times by my recent perusal of James Rhoades' Æneid, a translation never before read by me, & more faithful to P. Maro than any other version I have ever seen—including that of my late uncle Dr. Clark, which did not attain publication. This Virgilian diversion, together with the spectral thoughts incident to All Hallows' Eve with its Witch-Sabbaths on the hills, produced in me last Monday night a Roman dream of such supernal clearness & vividness, & such titanic adumbrations of hidden horror, that I verily believe I shall some day employ it in fiction. Roman dreams were no uncommon features of my youth—I used to follow the Divine Julius all over Gallia as a Tribunus Militum o'nights—but I had so long ceased to experience them, that the present one impressed me with extraordinary force.

It was a flaming sunset or late afternoon in the tiny provincial town of Pompelo, at the foot of the Pyrenees in Hispania Citerior. The year must have been in the late republic, for the province was still ruled by a senatorial proconsul instead of a praetorian legate of the Augustus, & the day was the first before the Kalends of November. The hills rose scarlet & gold to the north of the little town, & the westering sun shone ruddily & mystically on the crude new stone & plaster buildings of the dusty forum & the wooden walls of the circus

Editor's Note: This text is an extract from a letter to Donald Wandrei (2 November 1927), recording HPL's "Roman dream" of Halloween. Similar letters were written to Bernard Austin Dwyer and Frank Belknap Long; the latter was incorporated directly into Long's novel *The Horror from the Hills* (1931). The Wandrei letter was printed, with some letters, with the title "The Very Old Folk" in *Scienti-Snaps* 3, No. 3 (Summer 1940): 4–8. This text contained numerous errors. The present text is derived from the A.L.S., which was first printed in unaltered form in *Mysteries of Time and Spirit: The Letters of H. P. Lovecraft and Donald Wandrei*, ed. S. T. Joshi and David E. Schultz (San Francisco: Night Shade, 2002). No textual variants are presented for this text.

some distance to the east. Groups of citizens—broad-browed Roman colonists & coarse-haired Romanised natives, together with obvious hybrids of the two strains, alike clad in cheap woollen togas—& sprinklings of helmeted legionaries & coarse-mantled, black-bearded tribesmen of the circumambient Vascones—all thronged the few paved streets & forum; moved by some vague & ill-defined uneasiness. I myself had just alighted from a litter, which the Illyrian bearers seemed to have brought in some haste from Calagurris, across the Iberus to the southward. It appeared that I was a provincial quaestor named L. Caelius Rufus, & that I had been summoned by the proconsul, P. Scribonius Libo, who had come from Tarraco some days before. The soldiers were the fifth cohort of the XIIth legion, under the military tribune Sex. Asellius; & the legatus of the whole legion, Cn. Balbutius, had also come from Calagurris, where the permanent station was. The cause of the conference was a horror that brooded on the hills. All the townsfolk were frightened, & had begged the presence of a cohort from Calagurris. It was the Terrible Season of the autumn, & the wild people in the mountains were preparing for the frightful ceremonies which only rumour told of in the towns. They were the very old folk who dwelt higher up in the hills & spoke a choppy language which the Vascones could not understand. One seldom saw them; but a few times a year they sent down little yellow squint-eyed messengers (who looked like Scythians) to trade with the merchants by means of gestures, & every spring & autumn they held the infamous rites on the peaks, their howlings & altar-fires throwing terror into the villages. Always the same—the night before the Kalends of Maius & the night before the Kalends of November. Townsfolk would disappear just before these nights, & never be heard of again. And there were whispers that the native shepherds & farmers were not ill-disposed toward the very old folk—that more than one thatched hut was vacant before midnight on the two hideous Sabbaths. This year the horror was very great, for the people knew that the wrath of the very old folk was upon Pompelo. Three months previously five of the little squint-eyed traders had come down from the hills, & in a market brawl three of them had been killed. The remaining two had gone back wordlessly to their mountains—*and this autumn not a single villager had disappeared.* There was a menace in this immunity. It was not like the very old folk to spare their victims at the Sabbath. It was too good to be normal, & the villagers were afraid. For many nights there had been a hollow drumming on the hills, & at last the aedile Tib. Annaeus Stilpo (half native in blood) had sent to Balbutius at Calagurris for a cohort to stamp out the Sabbath on the terrible night. Balbutius had carelessly refused, on the ground that the villagers' fears were empty, & that the loathsome rites of hill folk were of no concern to the Roman People unless our own citizens were menaced. I, however, who seemed to be a close friend of Balbutius, had disagreed with him; averring that I had studied deeply in the black forbidden lore, & that I believed the very old folk capable of visiting almost any nameless doom upon the town, which after all was a Roman settlement & contained a great number of our citizens. The complaining aedile's own mother Helvia was a pure Roman, the daughter of M. Helvius Cinna, who had come over with Scipio's army. Accordingly I had sent a slave—a nimble little Greek called Antipater—to the proconsul with letters, & Scribonius had heeded my plea & ordered Balbutius to send his fifth cohort, under Asellius, to Pompelo; entering the hills at dusk on the eve of November's Kalends & stamping out whatever nameless orgies he might find—bringing such prisoners as he might take to Tarraco for the next propraetor's court. Balbutius, however, had protested, so that more correspondence had ensued. I had written so much to the proconsul that he had become gravely interested, & had resolved to make a personal inquiry into the horror. He had at length proceeded to Pompelo with his lictors & attendants; there hearing enough rumours to be greatly impressed & disturbed, & standing firmly by his order for the Sabbath's extirpation. Desirous of conferring with one who had studied the subject, he ordered me to accompany Asellius' cohort—& Balbutius had also come along to press his adverse advice, for he honestly believed that drastic military action would stir up a dangerous sentiment of unrest among the Vascones both tribal & settled. So here we all were in the mystic sunset of the autumn hills—old Scribonius Libo in his toga praetexta, the golden light glancing on his shiny bald head & wrinkled hawk face, Balbutius with his gleaming helmet & breastplate, blue-shaven lips compressed in conscientiously dogged opposition, young Asellius with his polished greaves & superior sneer, & the curious throng of townsfolk, legionaries, tribesmen, peasants, lictors, slaves, & attendants. I myself seemed to wear a common toga, & to have no especially distinguishing characteristic. And everywhere horror brooded. The town & country folk scarcely dared speak aloud, & the men of Libo's entourage, who had been there nearly a week, seemed to have caught something of the nameless dread. Old Scribonius himself looked very grave, & the sharp voices of us later comers seemed to hold something of curious inappropriateness, as in a place of death or the temple of some mystic god. We entered the praetorium & held grave converse. Balbutius pressed his objections, & was sustained by Asellius, who appeared to hold all the natives in extreme contempt while at the same time deeming it inadvisable to excite them. Both soldiers maintained that we could better afford to antagonise the minority of colonists & civilised natives by inaction, than to antagonise a probable majority of tribesmen & cottagers by stamping out the dread rites. I, on the other hand, renewed my demand for action, & offered to accompany the cohort on any expedition it might undertake. I pointed out that the barbarous Vascones were at best turbulent & uncertain, so that skirmishes with them were inevitable sooner or later whichever course we might take; that they had not in the past proved dangerous adversaries to our legions, & that it would ill become the representatives of the Roman People to suffer barbarians to interfere with a course which the justice & prestige of the Republic demanded. That, on the other hand, the successful administration of a province depended primarily upon the safety & good-will of the civilised element in whose hands the local machinery of commerce & prosperity reposed, & in whose veins a large mixture of our own Italian blood coursed. These, though in numbers they might form a minority, were the stable element whose constancy might be relied on, & whose coöperation would most firmly bind the province to the Imperium of the Senate & the Roman People. It was at once a duty & an advantage to afford them the protection due to Roman citizens; even (& here I shot a sarcastic look at Balbutius & Asellius) at the expense of a little trouble & activity, & of a slight interruption of the draught-playing & cock-fighting at the camp in Calagurris. That the danger to the town and inhabitants of Pompelo was a real one, I could not from my studies doubt. I had read many scrolls out of Syria &

Ægyptus, & the cryptic towns of Etruria, & had talked at length with the bloodthirsty priest of Diana Aricina in his temple in the woods bordering Lacus Nemorensis. There were shocking dooms that might be called out of the hills on the Sabbaths; dooms which ought not to exist within the territories of the Roman People; & to permit orgies of the kind known to prevail at Sabbaths would be but little in consonance with the customs of those whose forefathers, A. Postumius being consul, had executed so many Roman citizens for the practice of the Bacchanalia—a matter kept ever in memory by the Senatus Consultum de Bacchanalibus, graven upon bronze & set open to every eye. Checked in time, before the progress of the rites might evoke anything with which the iron of a Roman pilum might not be able to deal, the Sabbath would not be too much for the powers of a single cohort. Only participants need be apprehended, & the sparing of a great number of mere spectators would considerably lessen the resentment which any of the sympathising country folk might feel. In short, both principle & policy demanded stern action; & I could not doubt but that Publius Scribonius, bearing in mind the dignity & obligations of the Roman People, would adhere to his plan of despatching the cohort, me accompanying, despite such objections as Balbutius & Asellius—speaking indeed more like provincials than Romans—might see fit to offer & multiply. The slanting sun was now very low, & the whole town seemed draped in an unreal & malign glamour. Then P. Scribonius the proconsul signified his approval of my words, & stationed me with the cohort in the provisional capacity of a centurio primipilus; Balbutius & Asellius assenting, the former with better grace than the latter. As twilight fell on the wild autumnal slopes, a measured, hideous beating of strange drums floated down from afar in terrible rhythm. Some few of the legionarii shewed timidity, but sharp commands brought them into line, & the whole cohort was soon drawn up on the open plain east of the circus. Libo himself, as well as Balbutius, insisted on accompanying the cohort; but great difficulty was suffered in getting a native guide to point out the paths up the mountain. Finally a young man named Vercellius, the son of pure Roman parents, agreed to take us at least past the foothills. We began to march in the new dusk, with the thin silvern sickle of a young moon trembling over the woods on our left. That which disquieted us most was *the fact that the Sabbath was to be held at all.* Reports of the coming cohort must have reached the hills, & even the lack of a final decision could not make the rumour less alarming—yet there were the sinister drums as of yore, as if the celebrants had some peculiar reason to be indifferent whether or not the forces of the Roman People marched against them. The sound grew louder as we entered a rising gap in the hills, steep wooded banks enclosing us narrowly on either side, & displaying curiously fantastic tree-trunks in the light of our bobbing torches. All were afoot save Libo, Balbutius, Asellius, two or three of the centuriones, & myself, & at length the way became so steep & narrow that those who had horses were forced to leave them; a squad of ten men being left to guard them, though robber bands were not likely to be abroad on such a night of terror. Once in a while it seemed as though we detected a skulking form in the woods nearby, & after a half-hour's climb the steepness & narrowness of the way made the advance of so great a body of men—over 300, all told— exceedingly cumbrous & difficult. Then with utter & horrifying suddenness we heard a frightful sound from below. It was from the tethered horses—they had *screamed* .... not neighed, but *screamed* ...... & there was no light down there, nor the sound of any human thing, to shew why they had done so. At the same moment bonfires blazed out on all the peaks ahead, so that terror seemed to lurk equally before & behind us. Looking for the young Vercellius, our guide, we found only a crumpled heap weltering in a pool of blood. In his hand was a short sword snatched from the belt of D. Vibulanus, a subcenturio, & on his face was such a look of terror that the stoutest veterans turned pale at the sight. He had killed himself when the horses screamed .... he, who had been born & lived all his life in that region, & knew what men whispered about the hills. All the torches now began to dim, & the cries of frightened legionaries mingled with the unceasing screams of the tethered horses. The air grew perceptibly colder, more suddenly so than is usual at November's brink, & seemed stirred by terrible undulations which I could not help connecting with the beating of huge wings. The whole cohort now remained at a standstill, & as the torches faded I watched what I thought were fantastic shadows outlined in the sky by the spectral luminosity of the Via Lactea as it flowed through Perseus, Cassiopeia, Cepheus, &

Cygnus. Then suddenly all the stars were blotted from the sky—even bright Deneb & Vega ahead, & the lone Altair & Fomalhaut behind us. And as the torches died out altogether, there remained above that stricken & shrieking cohort only the noxious & horrible altar-flames on the towering peaks; hellish & red, & now silhouetting the mad, leaping, & colossal forms of such nameless beasts as had never a Phrygian priest or Campanian grandam whispered of in the wildest of furtive tales. And above the nighted screaming of men & horses that daemoniac drumming rose to louder pitch, whilst an ice-cold wind of shocking sentience & deliberateness swept down from those forbidden heights & coiled about each man separately, till all the cohort was struggling & screaming in the dark, as if acting out the fate of Laocoön & his sons. Only old Scribonius Libo seemed resigned. He uttered words amidst the screaming, & they echo still in my ears. *"Malitia vetus—malitia vetus est . . . . . venit . . . . tandem venit. . . ."*

And then I waked. It was the most vivid dream in years, drawing upon wells of the subconscious long untouched & forgotten. Of the fate of that cohort no record exists, but the town at least was saved—for encyclopaedias tell of the survival of Pompelo to this day, under the modern Spanish name of Pampelona. I shall have to look up Pampelona in some guidebook or travel volume, & see what its ancient tales & superstitions may be. But I shall never go near it on the night of All Hallows'—the night before the Kalends of November. In the genial summer it would be interesting to dig in those archaic hills, & to search a certain pass for the long-buried & encrusted eagles of a certain forgotten cohort.

Discarded Draft of
"The Shadow over Innsmouth"

[pp. 1–6:]

I
t was in the summer of 1927 that I suddenly cut short my sightseeing tour of New England and returned to Cleveland under a nervous strain. I have seldom mentioned the particulars of this trip, and hardly know why I do so now except that a recent newspaper cutting has somehow relieved the tension which formerly existed. A sweeping fire, it appears, has wiped out most of the empty ancient houses along the deserted Innsmouth waterfront as well as a certain number of buildings farther inland; while a singularly simultaneous explosion, heard for many miles around, has destroyed to a vast depth the great black reef a mile and a half out from shore where the sea-bottom abruptly falls to form an incalculable abyss. For certain reasons I take great satisfaction in these occurrences, even the first of which seems to me a blessing rather than a disaster. Especially am I glad that the old brick jewellery factory and the pillared Order of Dagon Hall have gone along with the rest. There is talk of incendiarism, and I suppose old Father Iwanicki could tell much if he chose; but what I know gives a very unusual angle to my opinion.

I never heard of Innsmouth till the day before I saw it for the first and last time. It does not seem to be mentioned on any modern map, and I was planning to go directly from Newburyport to Arkham, and thence to Gloucester, if I could find transportation. I had no car, but was travelling by motor coach, train,[a] and trolley, always seeking the

Editor's Note: This text derives from the versos of the A.Ms. of the story (JHL). It was first printed, as "Discarded Draught: The Shadow over Innsmouth," in *Acolyte* 2, No. 2 (Spring 1944): 3–7. It is unclear who prepared the text of this appearance. It was then reprinted in *Something about Cats and Other Pieces* (Arkham House, 1949), 176–84, and several later editions. Only divergences from the A.Ms. are presented here.

Text: A = A.Ms.

[a] train,] train A

cheapest possible route. In Newburyport they told me that the steam train was the thing to take to Arkham; and it was only at the station ticket office, when I demurred at the high fare, that I heard about Innsmouth. The agent, whose speech shewed him to be no local man, seemed sympathetic toward my efforts at economy, and made a suggestion that none of my other informants had offered.

"You could take that old bus, I suppose," he said with a certain hesitation, "but it isn't thought much of hereabouts. It goes through Innsmouth—you may have heard about that—and so the people don't like it. Run by an Innsmouth man—Joe Sargent—but never gets any custom from here, or from Arkham either, I guess. Wonder it keeps running at all. I suppose it's cheap enough, but I never see more than two or three people in it—nobody but those Innsmouth folks. Leaves the Square—front of Hammond's Drug Store—at 10 a.m. and 7 p.m. unless they've changed lately. Looks like a terrible rattletrap—I've never been on it."

That was the first I ever heard of Innsmouth. Any reference to a town not listed in the guide-books[a] would have interested me, and the agent's odd manner of allusion roused something like real curiosity. A town able to inspire such dislike in its neighbours, I thought, must be at least rather unusual, and worthy of a sightseer's attention. If it came before Arkham I would stop off there—and so I asked the agent to tell me something about it.

He was very deliberate, and spoke with an air of feeling somewhat superior to what he said.

"Innsmouth? Well, it's a queer kind of a town down at the mouth of the Manuxet. It used to be almost a city—quite a seaport before the War of 1812—but the place has all gone to pieces in the last hundred years or so. No railroad now—the B & M never went through there, and the branch line from Rowley was given up years ago. More empty houses than there are people, I guess, and no business to speak of. Everybody trades either here or in Arkham or Ipswich. At one time they had quite a number of mills there, but nothing's left now but one jewellery refinery.

[a] guide-books] guidebooks A

"That's a pretty prominent proposition, though—all the travelling salesmen seem to know about it. Makes a special kind of fancy jewellery out of a secret alloy that nobody can analyse very well. They say it's platinum, silver, and gold—but these people sell it so cheap that you can hardly believe it. Guess they have a corner on that kind of goods.

"Old man Marsh, who owns the thing, must be richer than Croesus. Queer old duck, though, and sticks pretty close around the town. He's the grandson of Captain[a] Obed Marsh, who founded the business. His mother was some kind of foreigner—they say a South Sea native—so everybody raised Cain when he married an Ipswich girl fifty years ago. They always do that about Innsmouth people. But his children and grandchildren look just like anybody else so far as I can see. I've had 'em pointed out to me here. Never saw the old man.

"And why is everybody so down on Innsmouth? Well—you mustn't take too much stock in what people around here say. They're hard to get started, but once they do get started they never stop. They've been telling things about Innsmouth—whispering 'em, mostly—for the last hundred years, I guess, and I gather they're more scared than anything else. Some of the stories would make you laugh—about old Captain Marsh driving bargains with the devil and bringing imps out of hell to live in Innsmouth, or about some kind of devil-worship and awful sacrifices in some place near the wharves that people stumbled on around 1850 or thereabouts—but I come from Panton, Vermont, and that kind of story doesn't go down with me.

"The real thing behind all this is simply race prejudice—and I don't say I'm blaming those that hold it. I hate those Innsmouth folks myself, and I wouldn't care to go to their town. I suppose you know— though I can see you're a Westerner by the way you talk—what a lot our New England ships used to have to do with queer ports in Asia, Africa, the South Seas, and everywhere else, and what queer kinds of people they sometimes brought back with them. You've probably heard about the Salem man that came back with a Chinese wife, and maybe you know there's still a colony of Fiji Islanders somewhere around Cape Cod.

[a] Captain] Capt. A

"Well, there must be something like that back of the Innsmouth people. The place was always badly cut off from the rest of the country by salt marshes and inlets, and we can't be sure about the ins and outs of the matter, but it's pretty plain that old Captain Marsh must have brought home some odd specimens when he had all three of his ships in commission back in the 1830's and 1840's. There certainly is a strange kind of a streak in the Innsmouth folks today—I don't know how to express it, but it sort of makes me crawl. You'll notice it a little in Joe Sargent if you take his bus. Some of them have flat noses, big mouths, weak retreating chins, and a funny kind of rough grey skin. The sides of their necks are sort of shrivelled or creased up, and they get bald very young. Nobody around here or in Arkham will have anything to do with them, and they act kind of offish themselves when they come to town. They used to ride on the railroad, walking and taking the train at Rowley or Ipswich, but now they use that bus.

"Yes, there's a hotel in Innsmouth—called the Gilman House— but I don't believe it can amount to much. I wouldn't advise you to try it. Better stay over here and take the ten o'clock bus tomorrow morning. Then you can get an evening bus there for Arkham at eight[a] o'clock. There was a factory inspector who stopped at the Gilman a couple of years ago, and he had a lot of unpleasant hints about the place. It seems they get a queer crowd there, for this fellow heard voices in other rooms that gave him the shivers. It was foreign talk, but he said the bad thing about it was the kind of voice that sometimes spoke. It sounded so unnatural—slopping-like, he said—that he didn't dare go to sleep. Just kept dressed and lit out early in the morning. The talk went on most of the night.

"This man—Casey, his name was—had a lot to say about the old Marsh factory, and what he said fitted in very well with some of the wild stories. The books were in no kind of shape, and the machinery looked old and almost abandoned, as if it hadn't been run a great deal. The place still used water power from the Lower Falls of the Manuxet. There were only a few employees, and they didn't seem to be doing much. It made me think, when he told me, about the local rumours that Marsh doesn't actually make the stuff he sells. Many people say he

[a] eight] 8 A

doesn't get enough factory supplies to be really running the place, and that he must be importing those queer ornaments from somewhere— heaven knows where. I don't believe that, though. The Marshes have been selling those outlandish rings and armlets and tiaras and things for nearly a hundred years; and if there were anywhere else where they got 'em, the general public would have found out all about it by this time. Then, too, there's no shipping or in-bound trucking around Innsmouth that would account for such imports. What does get imported is the queerest sort of glass and rubber trinkets—makes you think of what they used to buy in the old days to trade with savages. But it's a straight fact that all inspectors run up against queer things at the plant. Twenty odd years ago one of them disappeared at Innsmouth—never heard of again—and I myself knew George Cole, who went insane down there one night, and had to be lugged away by two men from the Danvers asylum, where he is now. He talks of some kind of sound and shrieks things about 'scaly water-devils'.

"And that makes me think of another of the old stories—about the black reef off the coast. Devil's Reef, they call it. It's almost above water a good part of the time, but at that you could hardly call it a real island. The story is that there's a whole legion of devils seen sometimes on that reef—sprawled about, or darting in and out of some kind of caves near the top. It's a rugged, uneven thing, a good bit over a mile out, and sailors used to make great detours just to avoid it. One of the things they had against Captain Marsh was that he used to land on it sometimes when it was fairly dry. Probably the rock formation interested him, but there was talk about his having dealings with daemons.[a] That was before the big epidemic of 1846, when over half the people in Innsmouth were carried off. They never did quite figure out what the trouble was, but it was probably some foreign kind of disease brought from China or somewhere by the shipping.

"Maybe that plague took off the best blood in Innsmouth. Anyway, they're a doubtful lot now—and there can't be more than 500 or 600 of them. The rich Marshes are as bad as any. I guess they're all what people call 'white trash'[b] down South—lawless and sly, and full

[a] daemons.] demons. A
[b] 'white trash'] "white trash" A

of secret doings. Lobster fishermen, mostly—exporting by truck. Nobody can ever keep track of 'em, and state school officials and census people have a devil of a time. That's why I wouldn't go at night if I were you. I've never been there and have no wish to go, but I guess a daytime trip wouldn't hurt you—even though the people here will advise you not to take it. If you're just sightseeing, Innsmouth ought to be quite a place for you."

And so I spent that evening at the Newburyport Public Library looking up data about Innsmouth. When I had tried to question natives in the shops, the lunch room, and the fire station I had found them even harder to get started than the ticket agent had predicted, and realised that I could not spare the time to overcome their first instinctive reticence. They had a kind of obscure suspiciousness. At the YMCA the clerk merely discouraged my going to such a dismal, decadent place, and the people at the library shewed much the same attitude, holding Innsmouth to be merely an exaggerated case of civic degeneration.

The Essex County histories on the shelves had very little to say, except that the town was founded in 1643, noted for shipbuilding before the Revolution, a seat of great marine prosperity in the early nineteenth[a] century, and later on a minor factory centre using the Manuxet as power. References to decline were very few, though the significance of the later records was unmistakable. After the Civil War all industrial life centred in the Marsh Refining Company at the Lower Falls, and the marketing of its products formed the only remaining bit of major commerce. There were very few foreigners; mostly Poles and Portuguese[b] on the southern fringe of the town. Local finances were very bad, and but for the Marsh factory the place would have been bankrupt.

I saw a good many booklets and catalogues and advertising calendars of the Marsh Refining Company in the business department of the library, and began to realise what a striking thing that lone industry was. The jewels and ornaments it sold were of the finest possible artistry and the most extreme originality; so delicately

[a] nineteenth] 19th A
[b] Portuguese] Portugese A

wrought, indeed, that one could not doubt but that handicraft played a large part in at least their final stages of manufacture. Some of the half-tone pictures of them interested me profoundly, for the strangeness and beauty of the designs seemed to my eye indicative of a profound and exotic genius—a genius so spectacular and bizarre that one could not help wondering whence the inspiration had come. It was easy to credit the boast of one of the booklets that this jewellery was a favourite with persons of sophisticated taste, and that several specimens were exhibited in museums of modern craftsmanship.

Large pieces predominated—armlets, tiaras, and elaborate pendants—but rings and lesser items were numerous. The raised or incised designs—partly conventional and partly with a curious marine motif—were wrought in a style of tremendous distinctiveness and of utter dissimilarity to the art traditions of any race or epoch I knew about. This other-worldly character was emphasised by the oddness of the precious alloy, whose general effect was suggested in several colour-plates. Something about these pictured things fascinated me intensely—almost disproportionately—and I resolved to see as many original specimens as possible both at Innsmouth and in shops and museums elsewhere. Yet there was a distinct element of repulsion mixed with the fascination; proceeding, perhaps, from the evil and silly old legends about the founder of the business which the ticket-agent had told me.

[p. 17:]

The door of the Marsh retail office was open, and I walked in with considerable expectancy. The interior was shabby and ill-lighted, but contained a large number of display cases of solid and capable workmanship. A youngish man came forward to meet me, and as I studied his face a fresh wave of disturbance passed over me. He was not unhandsome, but there was something subtly bizarre and aberrant about his features and vocal timbre. I could not stifle a keen sudden aversion, and acquired an unexplained reluctance to seem like any sort of curious investigator. Before I knew it I found myself telling the fellow that I was a jewellery buyer for a Cleveland firm, and preparing myself to shew a merely professional interest in what I should see.

It was hard, though, to carry out this policy. The clerk switched on more lights and began to lead me from case to case, but when I beheld the glittering marvels before me I could scarcely walk steadily or talk coherently. It took no excessive sensitiveness to beauty to make one literally gasp at the strange, alien loveliness of these opulent objects, and as I gazed fascinatedly I saw how little justice even the colour-plates[a] had done them. Even now I can hardly describe what I saw— though those who own such pieces or have seen them in shops and museums can supply the missing data. The massed effect of so many elaborate samples was what produced my especial feeling of awe and unrest. For somehow or other, these singular grotesques and arabesques did not seem to be the product of any earthly handiwork— least of all a factory only a stone's throw away. The patterns and traceries all hinted of remote spaces and unimaginable abysses, and the aquatic nature of the occasional pictorial items added to the general unearthliness. Some of the fabulous monsters filled me with an uncomfortable sense of dark pseudo-memory which I tried

[p. 21:]
the taint and blasphemy of furtive Innsmouth. He, like me, was a normal being outside the pall of decay and normally terrified by it. But because he was so inextricably close to the thing, he had been broken in a way that I was not yet broken.

Shaking off the hands of the firemen who sought to detain him, the ancient rose to his feet and greeted me as if I were an acquaintance. The grocery youth had told me where most of Uncle Zadok's liquor was obtained, and without a word I began leading him in that direction—through the Square and around into Eliot Street. His step was astonishingly brisk for one of his age and bibulousness, and I marvelled at the original strength of his constitution. My haste to leave Innsmouth had abated for the moment, and I felt instead a queer curiosity to dip into this mumbling patriarch's chaotic store of extravagant myth.

When we had bought a quart of whiskey in the rear of a dismal variety store, I led Uncle Zadok along South Street to the utterly

---

[a] colour-plates] colour plates A

abandoned section of the waterfront, and still farther southward to a point where even the fishermen on the distant breakwater could not see us, where I knew we could talk undisturbed. For some reason or other he seemed to dislike this arrangement—casting nervous glances out to sea in the direction of Devil Reef—but the lure of the whiskey was too strong for him to resist. After we had found a seat on the edge of a rotting wharf I gave him a pull at the bottle and waited for it to take effect. Naturally I graduated the doses very carefully, for I did not wish the old man's loquacity to turn into a stupor. As he grew more mellow, I began to venture some remarks and inquiries about Innsmouth, and was really startled by the terrible and sincere portentousness of his lowered voice. He did not seem as crazy as his wild tales would indicate, and I found myself shuddering even when I could not believe his fantastic inventions. I hardly wondered at the naive credulity of superstitious Father Iwanicki.

The Evil Clergyman

I was shewn[a] into the attic chamber by a grave, intelligent-looking man with quiet clothes and an iron-grey[b] beard, who spoke to me in this fashion:

"Yes, *he* lived here—but I don't advise your doing anything. Your curiosity makes you irresponsible. *We* never come here at night, and it's only because of *his* will that we keep it this way. You know what *he* did. That abominable society took charge at last, and we don't know where *he* is buried. There was no way the law or anything else could reach the society.

"I hope you won't stay till after dark. And I beg of you to let that thing on the table—the thing that looks like a match-box—alone. We don't know what it is, but we suspect it has something to do with what *he* did. We even avoid looking at it very steadily."

After a time the man left me alone in the attic room. It was very dingy and dusty, and only primitively furnished, but it had a neatness which shewed[c] it was not a slum-denizen's quarters. There were shelves full of theological and classical books, and another bookcase containing treatises on magic—Paracelsus, Albertus Magnus, Trithemius,

Editor's Note: This text is derived from a letter to Bernard Austin Dwyer, probably written in the summer or fall of 1933. The original A.L.S. has not surfaced, and the letter does not exist even as a transcript in the Arkham House Transcripts. Dwyer submitted the text to *Weird Tales*, where it was published as "The Wicked Clergyman." August Derleth reprinted the text under its present title in several editions.

Texts: A = *Weird Tales* 33, No. 4 (April 1939): 135–37 (as "The Wicked Clergyman"); B = *Dagon and Other Macabre Tales* (Arkham House, 1965), 297–301. Copy-text: A.

[a] shewn] shown A, B
[b] iron-grey] iron-gray A, B
[c] shewed] showed A, B

Hermes Trismegistus, Borellus, and others in strange alphabets whose titles I could not decipher. The furniture was very plain. There was a door, but it led only into a closet. The only egress was the aperture in the floor up to which the crude, steep staircase led. The windows were of bull's-eye pattern, and the black oak beams bespoke unbelievable antiquity. Plainly, this house was of the Old World. I seemed to know where I was, but cannot recall what I then knew. Certainly the town was *not* London. My impression is of a small seaport.

The small object on the table fascinated me intensely. I seemed to know what to do with it, for I drew a pocket electric light—or what looked like one—out of my pocket and nervously tested its flashes. The light was not white but violet, and seemed less like true light than like some radio-active bombardment. I recall that I did not regard it as a common flashlight—indeed, I *had* a common flashlight in another pocket.

It was getting dark, and the ancient roofs and chimney-pots outside looked very queer through the bull's-eye window-panes. Finally I summoned up courage and propped the small object up on the table against a book—then turned the rays of the peculiar violet light upon it. The light seemed now to be more like a rain or hail of small violet particles than like a continuous beam. As the particles struck the glassy surface at the centre[a] of the strange device, they seemed to produce a crackling noise like the sputtering of a vacuum tube through which sparks are passed. The dark glassy surface displayed a pinkish glow, and a vague white shape seemed to be taking form at its centre.[b] Then I noticed that I was not alone in the room—and put the ray-projector back in my pocket.

But the newcomer did not speak—nor did I hear any sound whatever during all the immediately following moments. Everything was shadowy pantomime, as if seen at a vast distance through some intervening haze—although on the other hand the newcomer and all subsequent comers loomed large and close, as if both near and distant, according to some abnormal geometry.

The newcomer was a thin, dark man of medium height attired in the clerical garb of the Anglican church. He was apparently about

[a] centre] center A, B
[b] centre.] center. A, B

thirty years old, with a sallow, olive complexion and fairly good features, but an abnormally high forehead. His black hair was well cut and neatly brushed, and he was clean-shaven though blue-chinned with a heavy growth of beard. He wore rimless spectacles with steel bows. His build and lower facial features were like other clergymen I had seen, but he had a vastly higher forehead, and was darker and more intelligent-looking—also more subtly and concealedly *evil*-looking. At the present moment—having just lighted a faint oil lamp—he looked nervous, and before I knew it he was casting all his magical books into a fireplace on the window side of the room (where the wall slanted sharply) which I had not noticed before. The flames devoured the volumes greedily—leaping up in strange colours[a] and emitting indescribably hideous odours[b] as the strangely hieroglyphed leaves and wormy bindings succumbed to the devastating element. All at once I saw there were others in the room—grave-looking men in clerical costume, one of whom wore the bands and knee-breeches of a bishop. Though I could hear nothing, I could see that they were bringing a decision of vast import to the first-comer. They seemed to hate and fear him at the same time, and he seemed to return these sentiments. His face set itself into a grim expression, but I could see his right hand shaking as he tried to grip the back of a chair. The bishop pointed to the empty case and to the fireplace (where the flames had died down amidst a charred, non-committal mass), and seemed filled with a peculiar loathing. The first-comer then gave a wry smile and reached out with his left hand toward the small object on the table. Everyone then seemed frightened. The procession of clerics began filing down the steep stairs through the trap-door in the floor, turning and making menacing gestures as they left. The bishop was last to go.

The first-comer now went to a cupboard on the inner side of the room and extracted a coil of rope. Mounting a chair, he attached one end of the rope to a hook in the great exposed central beam of black oak, and began making a noose with the other end. Realising[c] he was about to hang himself, I started forward to dissuade or save him. He

---

[a] colours] colors A, B
[b] odours] odors A, B
[c] Realising] Realizing A, B

saw me and ceased his preparations, looking at me with a kind of *triumph* which puzzled and disturbed me. He slowly stepped down from the chair and began gliding toward me with a positively wolfish grin on his dark, thin-lipped face.

I felt somehow in deadly peril, and drew out the peculiar ray-projector as a weapon of defence.[a] Why I thought it could help me, I do not know. I turned it on—full in his face, and saw the sallow features glow first with violet and then with pinkish light. His expression of wolfish exultation began to be crowded aside by a look of profound fear—which did not, however, wholly displace the exultation. He stopped in his tracks—then, flailing his arms wildly in the air, began to stagger backward. I saw he was edging toward the open stair-well in the floor, and tried to shout a warning, but he did not hear me. In another instant he had lurched backward through the opening and was lost to view.

I found difficulty in moving toward the stair-well, but when I did get there I found no crushed body on the floor below. Instead there was a clatter of people coming up with lanterns, for the spell of phantasmal silence had broken, and I once more heard sounds and saw figures as normally tri-dimensional. Something had evidently drawn a crowd to this place. Had there been a noise I had not heard? Presently the two people (simple villagers, apparently) farthest in the lead saw me—and stood paralysed.[b] One of them shrieked loudly and reverberantly:

"Ahrrh! . . . It be 'ee, zur? Again?"

Then they all turned and fled frantically. All, that is, but one. When the crowd was gone I saw the grave-bearded man who had brought me to this place—standing alone with a lantern. He was gazing at me gaspingly and fascinatedly, but did not seem afraid. Then he began to ascend the stairs, and joined me in the attic. He spoke:

"So you *didn't* let it alone! I'm sorry. I know what has happened. It happened once before, but the man got frightened and shot himself. You ought not to have made *him* come back. You know what *he* wants. But you mustn't get frightened like the other man he got. Something very strange and terrible has happened to you, but it didn't get far

[a] defence.] defense. A, B
[b] paralysed.] paralyzed. A, B

enough to hurt your mind and personality. If you'll keep cool, and accept the need for making certain radical readjustments in your life, you can keep right on enjoying the world, and the fruits of your scholarship. But you can't live here—and I don't think you'll wish to go back to London. I'd advise America.

"You mustn't try anything more with that—thing. Nothing can be put back now. It would only make matters worse to do—or summon—anything. You are not as badly off as you might be—but you must get out of here at once and stay away. You'd better thank heaven[a] it didn't go further. . . .

"I'm going to prepare you as bluntly as I can. There's been a certain change—in your personal appearance. *He* always causes that. But in a new country you can get used to it. There's a mirror up at the other end of the room, and I'm going to take you to it. You'll get a shock—though you will see nothing repulsive."

I was now shaking with a deadly fear, and the bearded man almost had to hold me up as he walked me across the room to the mirror, the faint lamp (i.e., that formerly on the table, not the still fainter lantern he had brought) in his free hand. This is what I saw in the glass:

A thin, dark man of medium stature attired in the clerical garb of the Anglican church, apparently about thirty, and with rimless, steel-bowed glasses glistening beneath a sallow, olive forehead of abnormal height.

It was the silent first-comer who had burned his books.

For all the rest of my life, in outward form, I was to be that man!

[a] heaven] Heaven A, B

[Cigarette Characterizations]

T he oddly unnatural face disclosed by the match's glow gave even this common cigarette an indefinable strangeness. Its newly lit[a] point pulsed in a feverish rhythm curiously unlike the puffs of the normal smoker, and when it blazed brightest one could see the whole white cylinder protruding like a fungoid excrescence from the thin, pallid lips. The smoke, when glimpsed, seemed to weave fantastic designs; and a long ash appeared with anomalous rapidity.

Editor's Note: This brief item was published in *Fantasy Magazine* (June 1934), as part of a series commissioned by the magazine's editor, Julius Schwartz, in which leading science fiction and weird authors—including Ralph Milne Farley, David H. Keller, Clark Ashton Smith, Harl Vincent, E. E. Smith, Otis Adelbert Kline, and Stanton A. Coblentz—were asked to parody to their own styles in describing a cigarette.

Text: A = *Fantasy Magazine* 3, No. 4 (June 1934), 15–16, 32.

[a] newly lit] newly-lit A

Of Evill Sorceries done in New England, of Daemons in No Humane Shape

B ut, not to speak at too great Length upon so horrid a Matter, I
will add onlie what is commonly reported concerning an
Happening in *New Plymouth*, fifty Years since, when Mr. *Bradford*
was Governour. 'Tis said, one *Richard Billington*, being instructed partly
by evill Books, and partly by an antient Wonder-Worker amongst yᵉ
Indian Salvages, so fell away from good *Christian* Practice that he not
only lay'd claim to Immortality in the Flesh, but sett up in the Woods a
Place of Dagon, namely great Ring of Stones, inside which he say'd
Prayers to yᵉ Divell, and sung certain Rites of Magick abominable by
Scripture. This being brought to the Notice of yᵉ Magistrates, he
deny'd all blasphemous Dealings; but not long after he privately
shew'd great Fear about some Thing he had call'd out of the Sky at
Night. There were in that year seven slayings in yᵉ Woods near to
Richard Billington's Stones, those slain being crushed and half-melted in
a Fashion outside all Experience. Upon Talk of a Tryall, *Billington* dropt
out of Sight, nor was any clear Word of him ever after heard.

Two months from then, by Night, there was heard a Band of
Wampanaug Salvages howling and singing in the Woods; and it
appeared, they took down the Ring of Stones and did much besides.
For their head Man *Misquamacus*, that same antient Wonder-Worker of

Editor's Note: This text exists as an A.Ms. at JHL. It is undated, but probably dates
to the mid-1930s. In a marginal note HPL identifies it as deriving from a fictitious
work, *"Thaumaturgicall Prodigies in the New-English Canaan,* by the Rev. Ward Phillips, Pastor of the Second Church in Arkham, in the Massachusetts-Bay—Boston,
1697." August Derleth found the text and incorporated it, with significant
alterations, in his "posthumous collaboration" *The Lurker at the Threshold* (Arkham
House, 1945). He also printed the altered text in *Some Notes on H. P. Lovecraft*
(Arkham House, 1959), xii–xv. where he misidentifies it as "the fragment titled
The Round Tower." No textual variants are presented for this text.

whom *Billington* had learnt some of his Sorceries, came shortly into the town and told Mr. *Bradford* some strange Things; namely, that *Billington* had done worse Evill than cou'd be well repair'd, and that he was no doubt eat up by what he had call'd out of the Sky. That there was no Way to send back that Thing he had summon'd, so the *Wampanaug* wise Men had caught and prison'd it where the Ring of Stones had been.

They had digg'd a Hole three Ells deep and two across, and had thither charmed yᵉ Daemon with Spells that they knew; covering it over with Great Rocks and setting on Top a flat Stone carved with what they call'd yᵉ Elder Sign. On this they made a Mound of the Earth digg'd from the Pit, sticking on it a tall Stone carv'd with a Warning. The old Salvage affirm'd, this Mound must on no Account be disturb'd, lest the Daemon come loose again which it wou'd if the bury'd flatt Stone with the Elder Sign shou'd get out of Place. On being ask'd what yᵉ Daemon look'd like, he gave a very curious and circumstantiall Relation, saying it was sometimes small and solid, like a great Toad the Bigness of a Ground-Hog, but sometimes big and cloudy, without any Shape at all.

It had yᵉ Name *Ossadagowah*, which signifys the child of *Sadogowah;* the last a frightful Spirit spoke of by old Men as coming down from the Stars and being formerly worshipt in Lands of the North. The *Wampanaugs,* and *Nansets* and *Nahiggansets,* knew how to draw it out of the Sky, but never did so because of the exceeding great Evilness of it. They knew also how to catch and prison it, tho' they cou'd not send it back whence it came. It was however declar'd, that the old Tribes of *Lamah,* who dwelt under the Great Bear and were antiently destroy'd for their Wickedness, knew how to manage it in all Ways. Many upstart Men pretended to a Knowledge of such antient Secrets, but none in these Parts cou'd give any Proof of truly having it. It was say'd by some, that Ossadogowah often went back to yᵉ Sky from choice without any sending, but that he cou'd not come back unless summon'd.

This much yᵉ antient Wizard *Misquamacus* told to Mr. *Bradford,* and ever after a great Mound in the Woods near the Pond southwest of *New-Plymouth* hath been straitly lett alone. The Tall Stone is these Twenty years gone, but the Mound is mark'd by the Circumstance, that nothing, neither Grass nor Brush, will grow upon it. Grave Men doubt that yᵉ evill *Billington* was eat up, as yᵉ Salvages believe, by what he call'd out of the Sky; notwithstanding certain Reports of the Idle, of his being since seen in divers places, and that no longer ago than the late monstrous Witchcraft in Essex-County, in the Year 1692.

But in respect of generall Infamy, no Report more terrible hath come to Notice, than of what Goodwife *Doten,* Relict of *John Doten* of *Duxbury* in the Old Colonie, brought out of the Woods near Candlemas of 1683. She affirm'd, and her good Neighbours likewise, that it had been borne that which was neither Beast nor Man, but like to a monstrous Bat with humane Face. The which was burnt by Order of the High-Sheriff on the 5th of June in the Year 1654.

Bibliography

I. Editions of H. P. Lovecraft's Stories

At the Mountains of Madness and Other Novels. Selected by August Derleth. Sauk City, WI: Arkham House, 1964. [Rev. ed. by S. T. Joshi, 1985.]

Beyond the Wall of Sleep. Edited by August Derleth and Donald Wandrei. Sauk City, WI: Arkham House, 1943.

The Cats of Ulthar. Cassia, FL: Dragon-Fly Press, 1935.

Dagon and Other Macabre Tales. Selected by August Derleth. Sauk City, WI: Arkham House, 1965. [Rev. ed. by S. T. Joshi, 1986.]

The Dunwich Horror and Others. Selected by August Derleth. Sauk City, WI: Arkham House, 1963. [Rev. ed. by S. T. Joshi, 1984.] [Prepared largely from plates of Lovecraft's *Best Supernatural Stories* (World Publishing Co., 1945). Text used for collation is the 4th printing (1973). The 5th printing (1981) contains some minor corrections of textual errors.]

Marginalia. Compiled by August Derleth. Sauk City, WI: Arkham House, 1944.

Miscellaneous Writings. Edited by S. T. Joshi. Sauk City, WI: Arkham House, 1995.

The Outsider and Others. Edited by August Derleth and Donald Wandrei. Sauk City, WI: Arkham House, 1939.

The Shadow over Innsmouth. Everett, PA: Visionary Publishing Co., 1936.

The Shunned House. Athol, MA: W. Paul Cook (The Recluse Press), 1928. [Printed but not bound or distributed.]

The Shuttered Room and Other Pieces. Compiled by August Derleth. Sauk City, WI: Arkham House, 1959.

The Weird Writings of H. P. Lovecraft. Mississauga, ON: Girasol, 2010. 2 vols. [Facsimiles of HPL's stories in *Weird Tales*.]

II. Other Editions

Essential Solitude: The Letters of H. P. Lovecraft and August Derleth. Edited by David E. Schultz and S. T. Joshi. New York: Hippocampus Press, 2008. 2 vols.

Letters to Elizabeth Toldridge and Anne Tillery Renshaw. Edited by David E. Schultz and S. T. Joshi. New York: Hippocampus Press, 2014.

Letters to James Ferdinand Morton. Edited by David E. Schultz and S. T. Joshi. New York: Hippocampus Press, 2011.

Letters to Robert Bloch and Others. Edited by David E. Schultz and S. T. Joshi. New York: Hippocampus Press, 2015.

A Means to Freedom: The Letters of H. P. Lovecraft and Robert E. Howard Edited by S. T. Joshi, David E. Schultz, and Rusty Burke. New York: Hippocampus Press, 2009. 2 vols.

Mysteries of Time and Spirit: The Letters of H. P. Lovecraft and Donald Wandrei. Edited by S. T. Joshi and David E. Schultz. San Francisco: Night Shade, 2002.

O Fortunate Floridian: H. P. Lovecraft's Letters to R. H. Barlow. Edited by S. T. Joshi and David E. Schultz. Tampa, FL: University of Tampa Press, 2007.

Selected Letters 1911–1937. Edited by August Derleth, Donald Wandrei, and James Turner. Sauk City, WI: Arkham House, 1965–76. 5 vols.